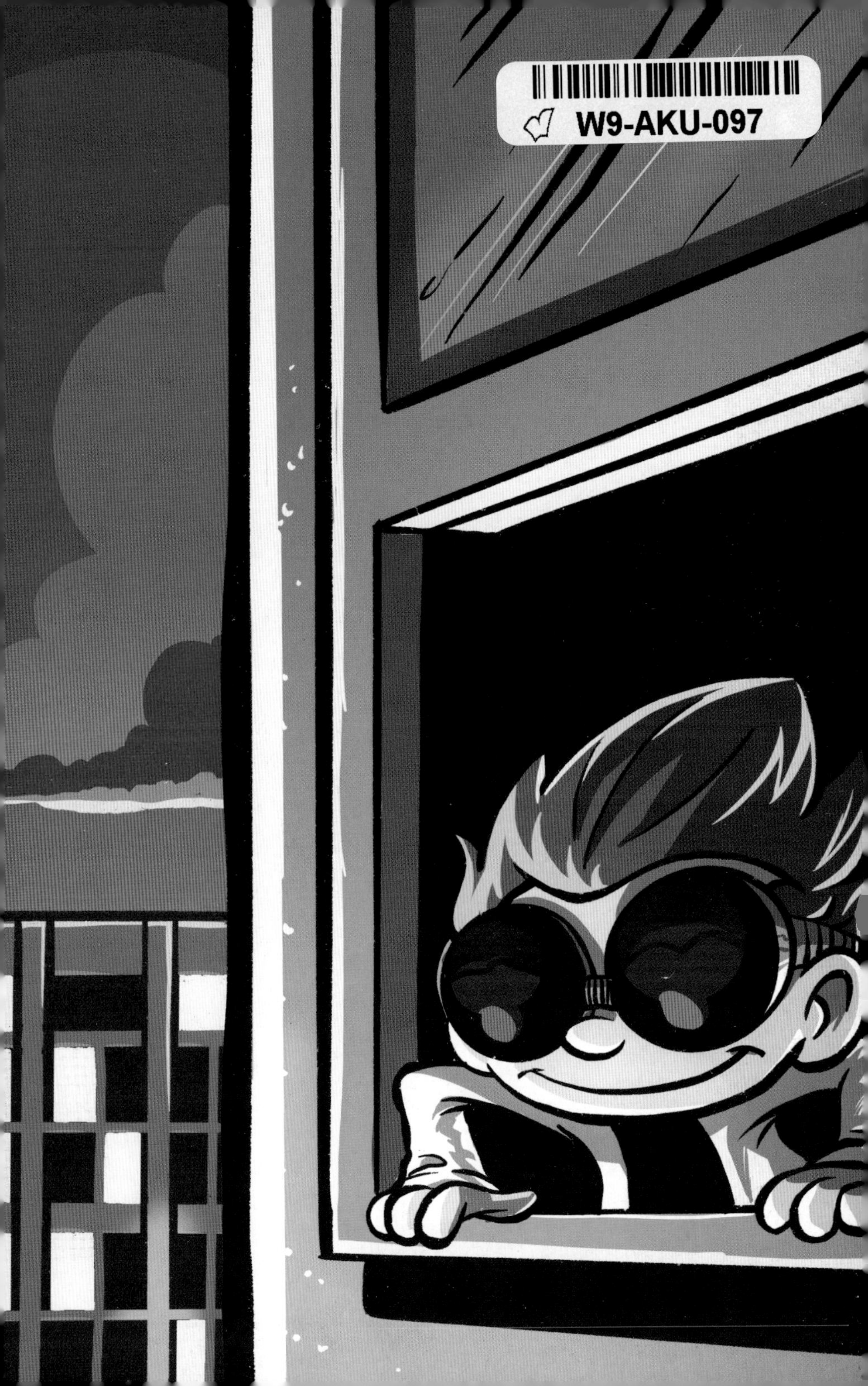

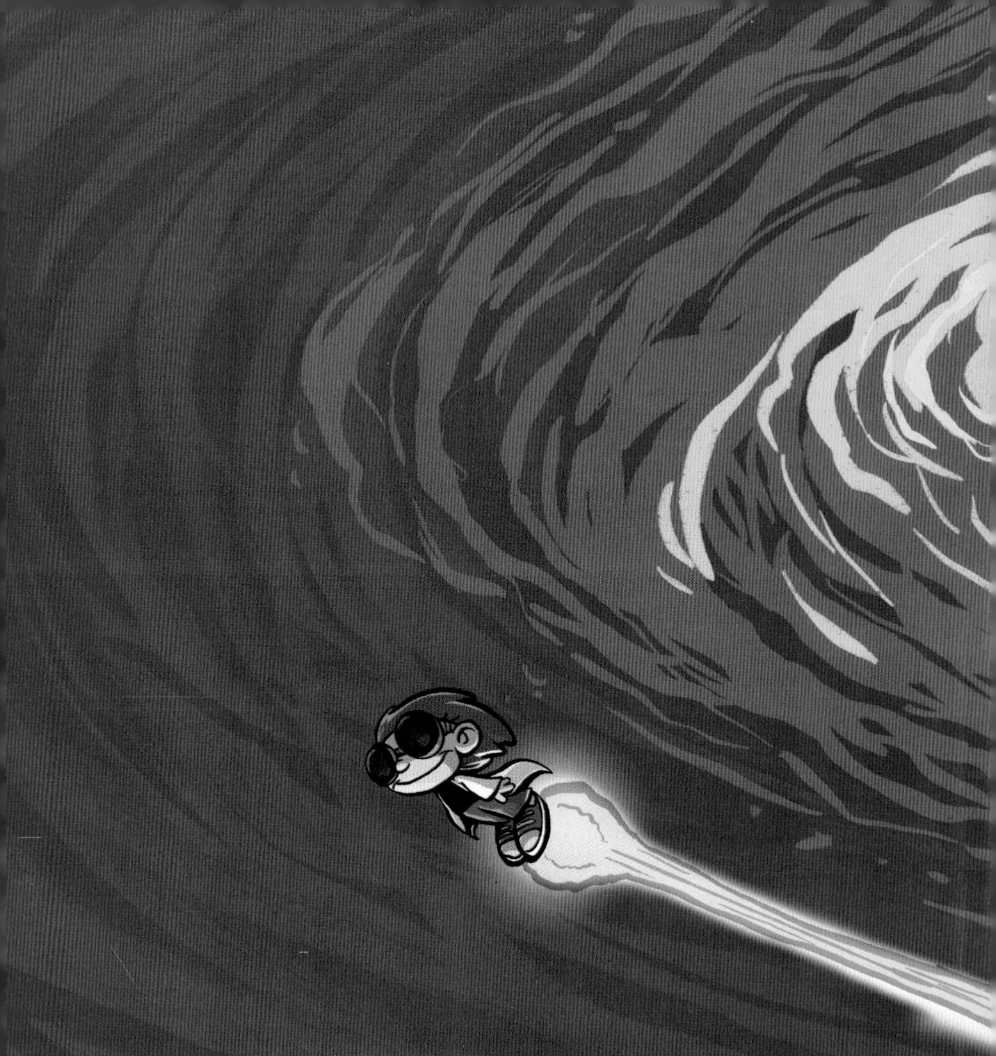

Also by
Lucas Turnbloom

STEVE L. McEVIL

STEVE L. McEVIL and the SECOND WIND

Lucas Turnbloom

Color by Marc Lapierre
and Lucas Turnbloom

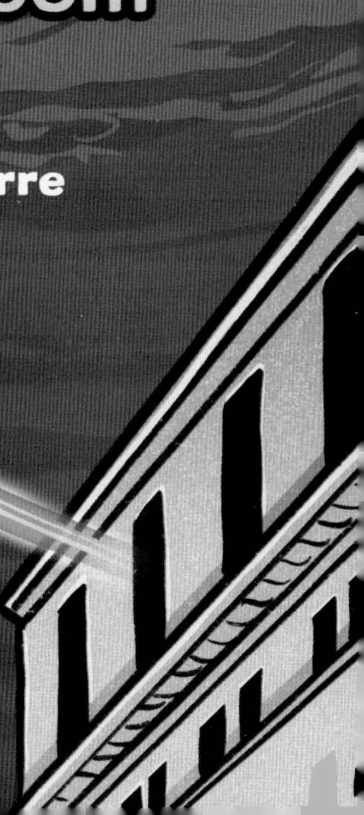

CROWN
BOOKS FOR YOUNG READERS
NEW YORK

**Huge thanks to Zoe Lapierre
for her coloring skills**

All rights reserved. Published in the United States by Crown Books for Young Readers,
an imprint of Random House Children's Books, a division of Penguin Random House LLC, New York.

Crown and the colophon are registered trademarks of Penguin Random House LLC.

RH Graphic with the book design is a trademark of Penguin Random House LLC.

Visit us on the Web! rhcbooks.com

Educators and librarians, for a variety of teaching tools, visit us at RHTeachersLibrarians.com

Library of Congress Cataloging-in-Publication Data is available upon request.

ISBN 978-0-593-30147-0 (hardcover) | ISBN 978-0-593-30149-4 (ebook)

Interior design by Bob Bianchini

MANUFACTURED IN CHINA

10 9 8 7 6 5 4 3 2 1

First Edition

FOR ALEX and AIDEN

PROLOGUE

In the Beginning...

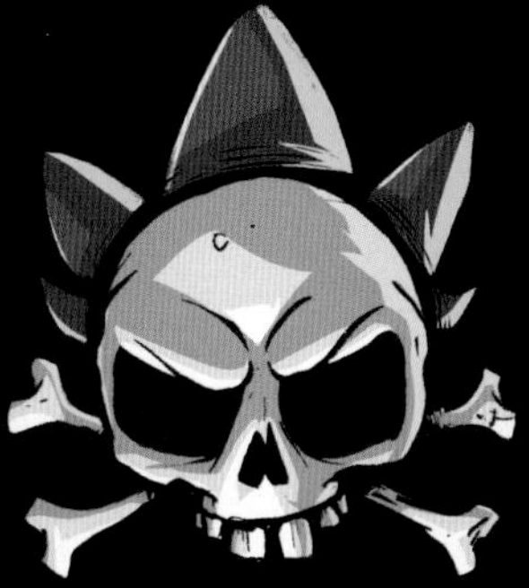

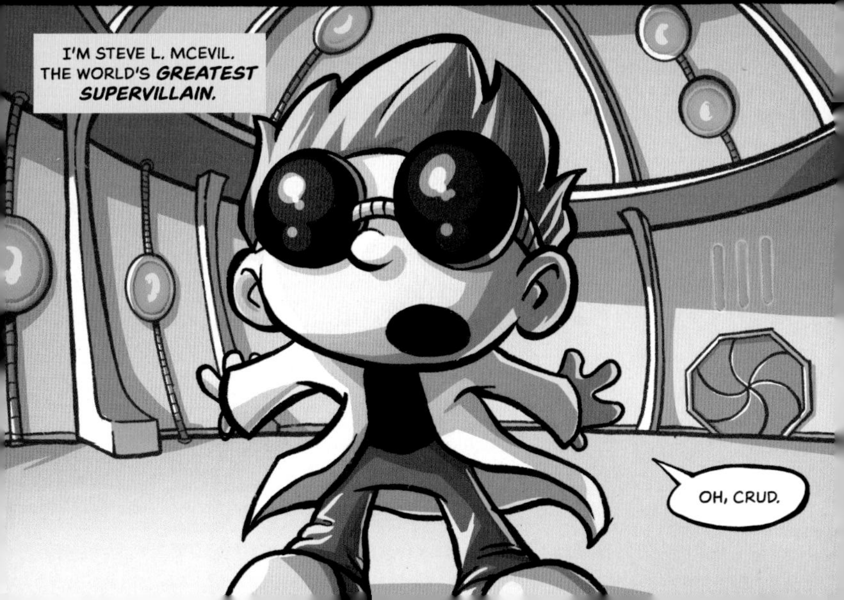
I'M STEVE L. MCEVIL. THE WORLD'S *GREATEST SUPERVILLAIN.*
OH, CRUD.

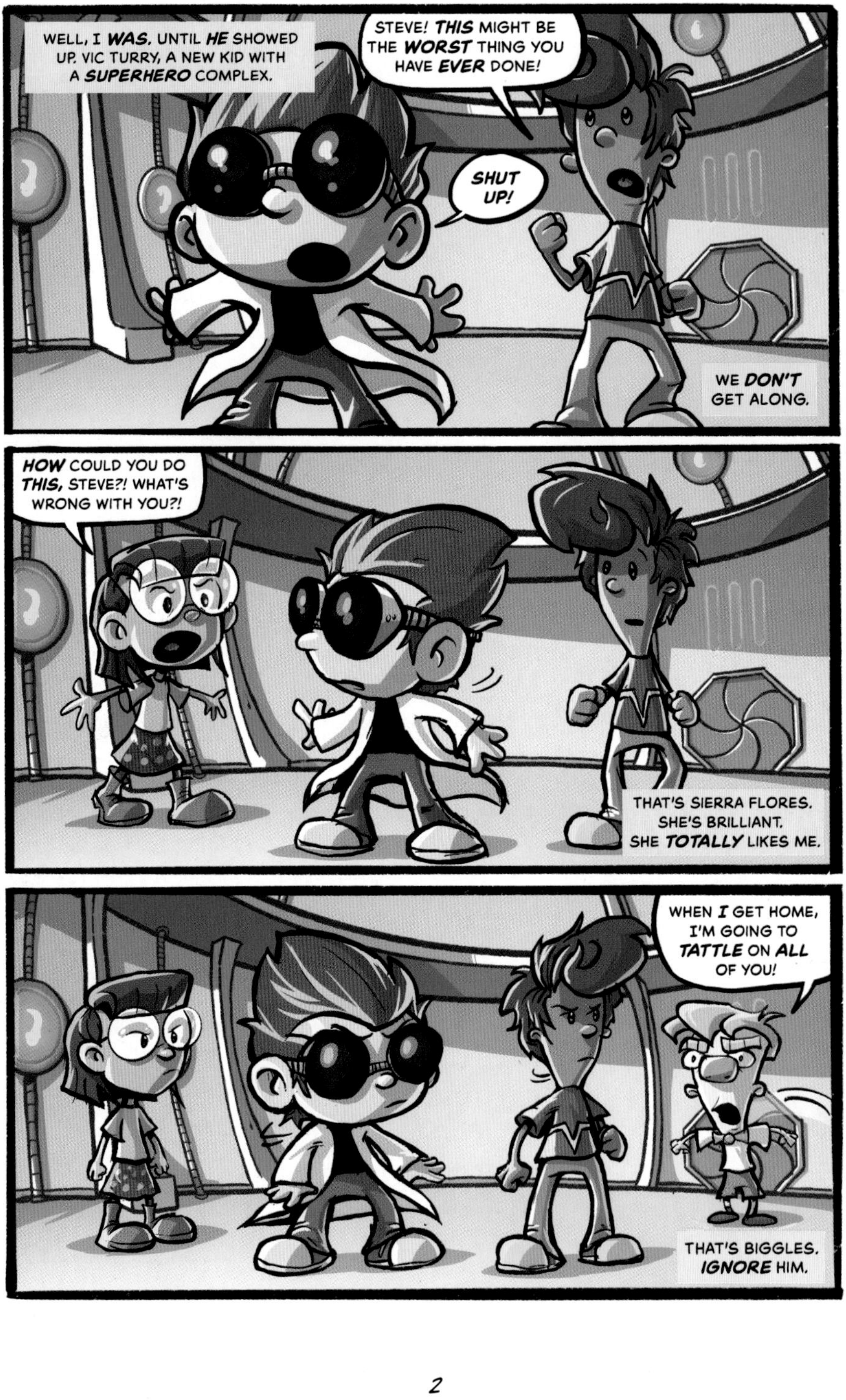

WELL, I **WAS**, UNTIL **HE** SHOWED UP. VIC TURRY, A NEW KID WITH A **SUPERHERO** COMPLEX.
STEVE! **THIS** MIGHT BE THE **WORST** THING YOU HAVE **EVER** DONE!
SHUT UP!
WE **DON'T** GET ALONG.
HOW COULD YOU DO **THIS,** STEVE?! WHAT'S WRONG WITH YOU?!
THAT'S SIERRA FLORES. SHE'S BRILLIANT. SHE **TOTALLY** LIKES ME.
WHEN **I** GET HOME, I'M GOING TO **TATTLE** ON **ALL** OF YOU!
THAT'S BIGGLES. **IGNORE** HIM.

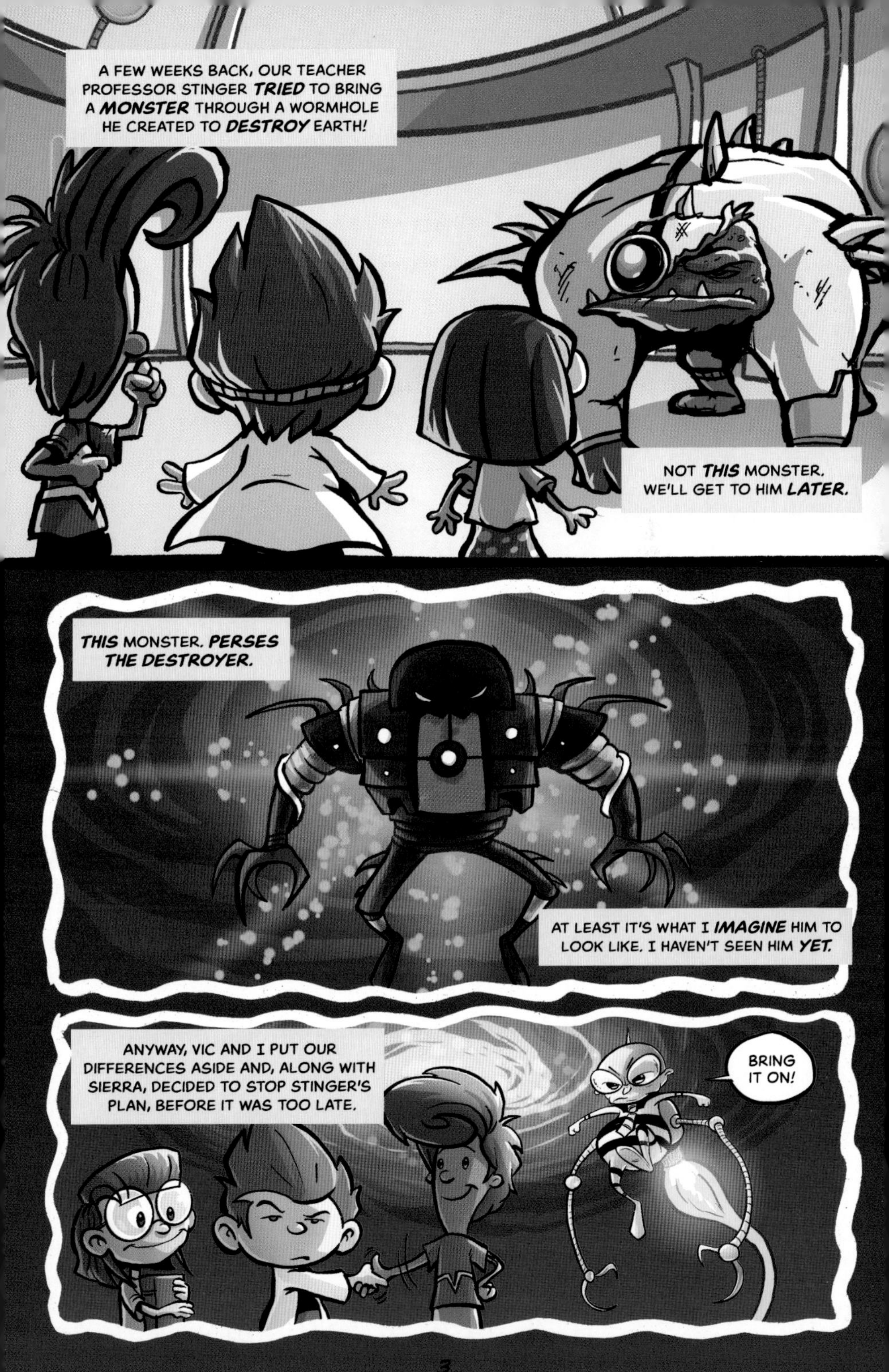
A FEW WEEKS BACK, OUR TEACHER PROFESSOR STINGER TRIED TO BRING A MONSTER THROUGH A WORMHOLE HE CREATED TO DESTROY EARTH!
NOT THIS MONSTER. WE'LL GET TO HIM LATER.
THIS MONSTER. PERSES THE DESTROYER.
AT LEAST IT'S WHAT I IMAGINE HIM TO LOOK LIKE. I HAVEN'T SEEN HIM YET.
ANYWAY, VIC AND I PUT OUR DIFFERENCES ASIDE AND, ALONG WITH SIERRA, DECIDED TO STOP STINGER'S PLAN, BEFORE IT WAS TOO LATE.
BRING IT ON!

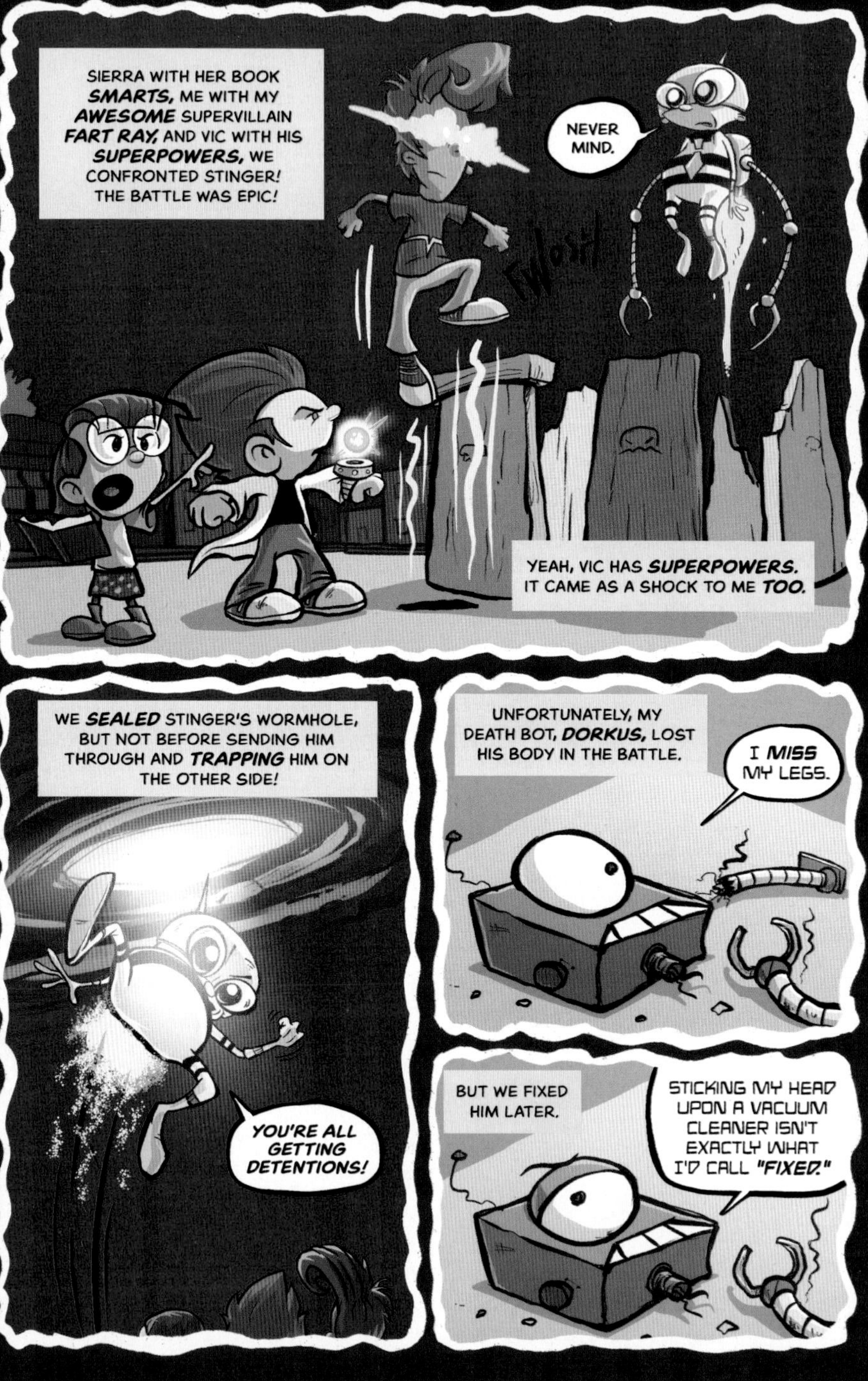

SIERRA WITH HER BOOK SMARTS, ME WITH MY AWESOME SUPERVILLAIN FART RAY, AND VIC WITH HIS SUPERPOWERS, WE CONFRONTED STINGER! THE BATTLE WAS EPIC!
NEVER MIND.
YEAH, VIC HAS SUPERPOWERS. IT CAME AS A SHOCK TO ME TOO.
WE SEALED STINGER'S WORMHOLE, BUT NOT BEFORE SENDING HIM THROUGH AND TRAPPING HIM ON THE OTHER SIDE!
YOU'RE ALL GETTING DETENTIONS!
UNFORTUNATELY, MY DEATH BOT, DORKUS, LOST HIS BODY IN THE BATTLE.
I MISS MY LEGS.
BUT WE FIXED HIM LATER.
STICKING MY HEAD UPON A VACUUM CLEANER ISN'T EXACTLY WHAT I'D CALL "FIXED."

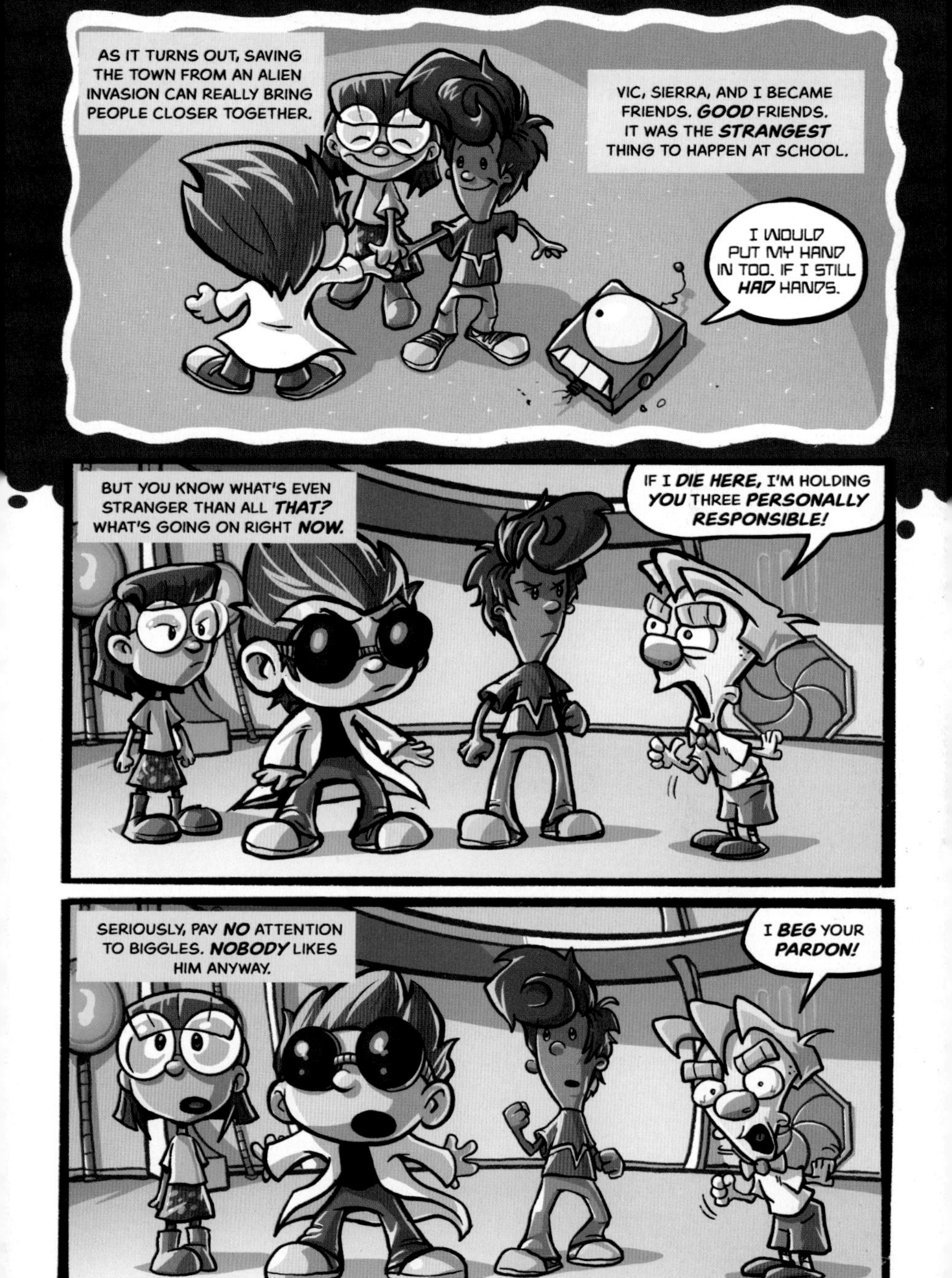
AS IT TURNS OUT, SAVING THE TOWN FROM AN ALIEN INVASION CAN REALLY BRING PEOPLE CLOSER TOGETHER.
VIC, SIERRA, AND I BECAME FRIENDS. **GOOD** FRIENDS. IT WAS THE **STRANGEST** THING TO HAPPEN AT SCHOOL.
I WOULD PUT MY HAND IN TOO. IF I STILL **HAD** HANDS.
BUT YOU KNOW WHAT'S EVEN STRANGER THAN ALL **THAT?** WHAT'S GOING ON RIGHT **NOW.**
IF I **DIE HERE,** I'M HOLDING **YOU** THREE **PERSONALLY RESPONSIBLE!**
SERIOUSLY, PAY **NO** ATTENTION TO BIGGLES. **NOBODY** LIKES HIM ANYWAY.
I **BEG** YOUR **PARDON!**

CHAPTER 1

Weird Science Fair

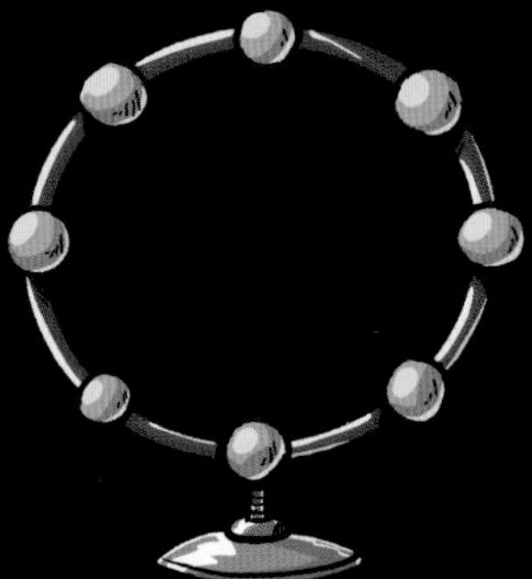

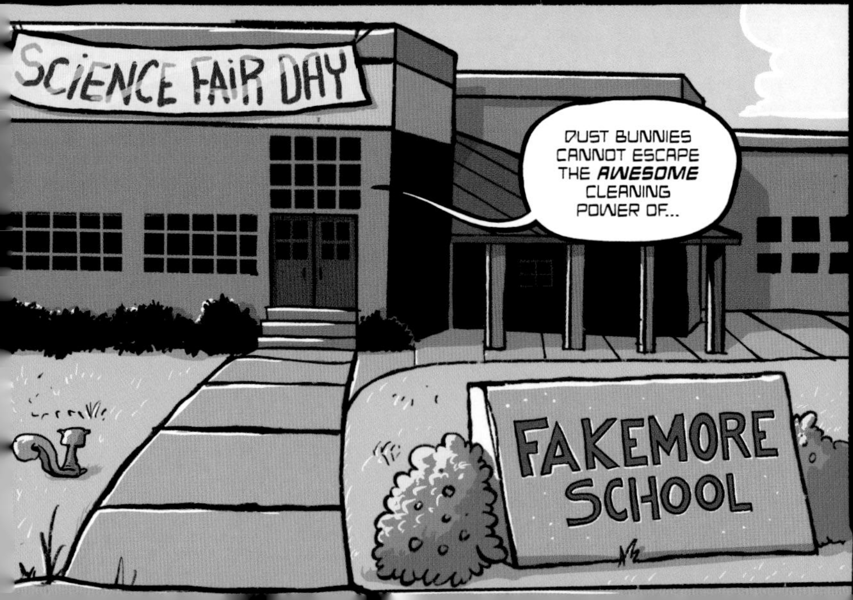
SCIENCE FAIR DAY
DUST BUNNIES CANNOT ESCAPE THE ***AWESOME*** CLEANING POWER OF...
FAKEMORE SCHOOL

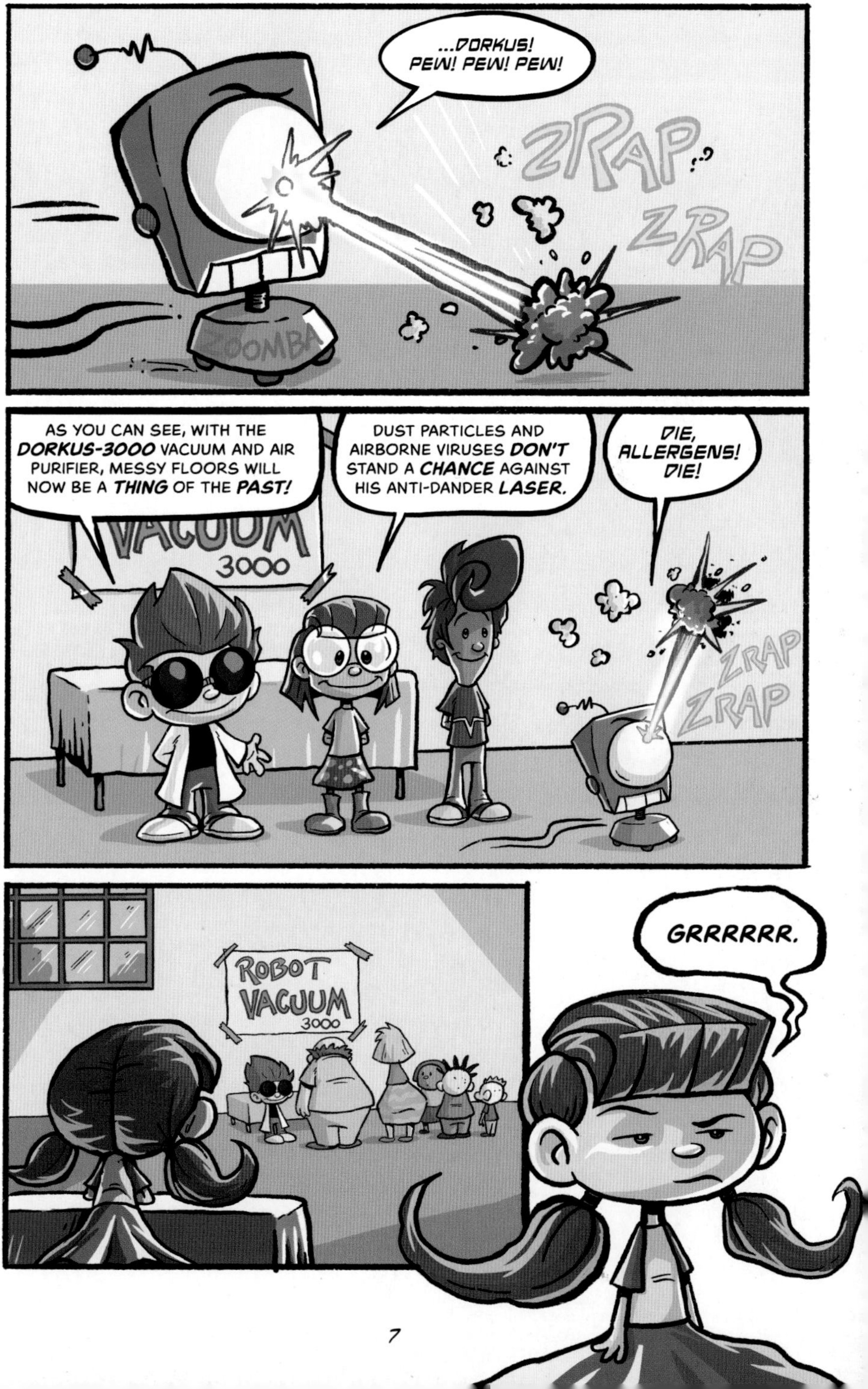
...DORKUS!
PEW! PEW! PEW!
ZRAP
ZRAP
ZOOMBA
AS YOU CAN SEE, WITH THE ***DORKUS-3000*** VACUUM AND AIR PURIFIER, MESSY FLOORS WILL NOW BE A ***THING*** OF THE ***PAST!***
DUST PARTICLES AND AIRBORNE VIRUSES ***DON'T*** STAND A ***CHANCE*** AGAINST HIS ANTI-DANDER ***LASER.***
DIE, ALLERGENS! DIE!
VACUUM
3000
ZRAP
ZRAP
ROBOT
VACUUM
3000
GRRRRRR.

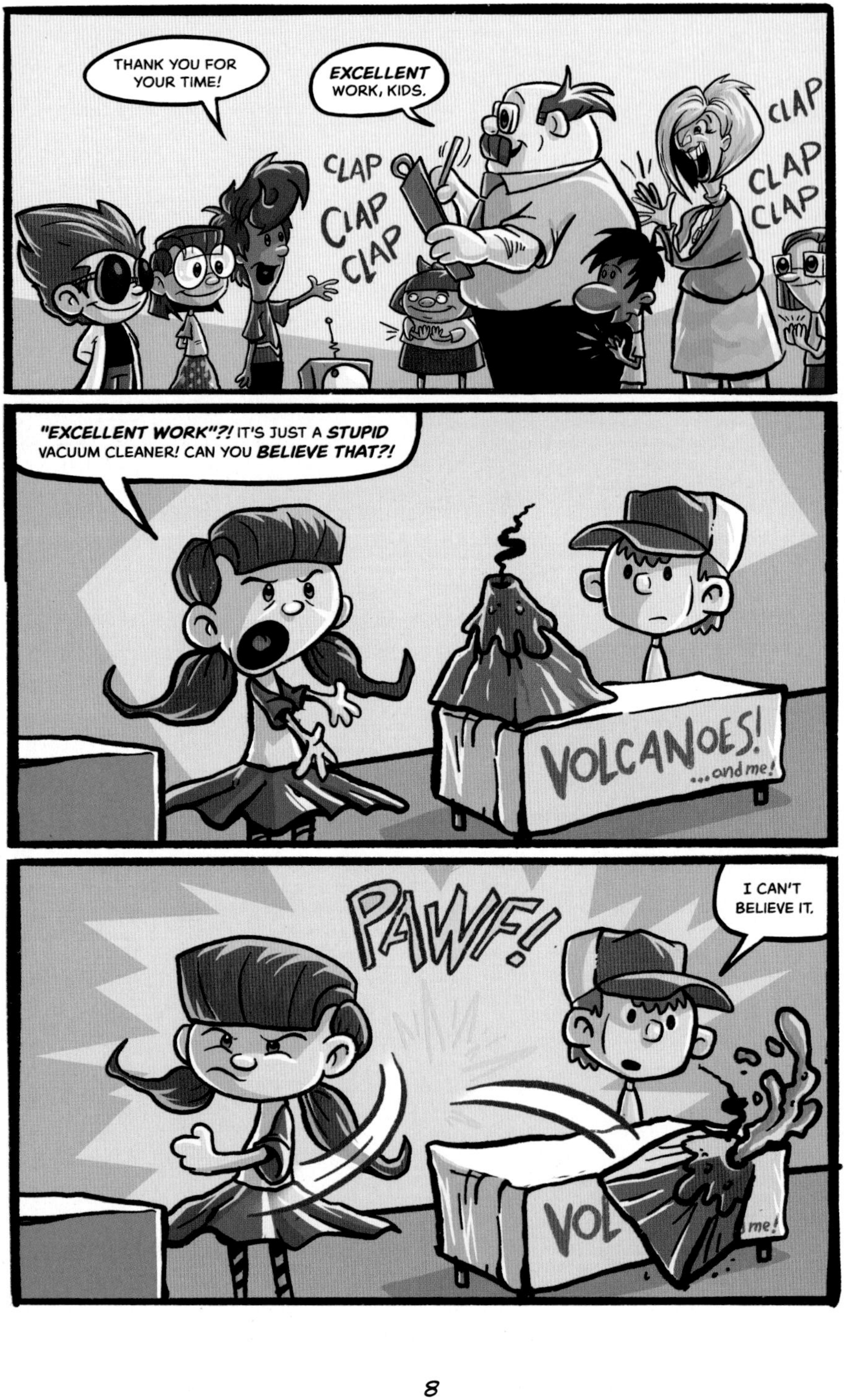
THANK YOU FOR YOUR TIME!
EXCELLENT WORK, KIDS.
CLAP CLAP CLAP
CLAP CLAP CLAP
"EXCELLENT WORK"?! IT'S JUST A STUPID VACUUM CLEANER! CAN YOU BELIEVE THAT?!
VOLCANOES! ...and me!
PAWF!
I CAN'T BELIEVE IT.
VOL
me!

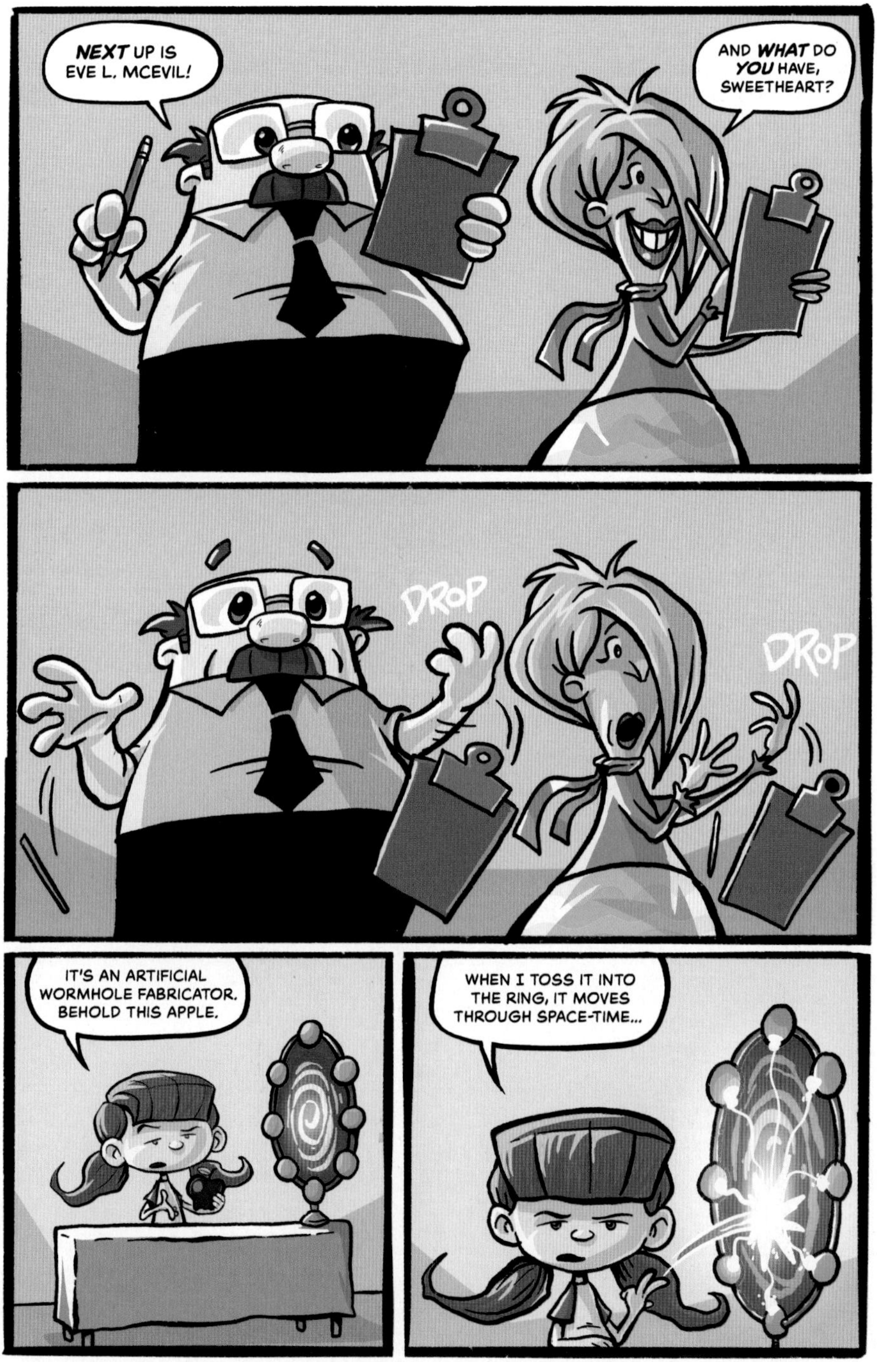
NEXT UP IS EVE L. MCEVIL!
AND WHAT DO YOU HAVE, SWEETHEART?
DROP
DROP
IT'S AN ARTIFICIAL WORMHOLE FABRICATOR. BEHOLD THIS APPLE.
WHEN I TOSS IT INTO THE RING, IT MOVES THROUGH SPACE-TIME...

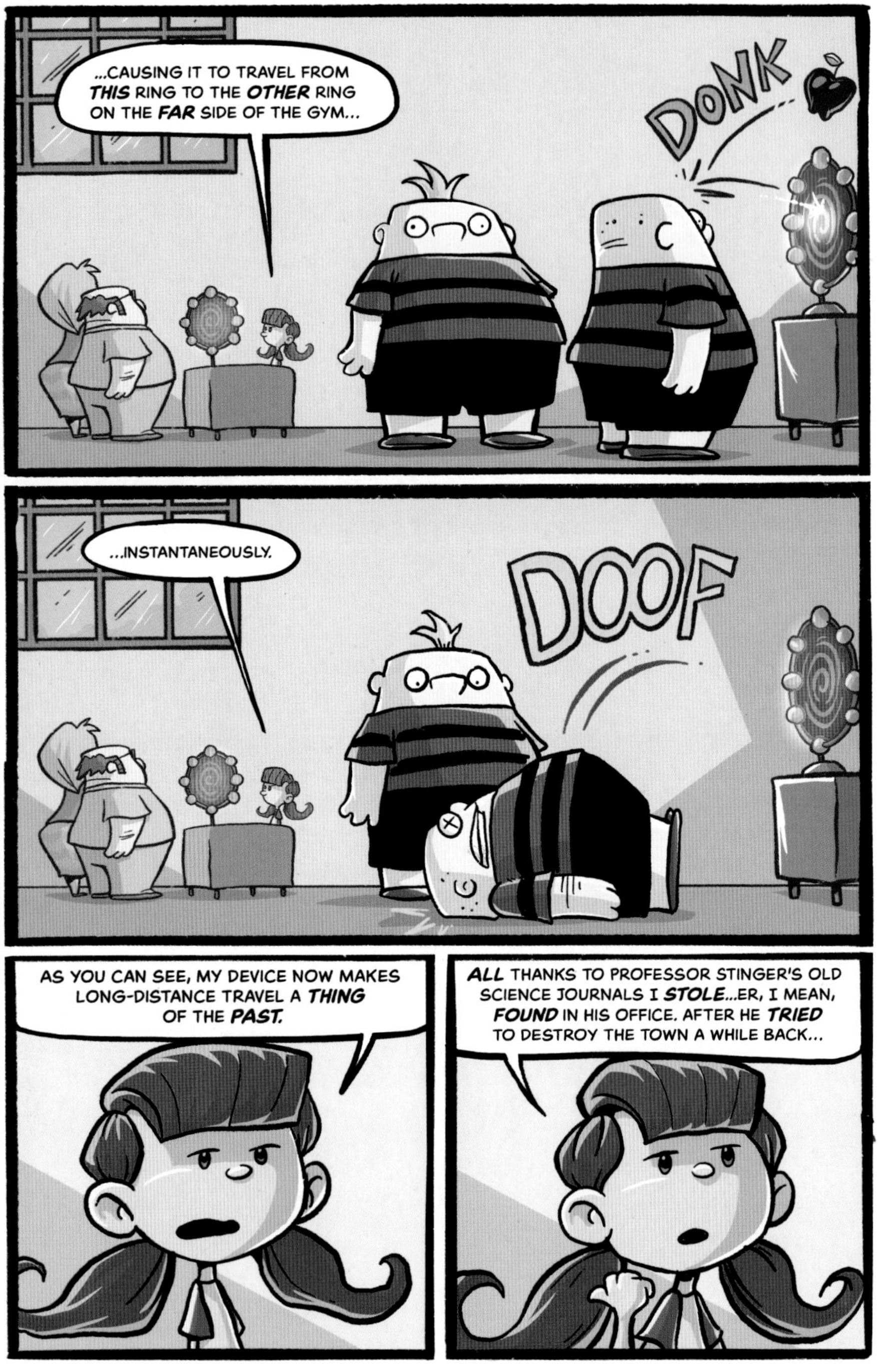
...CAUSING IT TO TRAVEL FROM THIS RING TO THE OTHER RING ON THE FAR SIDE OF THE GYM...
DONK
...INSTANTANEOUSLY.
DOOF
AS YOU CAN SEE, MY DEVICE NOW MAKES LONG-DISTANCE TRAVEL A THING OF THE PAST.
ALL THANKS TO PROFESSOR STINGER'S OLD SCIENCE JOURNALS I STOLE...ER, I MEAN, FOUND IN HIS OFFICE, AFTER HE TRIED TO DESTROY THE TOWN A WHILE BACK...

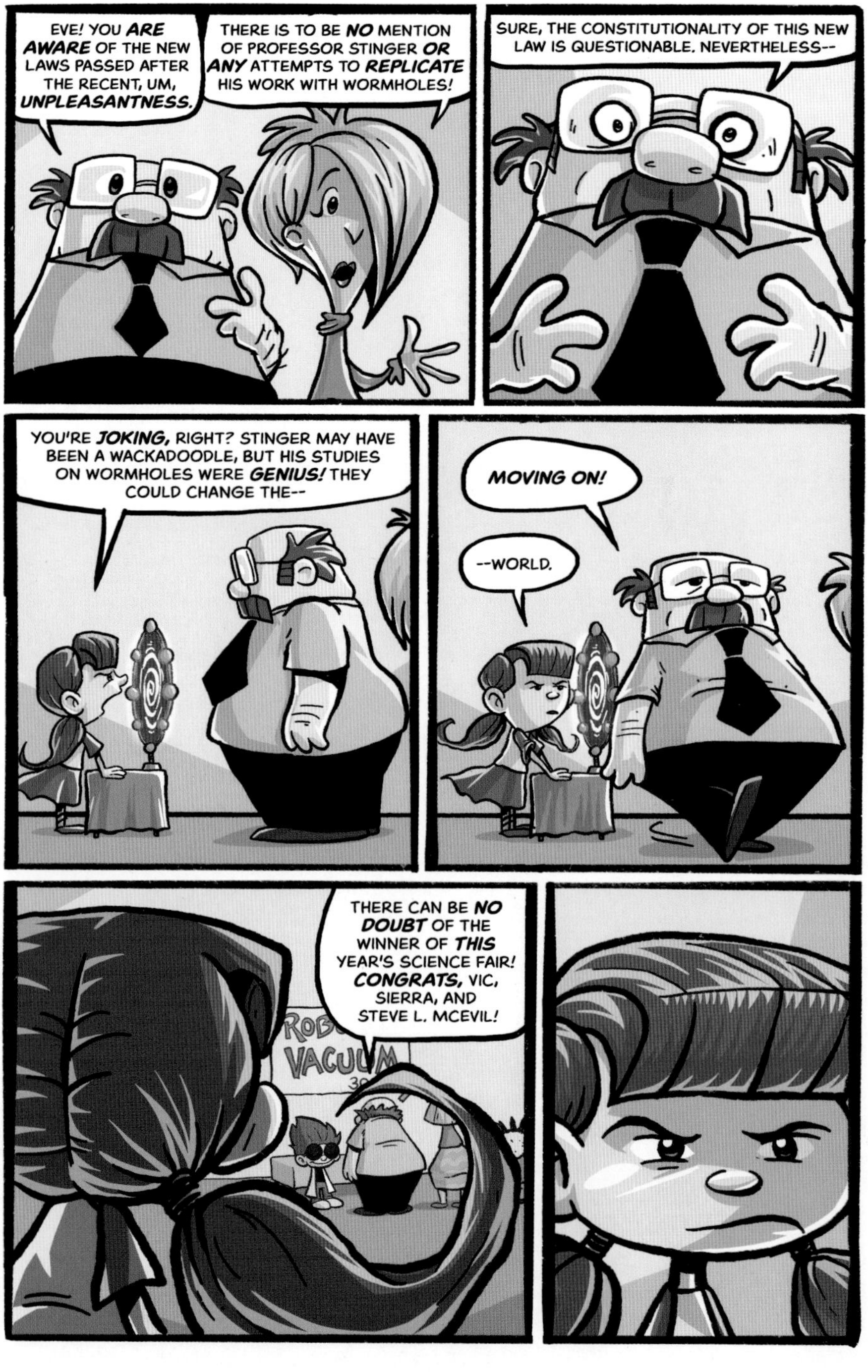
EVE! YOU ARE AWARE OF THE NEW LAWS PASSED AFTER THE RECENT, UM, UNPLEASANTNESS.
THERE IS TO BE NO MENTION OF PROFESSOR STINGER OR ANY ATTEMPTS TO REPLICATE HIS WORK WITH WORMHOLES!
SURE, THE CONSTITUTIONALITY OF THIS NEW LAW IS QUESTIONABLE. NEVERTHELESS--
YOU'RE JOKING, RIGHT? STINGER MAY HAVE BEEN A WACKADOODLE, BUT HIS STUDIES ON WORMHOLES WERE GENIUS! THEY COULD CHANGE THE--
MOVING ON!
--WORLD.
THERE CAN BE NO DOUBT OF THE WINNER OF THIS YEAR'S SCIENCE FAIR! CONGRATS, VIC, SIERRA, AND STEVE L. MCEVIL!

CHAPTER 2

Home Bittersweet Home

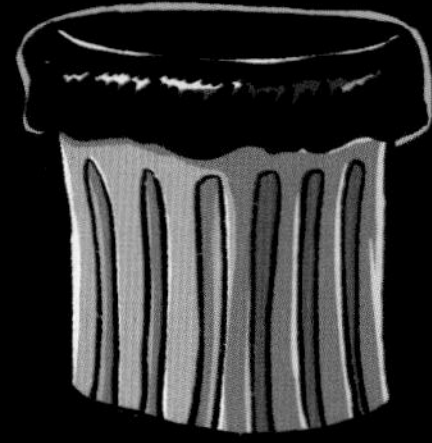

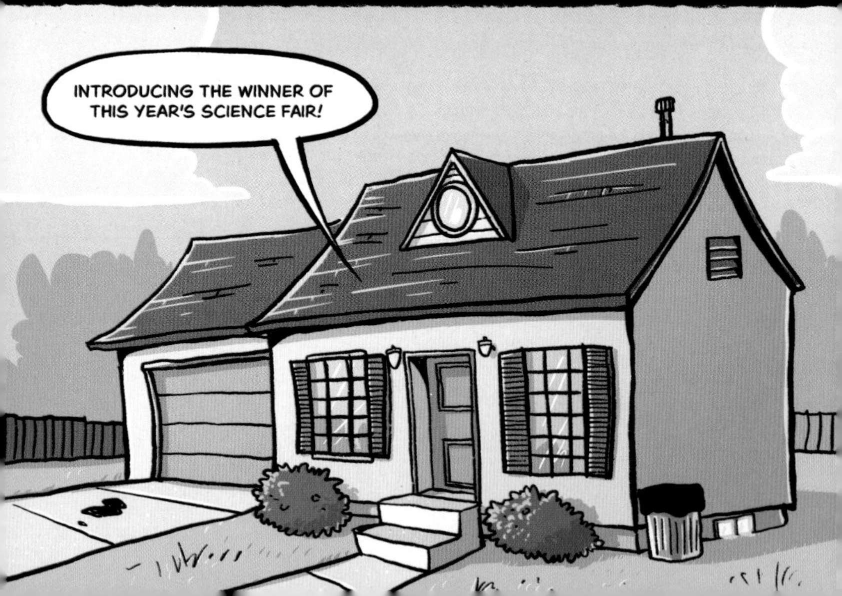
INTRODUCING THE WINNER OF THIS YEAR'S SCIENCE FAIR!

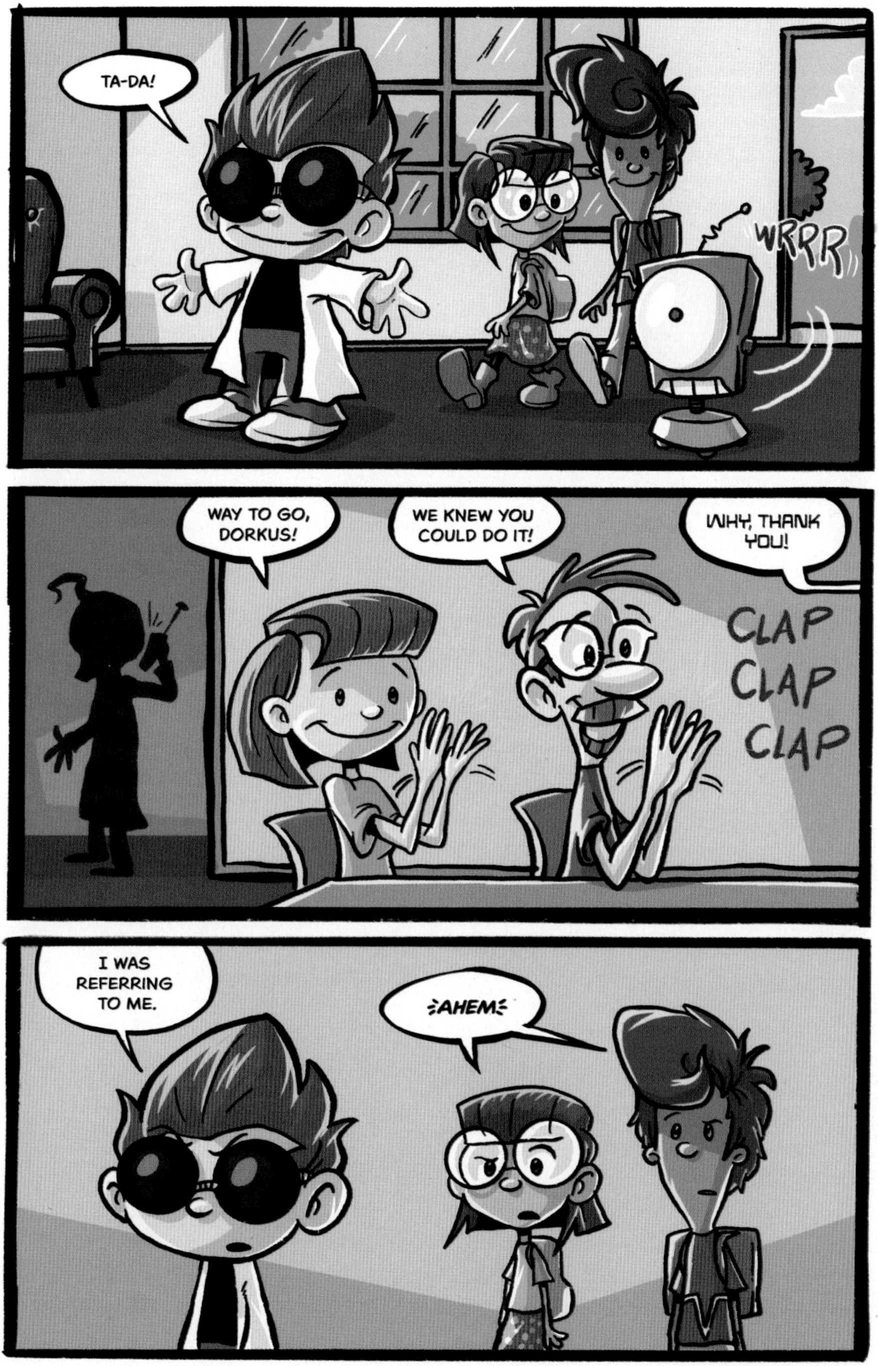
TA-DA!
WRRR
WAY TO GO, DORKUS!
WE KNEW YOU COULD DO IT!
WHY, THANK YOU!
CLAP CLAP CLAP
I WAS REFERRING TO ME.
AHEM

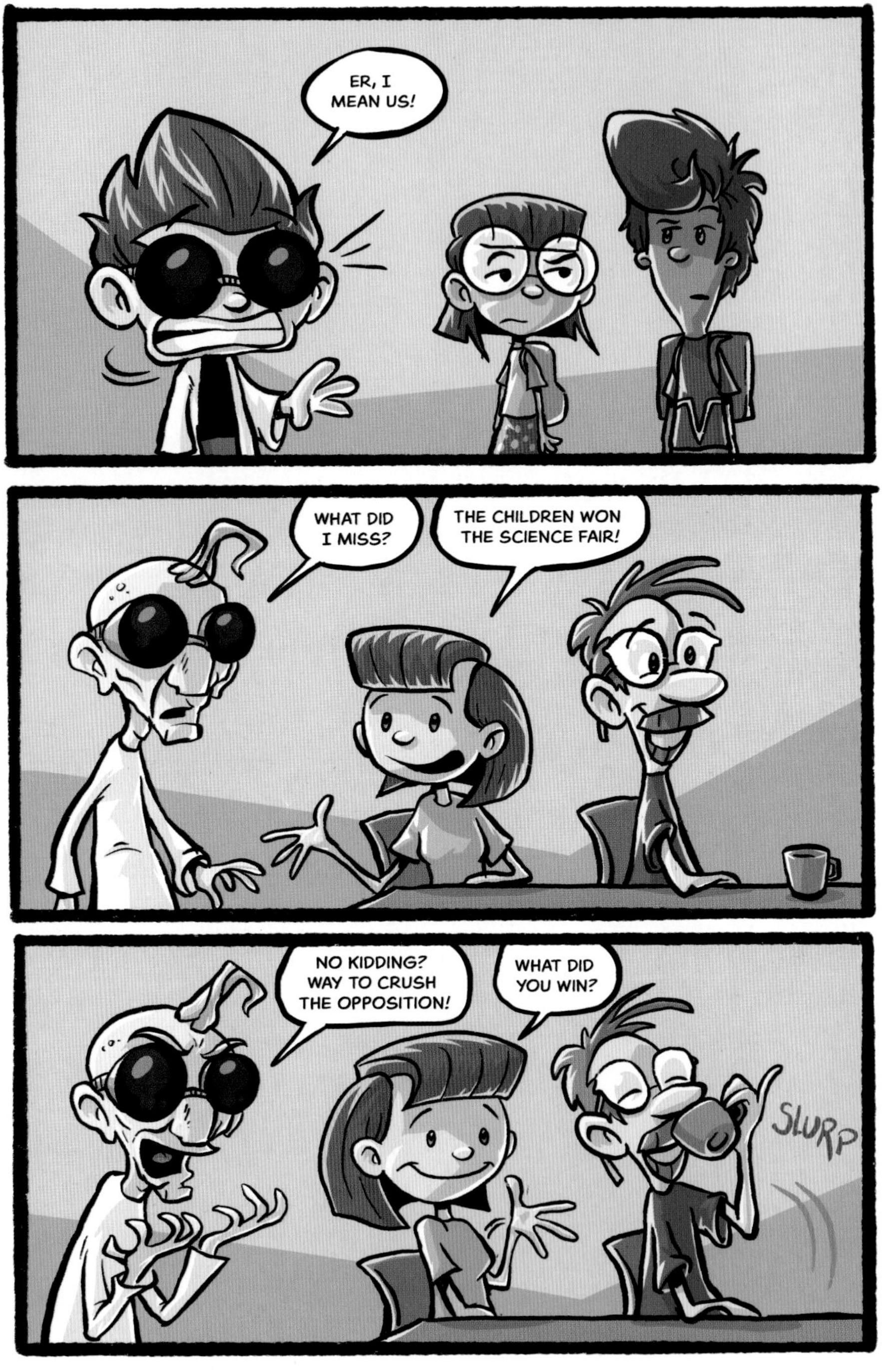
ER, I MEAN US!
WHAT DID I MISS?
THE CHILDREN WON THE SCIENCE FAIR!
NO KIDDING? WAY TO CRUSH THE OPPOSITION!
WHAT DID YOU WIN?
SLURP

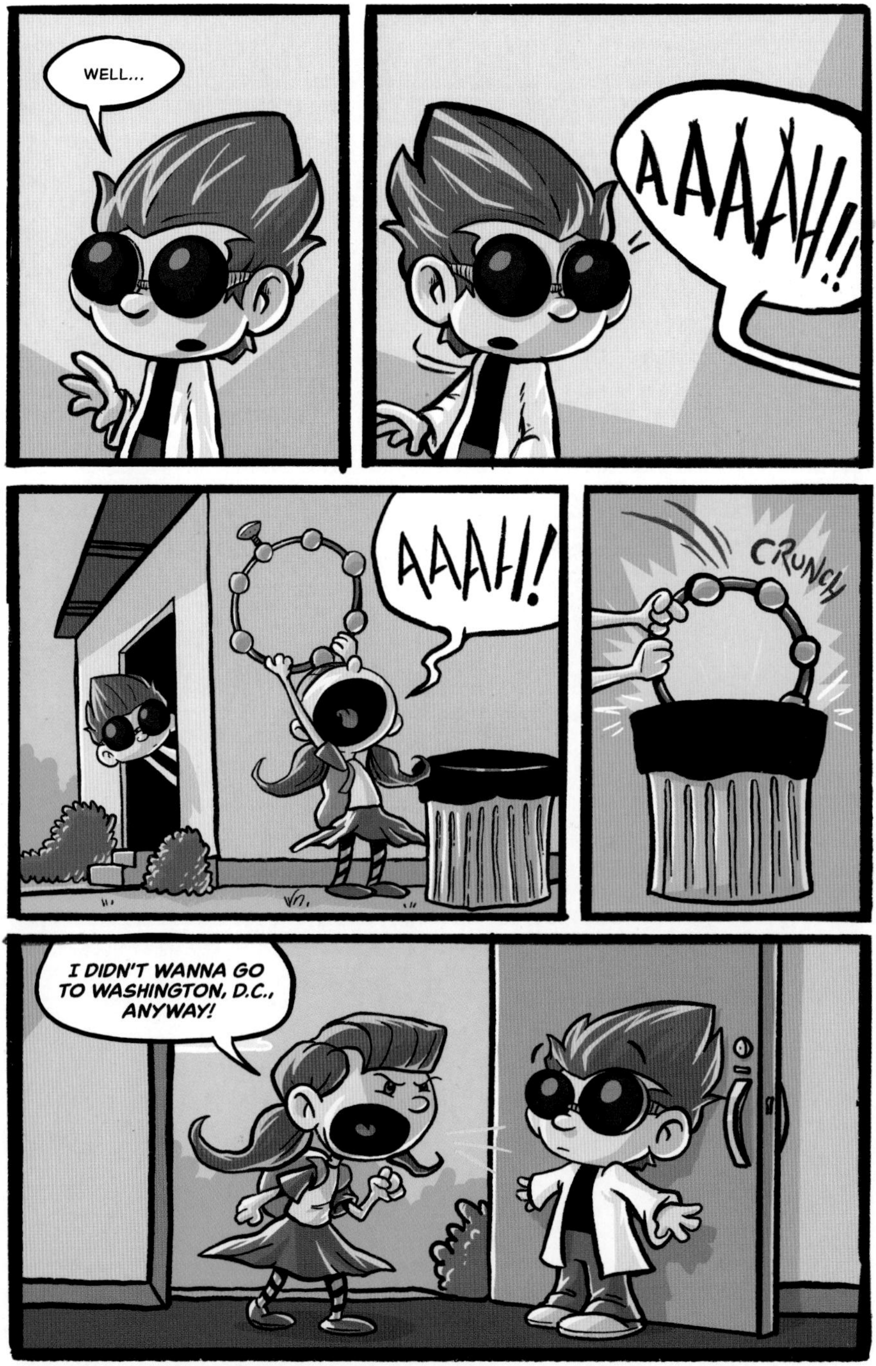
WELL...
AAAAH!!
AAAH!
CRUNCH
I DIDN'T WANNA GO TO WASHINGTON, D.C., ANYWAY!

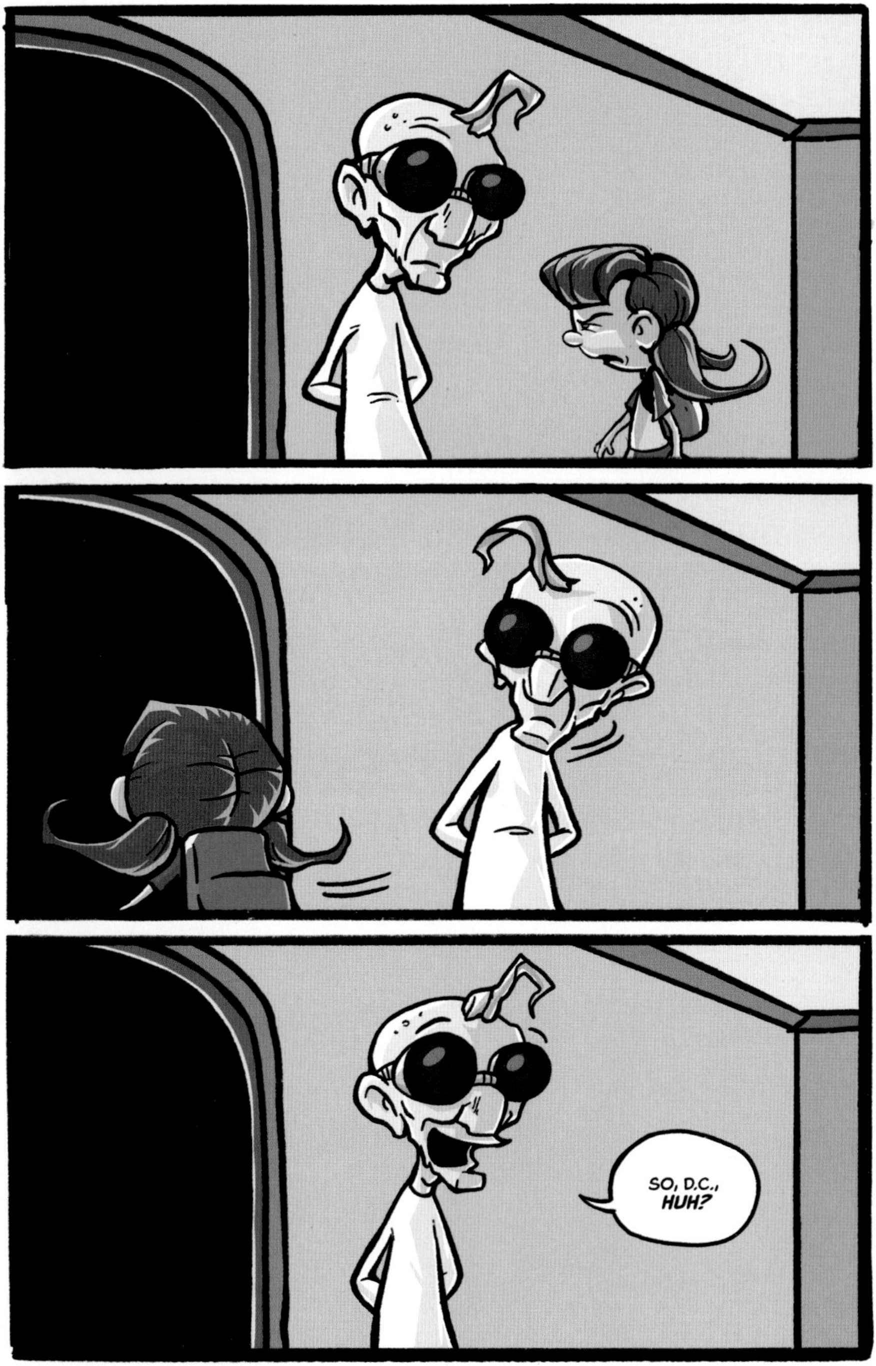
SO, D.C., HUH?

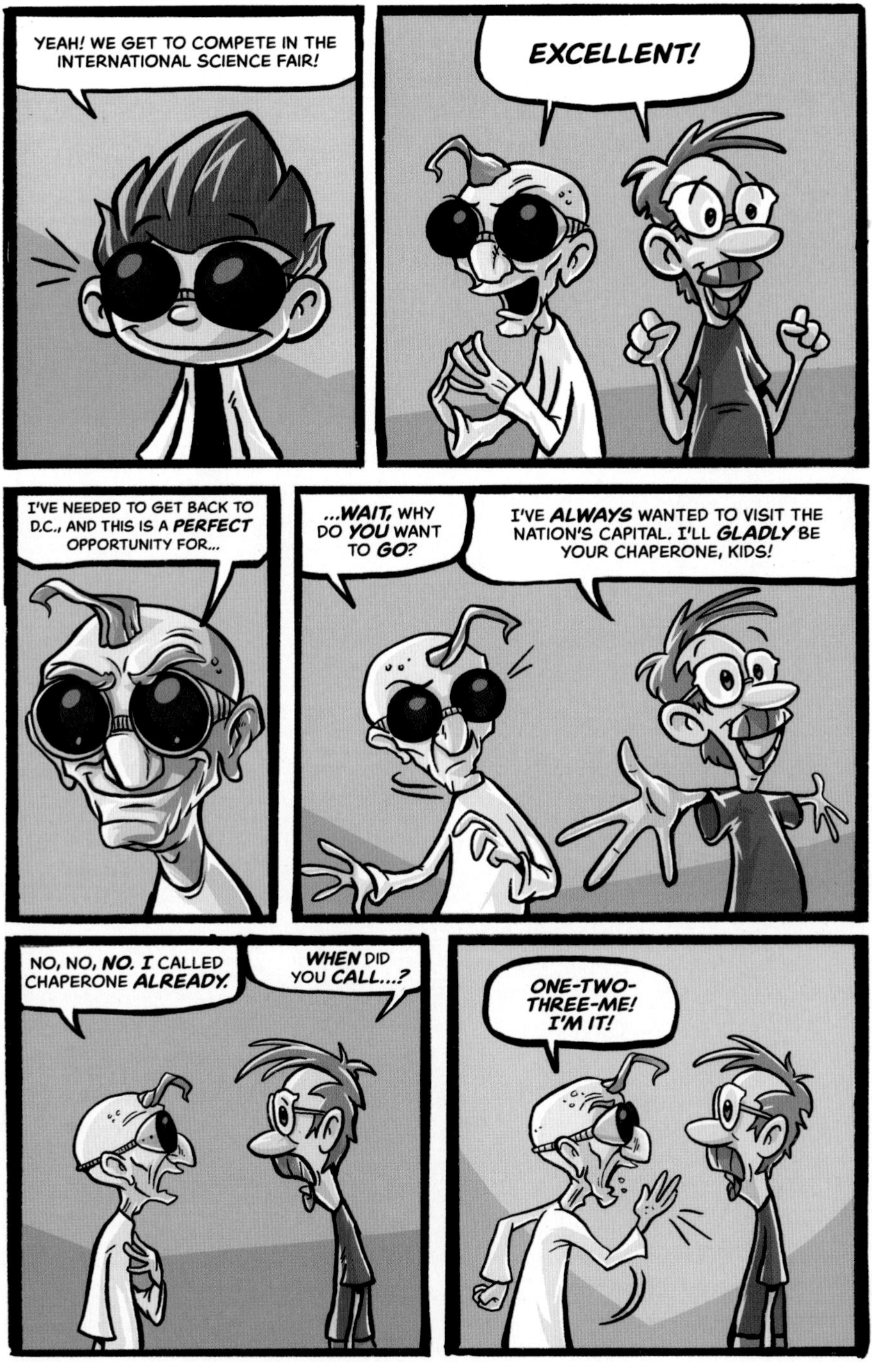
YEAH! WE GET TO COMPETE IN THE INTERNATIONAL SCIENCE FAIR!
EXCELLENT!
I'VE NEEDED TO GET BACK TO D.C., AND THIS IS A PERFECT OPPORTUNITY FOR...
...WAIT, WHY DO YOU WANT TO GO?
I'VE ALWAYS WANTED TO VISIT THE NATION'S CAPITAL. I'LL GLADLY BE YOUR CHAPERONE, KIDS!
NO, NO, NO. I CALLED CHAPERONE ALREADY.
WHEN DID YOU CALL...?
ONE-TWO-THREE-ME! I'M IT!

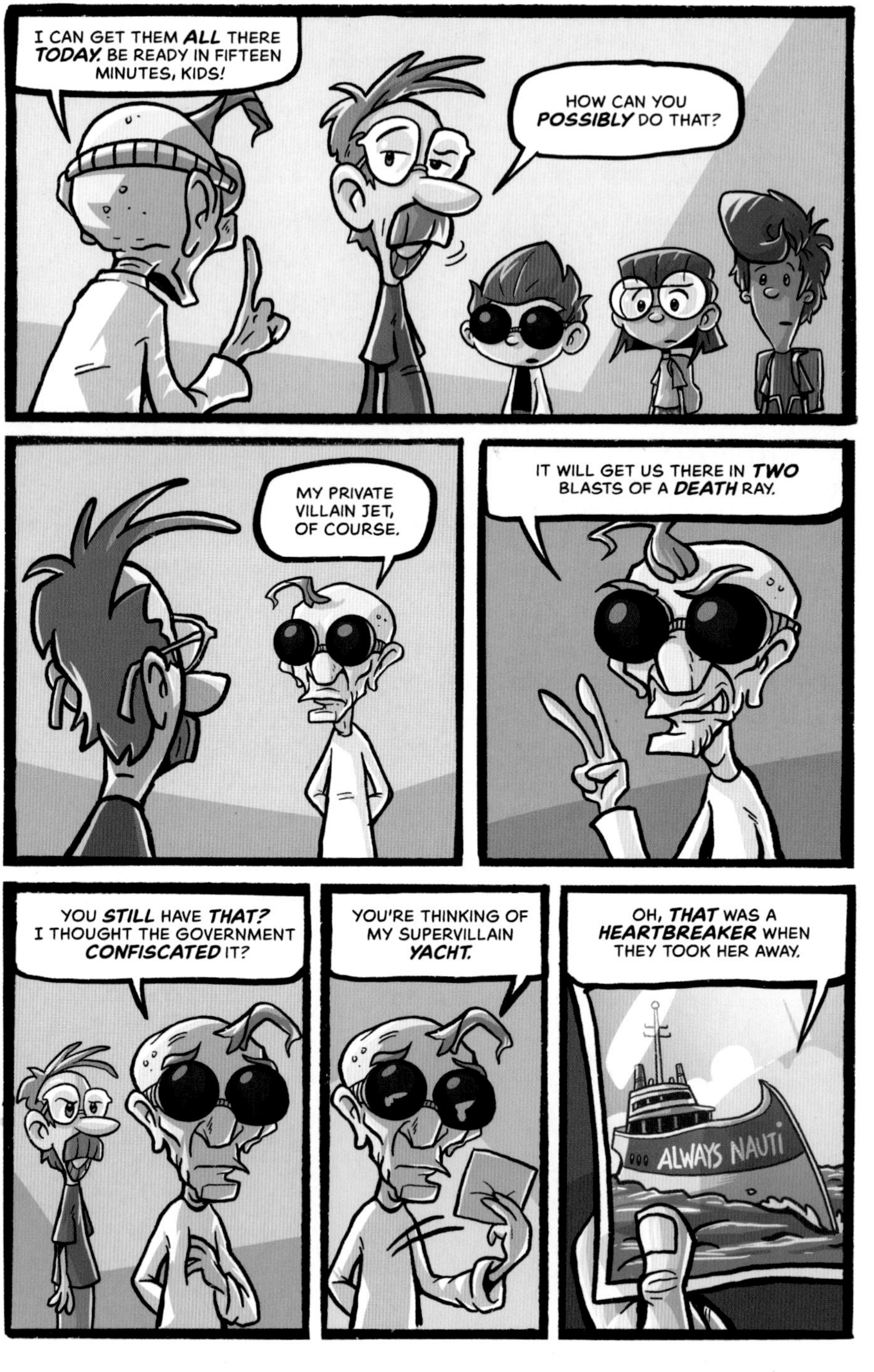

I CAN GET THEM ALL THERE TODAY. BE READY IN FIFTEEN MINUTES, KIDS!
HOW CAN YOU POSSIBLY DO THAT?
MY PRIVATE VILLAIN JET, OF COURSE.
IT WILL GET US THERE IN TWO BLASTS OF A DEATH RAY.
YOU STILL HAVE THAT? I THOUGHT THE GOVERNMENT CONFISCATED IT?
YOU'RE THINKING OF MY SUPERVILLAIN YACHT.
OH, THAT WAS A HEARTBREAKER WHEN THEY TOOK HER AWAY.
ALWAYS NAUTI

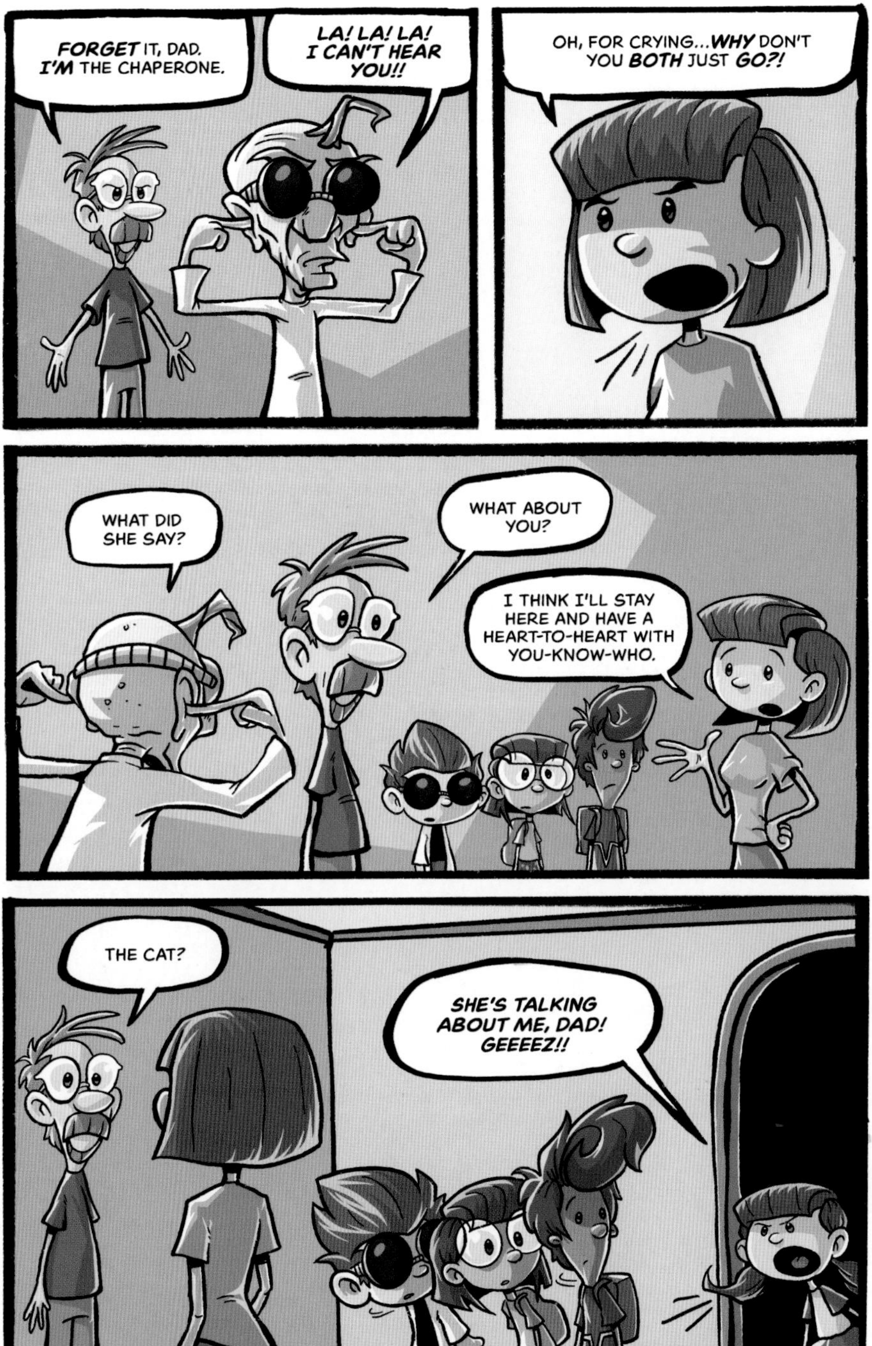
FORGET IT, DAD. I'M THE CHAPERONE.
LA! LA! LA! I CAN'T HEAR YOU!!
OH, FOR CRYING... WHY DON'T YOU BOTH JUST GO?!
WHAT DID SHE SAY?
WHAT ABOUT YOU?
I THINK I'LL STAY HERE AND HAVE A HEART-TO-HEART WITH YOU-KNOW-WHO.
THE CAT?
SHE'S TALKING ABOUT ME, DAD! GEEEEZ!!

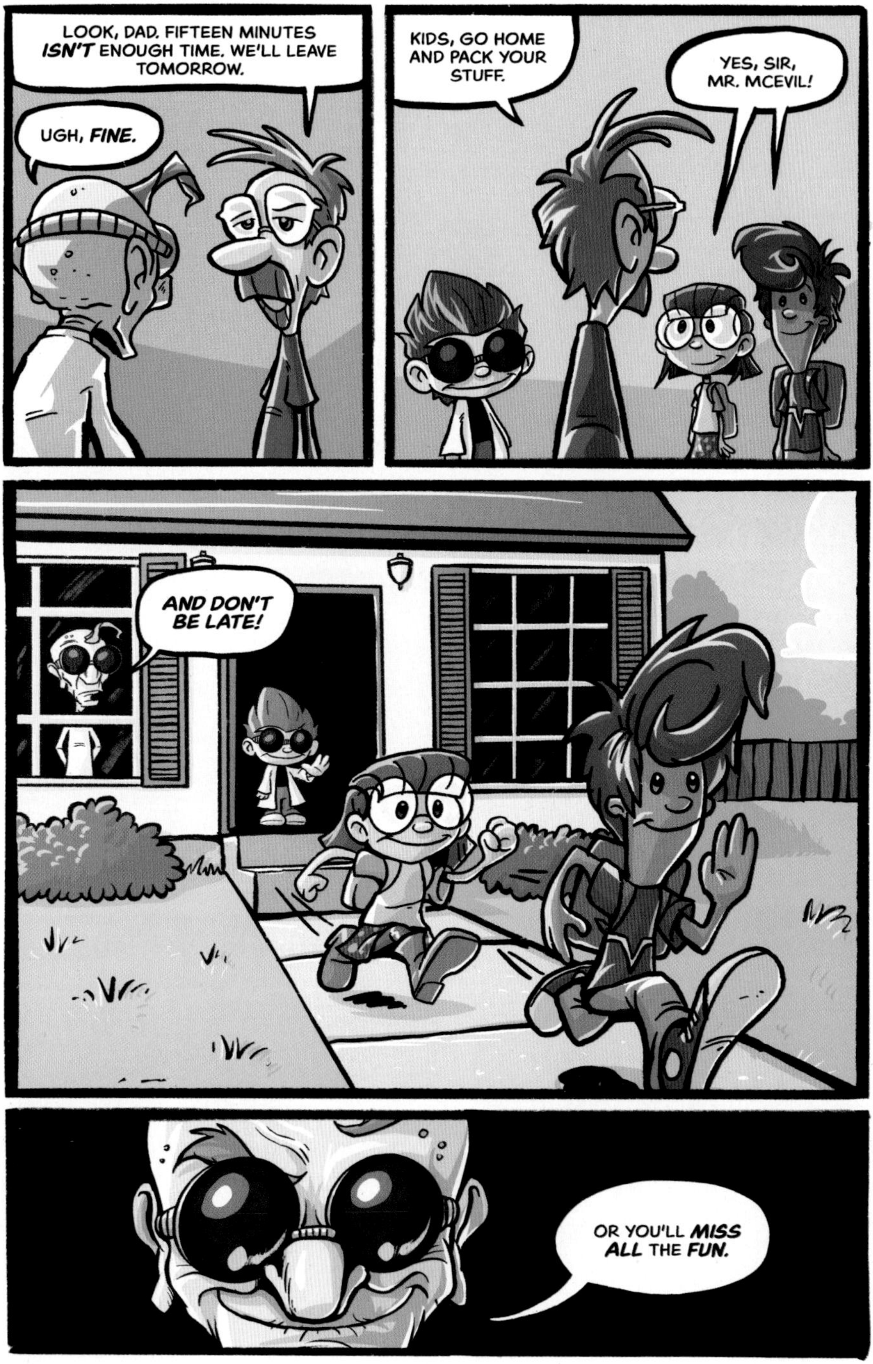
LOOK, DAD. FIFTEEN MINUTES ISN'T ENOUGH TIME. WE'LL LEAVE TOMORROW.
UGH, FINE.
KIDS, GO HOME AND PACK YOUR STUFF.
YES, SIR, MR. MCEVIL!
AND DON'T BE LATE!
OR YOU'LL MISS ALL THE FUN.

CHAPTER 3

You've Lost That Love of Stealing

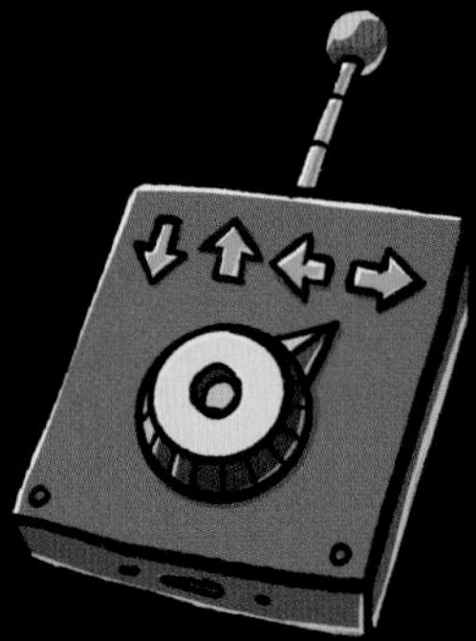

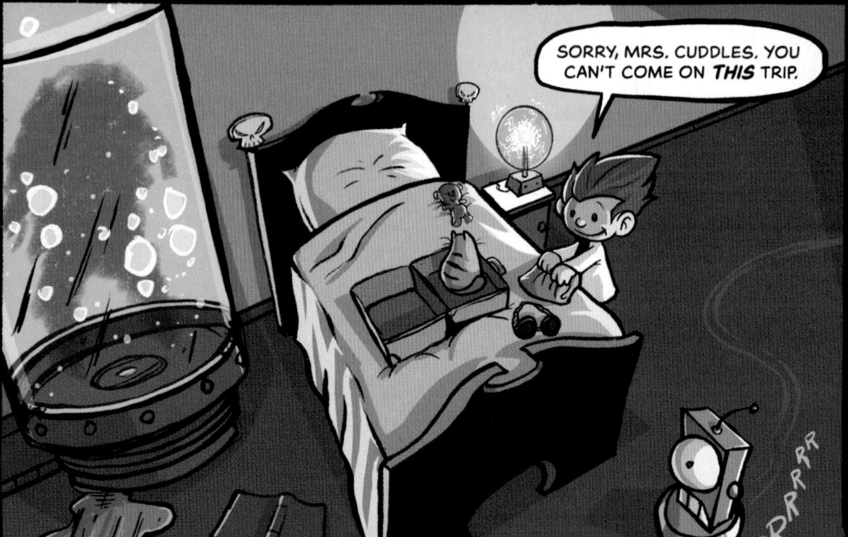

SORRY, MRS. CUDDLES. YOU CAN'T COME ON *THIS* TRIP.
WRRRRRRR

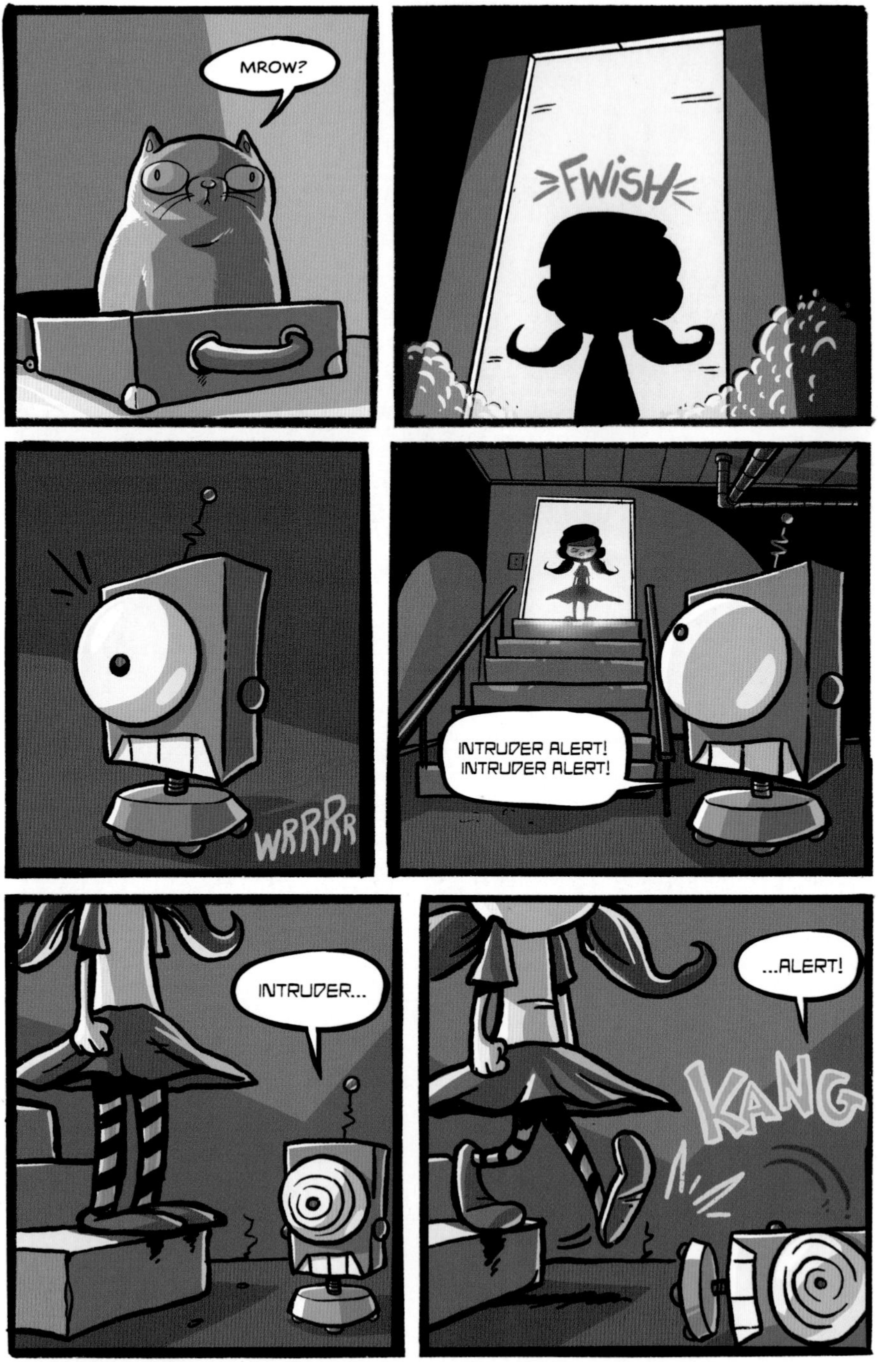
MROW?
FWISH
WRRRR
INTRUDER ALERT!
INTRUDER ALERT!
INTRUDER...
...ALERT!
KANG

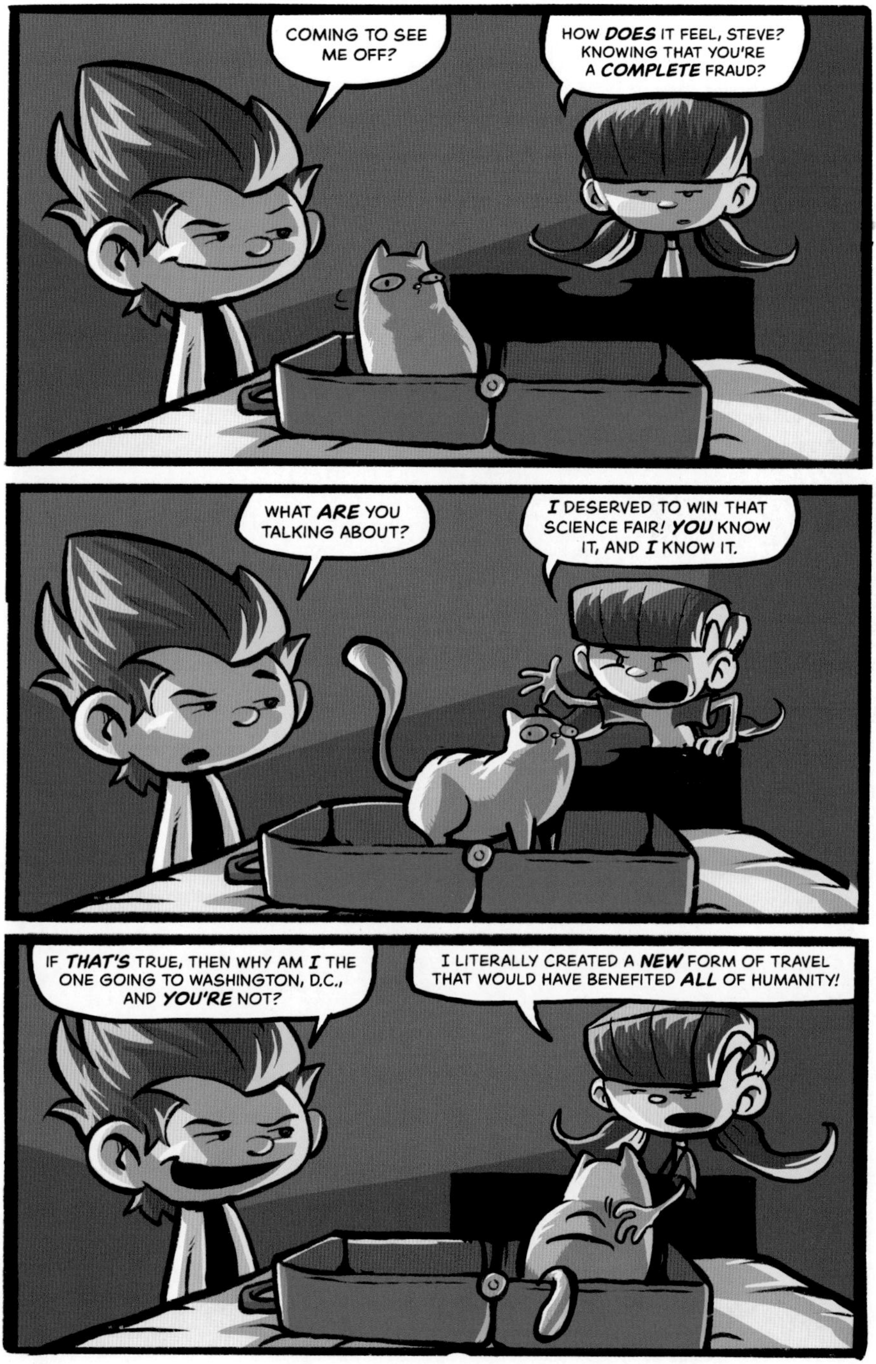
COMING TO SEE ME OFF?
HOW *DOES* IT FEEL, STEVE? KNOWING THAT YOU'RE A *COMPLETE* FRAUD?
WHAT *ARE* YOU TALKING ABOUT?
I DESERVED TO WIN THAT SCIENCE FAIR! *YOU* KNOW IT, AND *I* KNOW IT.
IF *THAT'S* TRUE, THEN WHY AM *I* THE ONE GOING TO WASHINGTON, D.C., AND *YOU'RE* NOT?
I LITERALLY CREATED A *NEW* FORM OF TRAVEL THAT WOULD HAVE BENEFITED *ALL* OF HUMANITY!

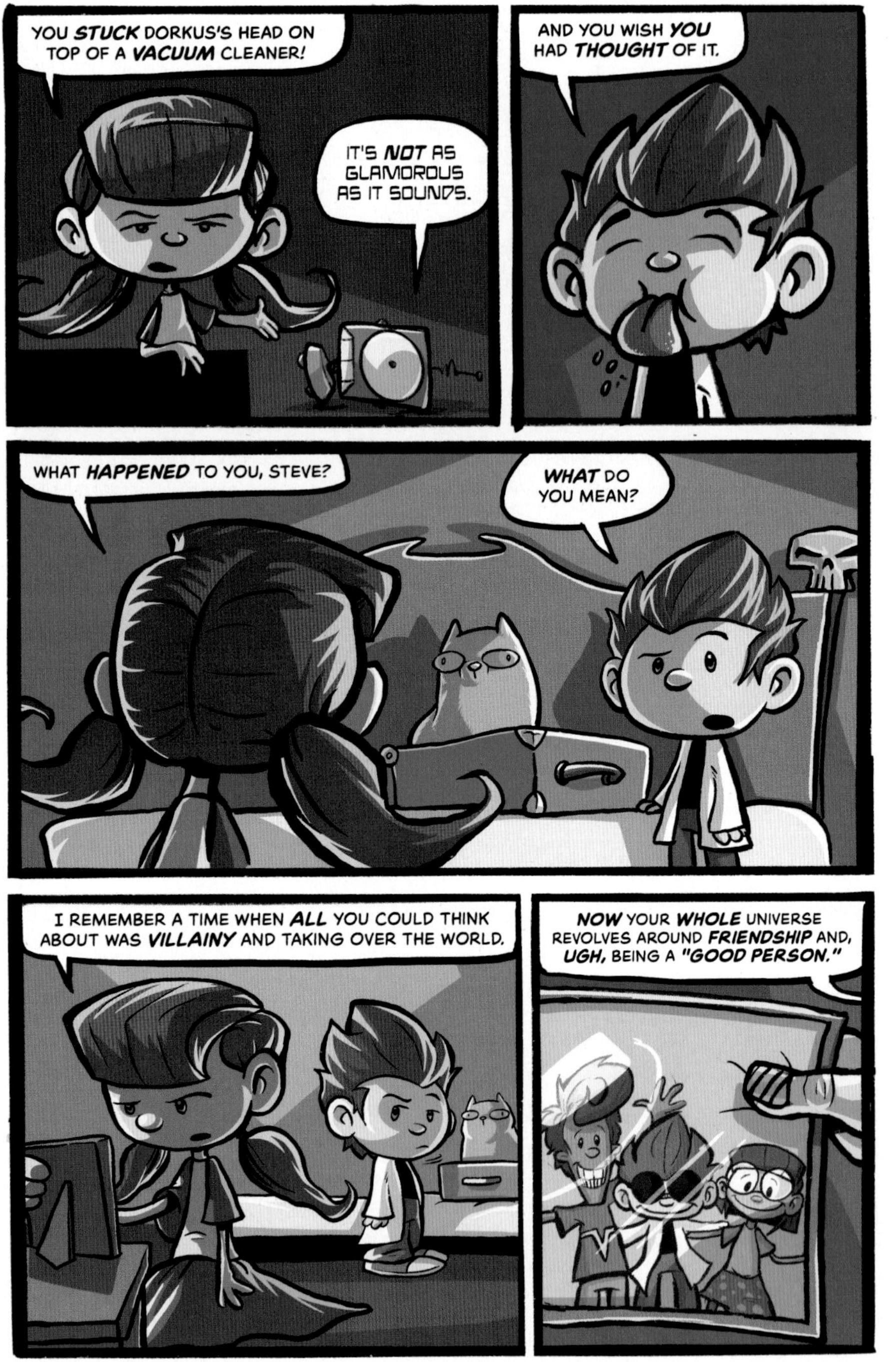

YOU **STUCK** DORKUS'S HEAD ON TOP OF A **VACUUM** CLEANER!
IT'S **NOT** AS GLAMOROUS AS IT SOUNDS.
AND YOU WISH **YOU** HAD **THOUGHT** OF IT.
WHAT **HAPPENED** TO YOU, STEVE?
WHAT DO YOU MEAN?
I REMEMBER A TIME WHEN **ALL** YOU COULD THINK ABOUT WAS **VILLAINY** AND TAKING OVER THE WORLD.
NOW YOUR **WHOLE** UNIVERSE REVOLVES AROUND **FRIENDSHIP** AND, **UGH,** BEING A **"GOOD PERSON."**

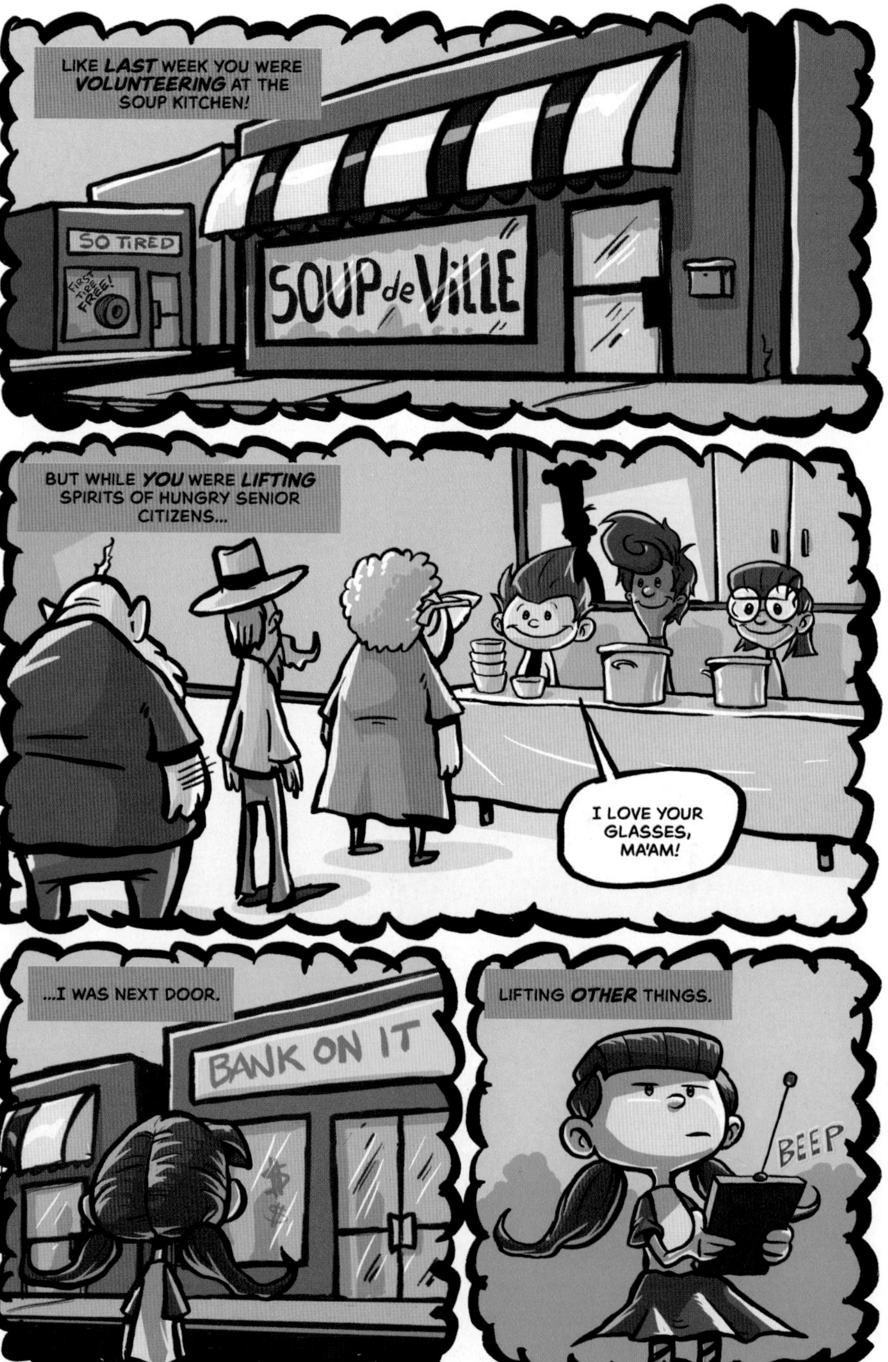
LIKE LAST WEEK YOU WERE VOLUNTEERING AT THE SOUP KITCHEN!
SO TIRED
FIRST TIRE FREE!
SOUP de VILLE
BUT WHILE YOU WERE LIFTING SPIRITS OF HUNGRY SENIOR CITIZENS...
I LOVE YOUR GLASSES, MA'AM!
...I WAS NEXT DOOR.
BANK ON IT
LIFTING OTHER THINGS.
BEEP

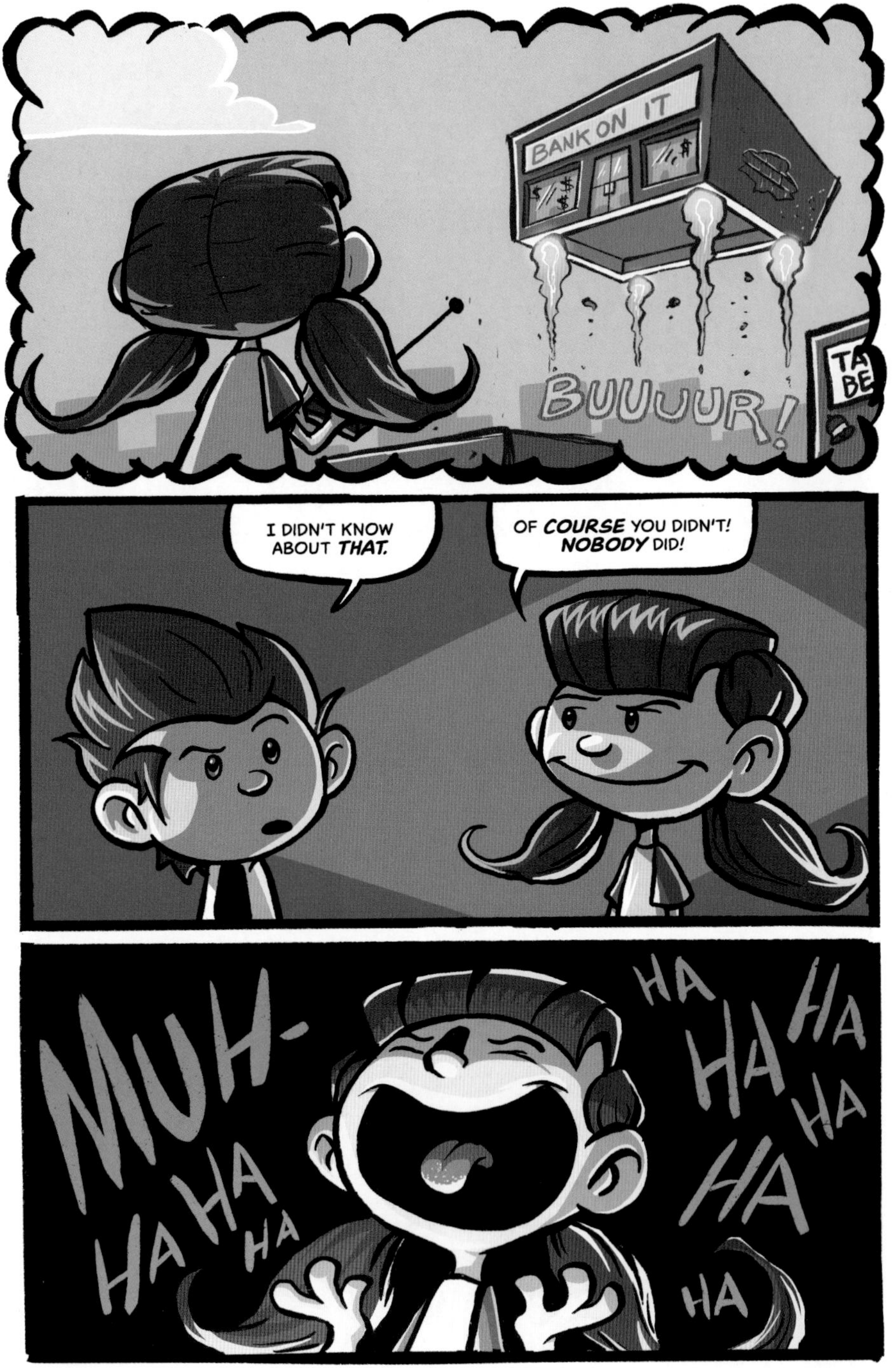
BANK ON IT
BUUUUR!
I DIDN'T KNOW ABOUT *THAT.*
OF ***COURSE*** YOU DIDN'T! ***NOBODY*** DID!
MUH-HA HA HA HA
HA HA HA HA HA HA

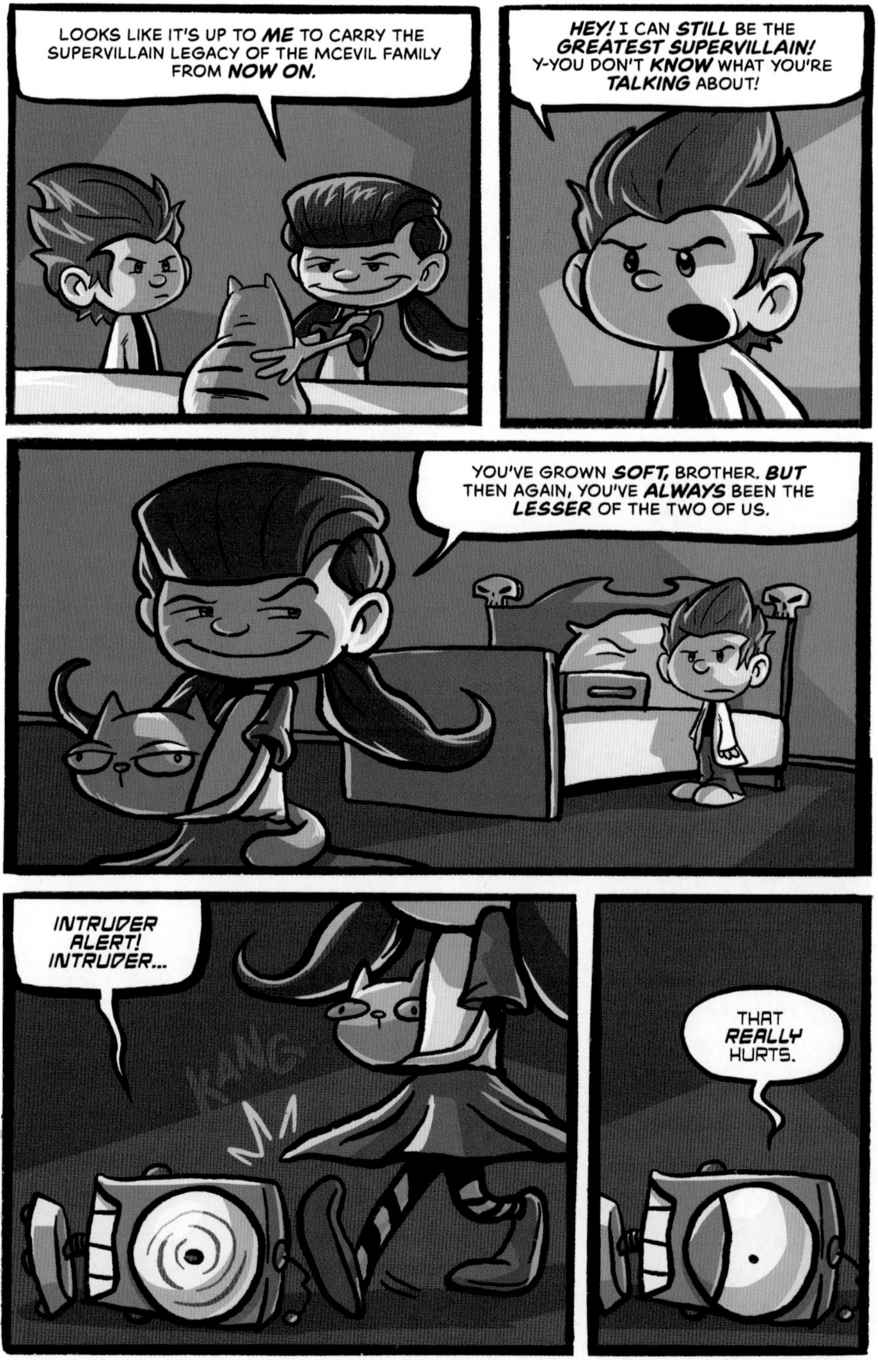
LOOKS LIKE IT'S UP TO **ME** TO CARRY THE SUPERVILLAIN LEGACY OF THE MCEVIL FAMILY FROM **NOW ON.**
HEY! I CAN **STILL** BE THE **GREATEST SUPERVILLAIN!** Y-YOU DON'T **KNOW** WHAT YOU'RE **TALKING** ABOUT!
YOU'VE GROWN **SOFT,** BROTHER. **BUT** THEN AGAIN, YOU'VE **ALWAYS** BEEN THE **LESSER** OF THE TWO OF US.
INTRUDER ALERT! INTRUDER...
KANG
THAT **REALLY** HURTS.

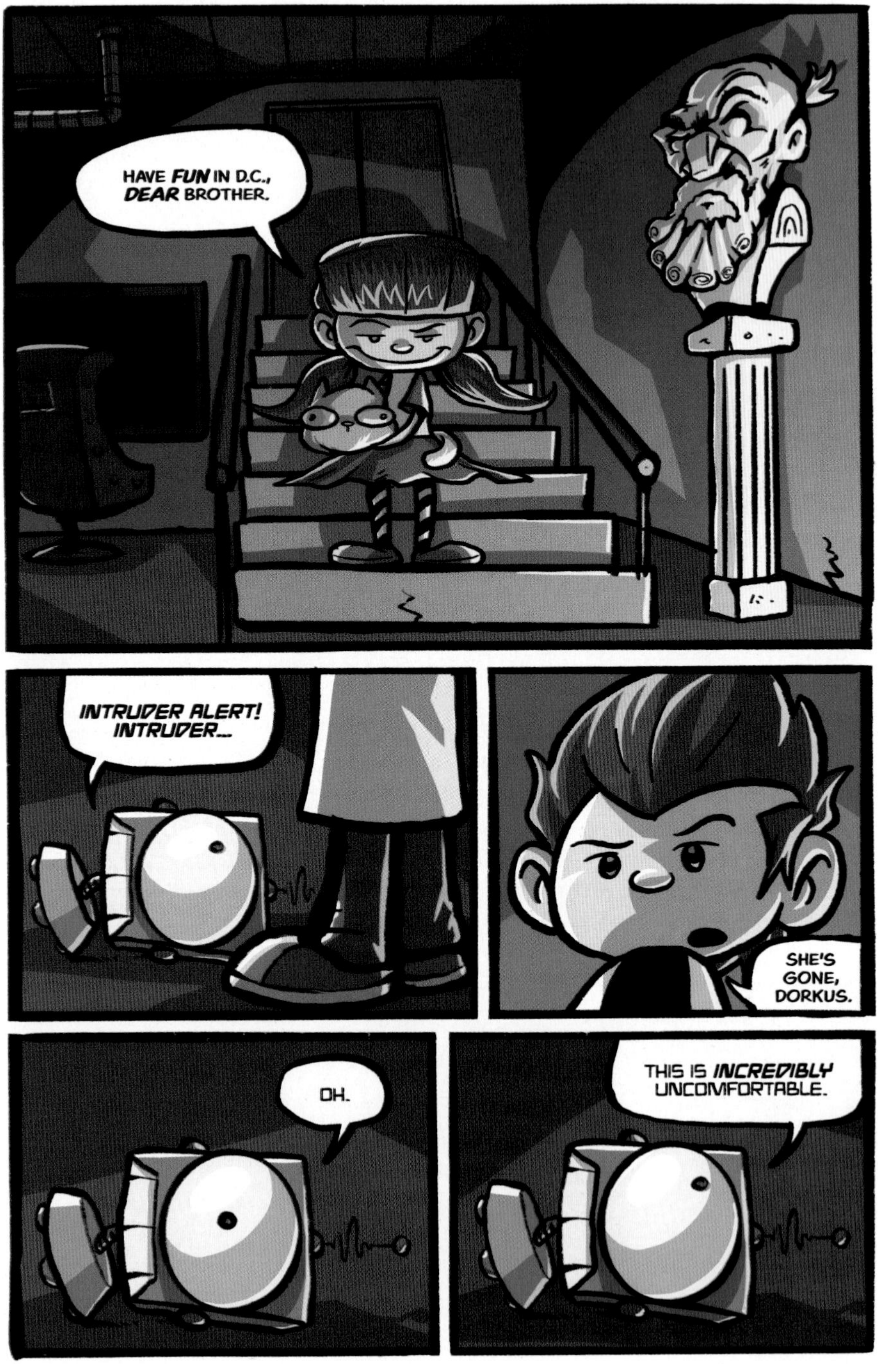
HAVE FUN IN D.C., DEAR BROTHER.
INTRUDER ALERT! INTRUDER...
SHE'S GONE, DORKUS.
OH.
THIS IS INCREDIBLY UNCOMFORTABLE.

CHAPTER 4

Family Matters

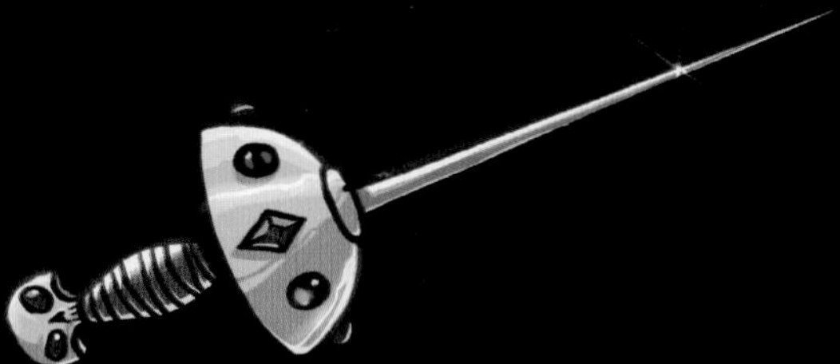

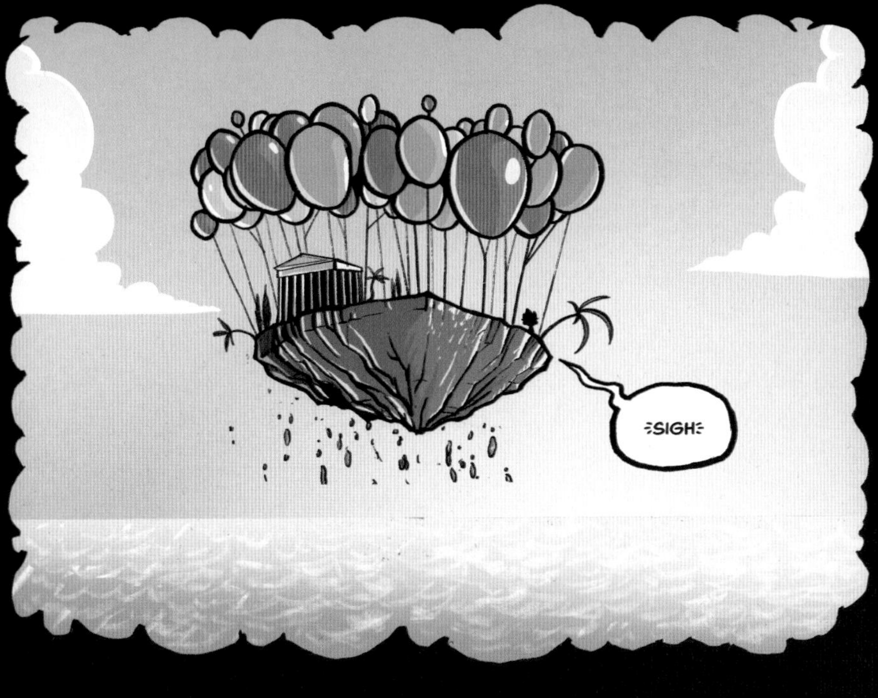
SIGH

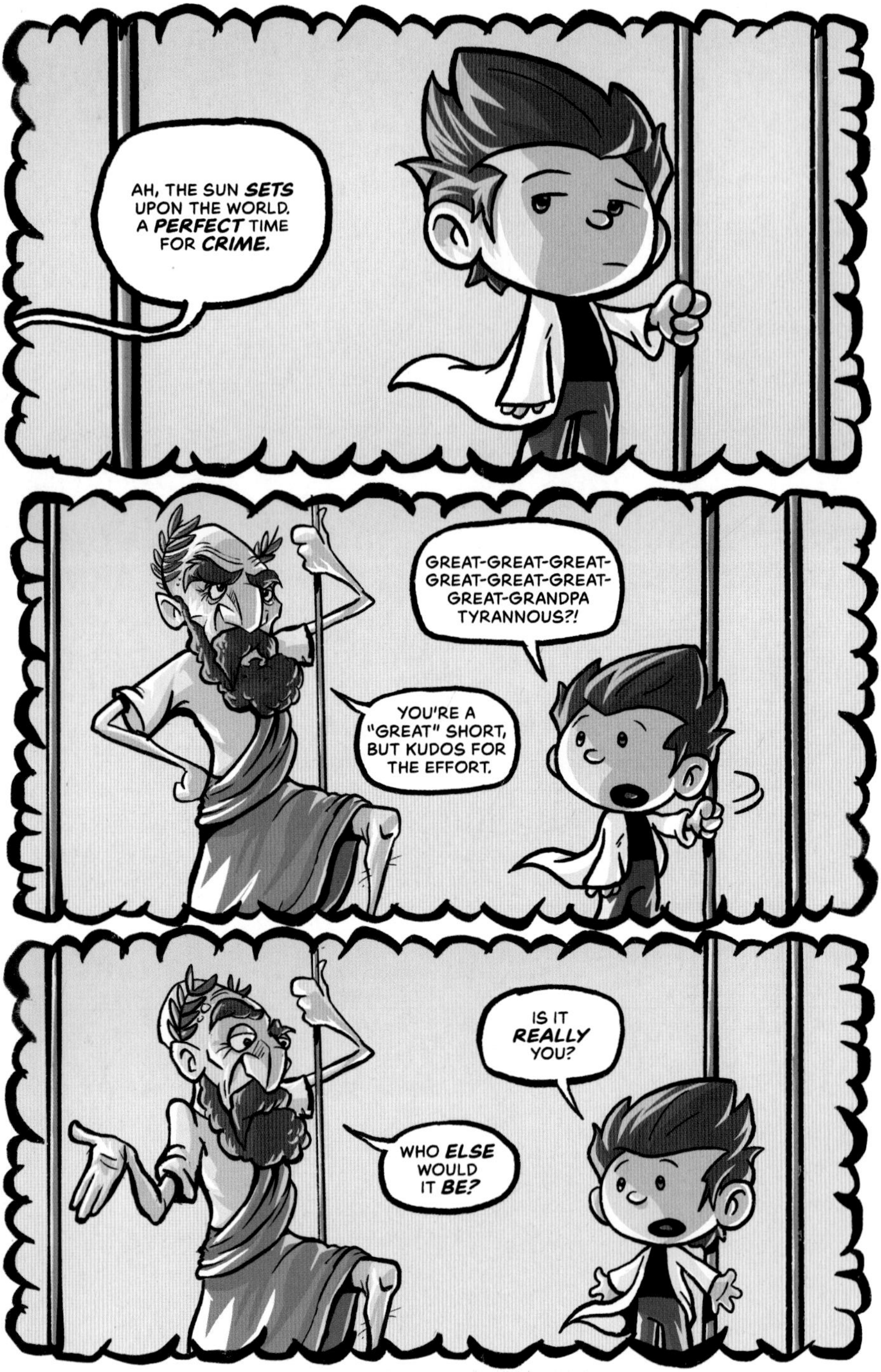
AH, THE SUN SETS UPON THE WORLD. A PERFECT TIME FOR CRIME.
GREAT-GREAT-GREAT-GREAT-GREAT-GREAT-GREAT-GRANDPA TYRANNOUS?!
YOU'RE A "GREAT" SHORT, BUT KUDOS FOR THE EFFORT.
IS IT REALLY YOU?
WHO ELSE WOULD IT BE?

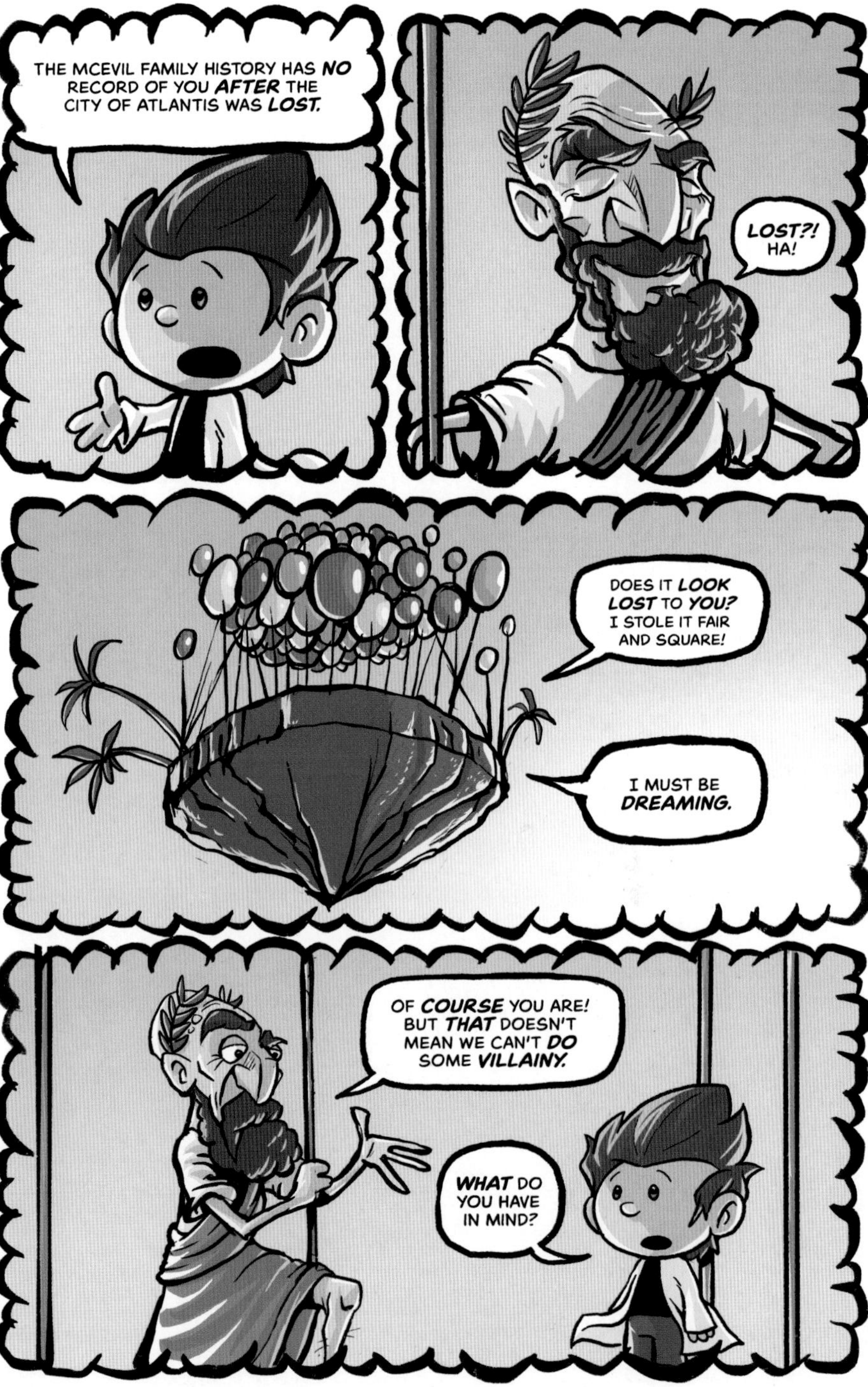
THE MCEVIL FAMILY HISTORY HAS NO RECORD OF YOU AFTER THE CITY OF ATLANTIS WAS LOST.
LOST?! HA!
DOES IT LOOK LOST TO YOU? I STOLE IT FAIR AND SQUARE!
I MUST BE DREAMING.
OF COURSE YOU ARE! BUT THAT DOESN'T MEAN WE CAN'T DO SOME VILLAINY.
WHAT DO YOU HAVE IN MIND?

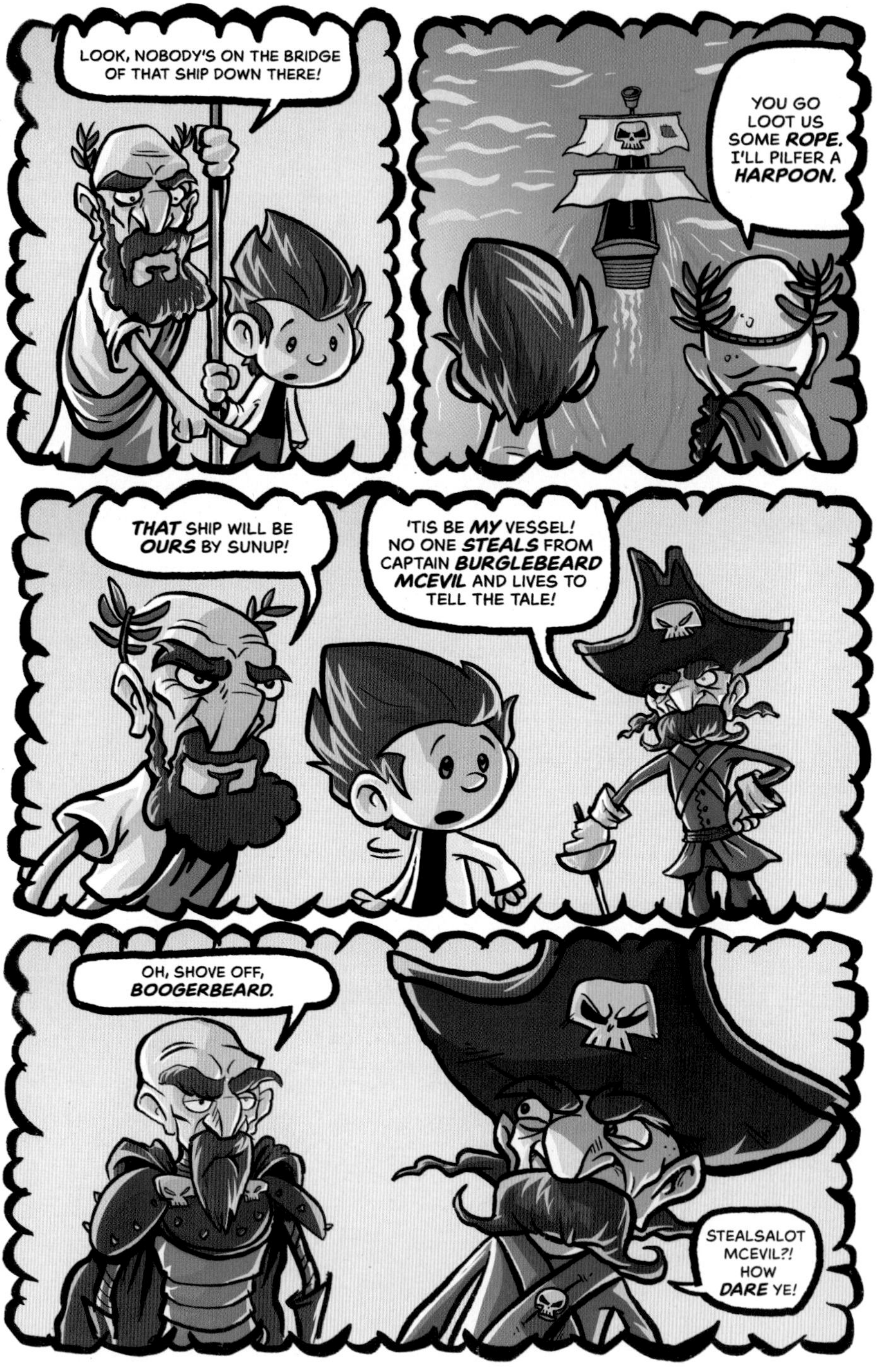
LOOK, NOBODY'S ON THE BRIDGE OF THAT SHIP DOWN THERE!
YOU GO LOOT US SOME **ROPE.** I'LL PILFER A **HARPOON.**
THAT SHIP WILL BE **OURS** BY SUNUP!
'TIS BE **MY** VESSEL! NO ONE **STEALS** FROM CAPTAIN **BURGLEBEARD MCEVIL** AND LIVES TO TELL THE TALE!
OH, SHOVE OFF, **BOOGERBEARD.**
STEALSALOT MCEVIL?! HOW **DARE** YE!

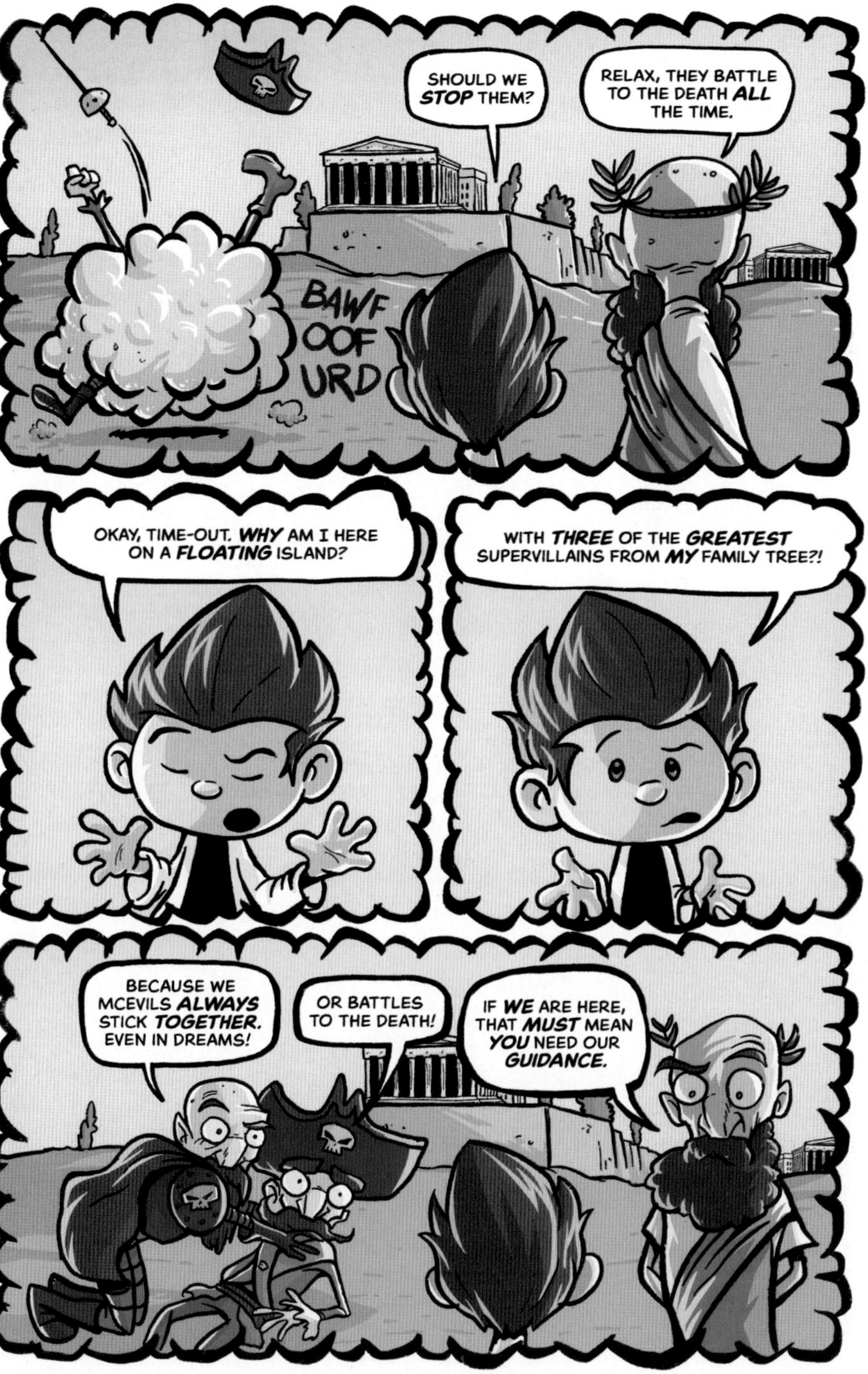
SHOULD WE STOP THEM?
RELAX, THEY BATTLE TO THE DEATH ALL THE TIME.
BAWF OOF URD
OKAY, TIME-OUT. WHY AM I HERE ON A FLOATING ISLAND?
WITH THREE OF THE GREATEST SUPERVILLAINS FROM MY FAMILY TREE?!
BECAUSE WE MCEVILS ALWAYS STICK TOGETHER. EVEN IN DREAMS!
OR BATTLES TO THE DEATH!
IF WE ARE HERE, THAT MUST MEAN YOU NEED OUR GUIDANCE.

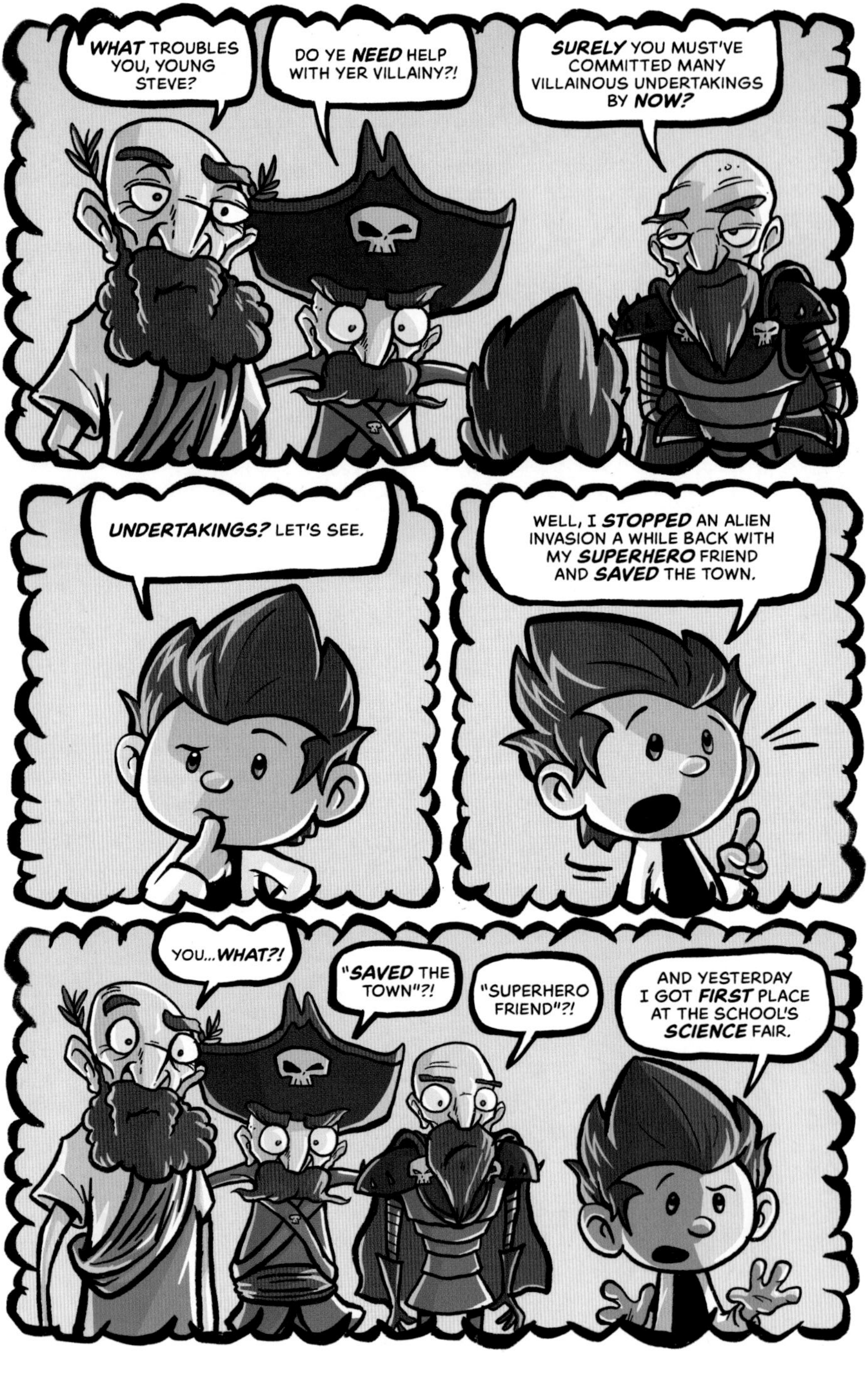
WHAT TROUBLES YOU, YOUNG STEVE?
DO YE NEED HELP WITH YER VILLAINY?!
SURELY YOU MUST'VE COMMITTED MANY VILLAINOUS UNDERTAKINGS BY NOW?
UNDERTAKINGS? LET'S SEE.
WELL, I STOPPED AN ALIEN INVASION A WHILE BACK WITH MY SUPERHERO FRIEND AND SAVED THE TOWN.
YOU...WHAT?!
"SAVED THE TOWN"?!
"SUPERHERO FRIEND"?!
AND YESTERDAY I GOT FIRST PLACE AT THE SCHOOL'S SCIENCE FAIR.

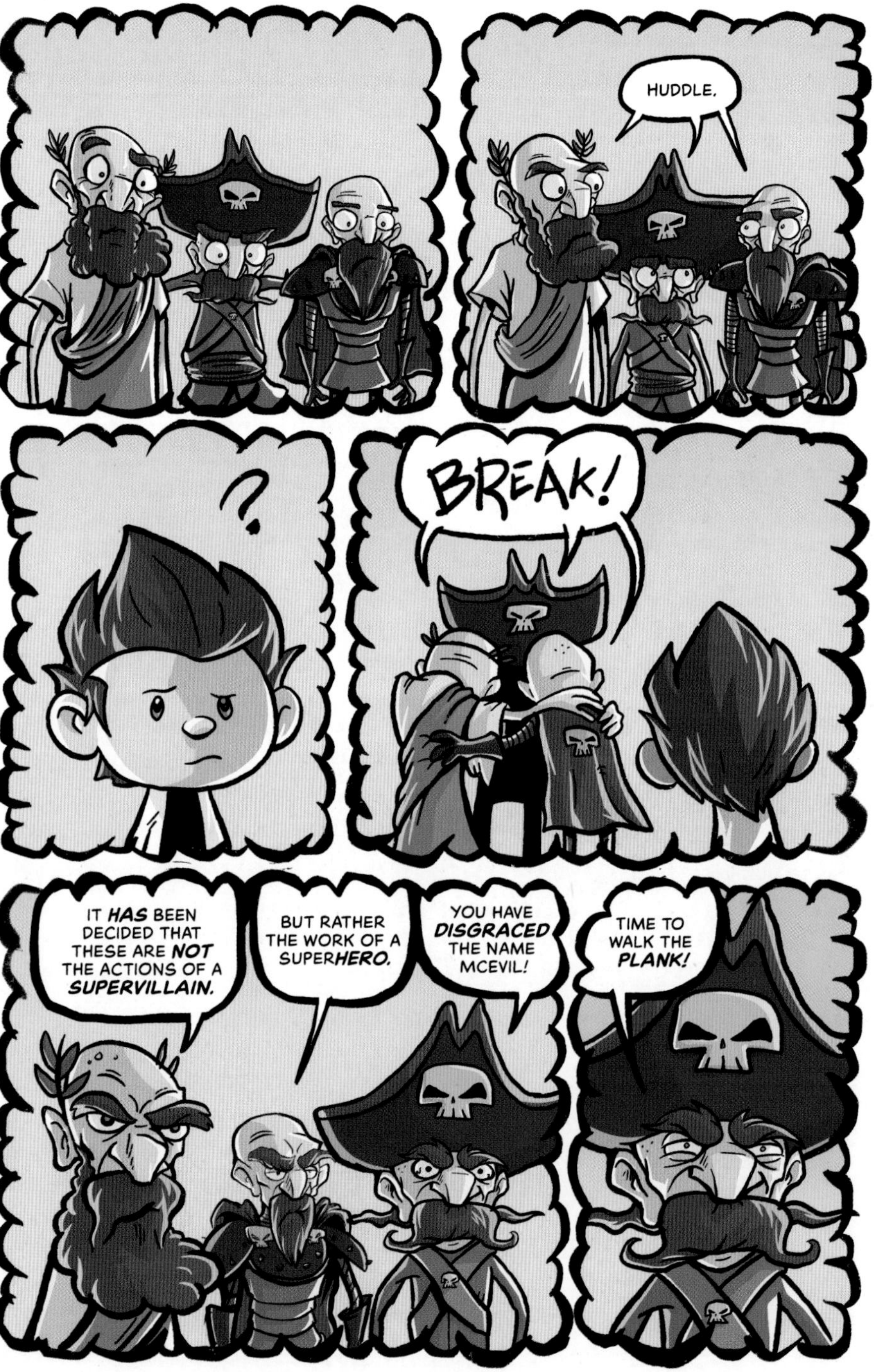
HUDDLE.
?
BREAK!
IT **HAS** BEEN DECIDED THAT THESE ARE **NOT** THE ACTIONS OF A **SUPERVILLAIN.**
BUT RATHER THE WORK OF A SUPER**HERO.**
YOU HAVE **DISGRACED** THE NAME MCEVIL!
TIME TO WALK THE **PLANK!**

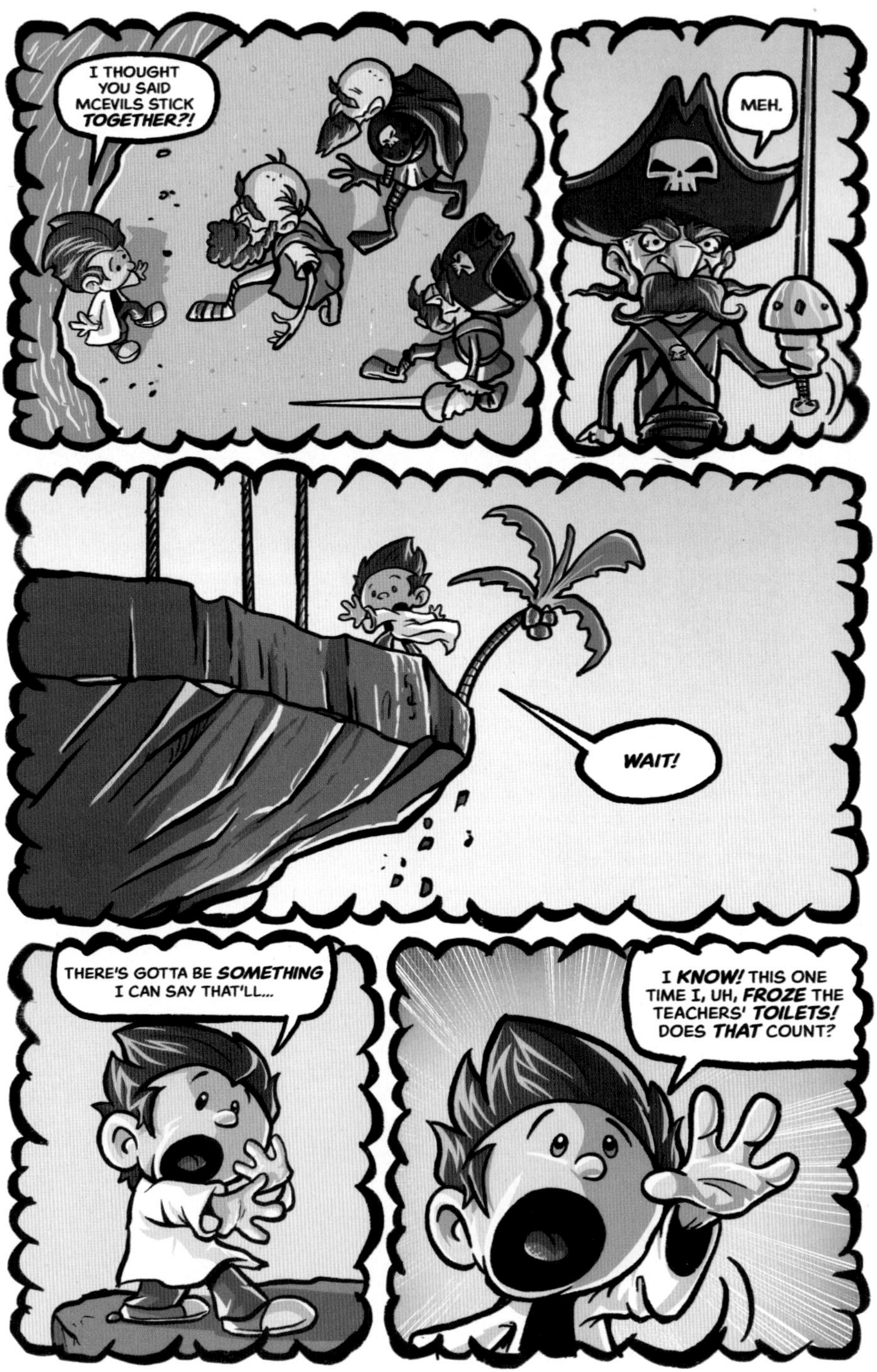
I THOUGHT YOU SAID MCEVILS STICK *TOGETHER?!*
MEH.
WAIT!
THERE'S GOTTA BE *SOMETHING* I CAN SAY THAT'LL...
I *KNOW!* THIS ONE TIME I, UH, *FROZE* THE TEACHERS' *TOILETS!* DOES *THAT* COUNT?

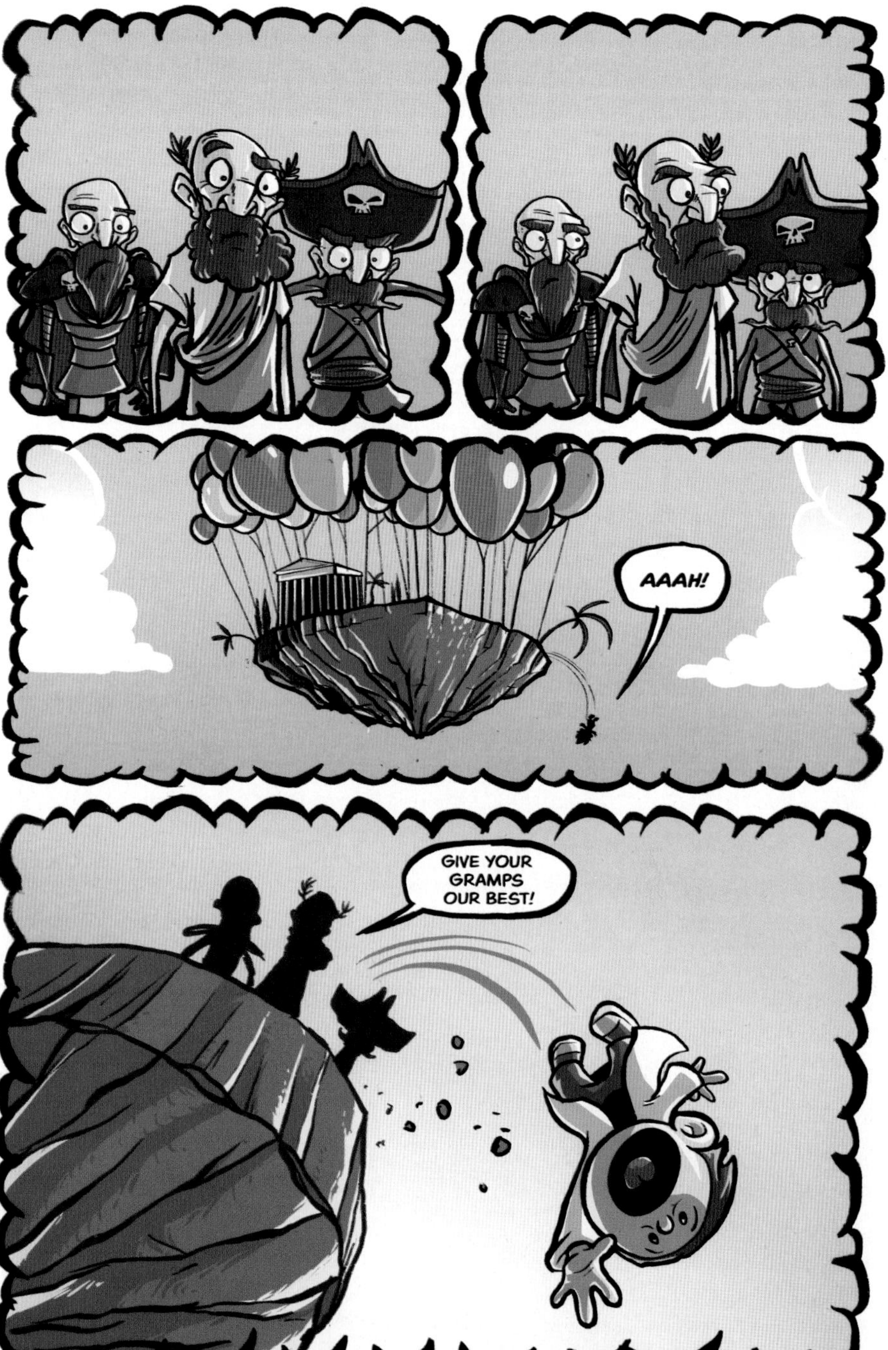
AAAH!
GIVE YOUR GRAMPS OUR BEST!

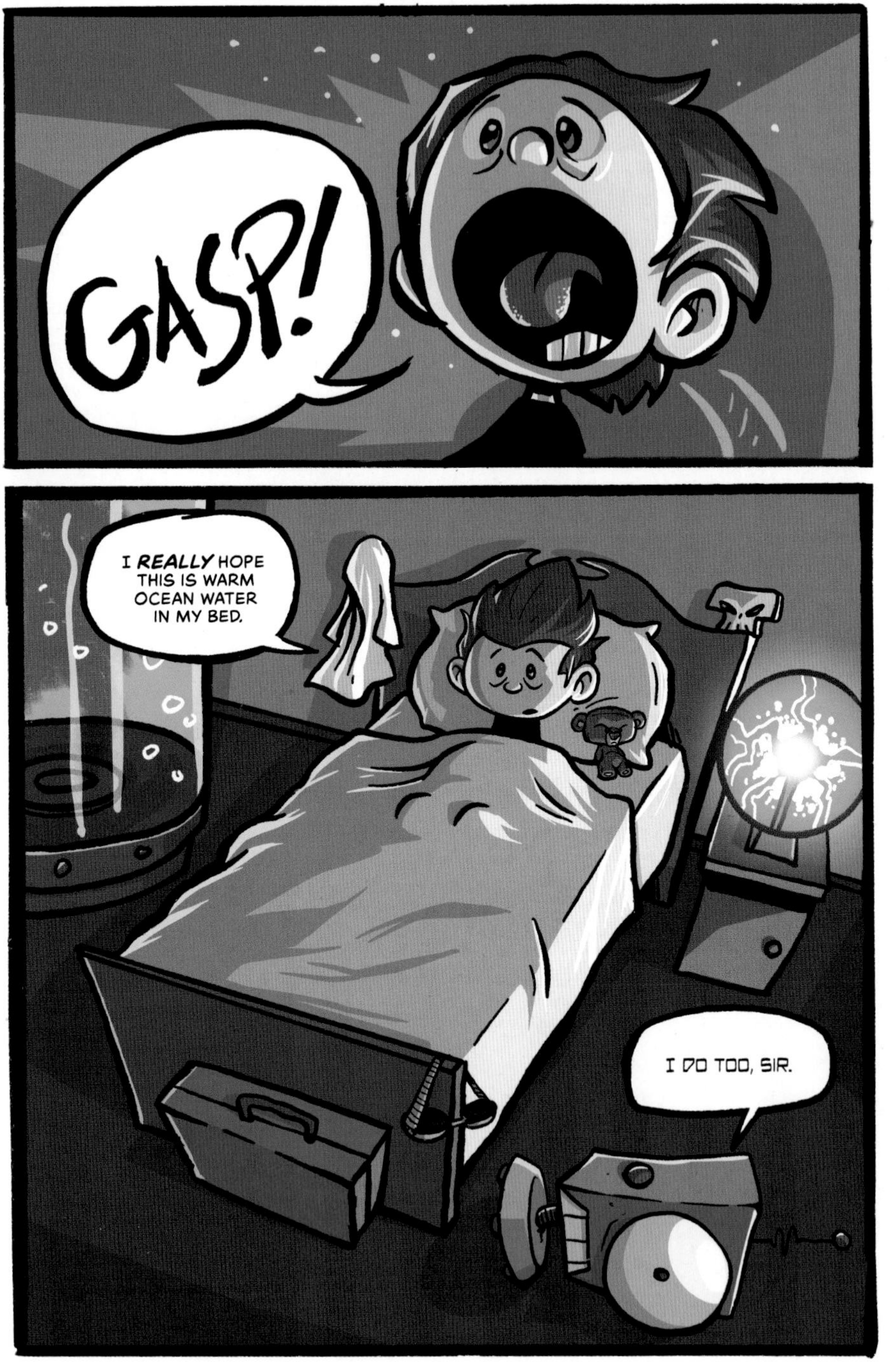
GASP!
I REALLY HOPE THIS IS WARM OCEAN WATER IN MY BED.
I DO TOO, SIR.

CHAPTER 5

Meet the New Steve, Same as the Old Steve

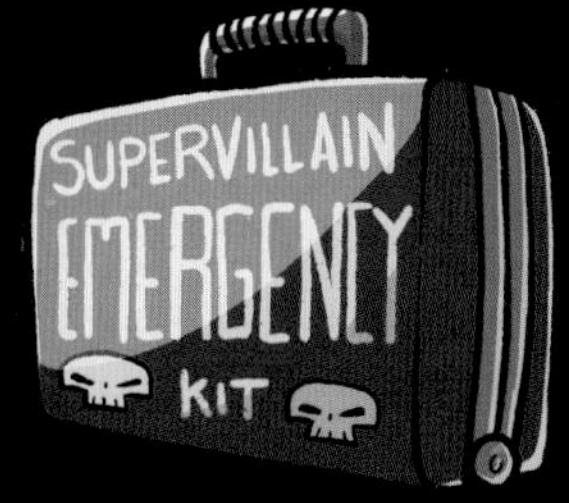
SUPERVILLAIN
EMERGENCY
KIT

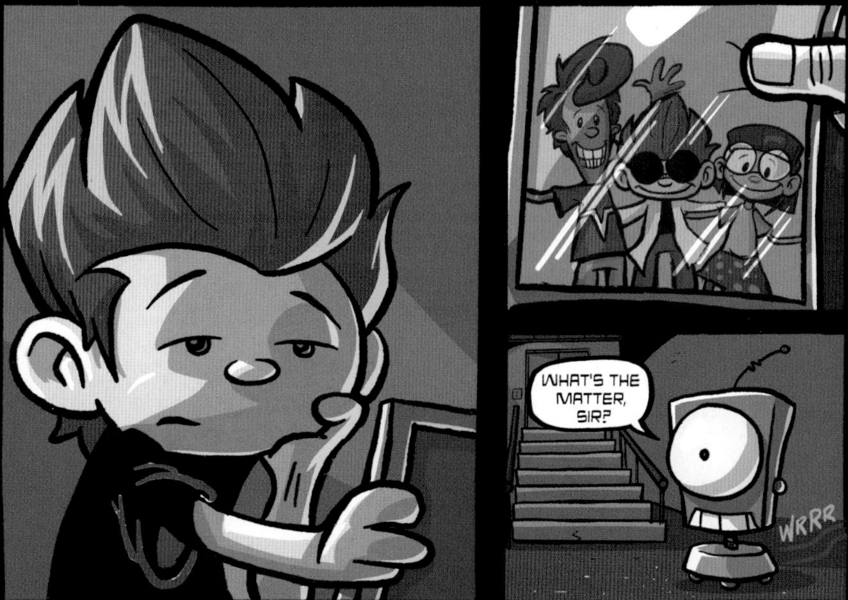
WHAT'S THE MATTER, SIR?
WRRR

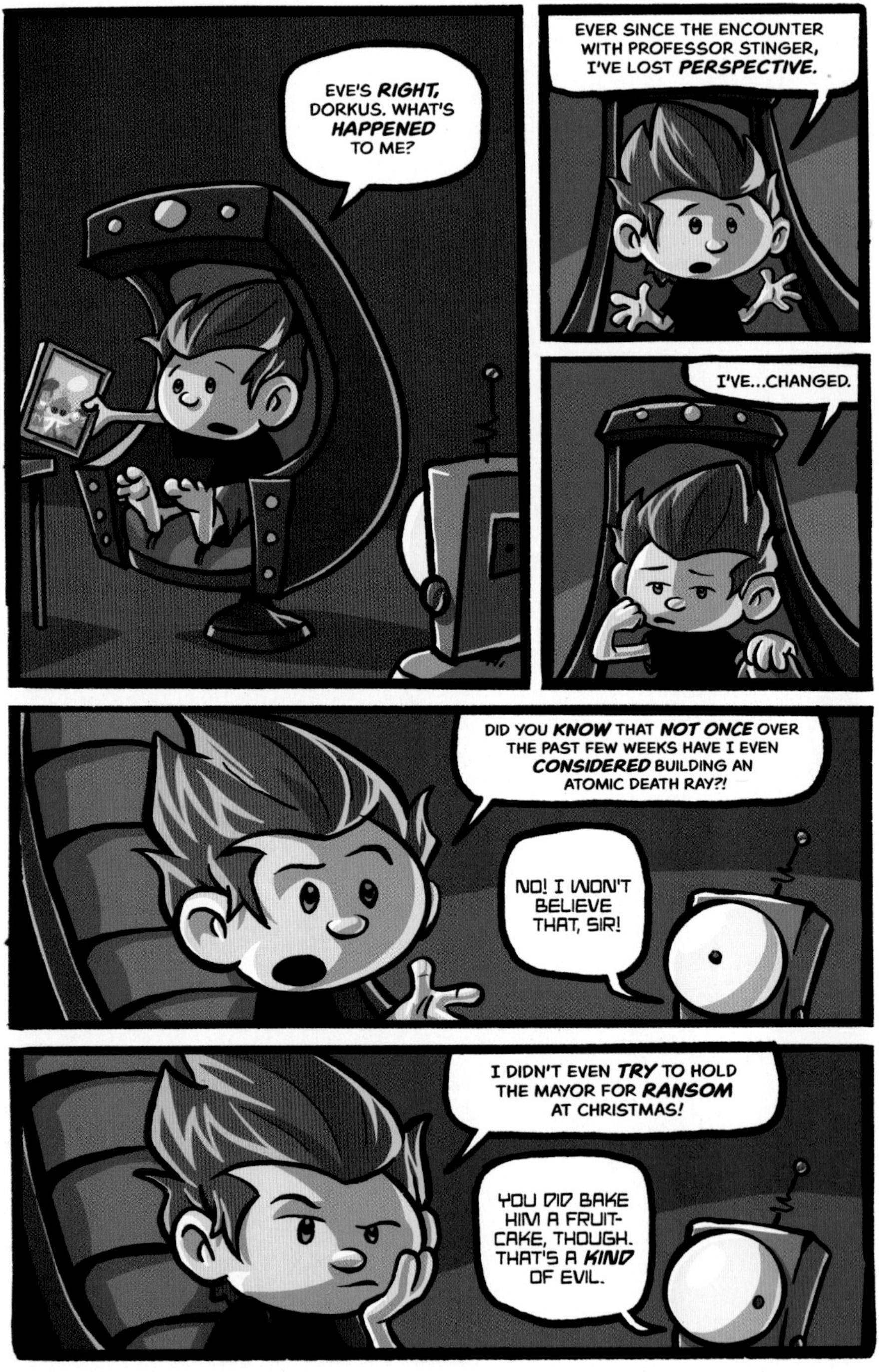
EVE'S RIGHT, DORKUS. WHAT'S HAPPENED TO ME?
EVER SINCE THE ENCOUNTER WITH PROFESSOR STINGER, I'VE LOST PERSPECTIVE.
I'VE...CHANGED.
DID YOU KNOW THAT NOT ONCE OVER THE PAST FEW WEEKS HAVE I EVEN CONSIDERED BUILDING AN ATOMIC DEATH RAY?!
NO! I WON'T BELIEVE THAT, SIR!
I DIDN'T EVEN TRY TO HOLD THE MAYOR FOR RANSOM AT CHRISTMAS!
YOU DID BAKE HIM A FRUIT-CAKE, THOUGH. THAT'S A KIND OF EVIL.

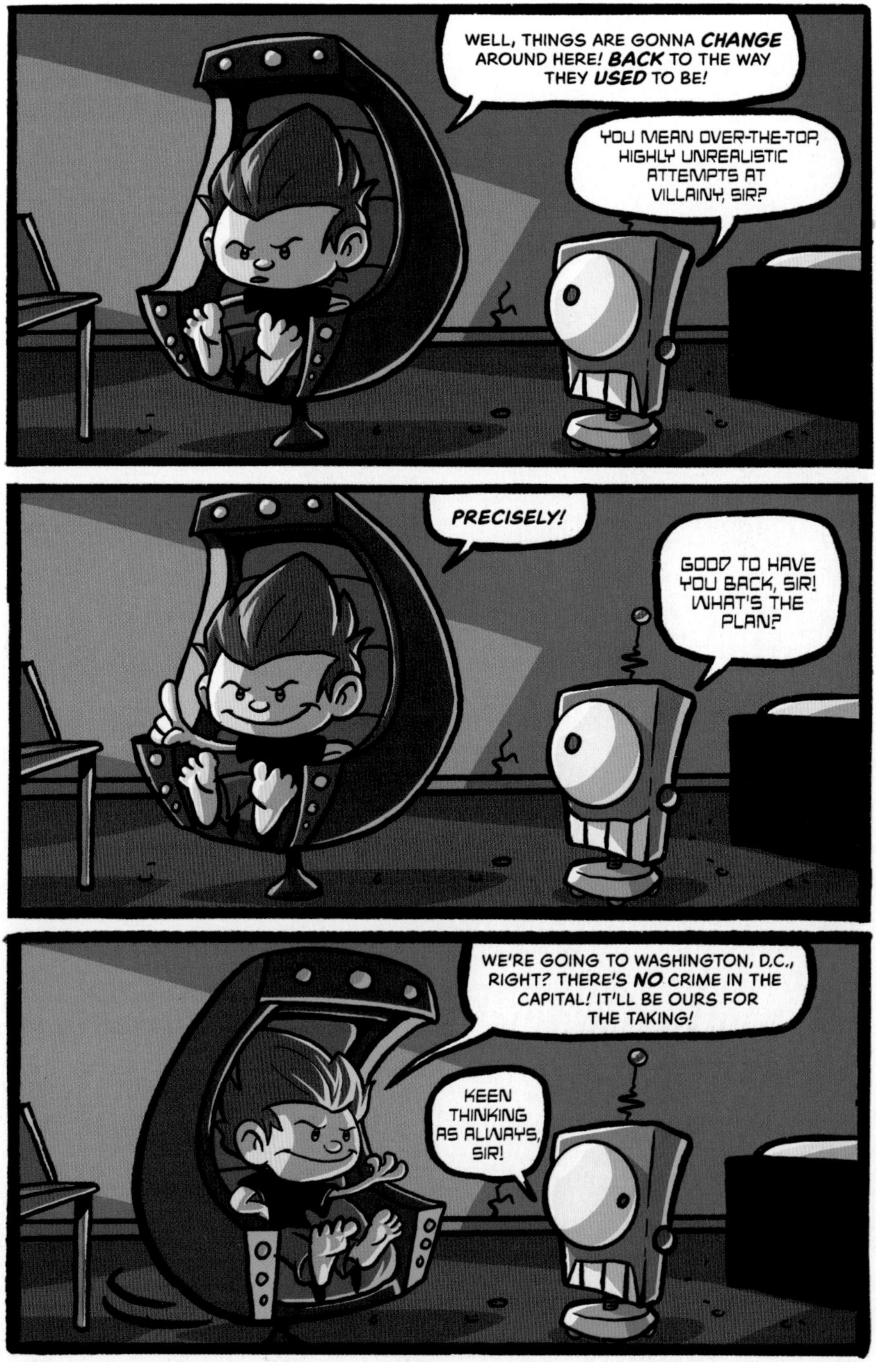
WELL, THINGS ARE GONNA *CHANGE* AROUND HERE! *BACK* TO THE WAY THEY *USED* TO BE!
YOU MEAN OVER-THE-TOP, HIGHLY UNREALISTIC ATTEMPTS AT VILLAINY, SIR?
PRECISELY!
GOOD TO HAVE YOU BACK, SIR! WHAT'S THE PLAN?
WE'RE GOING TO WASHINGTON, D.C., RIGHT? THERE'S *NO* CRIME IN THE CAPITAL! IT'LL BE OURS FOR THE TAKING!
KEEN THINKING AS ALWAYS, SIR!

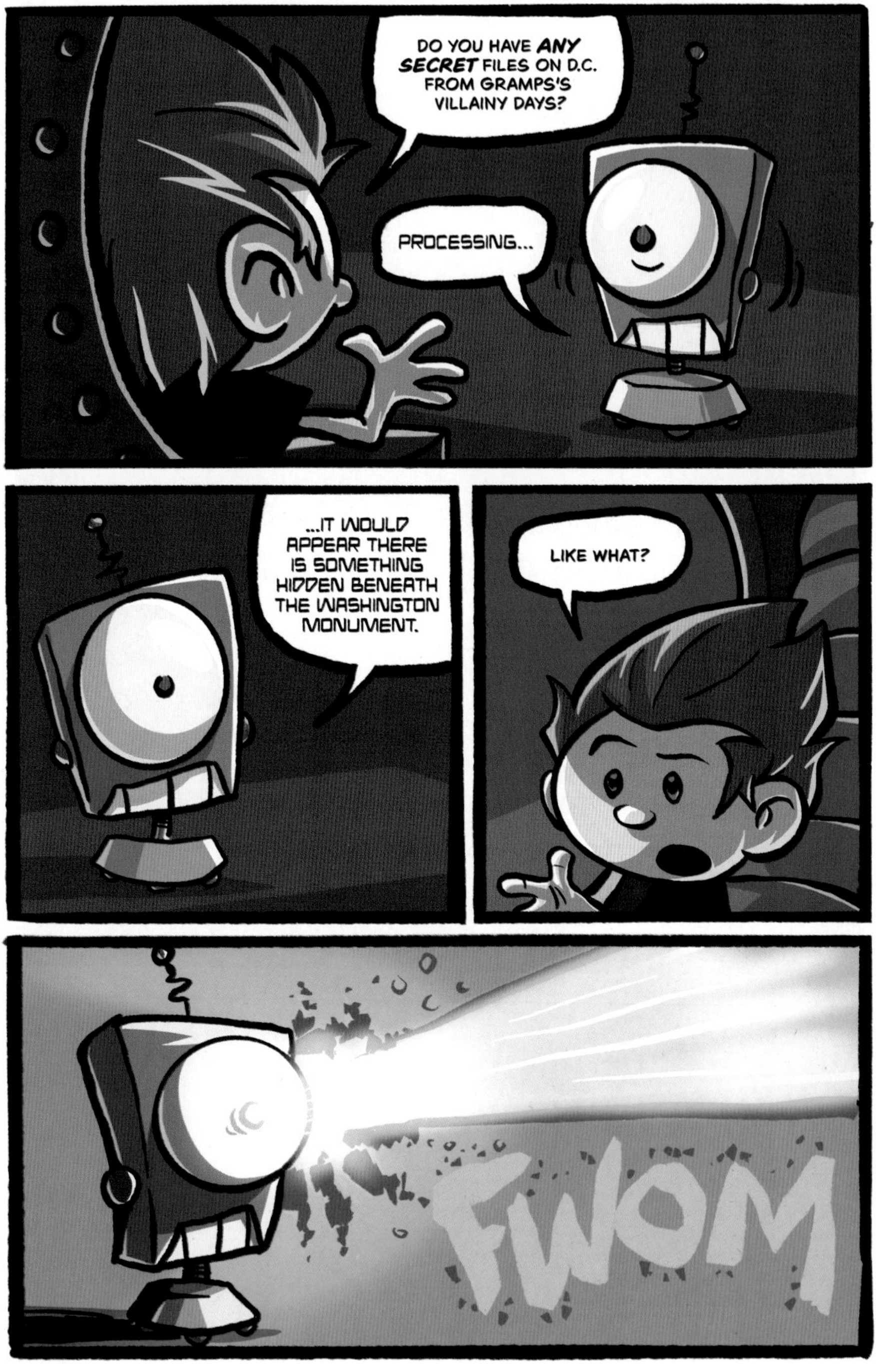
DO YOU HAVE ANY SECRET FILES ON D.C. FROM GRAMPS'S VILLAINY DAYS?
PROCESSING...
...IT WOULD APPEAR THERE IS SOMETHING HIDDEN BENEATH THE WASHINGTON MONUMENT.
LIKE WHAT?
FWOM

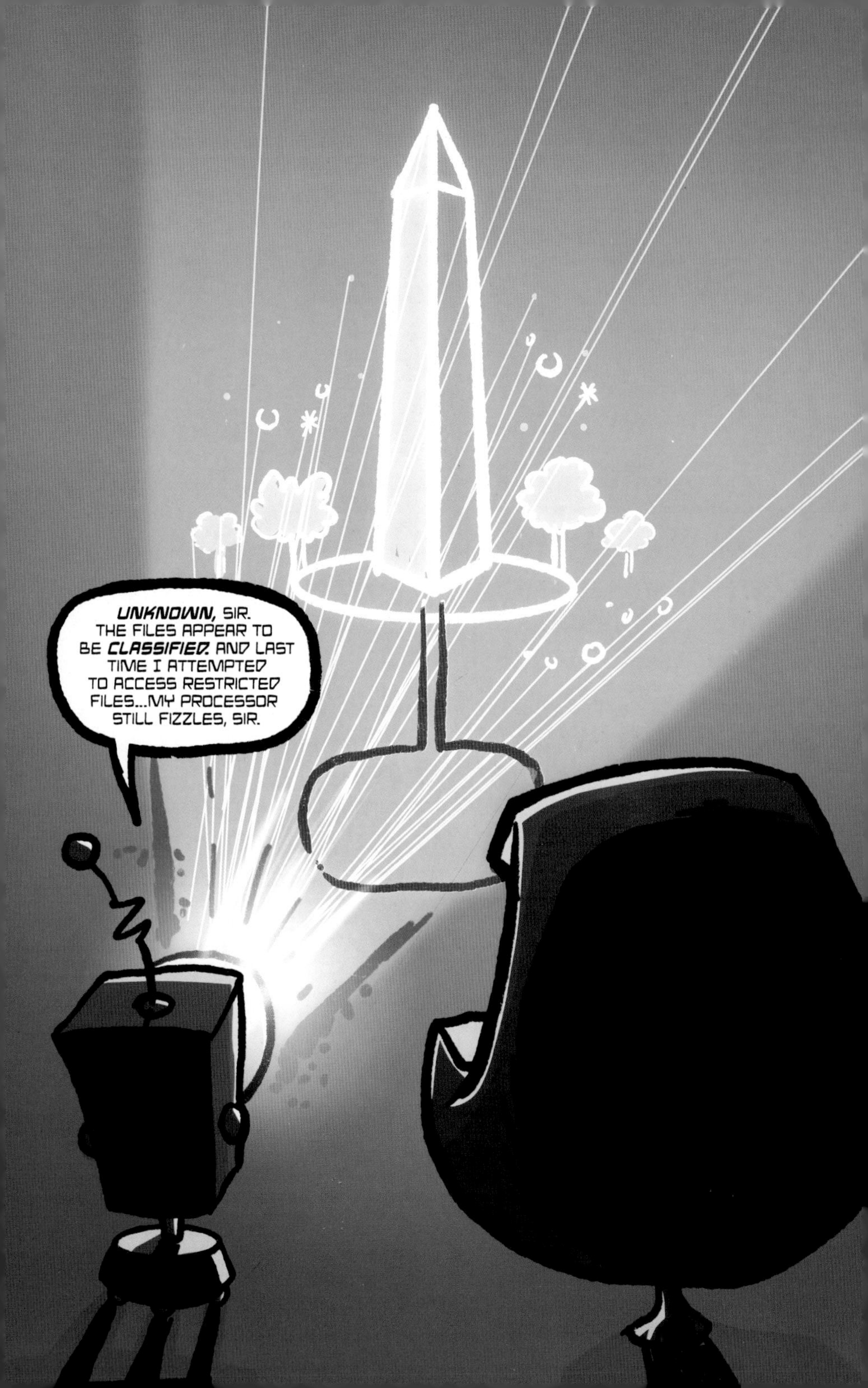
UNKNOWN, SIR. THE FILES APPEAR TO BE CLASSIFIED. AND LAST TIME I ATTEMPTED TO ACCESS RESTRICTED FILES...MY PROCESSOR STILL FIZZLES, SIR.

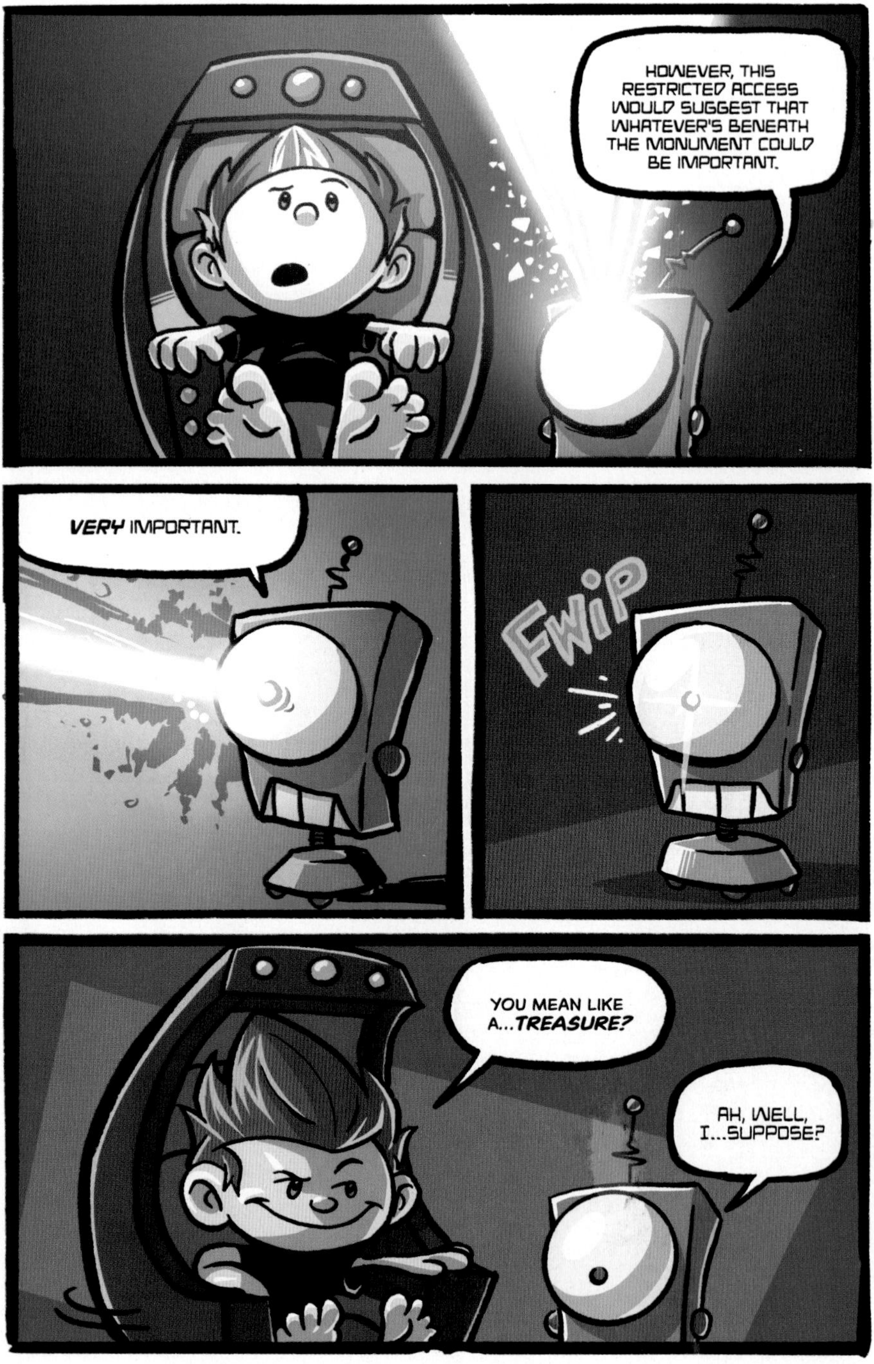
HOWEVER, THIS RESTRICTED ACCESS WOULD SUGGEST THAT WHATEVER'S BENEATH THE MONUMENT COULD BE IMPORTANT.
VERY IMPORTANT.
FWIP
YOU MEAN LIKE A...**TREASURE?**
AH, WELL, I...SUPPOSE?

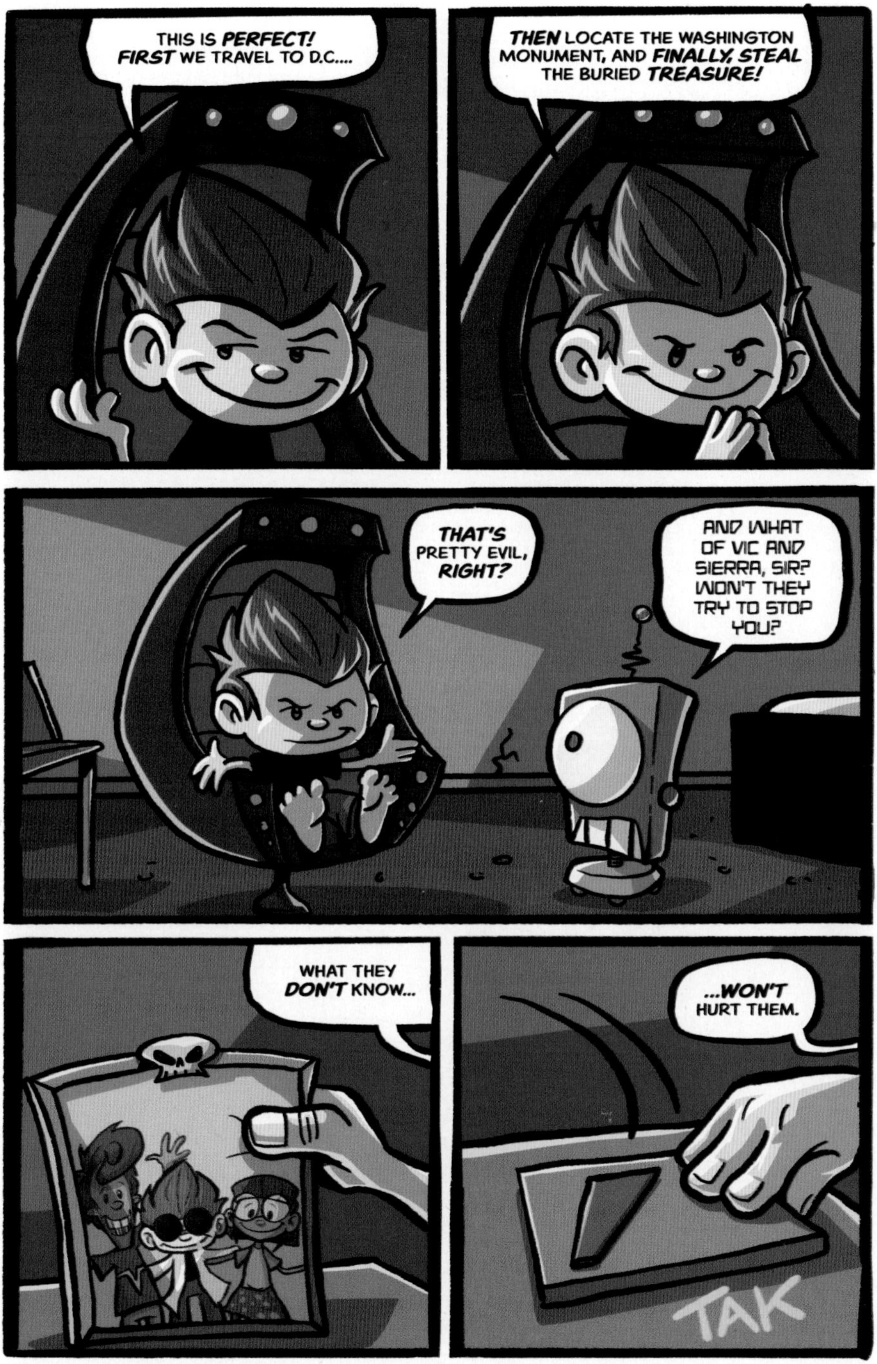
THIS IS PERFECT! FIRST WE TRAVEL TO D.C....
THEN LOCATE THE WASHINGTON MONUMENT, AND FINALLY, STEAL THE BURIED TREASURE!
THAT'S PRETTY EVIL, RIGHT?
AND WHAT OF VIC AND SIERRA, SIR? WON'T THEY TRY TO STOP YOU?
WHAT THEY DON'T KNOW...
...WON'T HURT THEM.
TAK

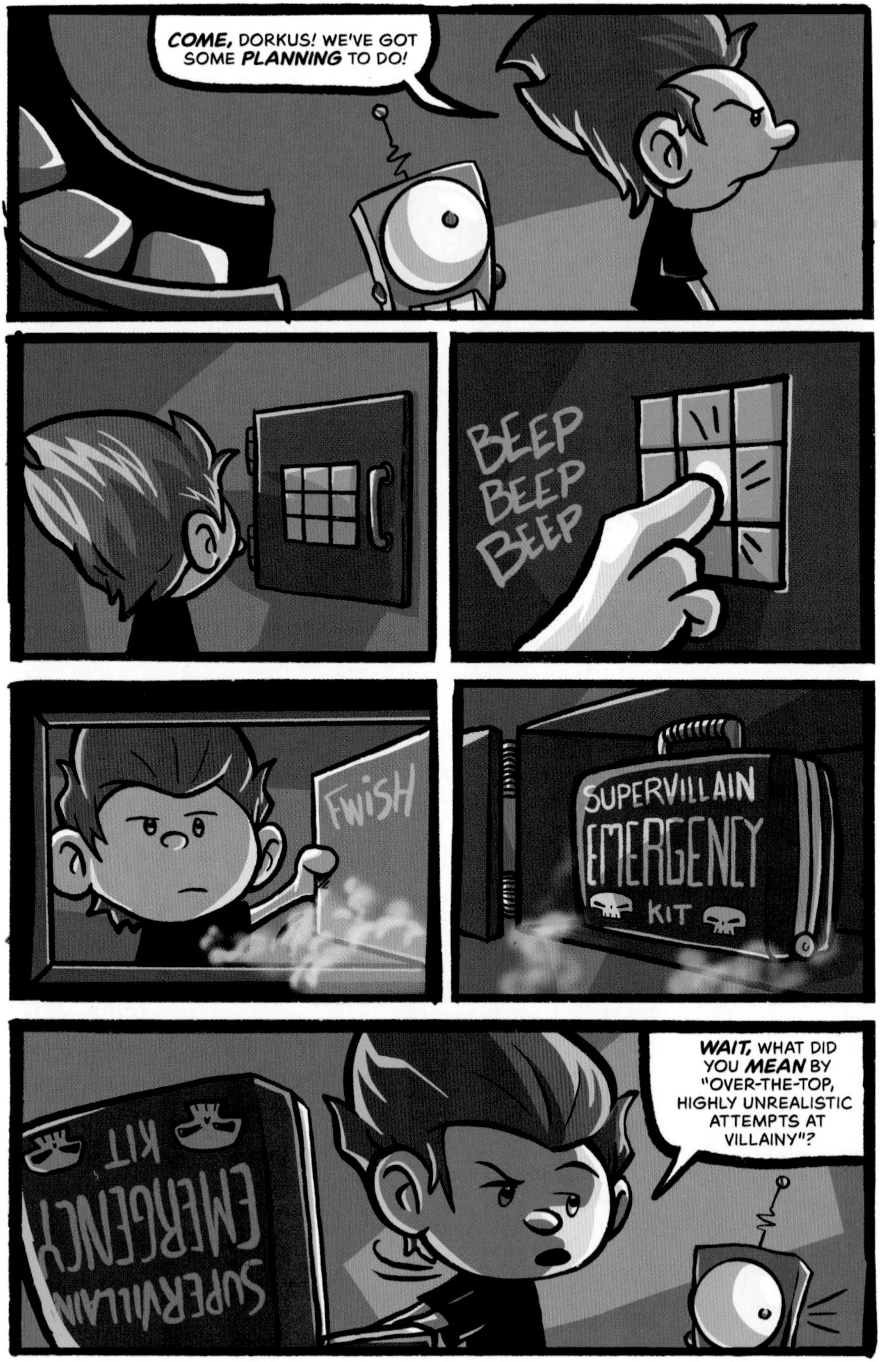
COME, DORKUS! WE'VE GOT SOME PLANNING TO DO!
BEEP BEEP BEEP
FWISH
SUPERVILLAIN EMERGENCY KIT
WAIT, WHAT DID YOU MEAN BY "OVER-THE-TOP, HIGHLY UNREALISTIC ATTEMPTS AT VILLAINY"?

CHAPTER 6

Leaving on a Threat Plane

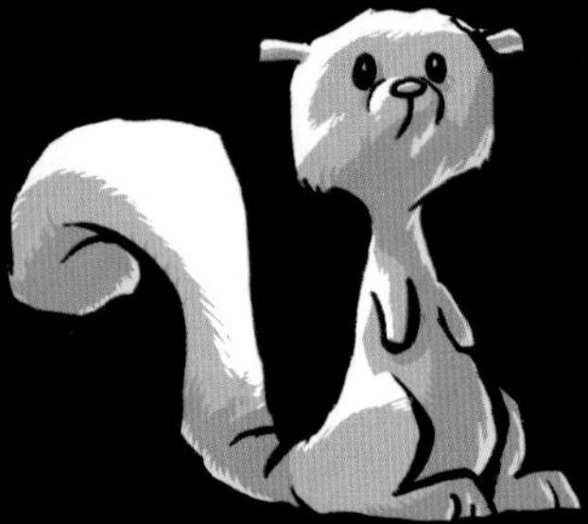

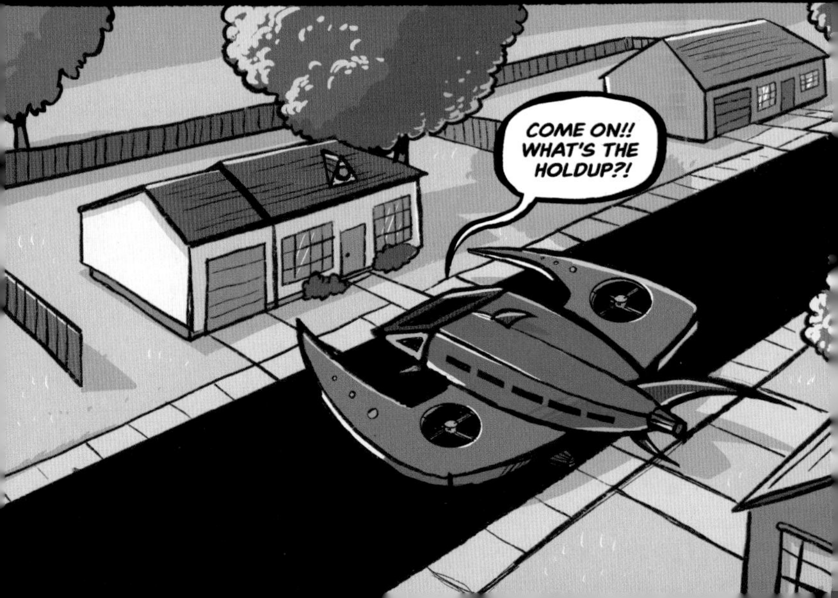
COME ON!! WHAT'S THE HOLDUP?!

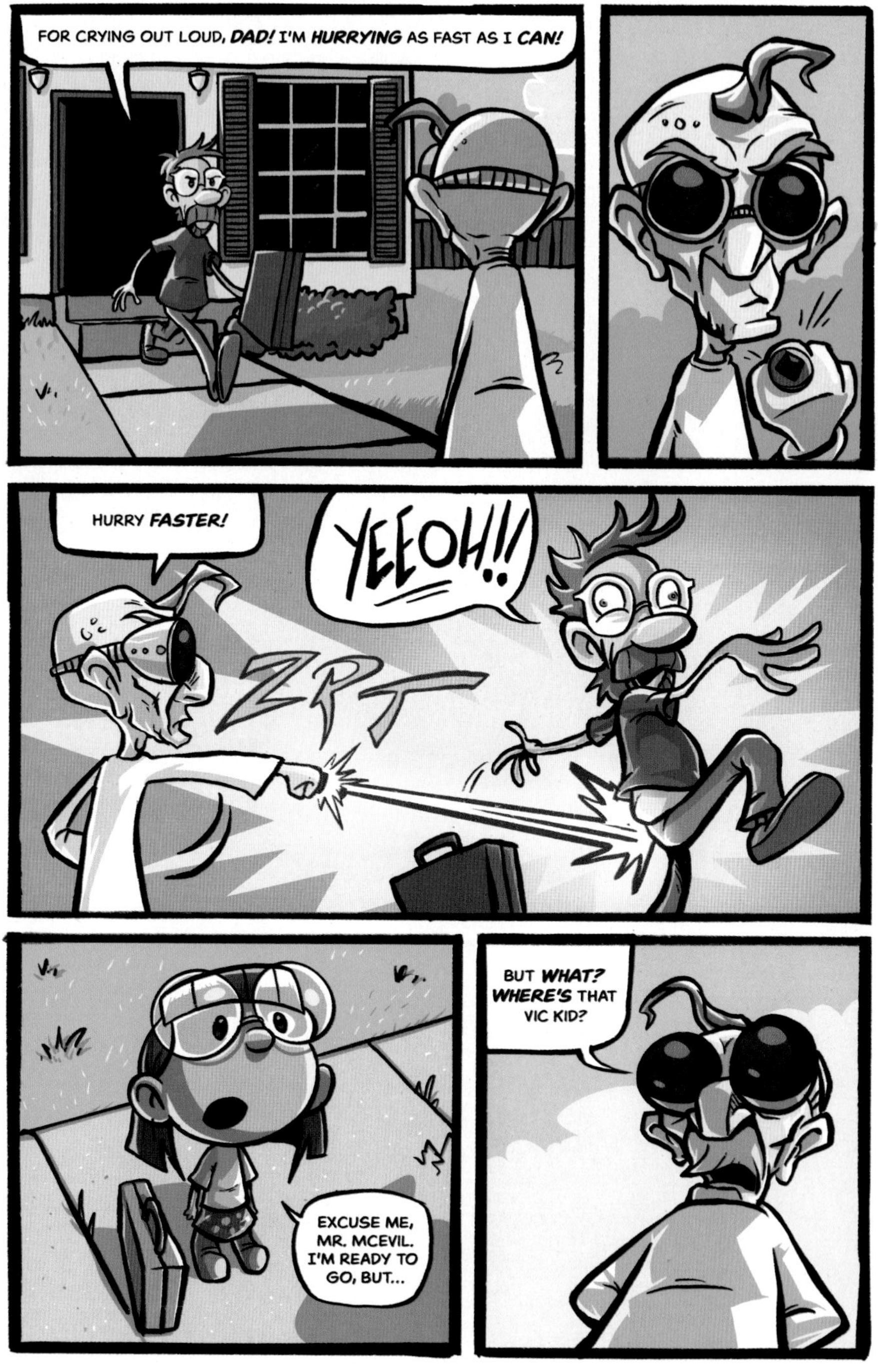
FOR CRYING OUT LOUD, DAD! I'M HURRYING AS FAST AS I CAN!
HURRY FASTER!
YEEOH!!
ZRT
EXCUSE ME, MR. MCEVIL. I'M READY TO GO, BUT...
BUT WHAT? WHERE'S THAT VIC KID?

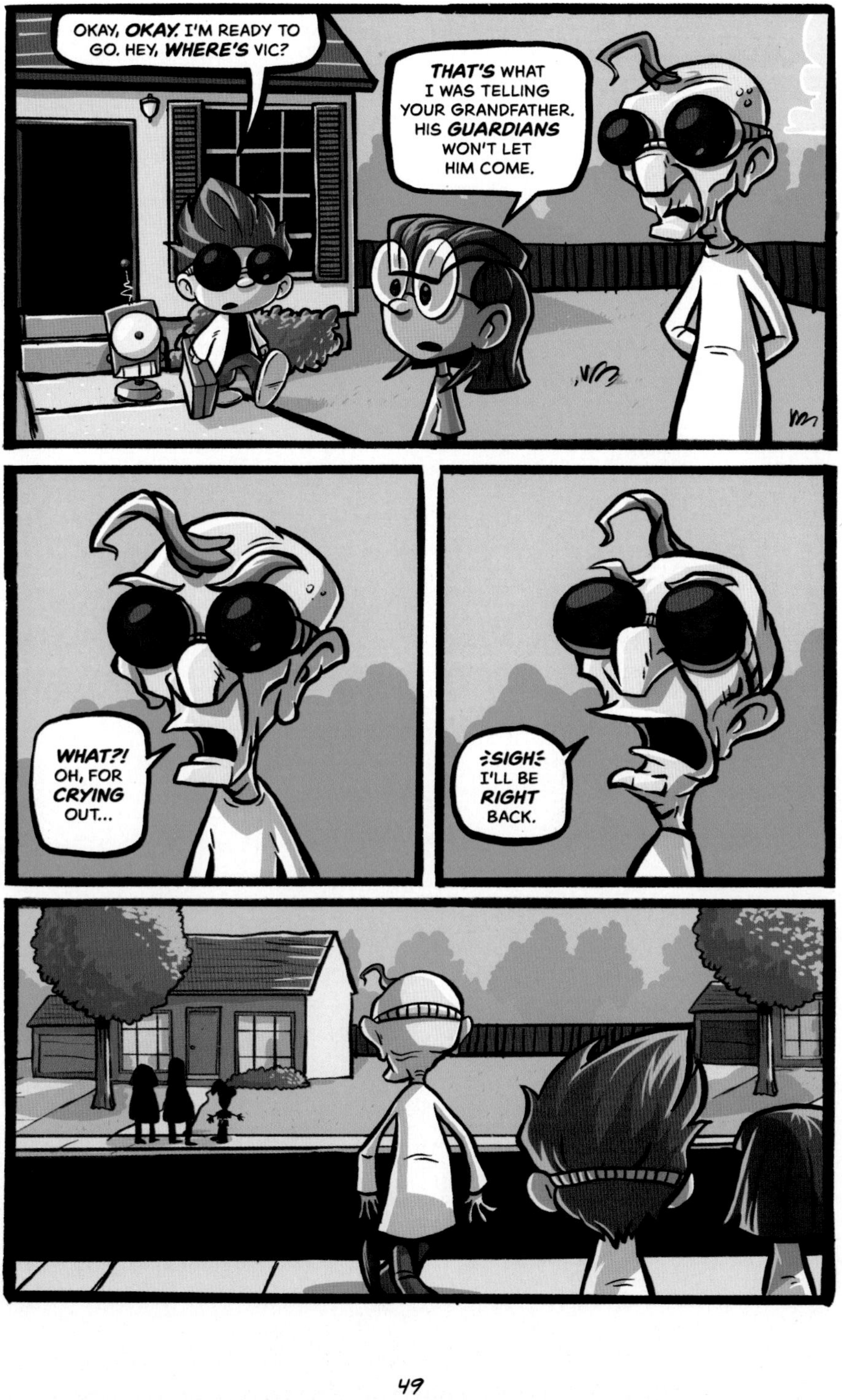
OKAY, OKAY. I'M READY TO GO. HEY, WHERE'S VIC?
THAT'S WHAT I WAS TELLING YOUR GRANDFATHER. HIS GUARDIANS WON'T LET HIM COME.
WHAT?! OH, FOR CRYING OUT...
SIGH I'LL BE RIGHT BACK.

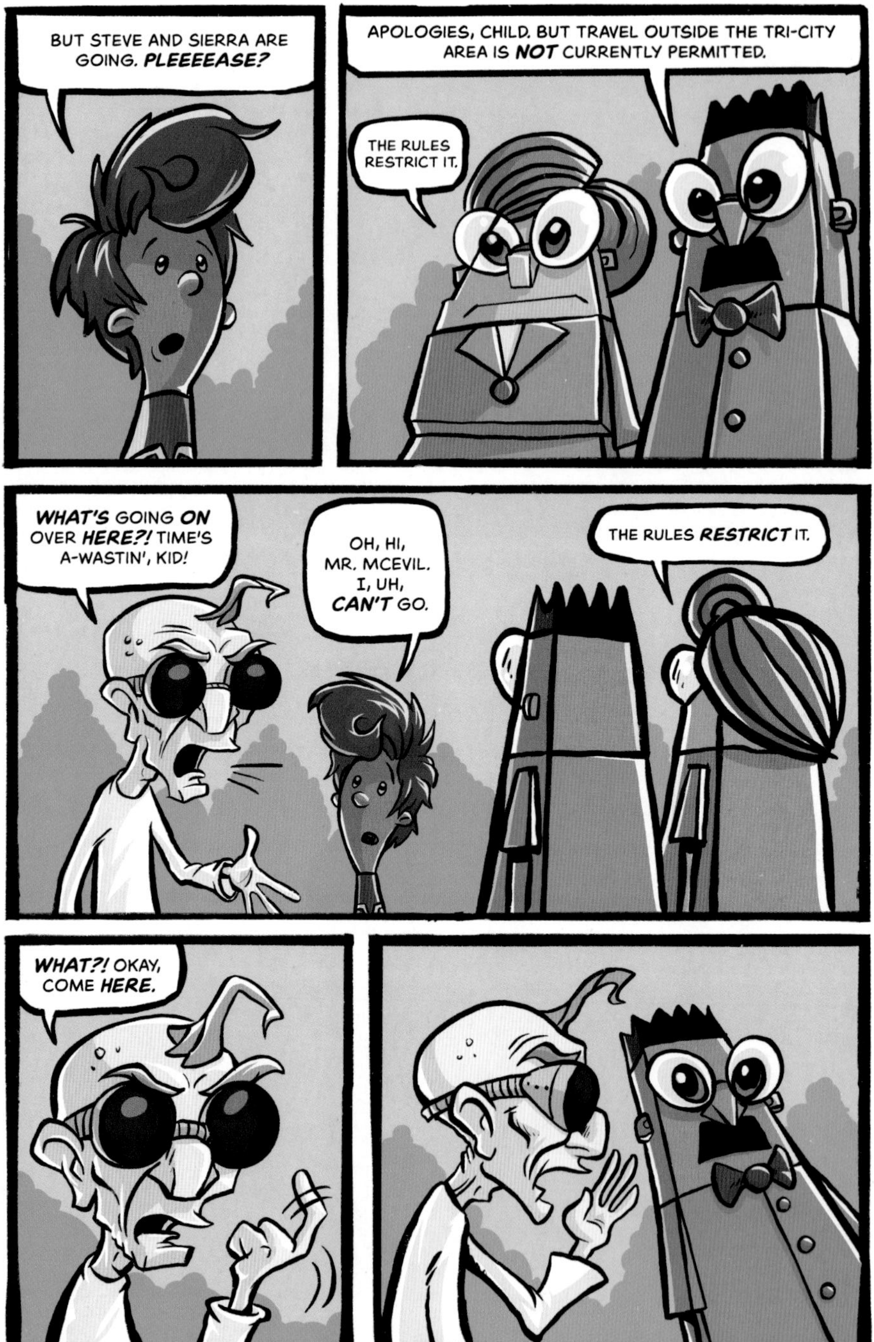

BUT STEVE AND SIERRA ARE GOING. PLEEEEASE?
APOLOGIES, CHILD. BUT TRAVEL OUTSIDE THE TRI-CITY AREA IS NOT CURRENTLY PERMITTED.
THE RULES RESTRICT IT.
WHAT'S GOING ON OVER HERE?! TIME'S A-WASTIN', KID!
OH, HI, MR. MCEVIL. I, UH, CAN'T GO.
THE RULES RESTRICT IT.
WHAT?! OKAY, COME HERE.

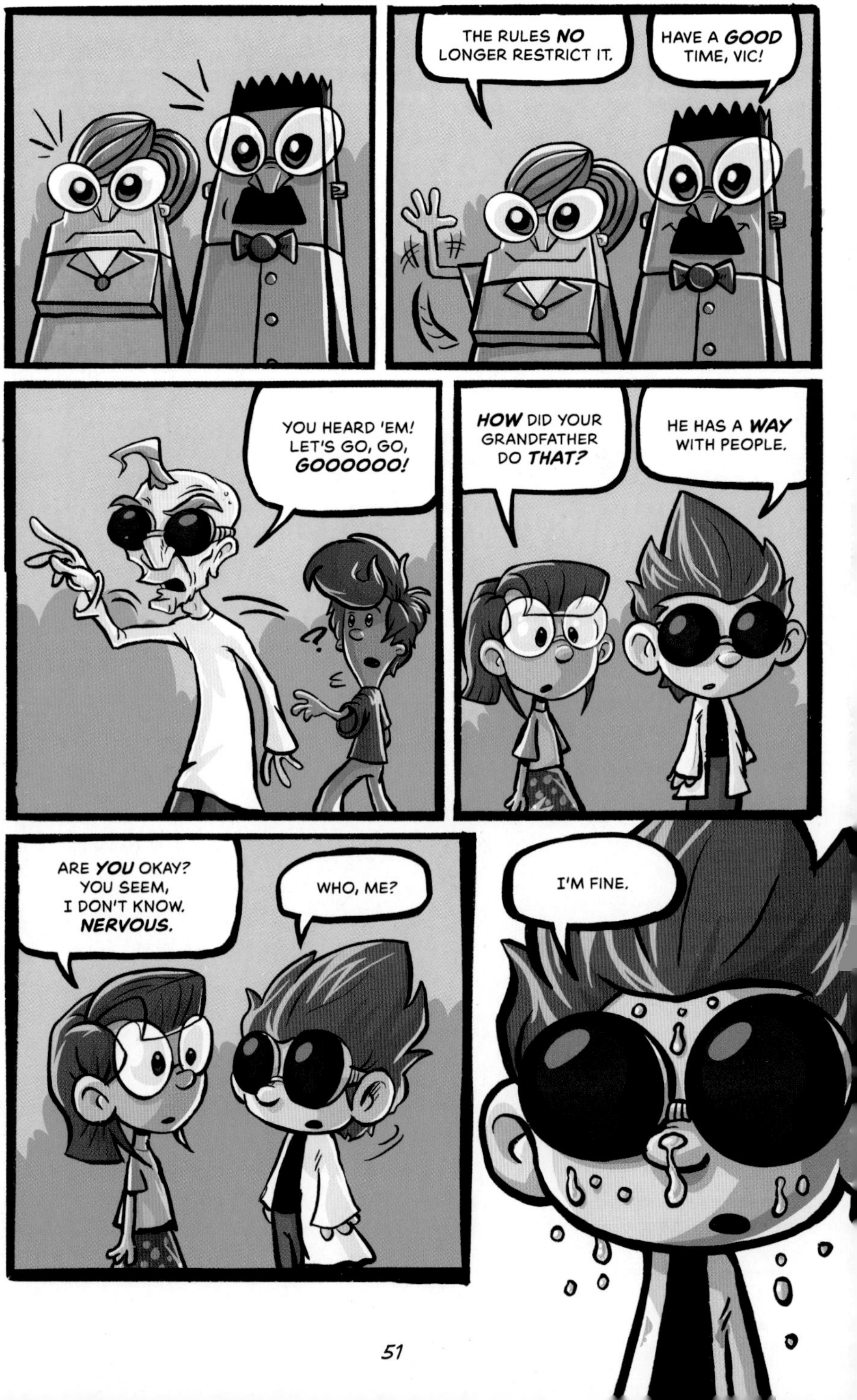
THE RULES NO LONGER RESTRICT IT.
HAVE A GOOD TIME, VIC!
YOU HEARD 'EM! LET'S GO, GO, GOOOOOO!
HOW DID YOUR GRANDFATHER DO THAT?
HE HAS A WAY WITH PEOPLE.
ARE YOU OKAY? YOU SEEM, I DON'T KNOW. NERVOUS.
WHO, ME?
I'M FINE.

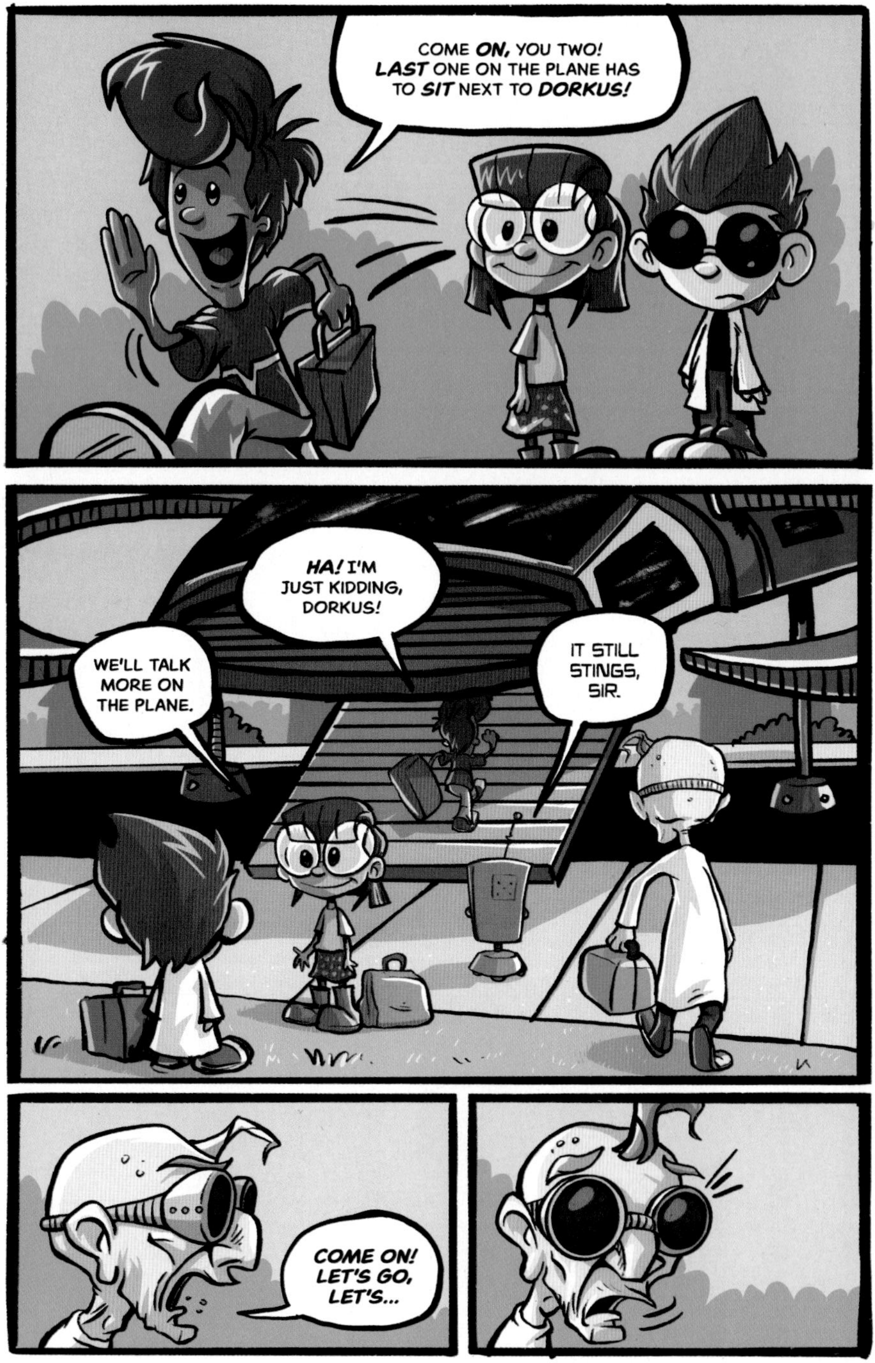
COME ON, YOU TWO! LAST ONE ON THE PLANE HAS TO SIT NEXT TO DORKUS!
HA! I'M JUST KIDDING, DORKUS!
WE'LL TALK MORE ON THE PLANE.
IT STILL STINGS, SIR.
COME ON! LET'S GO, LET'S...

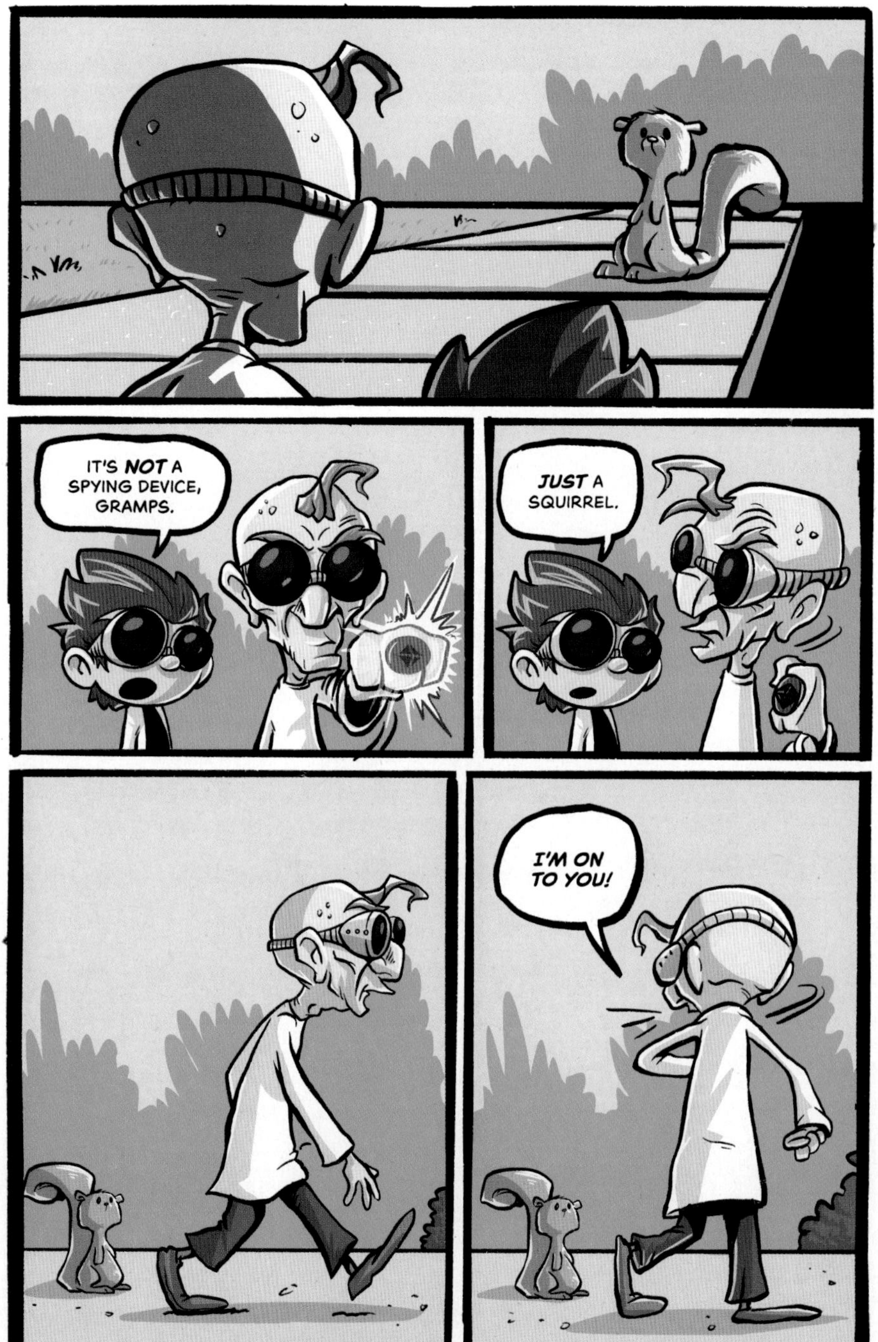
IT'S **NOT** A SPYING DEVICE, GRAMPS.
JUST A SQUIRREL.
I'M ON TO YOU!

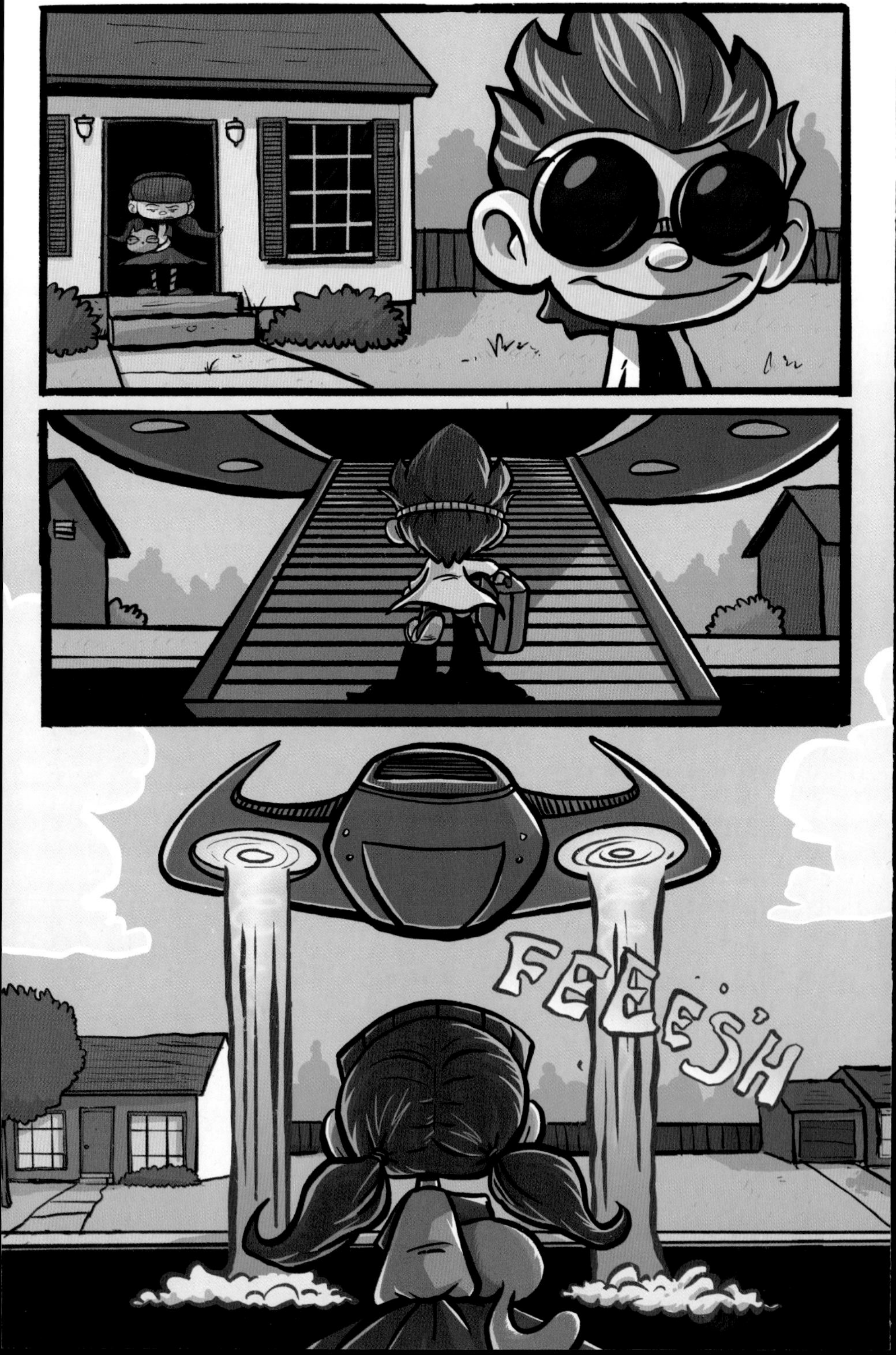
FEEESH

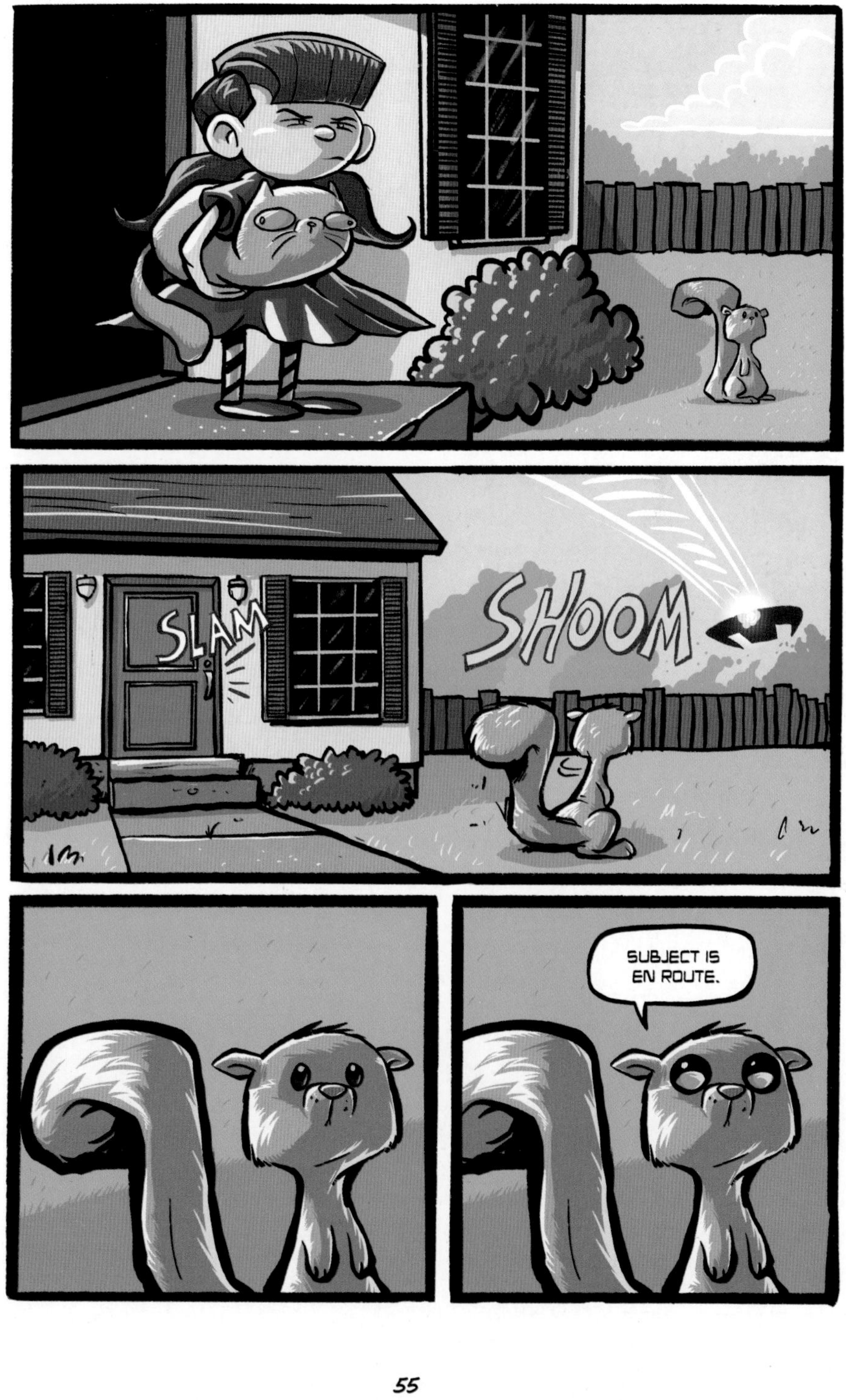
SLAM
SHOOM
SUBJECT IS EN ROUTE.

CHAPTER 7
The Unfriendly Skies

SO, DAD, YOU NEVER *TOLD* ME WHY YOU WANT TO GO TO WASHINGTON, D.C., SO *BADLY.*

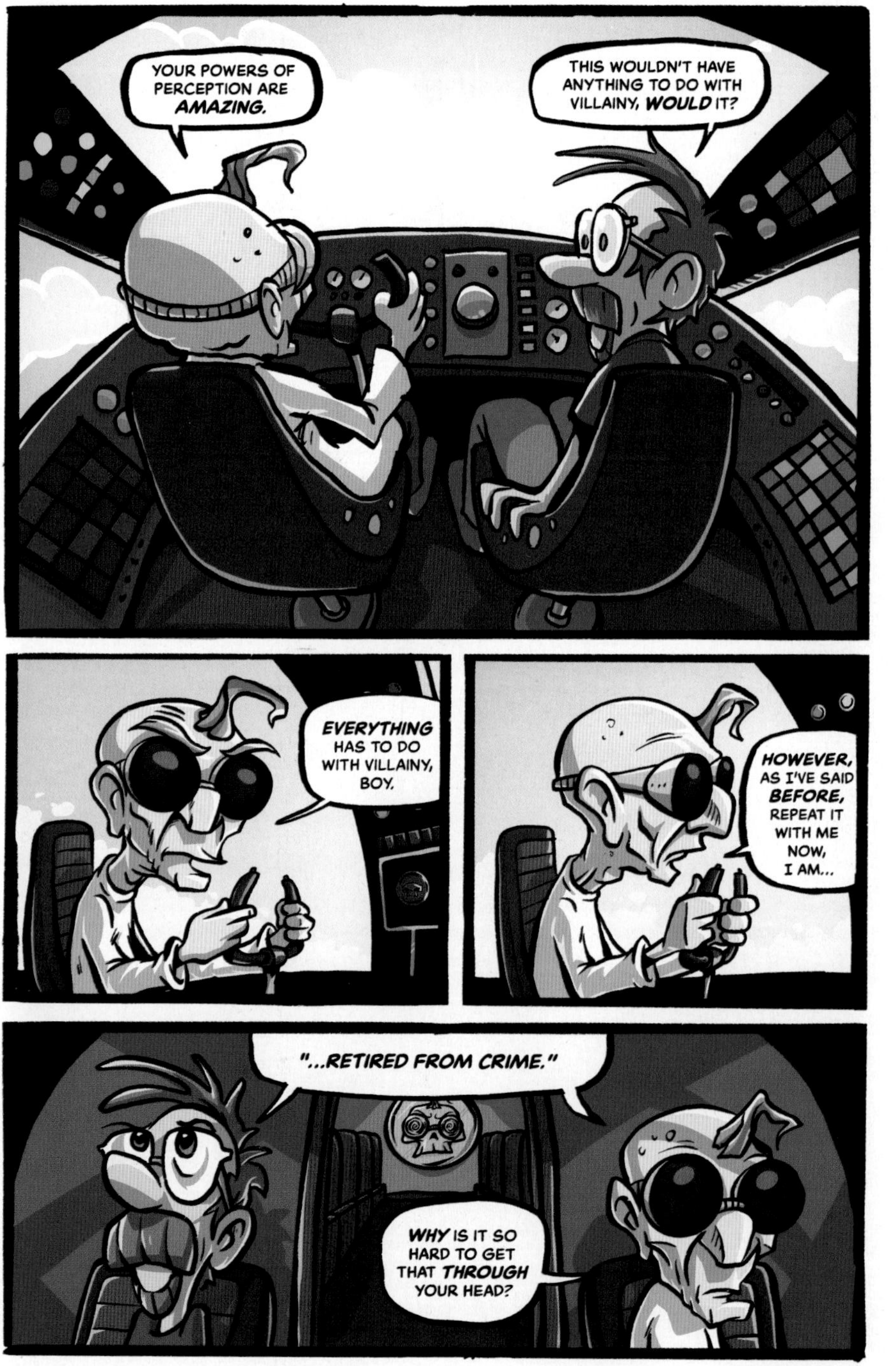
YOUR POWERS OF PERCEPTION ARE AMAZING.
THIS WOULDN'T HAVE ANYTHING TO DO WITH VILLAINY, WOULD IT?
EVERYTHING HAS TO DO WITH VILLAINY, BOY.
HOWEVER, AS I'VE SAID BEFORE, REPEAT IT WITH ME NOW, I AM...
"...RETIRED FROM CRIME."
WHY IS IT SO HARD TO GET THAT THROUGH YOUR HEAD?

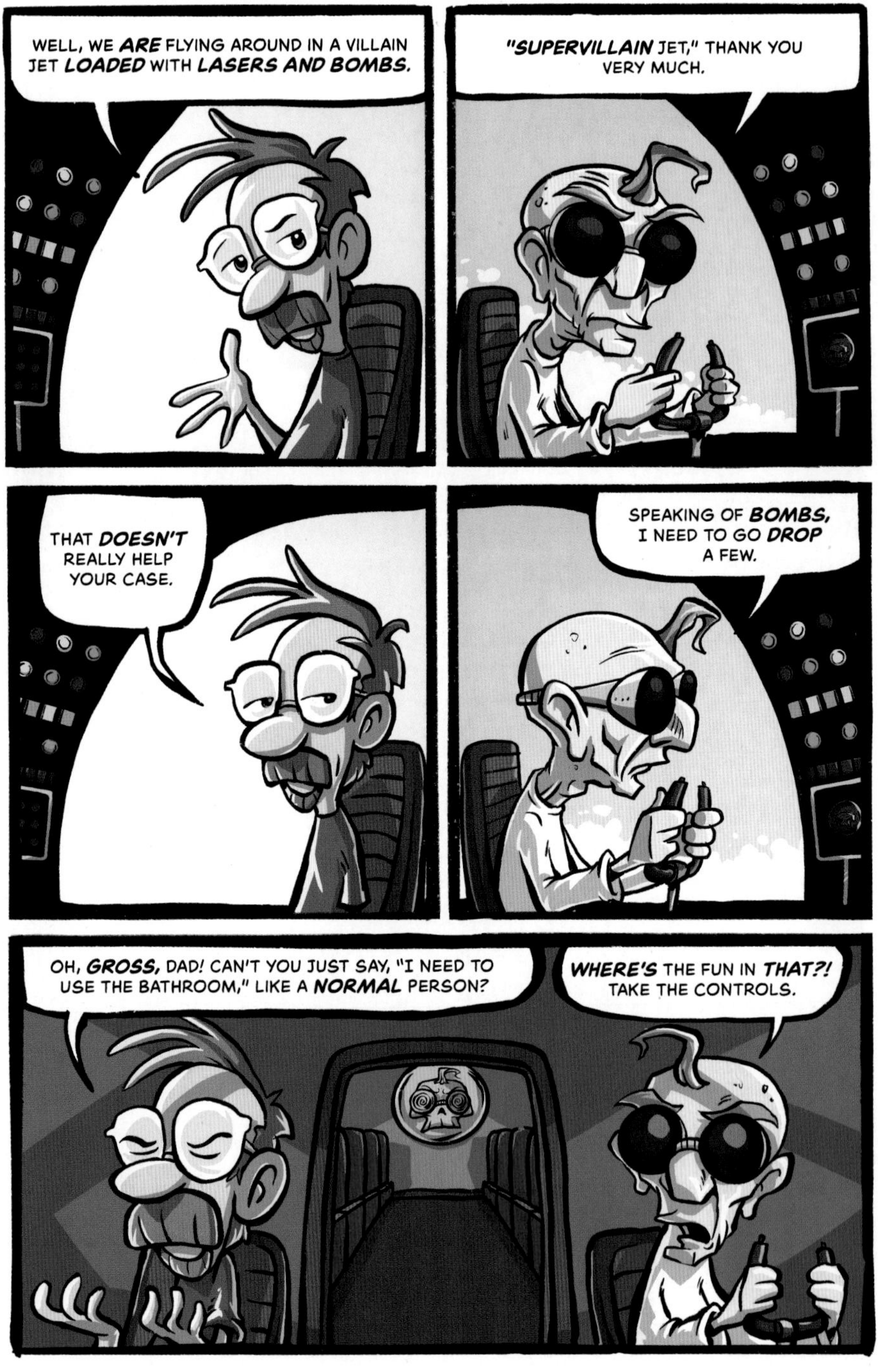

WELL, WE ARE FLYING AROUND IN A VILLAIN JET LOADED WITH LASERS AND BOMBS.
"SUPERVILLAIN JET," THANK YOU VERY MUCH.
THAT DOESN'T REALLY HELP YOUR CASE.
SPEAKING OF BOMBS, I NEED TO GO DROP A FEW.
OH, GROSS, DAD! CAN'T YOU JUST SAY, "I NEED TO USE THE BATHROOM," LIKE A NORMAL PERSON?
WHERE'S THE FUN IN THAT?! TAKE THE CONTROLS.

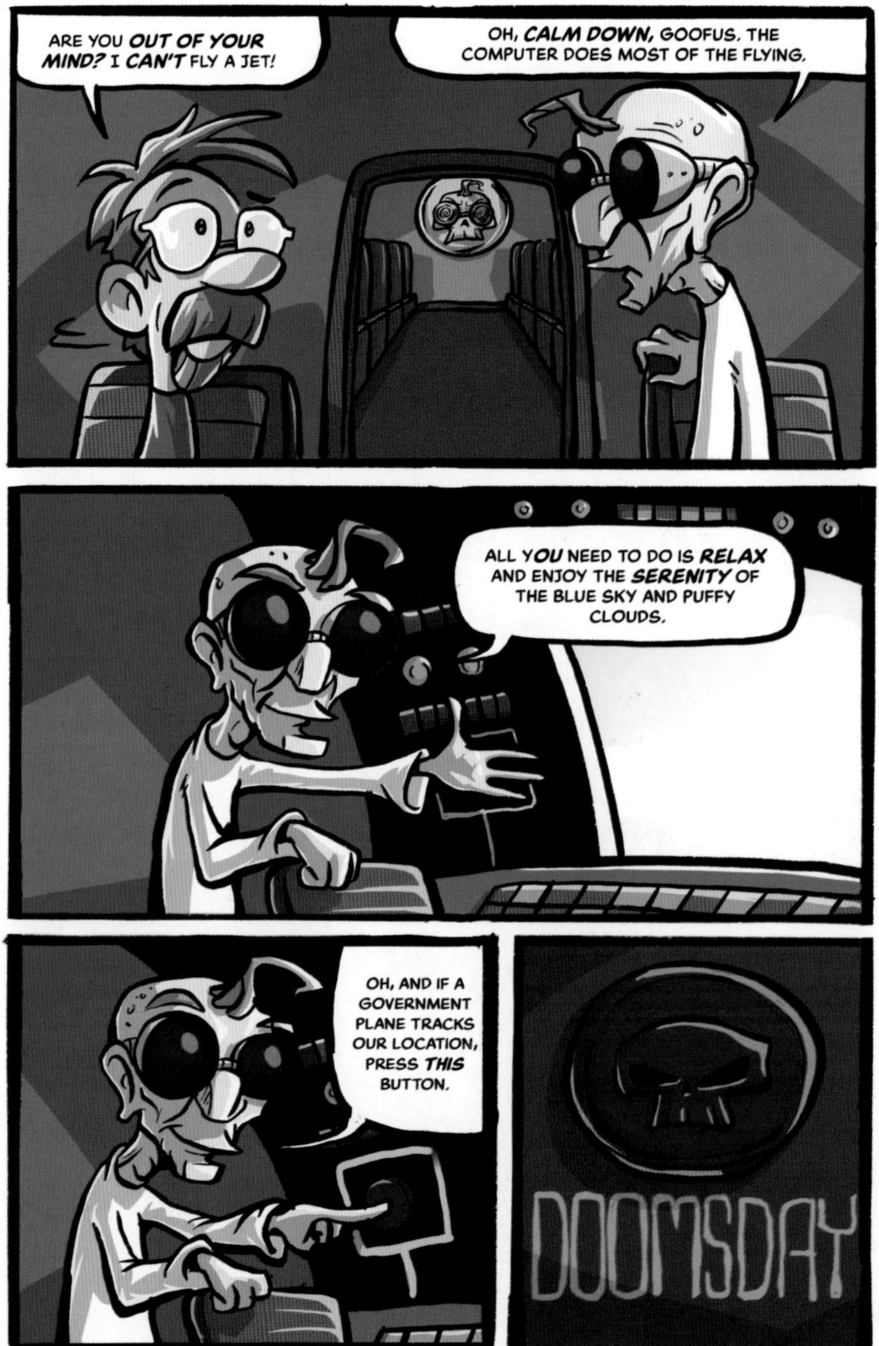
ARE YOU **OUT OF YOUR MIND?** I **CAN'T** FLY A JET!
OH, **CALM DOWN,** GOOFUS. THE COMPUTER DOES MOST OF THE FLYING.
ALL Y**OU** NEED TO DO IS **RELAX** AND ENJOY THE **SERENITY** OF THE BLUE SKY AND PUFFY CLOUDS.
OH, AND IF A GOVERNMENT PLANE TRACKS OUR LOCATION, PRESS **THIS** BUTTON.
DOOMSDAY

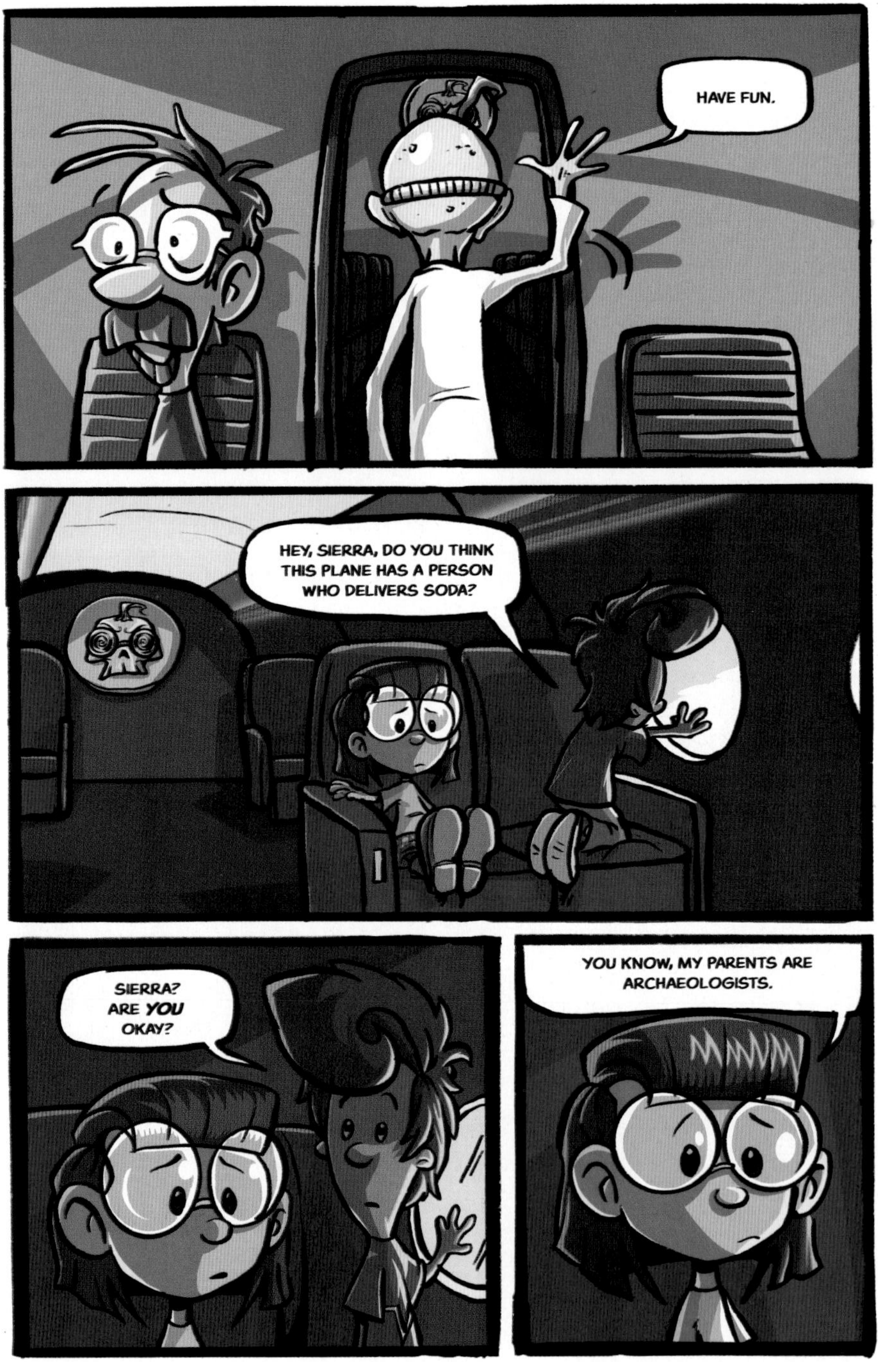
HAVE FUN.
HEY, SIERRA, DO YOU THINK THIS PLANE HAS A PERSON WHO DELIVERS SODA?
SIERRA? ARE *YOU* OKAY?
YOU KNOW, MY PARENTS ARE ARCHAEOLOGISTS.

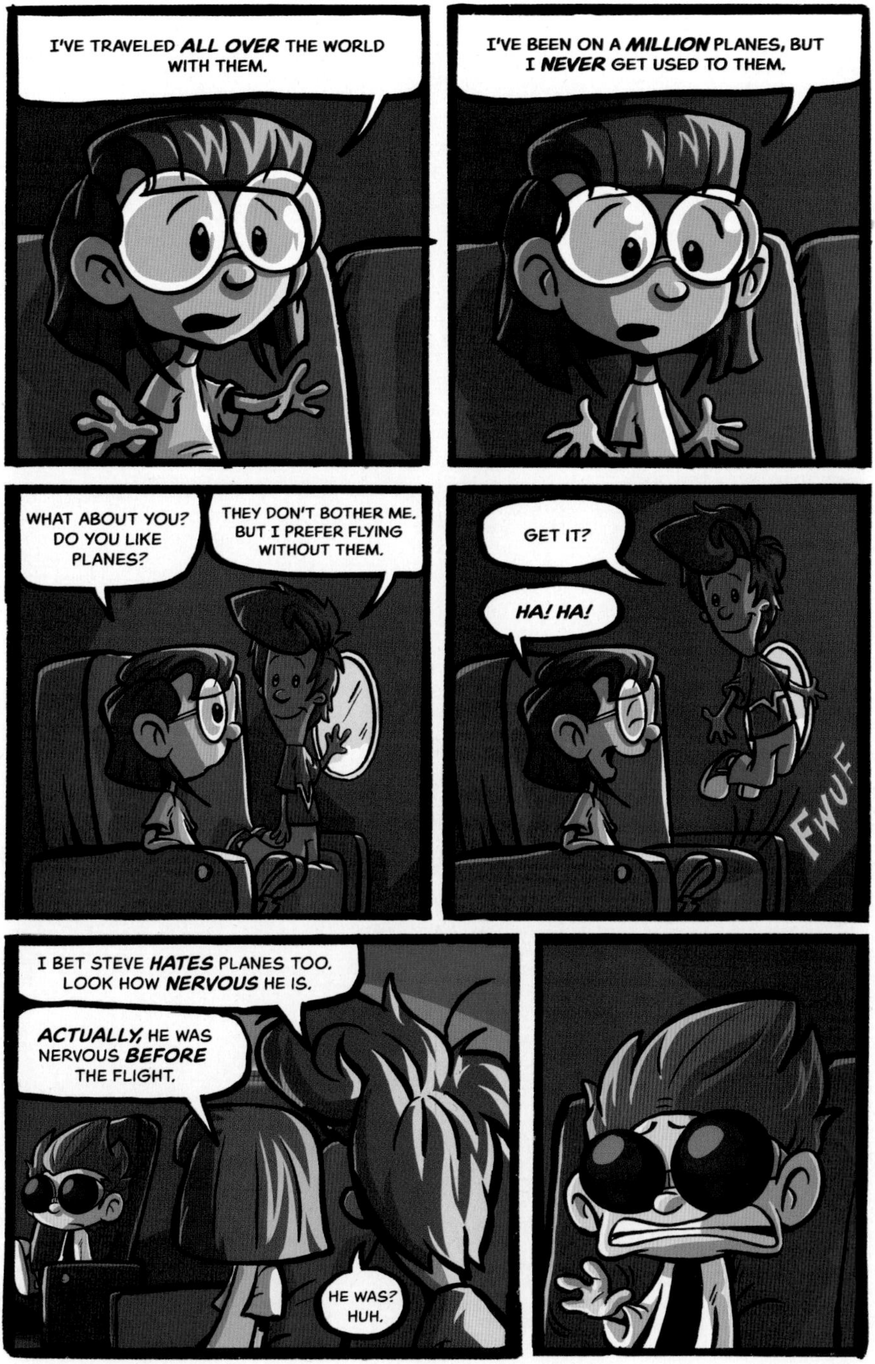
I'VE TRAVELED ALL OVER THE WORLD WITH THEM.
I'VE BEEN ON A MILLION PLANES, BUT I NEVER GET USED TO THEM.
WHAT ABOUT YOU? DO YOU LIKE PLANES?
THEY DON'T BOTHER ME. BUT I PREFER FLYING WITHOUT THEM.
GET IT?
HA! HA!
FWUF
I BET STEVE HATES PLANES TOO. LOOK HOW NERVOUS HE IS.
ACTUALLY, HE WAS NERVOUS BEFORE THE FLIGHT.
HE WAS? HUH.

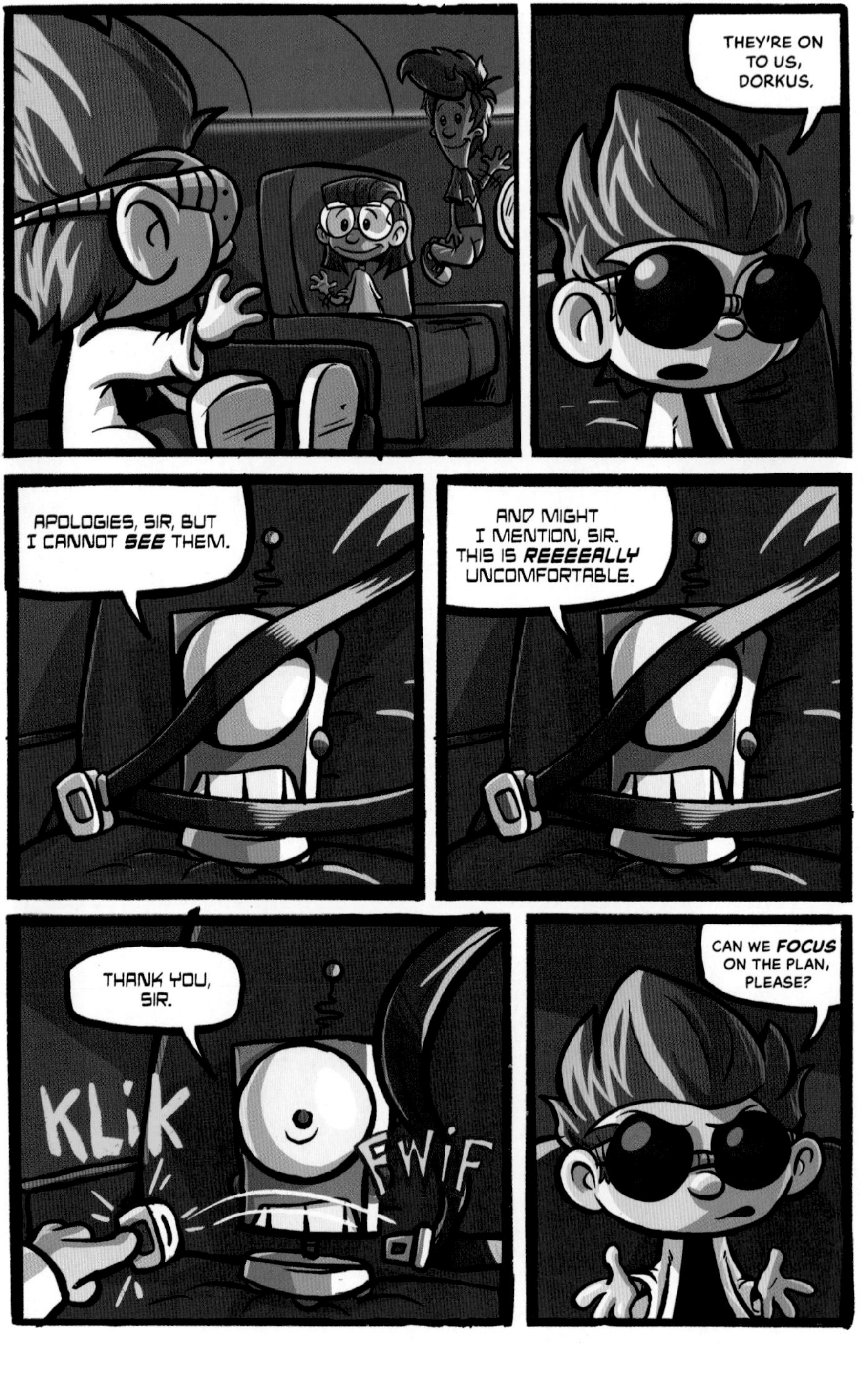
THEY'RE ON TO US, DORKUS.
APOLOGIES, SIR, BUT I CANNOT SEE THEM.
AND MIGHT I MENTION, SIR. THIS IS REEEEALLY UNCOMFORTABLE.
THANK YOU, SIR.
KLIK
FWIF
CAN WE FOCUS ON THE PLAN, PLEASE?

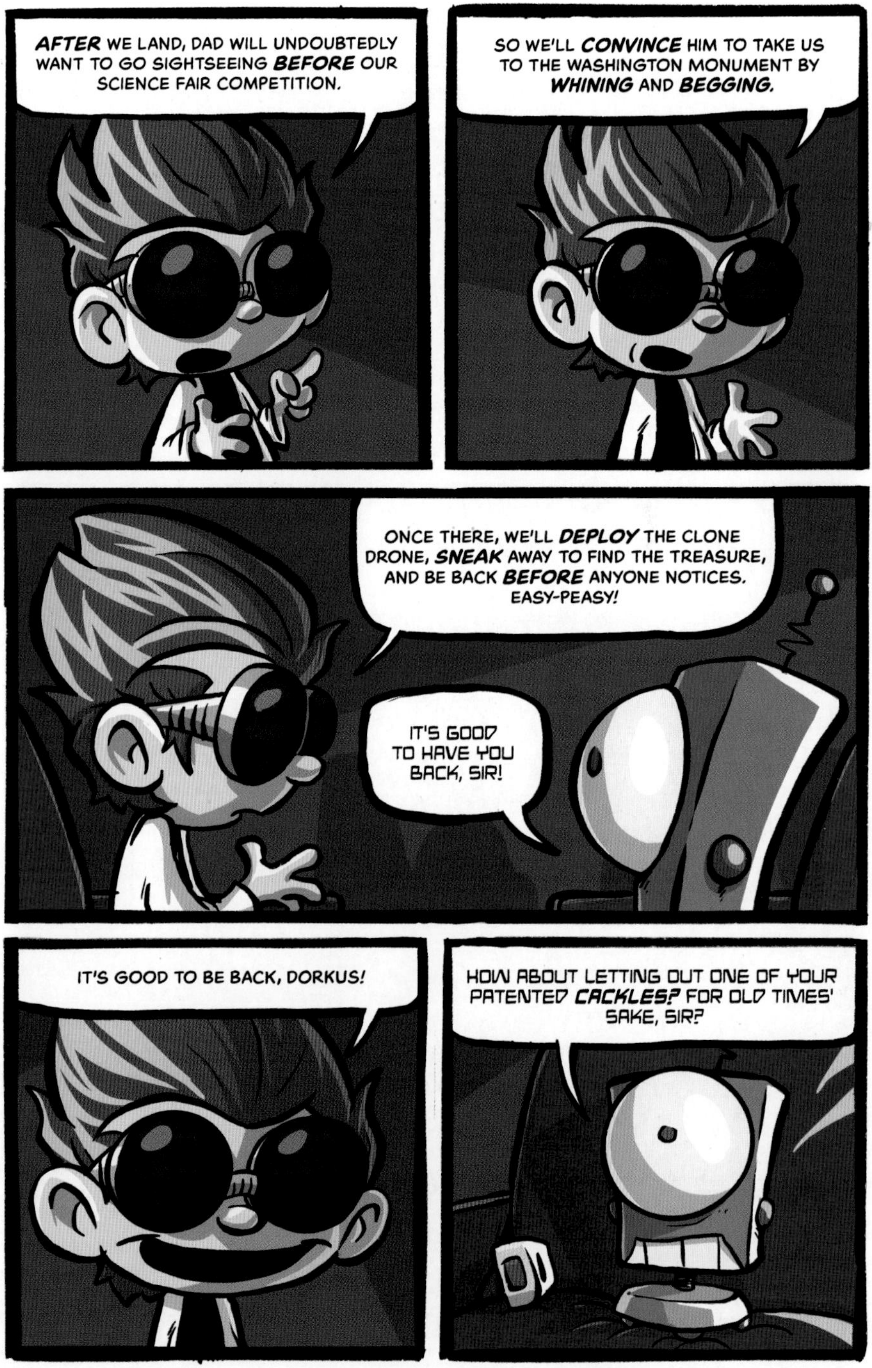
AFTER WE LAND, DAD WILL UNDOUBTEDLY WANT TO GO SIGHTSEEING BEFORE OUR SCIENCE FAIR COMPETITION.
SO WE'LL CONVINCE HIM TO TAKE US TO THE WASHINGTON MONUMENT BY WHINING AND BEGGING.
ONCE THERE, WE'LL DEPLOY THE CLONE DRONE, SNEAK AWAY TO FIND THE TREASURE, AND BE BACK BEFORE ANYONE NOTICES. EASY-PEASY!
IT'S GOOD TO HAVE YOU BACK, SIR!
IT'S GOOD TO BE BACK, DORKUS!
HOW ABOUT LETTING OUT ONE OF YOUR PATENTED CACKLES? FOR OLD TIMES' SAKE, SIR?

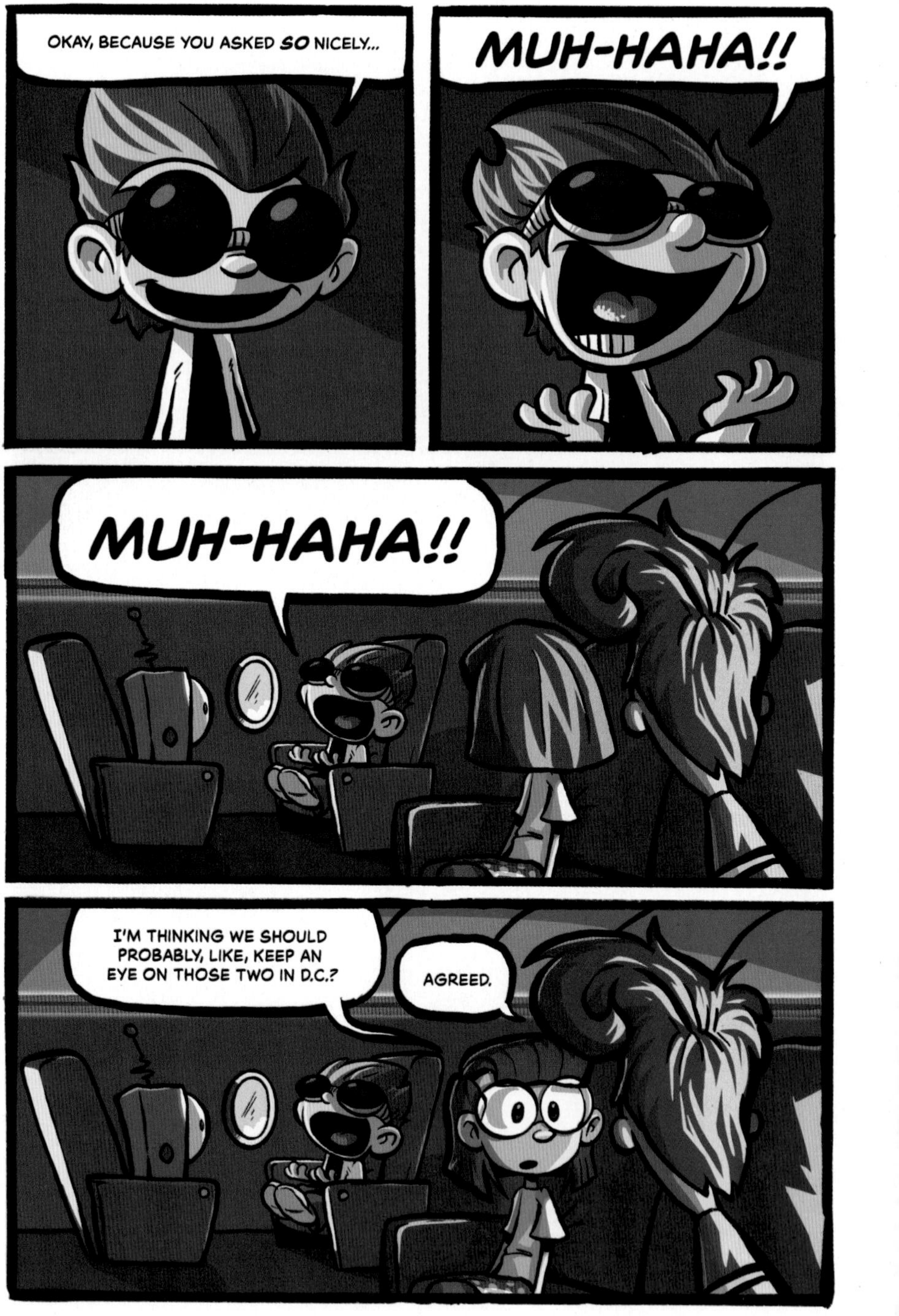
OKAY, BECAUSE YOU ASKED SO NICELY...
MUH-HAHA!!
MUH-HAHA!!
I'M THINKING WE SHOULD PROBABLY, LIKE, KEEP AN EYE ON THOSE TWO IN D.C.?
AGREED.

CHAPTER 8

"Across the Pond"

EVERYONE, REMEMBER *WHERE* WE'RE PARKED.
NO PARKING

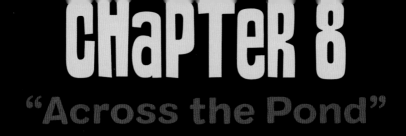

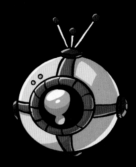

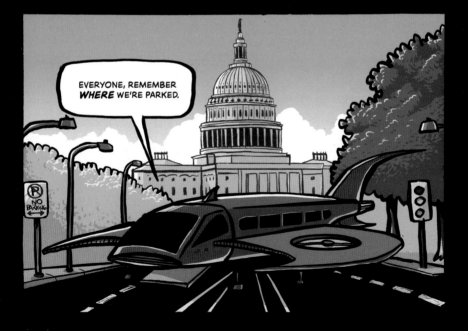

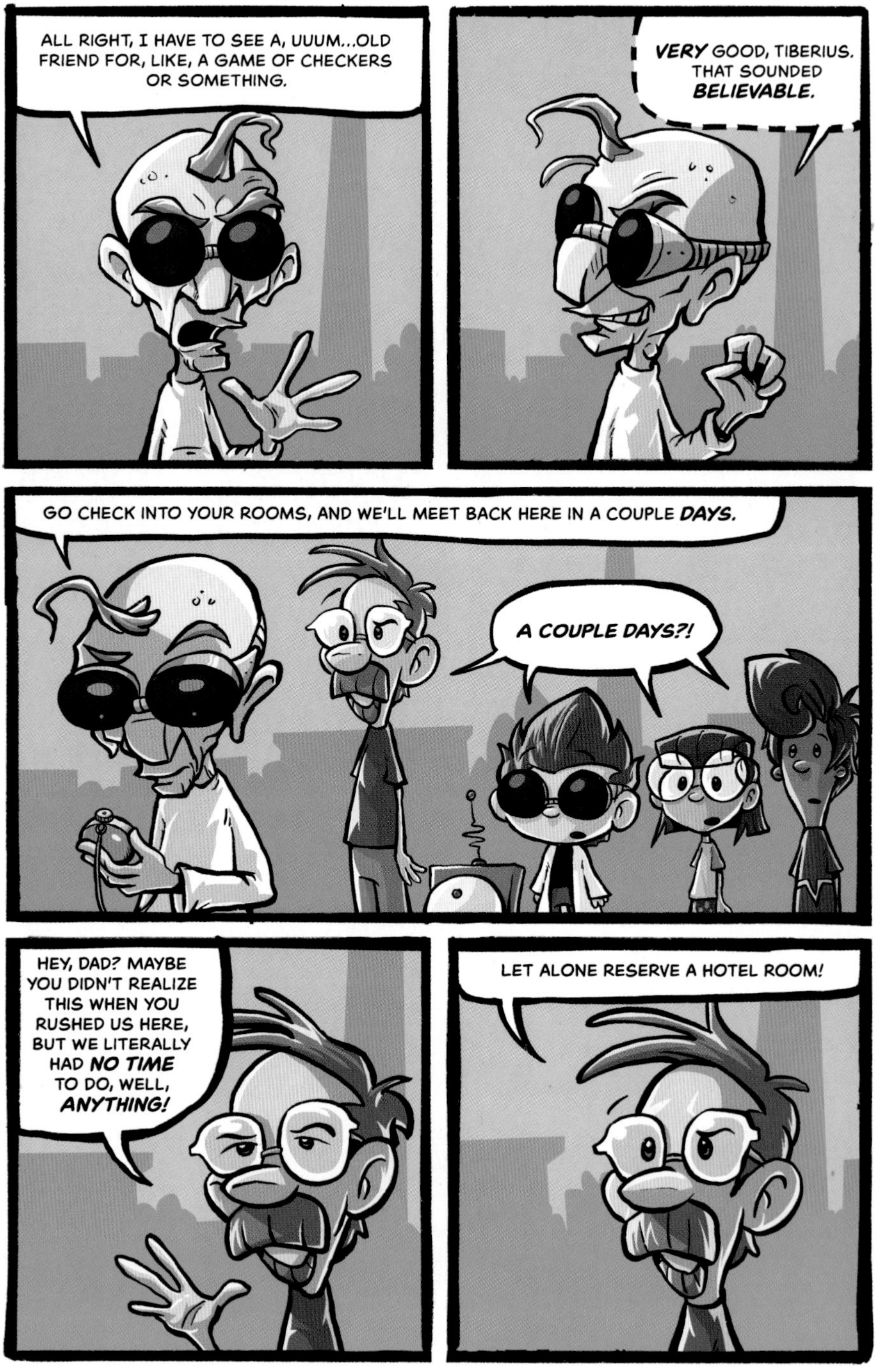
ALL RIGHT, I HAVE TO SEE A, UUUM...OLD FRIEND FOR, LIKE, A GAME OF CHECKERS OR SOMETHING.
VERY GOOD, TIBERIUS. THAT SOUNDED BELIEVABLE.
GO CHECK INTO YOUR ROOMS, AND WE'LL MEET BACK HERE IN A COUPLE DAYS.
A COUPLE DAYS?!
HEY, DAD? MAYBE YOU DIDN'T REALIZE THIS WHEN YOU RUSHED US HERE, BUT WE LITERALLY HAD NO TIME TO DO, WELL, ANYTHING!
LET ALONE RESERVE A HOTEL ROOM!

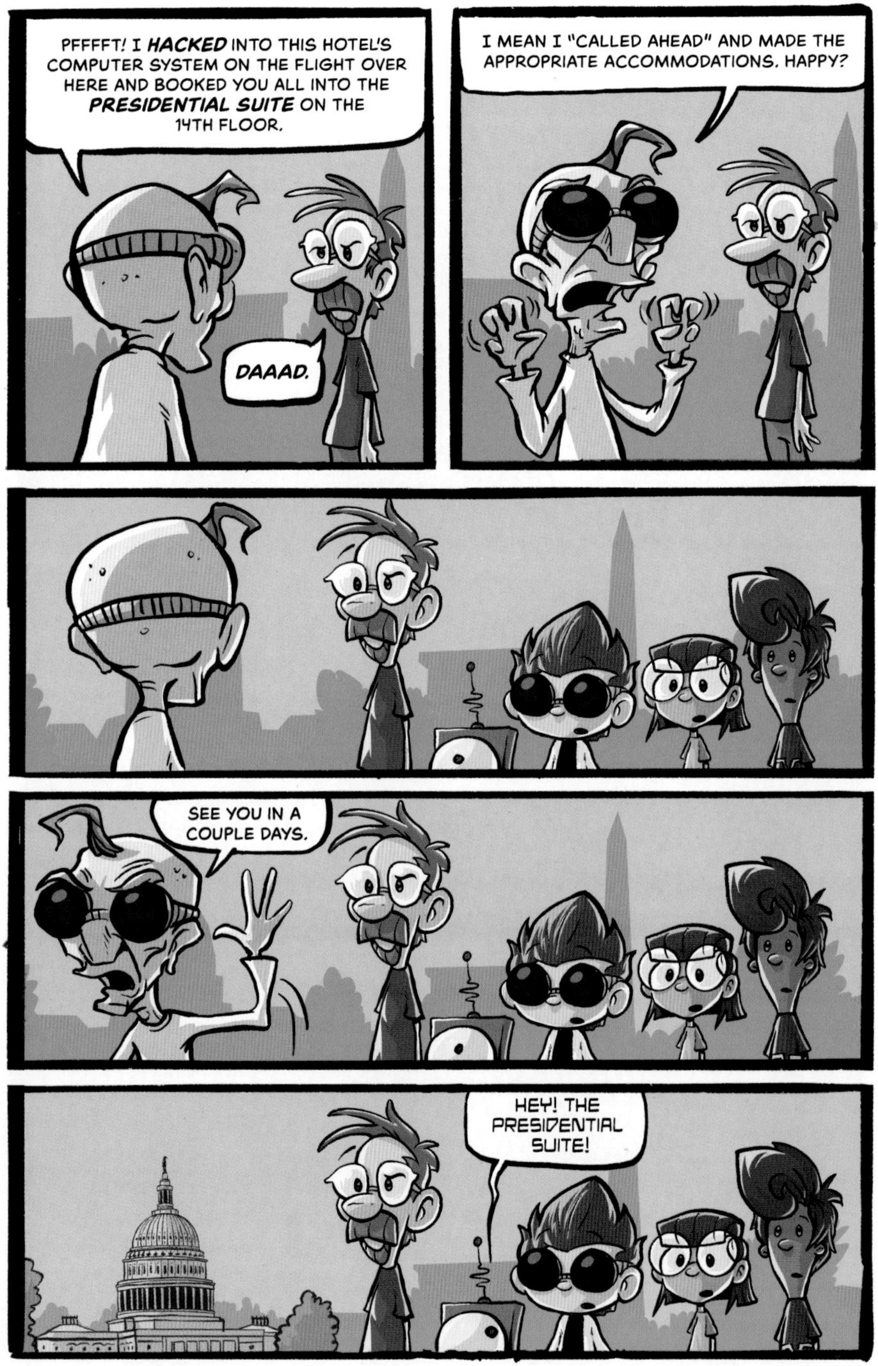
PFFFFT! I HACKED INTO THIS HOTEL'S COMPUTER SYSTEM ON THE FLIGHT OVER HERE AND BOOKED YOU ALL INTO THE PRESIDENTIAL SUITE ON THE 14TH FLOOR.
DAAAD.
I MEAN I "CALLED AHEAD" AND MADE THE APPROPRIATE ACCOMMODATIONS. HAPPY?
SEE YOU IN A COUPLE DAYS.
HEY! THE PRESIDENTIAL SUITE!

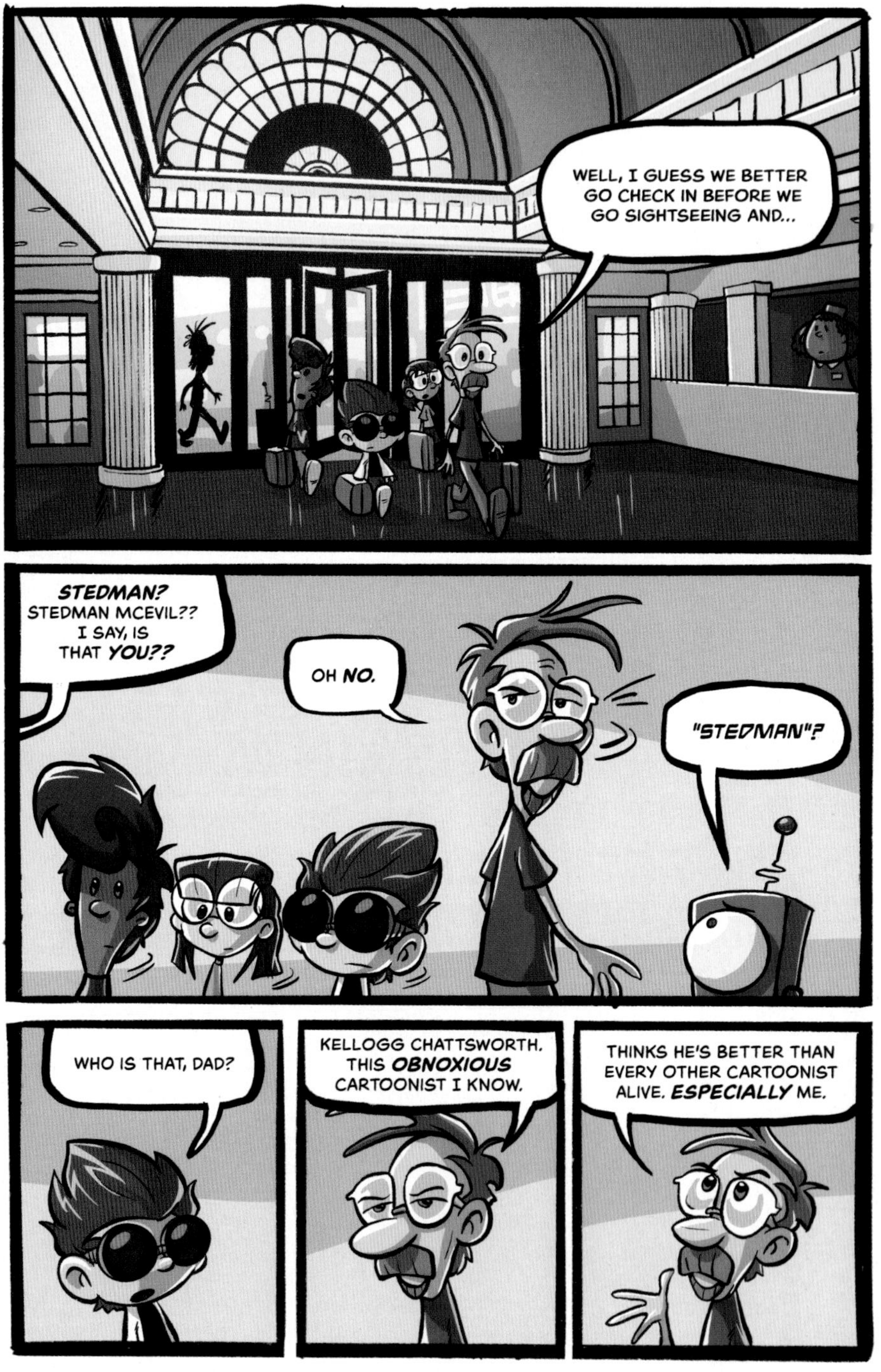
WELL, I GUESS WE BETTER GO CHECK IN BEFORE WE GO SIGHTSEEING AND...
STEDMAN? STEDMAN MCEVIL?? I SAY, IS THAT YOU??
OH NO.
"STEDMAN"?
WHO IS THAT, DAD?
KELLOGG CHATTSWORTH. THIS OBNOXIOUS CARTOONIST I KNOW.
THINKS HE'S BETTER THAN EVERY OTHER CARTOONIST ALIVE. ESPECIALLY ME.

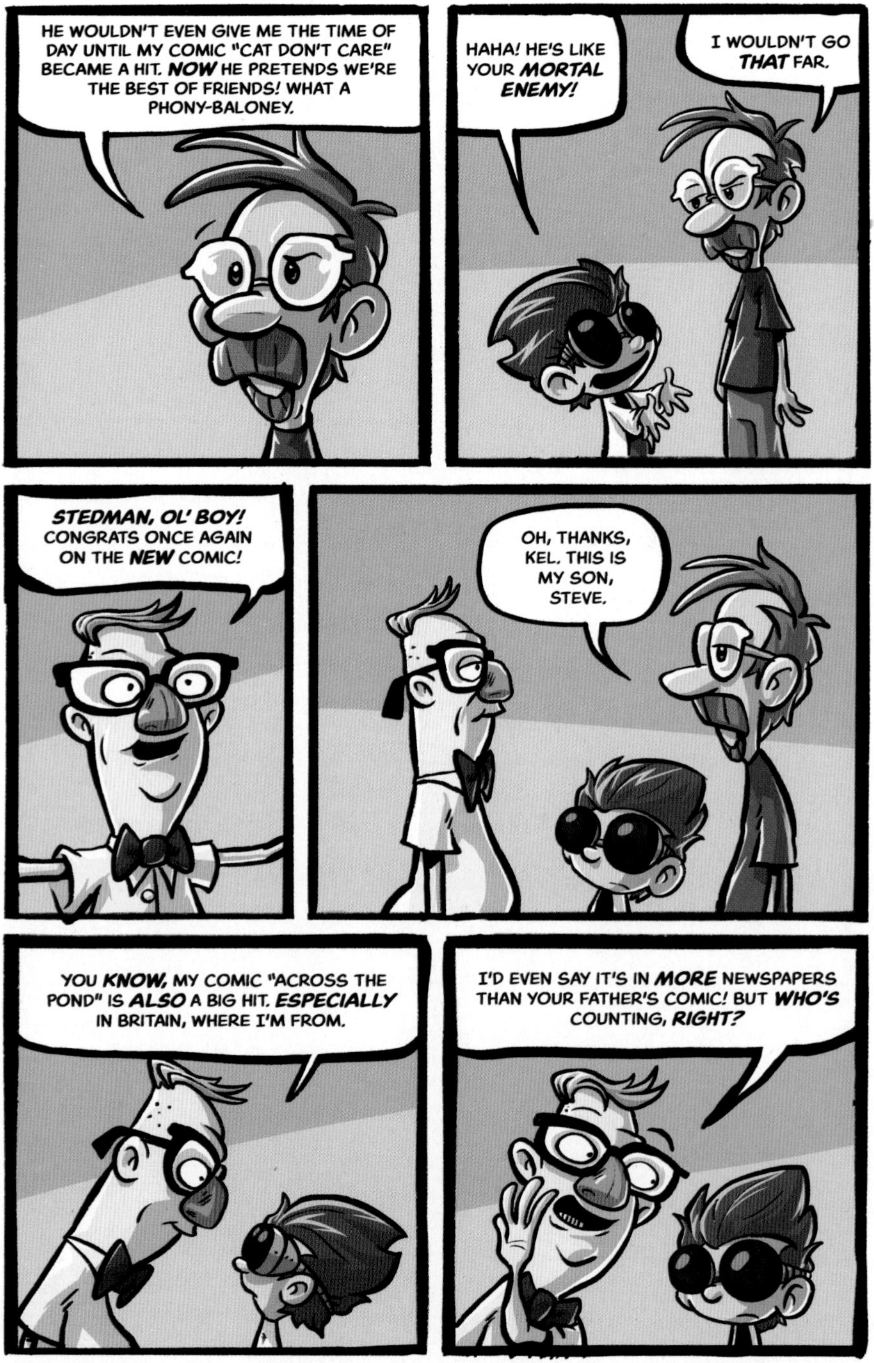

HE WOULDN'T EVEN GIVE ME THE TIME OF DAY UNTIL MY COMIC "CAT DON'T CARE" BECAME A HIT. NOW HE PRETENDS WE'RE THE BEST OF FRIENDS! WHAT A PHONY-BALONEY.
HAHA! HE'S LIKE YOUR MORTAL ENEMY!
I WOULDN'T GO THAT FAR.
STEDMAN, OL' BOY! CONGRATS ONCE AGAIN ON THE NEW COMIC!
OH, THANKS, KEL. THIS IS MY SON, STEVE.
YOU KNOW, MY COMIC "ACROSS THE POND" IS ALSO A BIG HIT. ESPECIALLY IN BRITAIN, WHERE I'M FROM.
I'D EVEN SAY IT'S IN MORE NEWSPAPERS THAN YOUR FATHER'S COMIC! BUT WHO'S COUNTING, RIGHT?

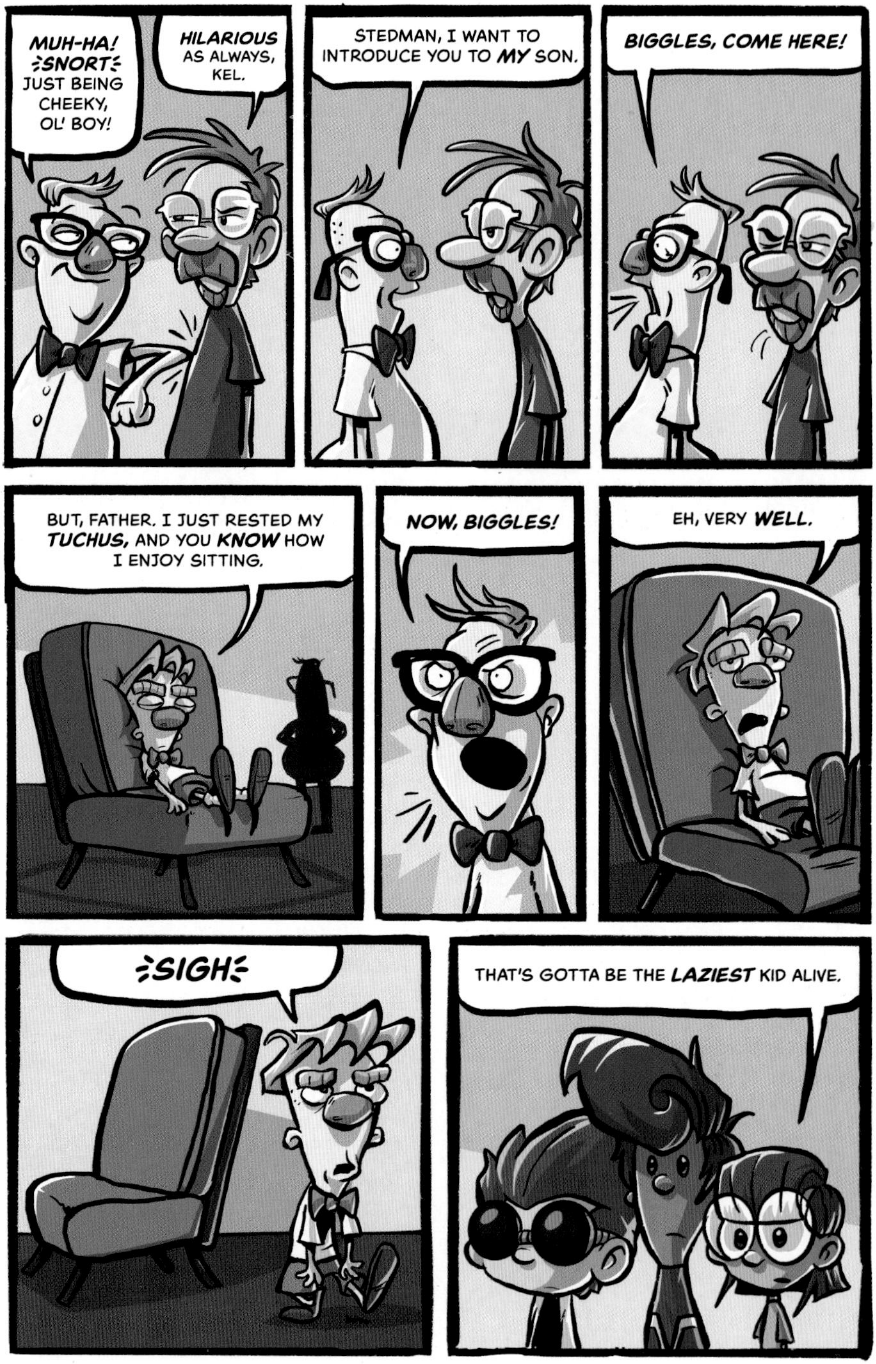
MUH-HA! SNORT JUST BEING CHEEKY, OL' BOY!
HILARIOUS AS ALWAYS, KEL.
STEDMAN, I WANT TO INTRODUCE YOU TO MY SON.
BIGGLES, COME HERE!
BUT, FATHER. I JUST RESTED MY TUCHUS, AND YOU KNOW HOW I ENJOY SITTING.
NOW, BIGGLES!
EH, VERY WELL.
SIGH
THAT'S GOTTA BE THE LAZIEST KID ALIVE.

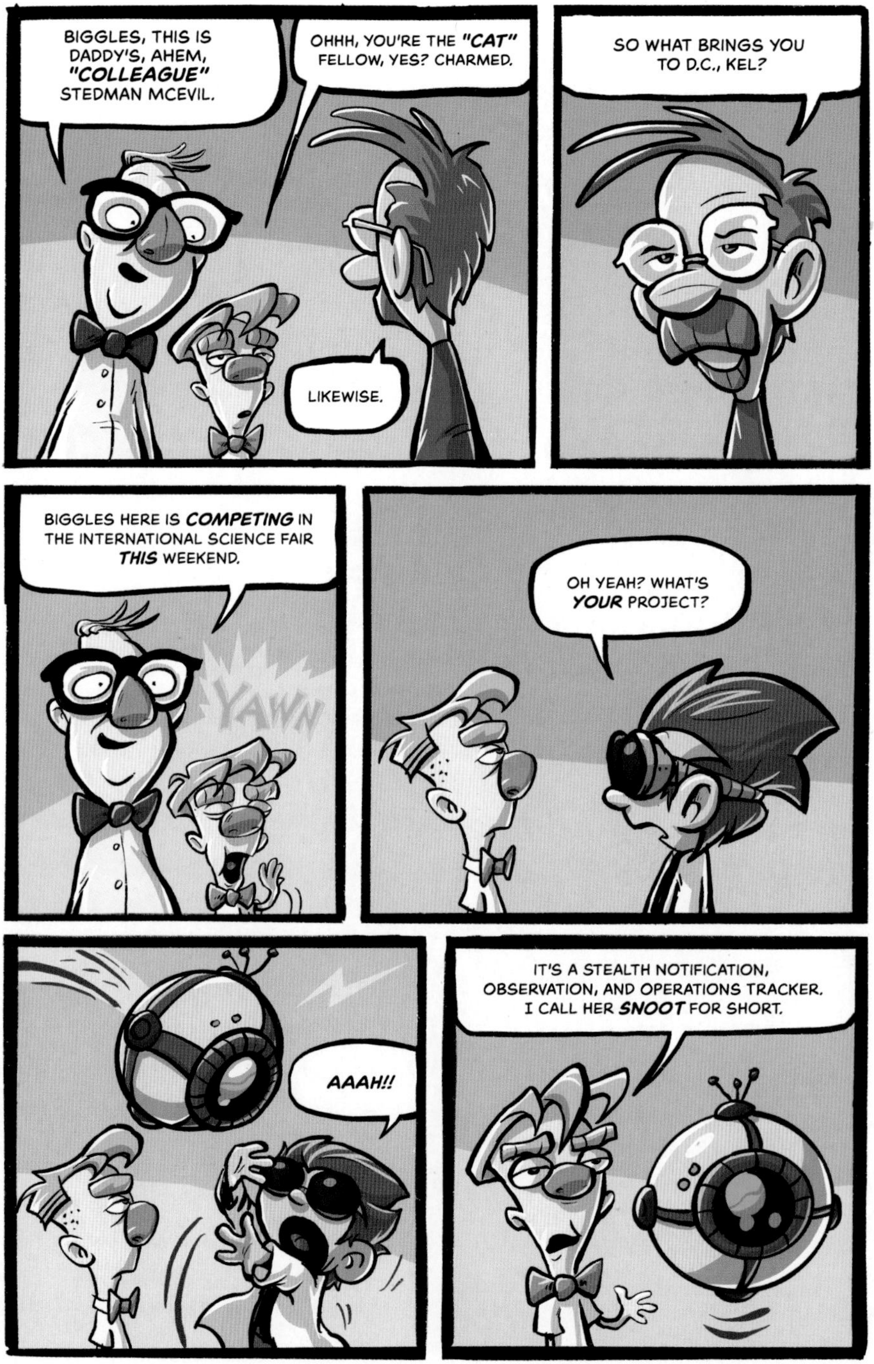
BIGGLES, THIS IS DADDY'S, AHEM, *"COLLEAGUE"* STEDMAN MCEVIL.
OHHH, YOU'RE THE *"CAT"* FELLOW, YES? CHARMED.
LIKEWISE.
SO WHAT BRINGS YOU TO D.C., KEL?
BIGGLES HERE IS *COMPETING* IN THE INTERNATIONAL SCIENCE FAIR *THIS* WEEKEND.
YAWN
OH YEAH? WHAT'S *YOUR* PROJECT?
AAAH!!
IT'S A STEALTH NOTIFICATION, OBSERVATION, AND OPERATIONS TRACKER. I CALL HER *SNOOT* FOR SHORT.

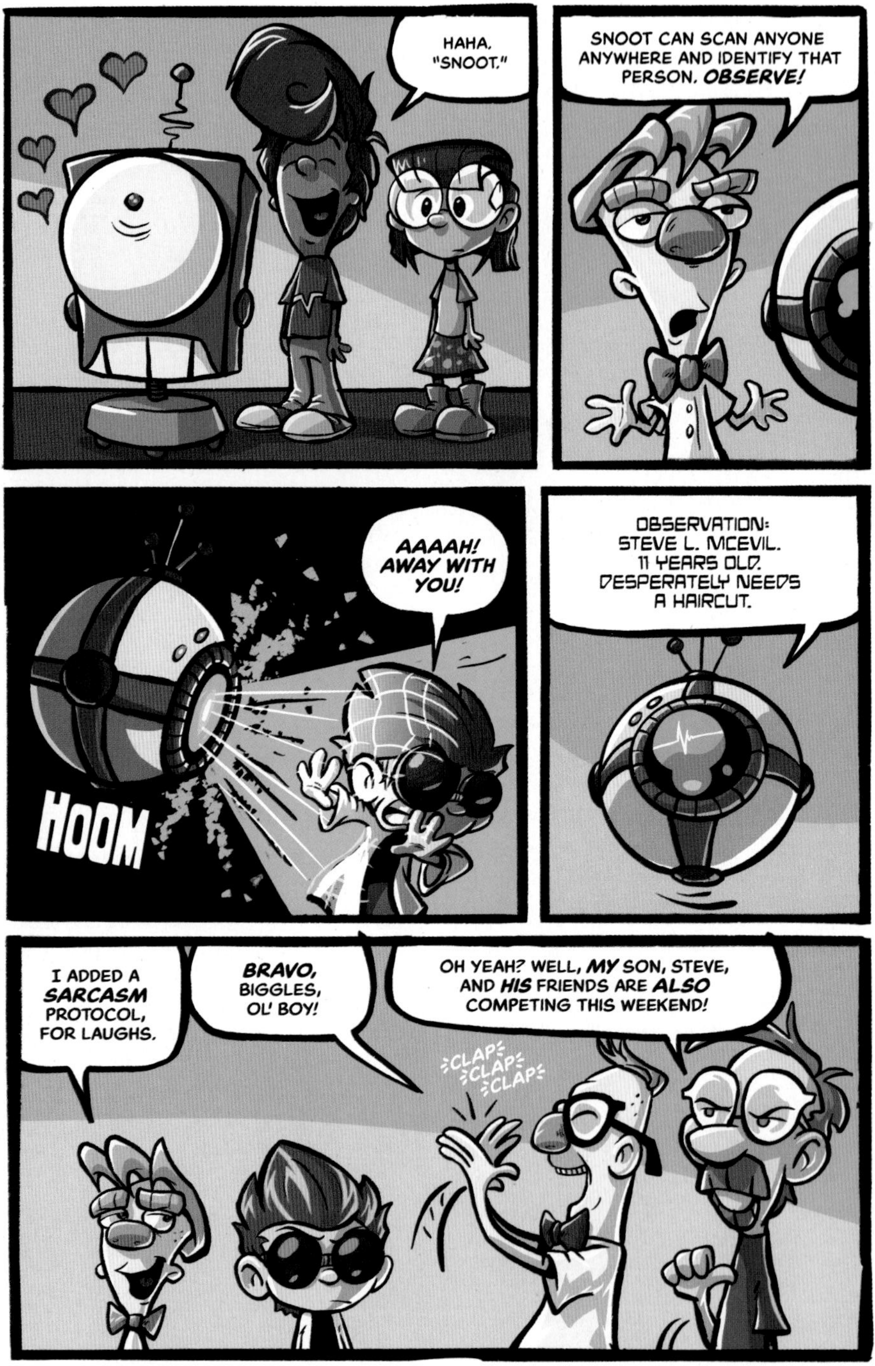
HAHA. "SNOOT."
SNOOT CAN SCAN ANYONE ANYWHERE AND IDENTIFY THAT PERSON. OBSERVE!
AAAAH! AWAY WITH YOU!
HOOM
OBSERVATION: STEVE L. MCEVIL. 11 YEARS OLD. DESPERATELY NEEDS A HAIRCUT.
I ADDED A SARCASM PROTOCOL, FOR LAUGHS.
BRAVO, BIGGLES, OL' BOY!
OH YEAH? WELL, MY SON, STEVE, AND HIS FRIENDS ARE ALSO COMPETING THIS WEEKEND!
CLAP CLAP CLAP

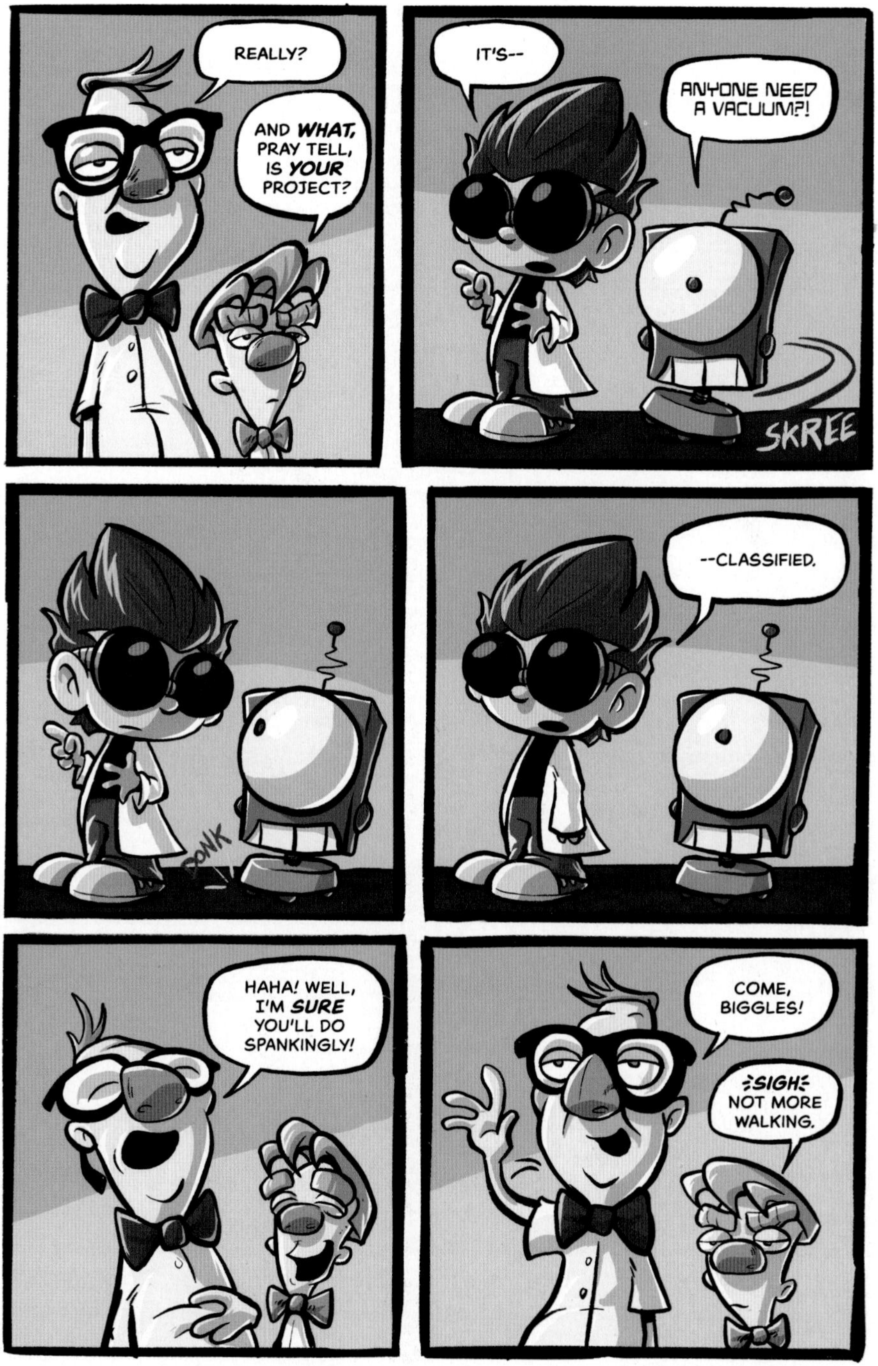
REALLY?
AND WHAT, PRAY TELL, IS YOUR PROJECT?
IT'S--
ANYONE NEED A VACUUM?!
SKREE
DONK
--CLASSIFIED.
HAHA! WELL, I'M SURE YOU'LL DO SPANKINGLY!
COME, BIGGLES!
SIGH NOT MORE WALKING.

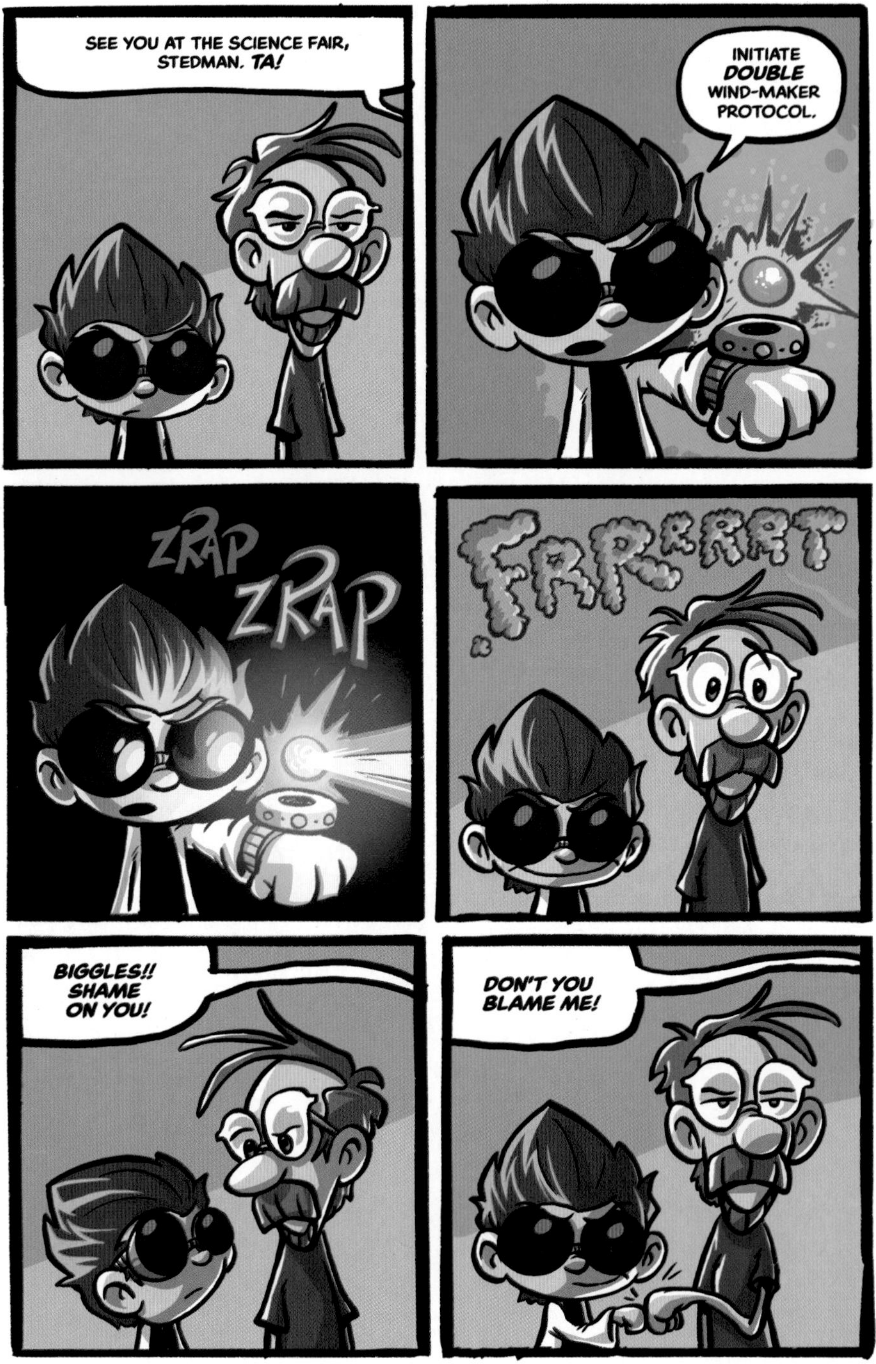
SEE YOU AT THE SCIENCE FAIR, STEDMAN. TA!
INITIATE DOUBLE WIND-MAKER PROTOCOL.
ZRAP
ZRAP
FRRERRRT
BIGGLES!! SHAME ON YOU!
DON'T YOU BLAME ME!

CHAPTER 9

Capital Capitol!

WELCOME TO WASHINGTON, D.C.! OUR FIRST STOP ON THE TOUR IS THE JEFFERSON MEMORIAL!
UM, THAT'S THE CAPITOL BUILDING.
CAPITAL OBSERVATION!

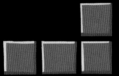

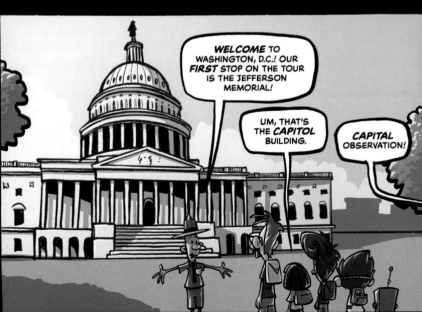

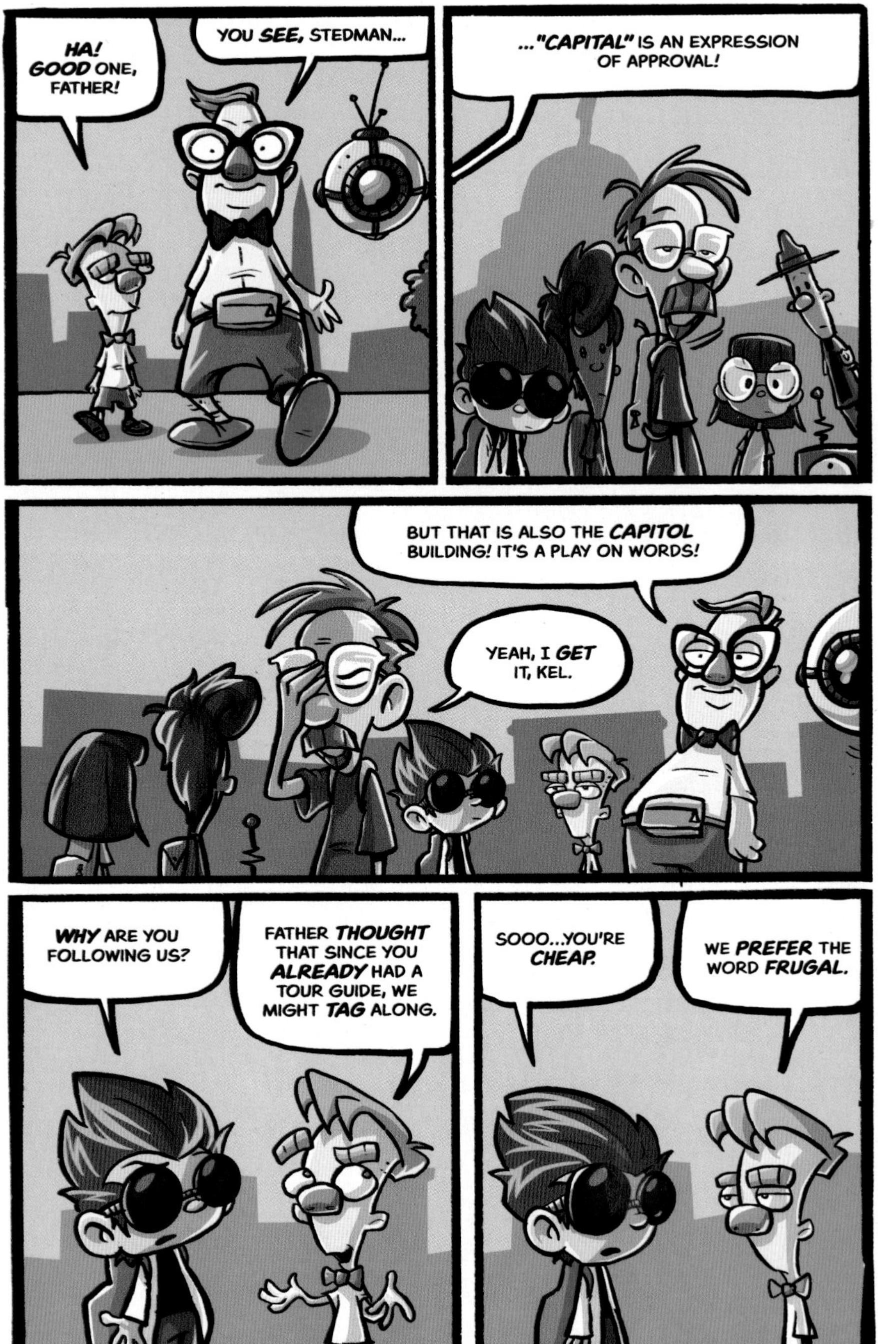
HA! GOOD ONE, FATHER!
YOU SEE, STEDMAN...
..."CAPITAL" IS AN EXPRESSION OF APPROVAL!
BUT THAT IS ALSO THE CAPITOL BUILDING! IT'S A PLAY ON WORDS!
YEAH, I GET IT, KEL.
WHY ARE YOU FOLLOWING US?
FATHER THOUGHT THAT SINCE YOU ALREADY HAD A TOUR GUIDE, WE MIGHT TAG ALONG.
SOOO...YOU'RE CHEAP.
WE PREFER THE WORD FRUGAL.

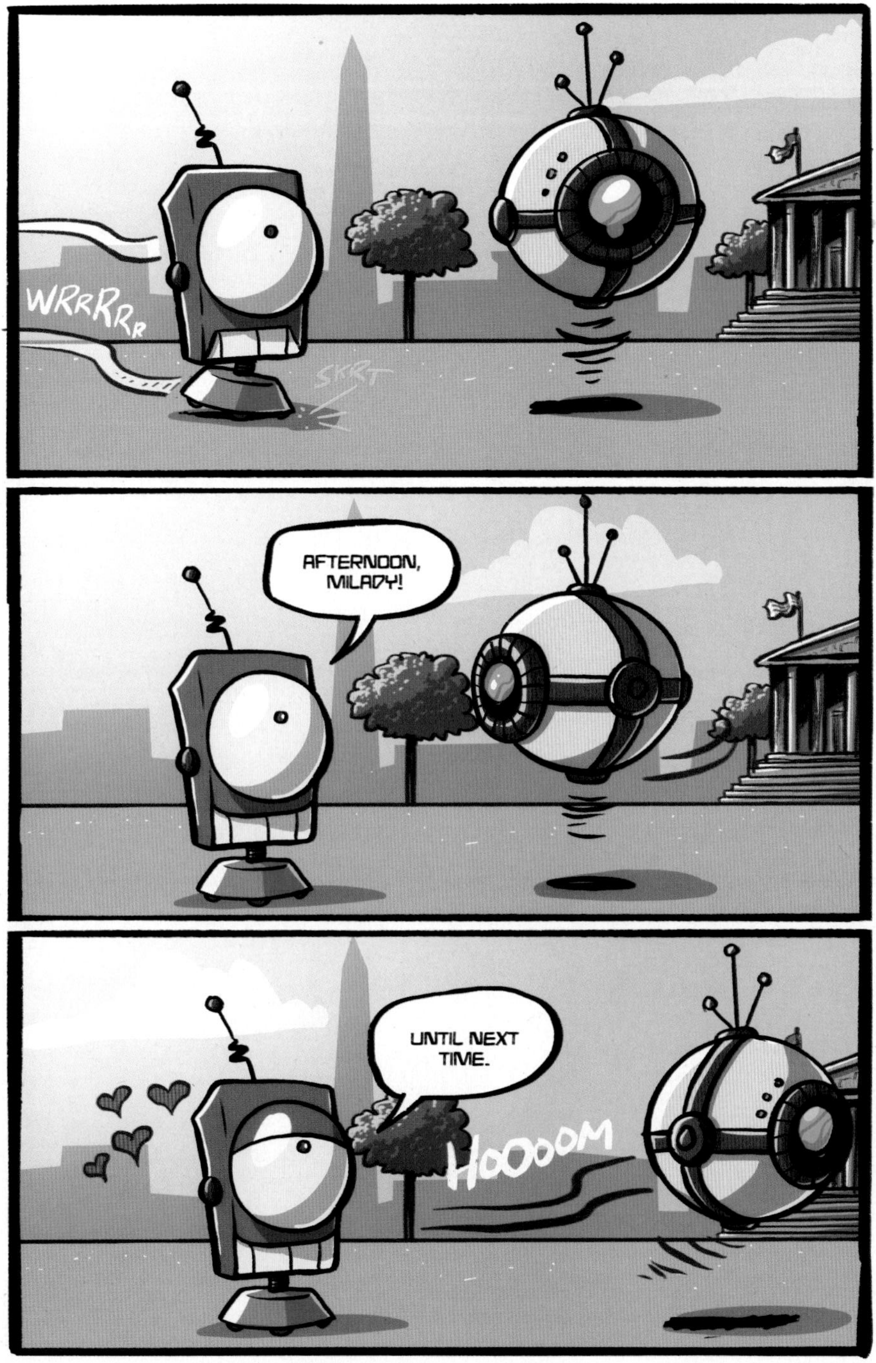
WRRRRR
SKRT
AFTERNOON, MILADY!
UNTIL NEXT TIME.
HOOOOM

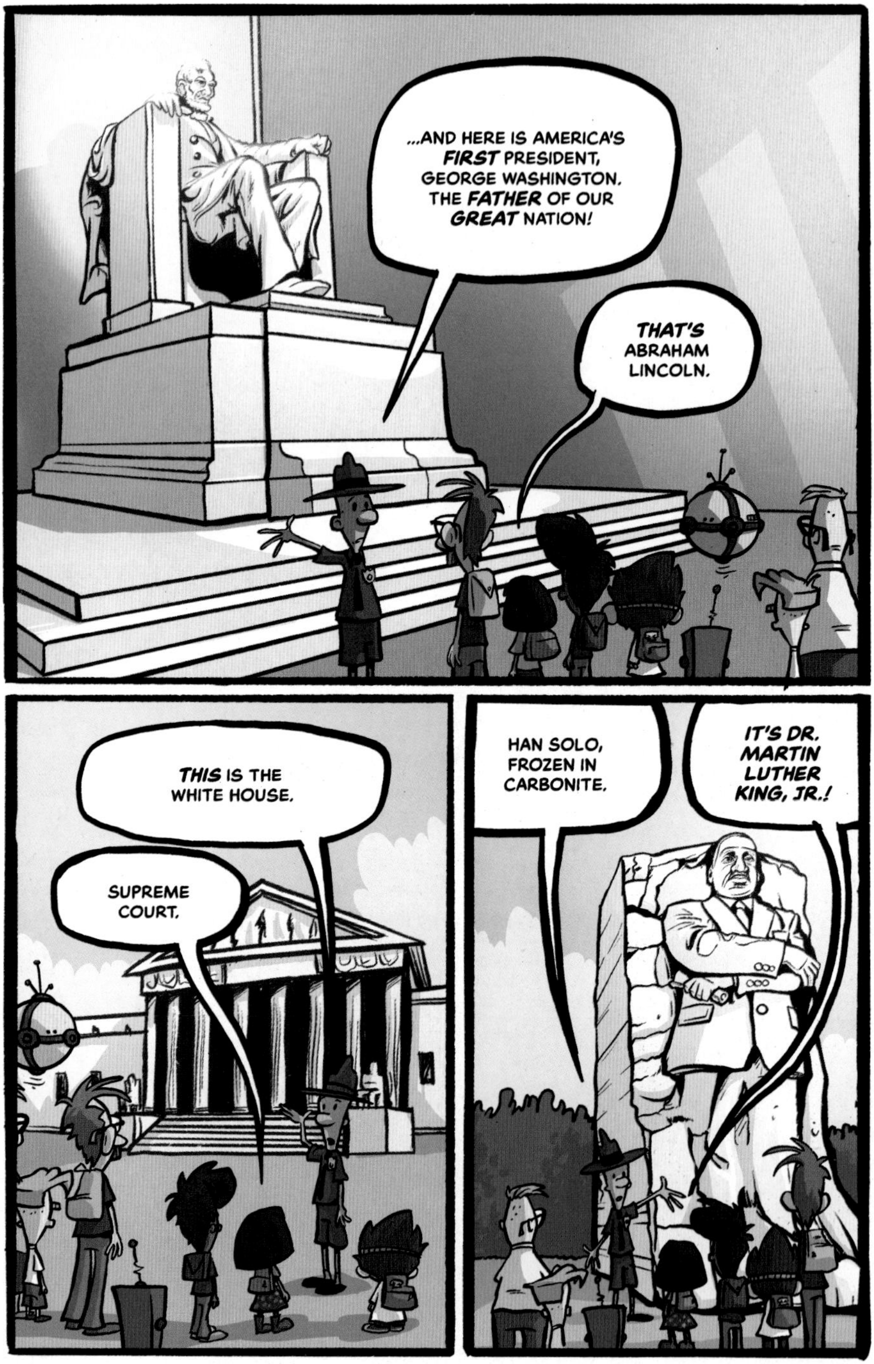
...AND HERE IS AMERICA'S FIRST PRESIDENT, GEORGE WASHINGTON. THE FATHER OF OUR GREAT NATION!
THAT'S ABRAHAM LINCOLN.
THIS IS THE WHITE HOUSE.
SUPREME COURT.
HAN SOLO, FROZEN IN CARBONITE.
IT'S DR. MARTIN LUTHER KING, JR.!

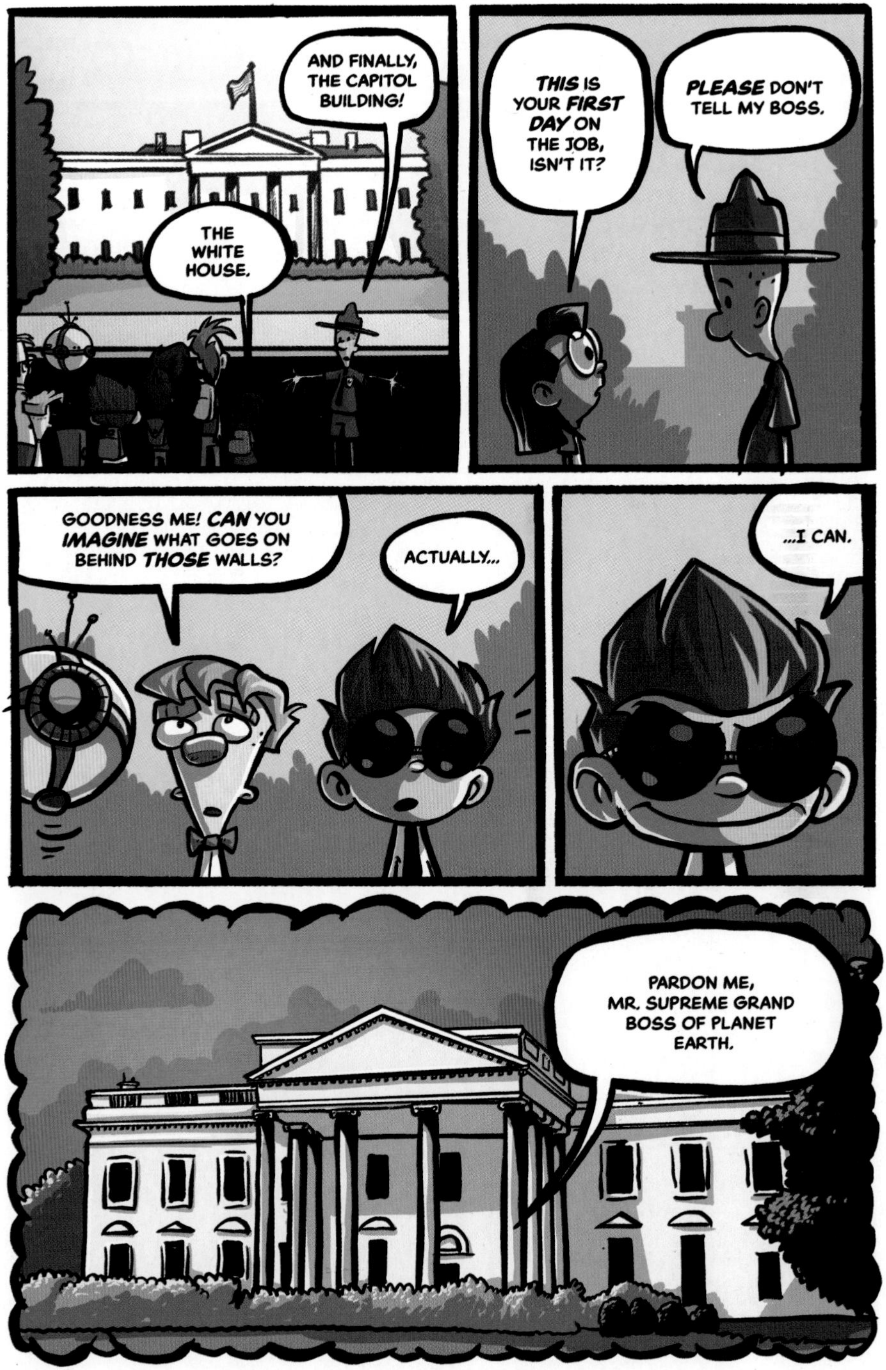
AND FINALLY, THE CAPITOL BUILDING!
THE WHITE HOUSE.
THIS IS YOUR FIRST DAY ON THE JOB, ISN'T IT?
PLEASE DON'T TELL MY BOSS.
GOODNESS ME! CAN YOU IMAGINE WHAT GOES ON BEHIND THOSE WALLS?
ACTUALLY...
...I CAN.
PARDON ME, MR. SUPREME GRAND BOSS OF PLANET EARTH.

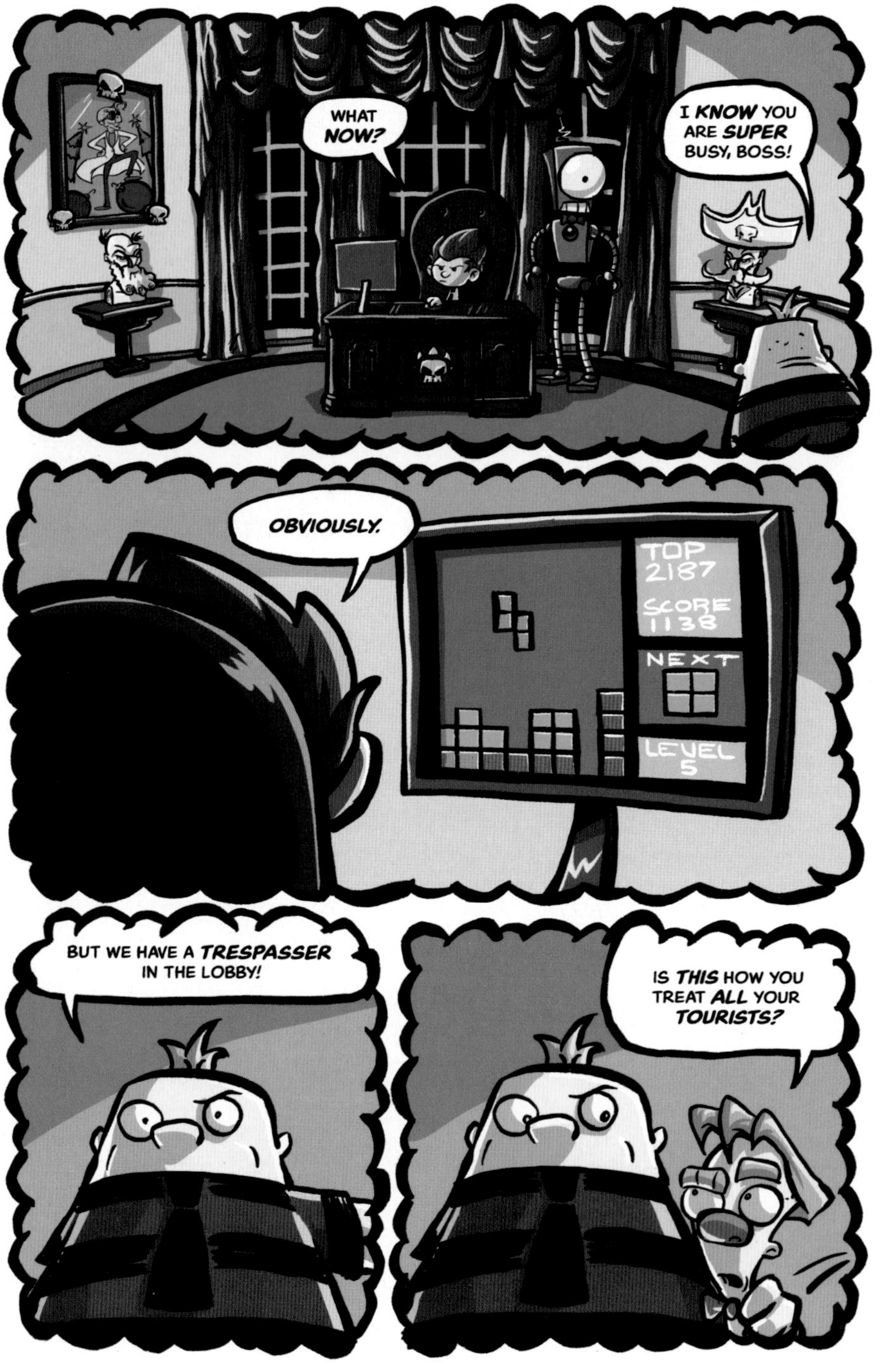
WHAT NOW?
I KNOW YOU ARE SUPER BUSY, BOSS!
OBVIOUSLY.
TOP 2187
SCORE 1138
NEXT
LEVEL 5
BUT WE HAVE A TRESPASSER IN THE LOBBY!
IS THIS HOW YOU TREAT ALL YOUR TOURISTS?

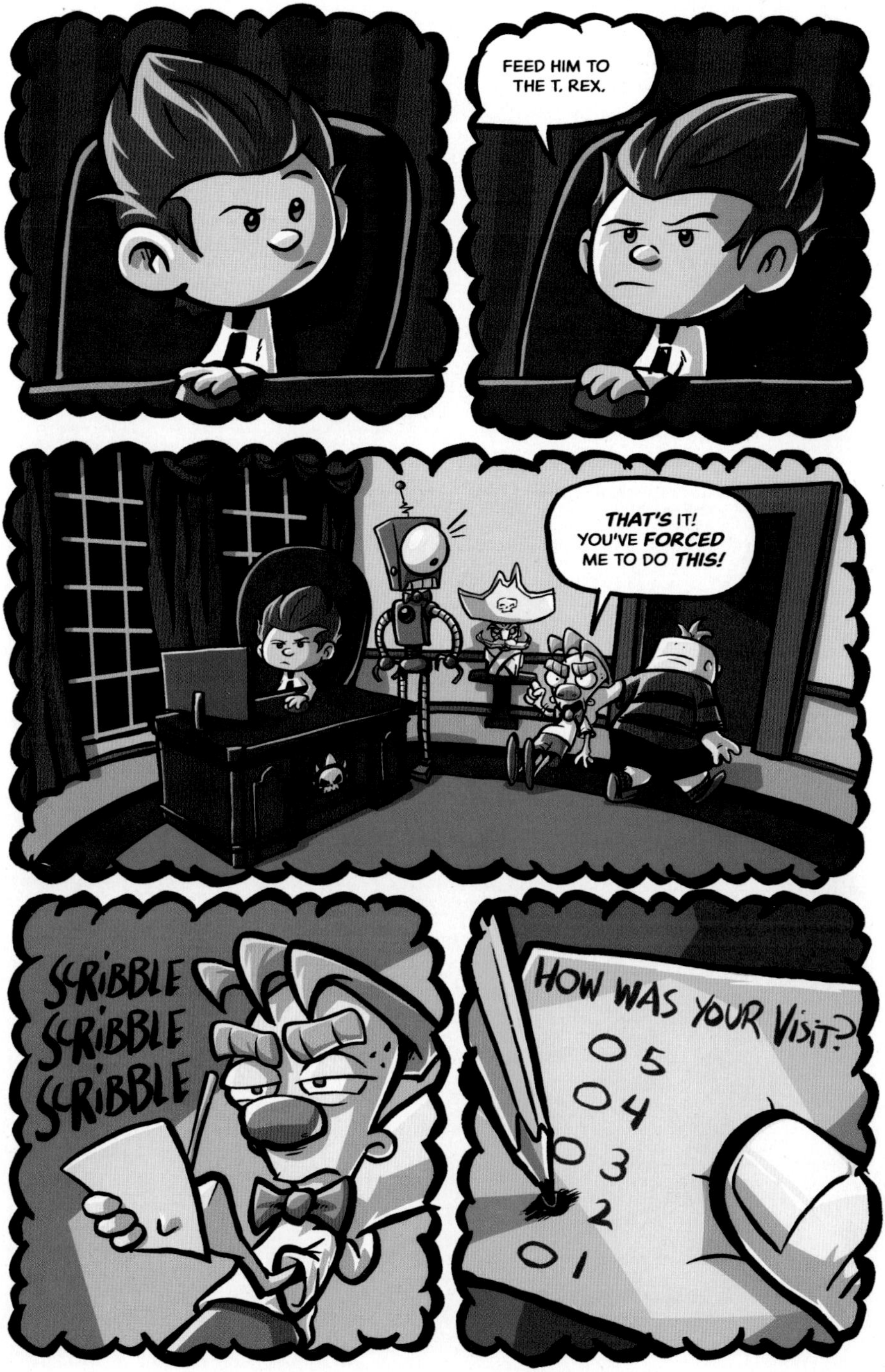
FEED HIM TO THE T. REX.
THAT'S IT! YOU'VE FORCED ME TO DO THIS!
SCRIBBLE SCRIBBLE SCRIBBLE
HOW WAS YOUR VISIT?
5
4
3
2
1

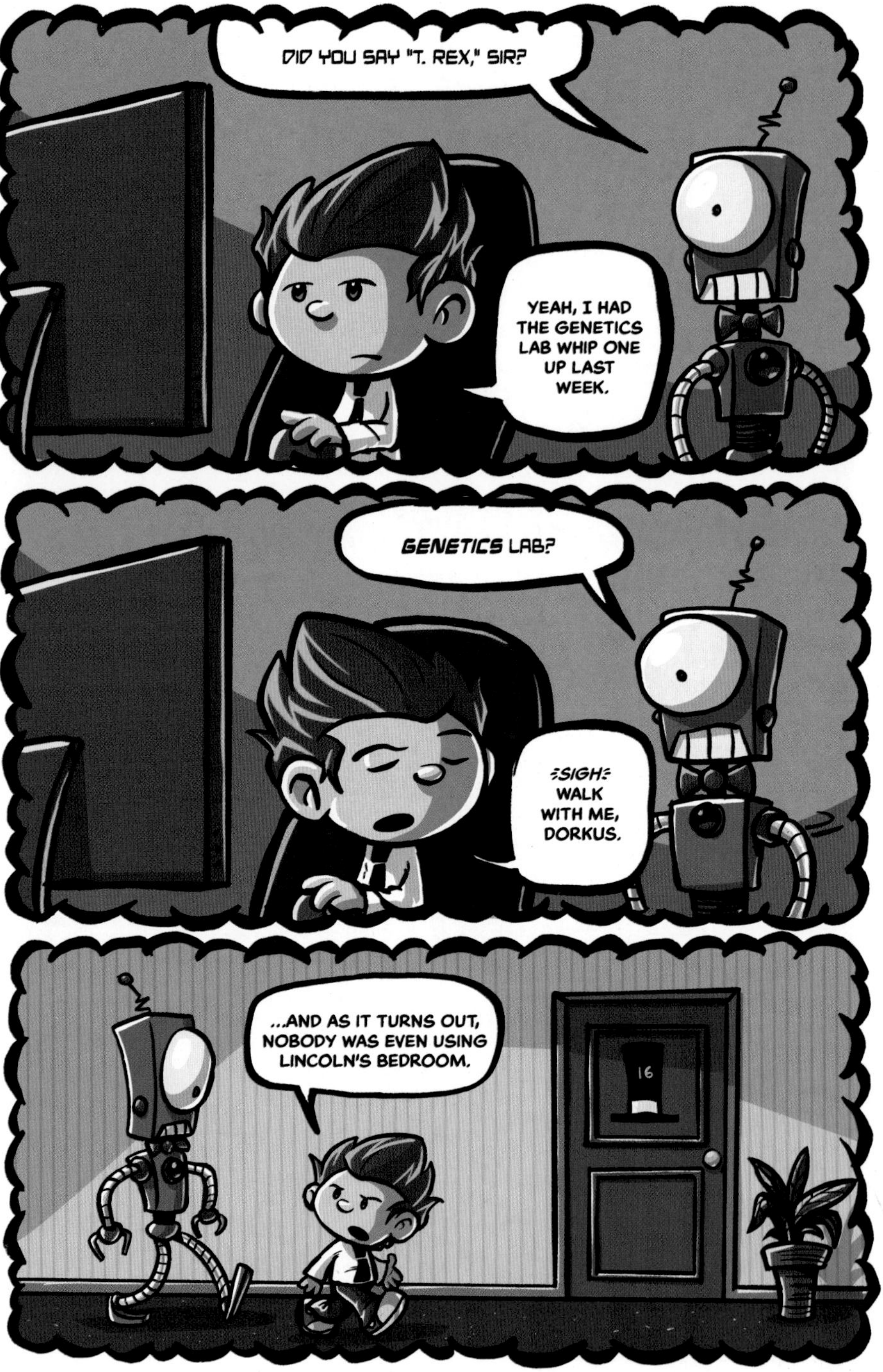
DID YOU SAY "T. REX," SIR?
YEAH, I HAD THE GENETICS LAB WHIP ONE UP LAST WEEK.
GENETICS LAB?
=SIGH= WALK WITH ME, DORKUS.
...AND AS IT TURNS OUT, NOBODY WAS EVEN USING LINCOLN'S BEDROOM.
16

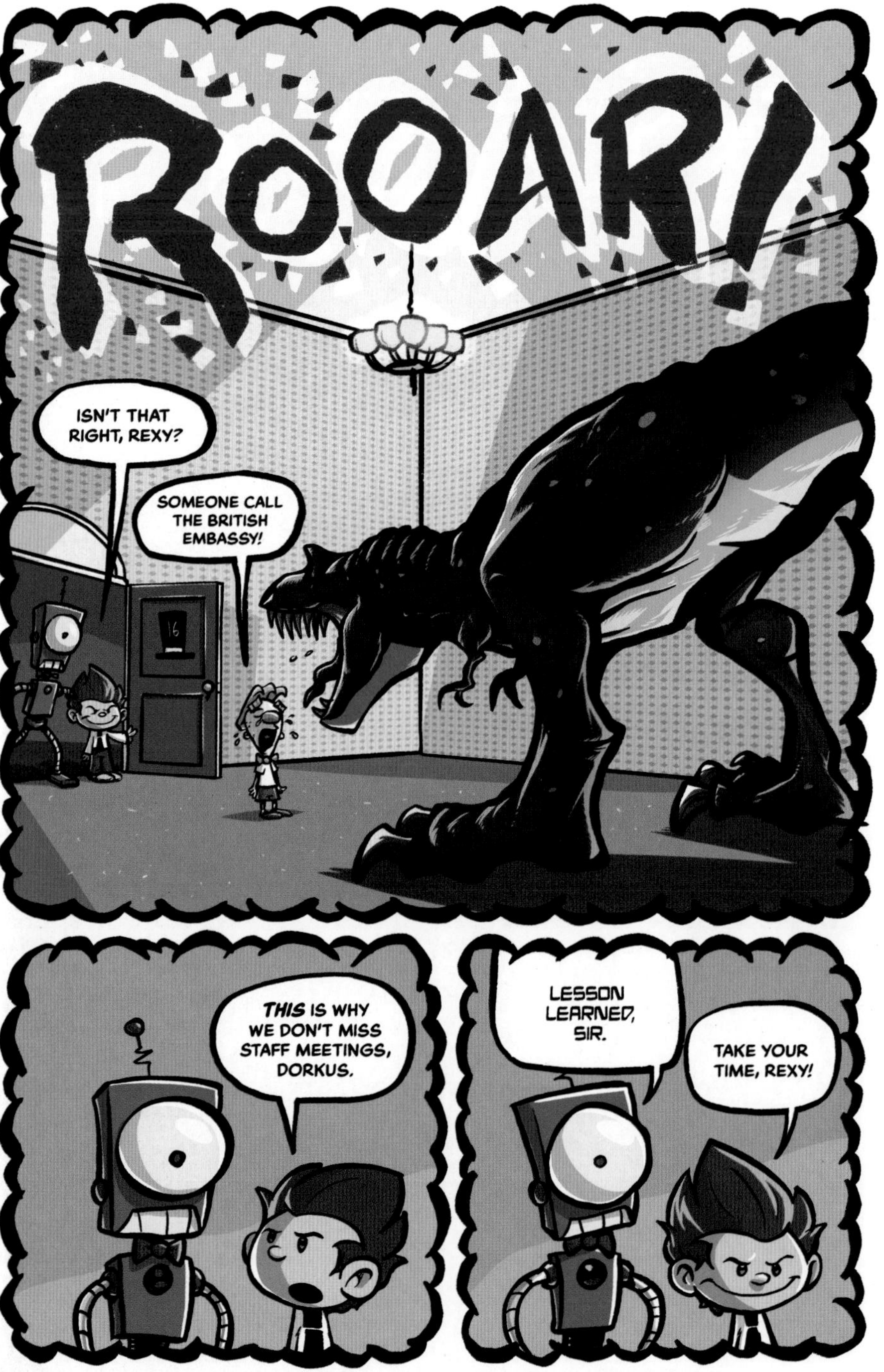
ROOAR!
ISN'T THAT RIGHT, REXY?
SOMEONE CALL THE BRITISH EMBASSY!
16
THIS IS WHY WE DON'T MISS STAFF MEETINGS, DORKUS.
LESSON LEARNED, SIR.
TAKE YOUR TIME, REXY!

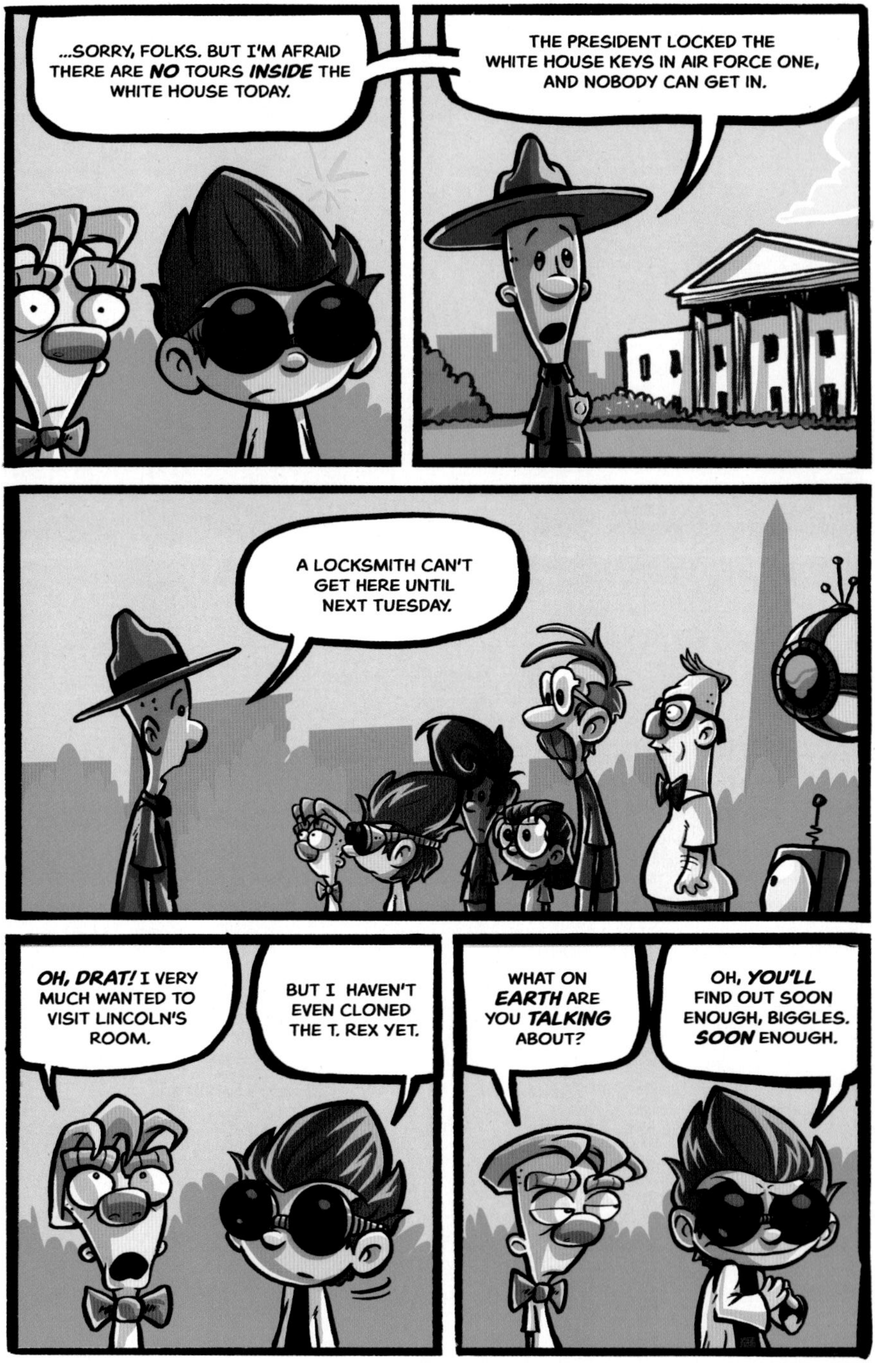
...SORRY, FOLKS. BUT I'M AFRAID THERE ARE NO TOURS INSIDE THE WHITE HOUSE TODAY.
THE PRESIDENT LOCKED THE WHITE HOUSE KEYS IN AIR FORCE ONE, AND NOBODY CAN GET IN.
A LOCKSMITH CAN'T GET HERE UNTIL NEXT TUESDAY.
OH, DRAT! I VERY MUCH WANTED TO VISIT LINCOLN'S ROOM.
BUT I HAVEN'T EVEN CLONED THE T. REX YET.
WHAT ON EARTH ARE YOU TALKING ABOUT?
OH, YOU'LL FIND OUT SOON ENOUGH, BIGGLES. SOON ENOUGH.

CHAPTER 10

Don't Bank on It

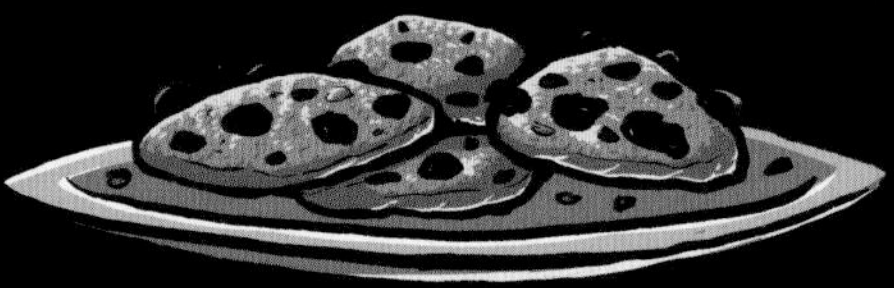

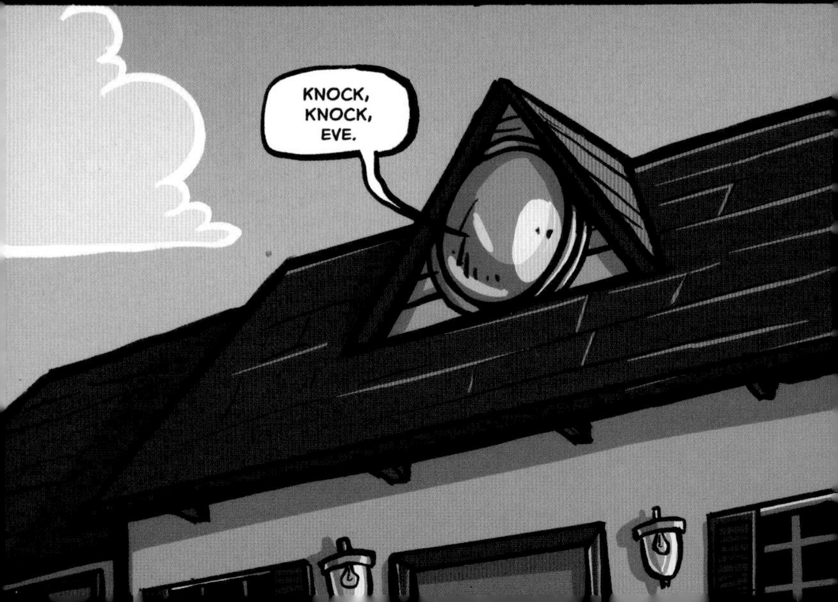
KNOCK, KNOCK, EVE.

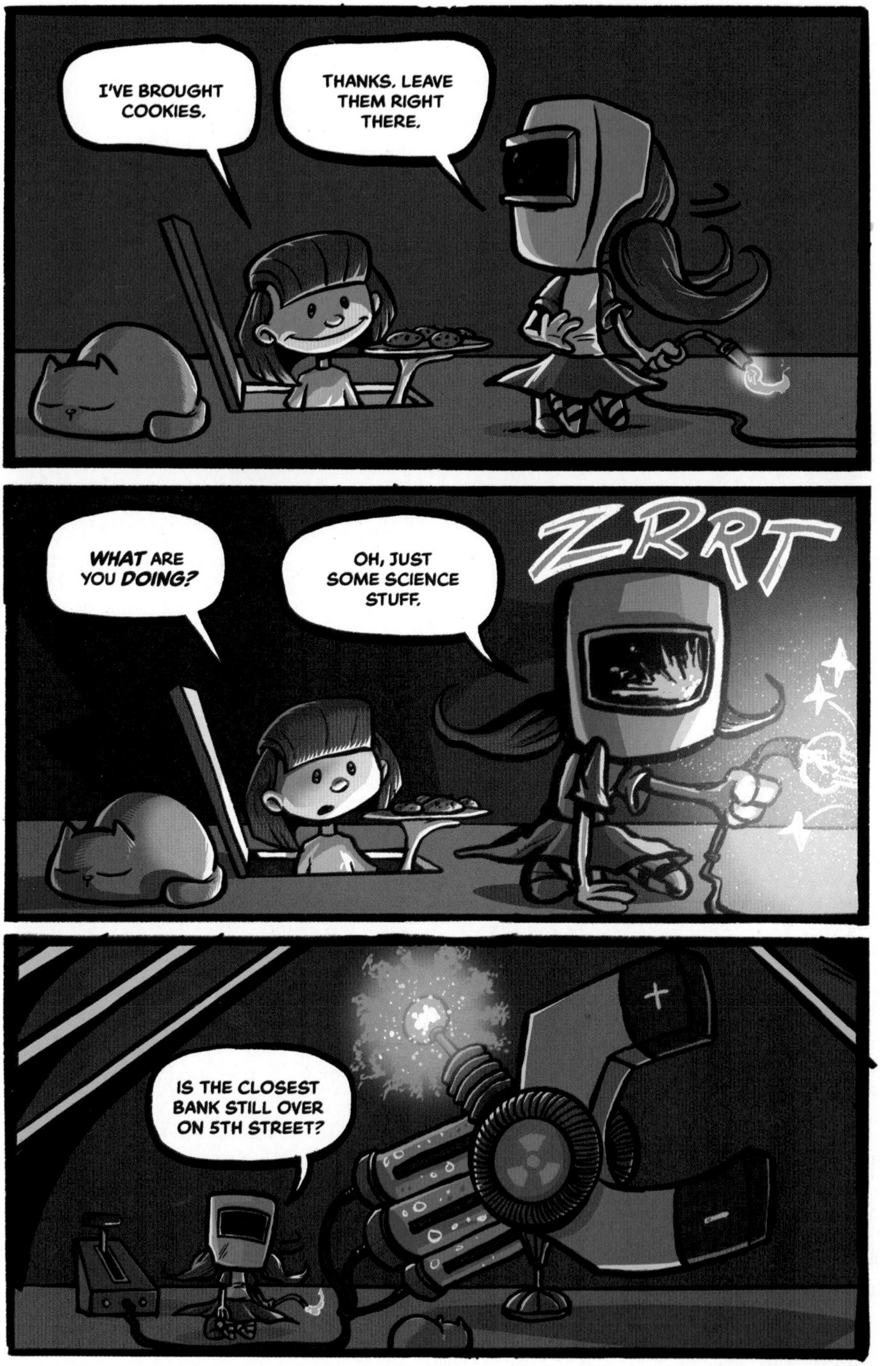
I'VE BROUGHT COOKIES.
THANKS. LEAVE THEM RIGHT THERE.
WHAT ARE YOU DOING?
OH, JUST SOME SCIENCE STUFF.
ZRRT
IS THE CLOSEST BANK STILL OVER ON 5TH STREET?

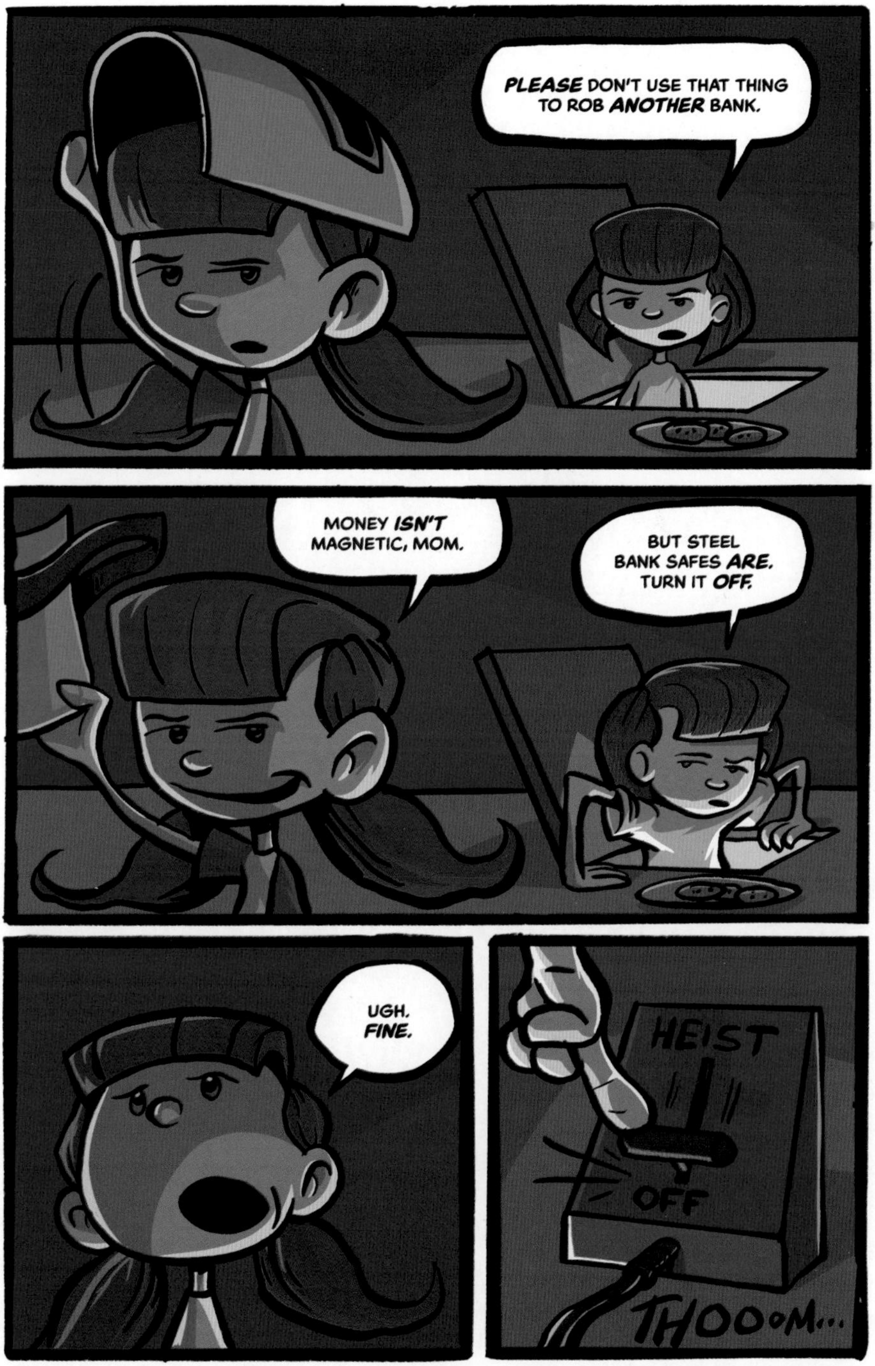
PLEASE DON'T USE THAT THING TO ROB ANOTHER BANK.
MONEY ISN'T MAGNETIC, MOM.
BUT STEEL BANK SAFES ARE. TURN IT OFF.
UGH. FINE.
HEIST
OFF
THOOoM...

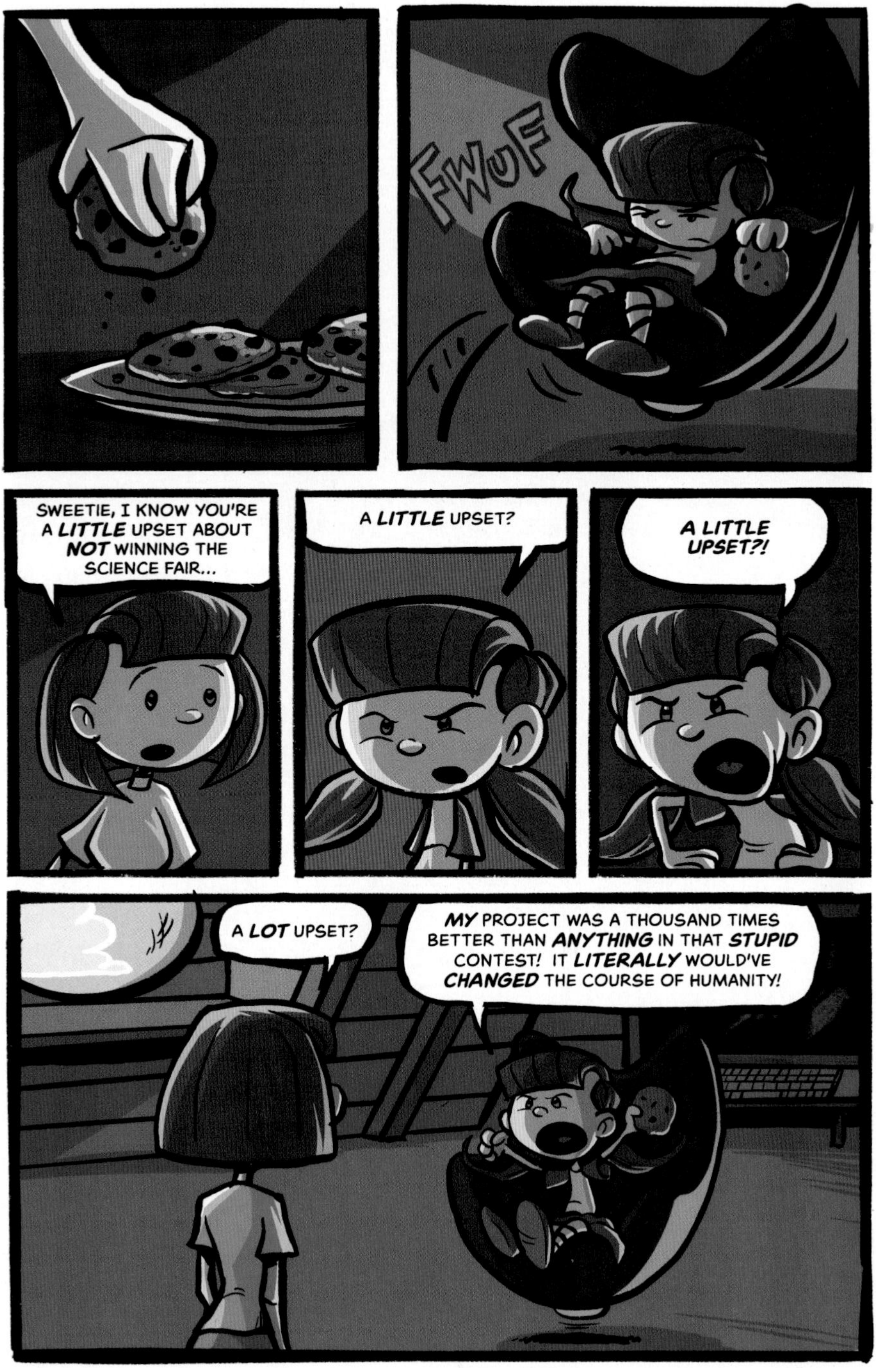
FWUF
SWEETIE, I KNOW YOU'RE A LITTLE UPSET ABOUT NOT WINNING THE SCIENCE FAIR...
A LITTLE UPSET?
A LITTLE UPSET?!
A LOT UPSET?
MY PROJECT WAS A THOUSAND TIMES BETTER THAN ANYTHING IN THAT STUPID CONTEST! IT LITERALLY WOULD'VE CHANGED THE COURSE OF HUMANITY!

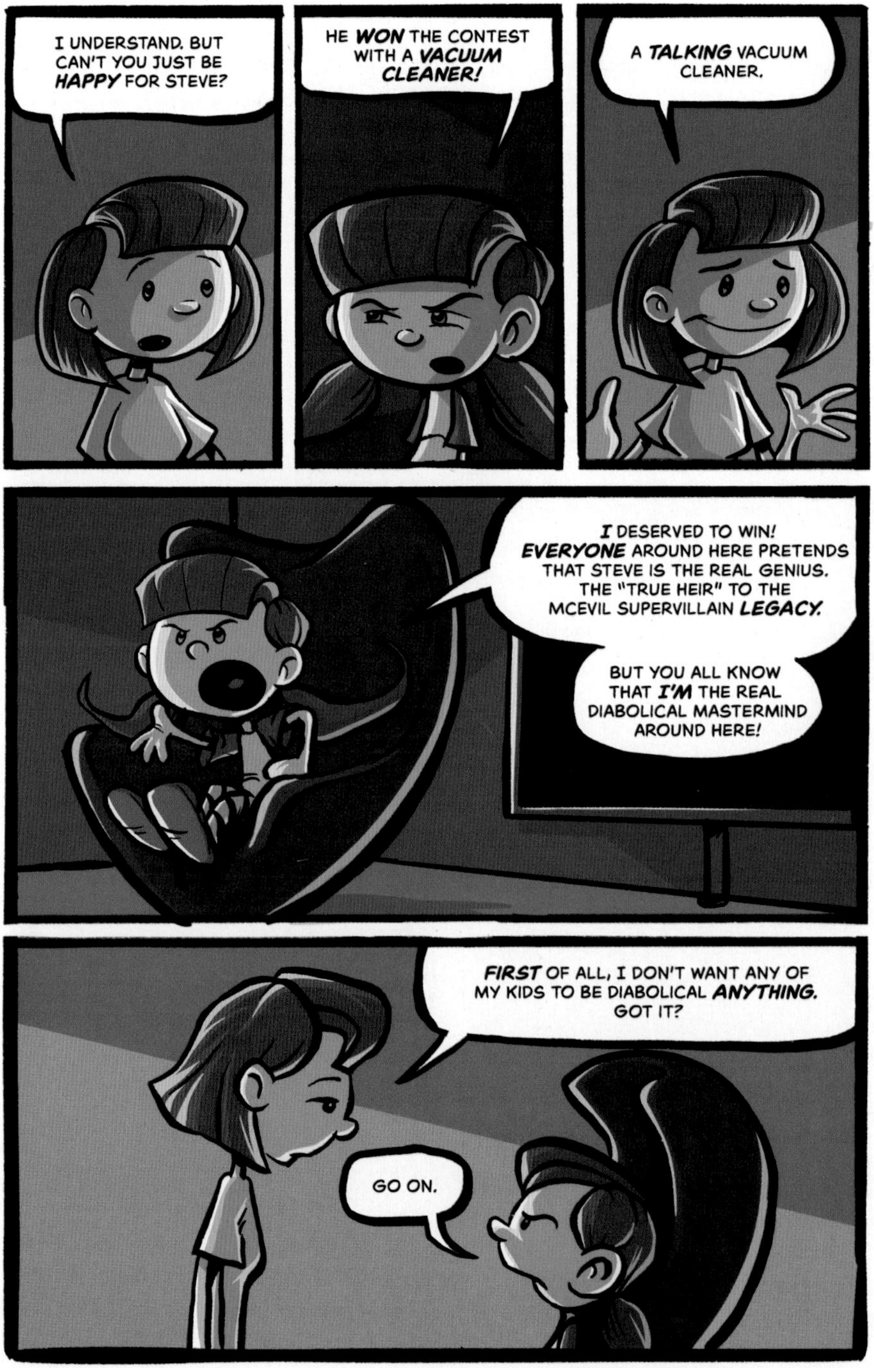
I UNDERSTAND. BUT CAN'T YOU JUST BE HAPPY FOR STEVE?
HE WON THE CONTEST WITH A VACUUM CLEANER!
A TALKING VACUUM CLEANER.
I DESERVED TO WIN! EVERYONE AROUND HERE PRETENDS THAT STEVE IS THE REAL GENIUS. THE "TRUE HEIR" TO THE MCEVIL SUPERVILLAIN LEGACY.
BUT YOU ALL KNOW THAT I'M THE REAL DIABOLICAL MASTERMIND AROUND HERE!
FIRST OF ALL, I DON'T WANT ANY OF MY KIDS TO BE DIABOLICAL ANYTHING. GOT IT?
GO ON.

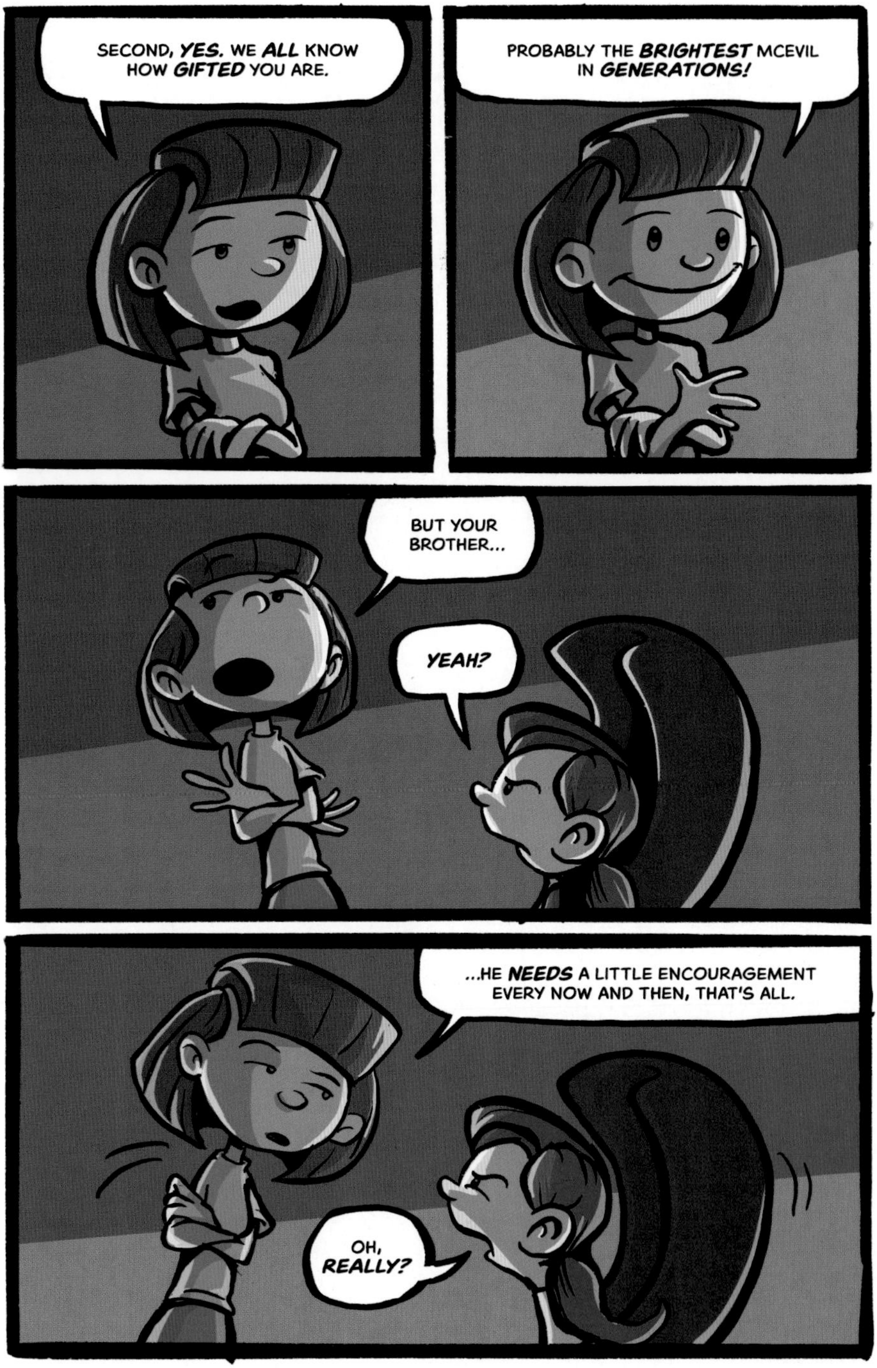
SECOND, YES. WE ALL KNOW HOW GIFTED YOU ARE.
PROBABLY THE BRIGHTEST MCEVIL IN GENERATIONS!
BUT YOUR BROTHER...
YEAH?
...HE NEEDS A LITTLE ENCOURAGEMENT EVERY NOW AND THEN, THAT'S ALL.
OH, REALLY?

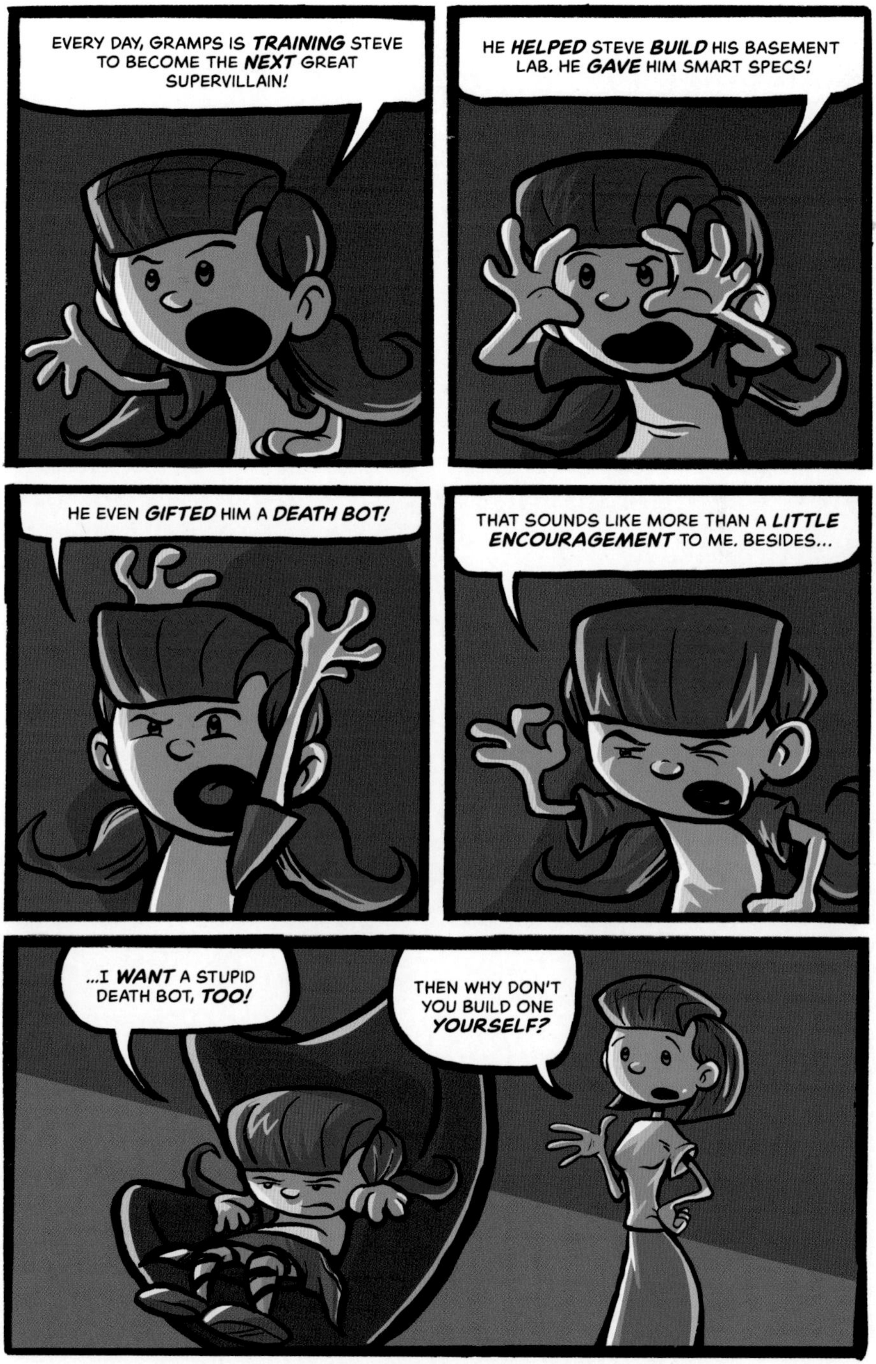
EVERY DAY, GRAMPS IS TRAINING STEVE TO BECOME THE NEXT GREAT SUPERVILLAIN!
HE HELPED STEVE BUILD HIS BASEMENT LAB. HE GAVE HIM SMART SPECS!
HE EVEN GIFTED HIM A DEATH BOT!
THAT SOUNDS LIKE MORE THAN A LITTLE ENCOURAGEMENT TO ME. BESIDES...
...I WANT A STUPID DEATH BOT, TOO!
THEN WHY DON'T YOU BUILD ONE YOURSELF?

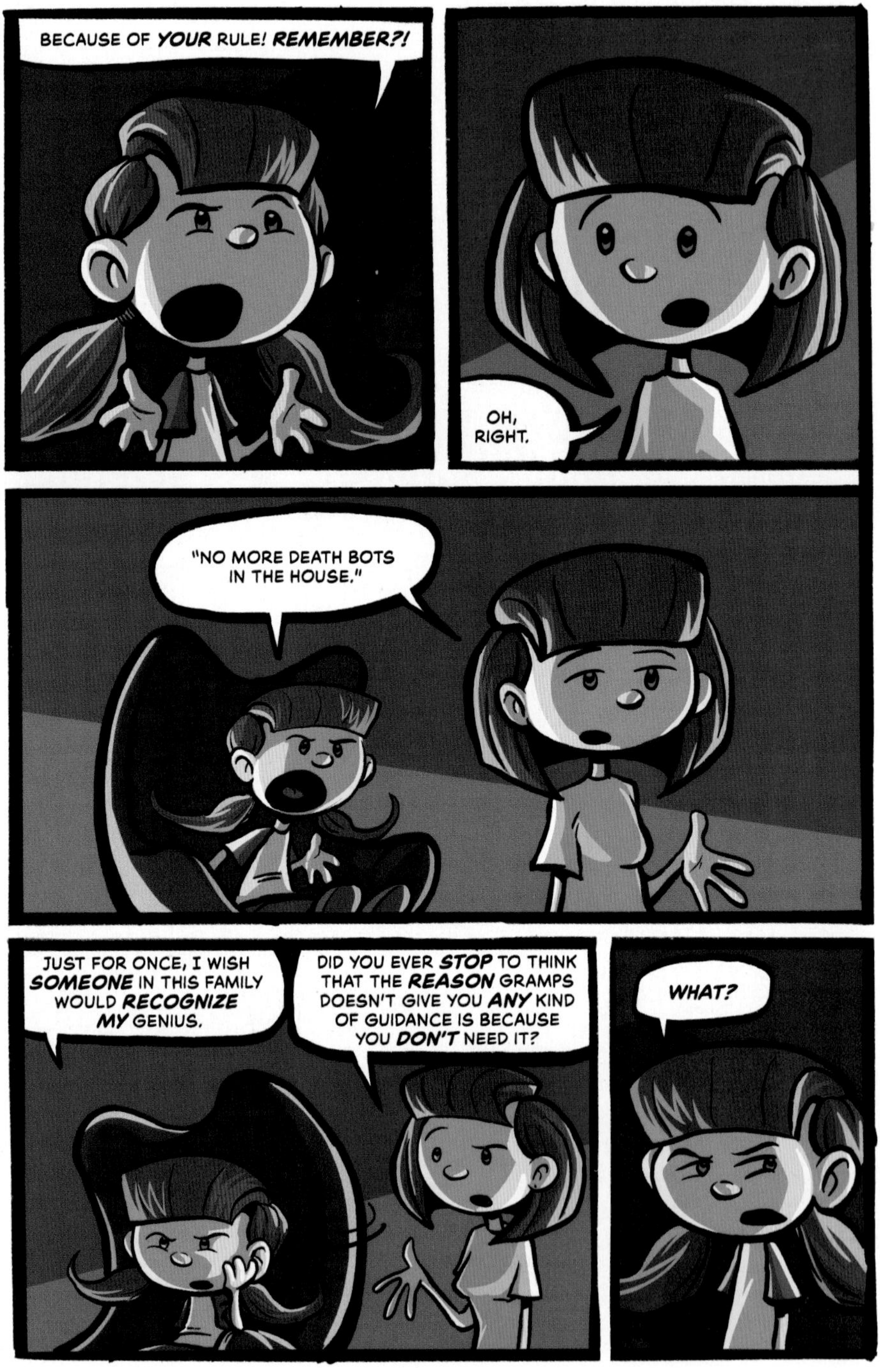
BECAUSE OF YOUR RULE! REMEMBER?!
OH, RIGHT.
"NO MORE DEATH BOTS IN THE HOUSE."
JUST FOR ONCE, I WISH SOMEONE IN THIS FAMILY WOULD RECOGNIZE MY GENIUS.
DID YOU EVER STOP TO THINK THAT THE REASON GRAMPS DOESN'T GIVE YOU ANY KIND OF GUIDANCE IS BECAUSE YOU DON'T NEED IT?
WHAT?

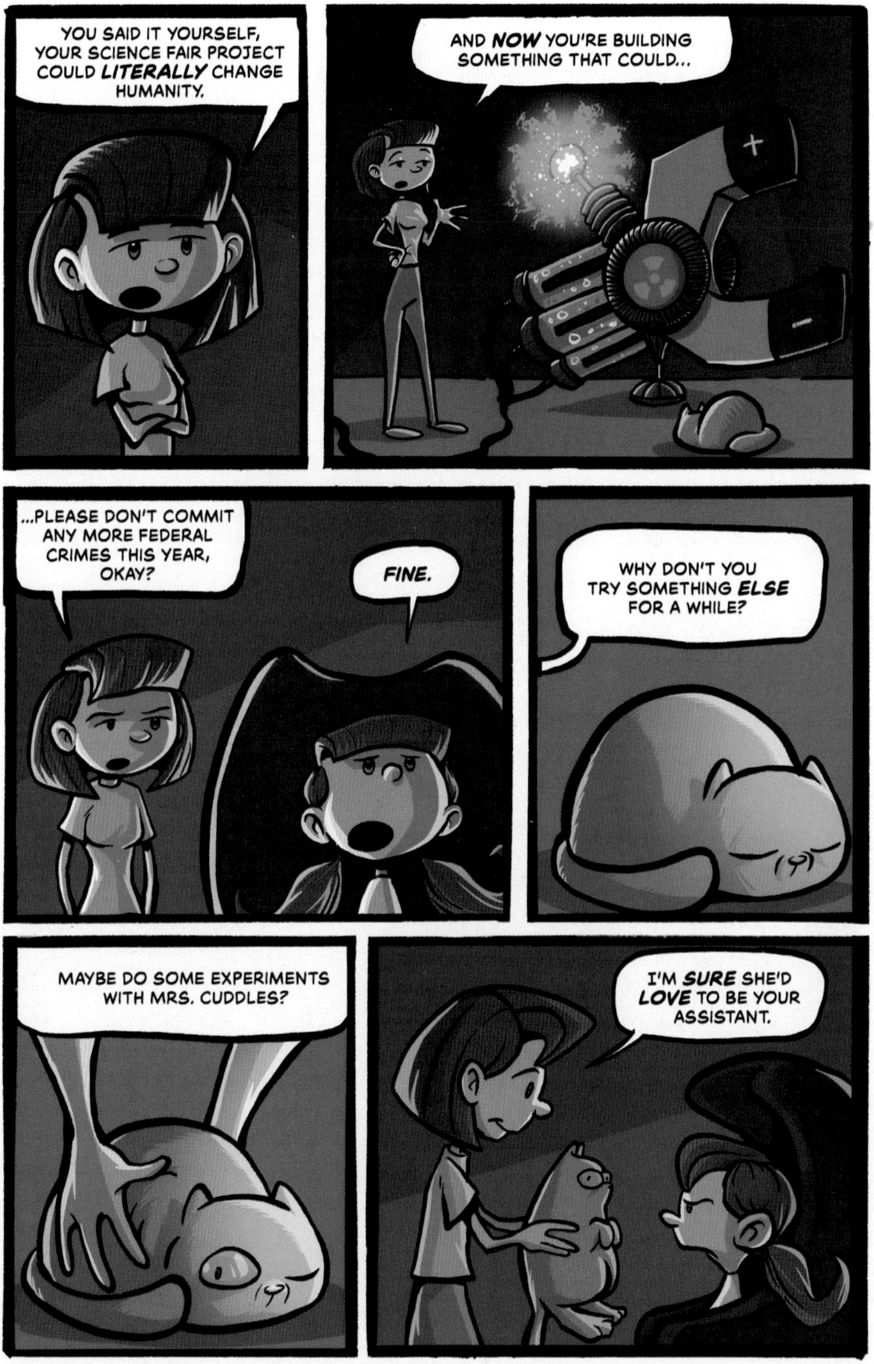
YOU SAID IT YOURSELF, YOUR SCIENCE FAIR PROJECT COULD LITERALLY CHANGE HUMANITY.
AND NOW YOU'RE BUILDING SOMETHING THAT COULD...
...PLEASE DON'T COMMIT ANY MORE FEDERAL CRIMES THIS YEAR, OKAY?
FINE.
WHY DON'T YOU TRY SOMETHING ELSE FOR A WHILE?
MAYBE DO SOME EXPERIMENTS WITH MRS. CUDDLES?
I'M SURE SHE'D LOVE TO BE YOUR ASSISTANT.

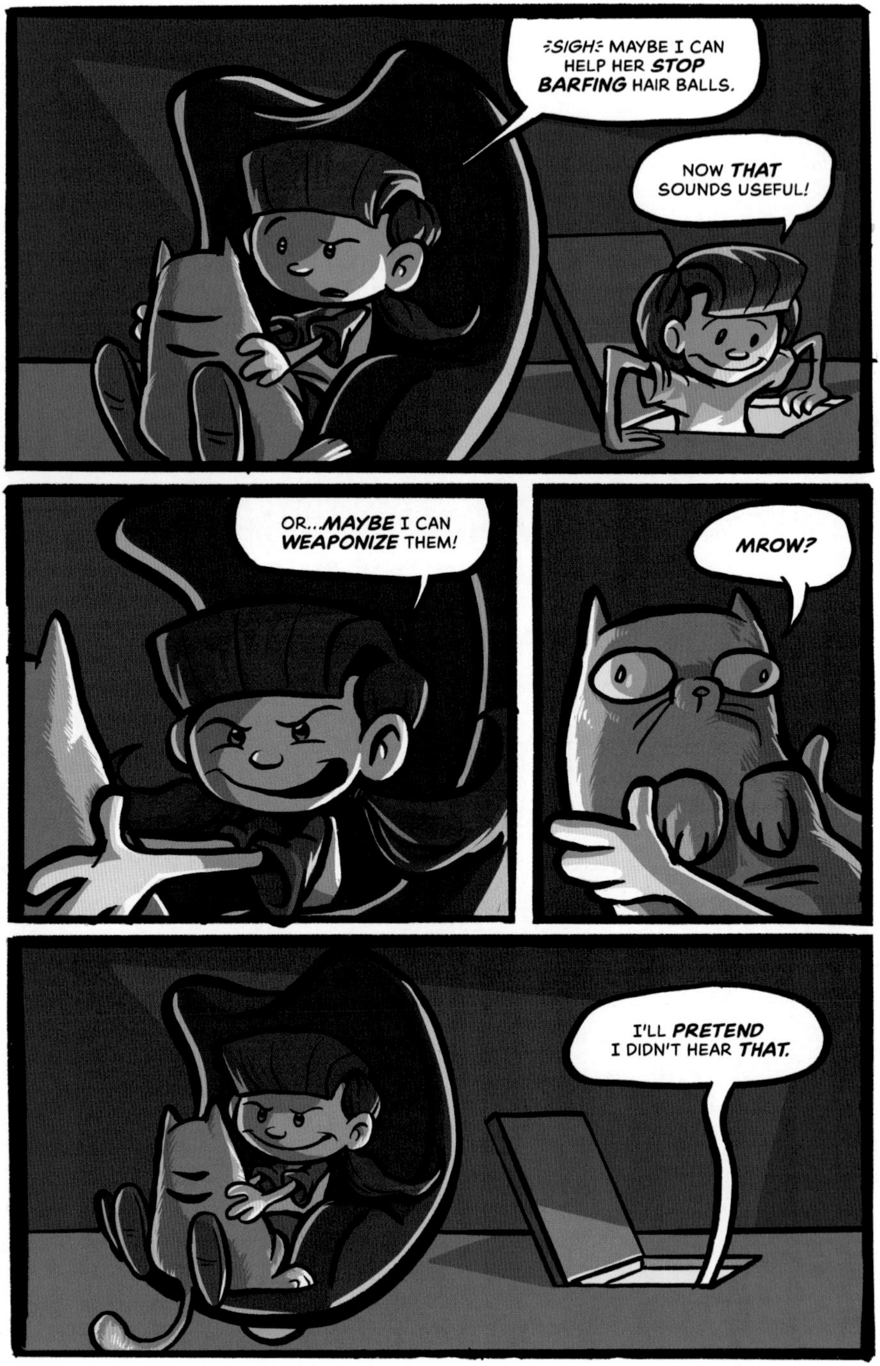

=SIGH= MAYBE I CAN HELP HER STOP BARFING HAIR BALLS.
NOW THAT SOUNDS USEFUL!
OR...MAYBE I CAN WEAPONIZE THEM!
MROW?
I'LL PRETEND I DIDN'T HEAR THAT.

CHAPTER 11

Plenty of Room at the Hotel's 14th Floor-ah

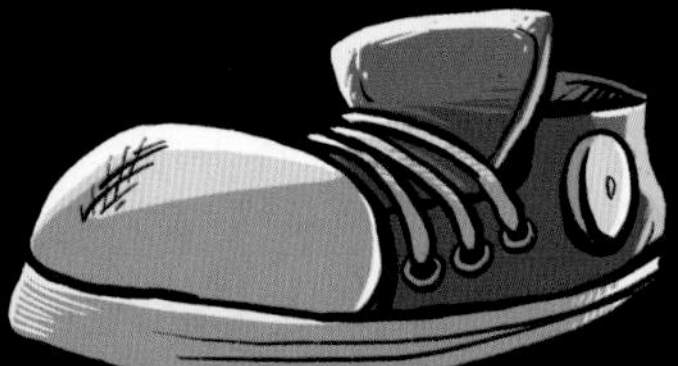

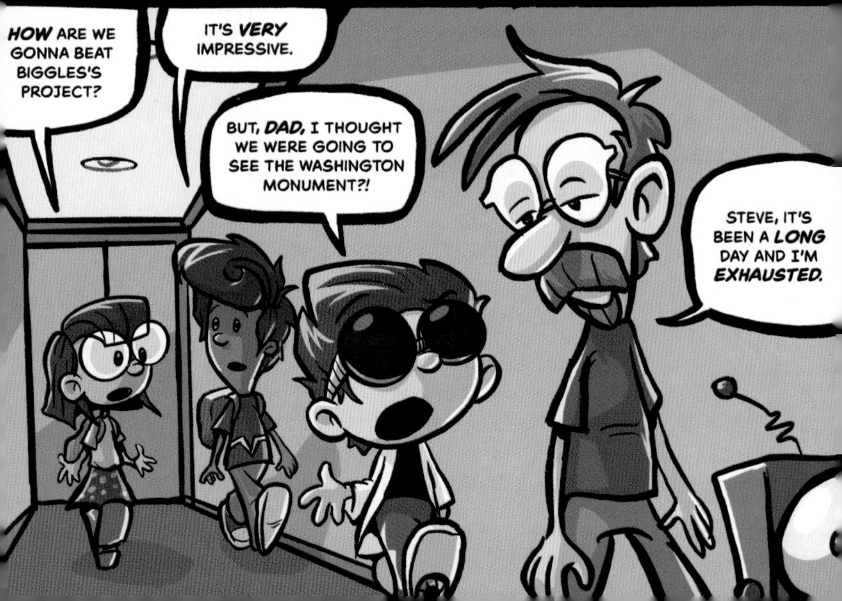

HOW ARE WE GONNA BEAT BIGGLES'S PROJECT?
IT'S VERY IMPRESSIVE.
BUT, DAD, I THOUGHT WE WERE GOING TO SEE THE WASHINGTON MONUMENT?!
STEVE, IT'S BEEN A LONG DAY AND I'M EXHAUSTED.

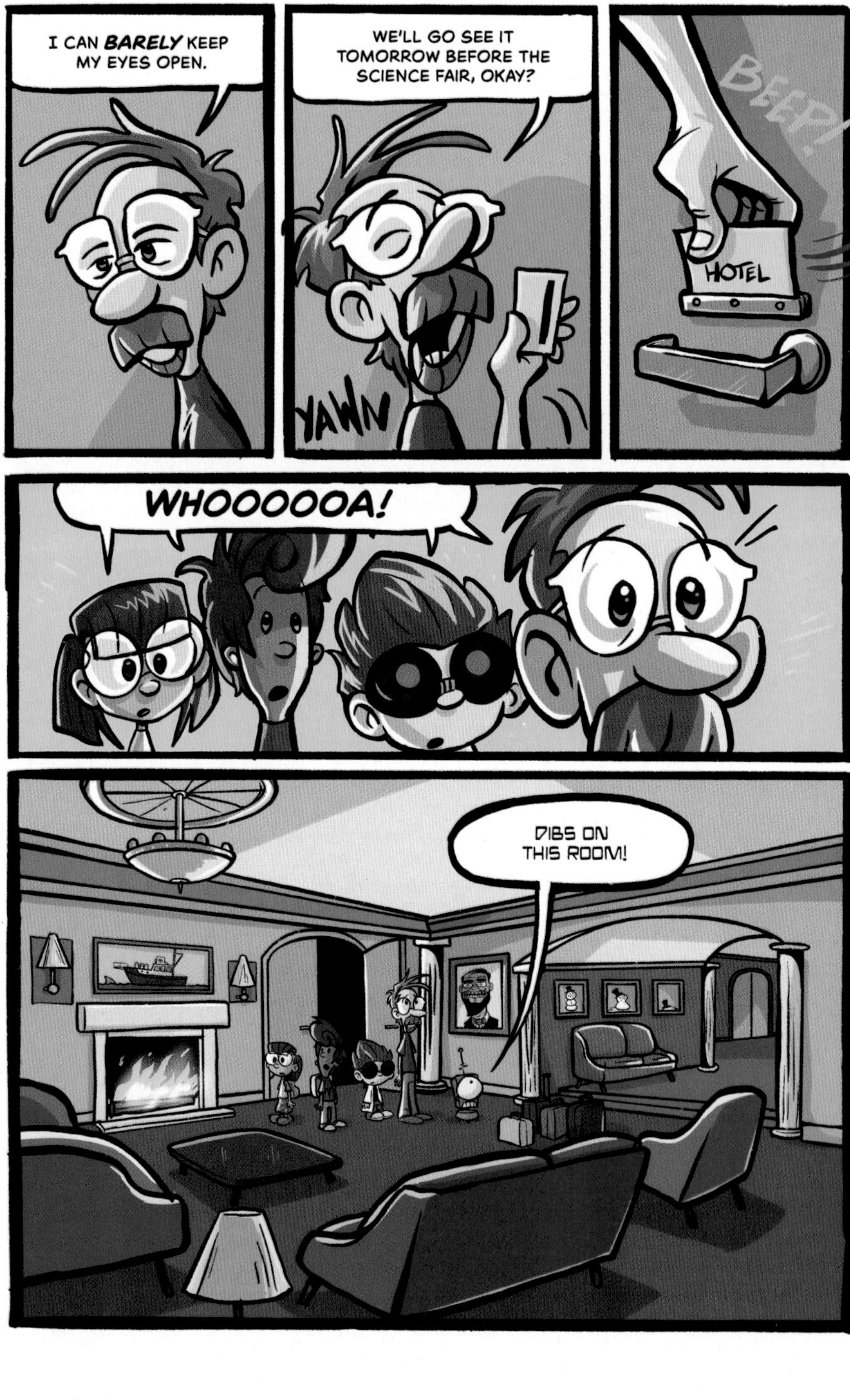
I CAN BARELY KEEP MY EYES OPEN.
WE'LL GO SEE IT TOMORROW BEFORE THE SCIENCE FAIR, OKAY?
YAWN
HOTEL
BEEP!
WHOOOOOA!
DIBS ON THIS ROOM!

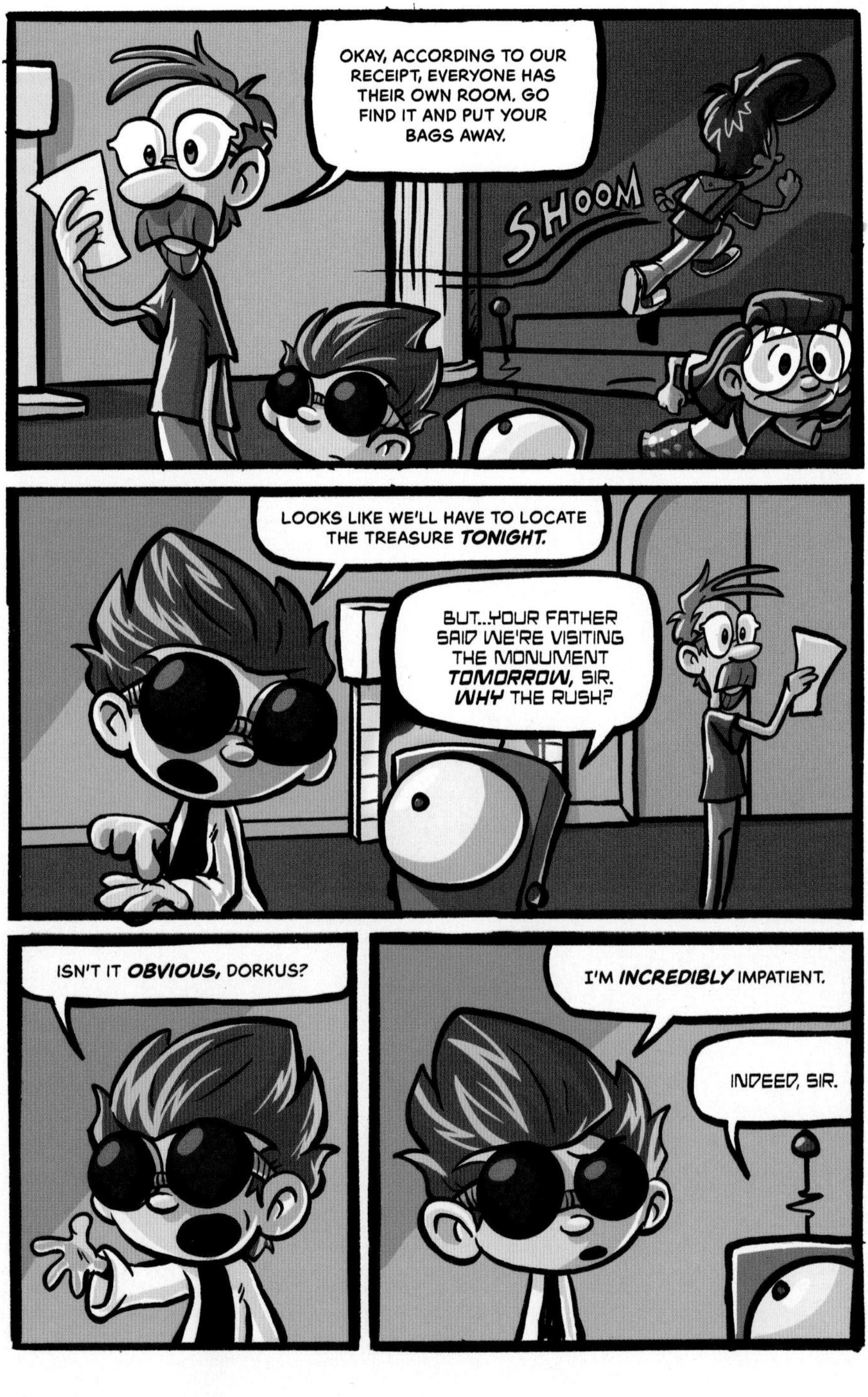
OKAY, ACCORDING TO OUR RECEIPT, EVERYONE HAS THEIR OWN ROOM. GO FIND IT AND PUT YOUR BAGS AWAY.
SHOOM
LOOKS LIKE WE'LL HAVE TO LOCATE THE TREASURE TONIGHT.
BUT...YOUR FATHER SAID WE'RE VISITING THE MONUMENT TOMORROW, SIR. WHY THE RUSH?
ISN'T IT OBVIOUS, DORKUS?
I'M INCREDIBLY IMPATIENT.
INDEED, SIR.

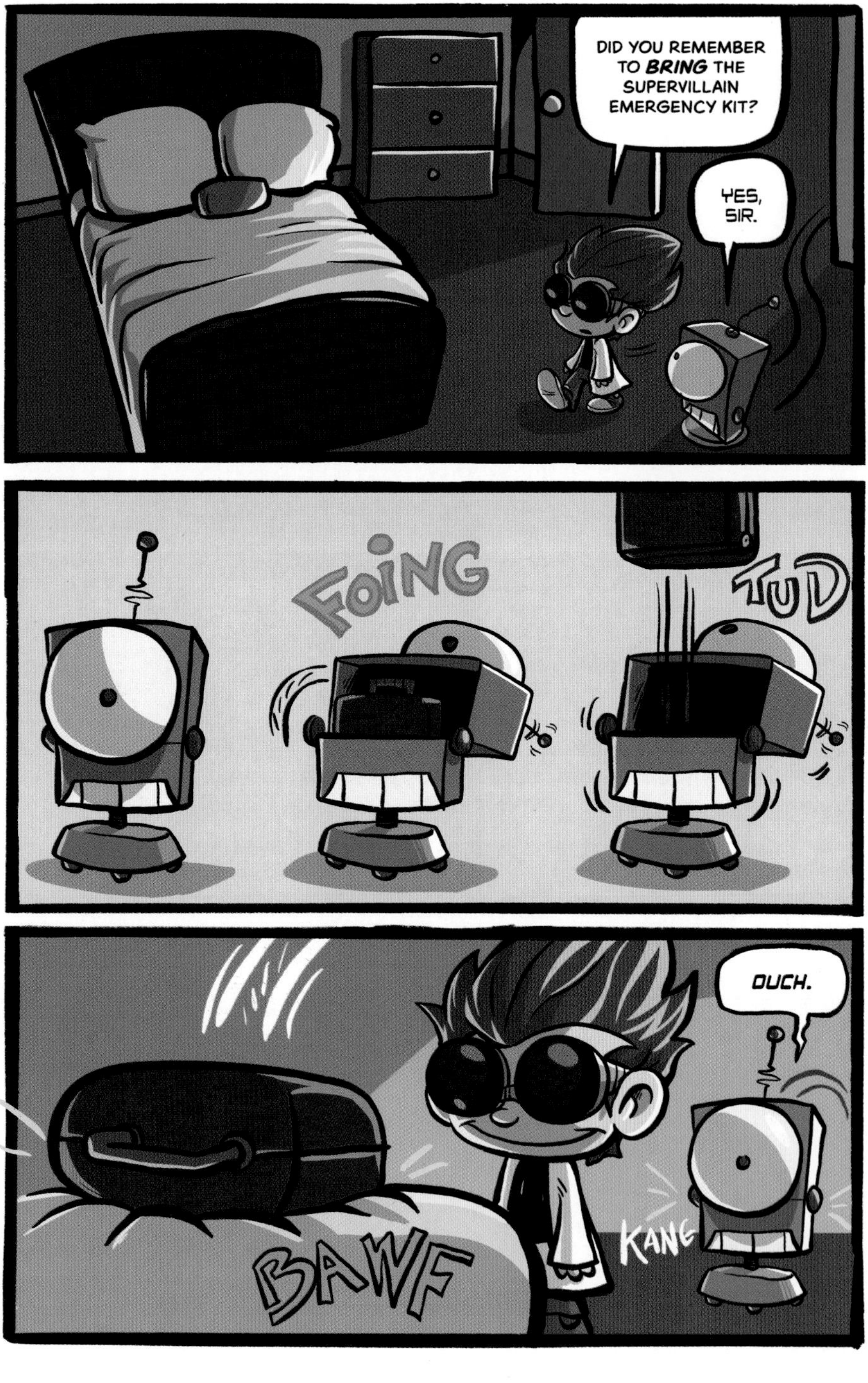
DID YOU REMEMBER TO *BRING* THE SUPERVILLAIN EMERGENCY KIT?
YES, SIR.
FOING
TUD
OUCH.
KANG
BAWF

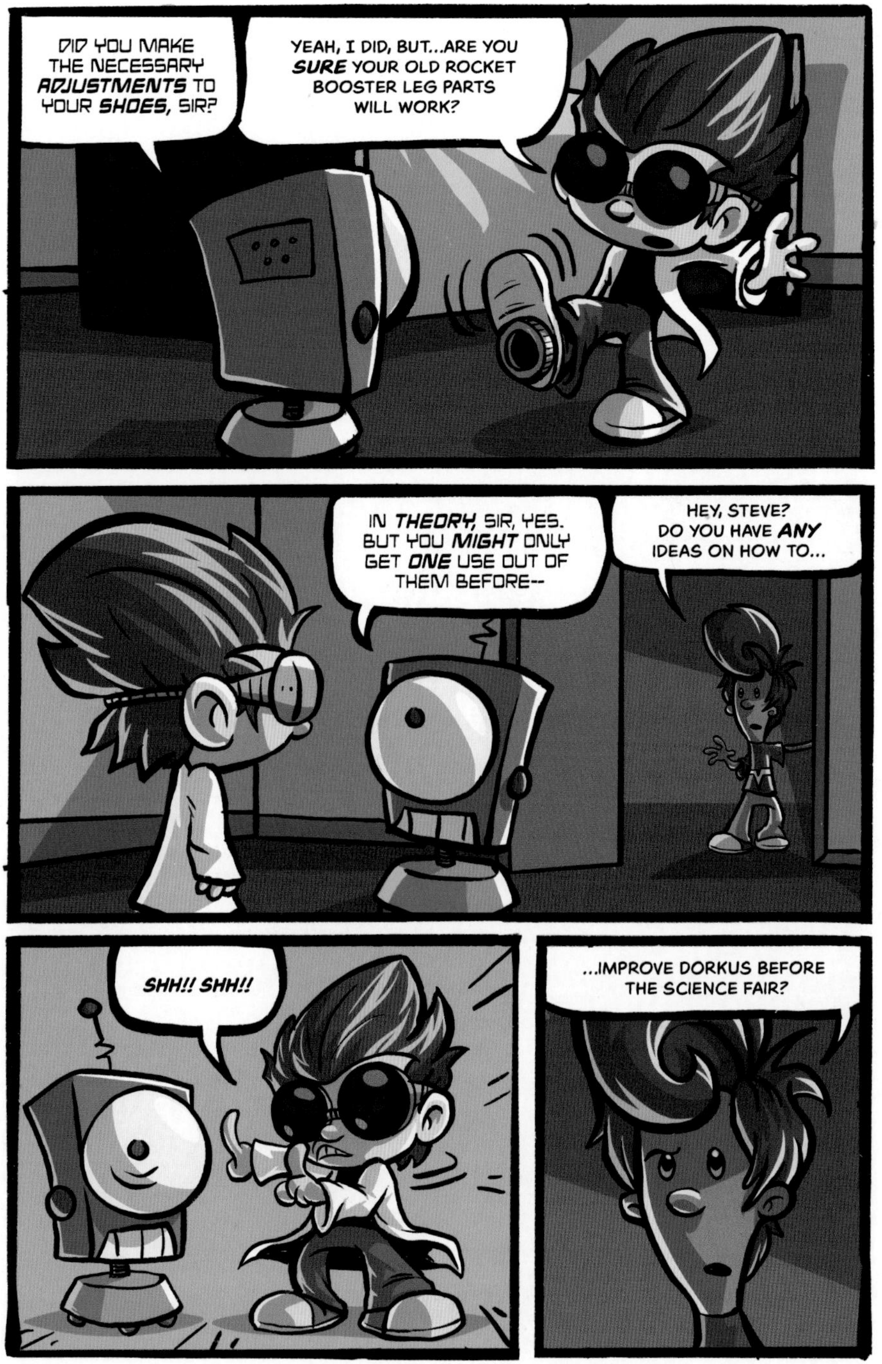
DID YOU MAKE THE NECESSARY ADJUSTMENTS TO YOUR SHOES, SIR?
YEAH, I DID, BUT...ARE YOU SURE YOUR OLD ROCKET BOOSTER LEG PARTS WILL WORK?
IN THEORY, SIR, YES. BUT YOU MIGHT ONLY GET ONE USE OUT OF THEM BEFORE--
HEY, STEVE? DO YOU HAVE ANY IDEAS ON HOW TO...
SHH!! SHH!!
...IMPROVE DORKUS BEFORE THE SCIENCE FAIR?

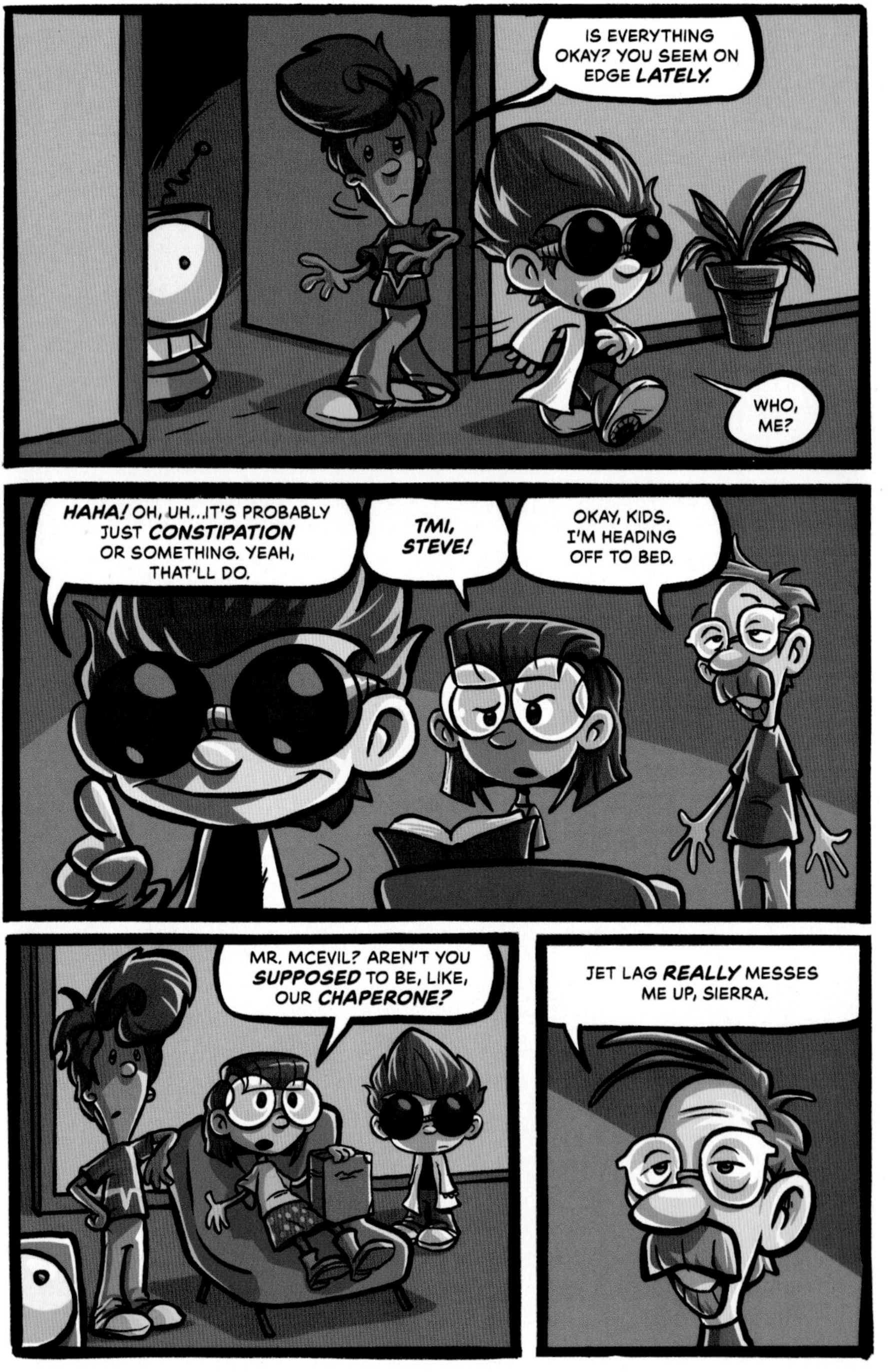
IS EVERYTHING OKAY? YOU SEEM ON EDGE LATELY.
WHO, ME?
HAHA! OH, UH...IT'S PROBABLY JUST CONSTIPATION OR SOMETHING. YEAH, THAT'LL DO.
TMI, STEVE!
OKAY, KIDS. I'M HEADING OFF TO BED.
MR. MCEVIL? AREN'T YOU SUPPOSED TO BE, LIKE, OUR CHAPERONE?
JET LAG REALLY MESSES ME UP, SIERRA.

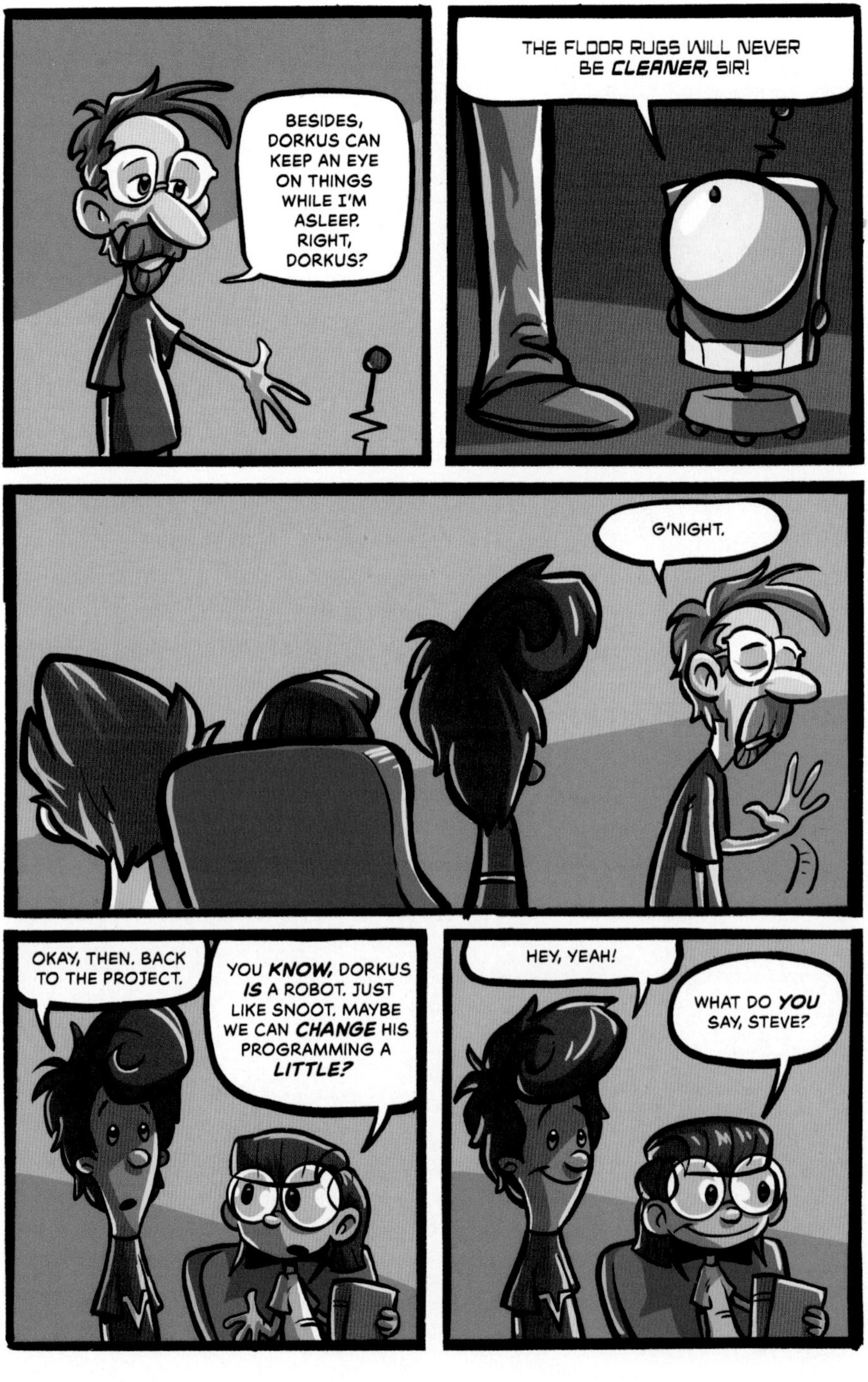
BESIDES, DORKUS CAN KEEP AN EYE ON THINGS WHILE I'M ASLEEP. RIGHT, DORKUS?
THE FLOOR RUGS WILL NEVER BE *CLEANER,* SIR!
G'NIGHT.
OKAY, THEN. BACK TO THE PROJECT.
YOU *KNOW,* DORKUS *IS* A ROBOT. JUST LIKE SNOOT. MAYBE WE CAN *CHANGE* HIS PROGRAMMING A *LITTLE?*
HEY, YEAH!
WHAT DO *YOU* SAY, STEVE?

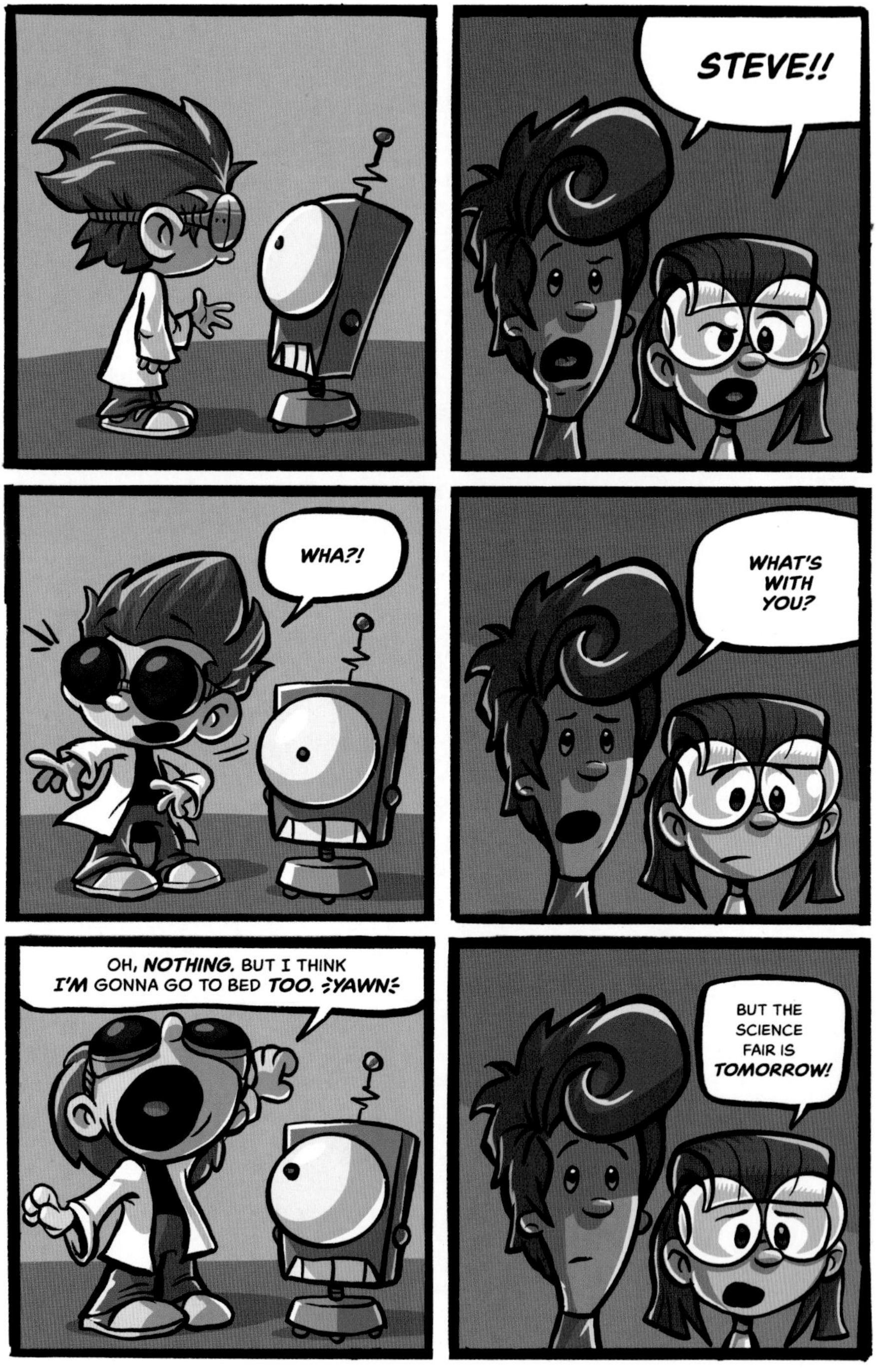
STEVE!!
WHA?!
WHAT'S WITH YOU?
OH, **NOTHING.** BUT I THINK ***I'M*** GONNA GO TO BED ***TOO.*** *YAWN*
BUT THE SCIENCE FAIR IS ***TOMORROW!***

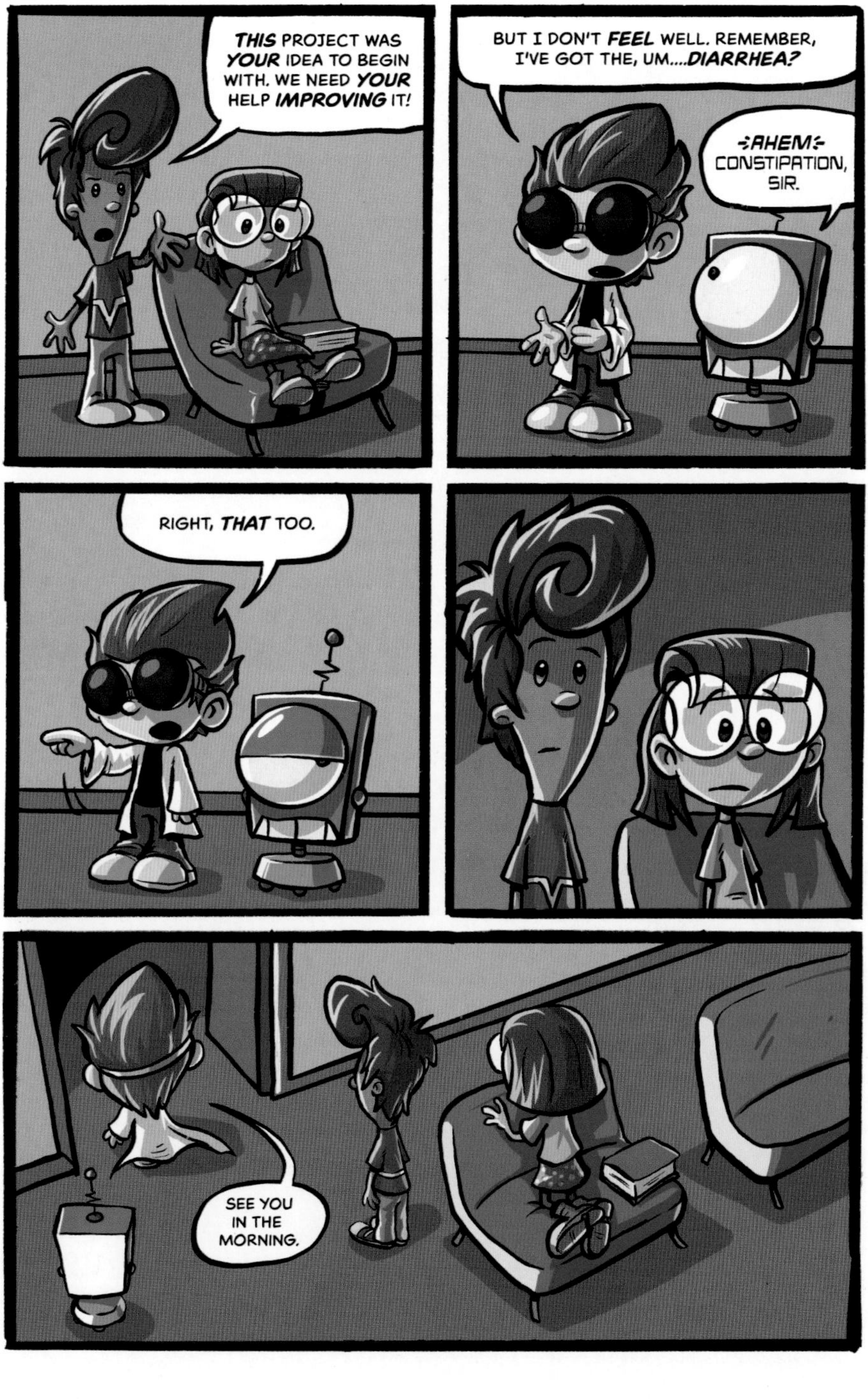
THIS PROJECT WAS YOUR IDEA TO BEGIN WITH. WE NEED YOUR HELP IMPROVING IT!
BUT I DON'T FEEL WELL. REMEMBER, I'VE GOT THE, UM....DIARRHEA?
AHEM CONSTIPATION, SIR.
RIGHT, THAT TOO.
SEE YOU IN THE MORNING.

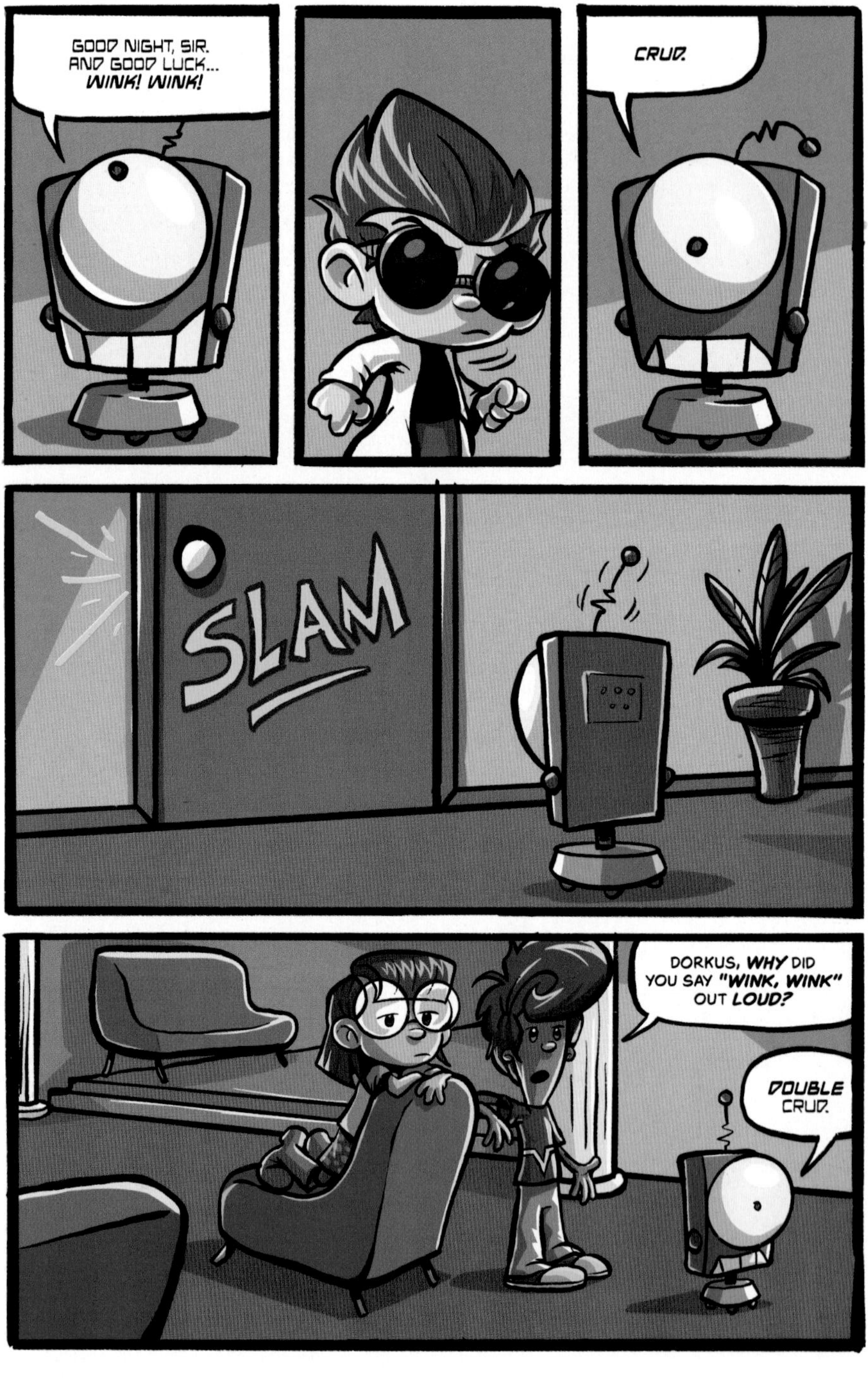
GOOD NIGHT, SIR. AND GOOD LUCK... WINK! WINK!
CRUD.
SLAM
DORKUS, WHY DID YOU SAY "WINK, WINK" OUT LOUD?
DOUBLE CRUD.

CHAPTER 12

Cloning Around

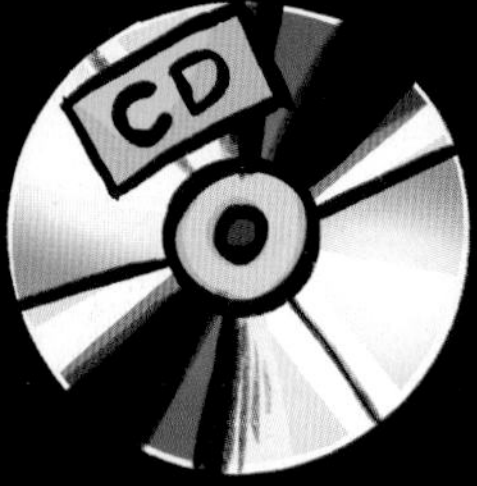
CD

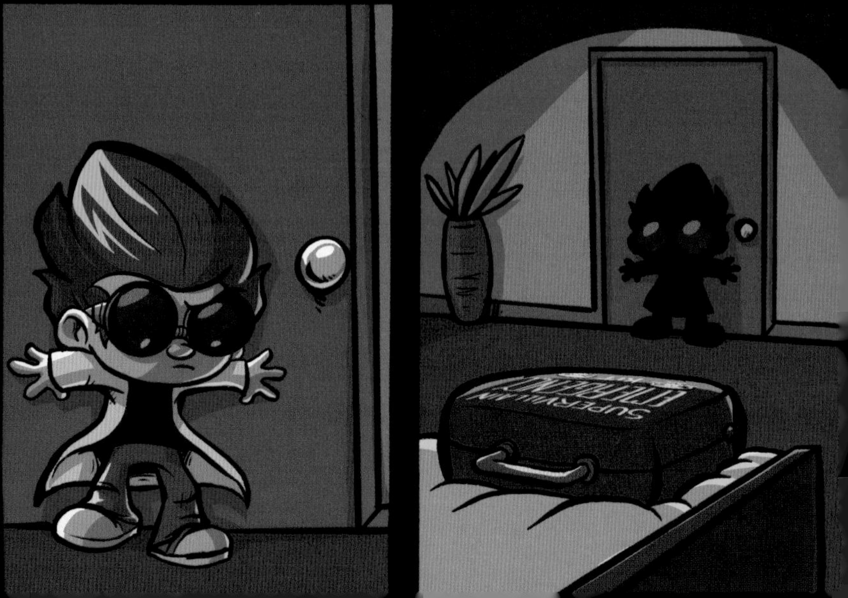

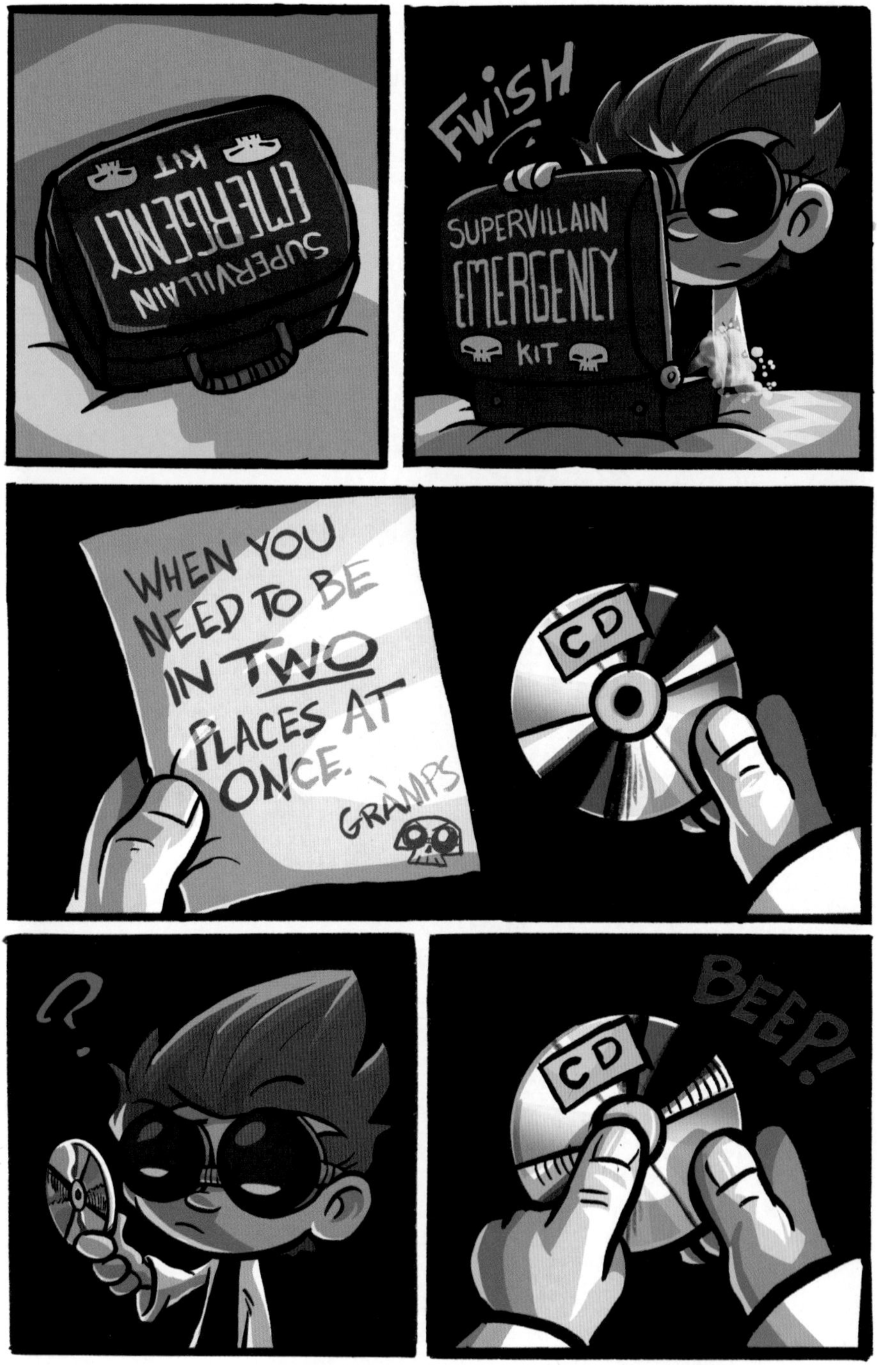
SUPERVILLAIN EMERGENCY KIT
FWISH
SUPERVILLAIN EMERGENCY KIT
WHEN YOU NEED TO BE IN TWO PLACES AT ONCE.
GRAMPS
CD
?
CD
BEEP!

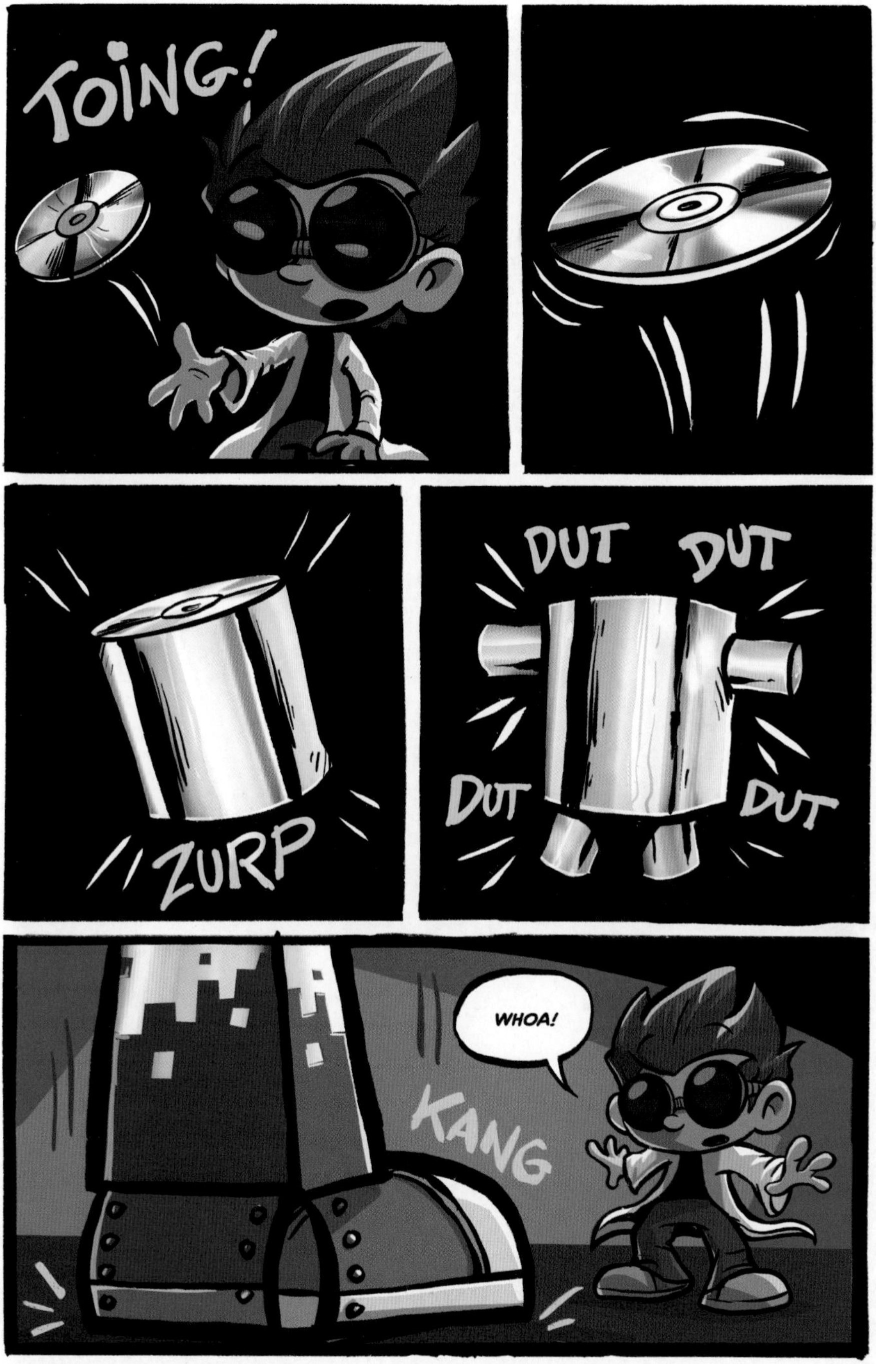
TOING!
ZURP
DUT DUT
DUT DUT
WHOA!
KANG

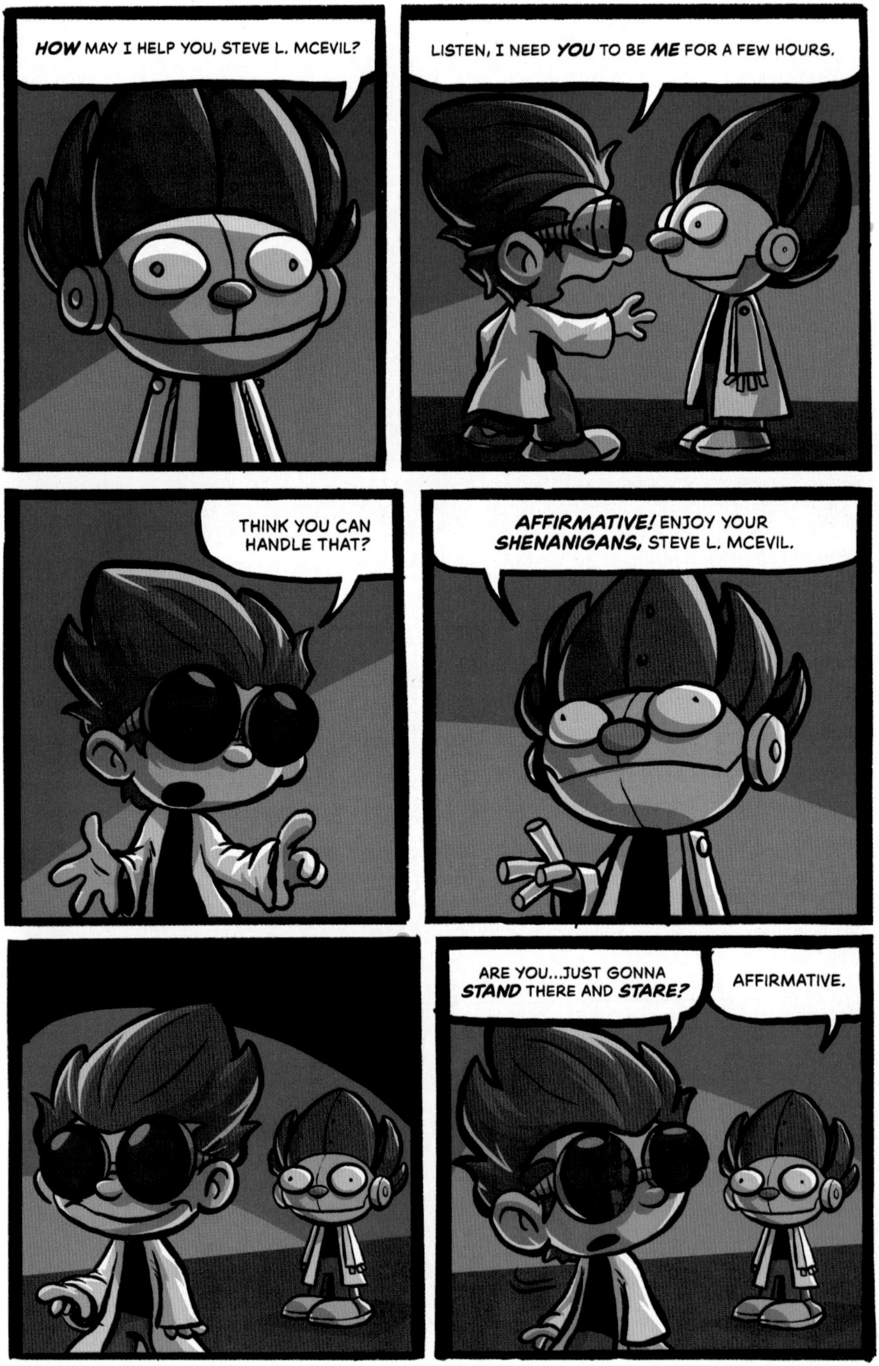
HOW MAY I HELP YOU, STEVE L. MCEVIL?
LISTEN, I NEED YOU TO BE ME FOR A FEW HOURS.
THINK YOU CAN HANDLE THAT?
AFFIRMATIVE! ENJOY YOUR SHENANIGANS, STEVE L. MCEVIL.
ARE YOU...JUST GONNA STAND THERE AND STARE?
AFFIRMATIVE.

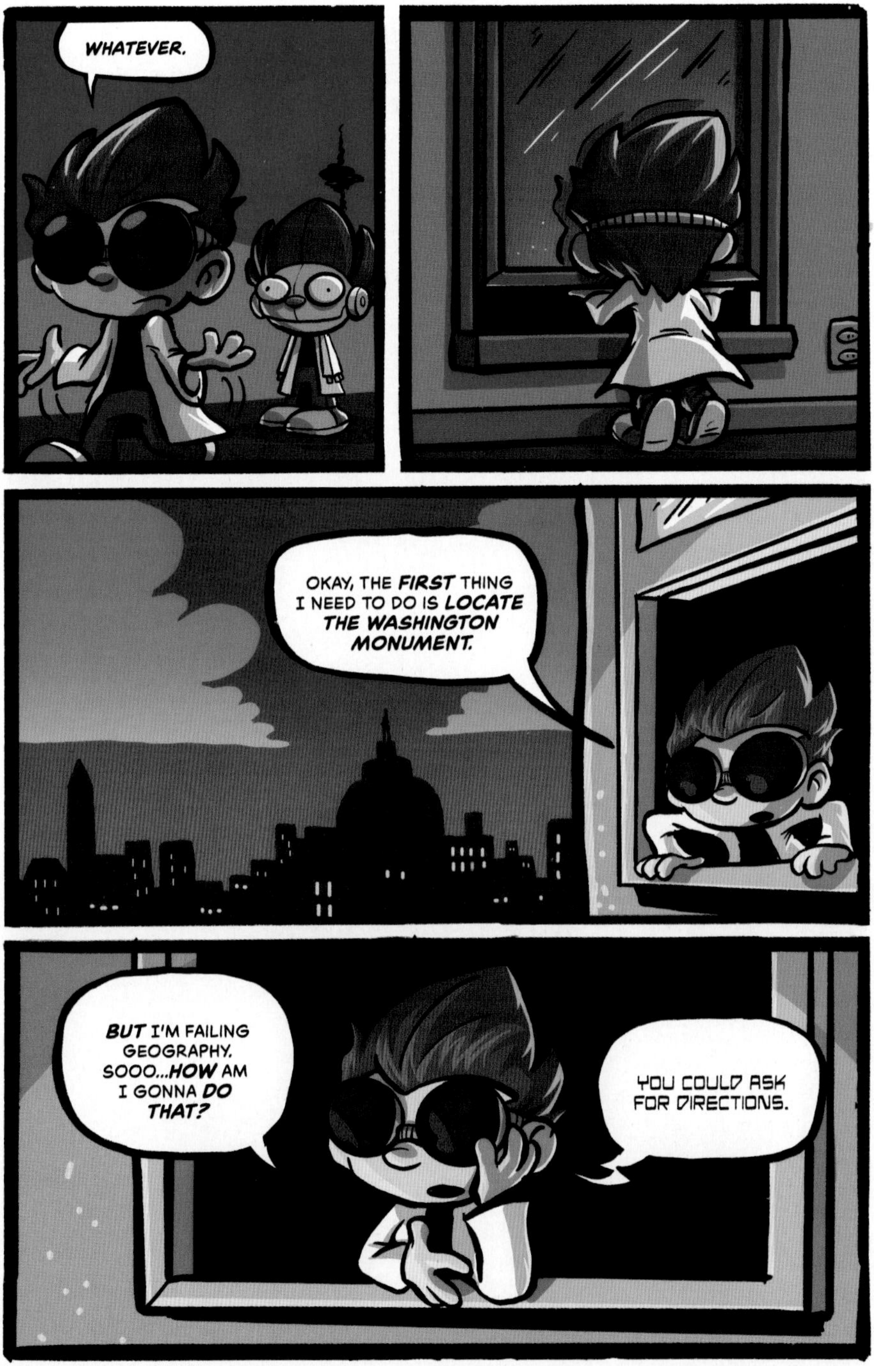
WHATEVER.
OKAY, THE FIRST THING I NEED TO DO IS LOCATE THE WASHINGTON MONUMENT.
BUT I'M FAILING GEOGRAPHY. SOOO...HOW AM I GONNA DO THAT?
YOU COULD ASK FOR DIRECTIONS.

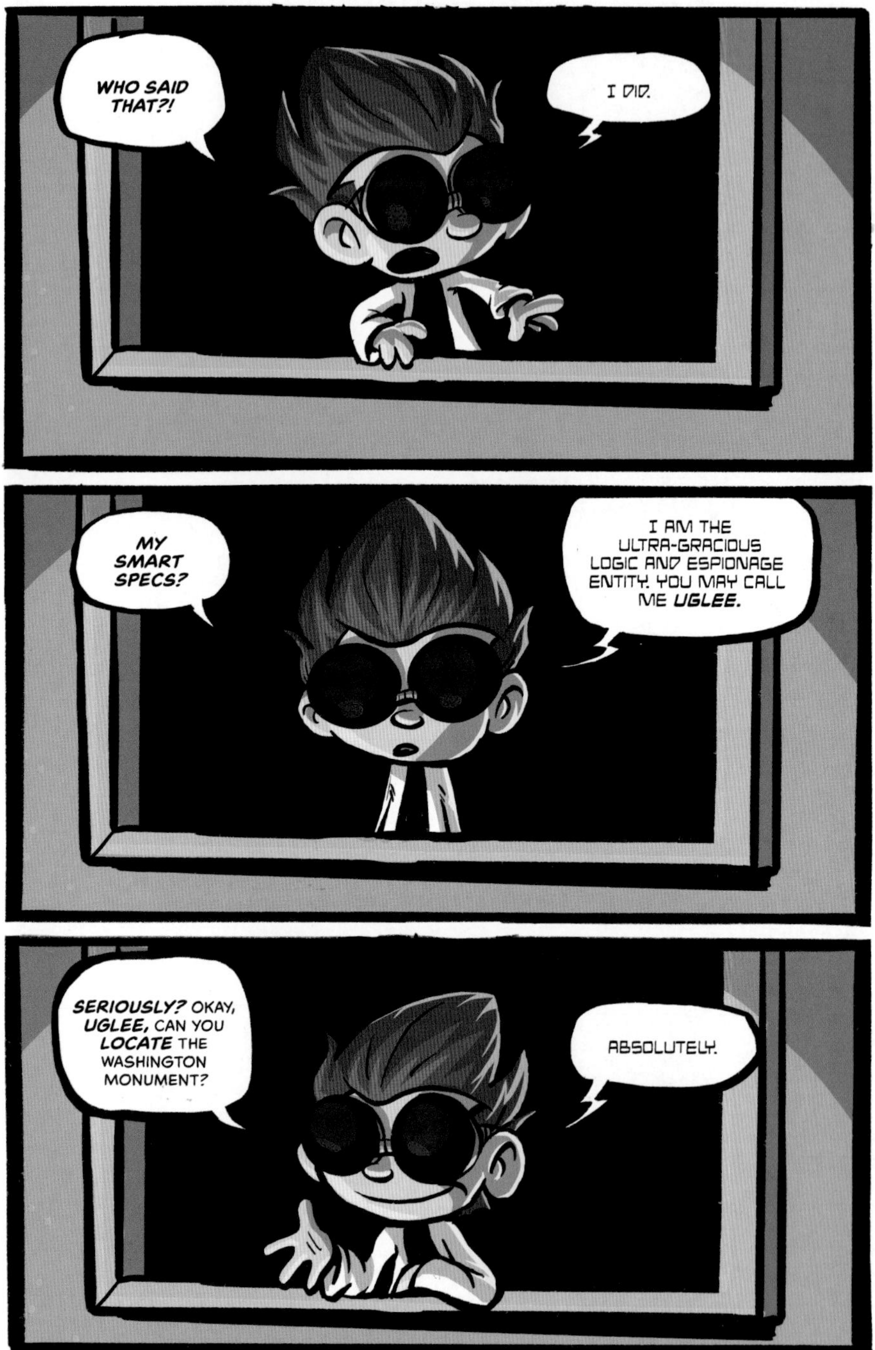
WHO SAID THAT?!
I DID.
MY SMART SPECS?
I AM THE ULTRA-GRACIOUS LOGIC AND ESPIONAGE ENTITY. YOU MAY CALL ME UGLEE.
SERIOUSLY? OKAY, UGLEE, CAN YOU LOCATE THE WASHINGTON MONUMENT?
ABSOLUTELY.

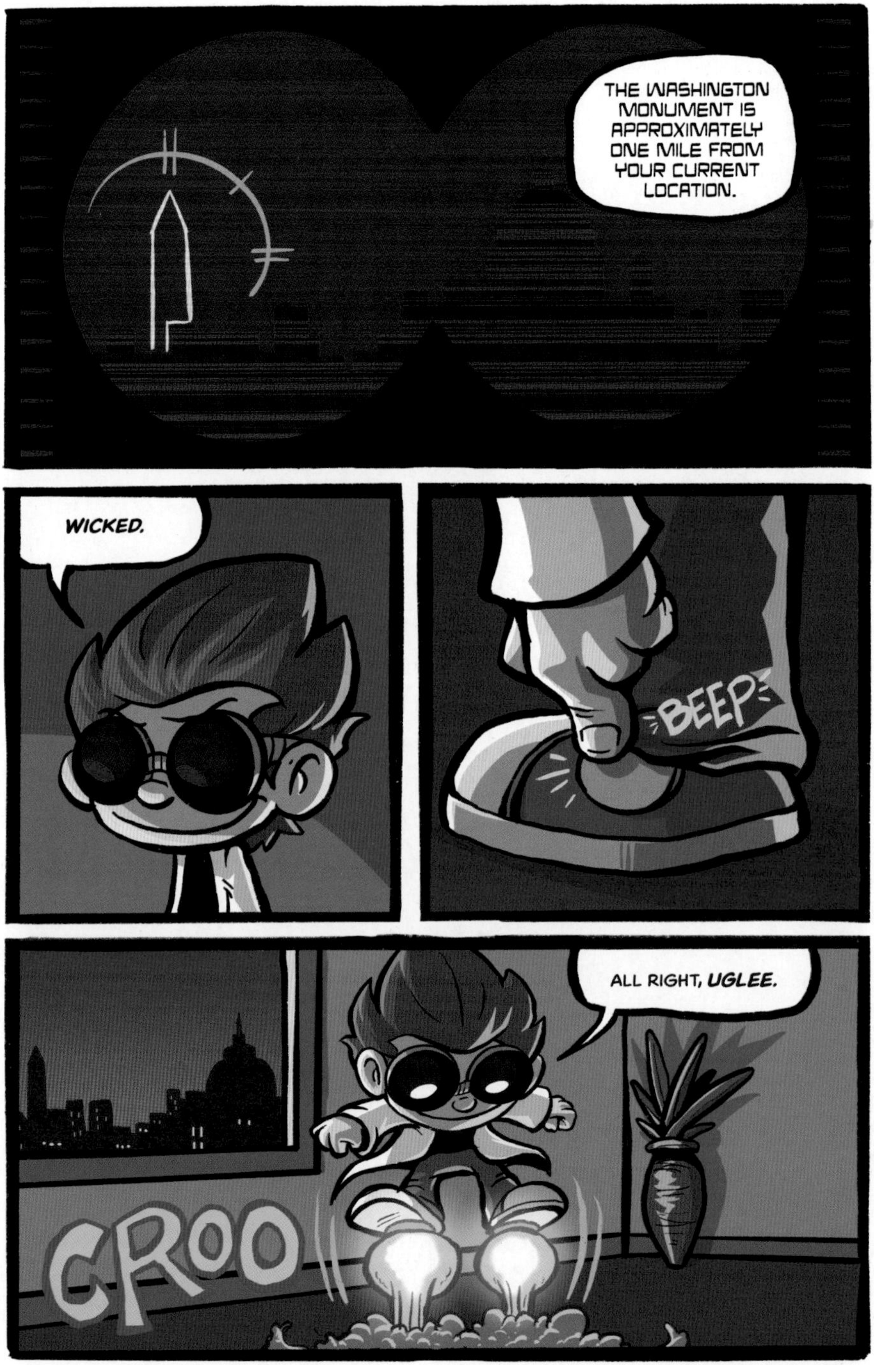
THE WASHINGTON MONUMENT IS APPROXIMATELY ONE MILE FROM YOUR CURRENT LOCATION.
WICKED.
BEEP
ALL RIGHT, UGLEE.
CROO

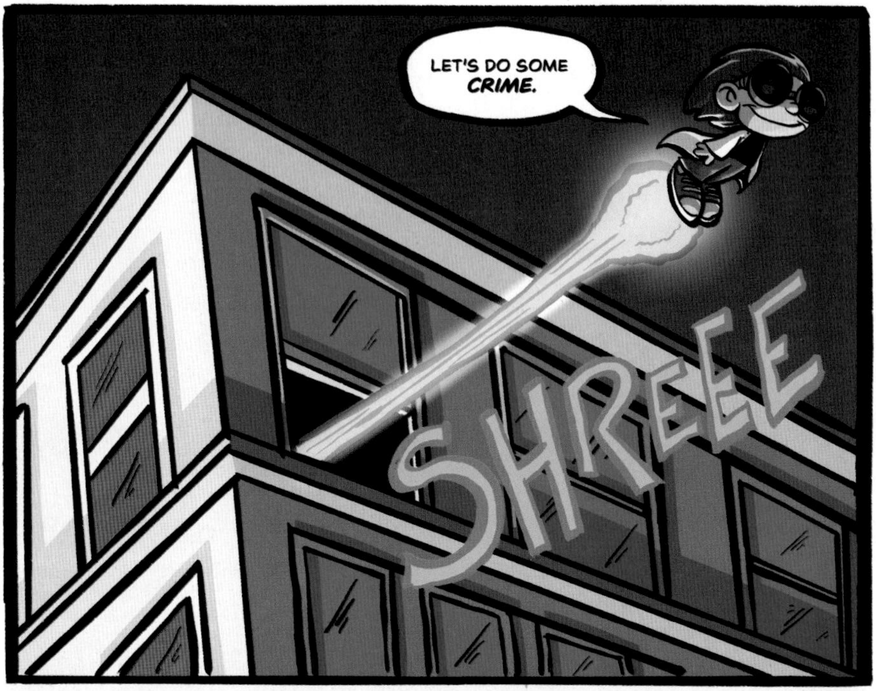
LET'S DO SOME CRIME.
SHREEE

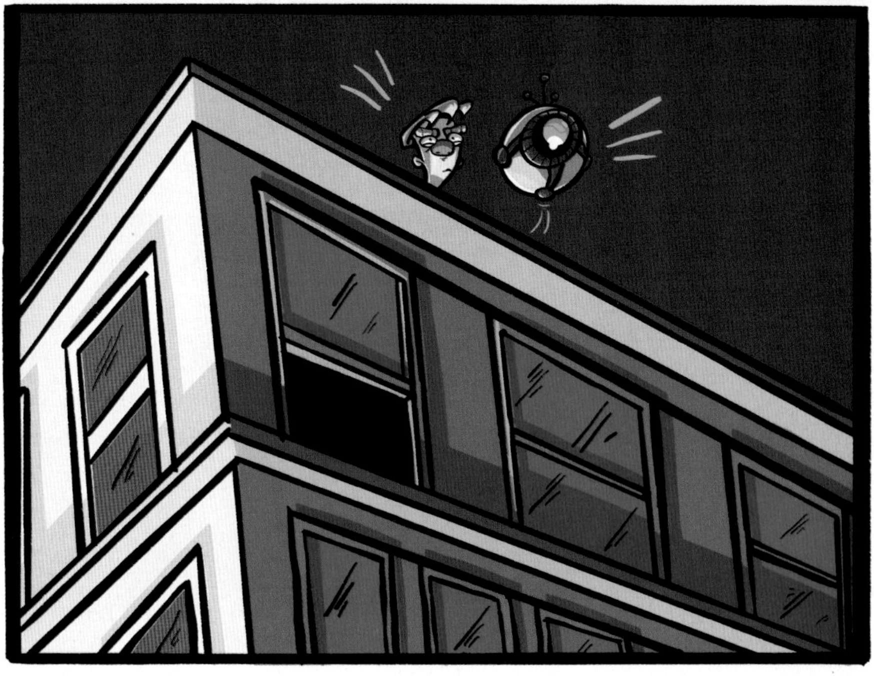

CHAPTER 13

One Person's Treasure

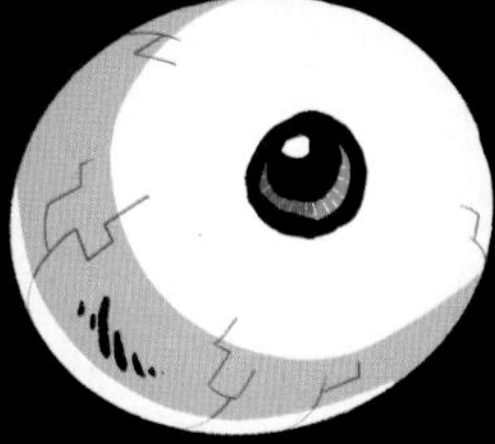

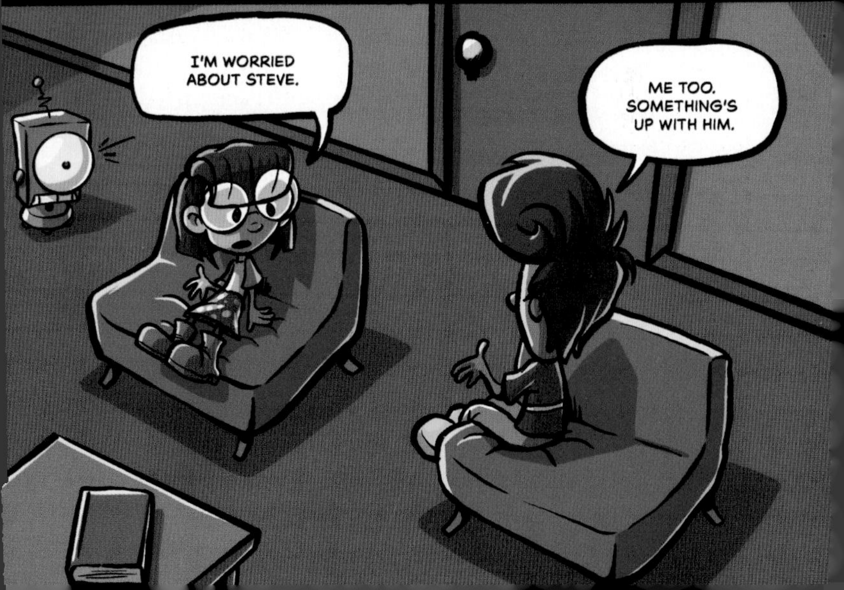
I'M WORRIED ABOUT STEVE.
ME TOO. SOMETHING'S UP WITH HIM.

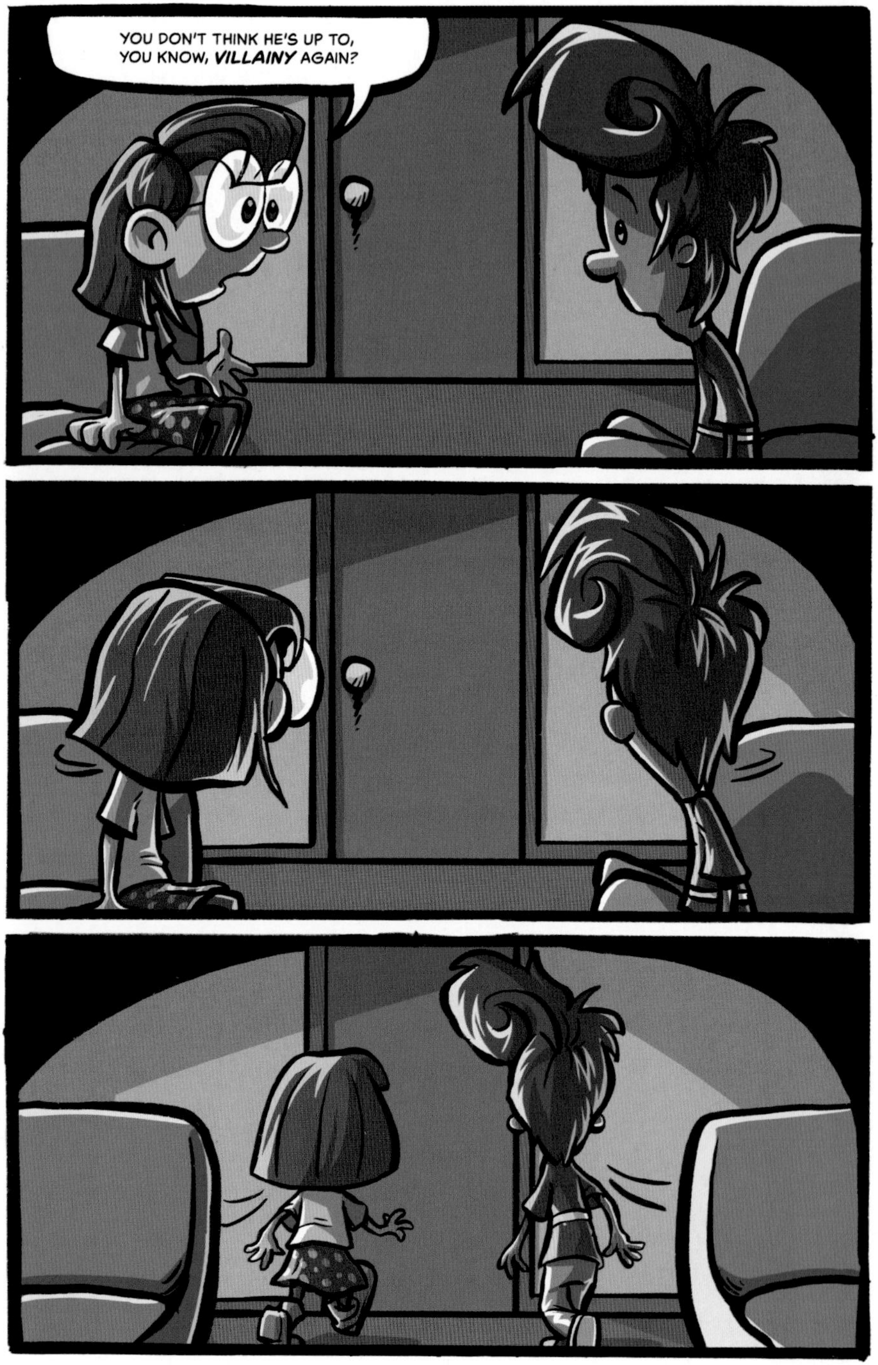
YOU DON'T THINK HE'S UP TO, YOU KNOW, VILLAINY AGAIN?

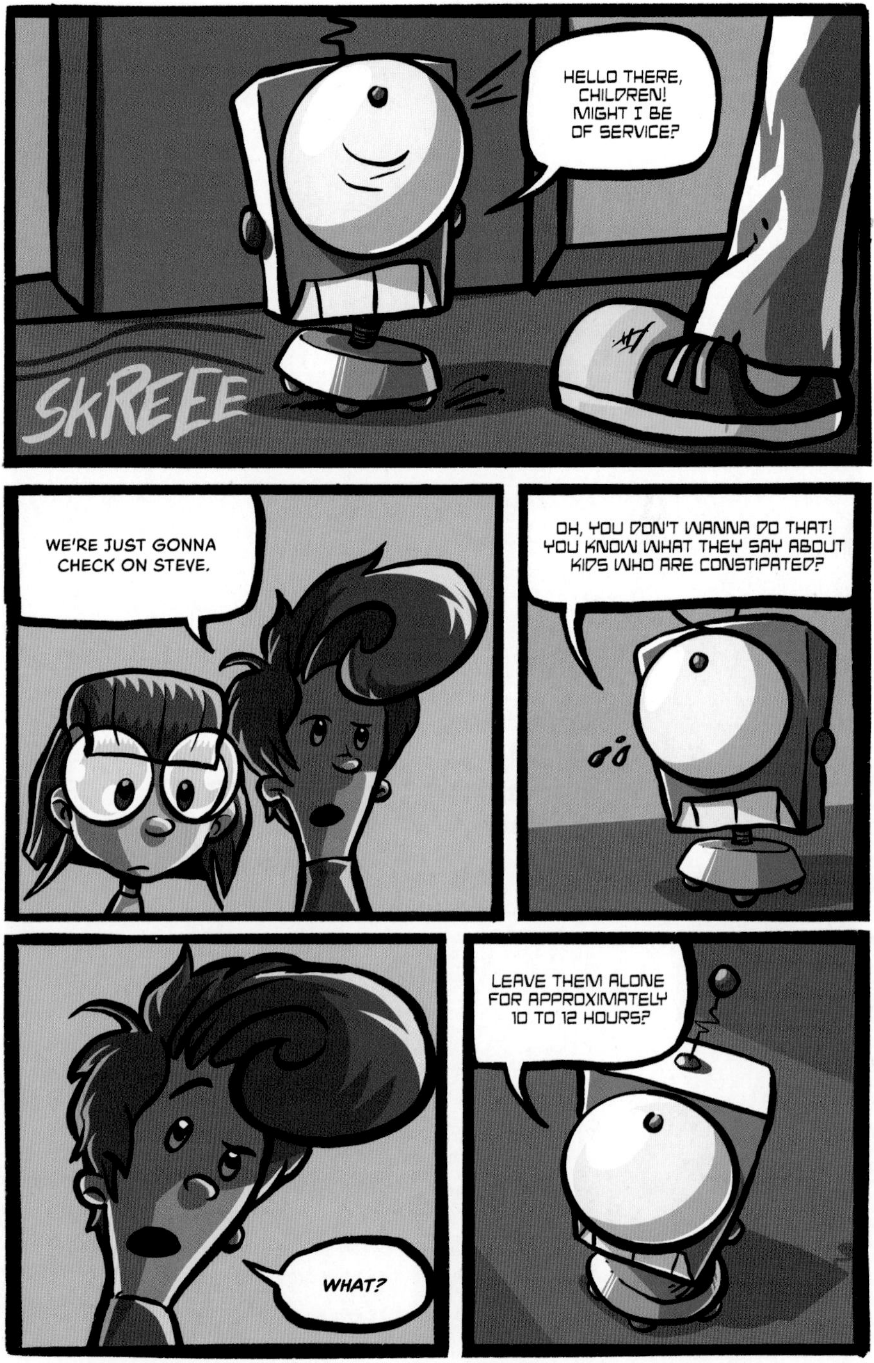
HELLO THERE, CHILDREN! MIGHT I BE OF SERVICE?
SKREEE
WE'RE JUST GONNA CHECK ON STEVE.
OH, YOU DON'T WANNA DO THAT! YOU KNOW WHAT THEY SAY ABOUT KIDS WHO ARE CONSTIPATED?
WHAT?
LEAVE THEM ALONE FOR APPROXIMATELY 10 TO 12 HOURS?

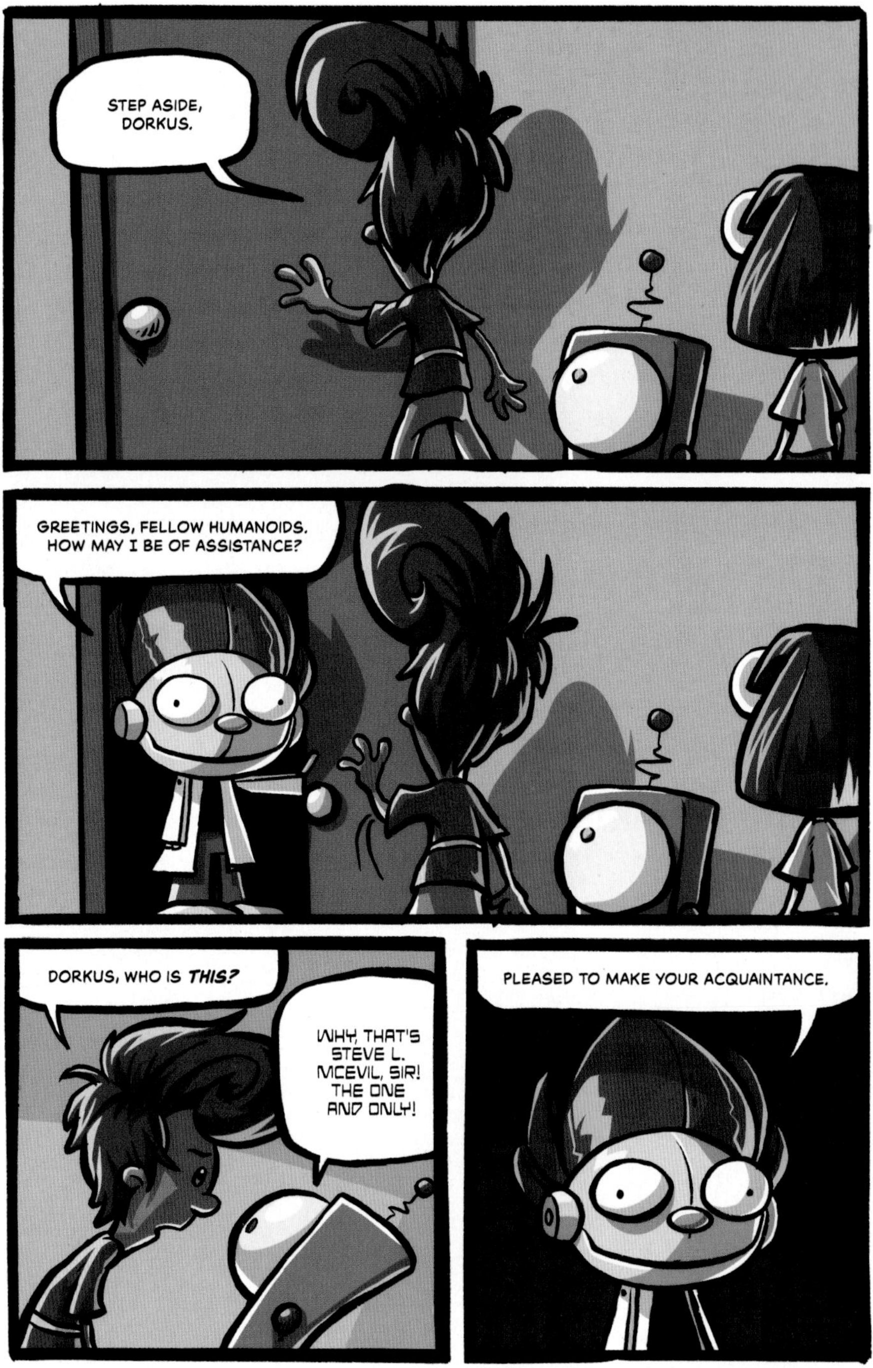
STEP ASIDE, DORKUS.
GREETINGS, FELLOW HUMANOIDS. HOW MAY I BE OF ASSISTANCE?
DORKUS, WHO IS *THIS?*
WHY, THAT'S STEVE L. MCEVIL, SIR! THE ONE AND ONLY!
PLEASED TO MAKE YOUR ACQUAINTANCE.

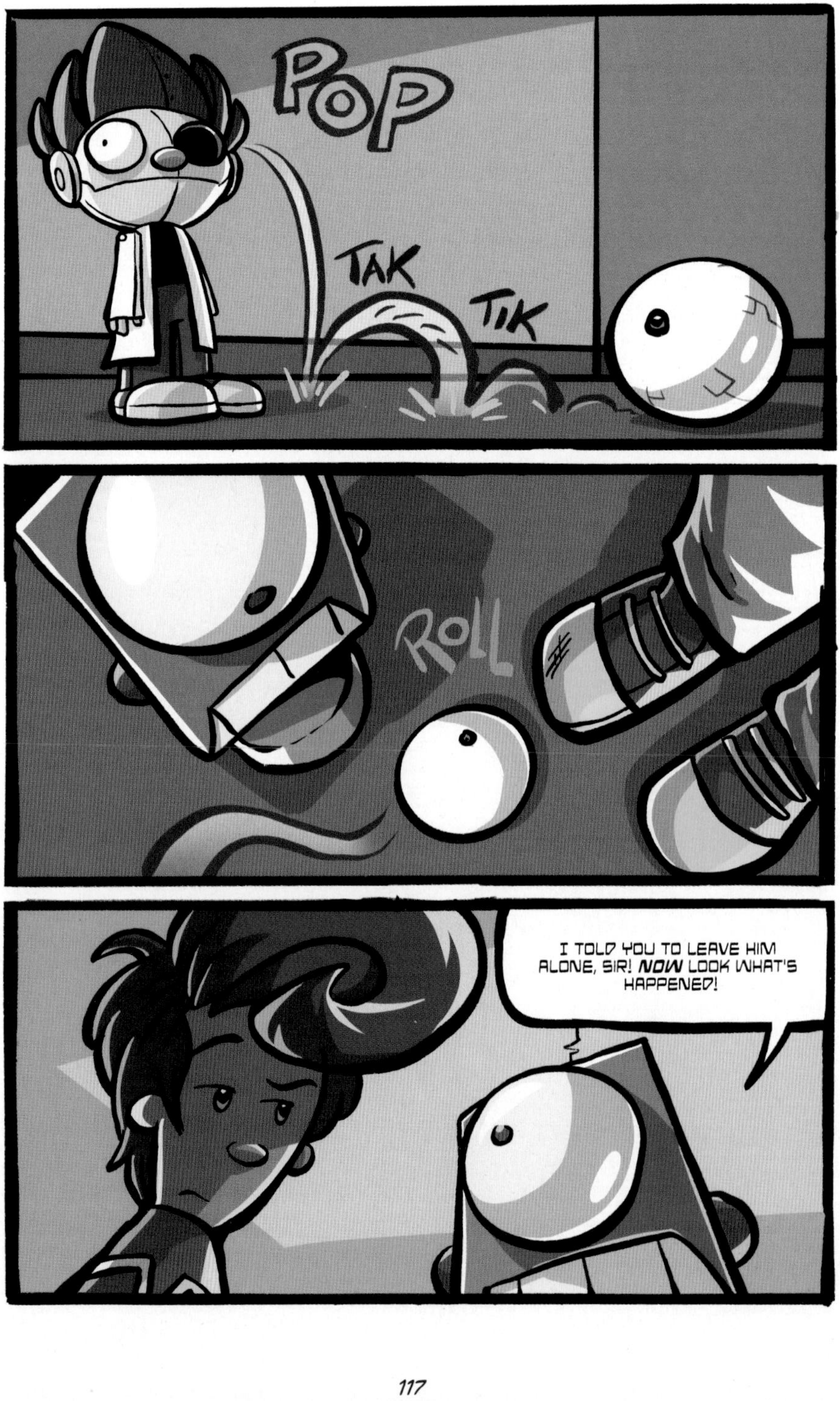
POP
TAK
TIK
ROLL
I TOLD YOU TO LEAVE HIM ALONE, SIR! *NOW* LOOK WHAT'S HAPPENED!

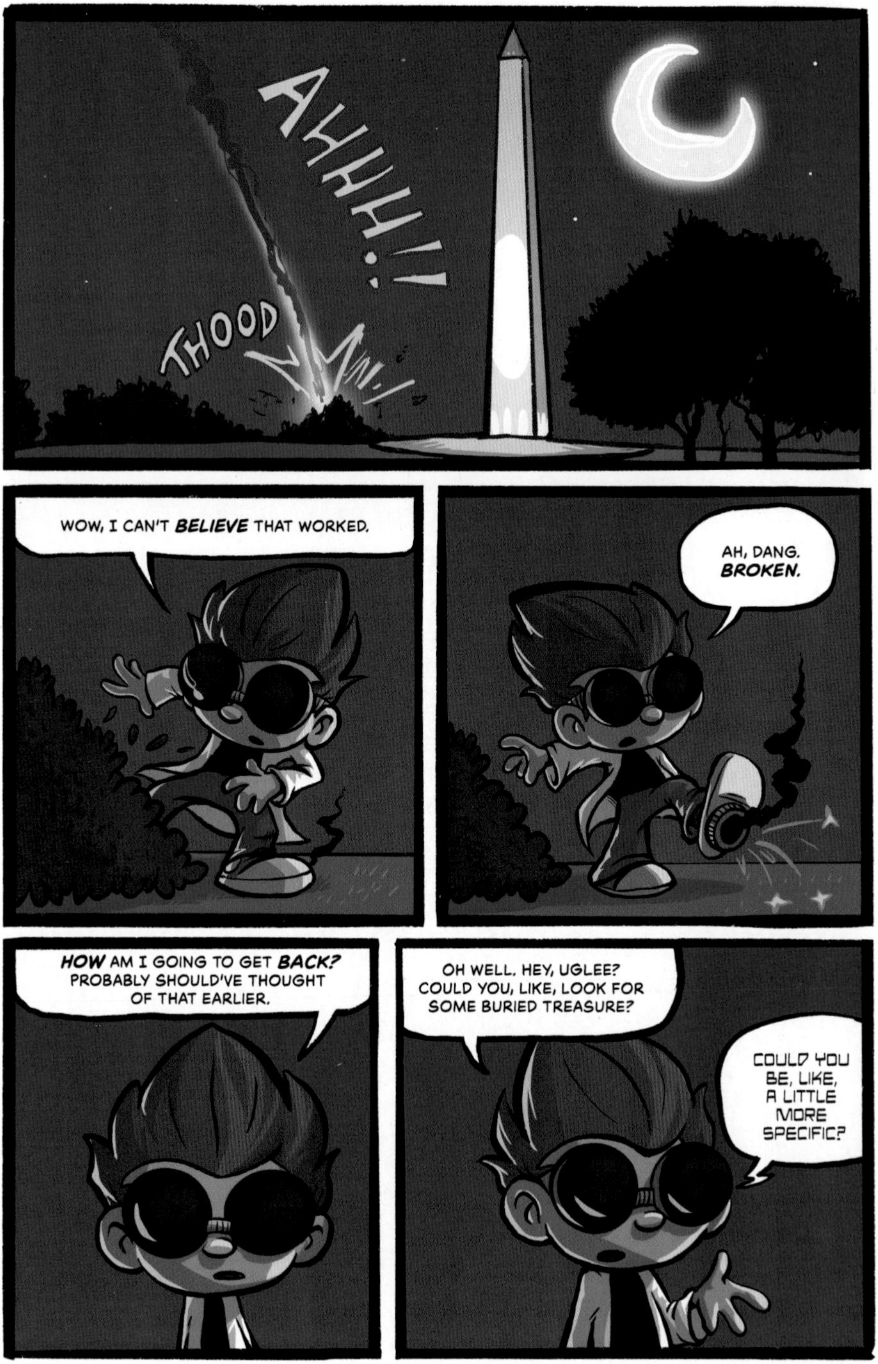
AHHH!!
THOOD
WOW, I CAN'T **BELIEVE** THAT WORKED.
AH, DANG. **BROKEN.**
HOW AM I GOING TO GET ***BACK?*** PROBABLY SHOULD'VE THOUGHT OF THAT EARLIER.
OH WELL. HEY, UGLEE? COULD YOU, LIKE, LOOK FOR SOME BURIED TREASURE?
COULD YOU BE, LIKE, A LITTLE MORE SPECIFIC?

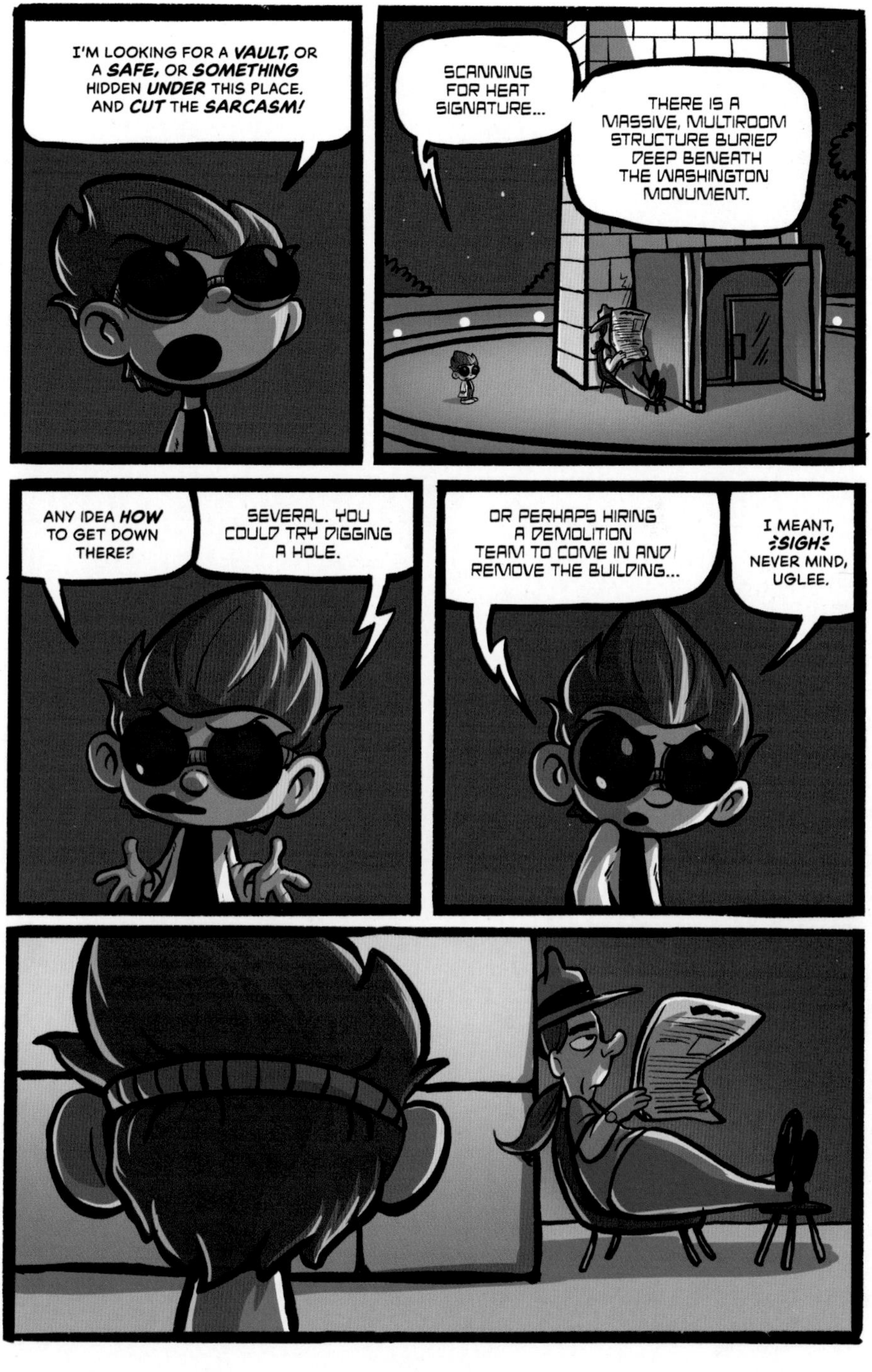
I'M LOOKING FOR A VAULT, OR A SAFE, OR SOMETHING HIDDEN UNDER THIS PLACE. AND CUT THE SARCASM!
SCANNING FOR HEAT SIGNATURE...
THERE IS A MASSIVE, MULTIROOM STRUCTURE BURIED DEEP BENEATH THE WASHINGTON MONUMENT.
ANY IDEA HOW TO GET DOWN THERE?
SEVERAL. YOU COULD TRY DIGGING A HOLE.
OR PERHAPS HIRING A DEMOLITION TEAM TO COME IN AND REMOVE THE BUILDING...
I MEANT, *SIGH* NEVER MIND, UGLEE.

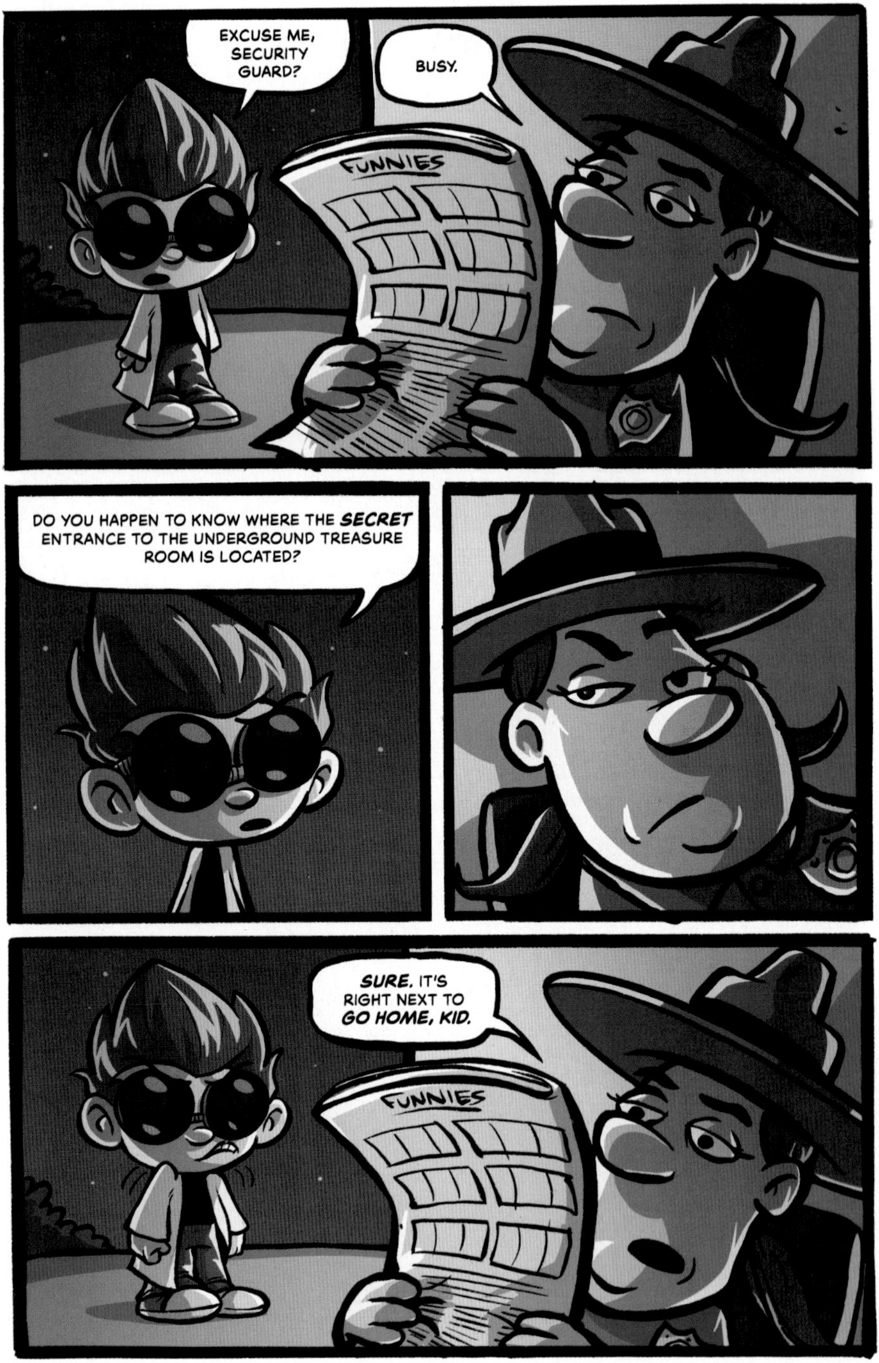
EXCUSE ME, SECURITY GUARD?
BUSY.
FUNNIES
DO YOU HAPPEN TO KNOW WHERE THE ***SECRET*** ENTRANCE TO THE UNDERGROUND TREASURE ROOM IS LOCATED?
SURE. IT'S RIGHT NEXT TO ***GO HOME, KID.***
FUNNIES

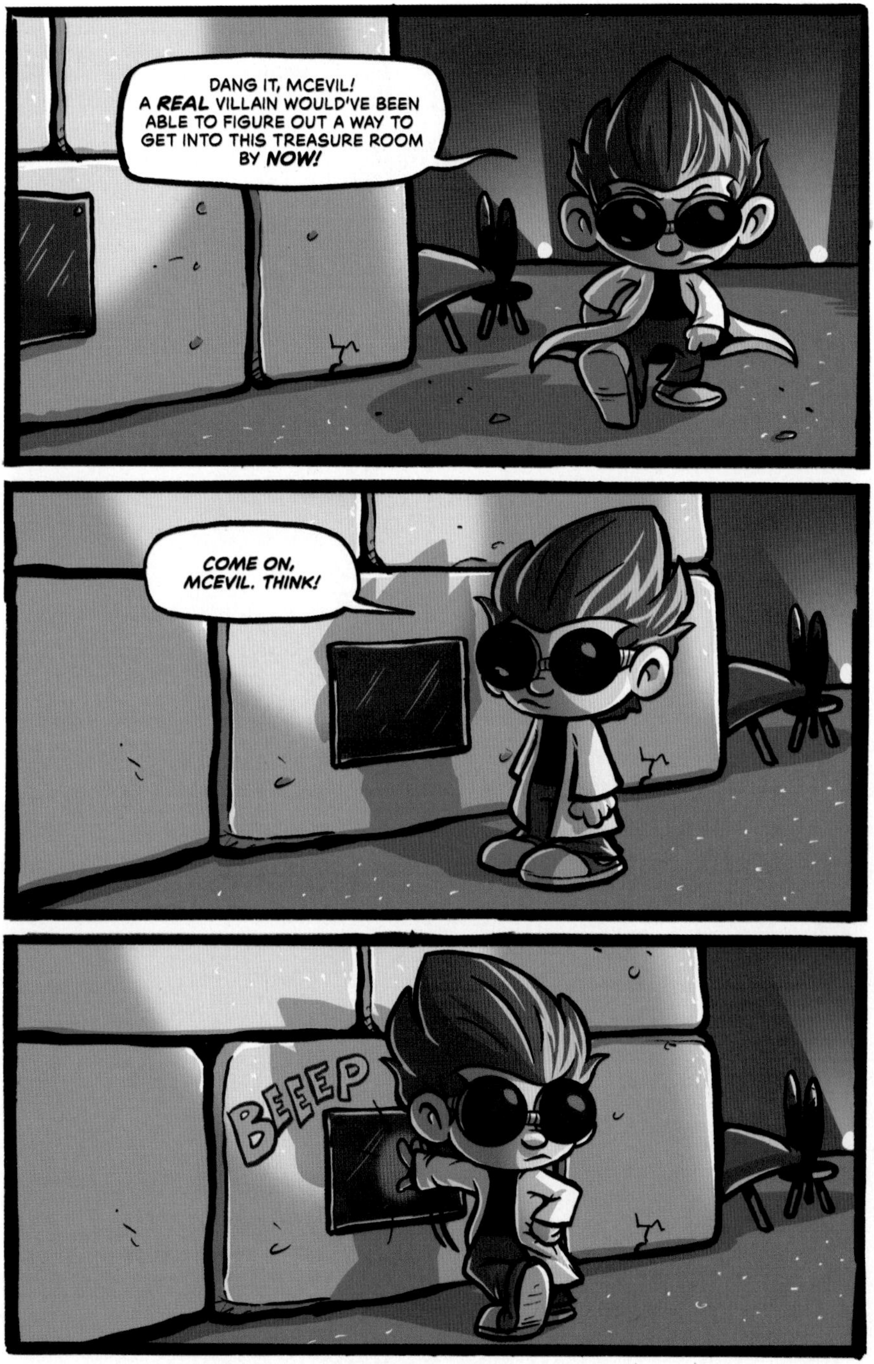
DANG IT, MCEVIL! A REAL VILLAIN WOULD'VE BEEN ABLE TO FIGURE OUT A WAY TO GET INTO THIS TREASURE ROOM BY NOW!
COME ON, MCEVIL. THINK!
BEEEP

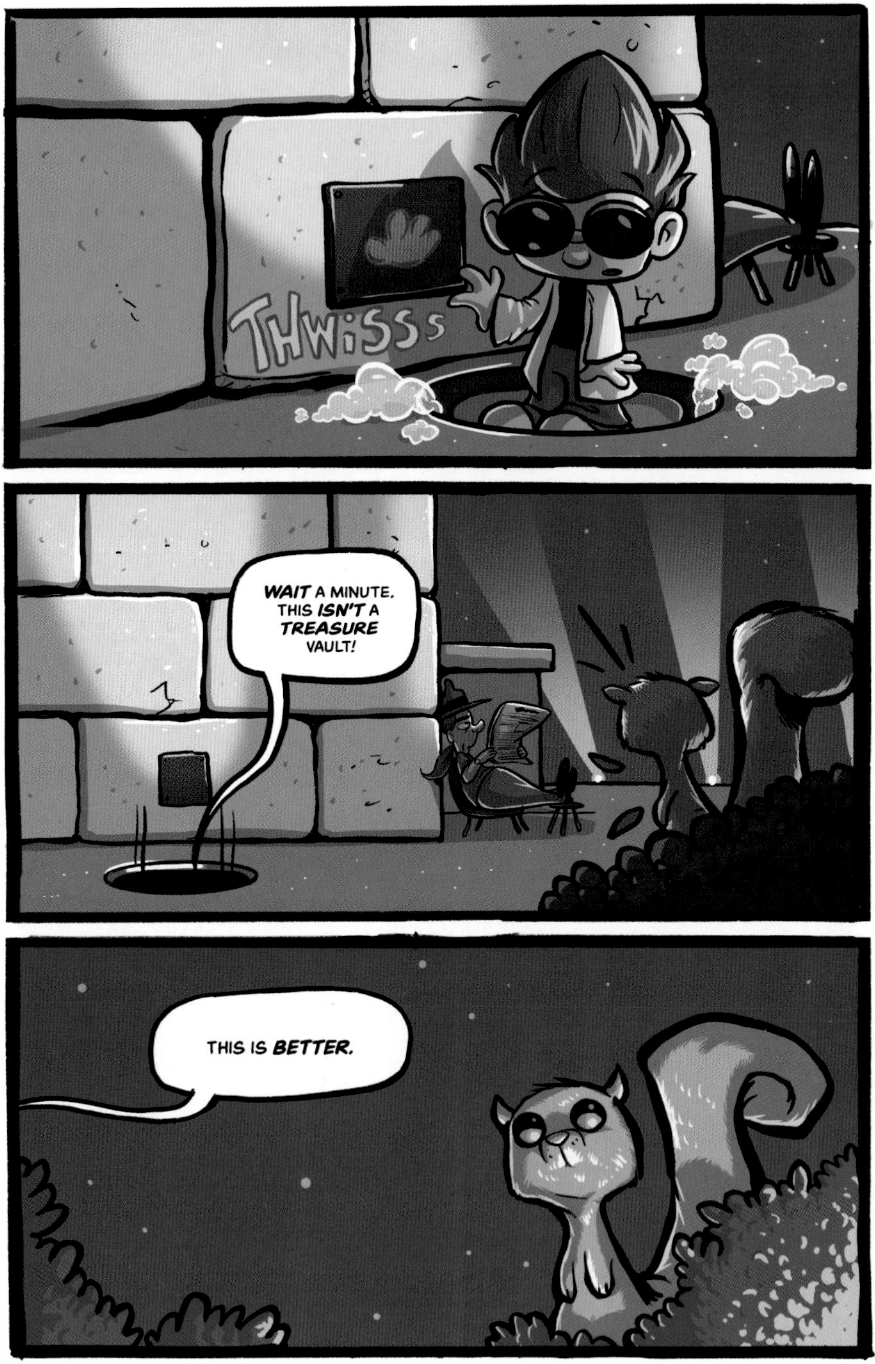
THWiSSS
WAIT A MINUTE. THIS ISN'T A TREASURE VAULT!
THIS IS BETTER.

CHAPTER 14

Send in the Clones

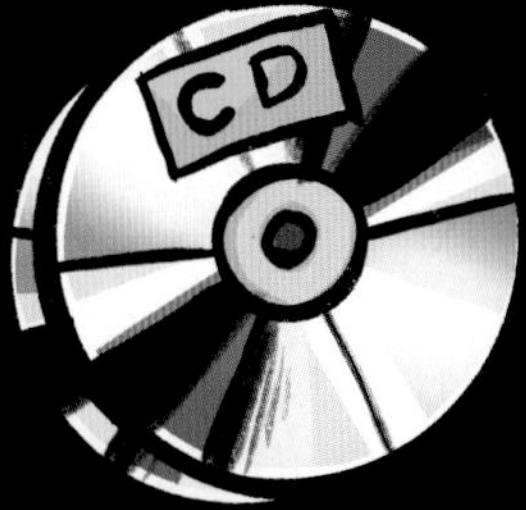
CD

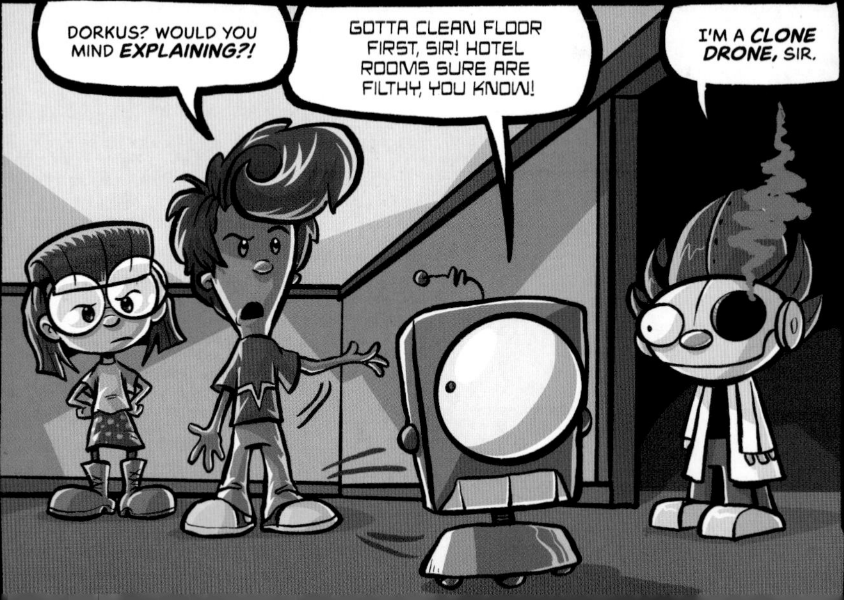
DORKUS? WOULD YOU MIND **EXPLAINING?!**
GOTTA CLEAN FLOOR FIRST, SIR! HOTEL ROOMS SURE ARE FILTHY, YOU KNOW!
I'M A ***CLONE DRONE,*** SIR.

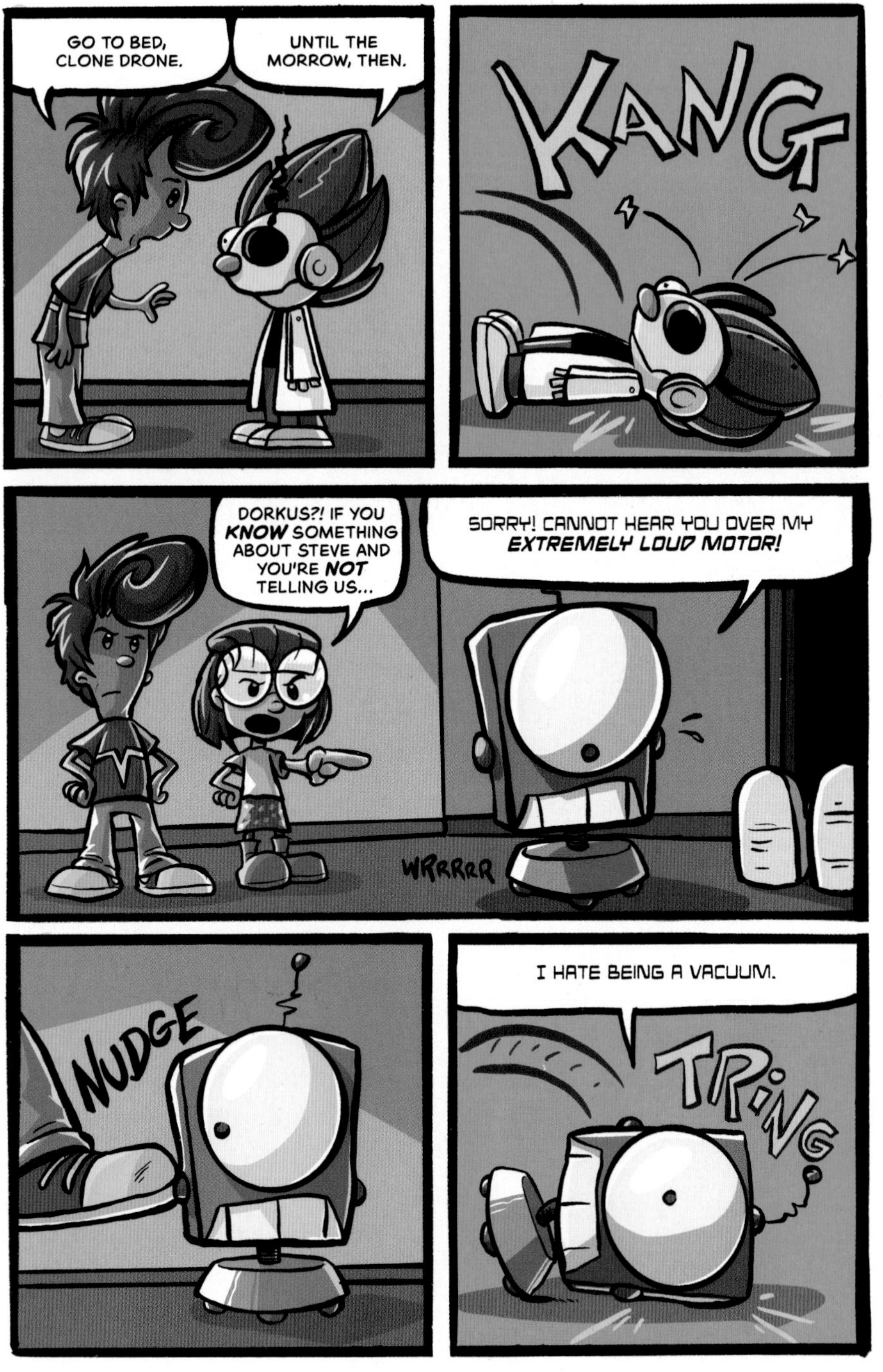
GO TO BED, CLONE DRONE.
UNTIL THE MORROW, THEN.
KANG
DORKUS?! IF YOU KNOW SOMETHING ABOUT STEVE AND YOU'RE NOT TELLING US...
SORRY! CANNOT HEAR YOU OVER MY EXTREMELY LOUD MOTOR!
WRRRRR
NUDGE
I HATE BEING A VACUUM.
TRING

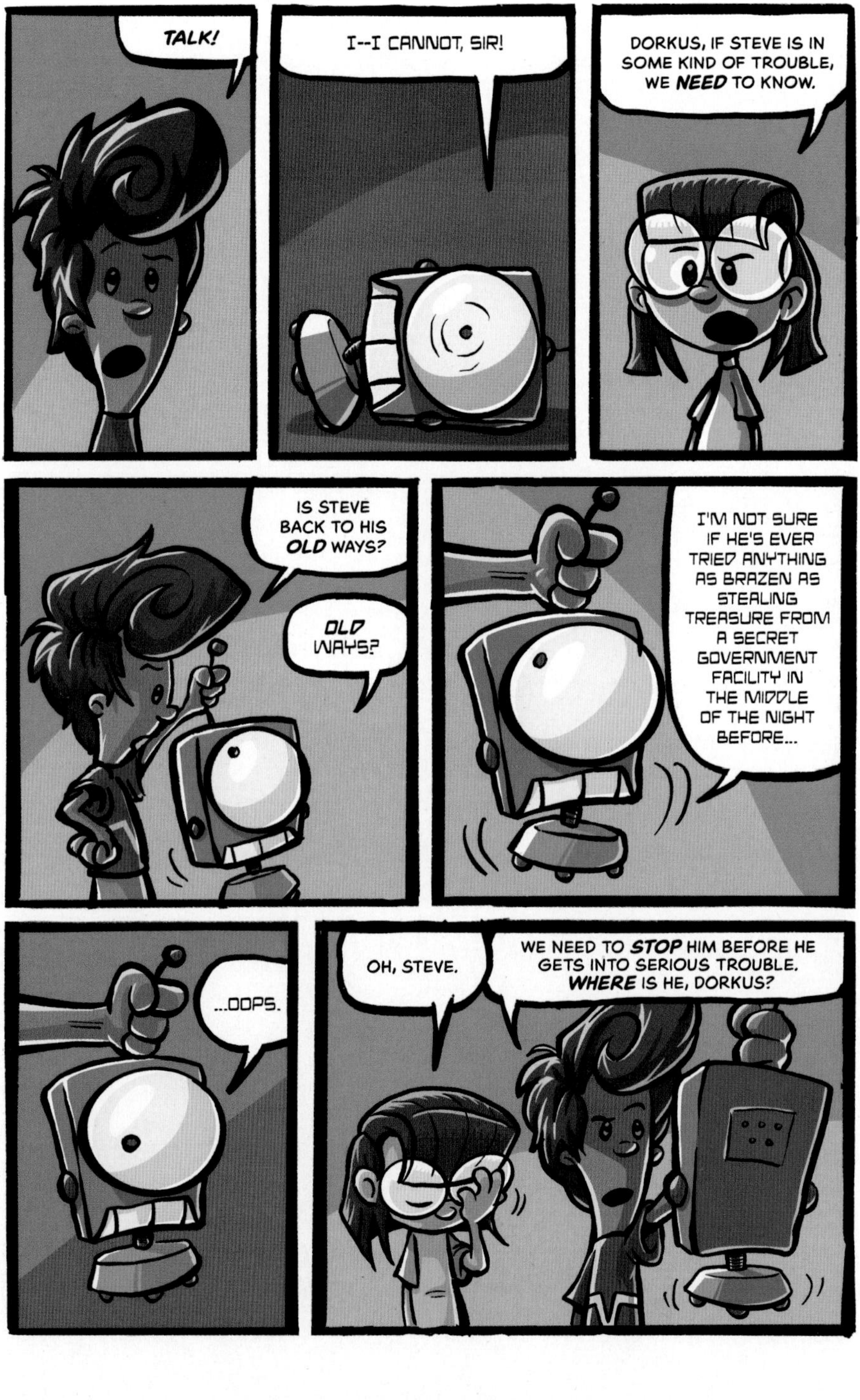
TALK!
I--I CANNOT, SIR!
DORKUS, IF STEVE IS IN SOME KIND OF TROUBLE, WE NEED TO KNOW.
IS STEVE BACK TO HIS OLD WAYS?
OLD WAYS?
I'M NOT SURE IF HE'S EVER TRIED ANYTHING AS BRAZEN AS STEALING TREASURE FROM A SECRET GOVERNMENT FACILITY IN THE MIDDLE OF THE NIGHT BEFORE...
...OOPS.
OH, STEVE.
WE NEED TO STOP HIM BEFORE HE GETS INTO SERIOUS TROUBLE. WHERE IS HE, DORKUS?

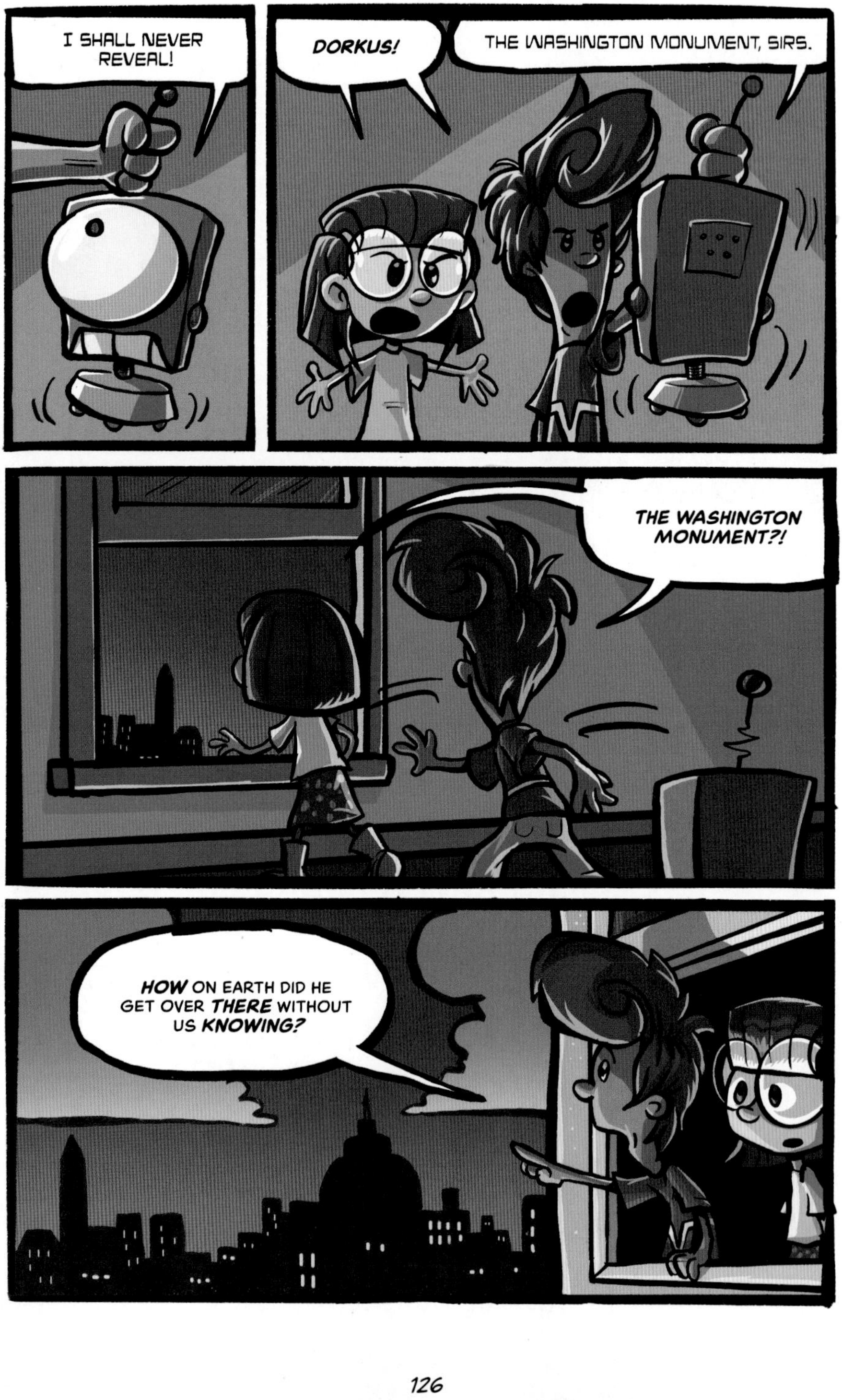
I SHALL NEVER REVEAL!
DORKUS!
THE WASHINGTON MONUMENT, SIRS.
THE WASHINGTON MONUMENT?!
HOW ON EARTH DID HE GET OVER THERE WITHOUT US KNOWING?

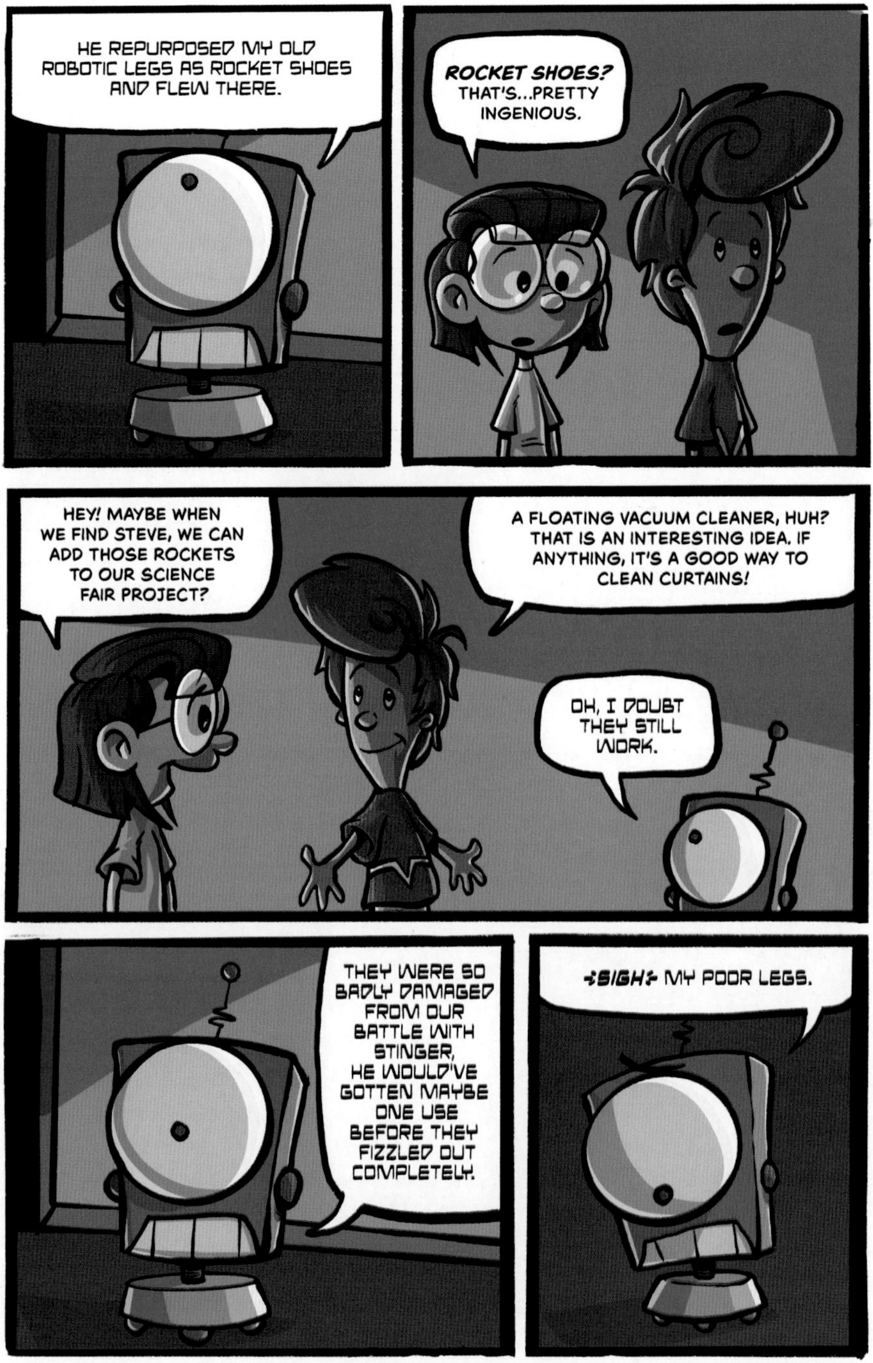
HE REPURPOSED MY OLD ROBOTIC LEGS AS ROCKET SHOES AND FLEW THERE.
ROCKET SHOES? THAT'S...PRETTY INGENIOUS.
HEY! MAYBE WHEN WE FIND STEVE, WE CAN ADD THOSE ROCKETS TO OUR SCIENCE FAIR PROJECT?
A FLOATING VACUUM CLEANER, HUH? THAT IS AN INTERESTING IDEA. IF ANYTHING, IT'S A GOOD WAY TO CLEAN CURTAINS!
OH, I DOUBT THEY STILL WORK.
THEY WERE SO BADLY DAMAGED FROM OUR BATTLE WITH STINGER, HE WOULD'VE GOTTEN MAYBE ONE USE BEFORE THEY FIZZLED OUT COMPLETELY.
SIGH MY POOR LEGS.

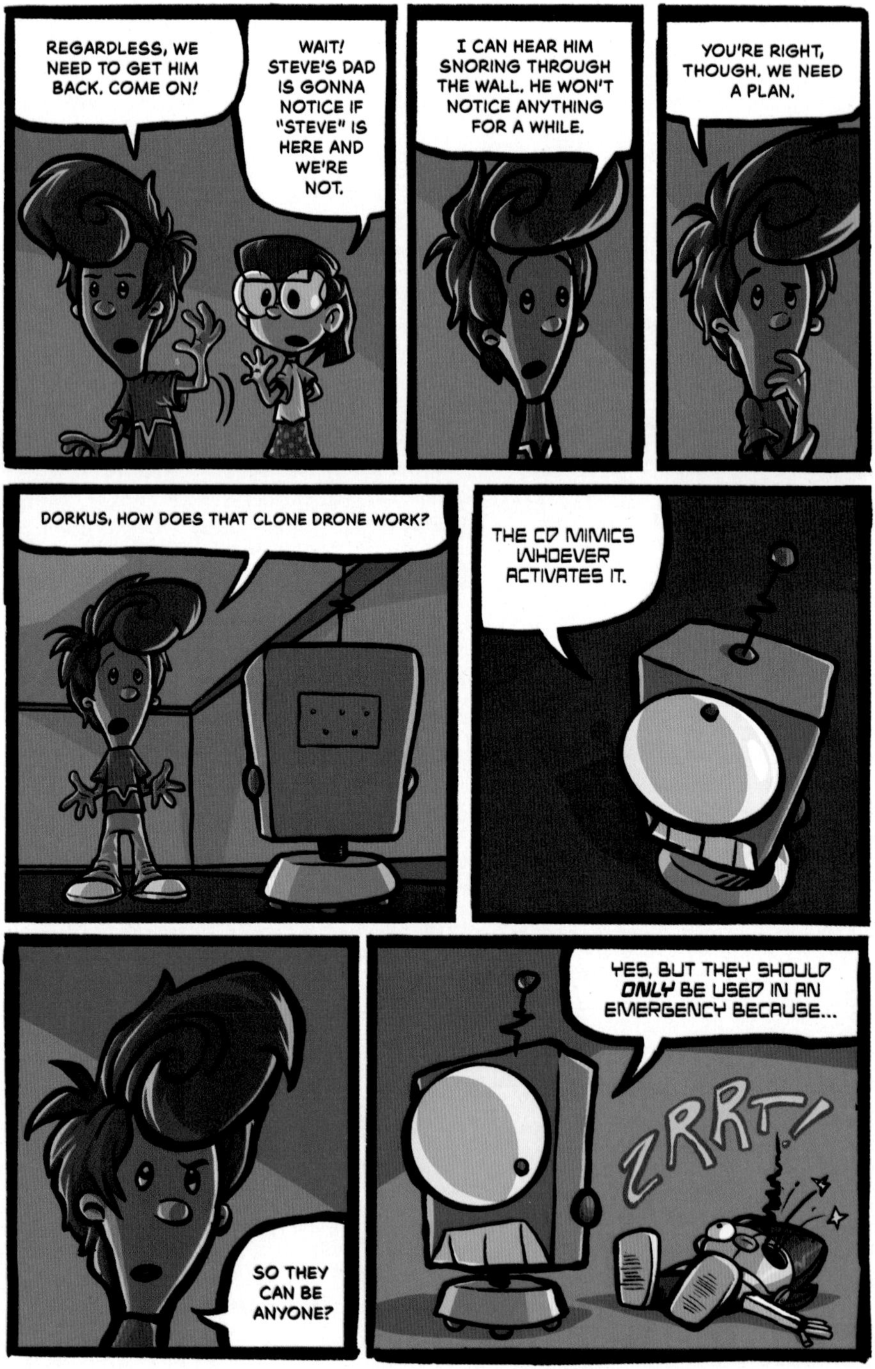

REGARDLESS, WE NEED TO GET HIM BACK. COME ON!
WAIT! STEVE'S DAD IS GONNA NOTICE IF "STEVE" IS HERE AND WE'RE NOT.
I CAN HEAR HIM SNORING THROUGH THE WALL. HE WON'T NOTICE ANYTHING FOR A WHILE.
YOU'RE RIGHT, THOUGH. WE NEED A PLAN.
DORKUS, HOW DOES THAT CLONE DRONE WORK?
THE CD MIMICS WHOEVER ACTIVATES IT.
SO THEY CAN BE ANYONE?
YES, BUT THEY SHOULD ONLY BE USED IN AN EMERGENCY BECAUSE...
ZRRT!

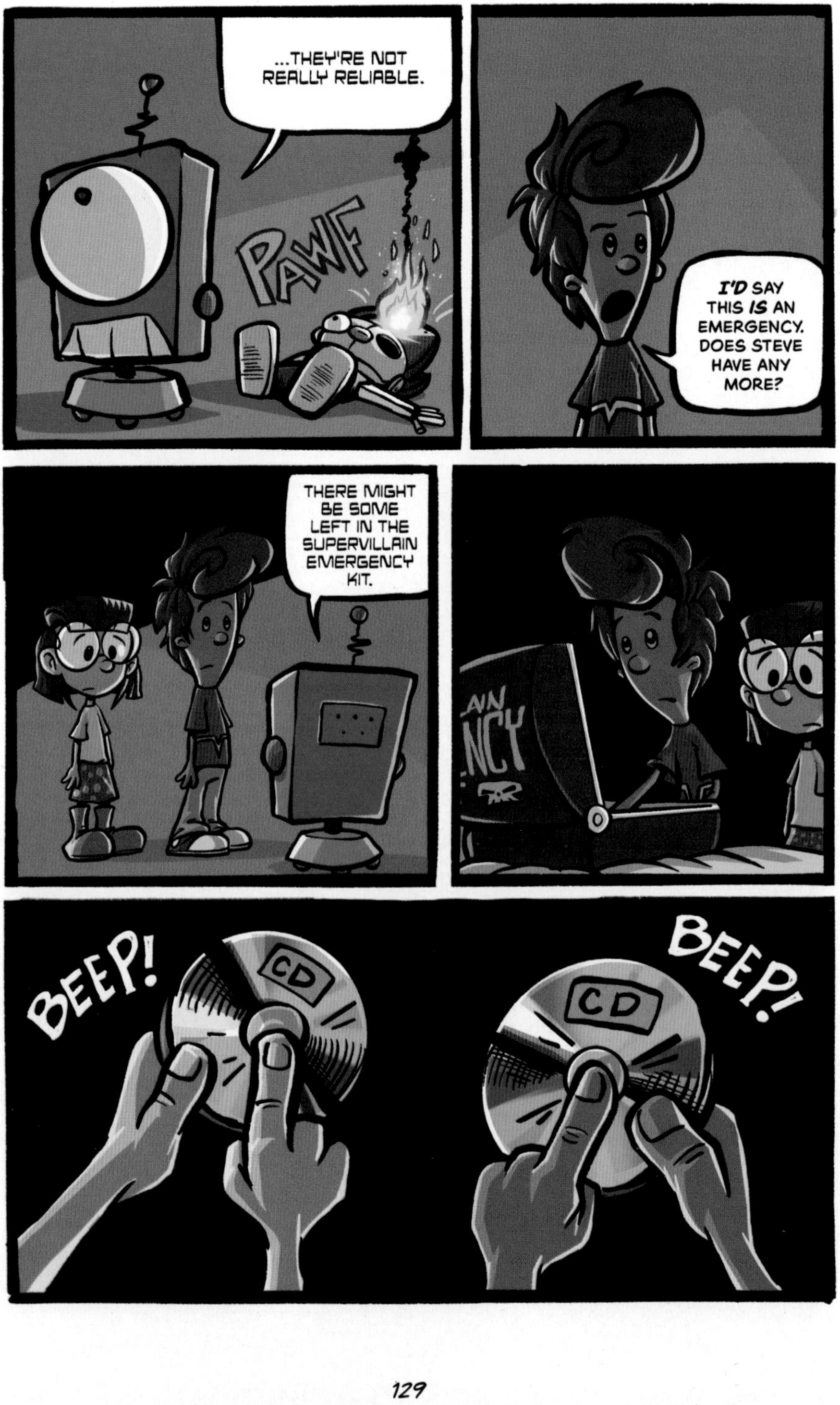
...THEY'RE NOT REALLY RELIABLE.
PAWF
I'D SAY THIS IS AN EMERGENCY. DOES STEVE HAVE ANY MORE?
THERE MIGHT BE SOME LEFT IN THE SUPERVILLAIN EMERGENCY KIT.
BEEP!
CD
BEEP!
CD

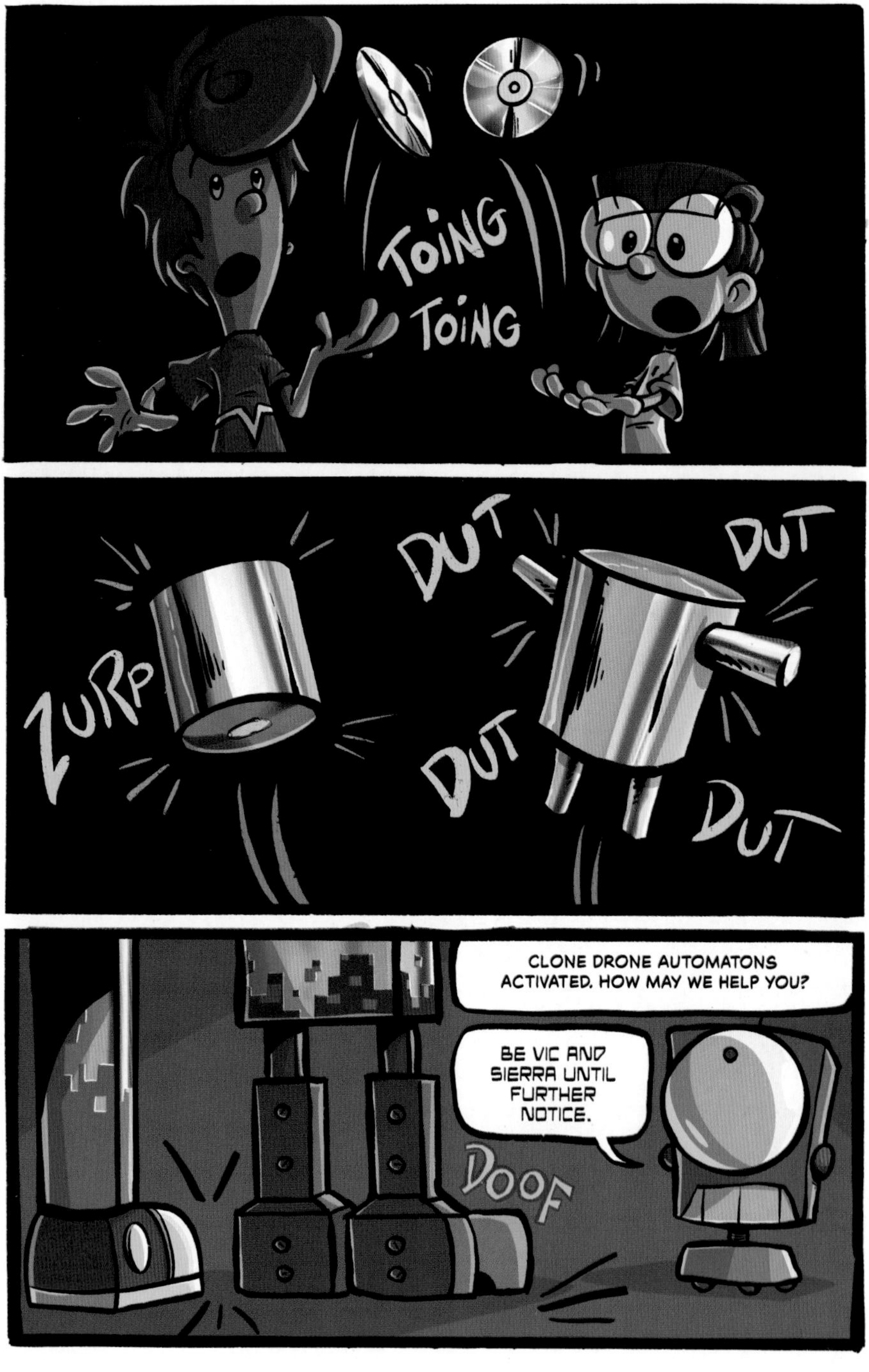
TOING
TOING
ZURP
DUT
DUT
DUT
DUT
CLONE DRONE AUTOMATONS ACTIVATED. HOW MAY WE HELP YOU?
BE VIC AND SIERRA UNTIL FURTHER NOTICE.
DOOF

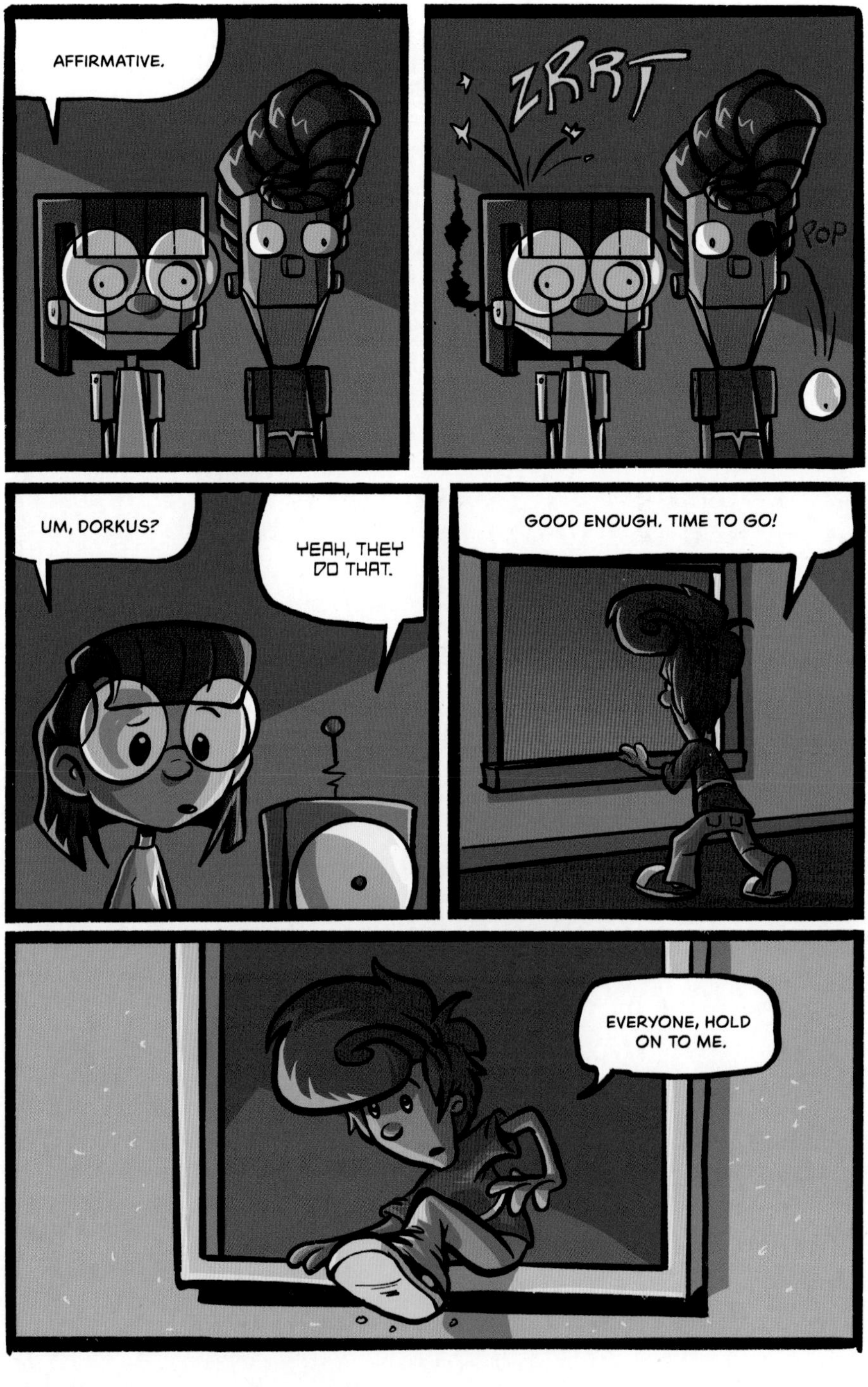
AFFIRMATIVE.
ZRRT
POP
UM, DORKUS?
YEAH, THEY DO THAT.
GOOD ENOUGH. TIME TO GO!
EVERYONE, HOLD ON TO ME.

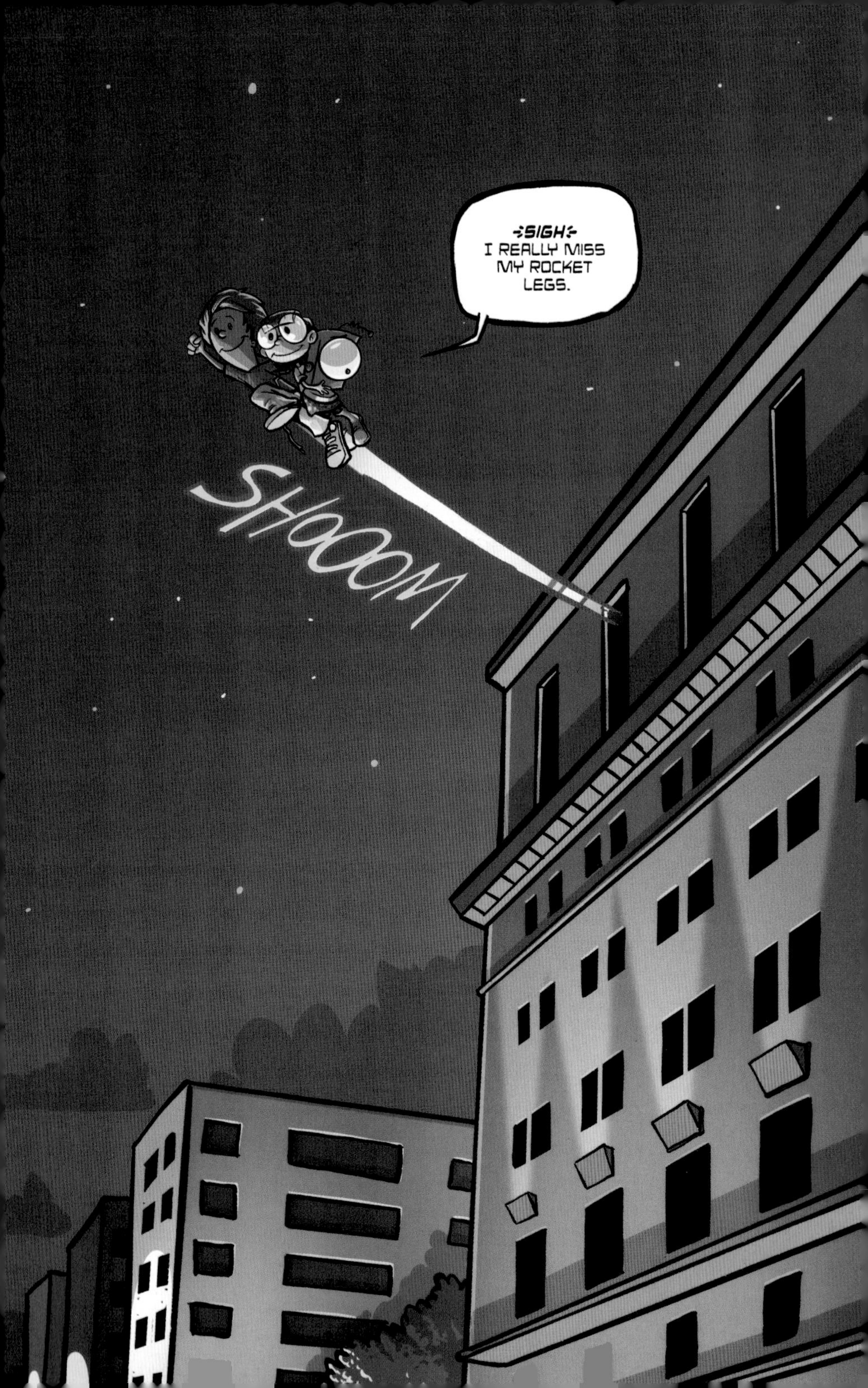

-SIGH- I REALLY MISS MY ROCKET LEGS.
SHOOOM

CHAPTER 15

The Spy Who Loathed We

STEVE!!
WHERE ARE YOU?!
WHY IS IT SO HARD FOR PEOPLE TO PUT TRASH IN THE RECEPTACLE?
WRRRR

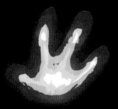

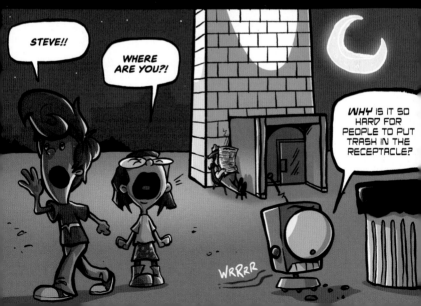

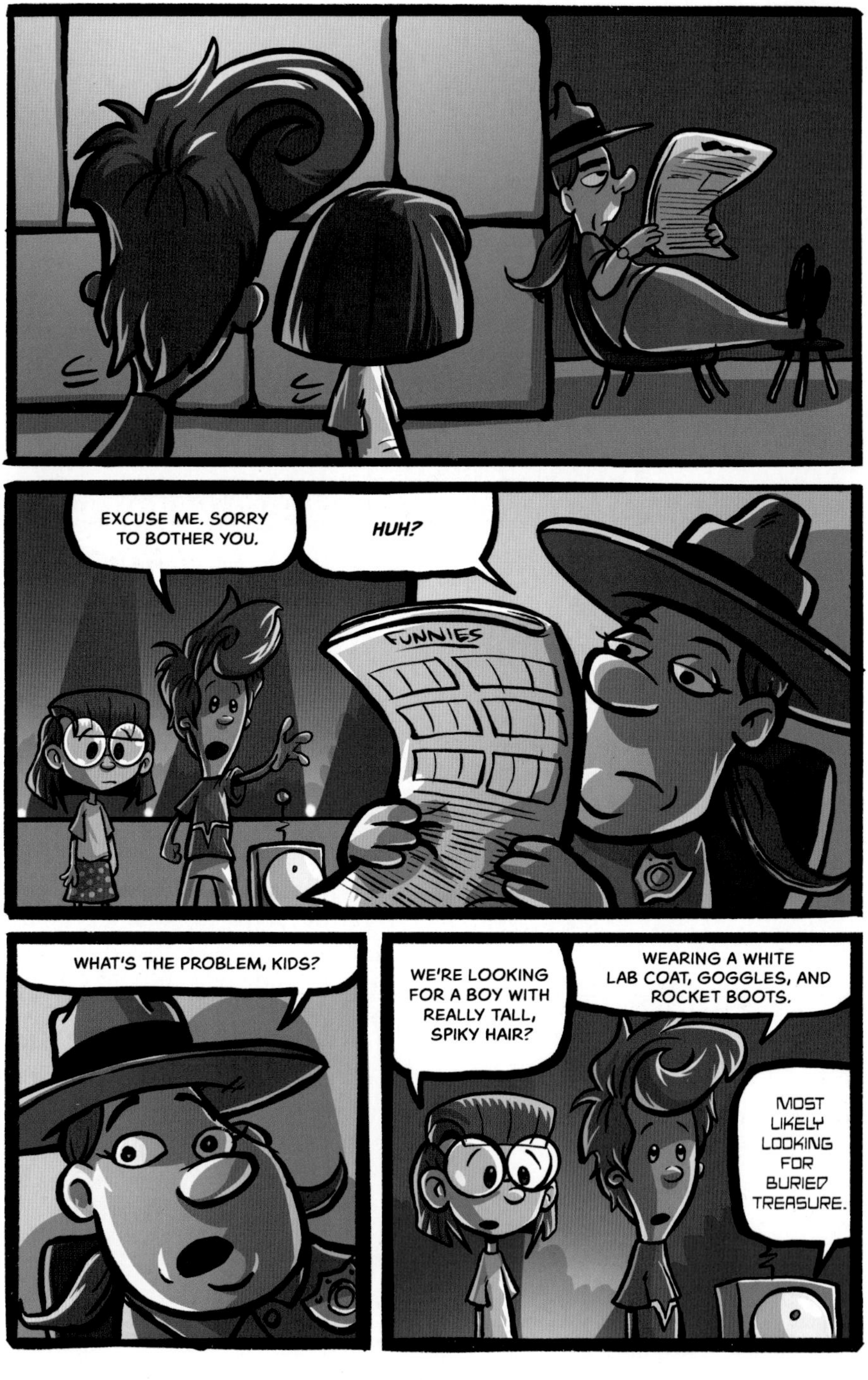
EXCUSE ME. SORRY TO BOTHER YOU.
HUH?
FUNNIES
WHAT'S THE PROBLEM, KIDS?
WE'RE LOOKING FOR A BOY WITH REALLY TALL, SPIKY HAIR?
WEARING A WHITE LAB COAT, GOGGLES, AND ROCKET BOOTS.
MOST LIKELY LOOKING FOR BURIED TREASURE.

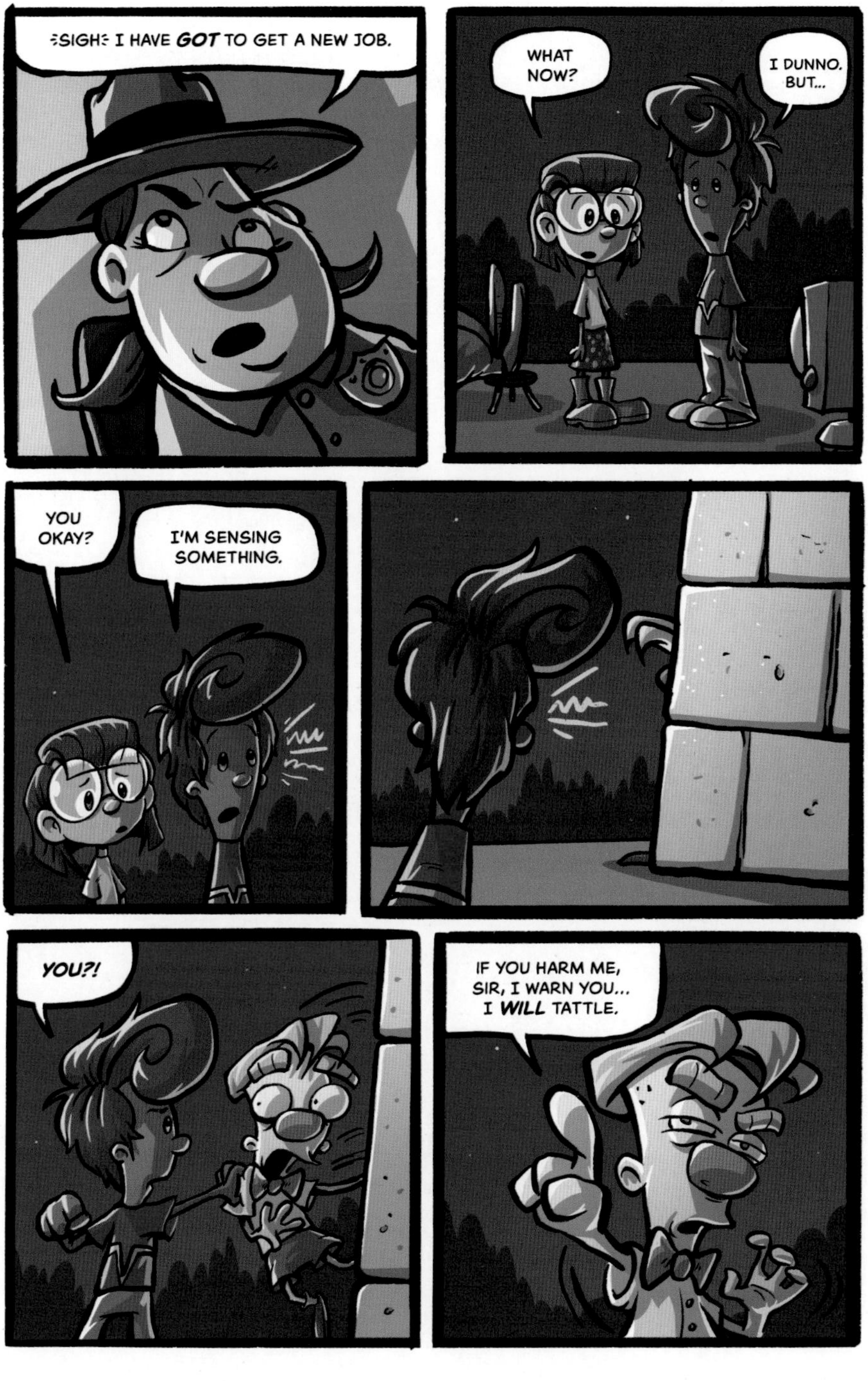

=SIGH= I HAVE *GOT* TO GET A NEW JOB.
WHAT NOW?
I DUNNO. BUT...
YOU OKAY?
I'M SENSING SOMETHING.
YOU?!
IF YOU HARM ME, SIR, I WARN YOU... I *WILL* TATTLE.

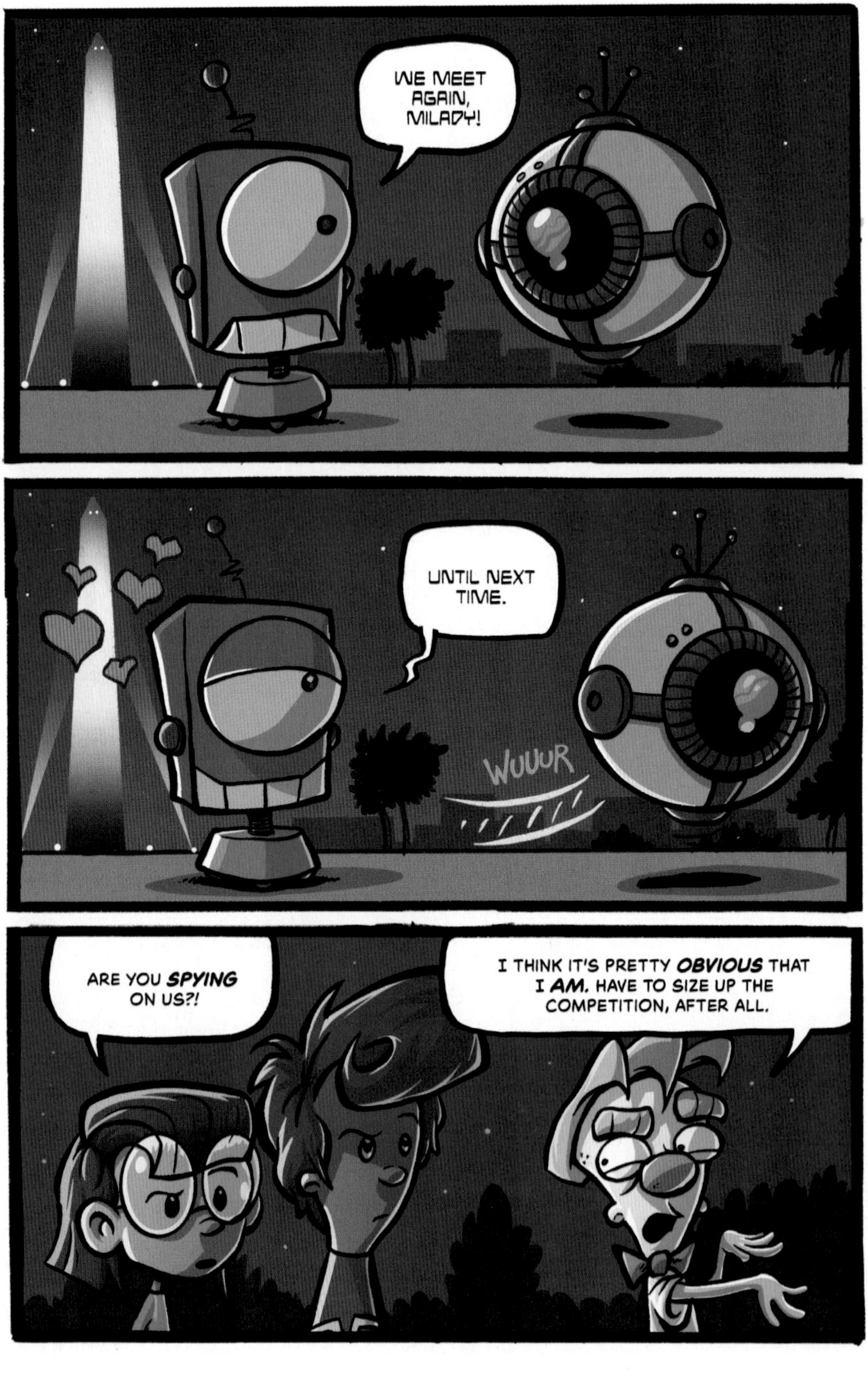
WE MEET AGAIN, MILADY!
UNTIL NEXT TIME.
WUUUR
ARE YOU SPYING ON US?!
I THINK IT'S PRETTY OBVIOUS THAT I AM. HAVE TO SIZE UP THE COMPETITION, AFTER ALL.

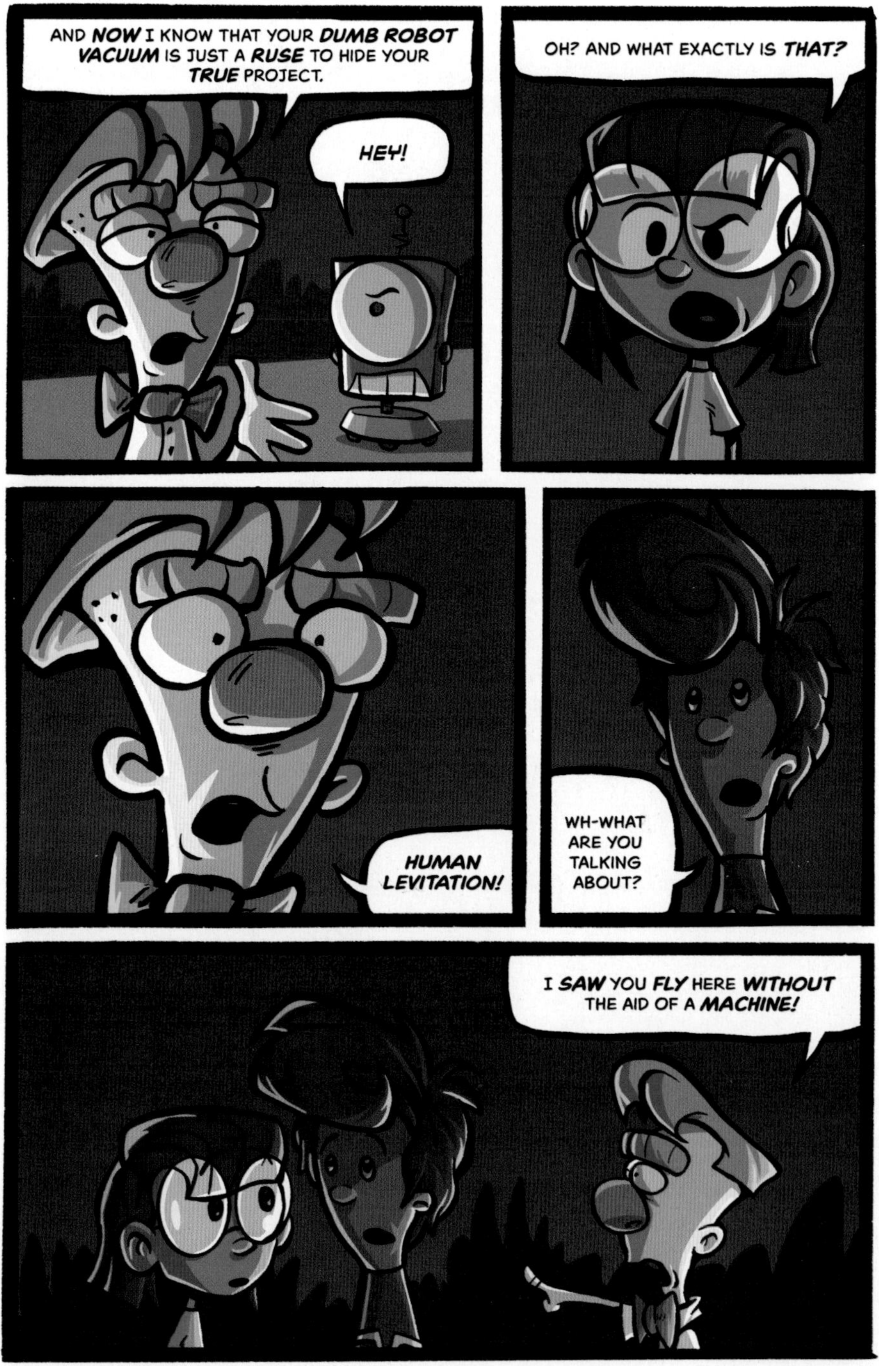
AND NOW I KNOW THAT YOUR DUMB ROBOT VACUUM IS JUST A RUSE TO HIDE YOUR TRUE PROJECT.
HEY!
OH? AND WHAT EXACTLY IS THAT?
HUMAN LEVITATION!
WH-WHAT ARE YOU TALKING ABOUT?
I SAW YOU FLY HERE WITHOUT THE AID OF A MACHINE!

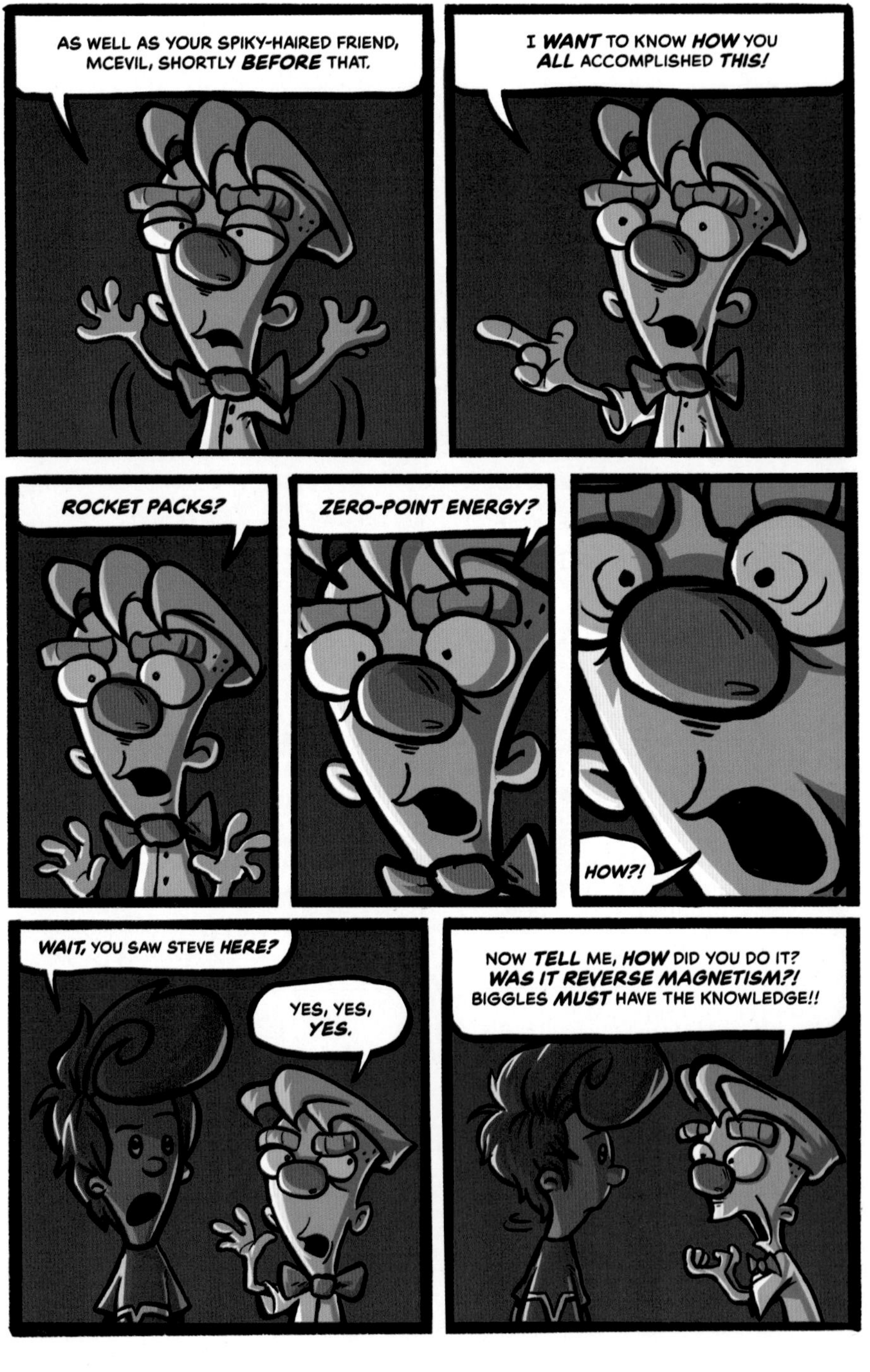
AS WELL AS YOUR SPIKY-HAIRED FRIEND, MCEVIL, SHORTLY BEFORE THAT.
I WANT TO KNOW HOW YOU ALL ACCOMPLISHED THIS!
ROCKET PACKS?
ZERO-POINT ENERGY?
HOW?!
WAIT, YOU SAW STEVE HERE?
YES, YES, YES.
NOW TELL ME, HOW DID YOU DO IT? WAS IT REVERSE MAGNETISM?! BIGGLES MUST HAVE THE KNOWLEDGE!!

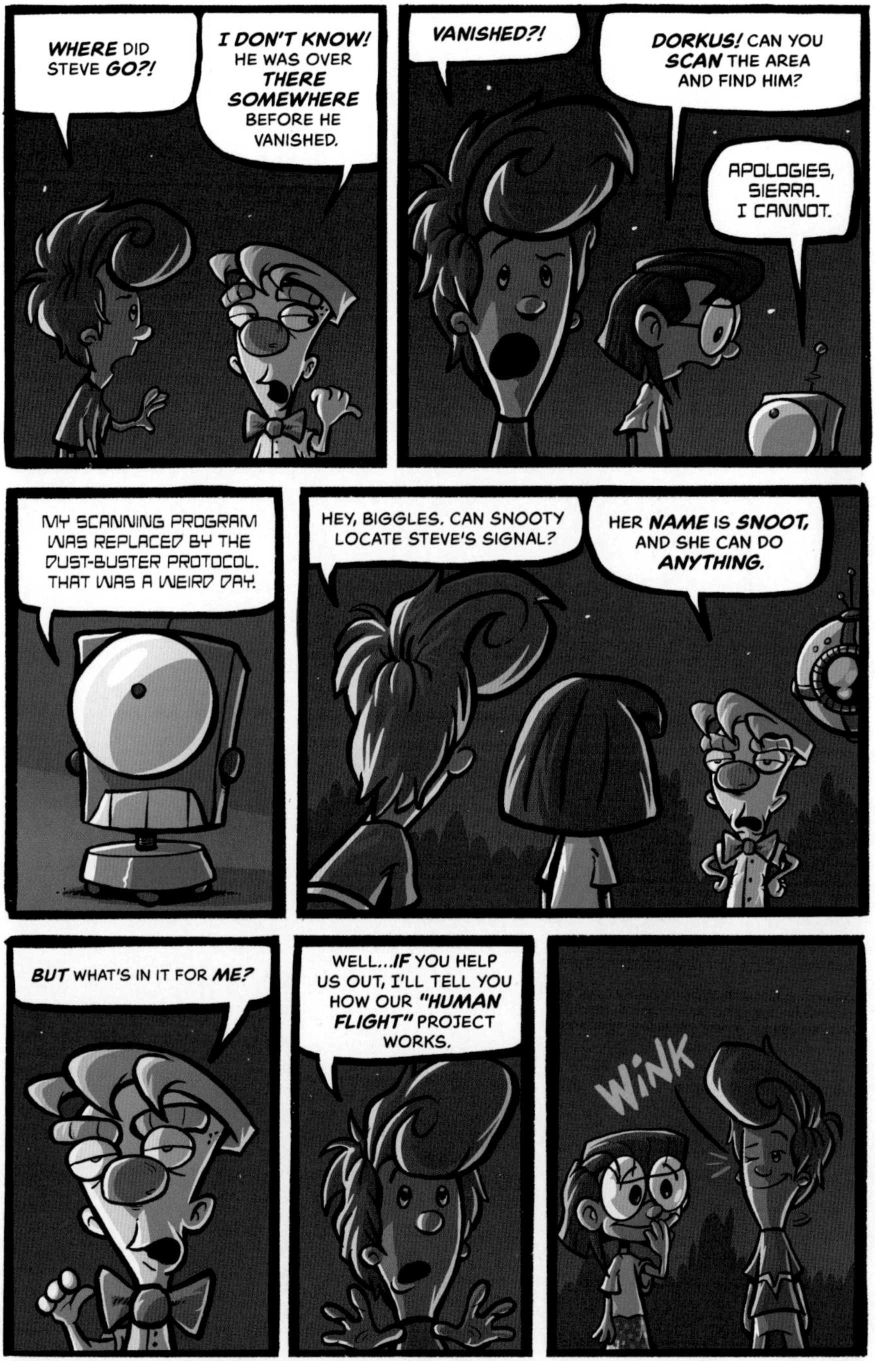
WHERE DID STEVE GO?!
I DON'T KNOW! HE WAS OVER THERE SOMEWHERE BEFORE HE VANISHED.
VANISHED?!
DORKUS! CAN YOU SCAN THE AREA AND FIND HIM?
APOLOGIES, SIERRA. I CANNOT.
MY SCANNING PROGRAM WAS REPLACED BY THE DUST-BUSTER PROTOCOL. THAT WAS A WEIRD DAY.
HEY, BIGGLES. CAN SNOOTY LOCATE STEVE'S SIGNAL?
HER NAME IS SNOOT, AND SHE CAN DO ANYTHING.
BUT WHAT'S IN IT FOR ME?
WELL...IF YOU HELP US OUT, I'LL TELL YOU HOW OUR "HUMAN FLIGHT" PROJECT WORKS.
WINK

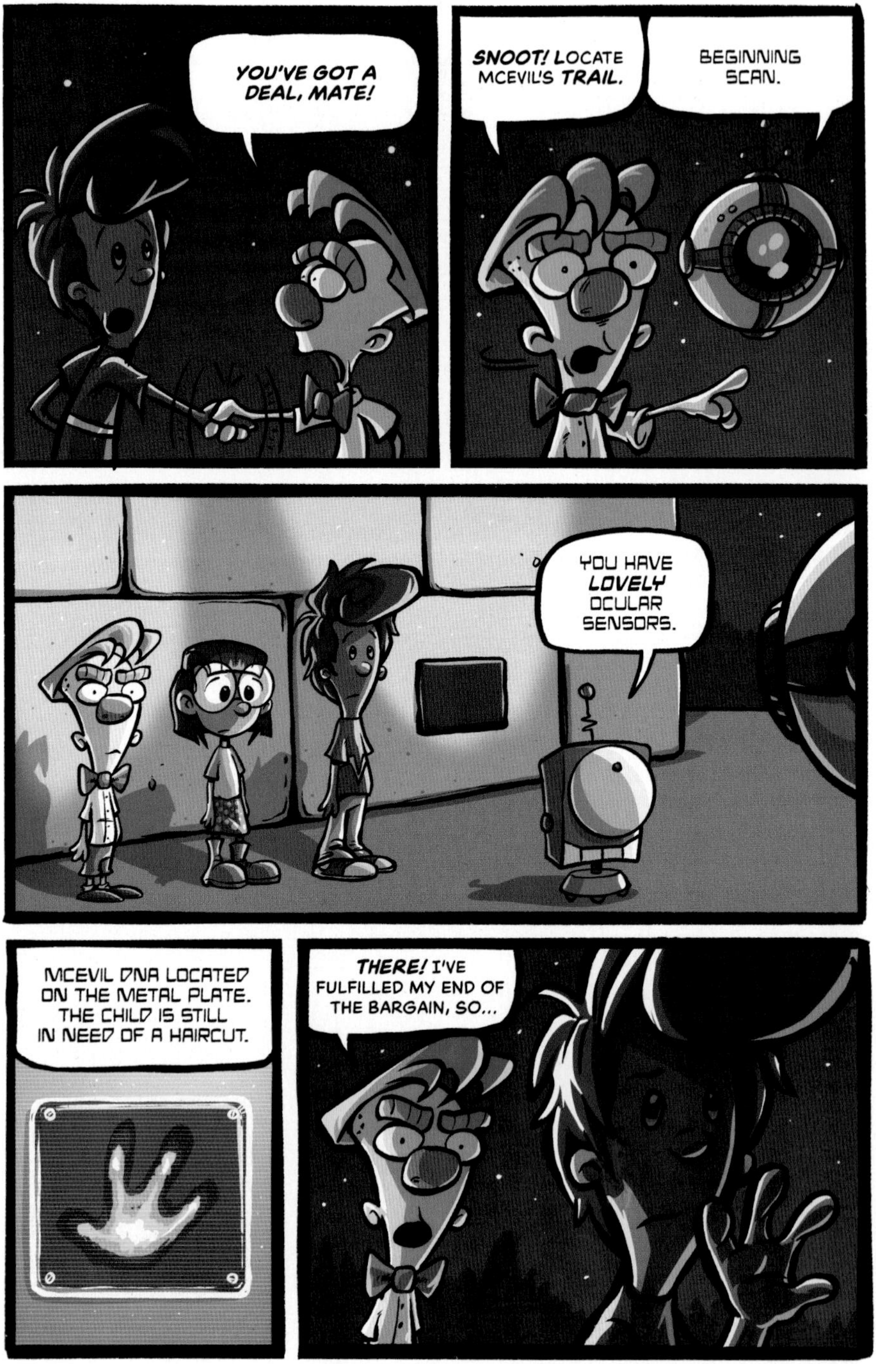
YOU'VE GOT A DEAL, MATE!
SNOOT! LOCATE MCEVIL'S TRAIL.
BEGINNING SCAN.
YOU HAVE LOVELY OCULAR SENSORS.
MCEVIL DNA LOCATED ON THE METAL PLATE. THE CHILD IS STILL IN NEED OF A HAIRCUT.
THERE! I'VE FULFILLED MY END OF THE BARGAIN, SO...

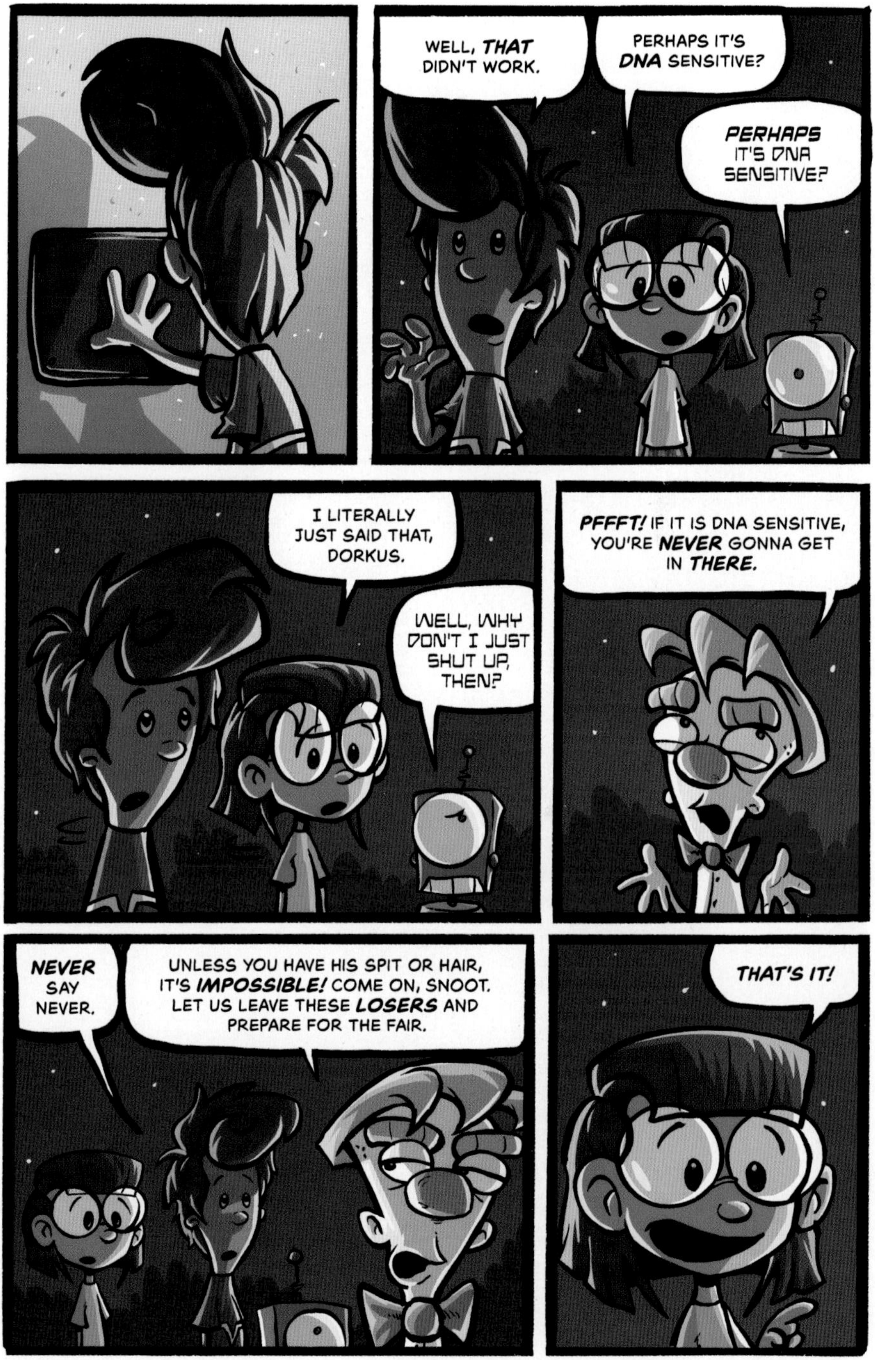
WELL, THAT DIDN'T WORK.
PERHAPS IT'S DNA SENSITIVE?
PERHAPS IT'S DNA SENSITIVE?
I LITERALLY JUST SAID THAT, DORKUS.
WELL, WHY DON'T I JUST SHUT UP, THEN?
PFFFT! IF IT IS DNA SENSITIVE, YOU'RE NEVER GONNA GET IN THERE.
NEVER SAY NEVER.
UNLESS YOU HAVE HIS SPIT OR HAIR, IT'S IMPOSSIBLE! COME ON, SNOOT. LET US LEAVE THESE LOSERS AND PREPARE FOR THE FAIR.
THAT'S IT!

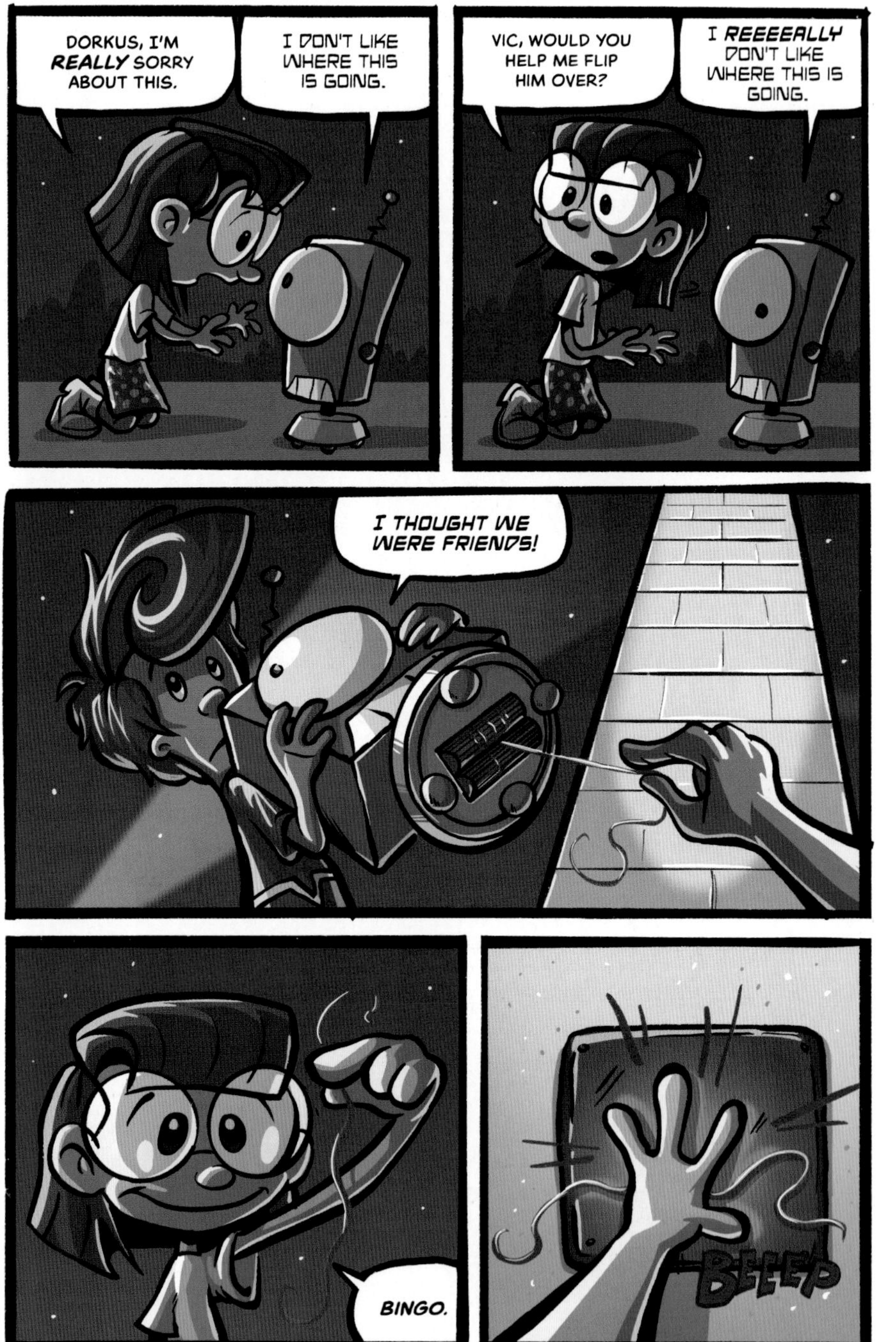
DORKUS, I'M REALLY SORRY ABOUT THIS.
I DON'T LIKE WHERE THIS IS GOING.
VIC, WOULD YOU HELP ME FLIP HIM OVER?
I REEEEALLY DON'T LIKE WHERE THIS IS GOING.
I THOUGHT WE WERE FRIENDS!
BINGO.
BEEEP

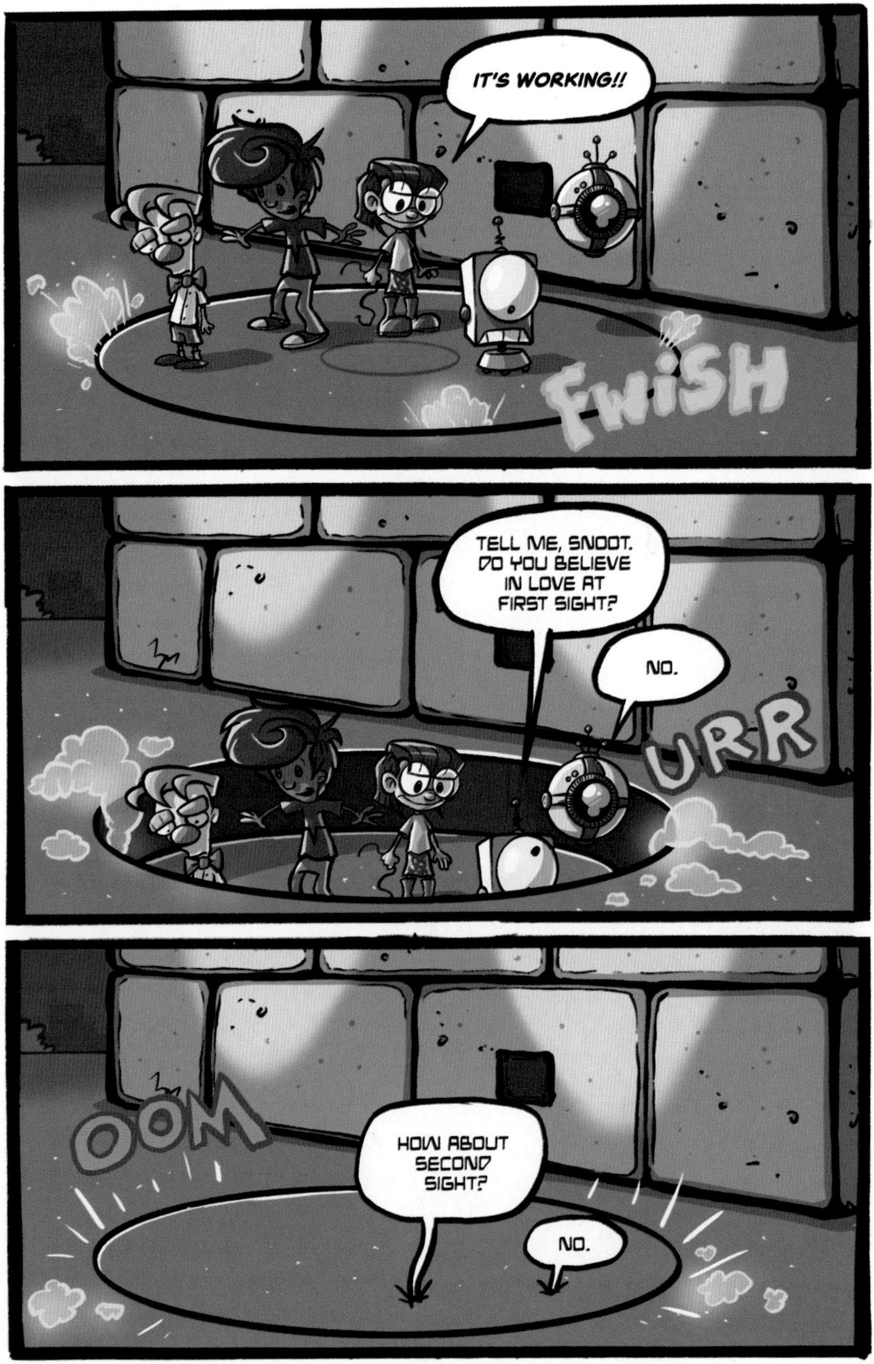
IT'S WORKING!!
FWISH
TELL ME, SNOOT. DO YOU BELIEVE IN LOVE AT FIRST SIGHT?
NO.
URR
OOM
HOW ABOUT SECOND SIGHT?
NO.

CHAPTER 16

Lab of Confusion

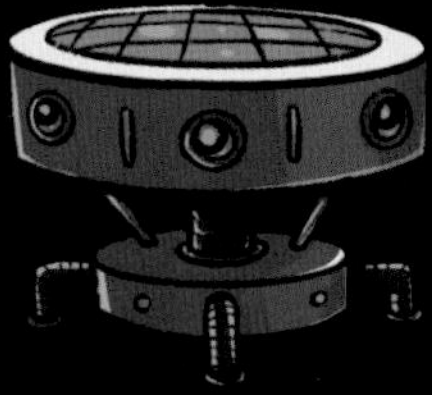

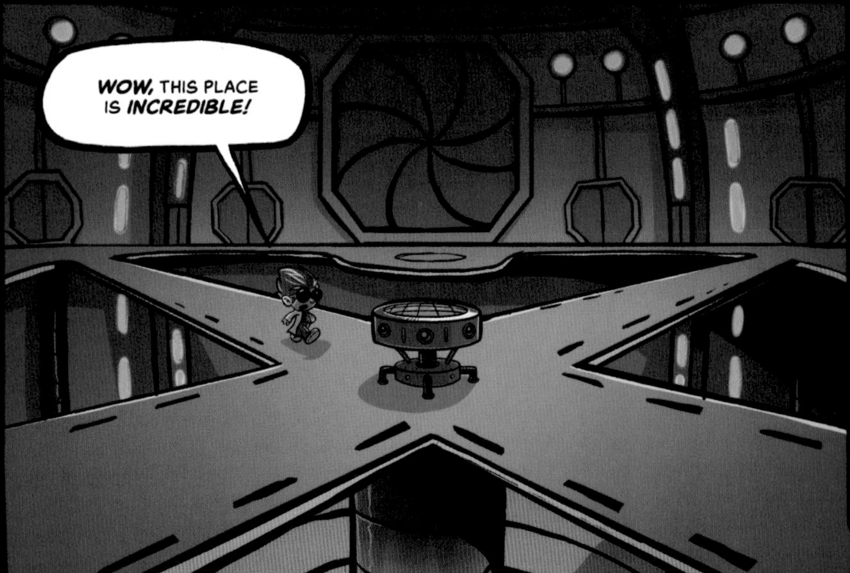
WOW, THIS PLACE IS INCREDIBLE!

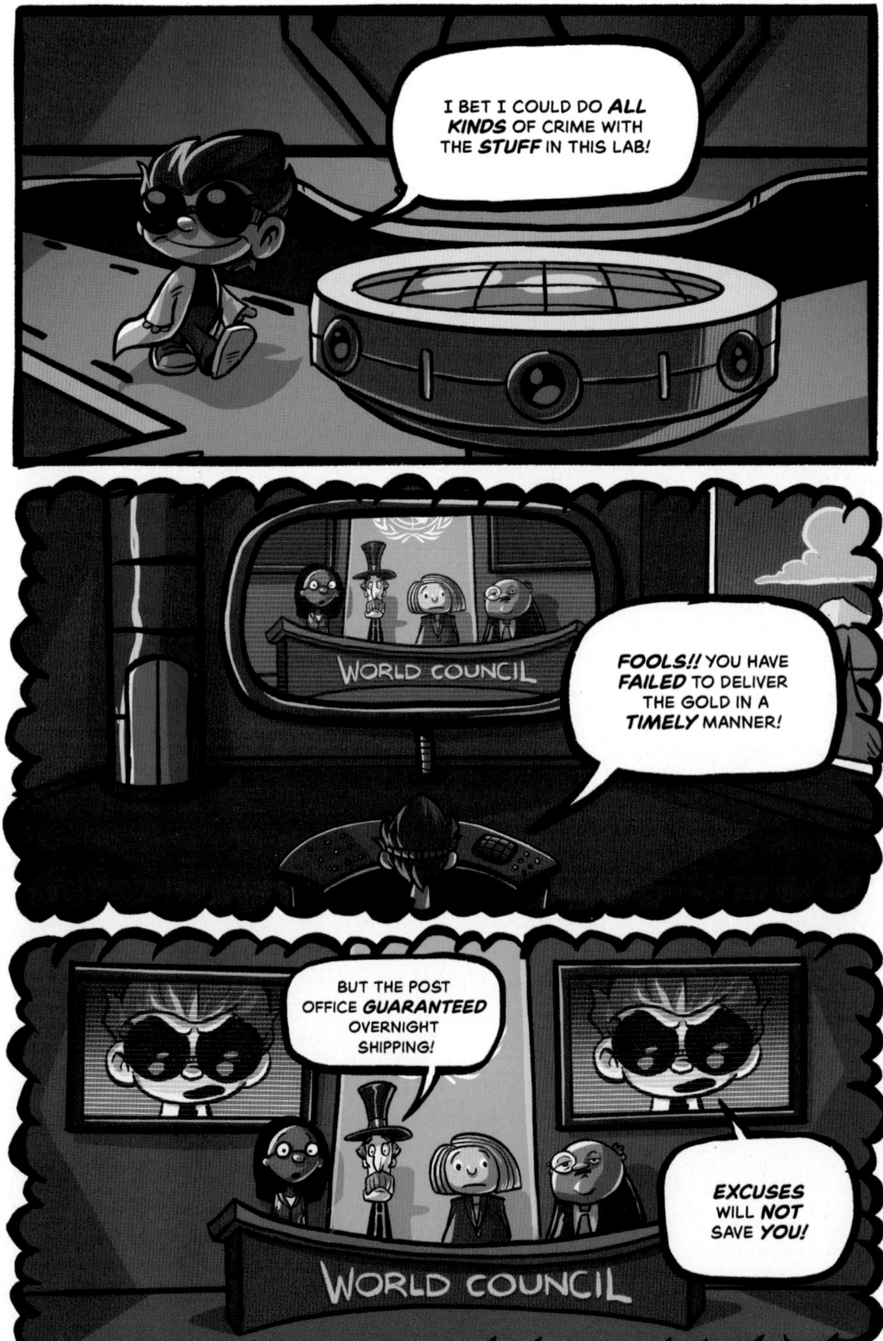
I BET I COULD DO ALL KINDS OF CRIME WITH THE STUFF IN THIS LAB!
WORLD COUNCIL
FOOLS!! YOU HAVE FAILED TO DELIVER THE GOLD IN A TIMELY MANNER!
BUT THE POST OFFICE GUARANTEED OVERNIGHT SHIPPING!
EXCUSES WILL NOT SAVE YOU!
WORLD COUNCIL

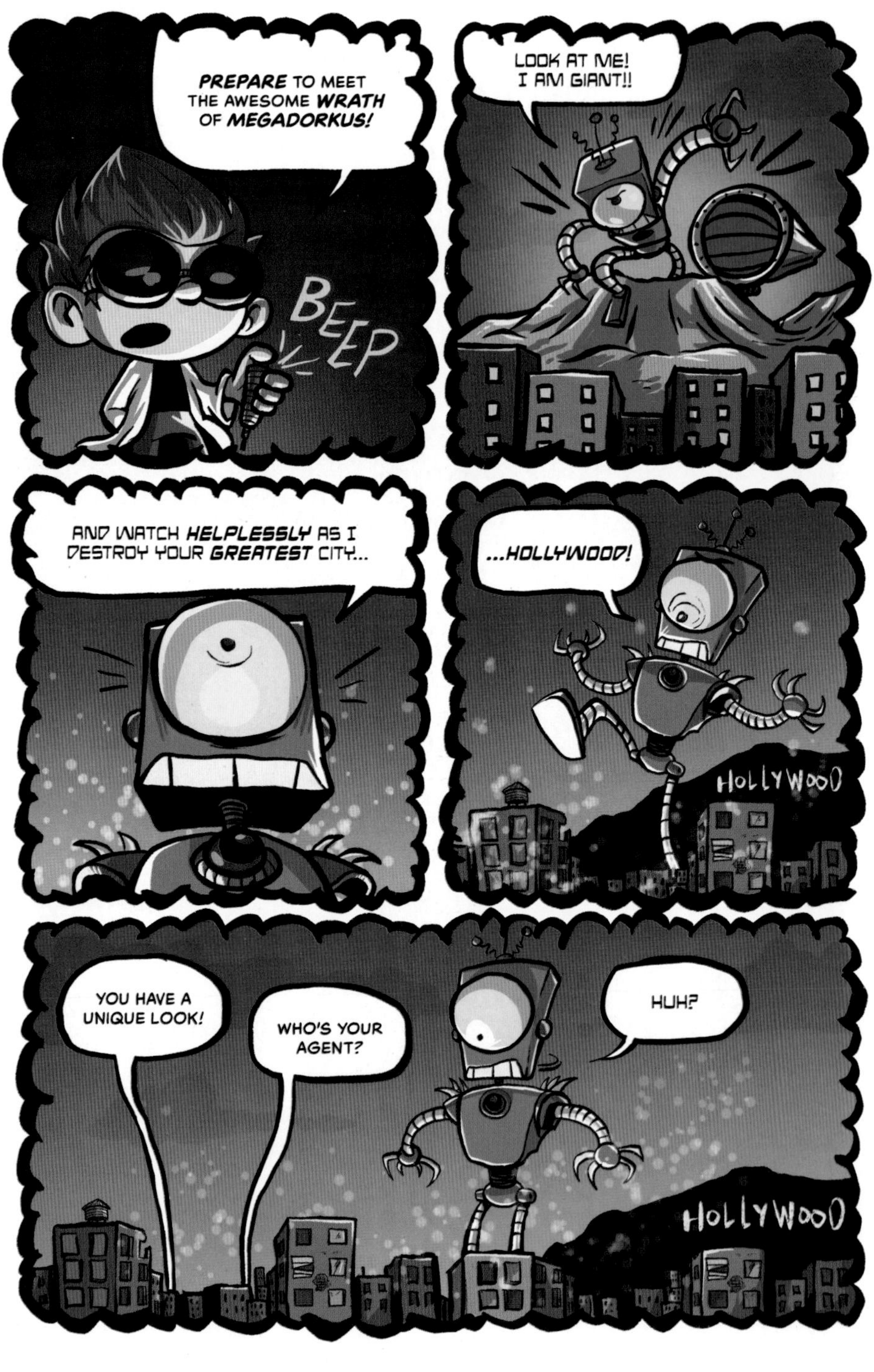
PREPARE TO MEET THE AWESOME WRATH OF MEGADORKUS!
BEEP
LOOK AT ME! I AM GIANT!!
AND WATCH HELPLESSLY AS I DESTROY YOUR GREATEST CITY...
...HOLLYWOOD!
HOLLYWOOD
YOU HAVE A UNIQUE LOOK!
WHO'S YOUR AGENT?
HUH?
HOLLYWOOD

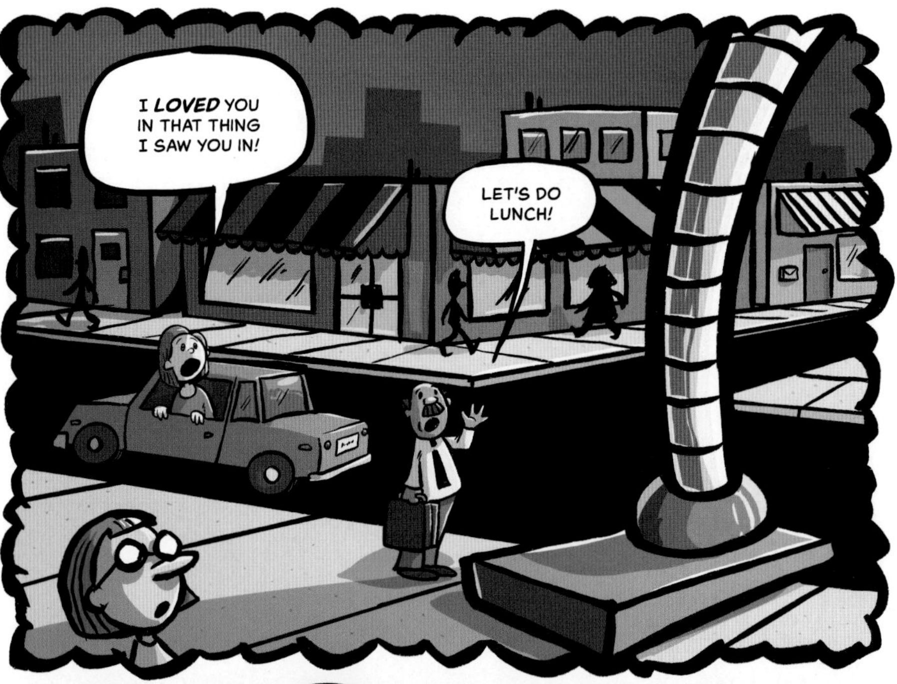
I LOVED YOU IN THAT THING I SAW YOU IN!
LET'S DO LUNCH!

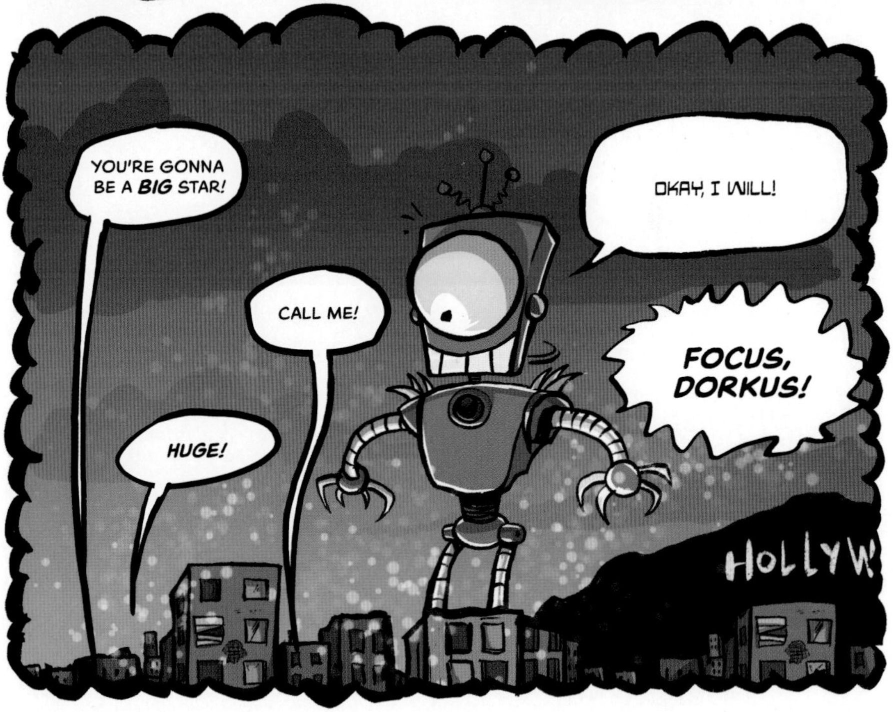
YOU'RE GONNA BE A BIG STAR!
HUGE!
CALL ME!
OKAY, I WILL!
FOCUS, DORKUS!
HOLLYW

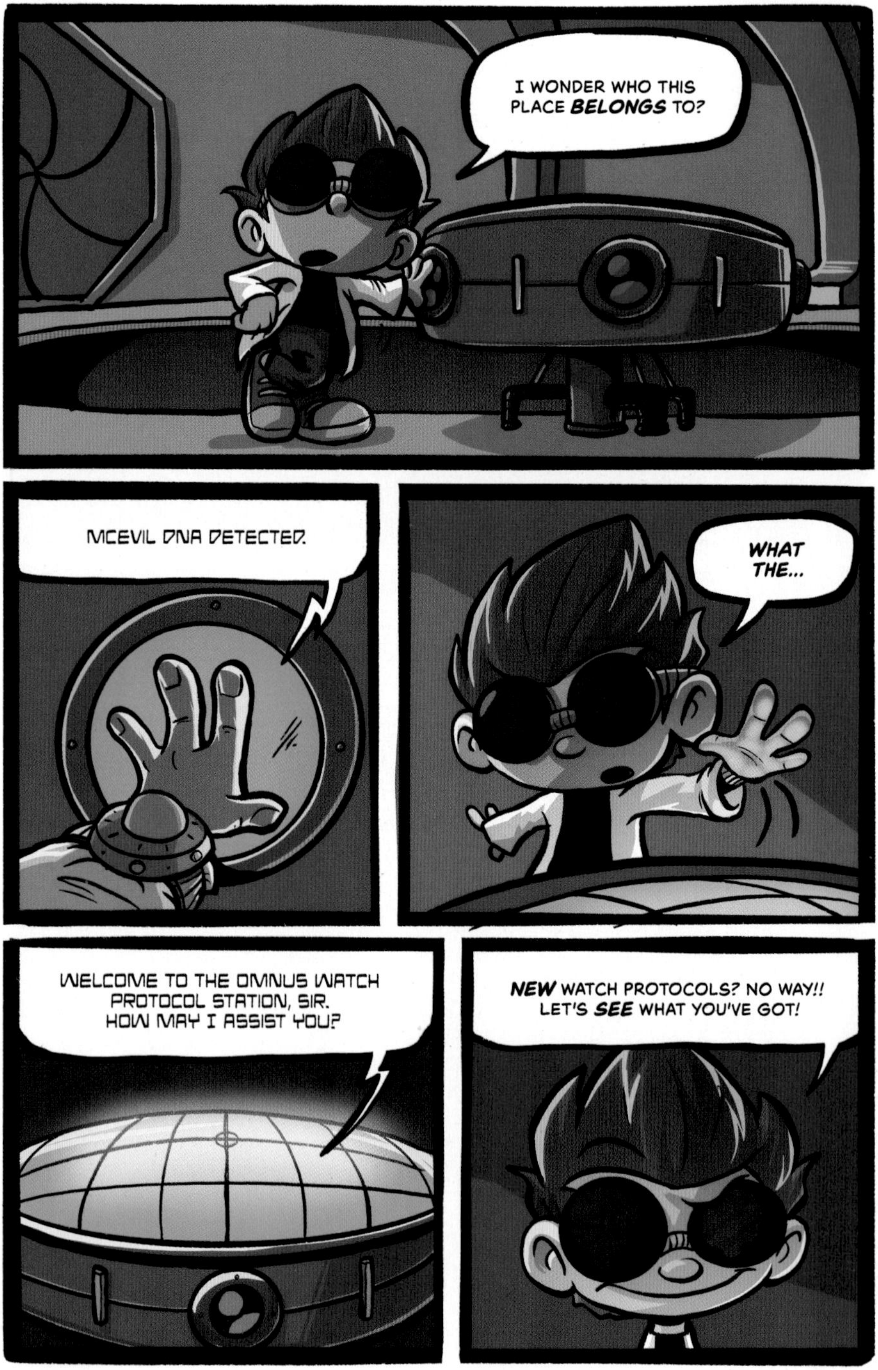
I WONDER WHO THIS PLACE BELONGS TO?
MCEVIL DNA DETECTED.
WHAT THE...
WELCOME TO THE OMNUS WATCH PROTOCOL STATION, SIR. HOW MAY I ASSIST YOU?
NEW WATCH PROTOCOLS? NO WAY!! LET'S SEE WHAT YOU'VE GOT!

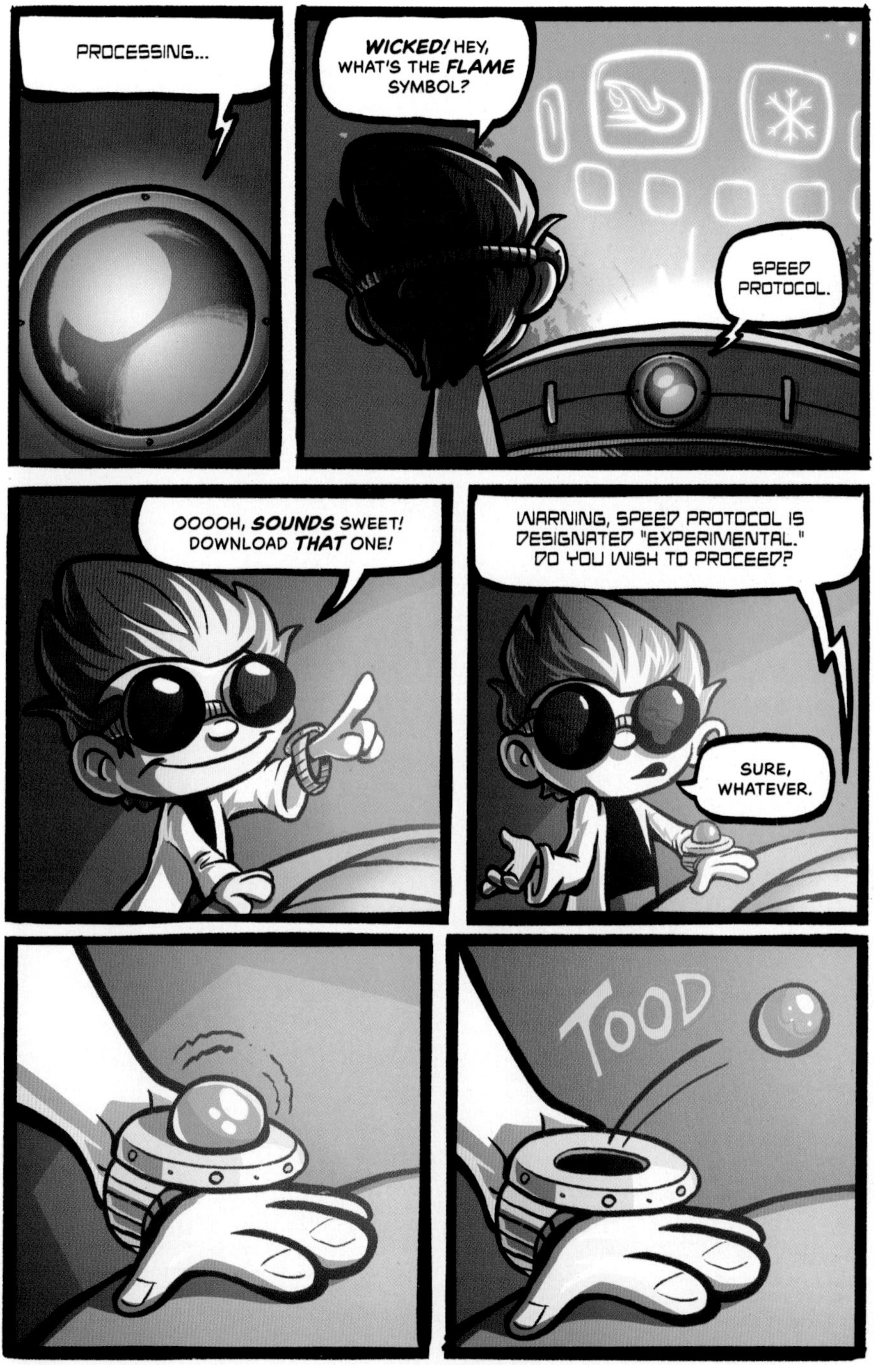
PROCESSING...
WICKED! HEY, WHAT'S THE FLAME SYMBOL?
SPEED PROTOCOL.
OOOOH, SOUNDS SWEET! DOWNLOAD THAT ONE!
WARNING, SPEED PROTOCOL IS DESIGNATED "EXPERIMENTAL." DO YOU WISH TO PROCEED?
SURE, WHATEVER.
TOOD

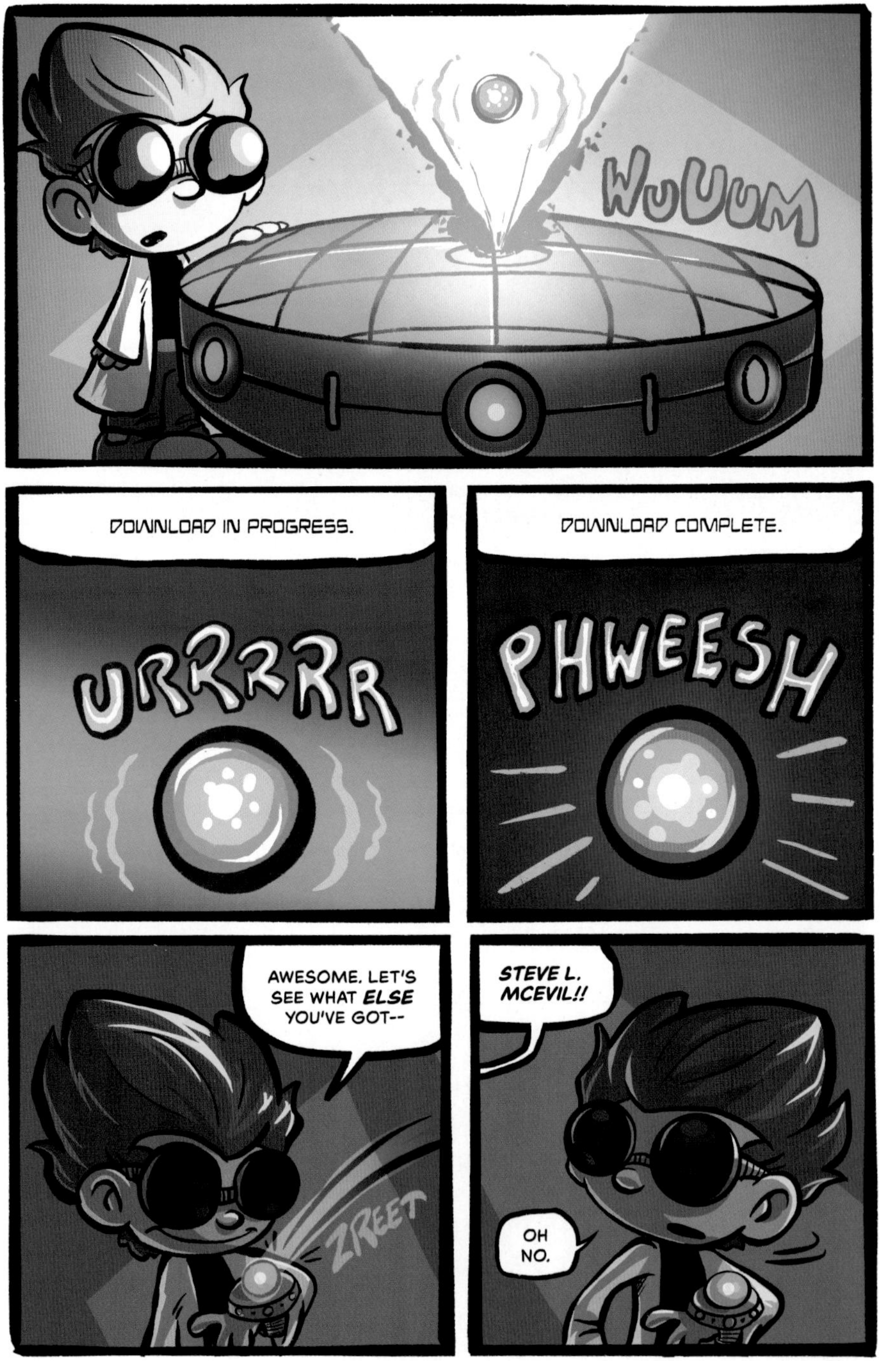
WUUUM
DOWNLOAD IN PROGRESS.
URRRRR
DOWNLOAD COMPLETE.
PHWEESH
AWESOME. LET'S SEE WHAT *ELSE* YOU'VE GOT--
ZREET
STEVE L. MCEVIL!!
OH NO.

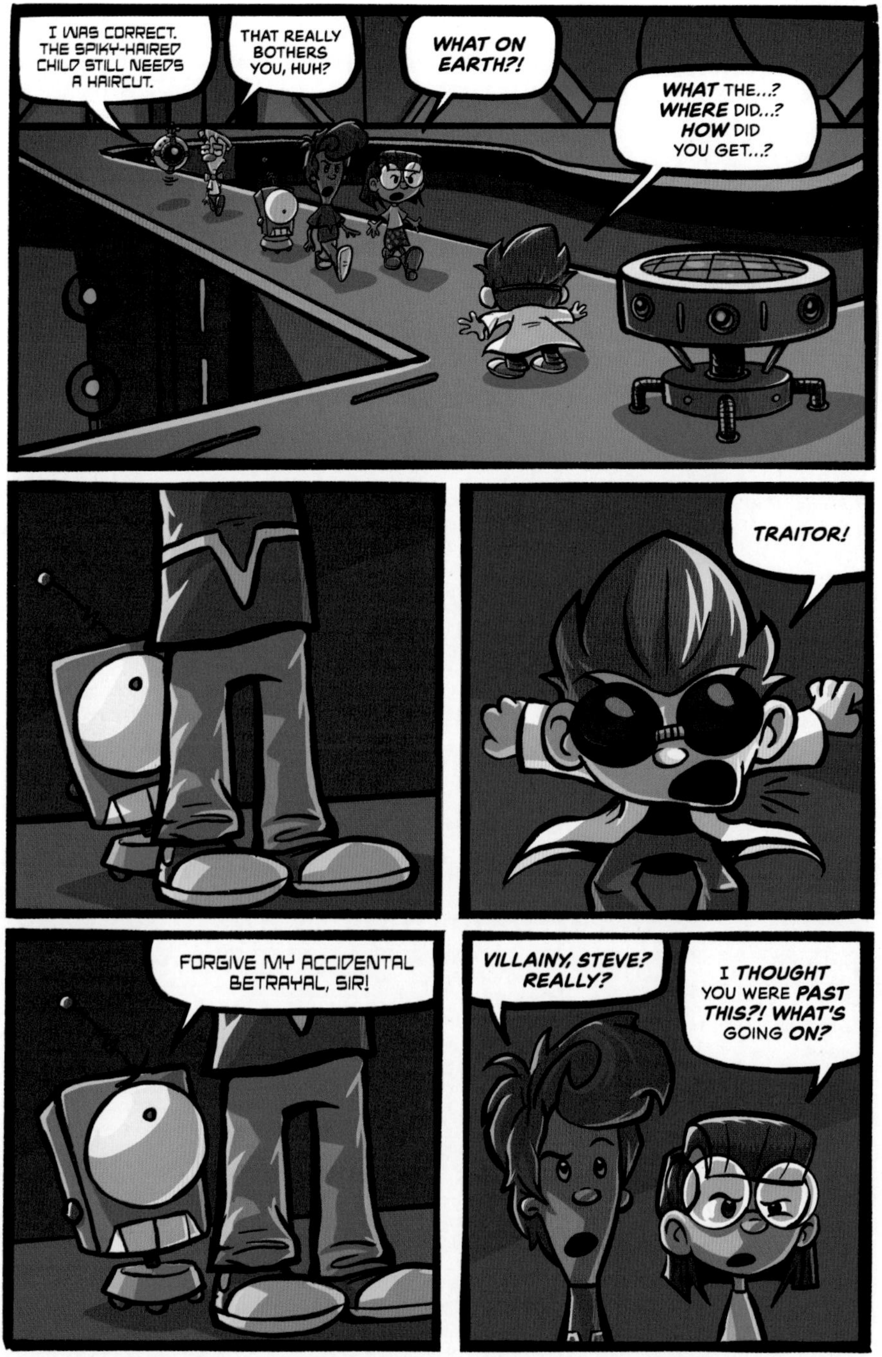
I WAS CORRECT. THE SPIKY-HAIRED CHILD STILL NEEDS A HAIRCUT.
THAT REALLY BOTHERS YOU, HUH?
WHAT ON EARTH?!
WHAT THE...? WHERE DID...? HOW DID YOU GET...?
TRAITOR!
FORGIVE MY ACCIDENTAL BETRAYAL, SIR!
VILLAINY, STEVE? REALLY?
I THOUGHT YOU WERE PAST THIS?! WHAT'S GOING ON?

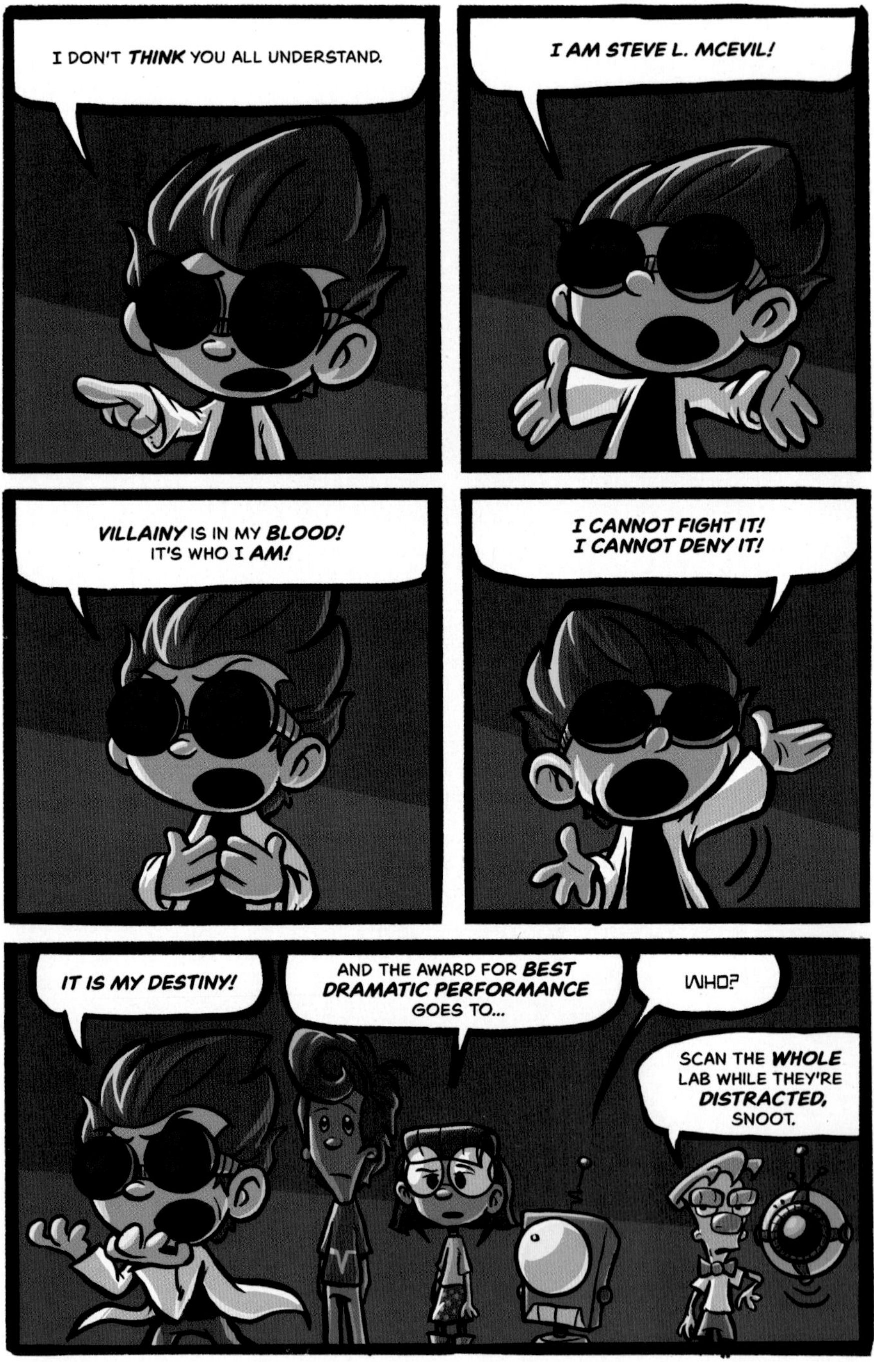
I DON'T *THINK* YOU ALL UNDERSTAND.
I AM STEVE L. MCEVIL!
VILLAINY IS IN MY *BLOOD!* IT'S WHO I *AM!*
I CANNOT FIGHT IT! I CANNOT DENY IT!
IT IS MY DESTINY!
AND THE AWARD FOR *BEST DRAMATIC PERFORMANCE* GOES TO...
WHO?
SCAN THE *WHOLE* LAB WHILE THEY'RE *DISTRACTED,* SNOOT.

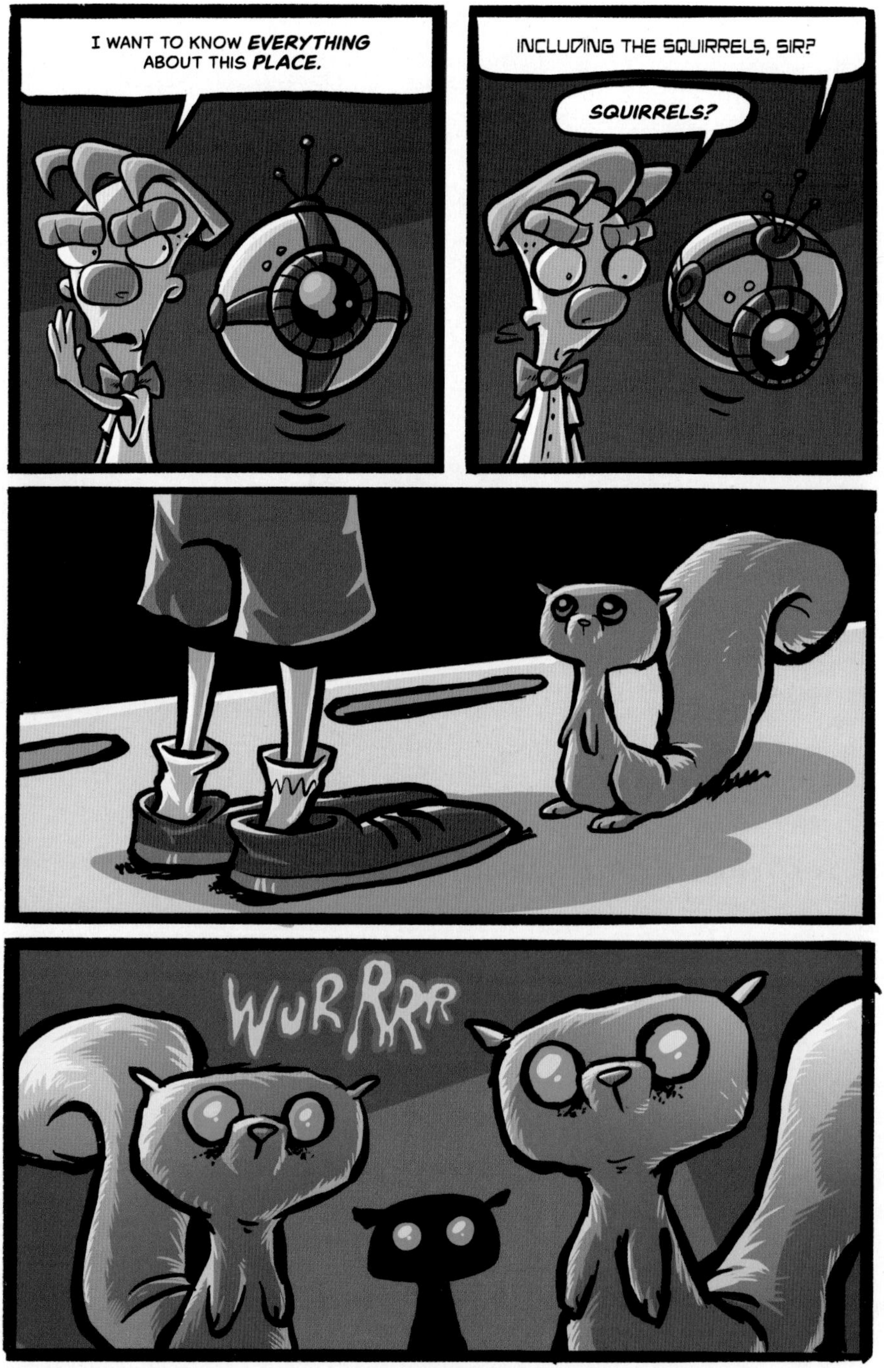
I WANT TO KNOW EVERYTHING ABOUT THIS PLACE.
INCLUDING THE SQUIRRELS, SIR?
SQUIRRELS?
WURRRR

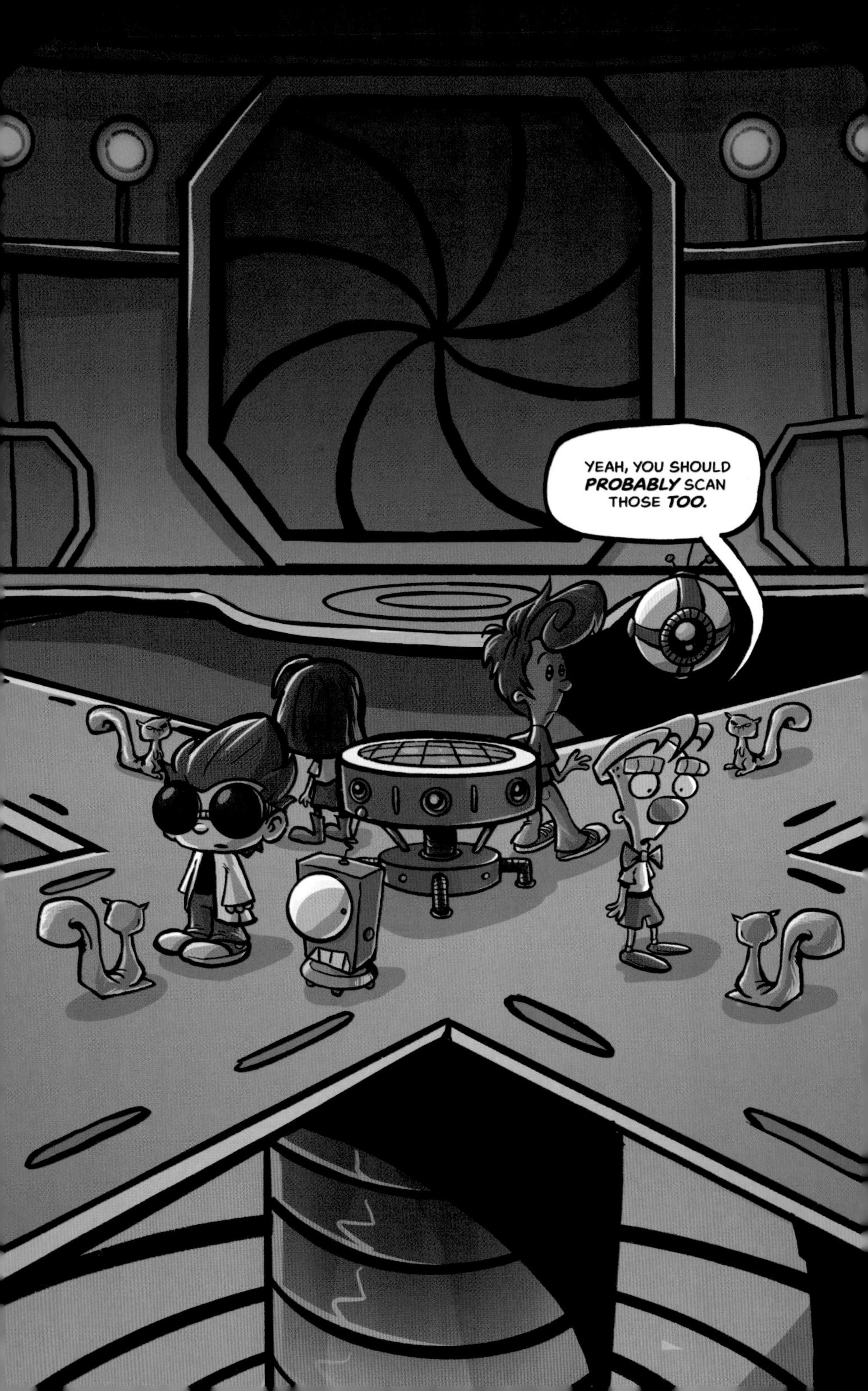
YEAH, YOU SHOULD ***PROBABLY*** SCAN THOSE ***TOO.***

CHAPTER 17

Smooth Criminal

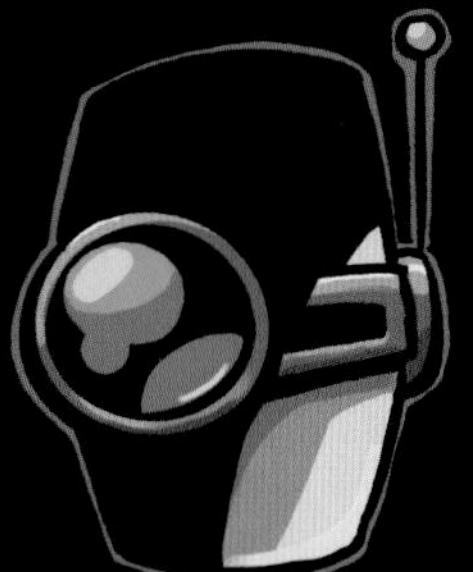

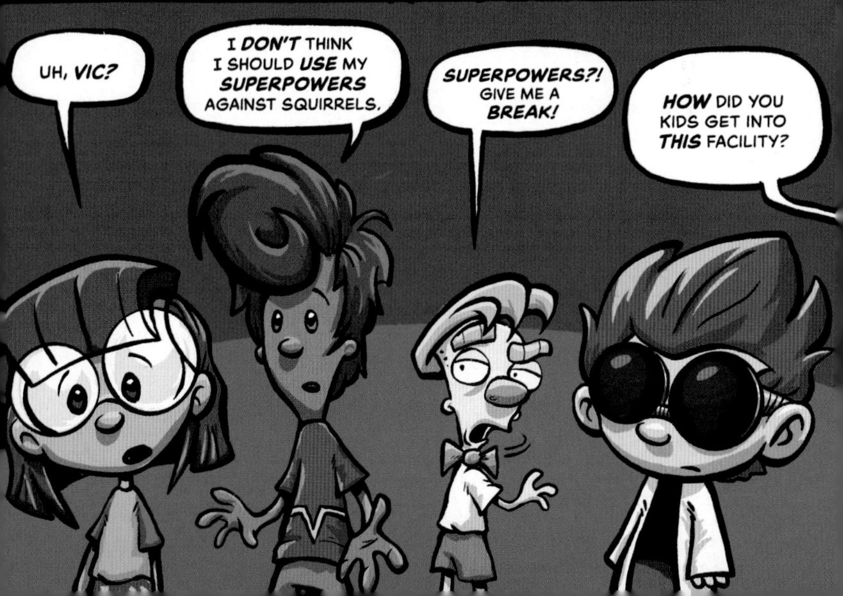
UH, VIC?
I DON'T THINK I SHOULD USE MY SUPERPOWERS AGAINST SQUIRRELS.
SUPERPOWERS?! GIVE ME A BREAK!
HOW DID YOU KIDS GET INTO THIS FACILITY?

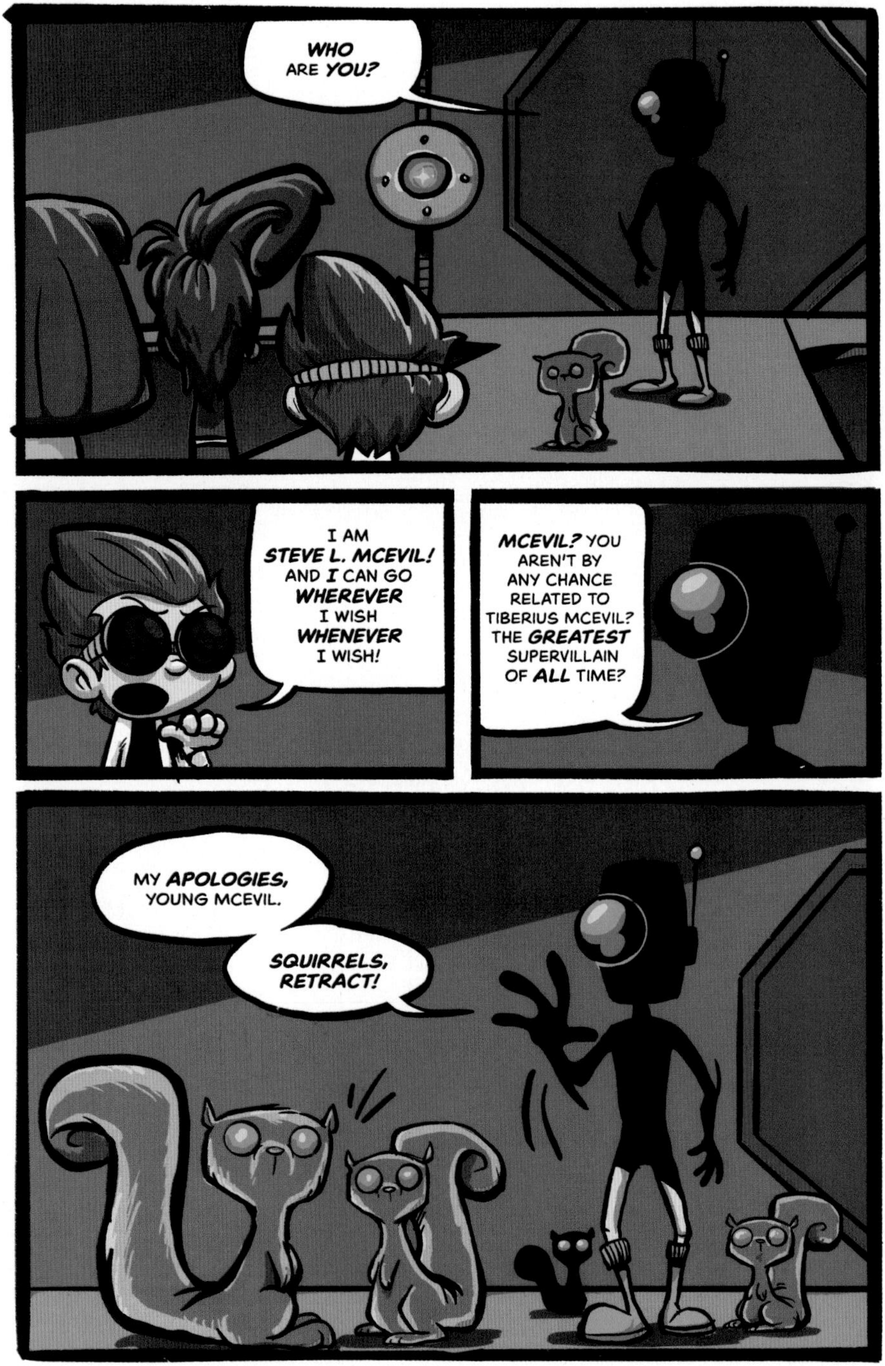
WHO ARE YOU?
I AM STEVE L. MCEVIL! AND I CAN GO WHEREVER I WISH WHENEVER I WISH!
MCEVIL? YOU AREN'T BY ANY CHANCE RELATED TO TIBERIUS MCEVIL? THE GREATEST SUPERVILLAIN OF ALL TIME?
MY APOLOGIES, YOUNG MCEVIL.
SQUIRRELS, RETRACT!

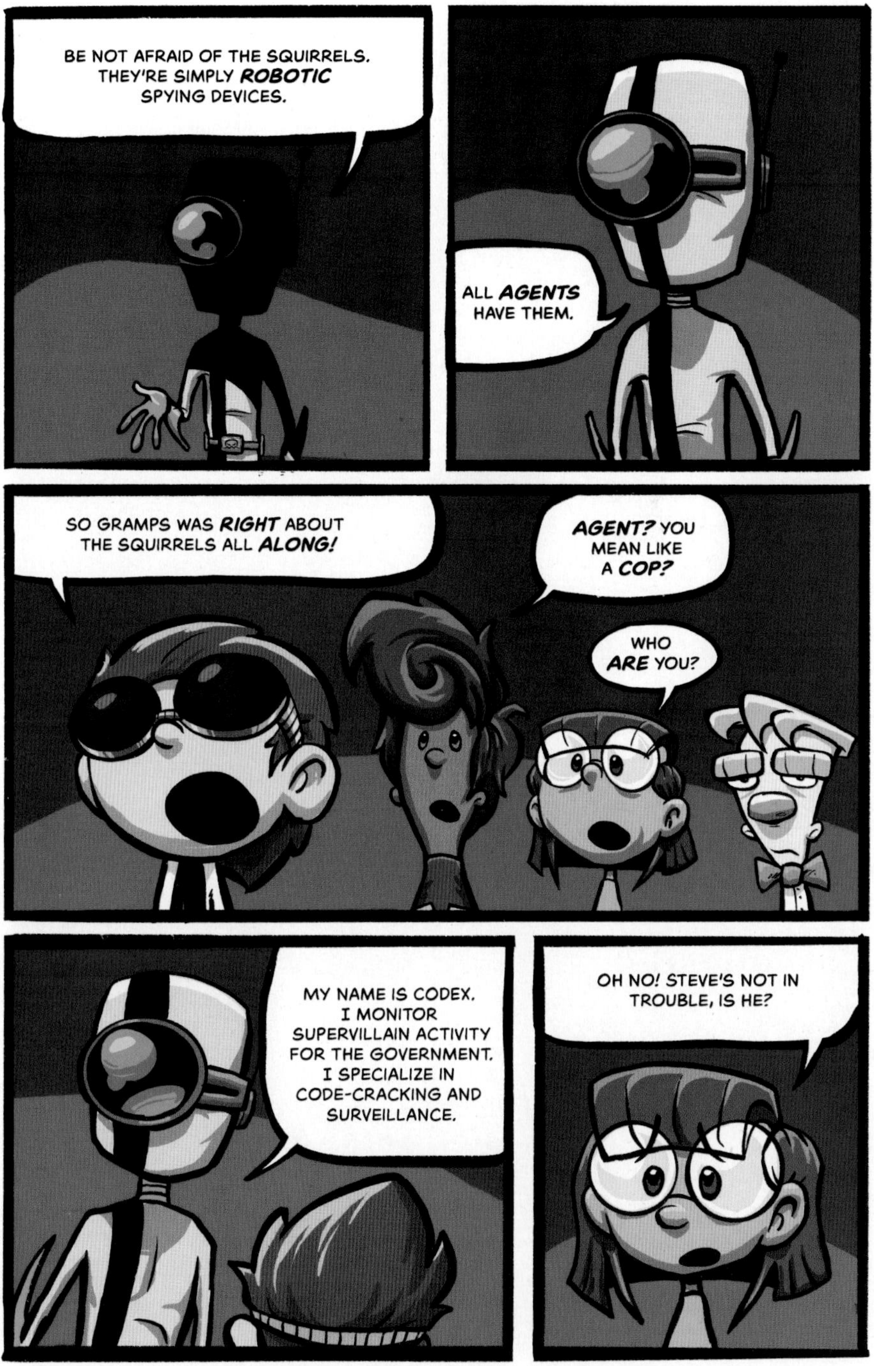
BE NOT AFRAID OF THE SQUIRRELS. THEY'RE SIMPLY ***ROBOTIC*** SPYING DEVICES.
ALL ***AGENTS*** HAVE THEM.
SO GRAMPS WAS ***RIGHT*** ABOUT THE SQUIRRELS ALL ***ALONG!***
AGENT? YOU MEAN LIKE A ***COP?***
WHO ***ARE*** YOU?
MY NAME IS CODEX. I MONITOR SUPERVILLAIN ACTIVITY FOR THE GOVERNMENT. I SPECIALIZE IN CODE-CRACKING AND SURVEILLANCE.
OH NO! STEVE'S NOT IN TROUBLE, IS HE?

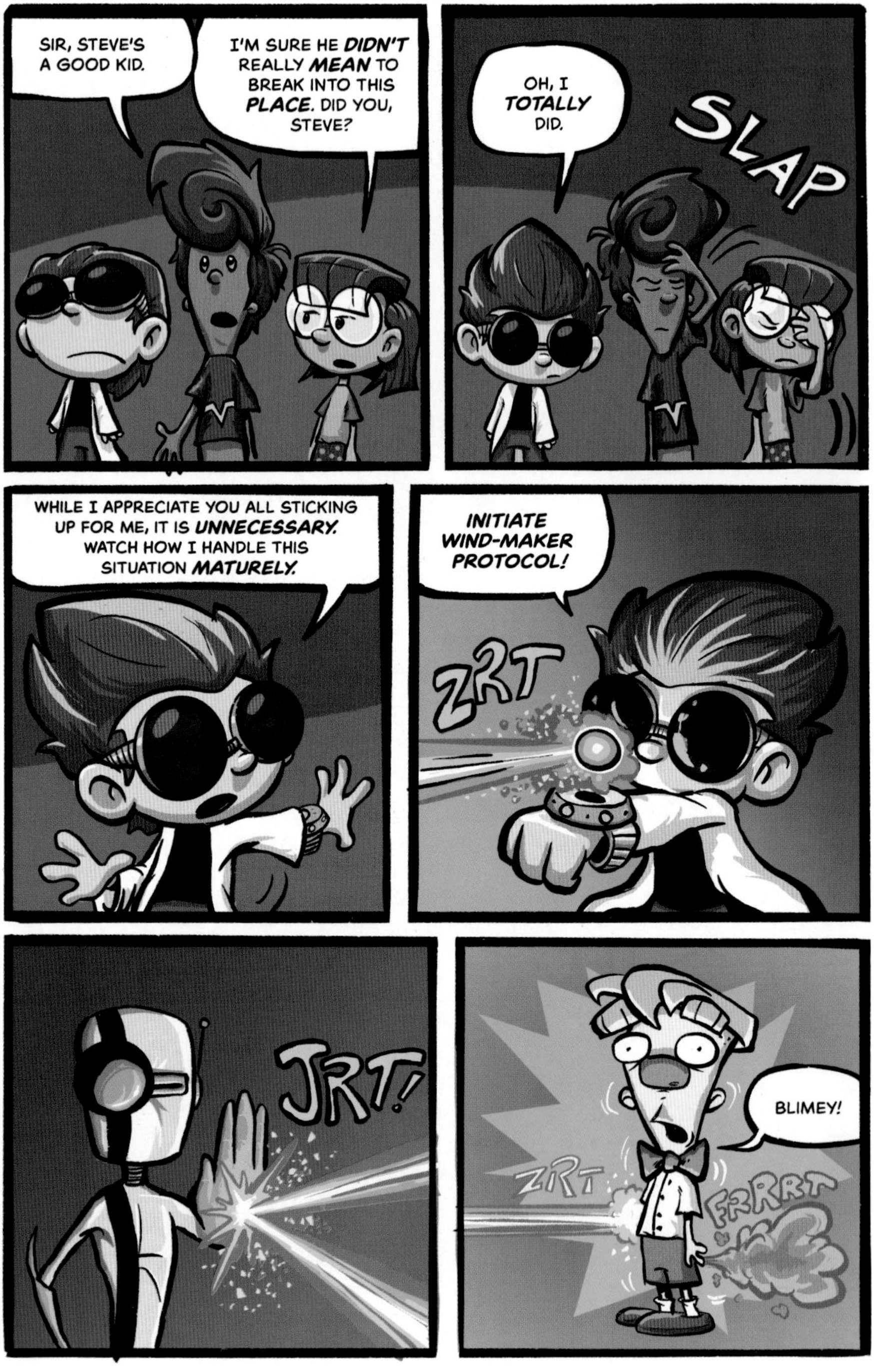
SIR, STEVE'S A GOOD KID.
I'M SURE HE DIDN'T REALLY MEAN TO BREAK INTO THIS PLACE. DID YOU, STEVE?
OH, I TOTALLY DID.
SLAP
WHILE I APPRECIATE YOU ALL STICKING UP FOR ME, IT IS UNNECESSARY. WATCH HOW I HANDLE THIS SITUATION MATURELY.
INITIATE WIND-MAKER PROTOCOL!
ZRT
JRT!
BLIMEY!
ZIRT
FRRRT

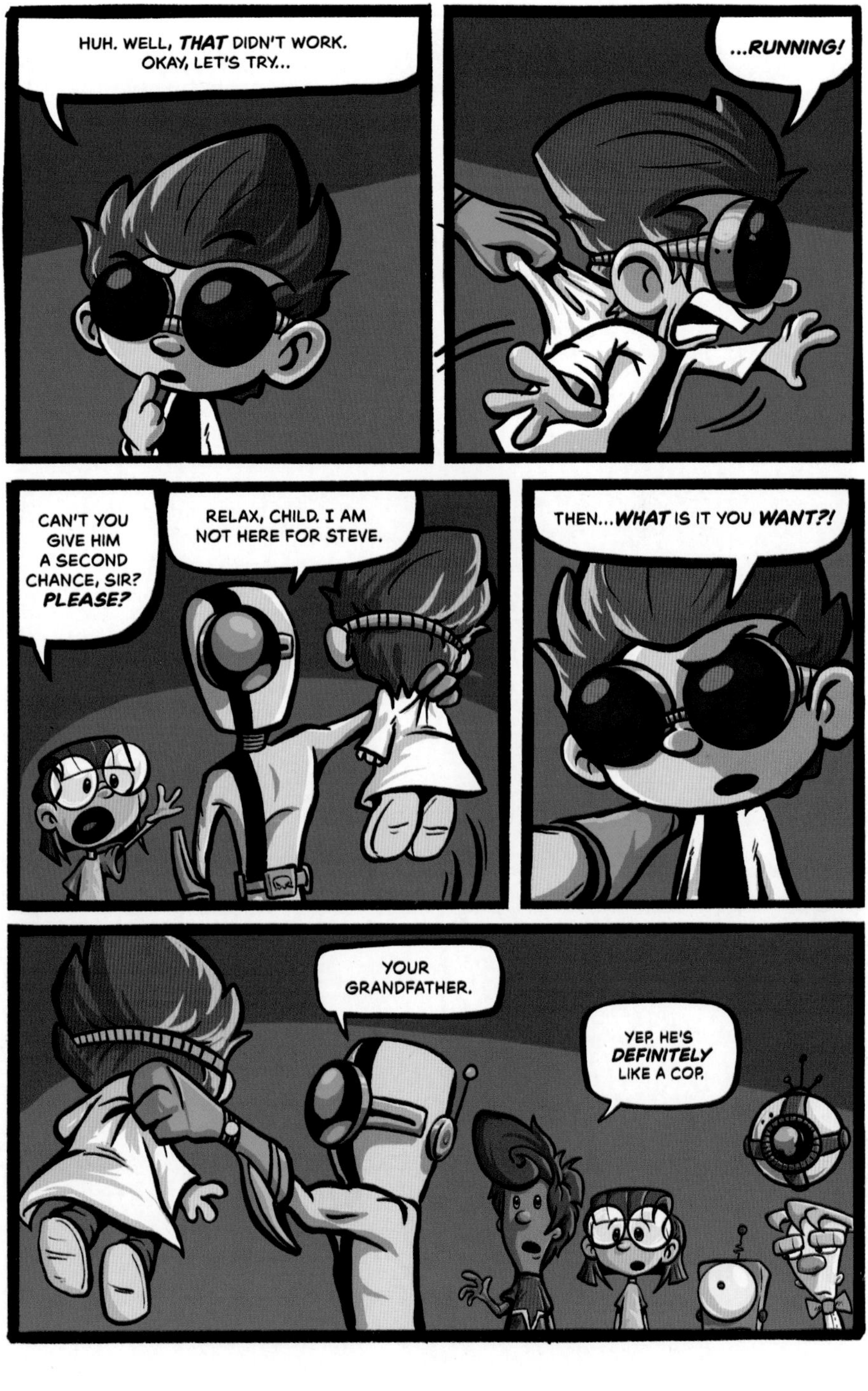
HUH. WELL, THAT DIDN'T WORK. OKAY, LET'S TRY...
...RUNNING!
CAN'T YOU GIVE HIM A SECOND CHANCE, SIR? PLEASE?
RELAX, CHILD. I AM NOT HERE FOR STEVE.
THEN...WHAT IS IT YOU WANT?!
YOUR GRANDFATHER.
YEP. HE'S DEFINITELY LIKE A COP.

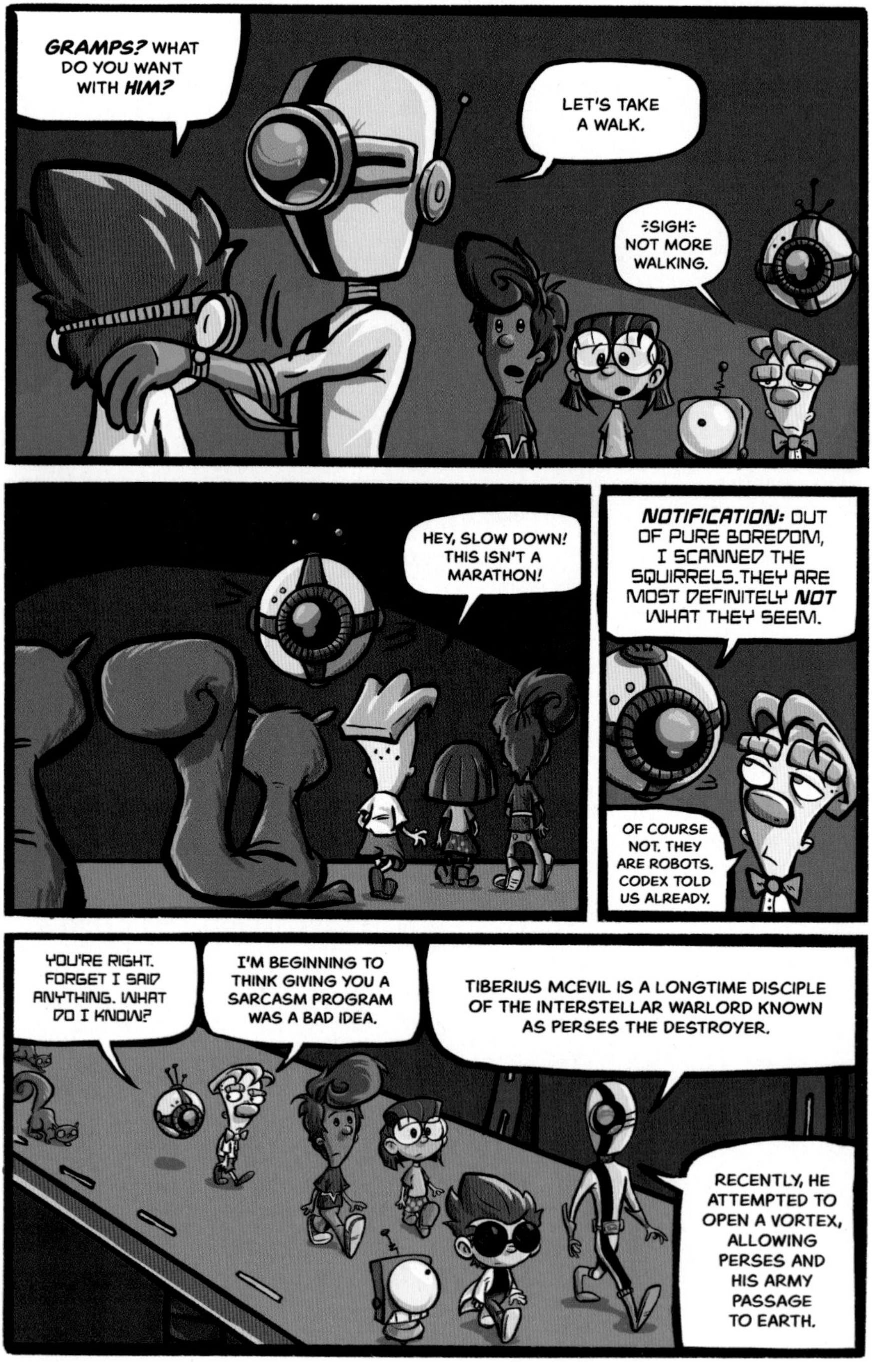
GRAMPS? WHAT DO YOU WANT WITH HIM?
LET'S TAKE A WALK.
SIGH NOT MORE WALKING.
HEY, SLOW DOWN! THIS ISN'T A MARATHON!
NOTIFICATION: OUT OF PURE BOREDOM, I SCANNED THE SQUIRRELS. THEY ARE MOST DEFINITELY NOT WHAT THEY SEEM.
OF COURSE NOT. THEY ARE ROBOTS. CODEX TOLD US ALREADY.
YOU'RE RIGHT. FORGET I SAID ANYTHING. WHAT DO I KNOW?
I'M BEGINNING TO THINK GIVING YOU A SARCASM PROGRAM WAS A BAD IDEA.
TIBERIUS MCEVIL IS A LONGTIME DISCIPLE OF THE INTERSTELLAR WARLORD KNOWN AS PERSES THE DESTROYER.
RECENTLY, HE ATTEMPTED TO OPEN A VORTEX, ALLOWING PERSES AND HIS ARMY PASSAGE TO EARTH.

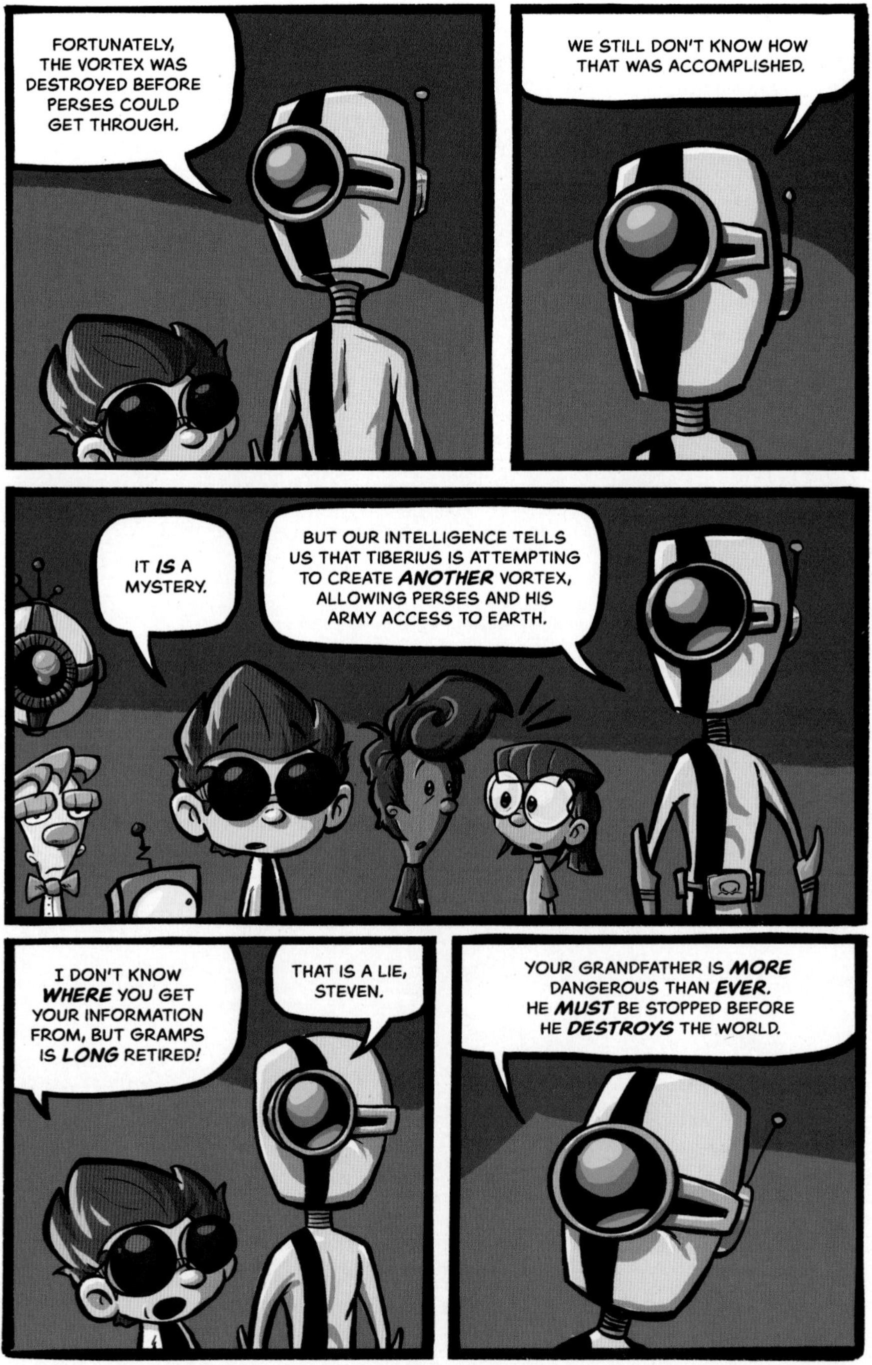
FORTUNATELY, THE VORTEX WAS DESTROYED BEFORE PERSES COULD GET THROUGH.
WE STILL DON'T KNOW HOW THAT WAS ACCOMPLISHED.
IT *IS* A MYSTERY.
BUT OUR INTELLIGENCE TELLS US THAT TIBERIUS IS ATTEMPTING TO CREATE *ANOTHER* VORTEX, ALLOWING PERSES AND HIS ARMY ACCESS TO EARTH.
I DON'T KNOW *WHERE* YOU GET YOUR INFORMATION FROM, BUT GRAMPS IS *LONG* RETIRED!
THAT IS A LIE, STEVEN.
YOUR GRANDFATHER IS *MORE* DANGEROUS THAN *EVER*. HE *MUST* BE STOPPED BEFORE HE *DESTROYS* THE WORLD.

CHAPTER 18
True Lies

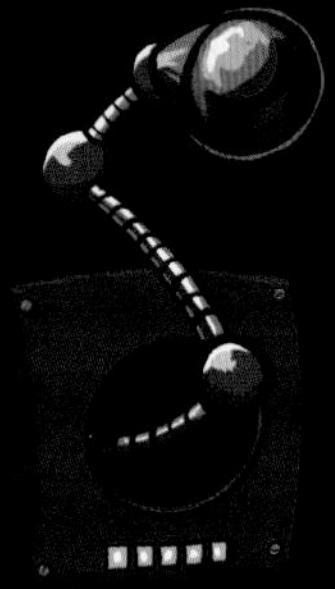

HAVEN'T YOU NOTICED ANYTHING SUSPICIOUS ABOUT YOUR GRANDFATHER LATELY? ACTING NERVOUS? ALWAYS PARANOID SOMEONE IS FOLLOWING HIM?

HE'S ALWAYS LIKE THAT!

BESIDES, HE WAS *RIGHT* ABOUT THE *SQUIRRELS!*

HE'S NEVER MENTIONED ANYTHING ABOUT AN "OPERATION PERSES" TO YOU? EVEN IN PASSING?

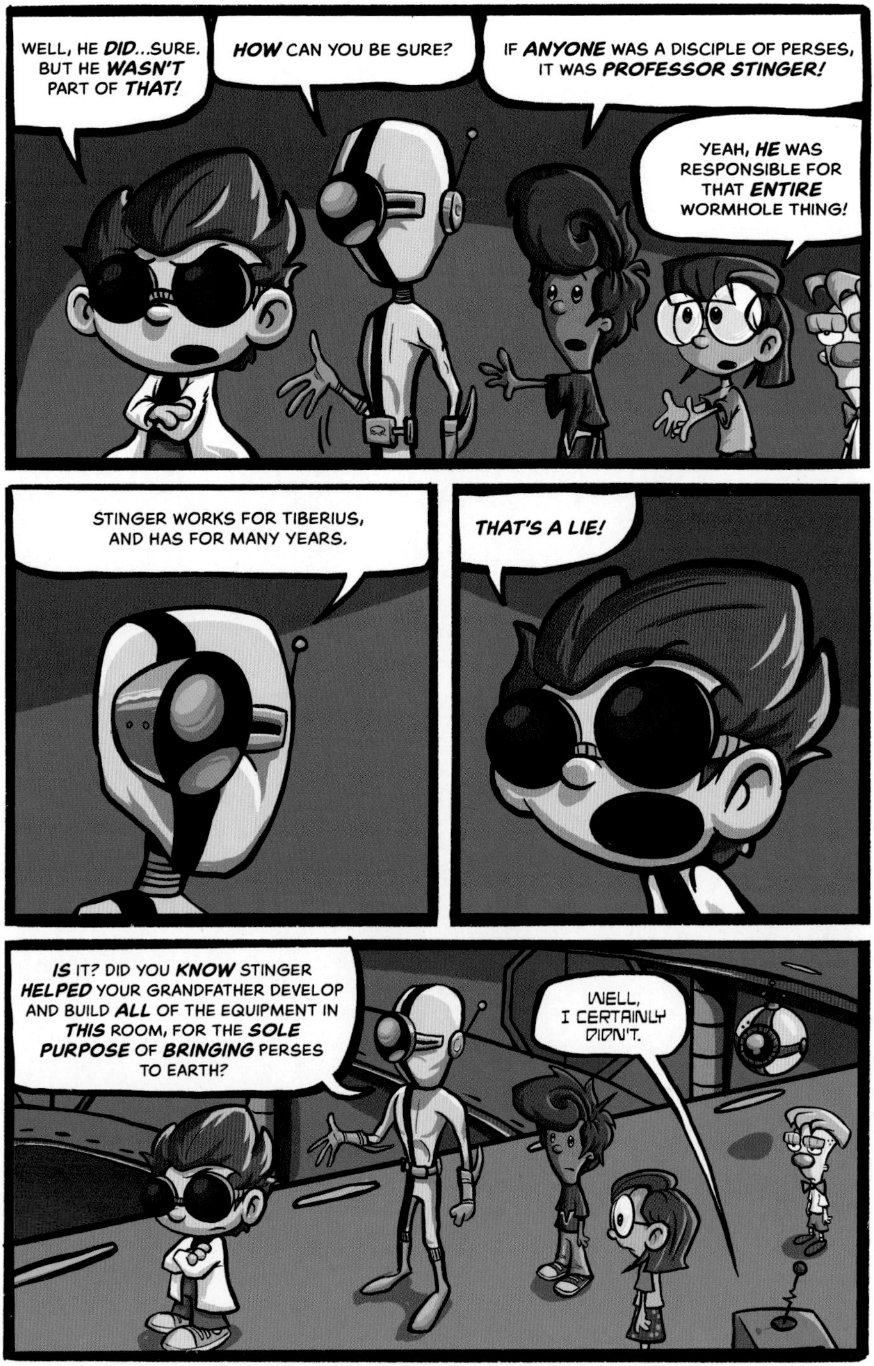
WELL, HE DID...SURE. BUT HE WASN'T PART OF THAT!
HOW CAN YOU BE SURE?
IF ANYONE WAS A DISCIPLE OF PERSES, IT WAS PROFESSOR STINGER!
YEAH, HE WAS RESPONSIBLE FOR THAT ENTIRE WORMHOLE THING!
STINGER WORKS FOR TIBERIUS, AND HAS FOR MANY YEARS.
THAT'S A LIE!
IS IT? DID YOU KNOW STINGER HELPED YOUR GRANDFATHER DEVELOP AND BUILD ALL OF THE EQUIPMENT IN THIS ROOM, FOR THE SOLE PURPOSE OF BRINGING PERSES TO EARTH?
WELL, I CERTAINLY DIDN'T.

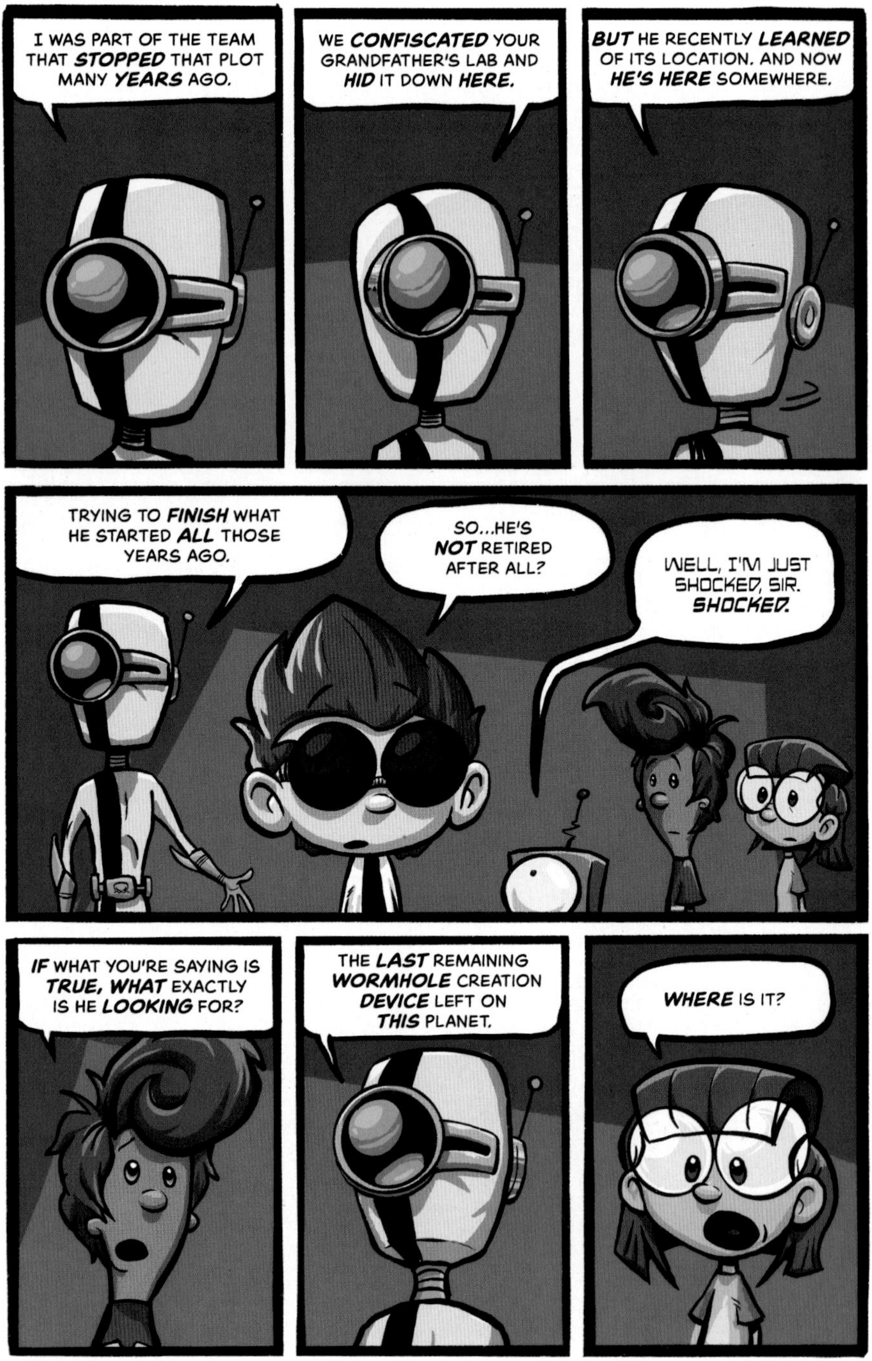
I WAS PART OF THE TEAM THAT STOPPED THAT PLOT MANY YEARS AGO.
WE CONFISCATED YOUR GRANDFATHER'S LAB AND HID IT DOWN HERE.
BUT HE RECENTLY LEARNED OF ITS LOCATION. AND NOW HE'S HERE SOMEWHERE.
TRYING TO FINISH WHAT HE STARTED ALL THOSE YEARS AGO.
SO...HE'S NOT RETIRED AFTER ALL?
WELL, I'M JUST SHOCKED, SIR. SHOCKED.
IF WHAT YOU'RE SAYING IS TRUE, WHAT EXACTLY IS HE LOOKING FOR?
THE LAST REMAINING WORMHOLE CREATION DEVICE LEFT ON THIS PLANET.
WHERE IS IT?

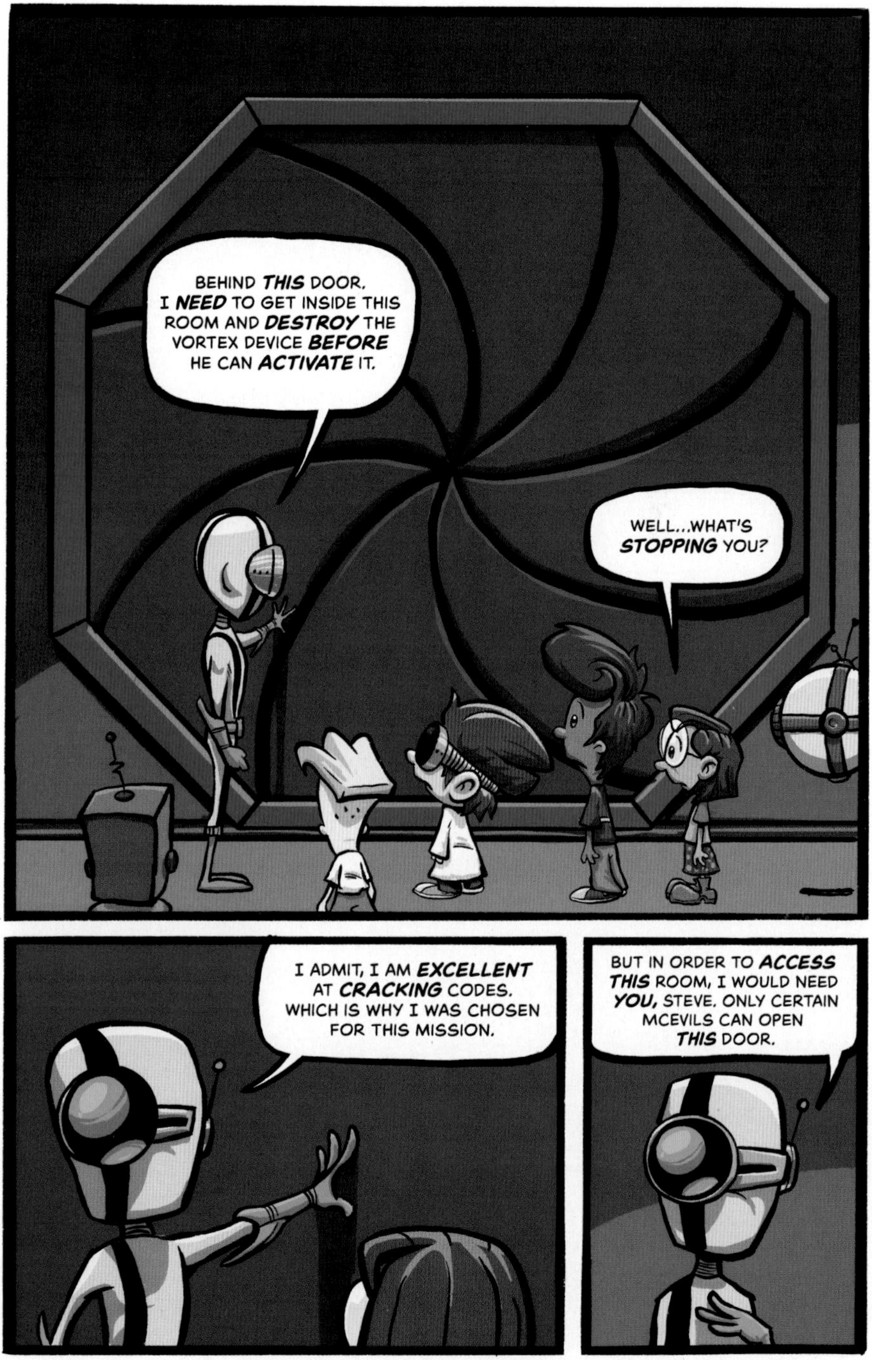
BEHIND THIS DOOR. I NEED TO GET INSIDE THIS ROOM AND DESTROY THE VORTEX DEVICE BEFORE HE CAN ACTIVATE IT.
WELL...WHAT'S STOPPING YOU?
I ADMIT, I AM EXCELLENT AT CRACKING CODES. WHICH IS WHY I WAS CHOSEN FOR THIS MISSION.
BUT IN ORDER TO ACCESS THIS ROOM, I WOULD NEED YOU, STEVE. ONLY CERTAIN MCEVILS CAN OPEN THIS DOOR.

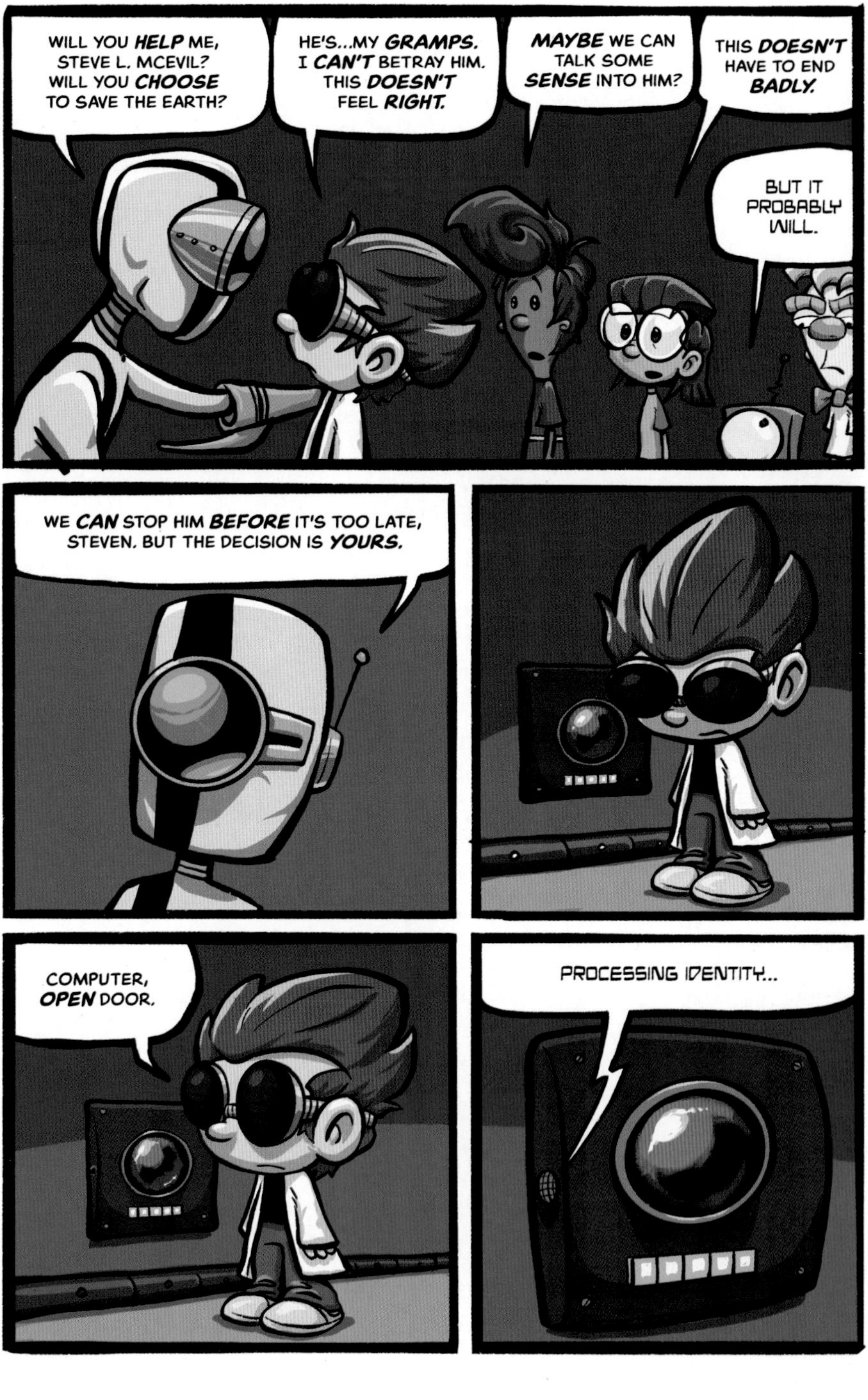
WILL YOU HELP ME, STEVE L. MCEVIL? WILL YOU CHOOSE TO SAVE THE EARTH?
HE'S...MY GRAMPS. I CAN'T BETRAY HIM. THIS DOESN'T FEEL RIGHT.
MAYBE WE CAN TALK SOME SENSE INTO HIM?
THIS DOESN'T HAVE TO END BADLY.
BUT IT PROBABLY WILL.
WE CAN STOP HIM BEFORE IT'S TOO LATE, STEVEN. BUT THE DECISION IS YOURS.
COMPUTER, OPEN DOOR.
PROCESSING IDENTITY...

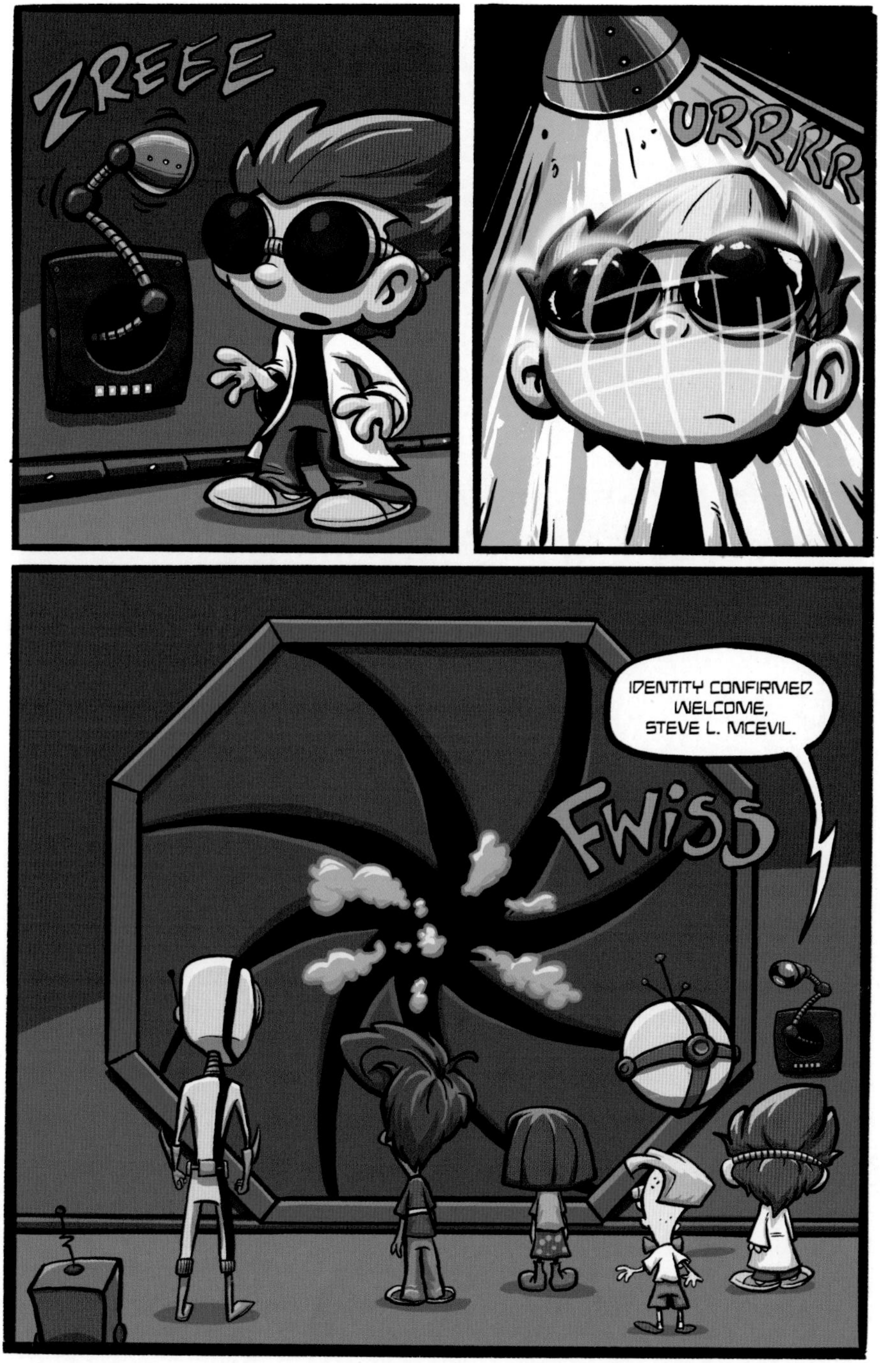
ZREEE
URRRRR
IDENTITY CONFIRMED. WELCOME, STEVE L. MCEVIL.
FWISS

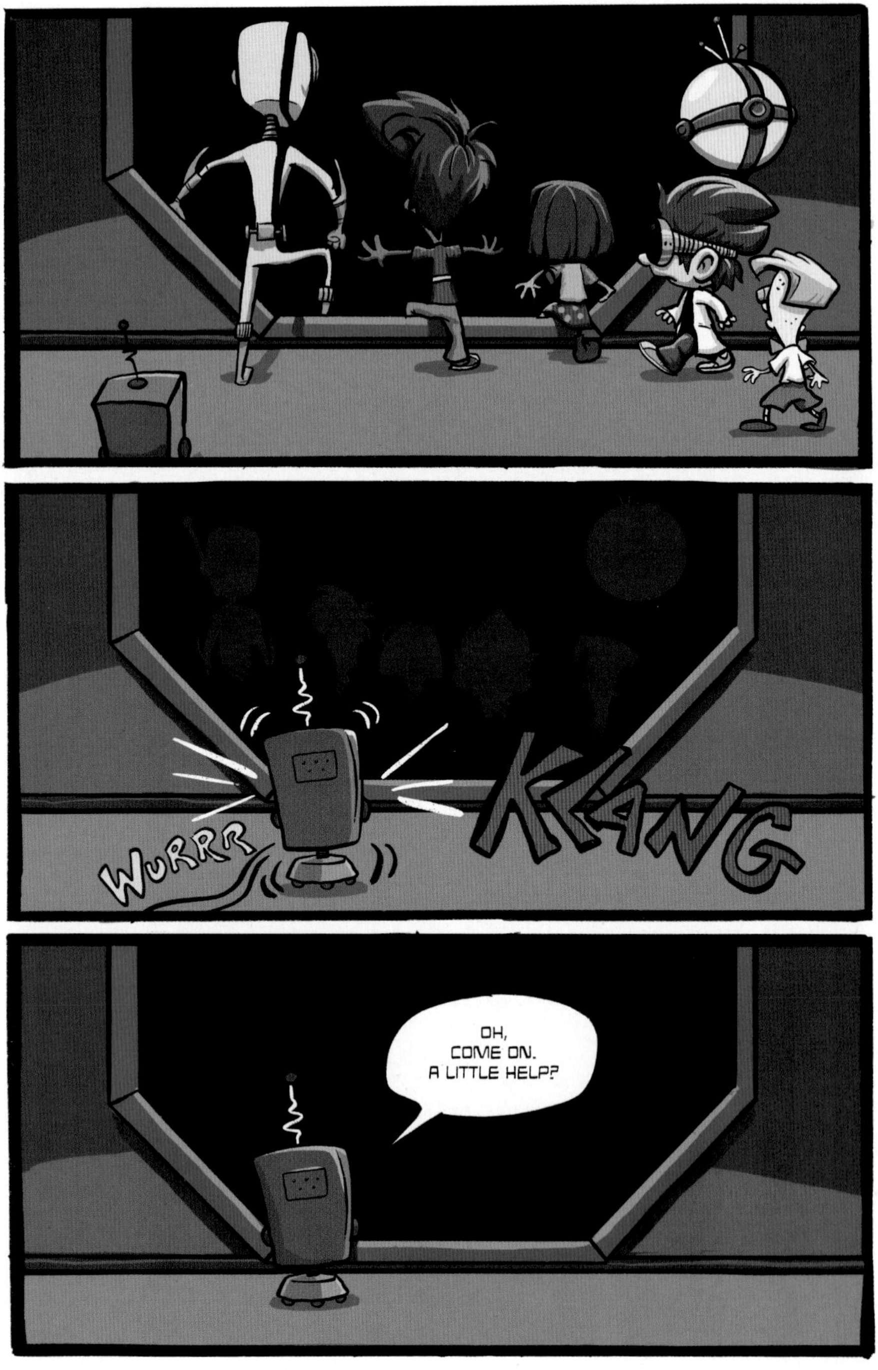
WURRR
KLANG
OH,
COME ON.
A LITTLE HELP?

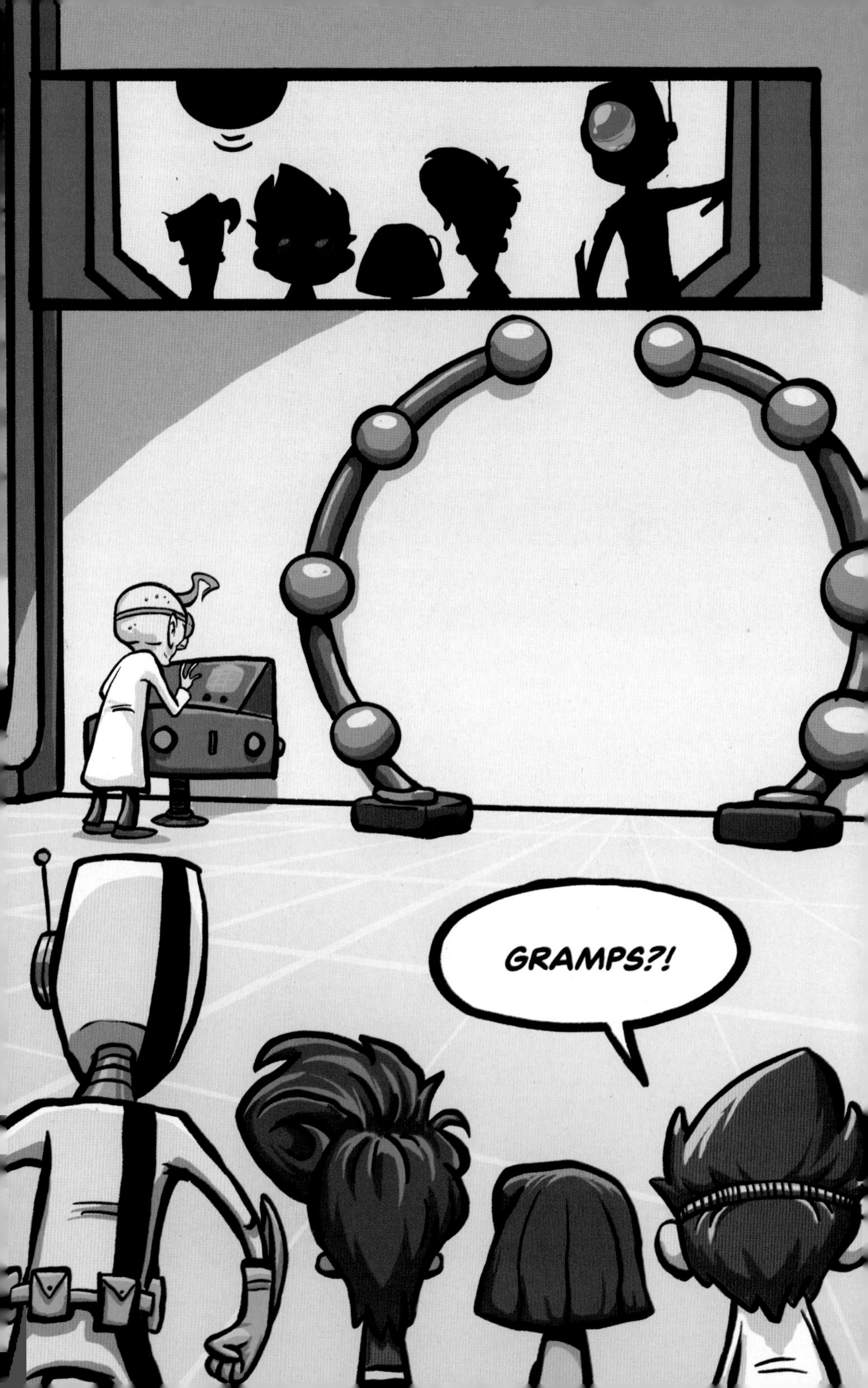
GRAMPS?!

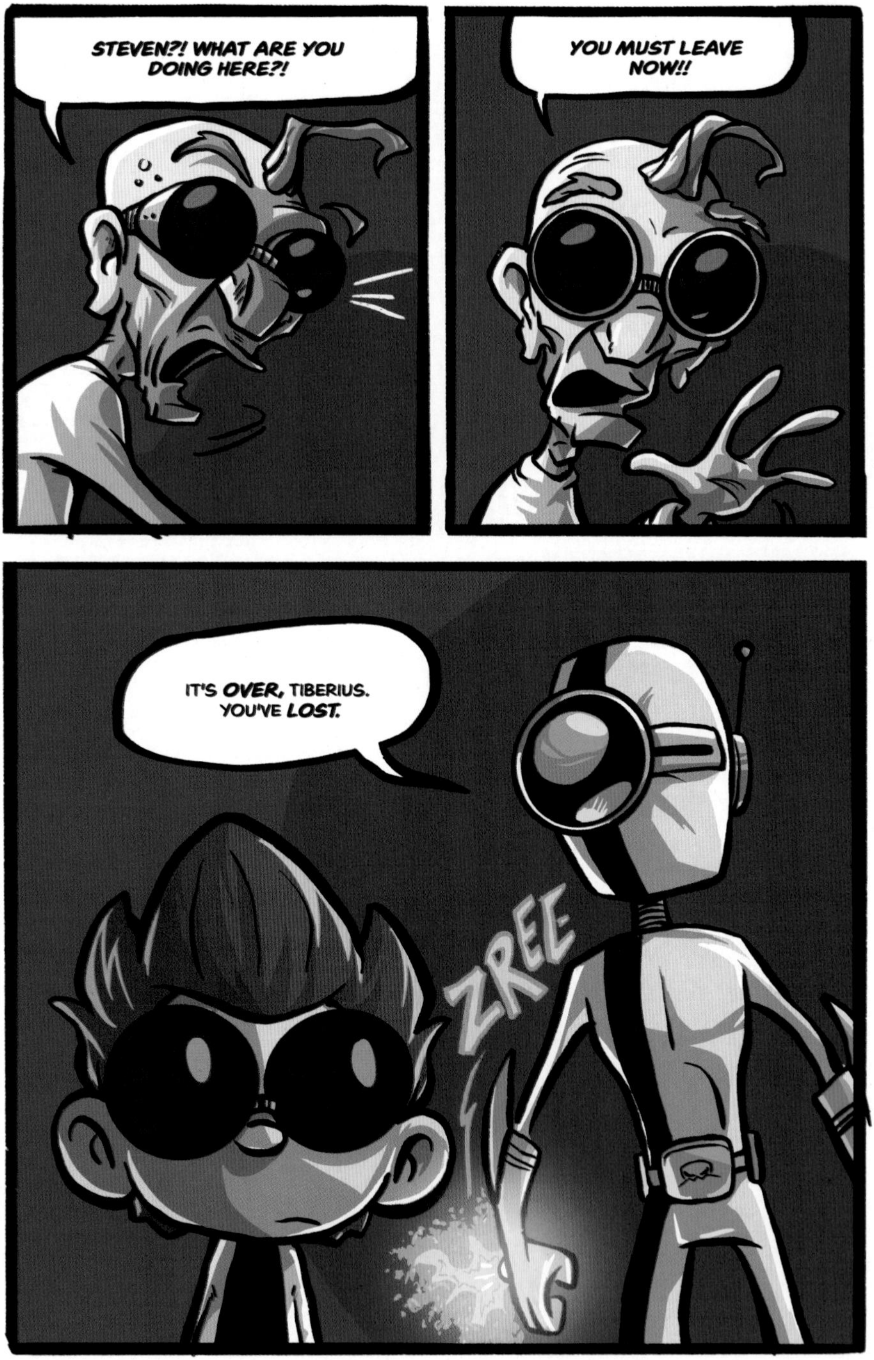
STEVEN?! WHAT ARE YOU DOING HERE?!
YOU MUST LEAVE NOW!!
IT'S *OVER,* TIBERIUS. YOU'VE *LOST.*
ZREE

CHAPTER 19
Lying in Wait

CODEX! I MIGHT HAVE KNOWN YOU'D SHOW UP!!
ZREEE

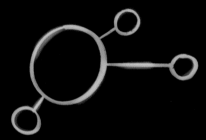

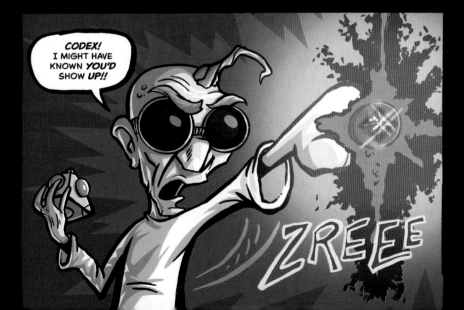

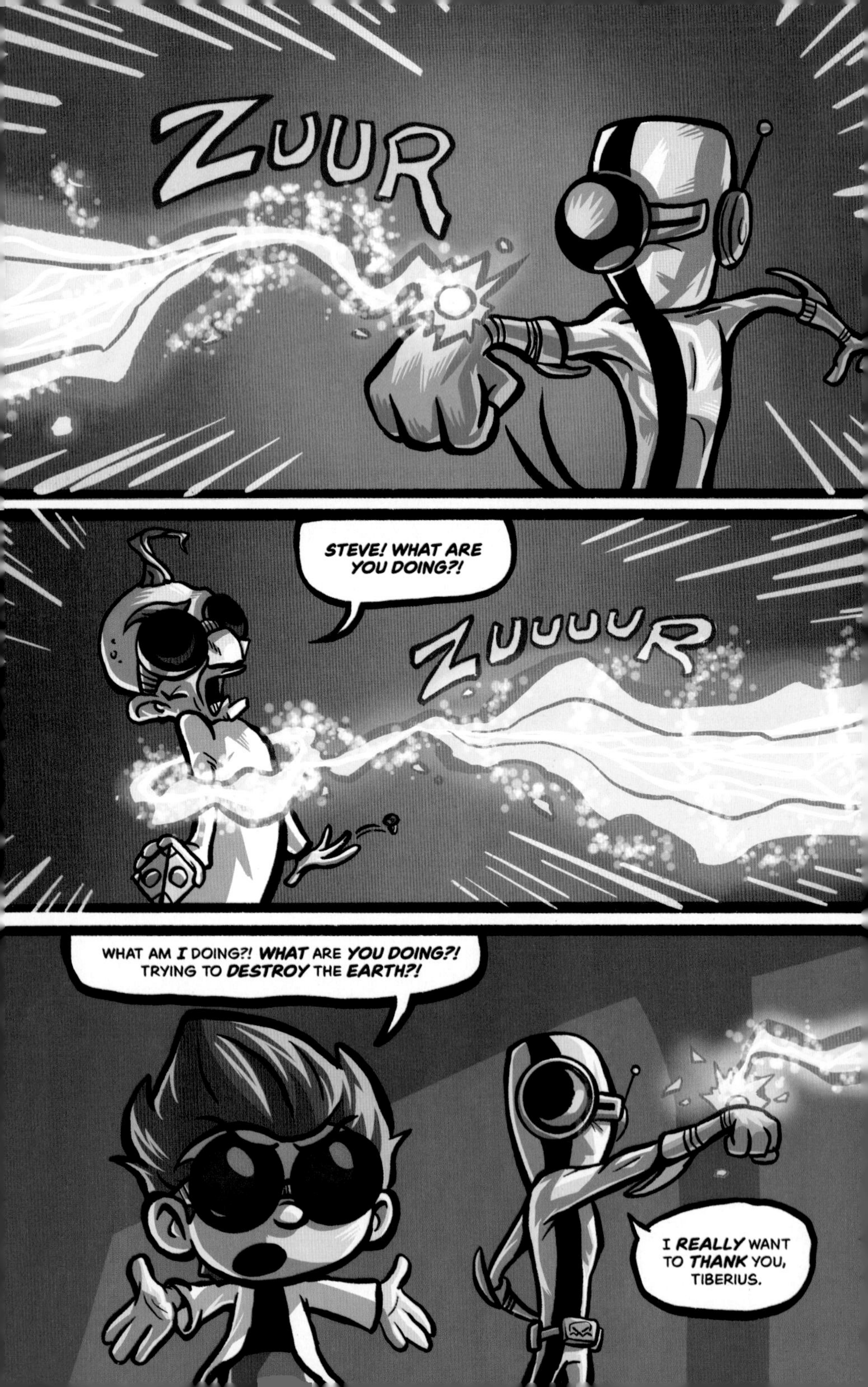
ZUUR
STEVE! WHAT ARE YOU DOING?!
ZUUUUR
WHAT AM I DOING?! WHAT ARE YOU DOING?! TRYING TO DESTROY THE EARTH?!
I REALLY WANT TO THANK YOU, TIBERIUS.

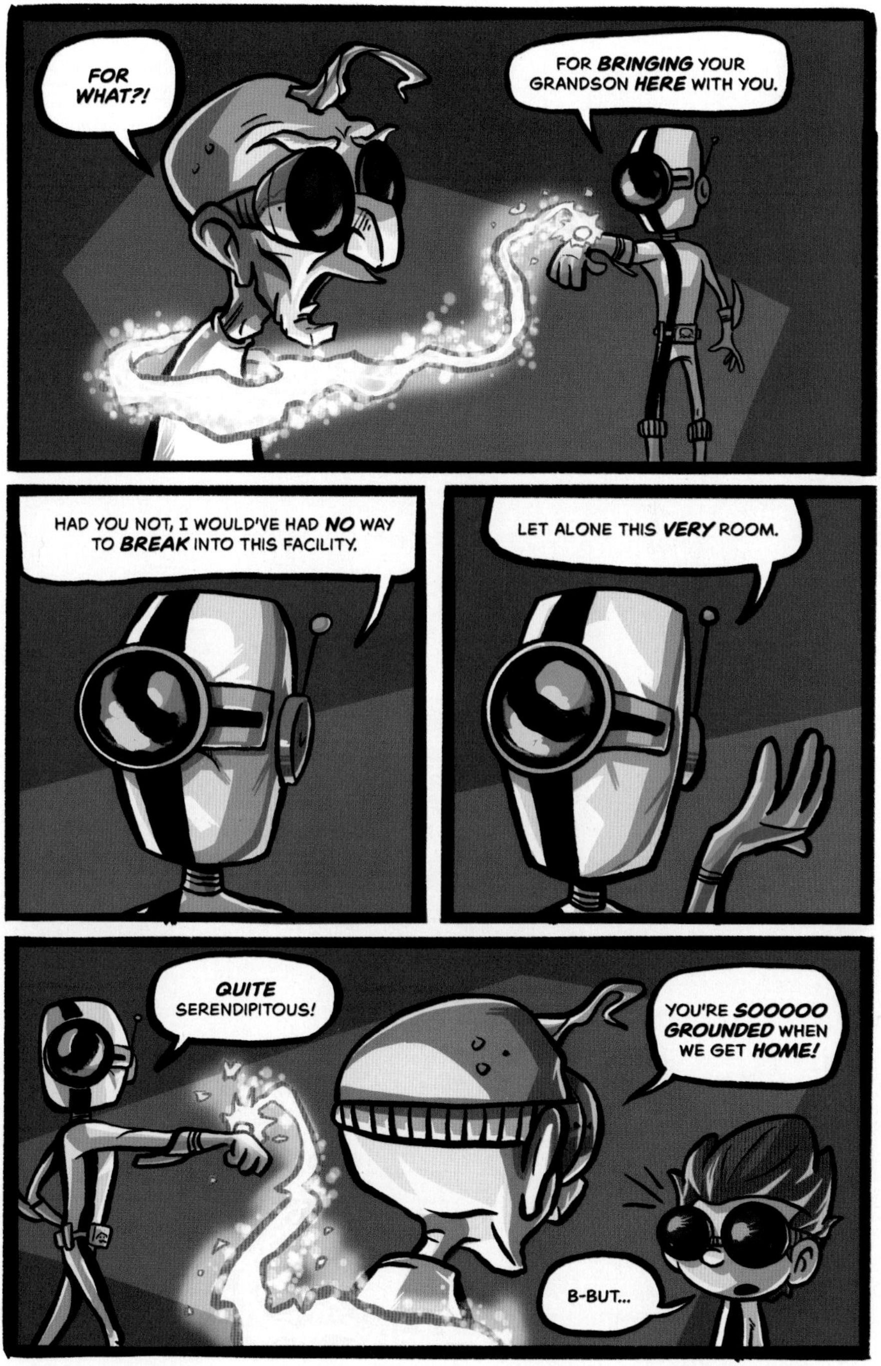
FOR WHAT?!
FOR BRINGING YOUR GRANDSON HERE WITH YOU.
HAD YOU NOT, I WOULD'VE HAD NO WAY TO BREAK INTO THIS FACILITY.
LET ALONE THIS VERY ROOM.
QUITE SERENDIPITOUS!
YOU'RE SOOOOO GROUNDED WHEN WE GET HOME!
B-BUT...

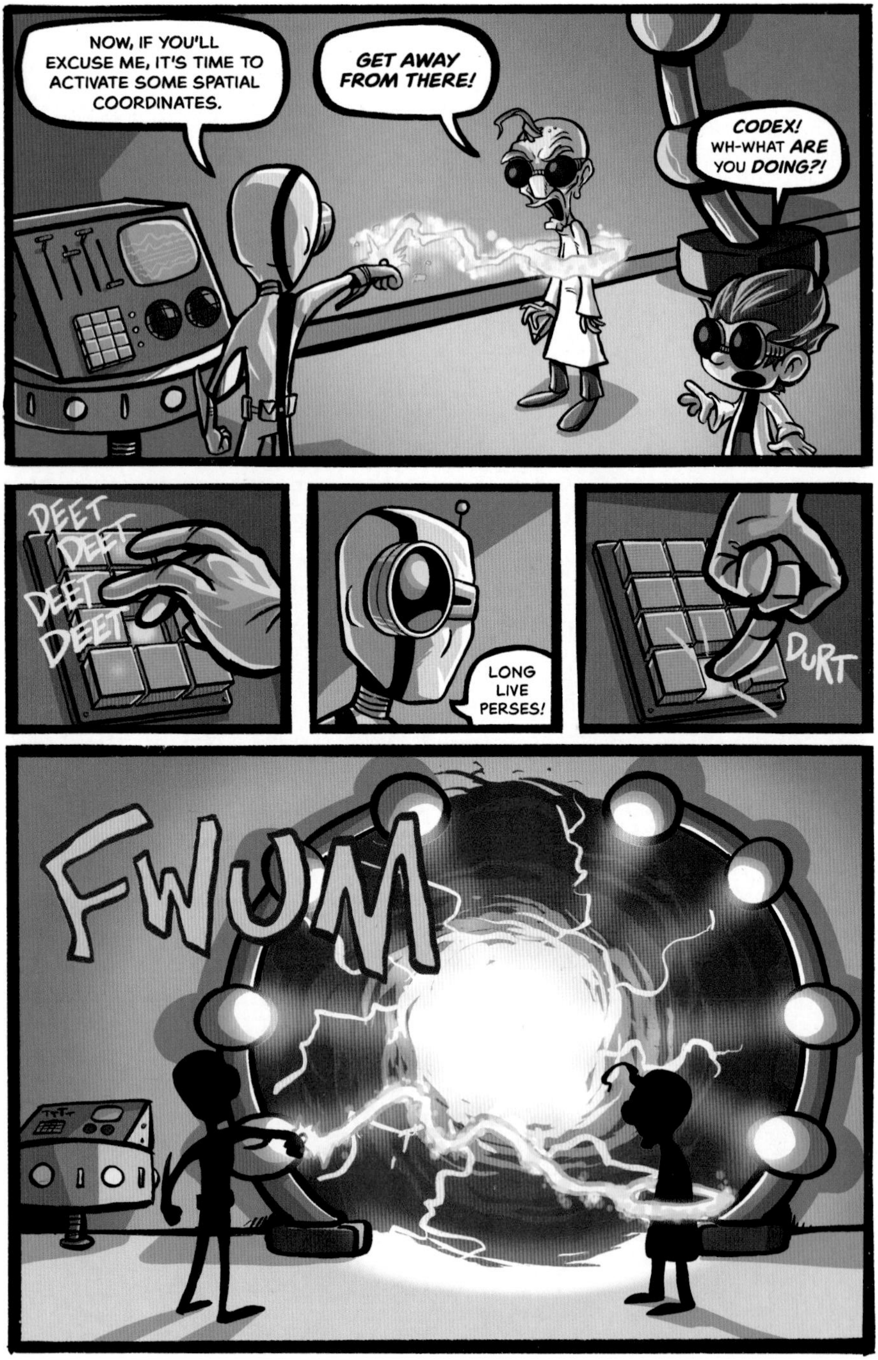

NOW, IF YOU'LL EXCUSE ME, IT'S TIME TO ACTIVATE SOME SPATIAL COORDINATES.
GET AWAY FROM THERE!
CODEX! WH-WHAT ARE YOU DOING?!
DEET DEET DEET DEET
LONG LIVE PERSES!
DURT
FWUM

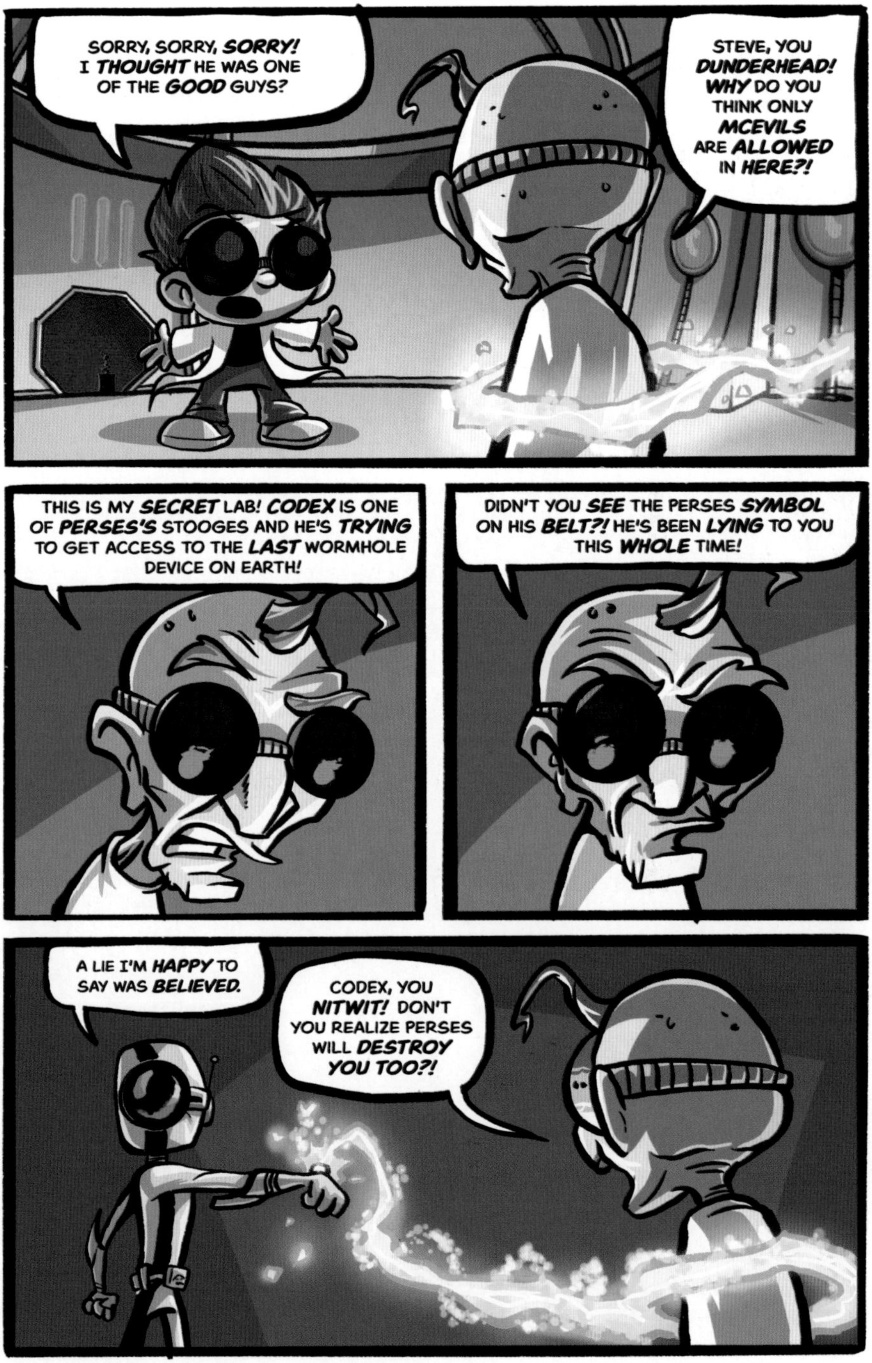
SORRY, SORRY, SORRY! I THOUGHT HE WAS ONE OF THE GOOD GUYS?
STEVE, YOU DUNDERHEAD! WHY DO YOU THINK ONLY MCEVILS ARE ALLOWED IN HERE?!
THIS IS MY SECRET LAB! CODEX IS ONE OF PERSES'S STOOGES AND HE'S TRYING TO GET ACCESS TO THE LAST WORMHOLE DEVICE ON EARTH!
DIDN'T YOU SEE THE PERSES SYMBOL ON HIS BELT?! HE'S BEEN LYING TO YOU THIS WHOLE TIME!
A LIE I'M HAPPY TO SAY WAS BELIEVED.
CODEX, YOU NITWIT! DON'T YOU REALIZE PERSES WILL DESTROY YOU TOO?!

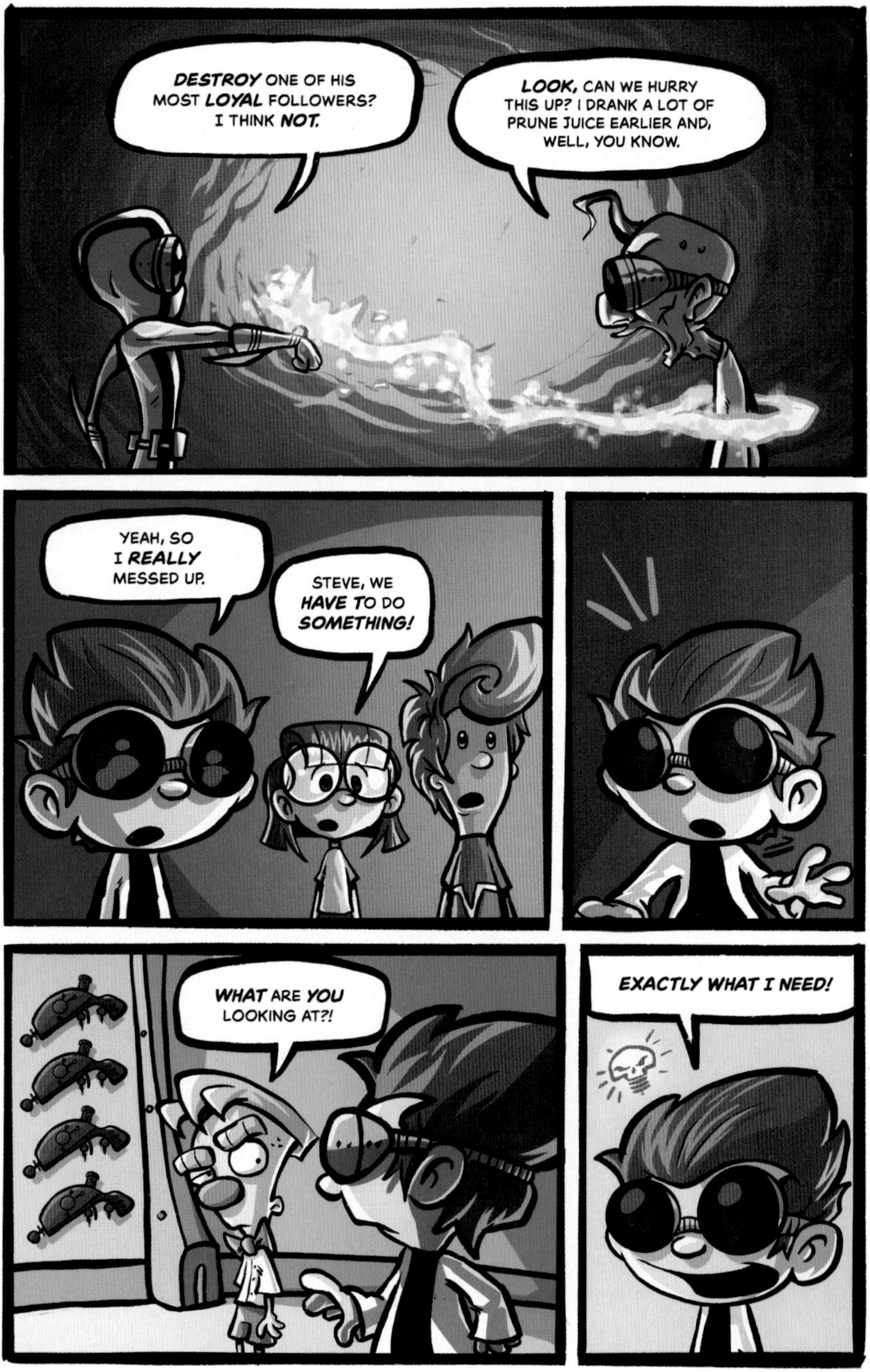

DESTROY ONE OF HIS MOST LOYAL FOLLOWERS? I THINK NOT.
LOOK, CAN WE HURRY THIS UP? I DRANK A LOT OF PRUNE JUICE EARLIER AND, WELL, YOU KNOW.
YEAH, SO I REALLY MESSED UP.
STEVE, WE HAVE TO DO SOMETHING!
WHAT ARE YOU LOOKING AT?!
EXACTLY WHAT I NEED!

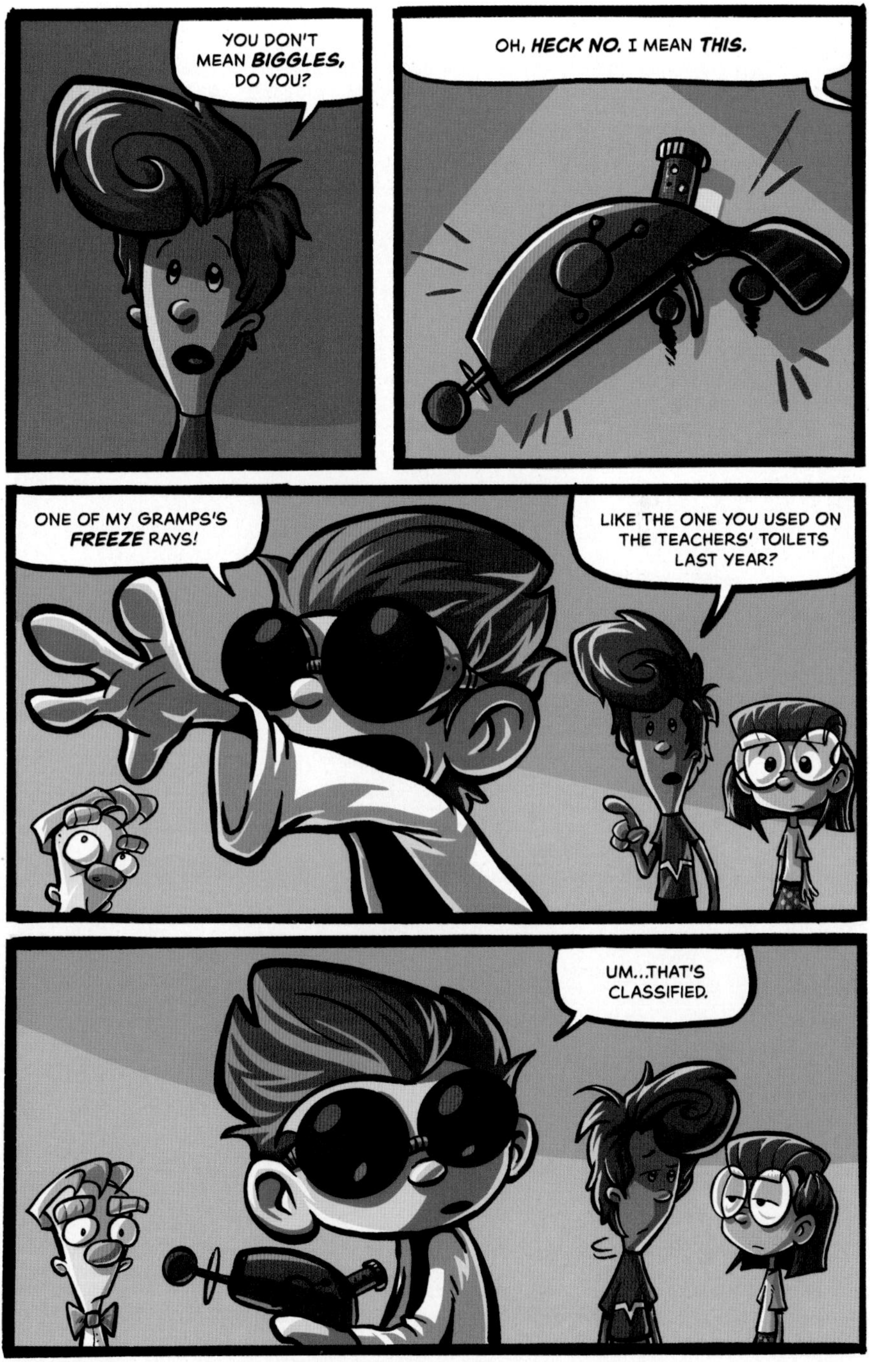
YOU DON'T MEAN *BIGGLES,* DO YOU?
OH, *HECK NO.* I MEAN *THIS.*
ONE OF MY GRAMPS'S *FREEZE* RAYS!
LIKE THE ONE YOU USED ON THE TEACHERS' TOILETS LAST YEAR?
UM...THAT'S CLASSIFIED.

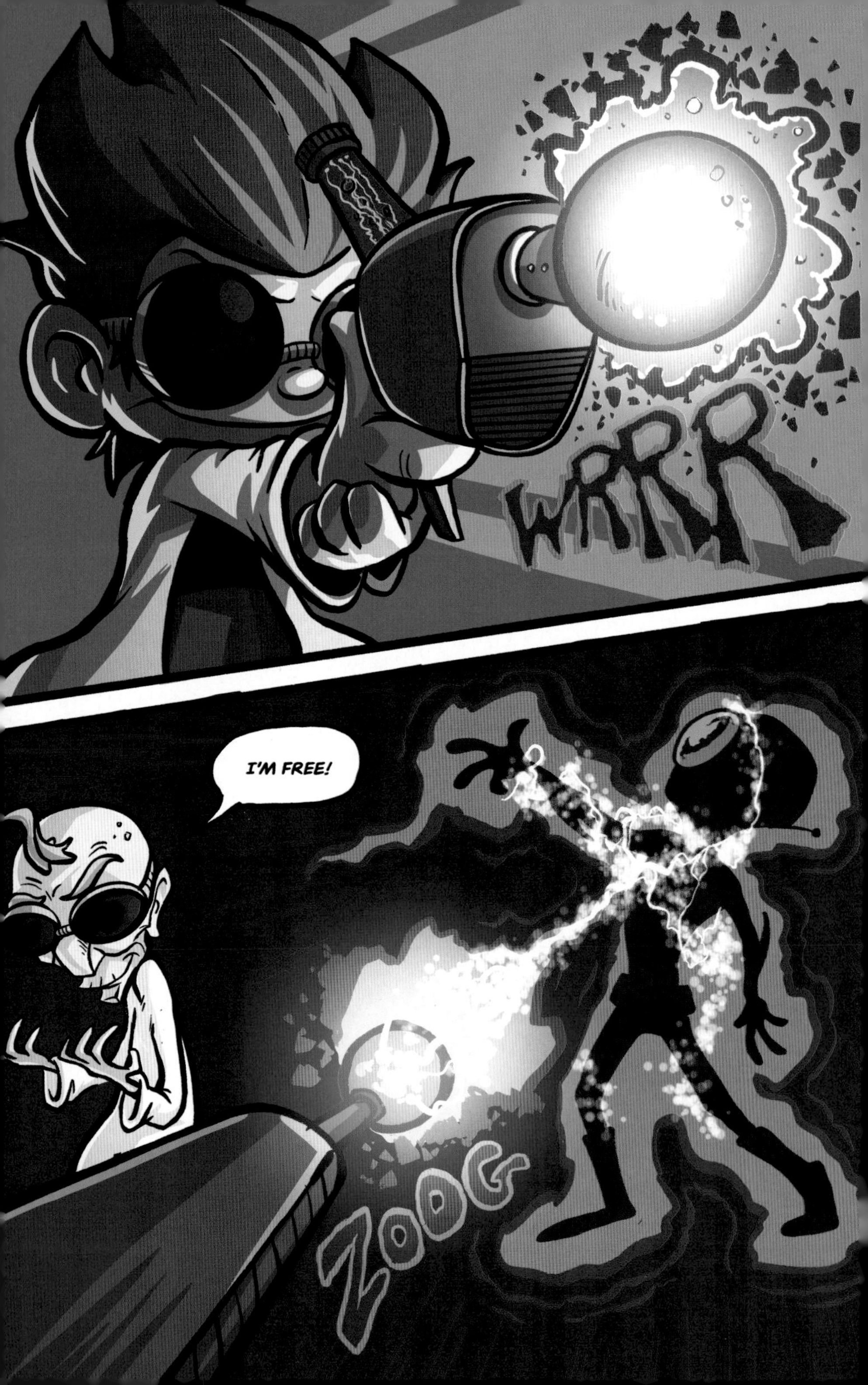
WRRR
I'M FREE!
ZOOG

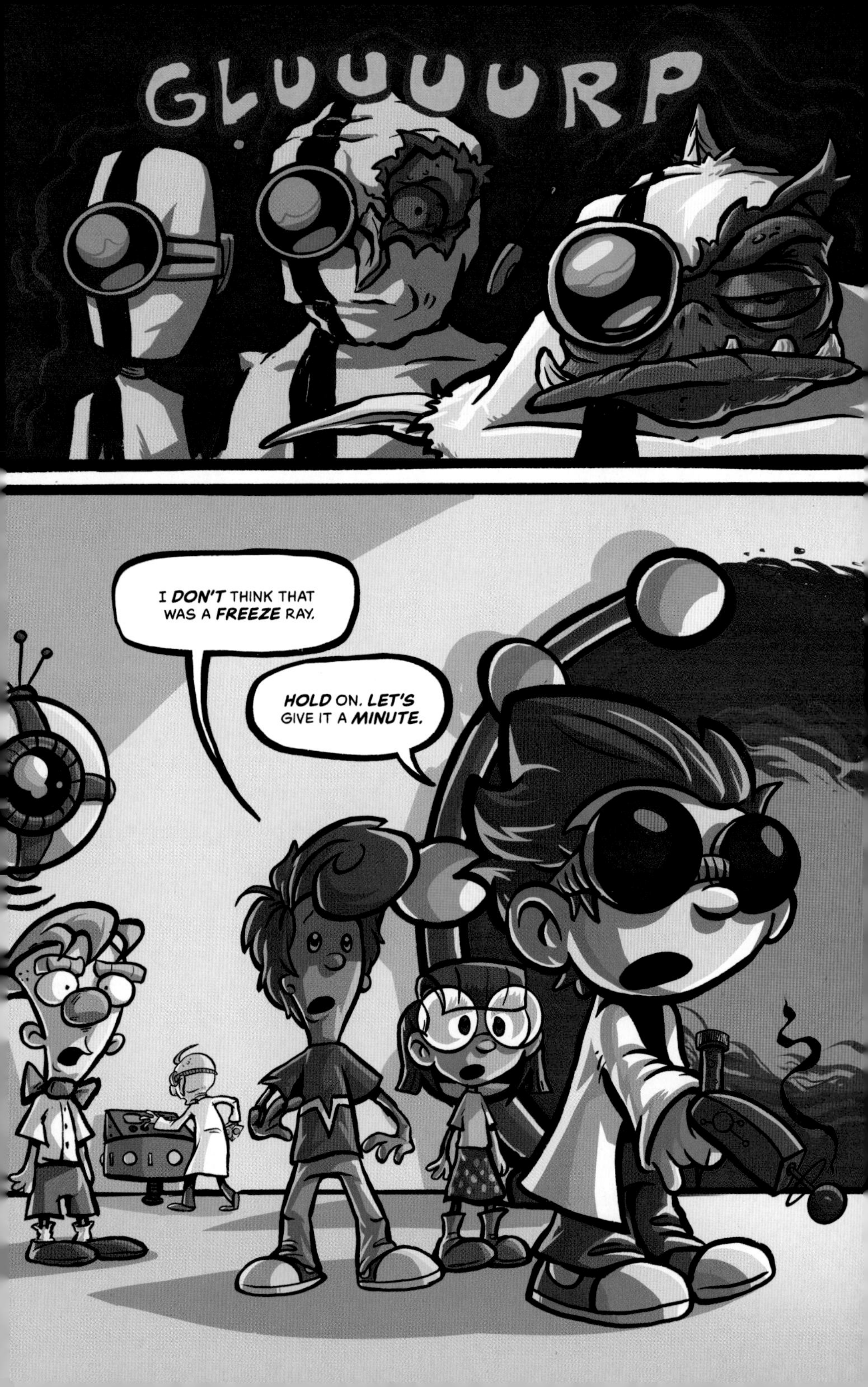
GLUUURP
I DON'T THINK THAT WAS A FREEZE RAY.
HOLD ON. LET'S GIVE IT A MINUTE.

CHAPTER 20

Monstrous Behavior

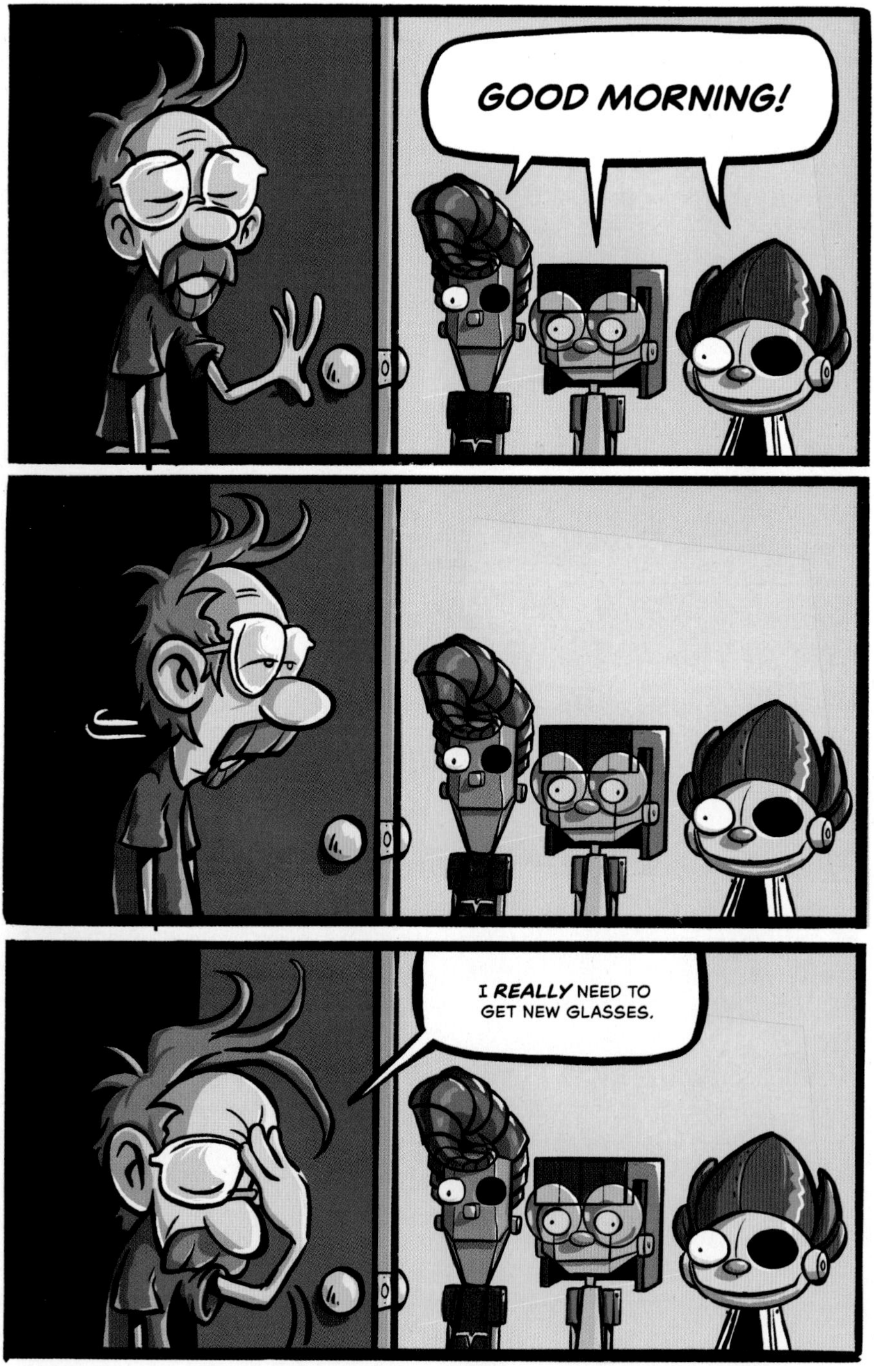
GOOD MORNING!
I *REALLY* NEED TO GET NEW GLASSES.

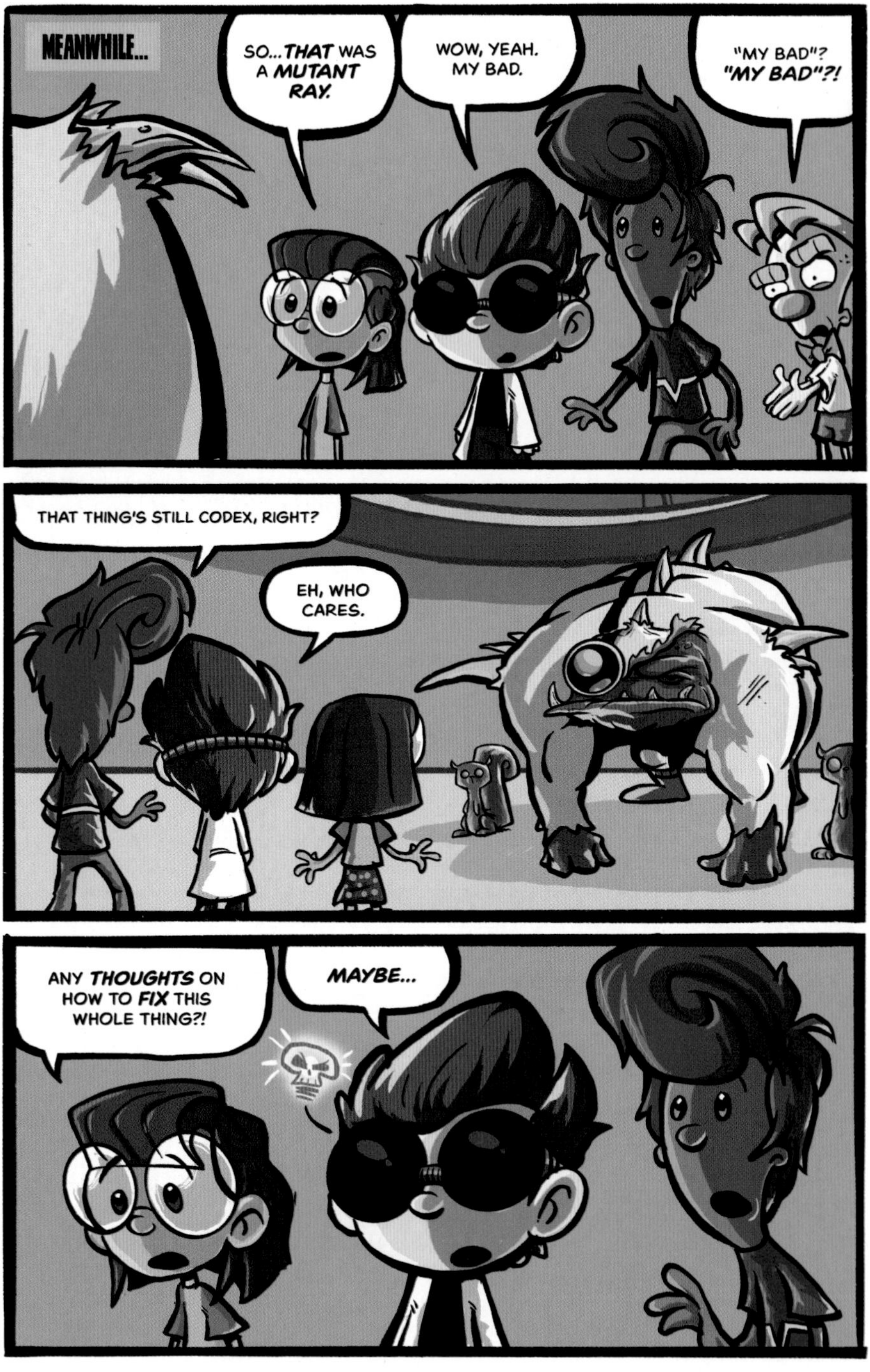
MEANWHILE...
SO...THAT WAS A MUTANT RAY.
WOW, YEAH. MY BAD.
"MY BAD"? "MY BAD"?!
THAT THING'S STILL CODEX, RIGHT?
EH, WHO CARES.
ANY THOUGHTS ON HOW TO FIX THIS WHOLE THING?!
MAYBE...

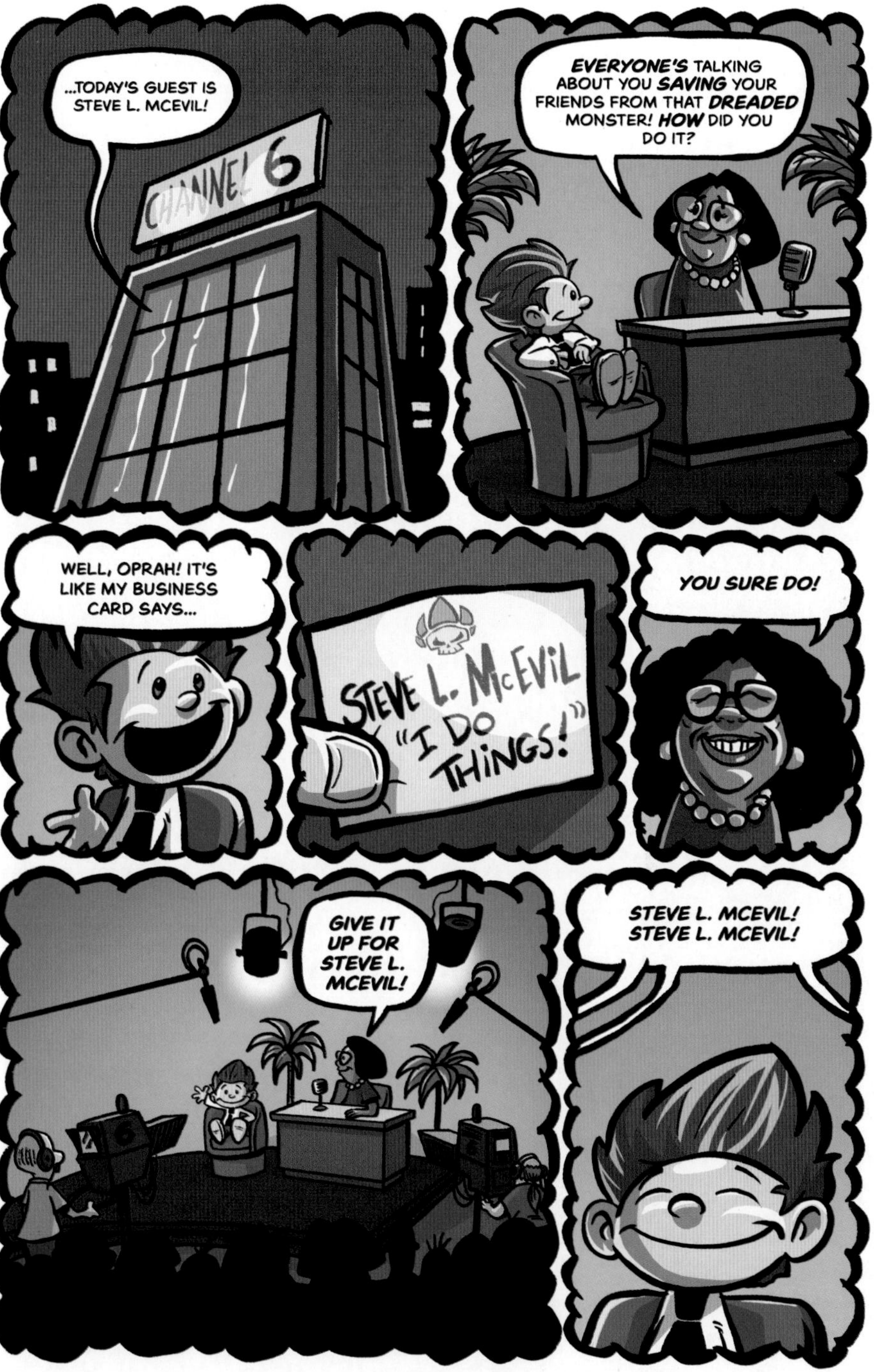
...TODAY'S GUEST IS STEVE L. MCEVIL!
CHANNEL 6
EVERYONE'S TALKING ABOUT YOU SAVING YOUR FRIENDS FROM THAT DREADED MONSTER! HOW DID YOU DO IT?
WELL, OPRAH! IT'S LIKE MY BUSINESS CARD SAYS...
STEVE L. McEVIL "I DO THINGS!"
YOU SURE DO!
GIVE IT UP FOR STEVE L. MCEVIL!
STEVE L. MCEVIL! STEVE L. MCEVIL!

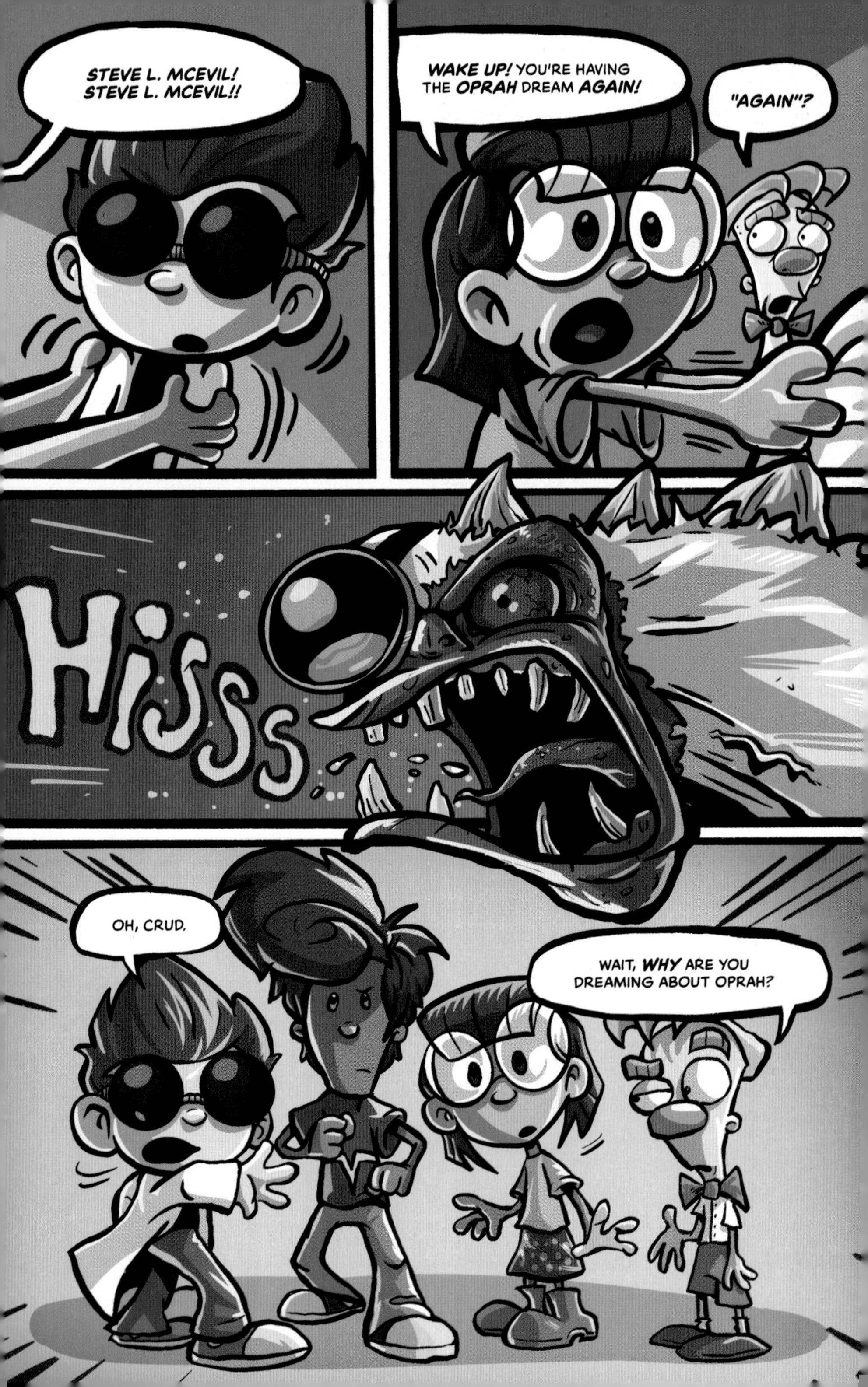
STEVE L. MCEVIL! STEVE L. MCEVIL!!
WAKE UP! YOU'RE HAVING THE OPRAH DREAM AGAIN!
"AGAIN"?
HISSS
OH, CRUD.
WAIT, WHY ARE YOU DREAMING ABOUT OPRAH?

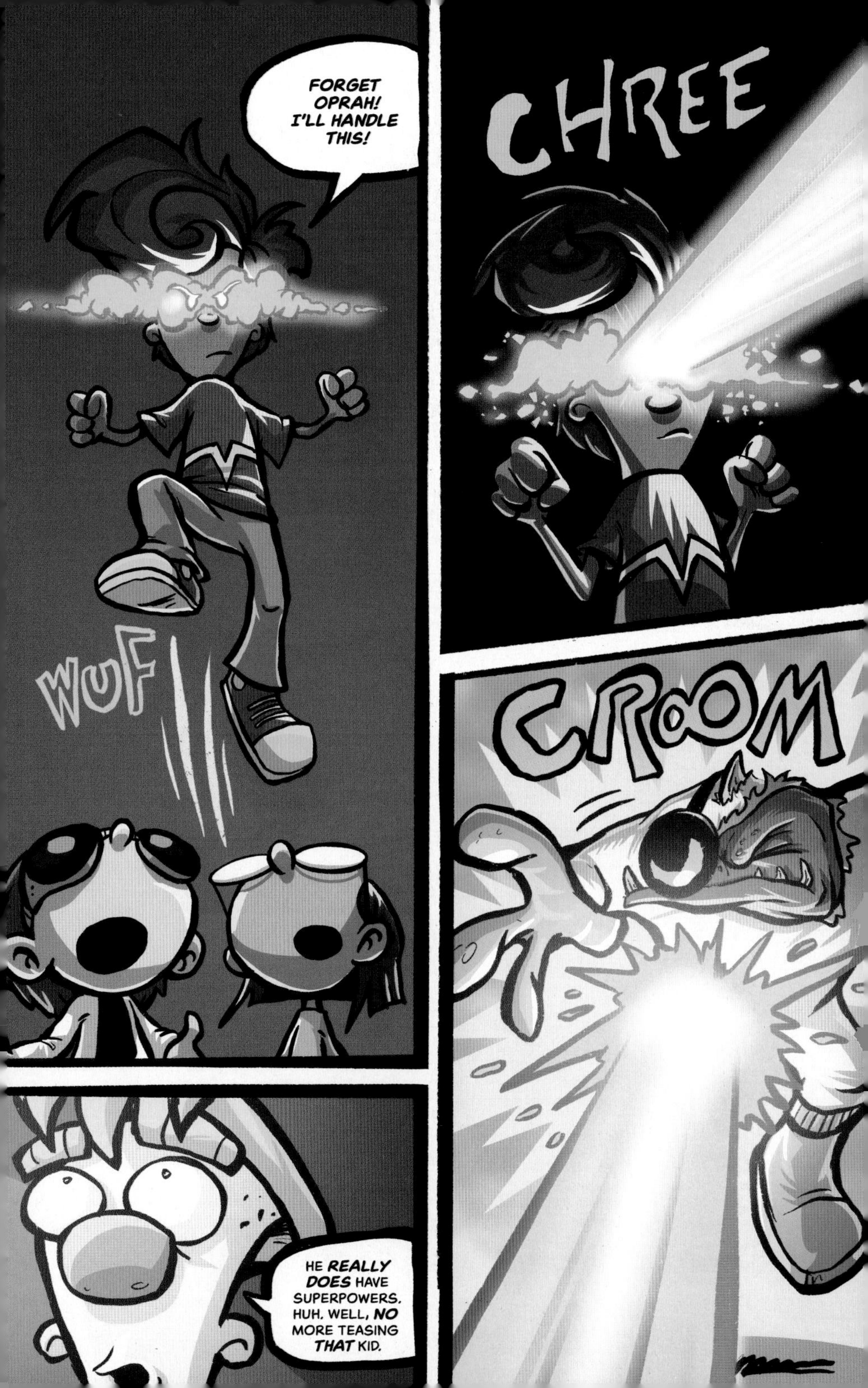
FORGET OPRAH! I'LL HANDLE THIS!
WUF
CHREE
CROOM
HE REALLY DOES HAVE SUPERPOWERS. HUH. WELL, NO MORE TEASING THAT KID.

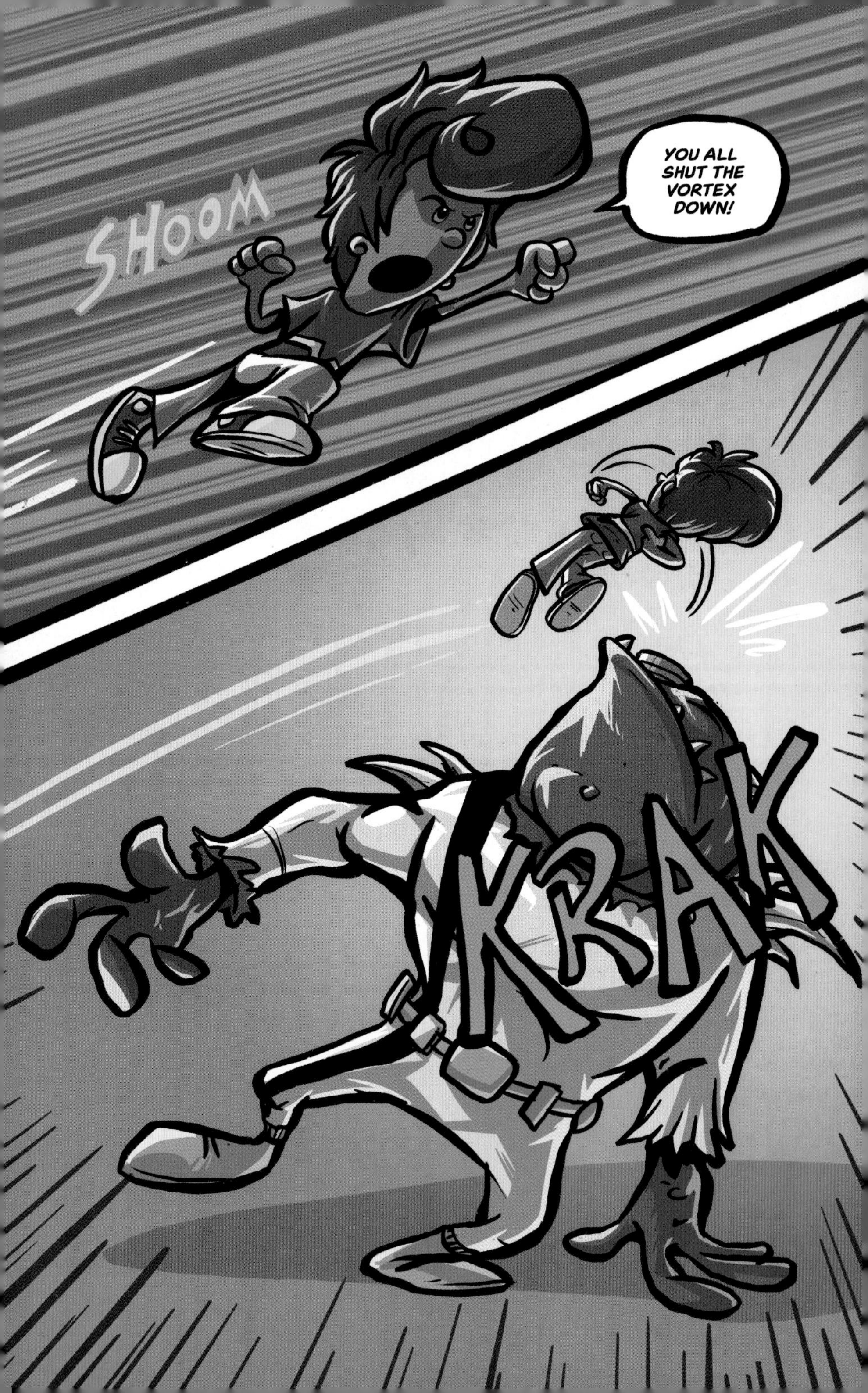
SHOOM
YOU ALL SHUT THE VORTEX DOWN!
KRAK

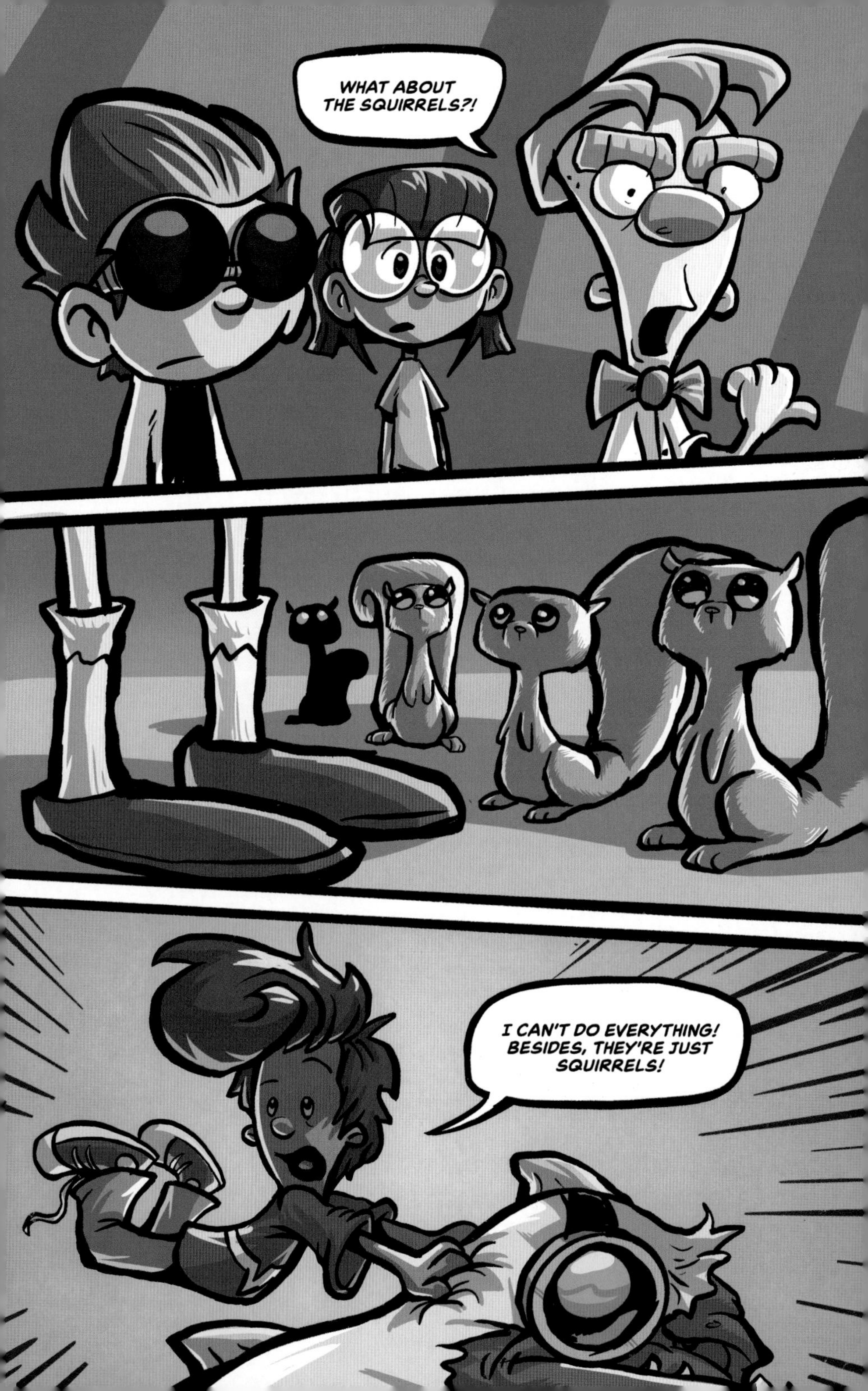
WHAT ABOUT THE SQUIRRELS?!
I CAN'T DO EVERYTHING! BESIDES, THEY'RE JUST SQUIRRELS!

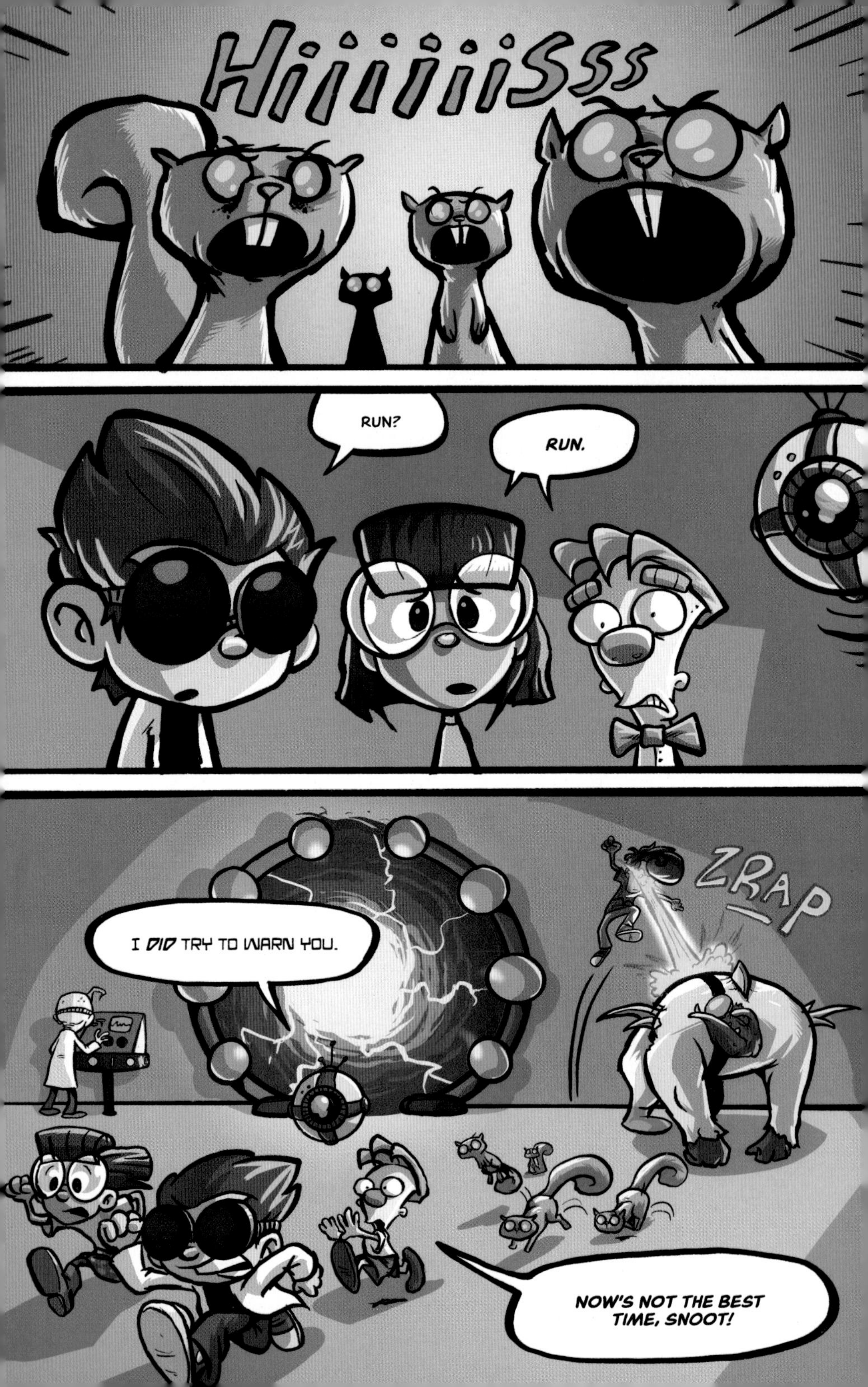
HiiiiiiSSS
RUN?
RUN.
I DID TRY TO WARN YOU.
ZRAP
NOW'S NOT THE BEST TIME, SNOOT!

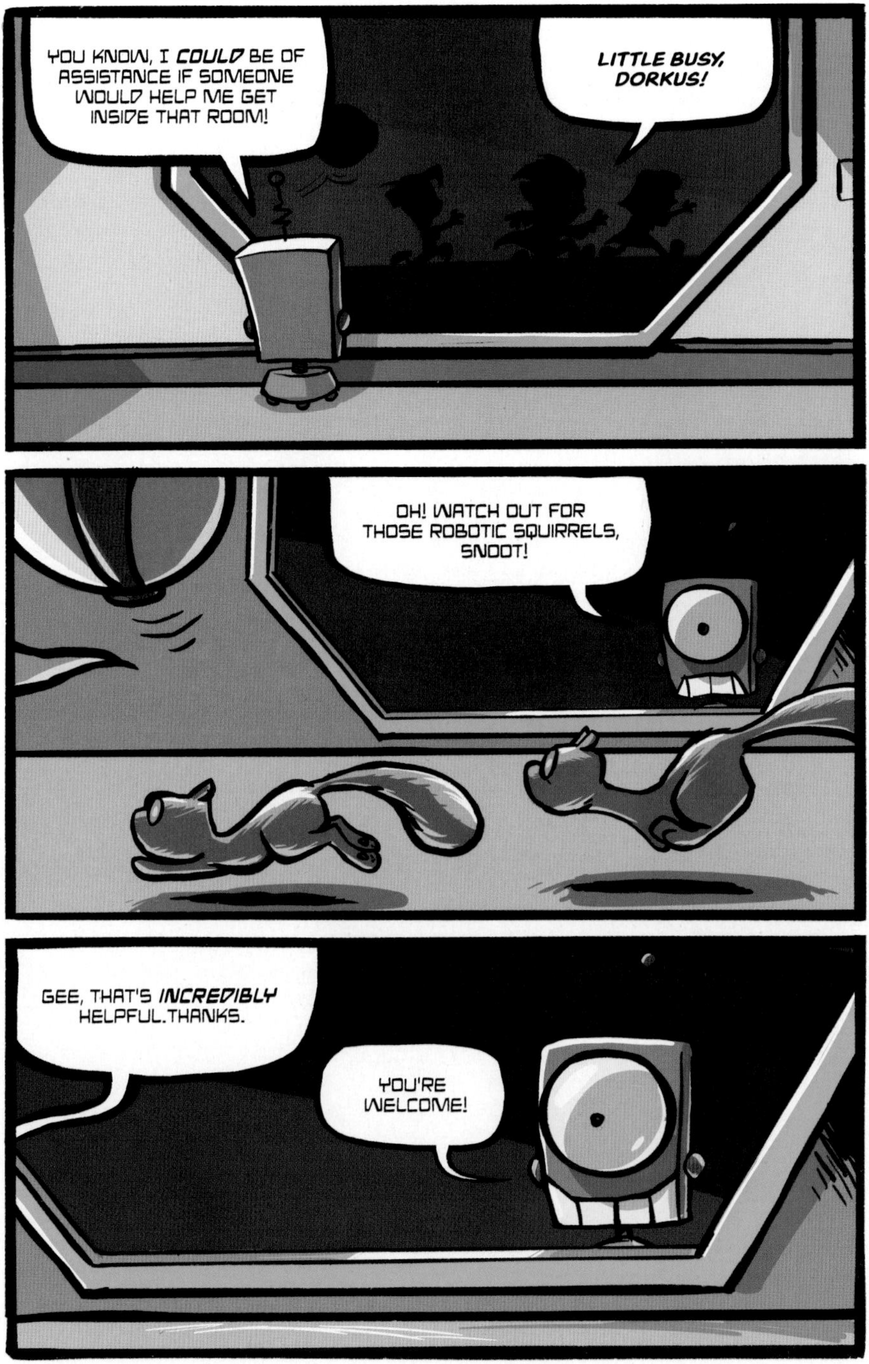
YOU KNOW, I *COULD* BE OF ASSISTANCE IF SOMEONE WOULD HELP ME GET INSIDE THAT ROOM!
LITTLE BUSY, DORKUS!
OH! WATCH OUT FOR THOSE ROBOTIC SQUIRRELS, SNOOT!
GEE, THAT'S *INCREDIBLY* HELPFUL.THANKS.
YOU'RE WELCOME!

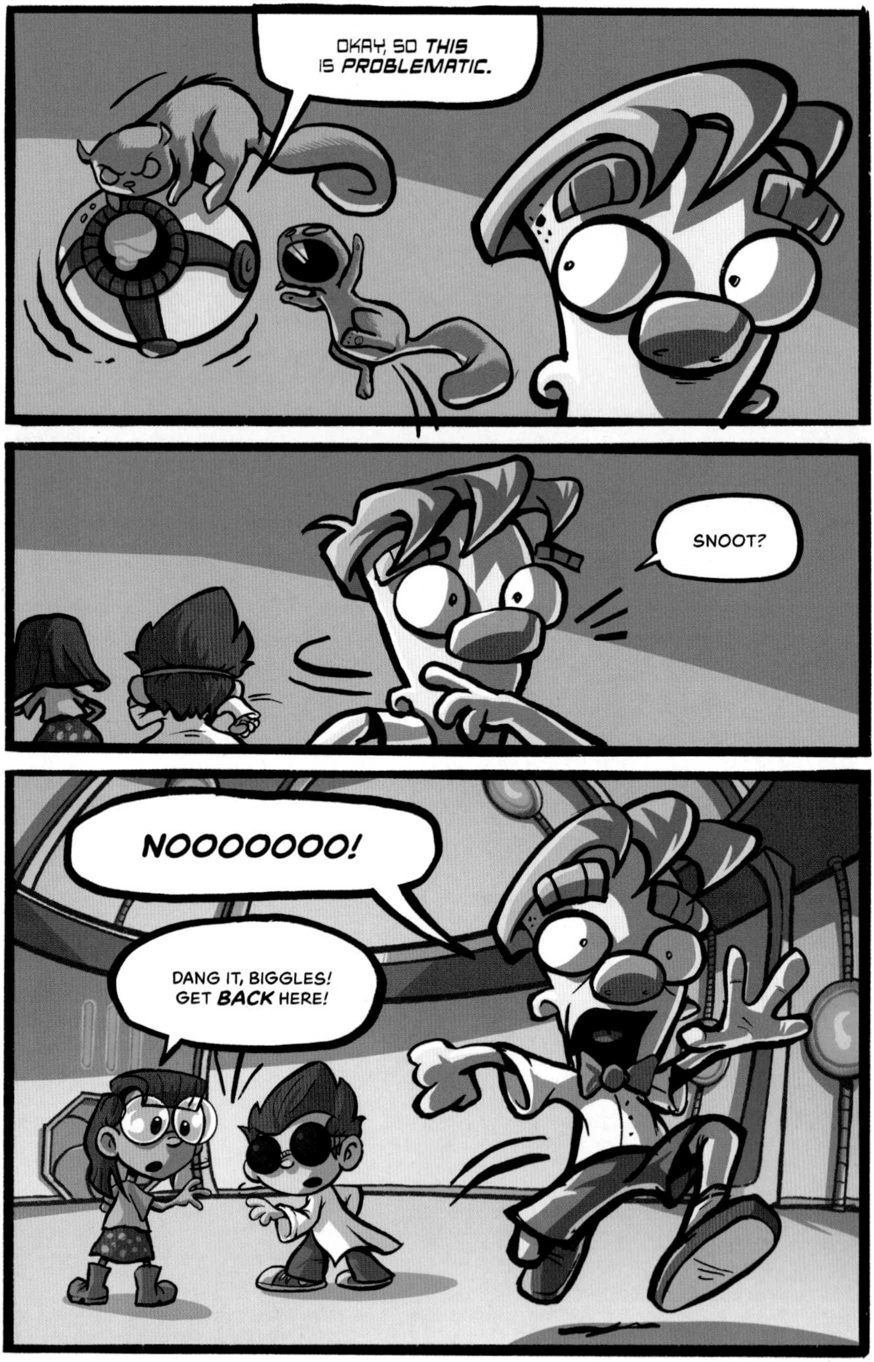
OKAY, SO THIS IS PROBLEMATIC.
SNOOT?
NOOOOOOO!
DANG IT, BIGGLES! GET BACK HERE!

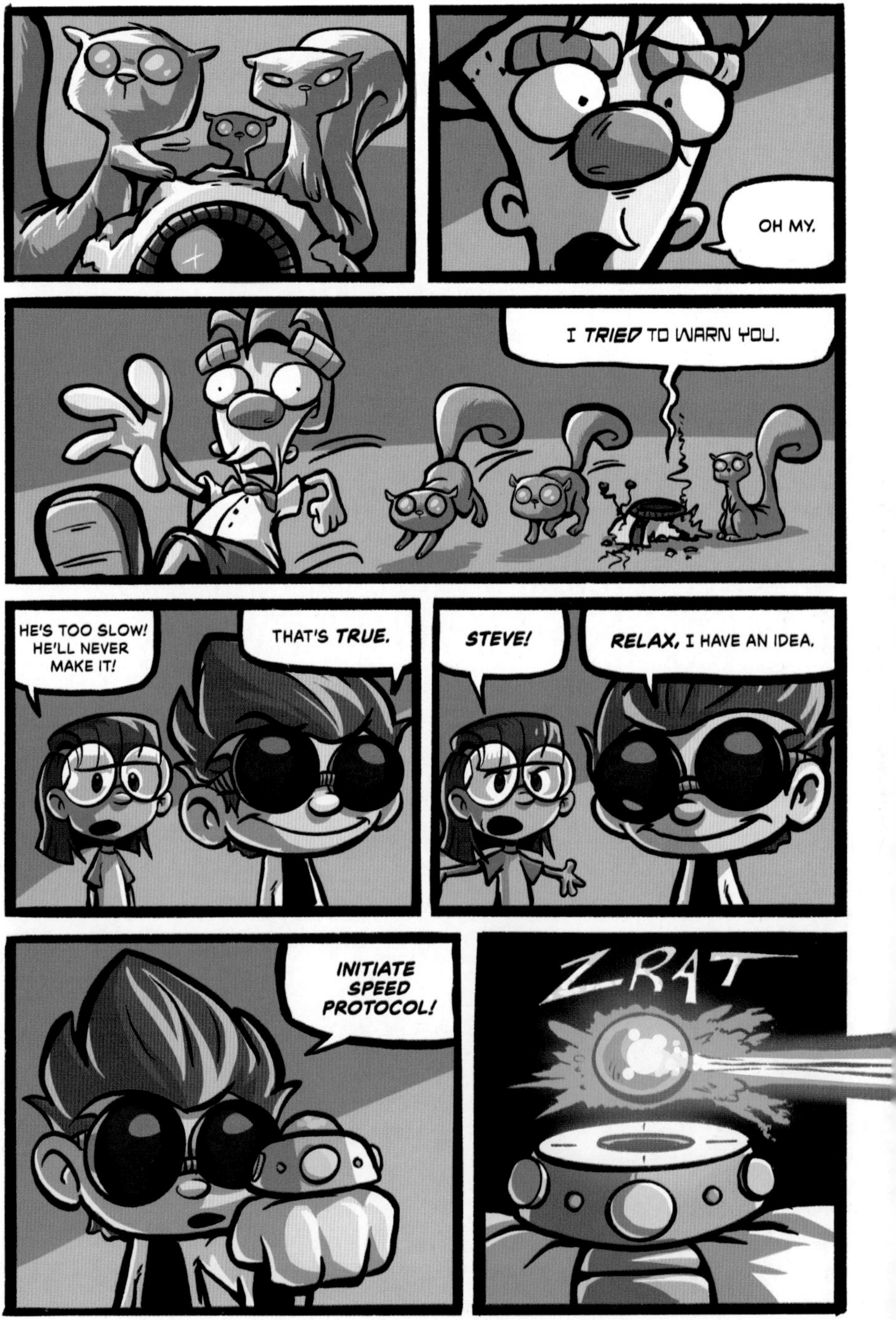
OH MY.
I TRIED TO WARN YOU.
HE'S TOO SLOW! HE'LL NEVER MAKE IT!
THAT'S TRUE.
STEVE!
RELAX, I HAVE AN IDEA.
INITIATE SPEED PROTOCOL!
ZRAT

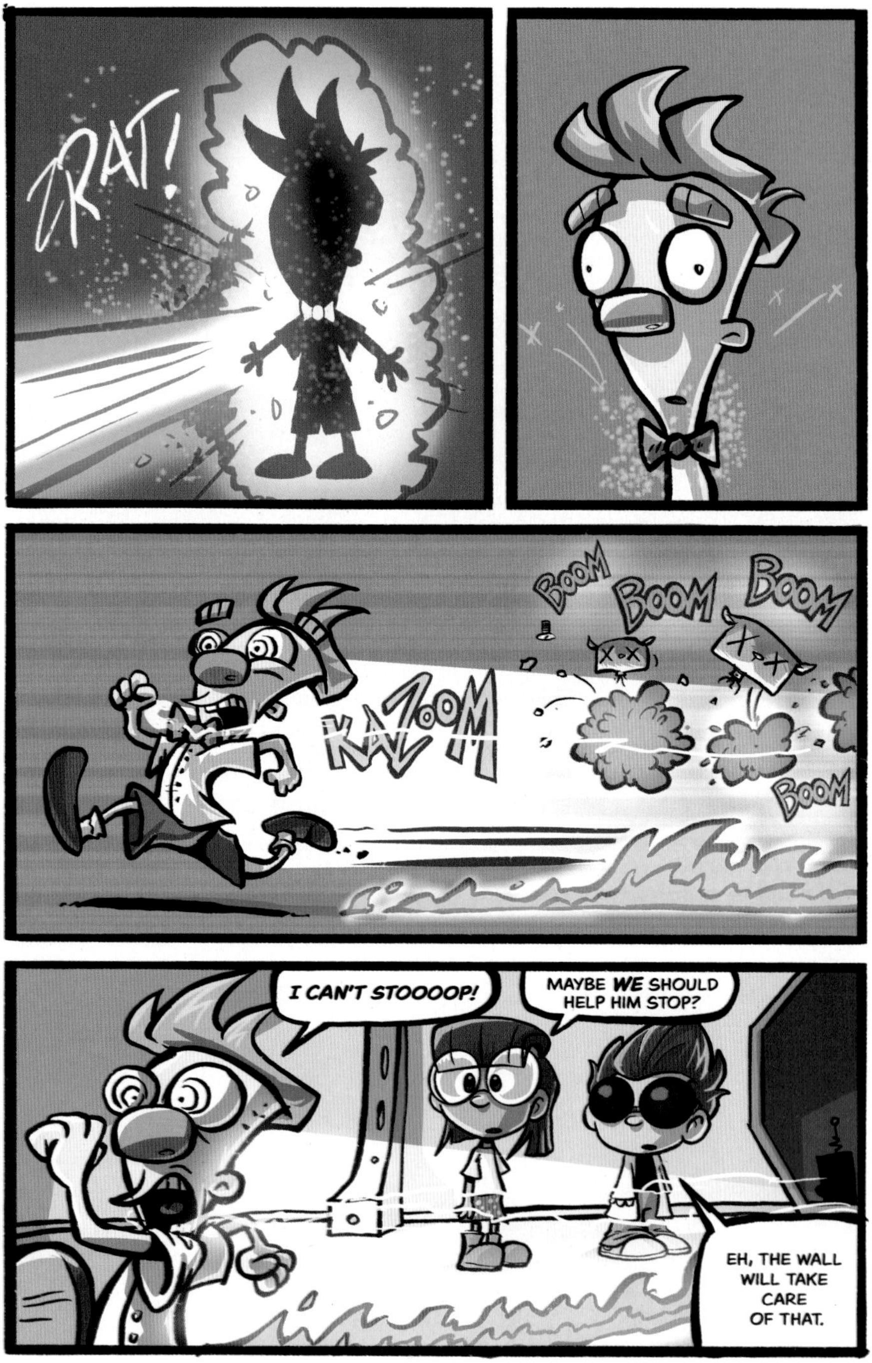
ZRAT!
BOOM
BOOM
BOOM
KAZOOM
BOOM
I CAN'T STOOOOP!
MAYBE WE SHOULD HELP HIM STOP?
EH, THE WALL WILL TAKE CARE OF THAT.

CHAPTER 21

Countdown to Extinction

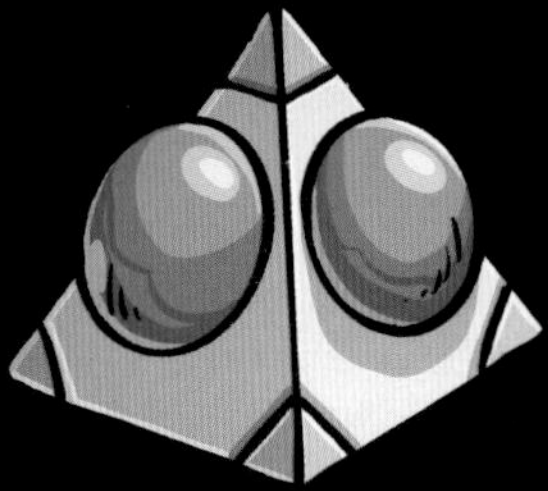

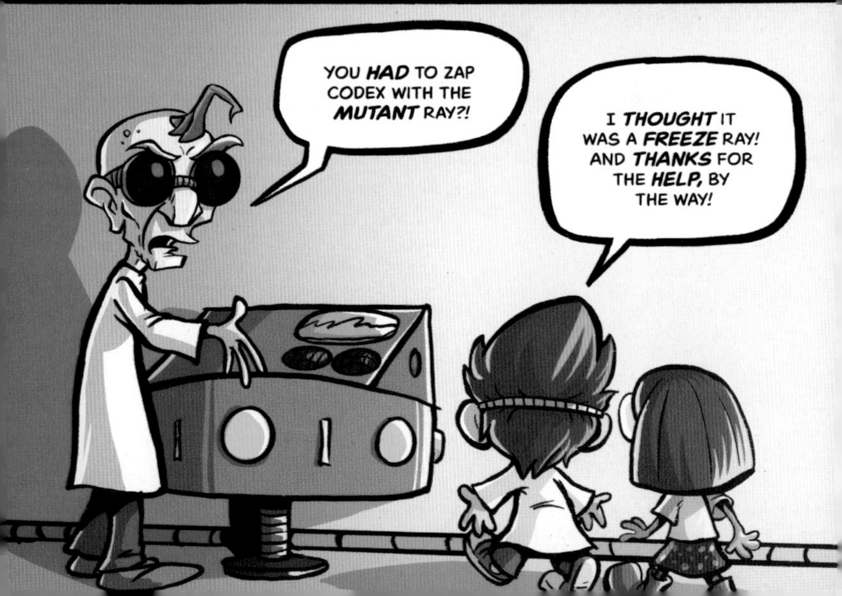
YOU *HAD* TO ZAP CODEX WITH THE *MUTANT* RAY?!
I *THOUGHT* IT WAS A *FREEZE* RAY! AND *THANKS* FOR THE *HELP,* BY THE WAY!

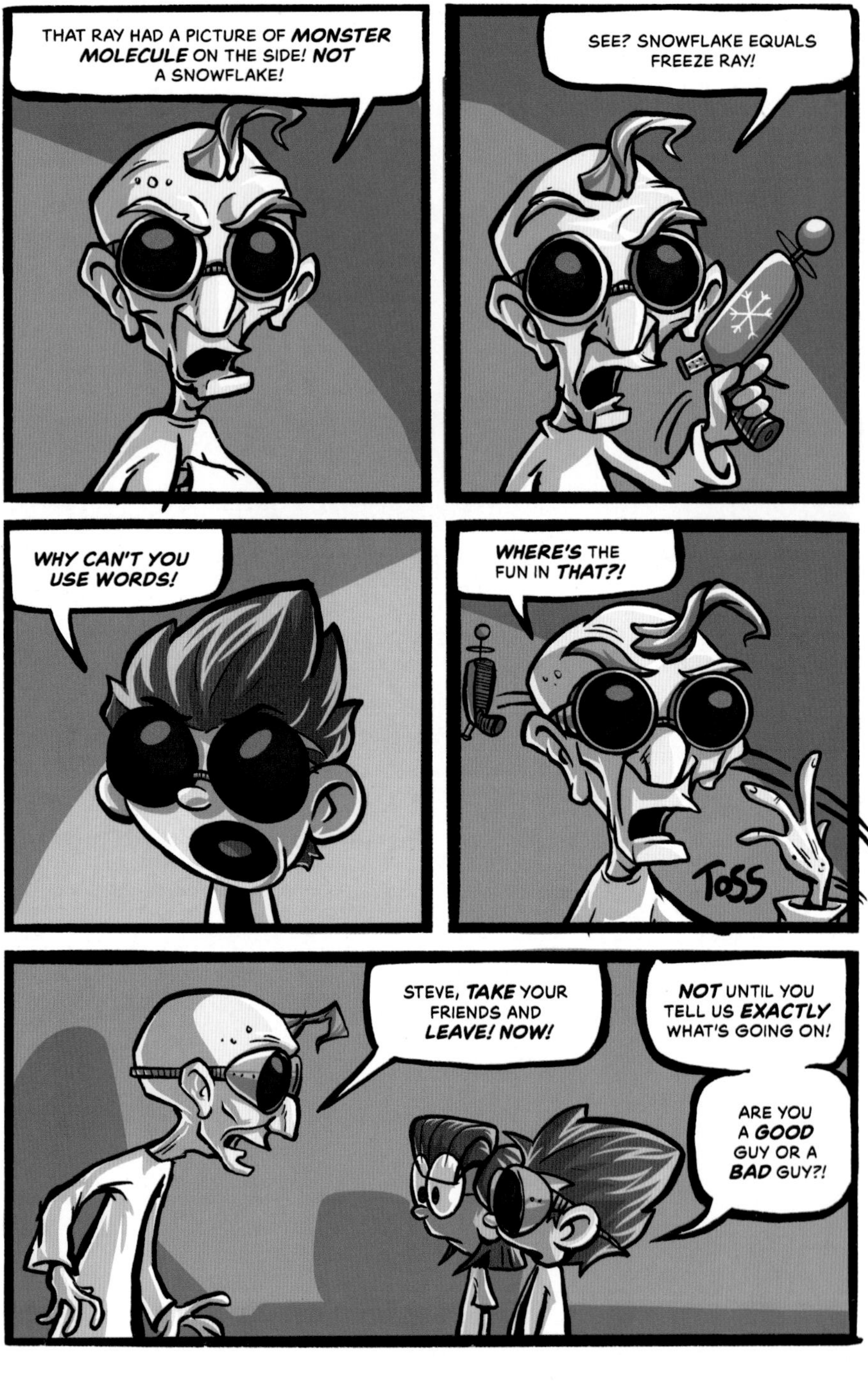
THAT RAY HAD A PICTURE OF **MONSTER MOLECULE** ON THE SIDE! **NOT** A SNOWFLAKE!
SEE? SNOWFLAKE EQUALS FREEZE RAY!
WHY CAN'T YOU USE WORDS!
WHERE'S THE FUN IN ***THAT?!***
TOSS
STEVE, ***TAKE*** YOUR FRIENDS AND ***LEAVE! NOW!***
NOT UNTIL YOU TELL US ***EXACTLY*** WHAT'S GOING ON!
ARE YOU A ***GOOD*** GUY OR A ***BAD*** GUY?!

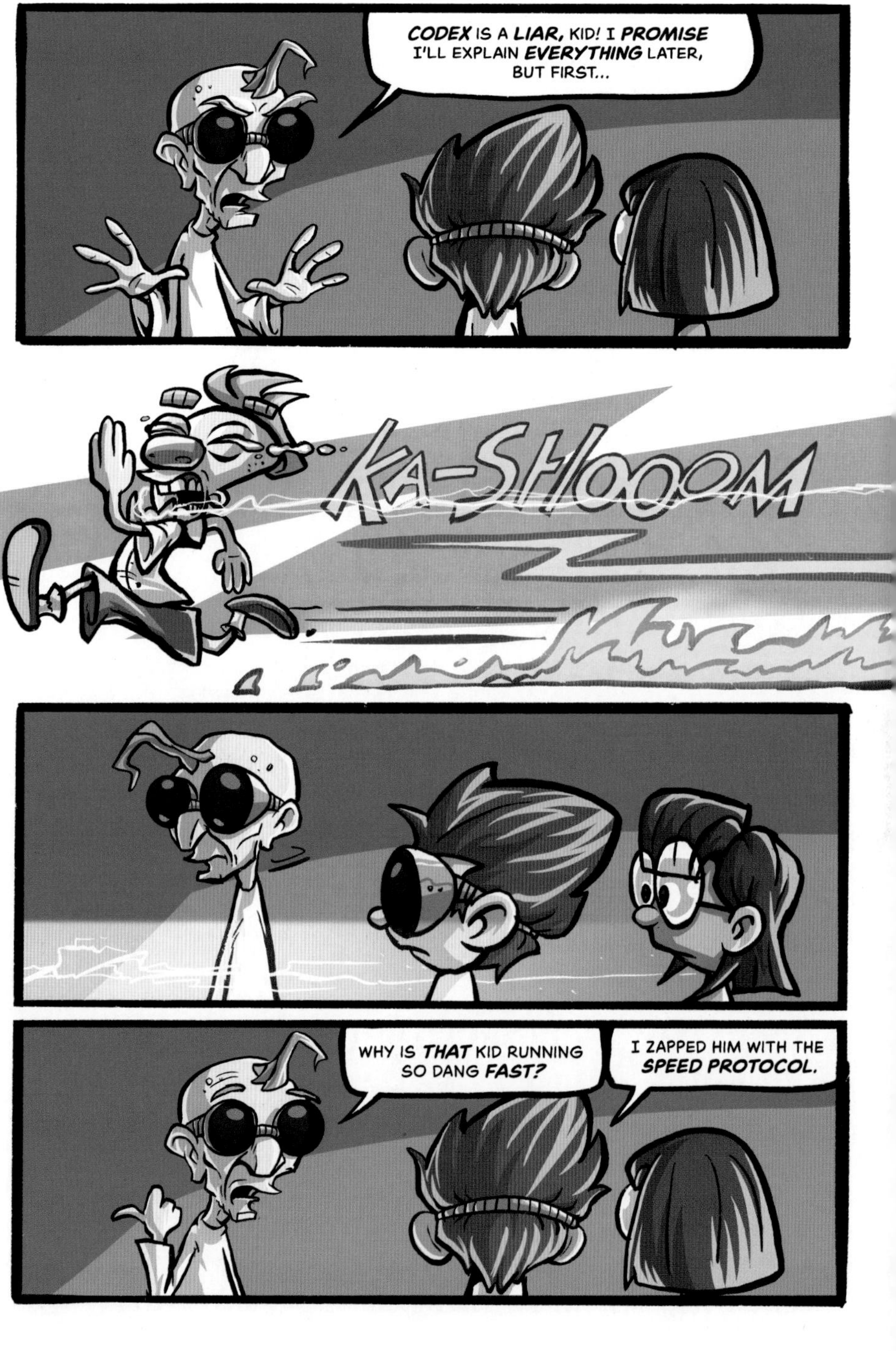
CODEX IS A LIAR, KID! I PROMISE I'LL EXPLAIN EVERYTHING LATER, BUT FIRST...
KA-SHOOOM
WHY IS THAT KID RUNNING SO DANG FAST?
I ZAPPED HIM WITH THE SPEED PROTOCOL.

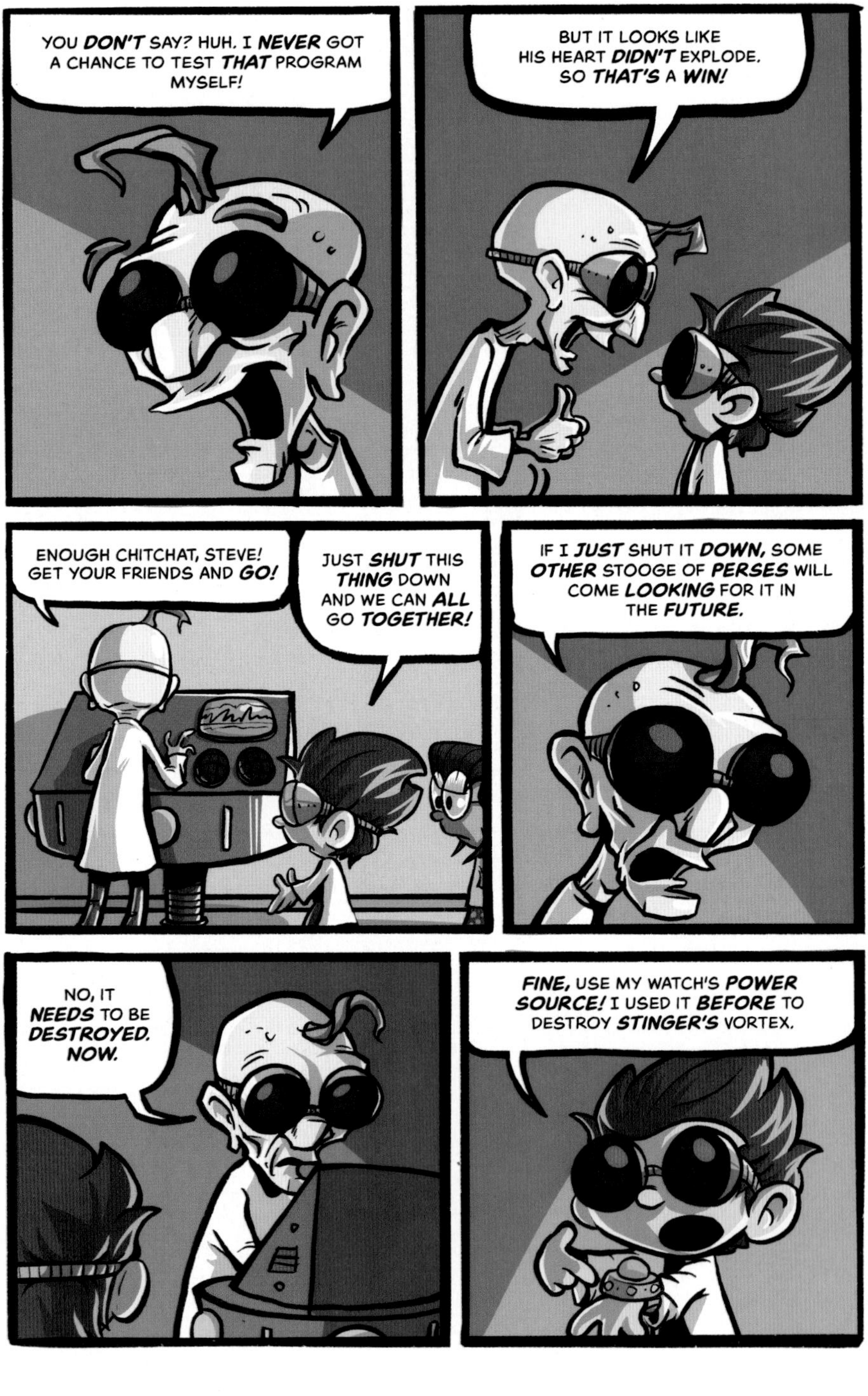
YOU DON'T SAY? HUH. I NEVER GOT A CHANCE TO TEST THAT PROGRAM MYSELF!
BUT IT LOOKS LIKE HIS HEART DIDN'T EXPLODE. SO THAT'S A WIN!
ENOUGH CHITCHAT, STEVE! GET YOUR FRIENDS AND GO!
JUST SHUT THIS THING DOWN AND WE CAN ALL GO TOGETHER!
IF I JUST SHUT IT DOWN, SOME OTHER STOOGE OF PERSES WILL COME LOOKING FOR IT IN THE FUTURE.
NO, IT NEEDS TO BE DESTROYED. NOW.
FINE, USE MY WATCH'S POWER SOURCE! I USED IT BEFORE TO DESTROY STINGER'S VORTEX.

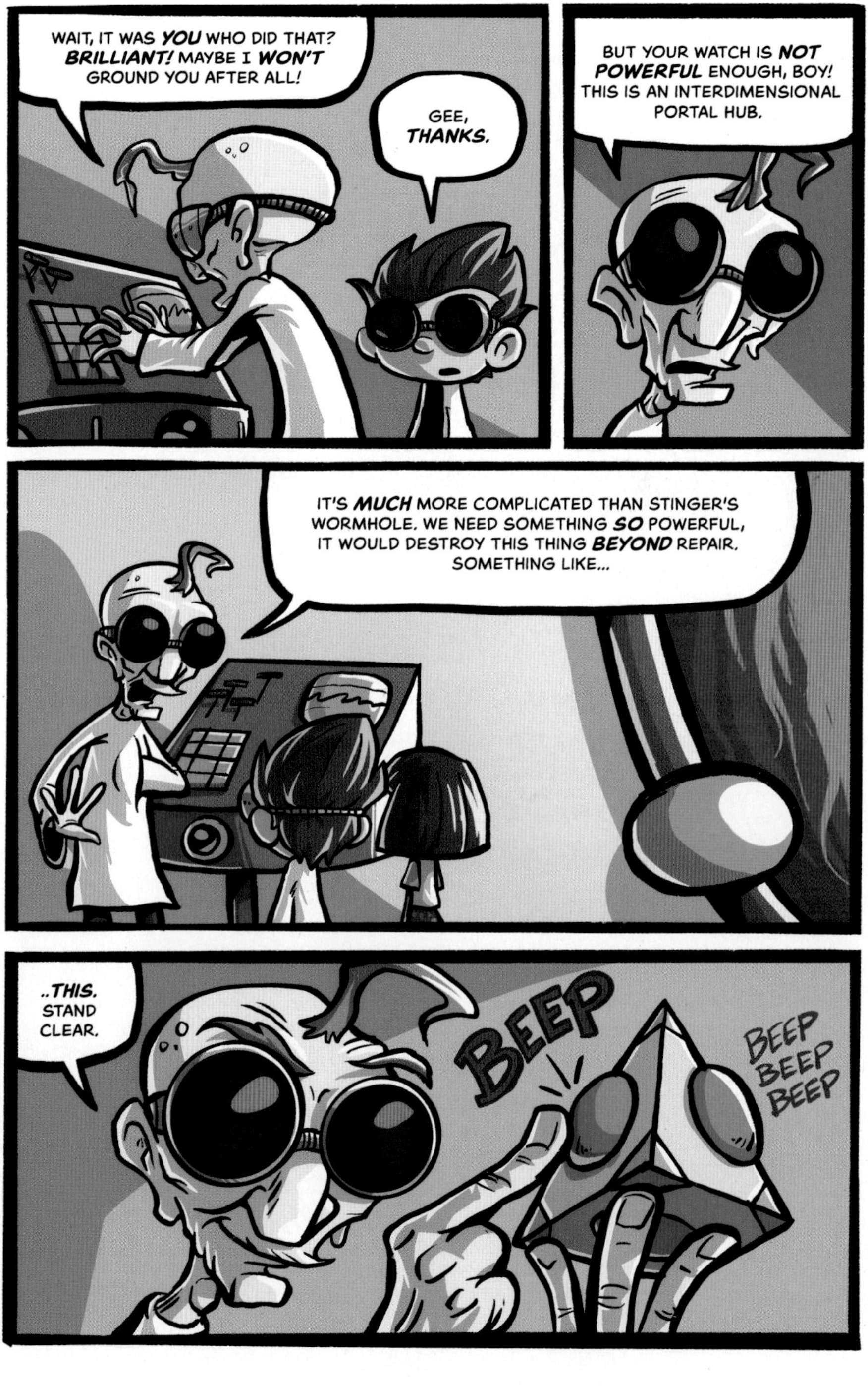

WAIT, IT WAS YOU WHO DID THAT? BRILLIANT! MAYBE I WON'T GROUND YOU AFTER ALL!
GEE, THANKS.
BUT YOUR WATCH IS NOT POWERFUL ENOUGH, BOY! THIS IS AN INTERDIMENSIONAL PORTAL HUB.
IT'S MUCH MORE COMPLICATED THAN STINGER'S WORMHOLE. WE NEED SOMETHING SO POWERFUL, IT WOULD DESTROY THIS THING BEYOND REPAIR. SOMETHING LIKE...
..THIS. STAND CLEAR.
BEEP
BEEP BEEP BEEP

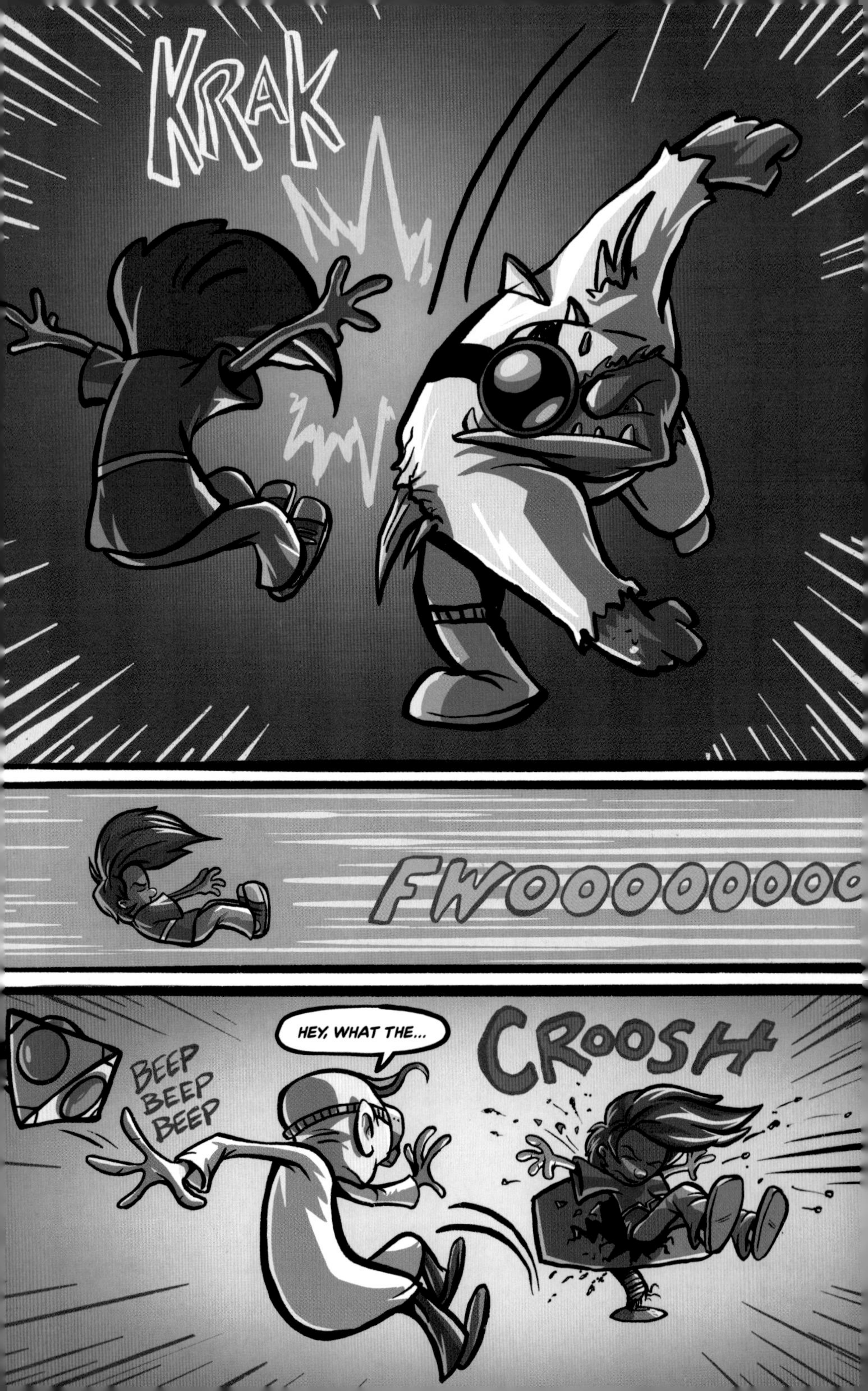
KRAK
FWOOOOOOOO
BEEP BEEP BEEP
HEY, WHAT THE...
CROOSH

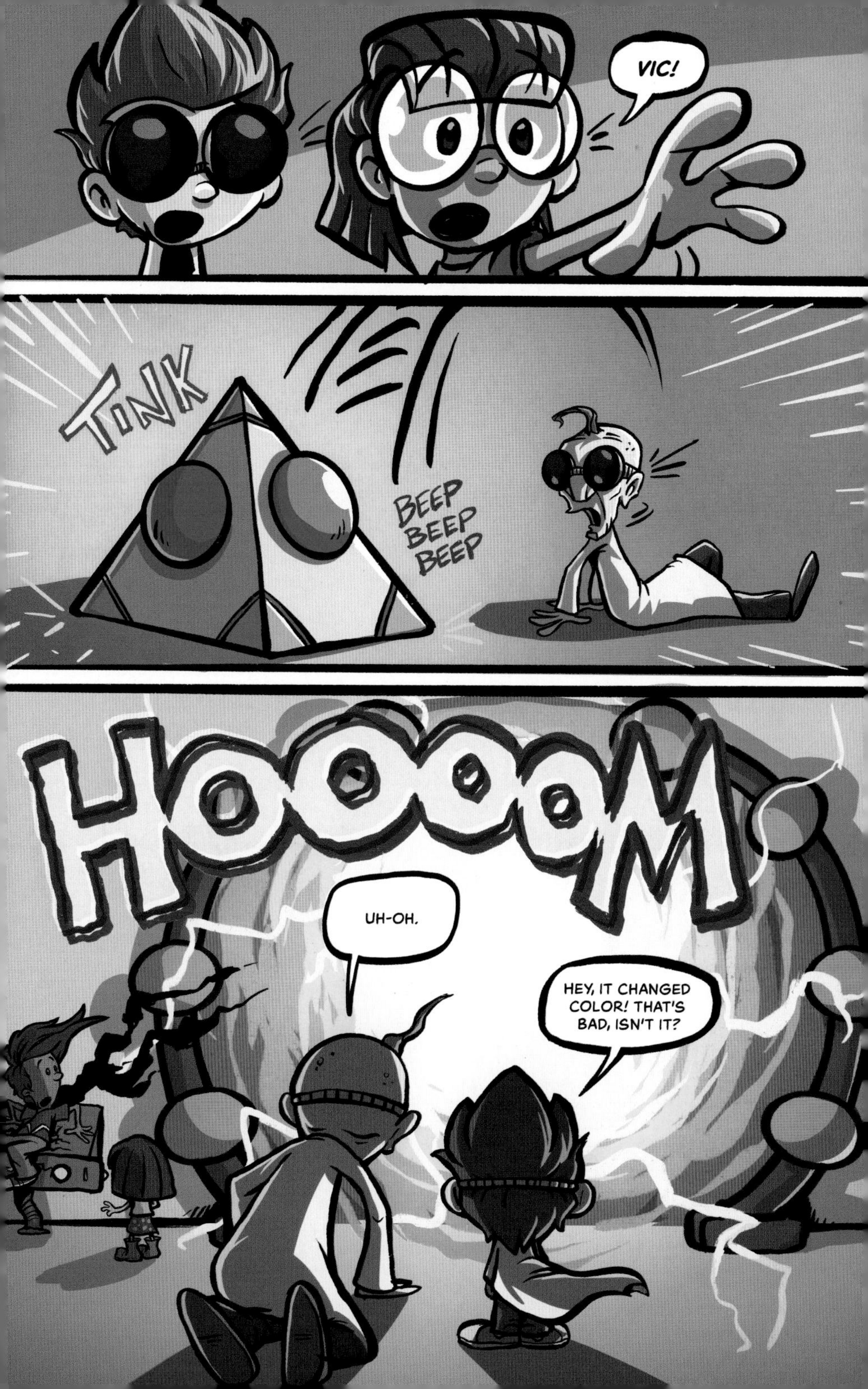
VIC!
TINK
BEEP BEEP BEEP
HOOOOM!
UH-OH.
HEY, IT CHANGED COLOR! THAT'S BAD, ISN'T IT?

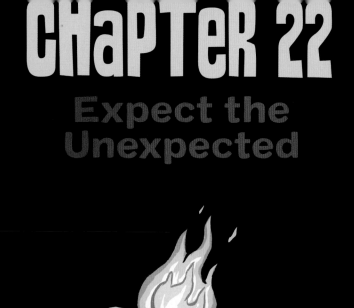

CHAPTER 22

Expect the Unexpected

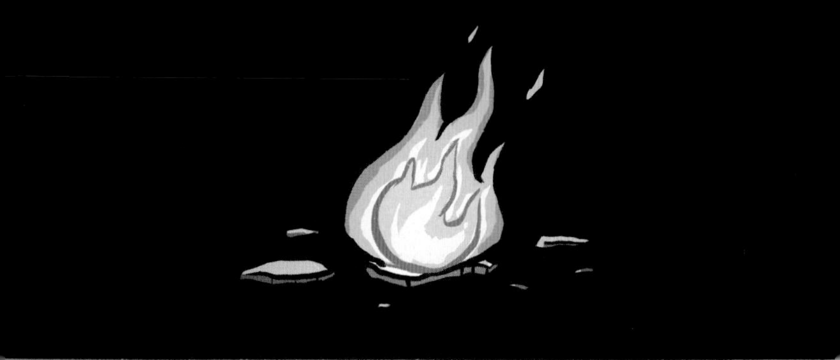

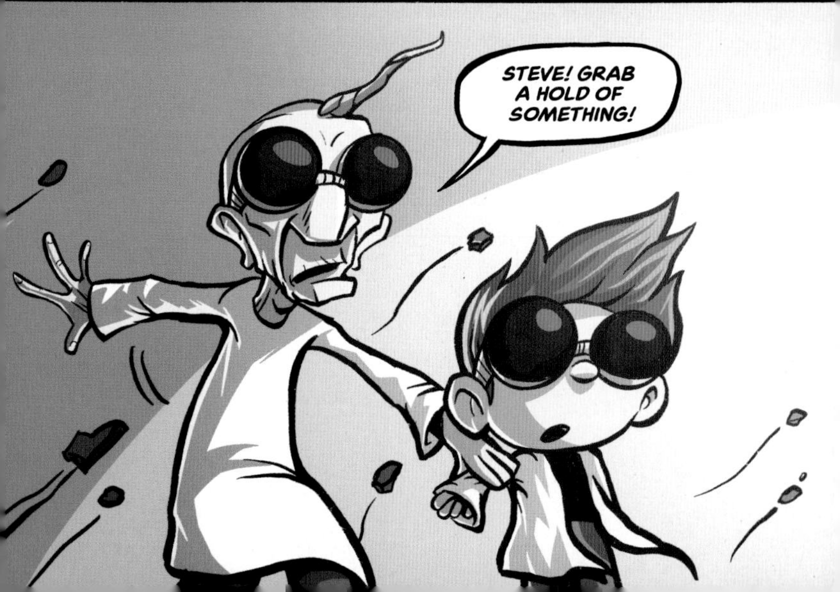
STEVE! GRAB A HOLD OF SOMETHING!

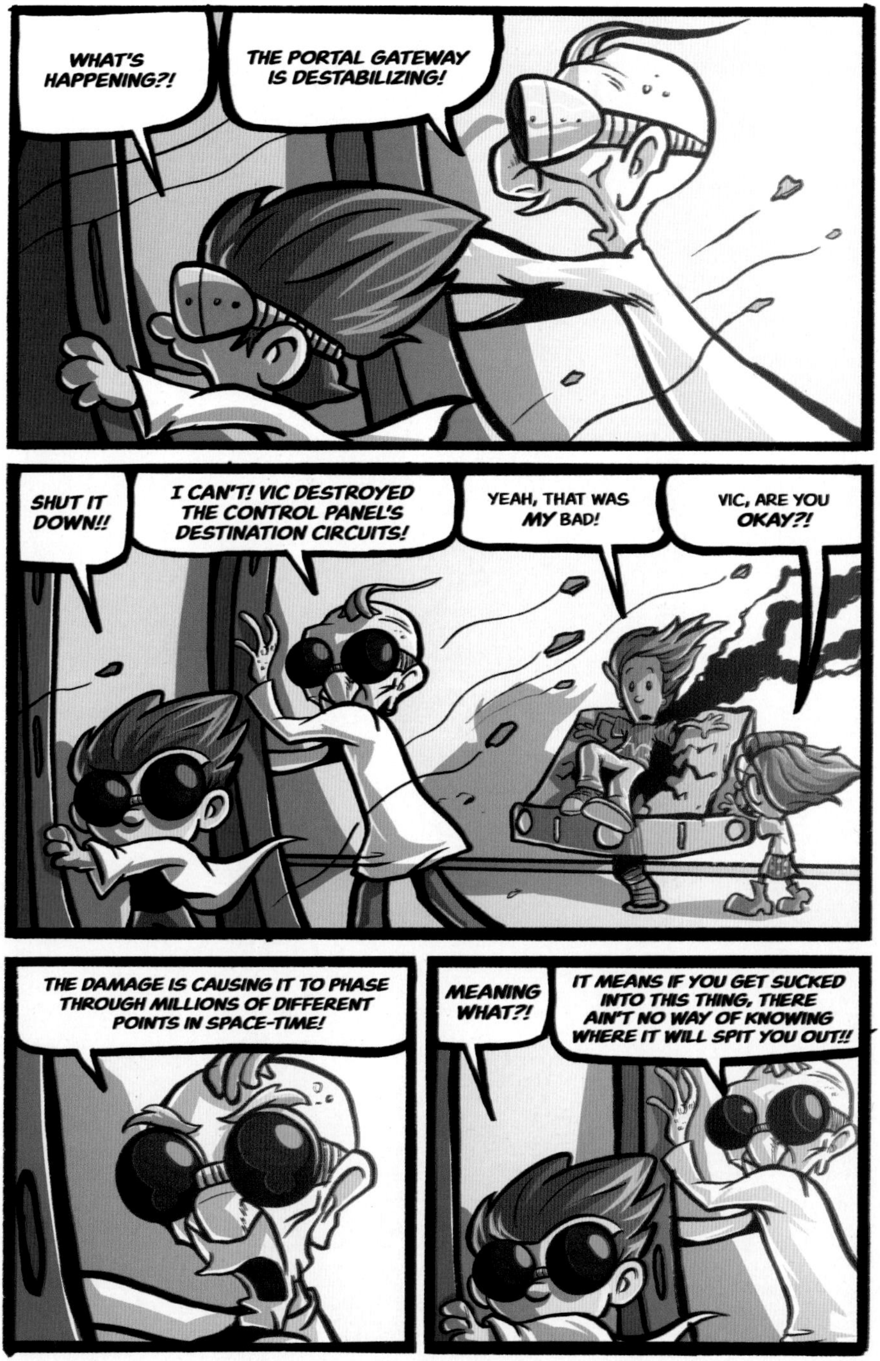
WHAT'S HAPPENING?!
THE PORTAL GATEWAY IS DESTABILIZING!
SHUT IT DOWN!!
I CAN'T! VIC DESTROYED THE CONTROL PANEL'S DESTINATION CIRCUITS!
YEAH, THAT WAS MY BAD!
VIC, ARE YOU OKAY?!
THE DAMAGE IS CAUSING IT TO PHASE THROUGH MILLIONS OF DIFFERENT POINTS IN SPACE-TIME!
MEANING WHAT?!
IT MEANS IF YOU GET SUCKED INTO THIS THING, THERE AIN'T NO WAY OF KNOWING WHERE IT WILL SPIT YOU OUT!!

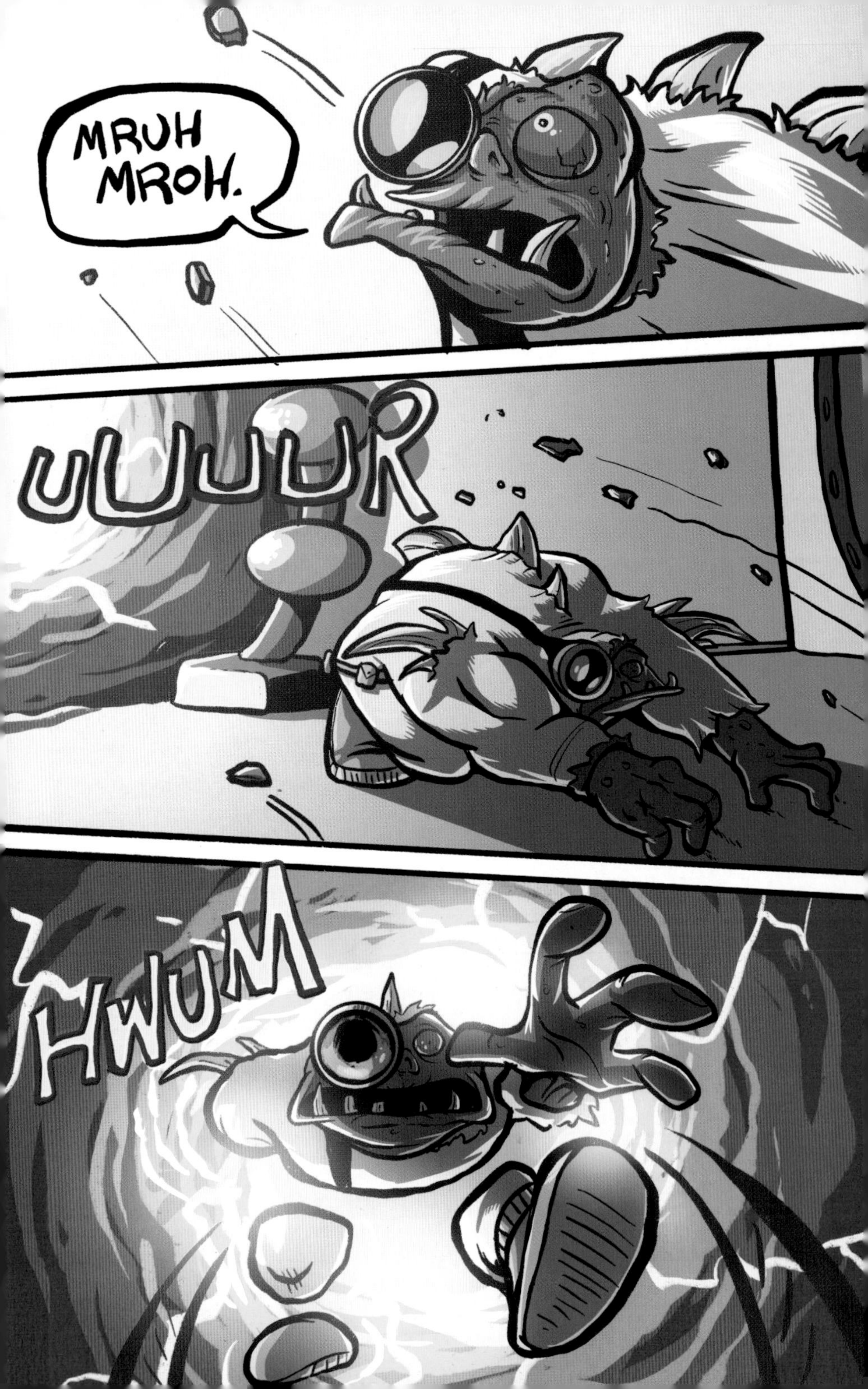
MRUH MROH.
UUUUR
HWUM

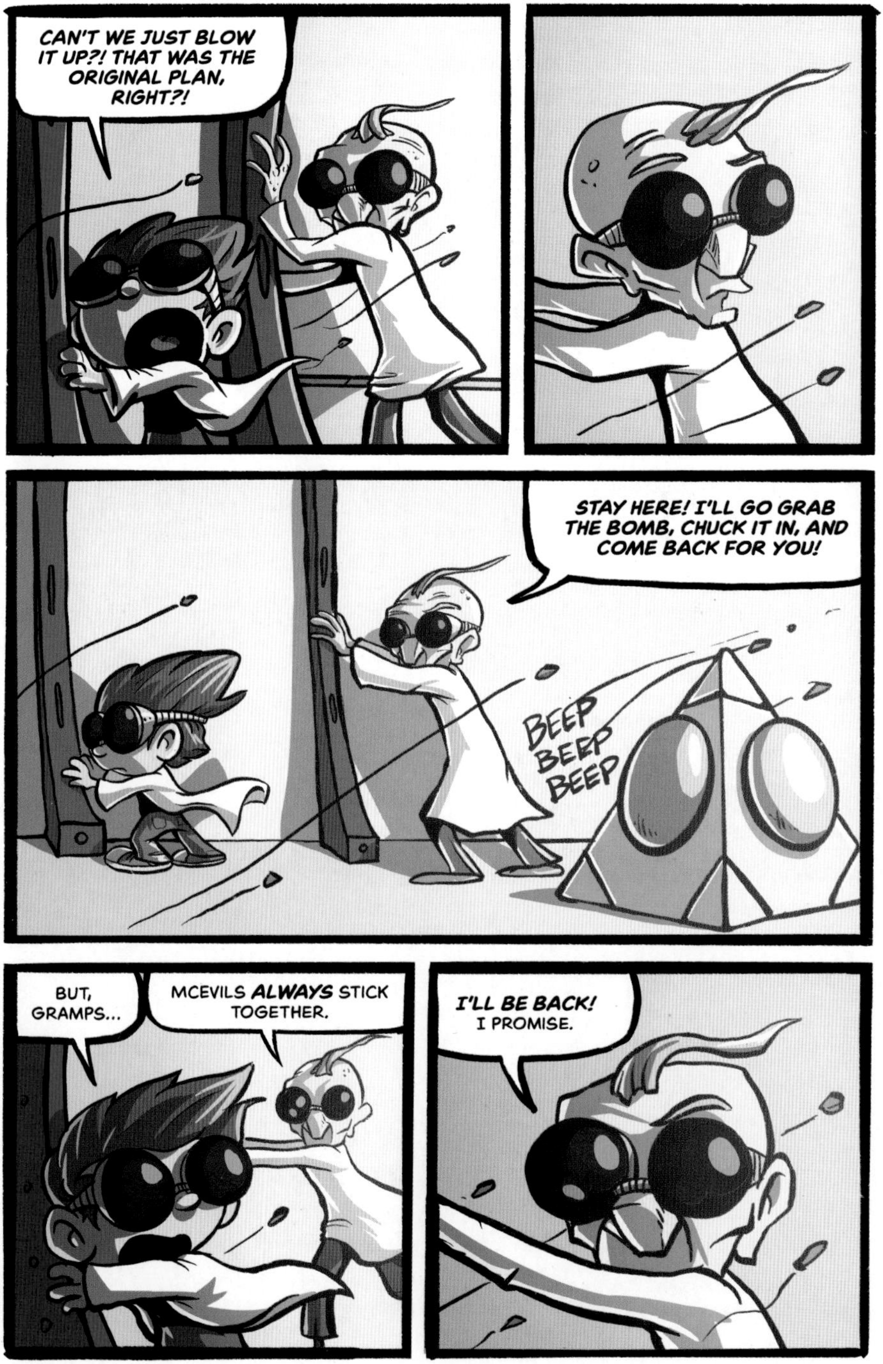

CAN'T WE JUST BLOW IT UP?! THAT WAS THE ORIGINAL PLAN, RIGHT?!
STAY HERE! I'LL GO GRAB THE BOMB, CHUCK IT IN, AND COME BACK FOR YOU!
BEEP BEEP BEEP
BUT, GRAMPS...
MCEVILS ALWAYS STICK TOGETHER.
I'LL BE BACK! I PROMISE.

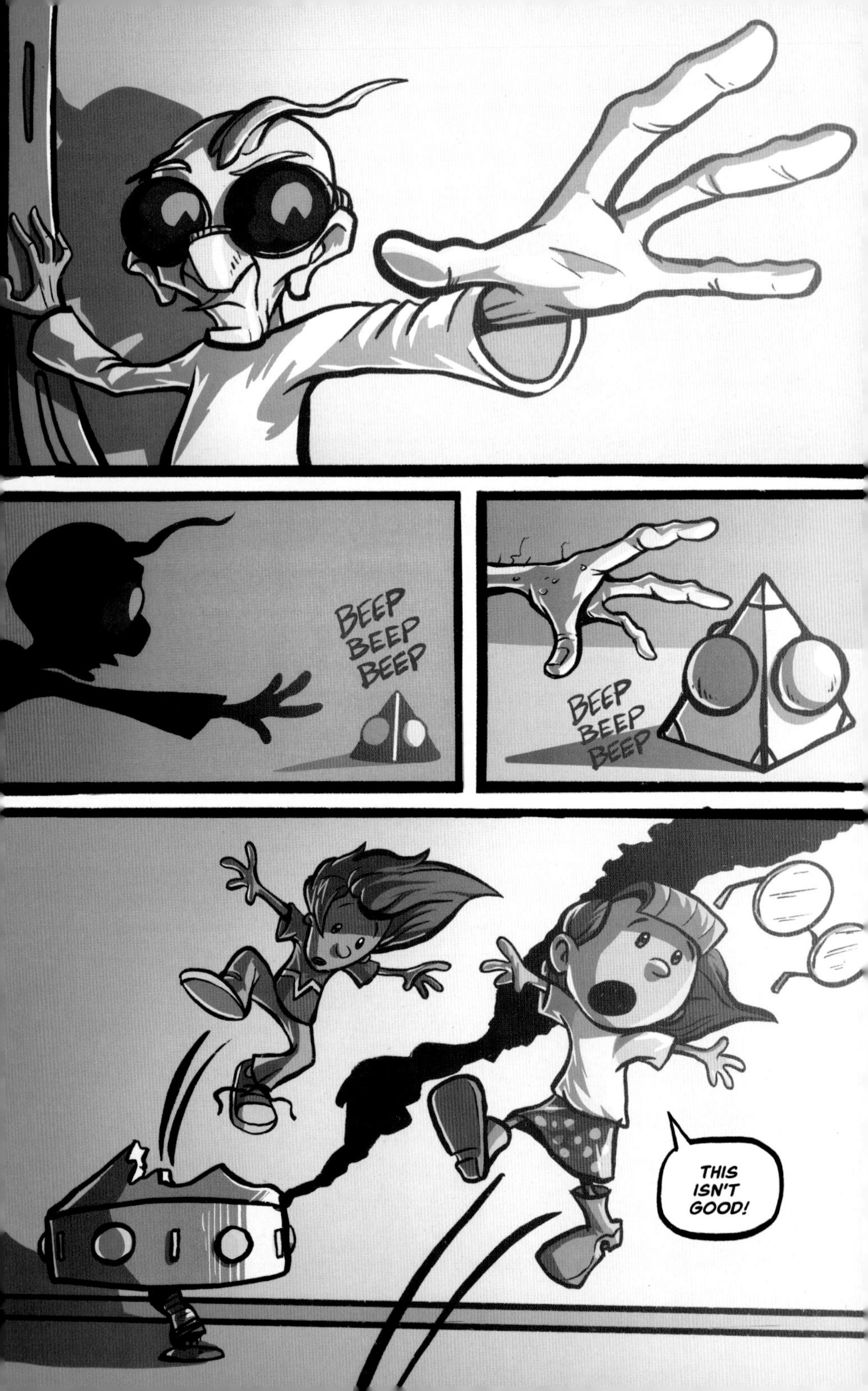
BEEP
BEEP
BEEP
BEEP
BEEP
BEEP
THIS ISN'T GOOD!

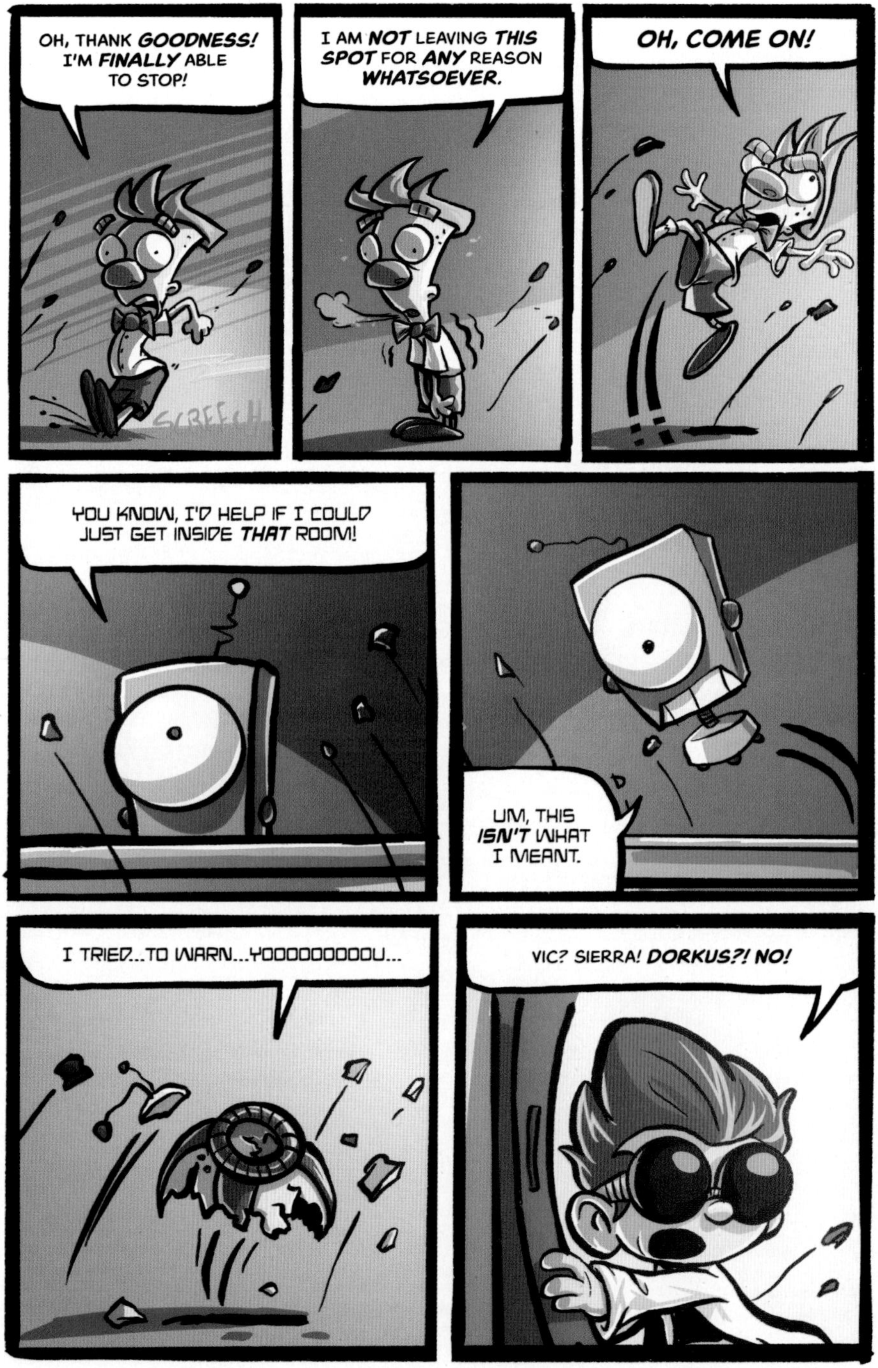
OH, THANK GOODNESS! I'M FINALLY ABLE TO STOP!
SCREECH
I AM NOT LEAVING THIS SPOT FOR ANY REASON WHATSOEVER.
OH, COME ON!
YOU KNOW, I'D HELP IF I COULD JUST GET INSIDE THAT ROOM!
UM, THIS ISN'T WHAT I MEANT.
I TRIED...TO WARN...YOOOOOOOOOU...
VIC? SIERRA! DORKUS?! NO!

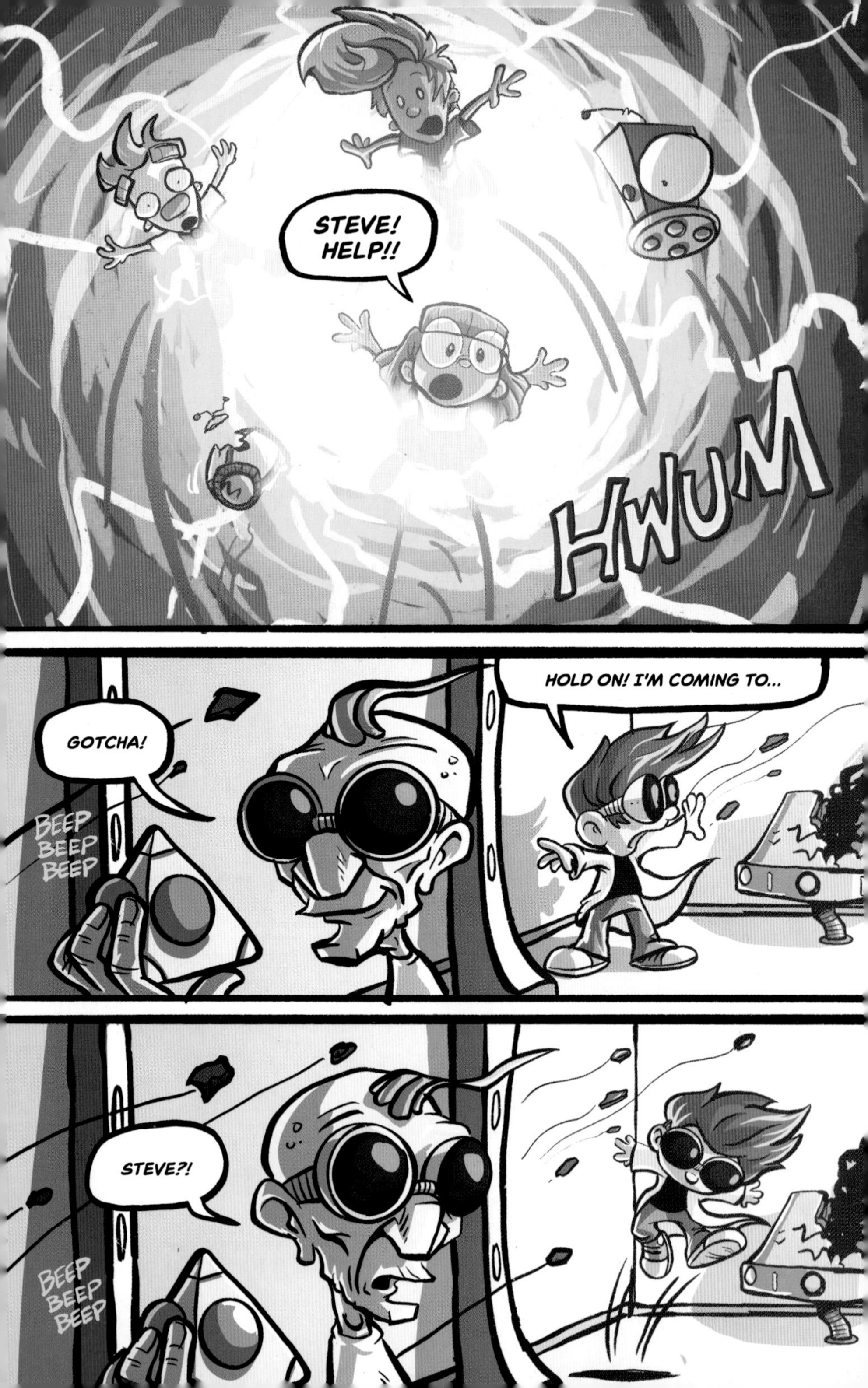

STEVE! HELP!!
HWUM
GOTCHA!
BEEP BEEP BEEP
HOLD ON! I'M COMING TO...
STEVE?!
BEEP BEEP BEEP

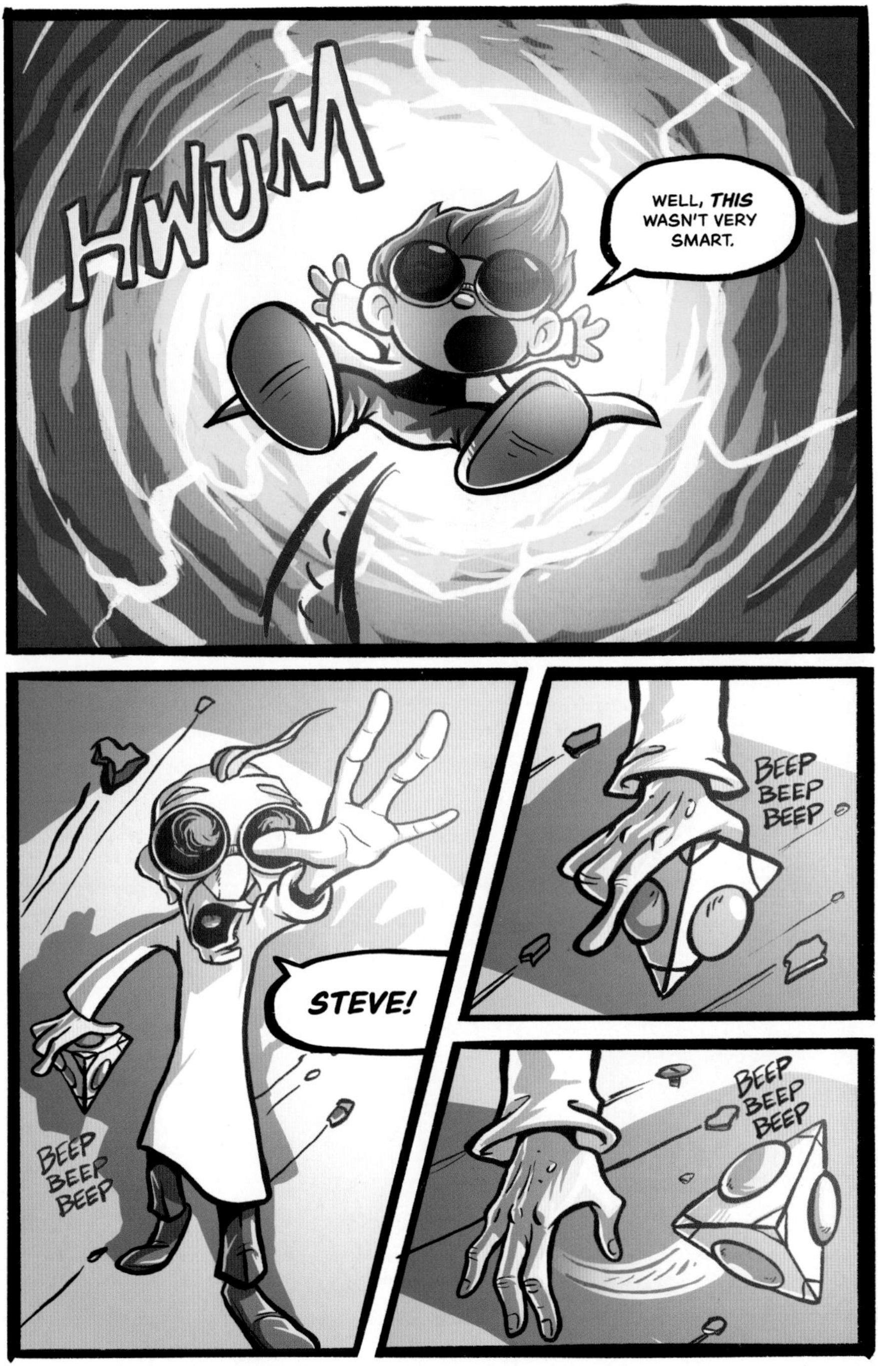
HWUM
WELL, THIS WASN'T VERY SMART.
STEVE!
BEEP BEEP BEEP
BEEP BEEP BEEP
BEEP BEEP BEEP

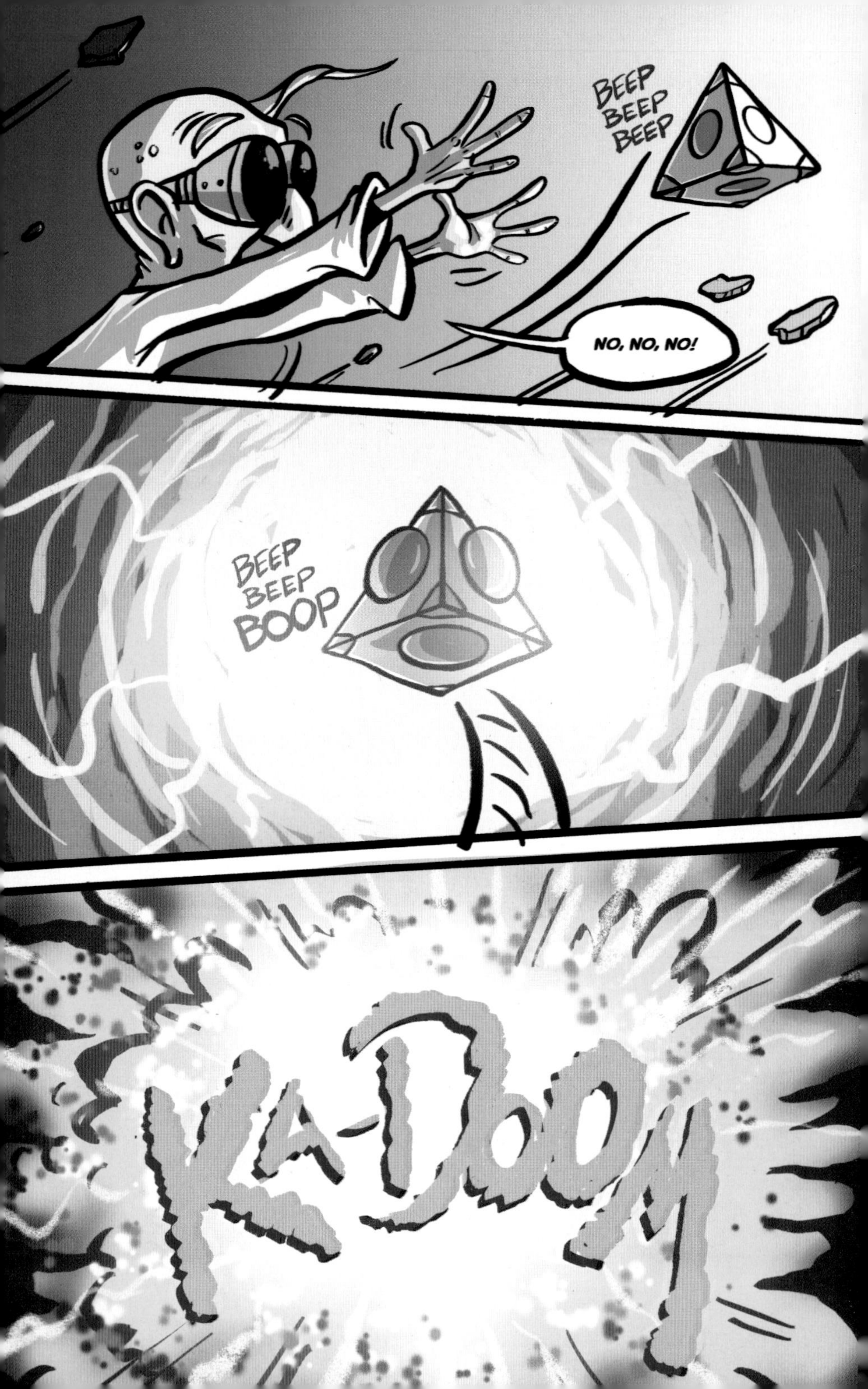
BEEP BEEP BEEP
NO, NO, NO!
BEEP BEEP BOOP
KA-DOOM

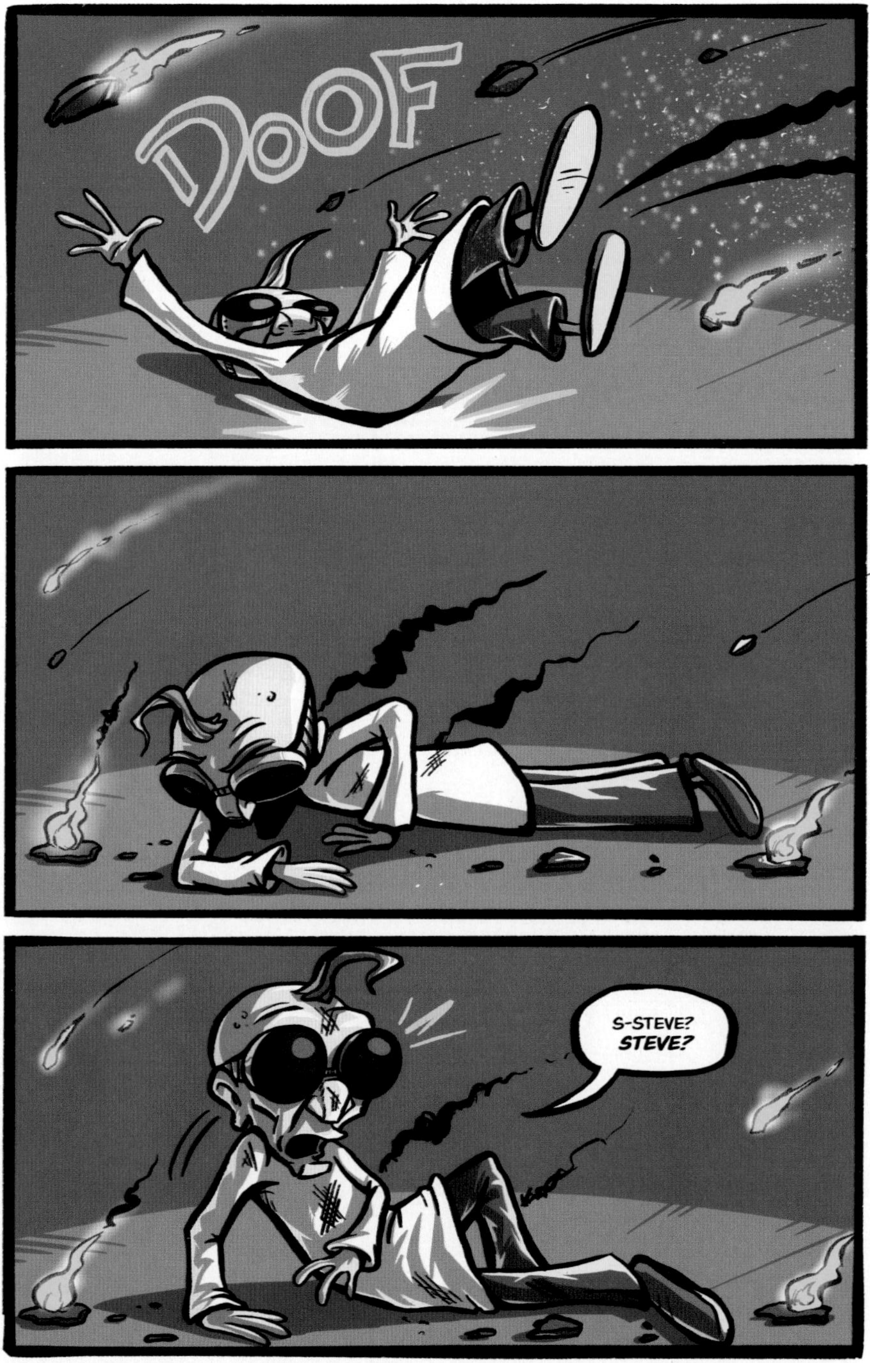
DOOF
S-STEVE? STEVE?

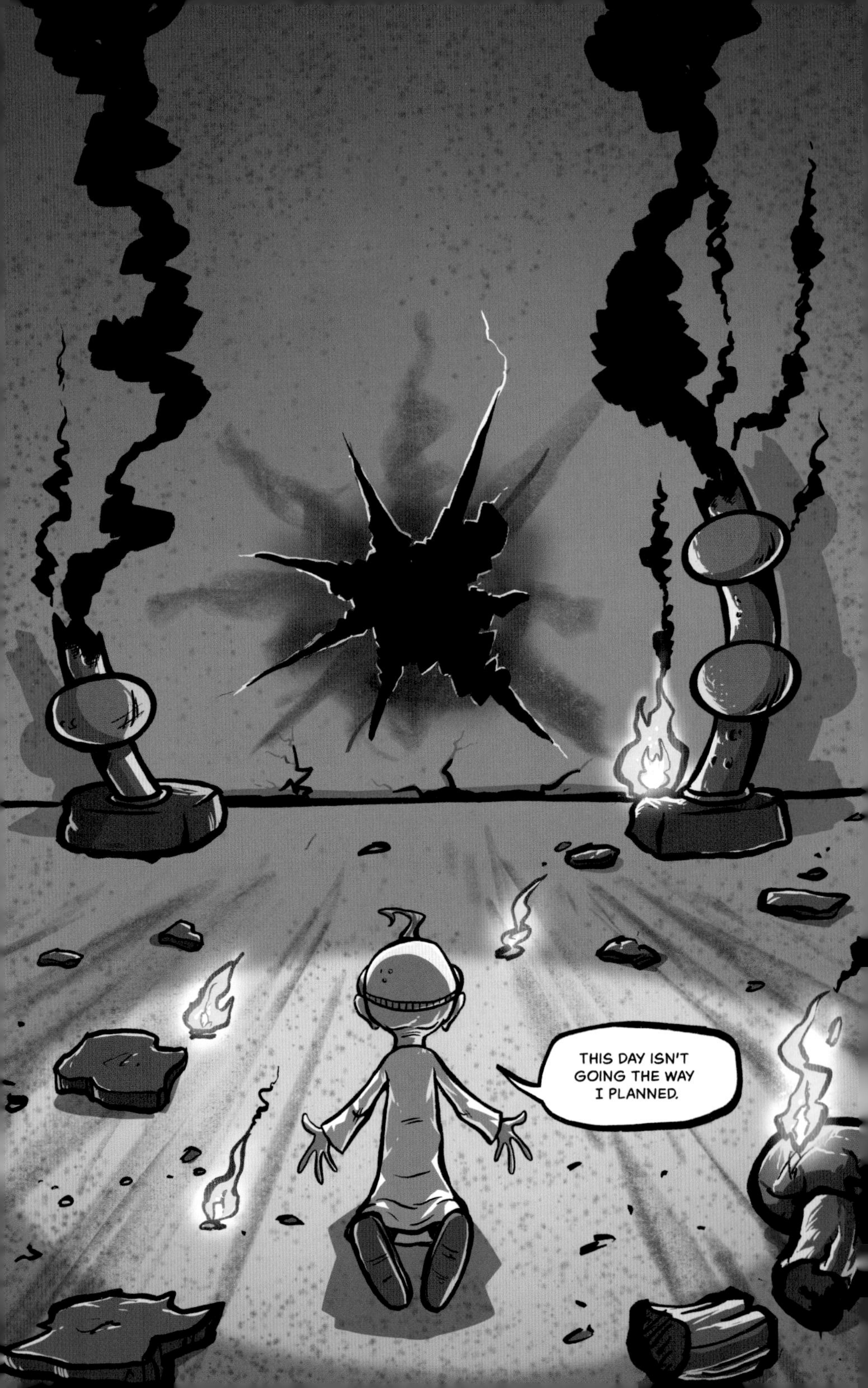
THIS DAY ISN'T GOING THE WAY I PLANNED.

CHAPTER 23

The Last Retort

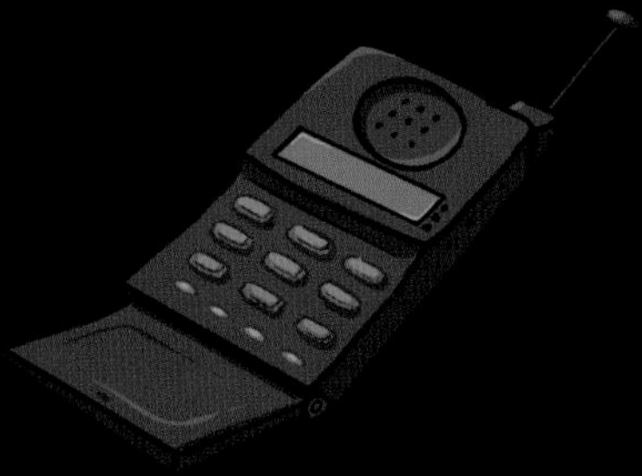

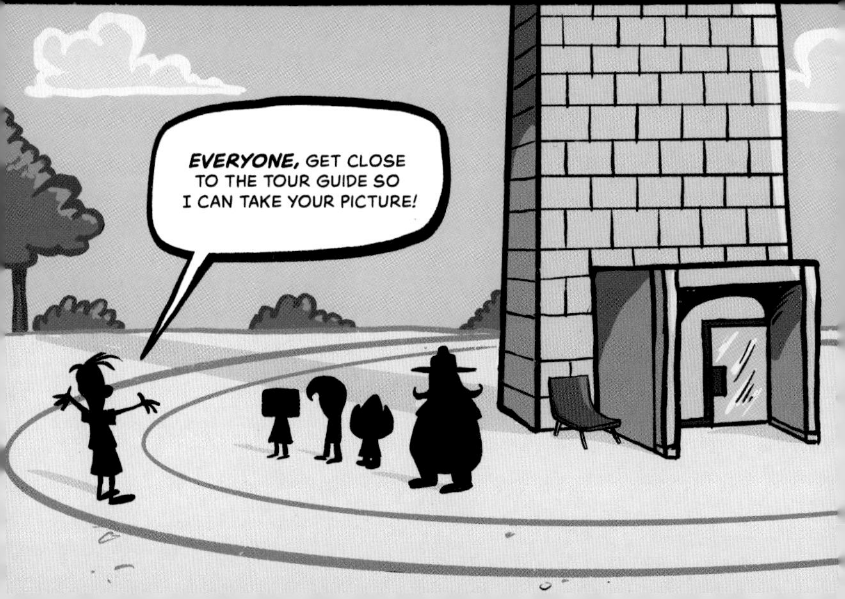
EVERYONE, GET CLOSE TO THE TOUR GUIDE SO I CAN TAKE YOUR PICTURE!

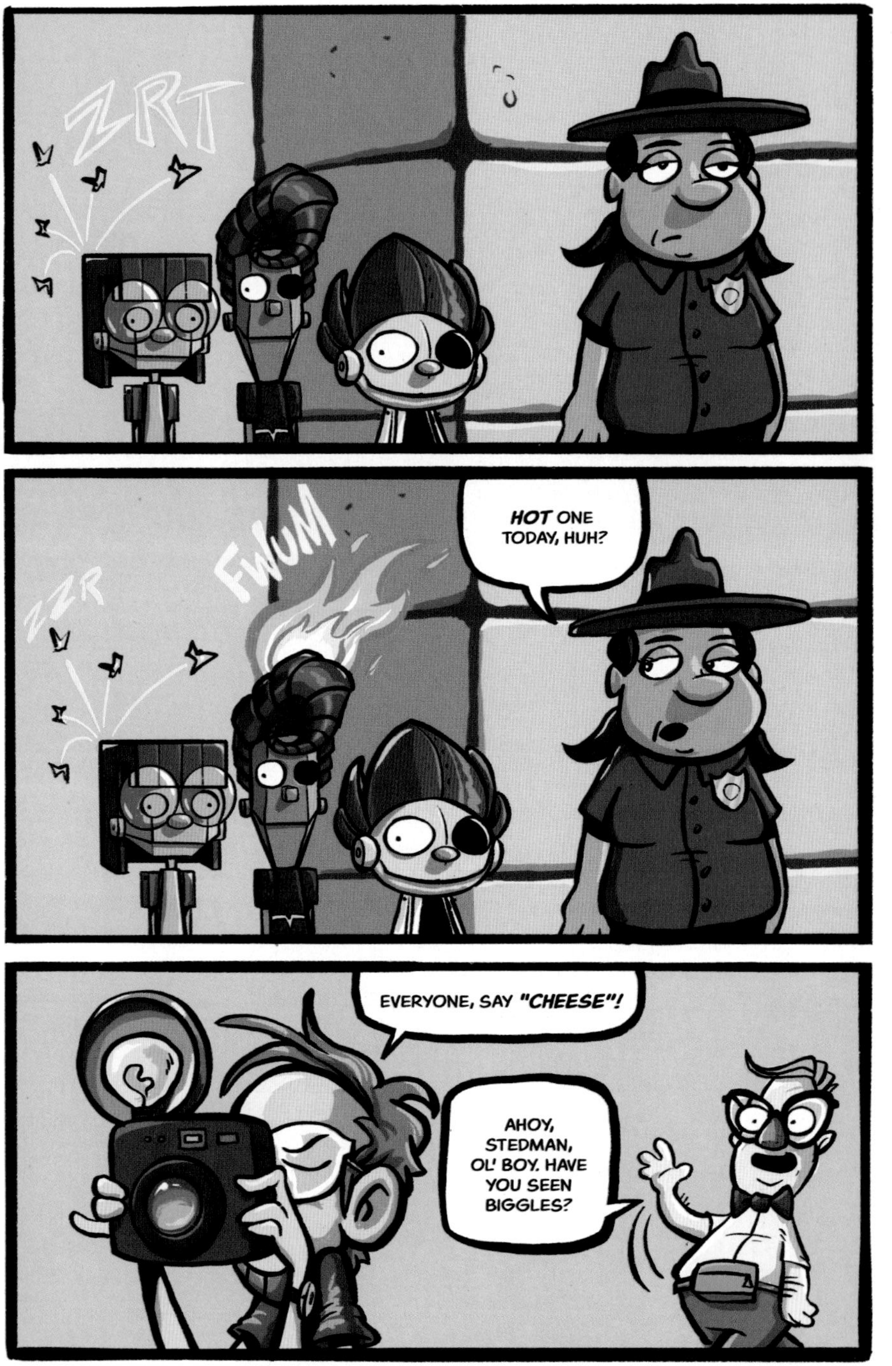
ZRT
ZZR
FWUM
HOT ONE TODAY, HUH?
EVERYONE, SAY "CHEESE"!
AHOY, STEDMAN, OL' BOY. HAVE YOU SEEN BIGGLES?

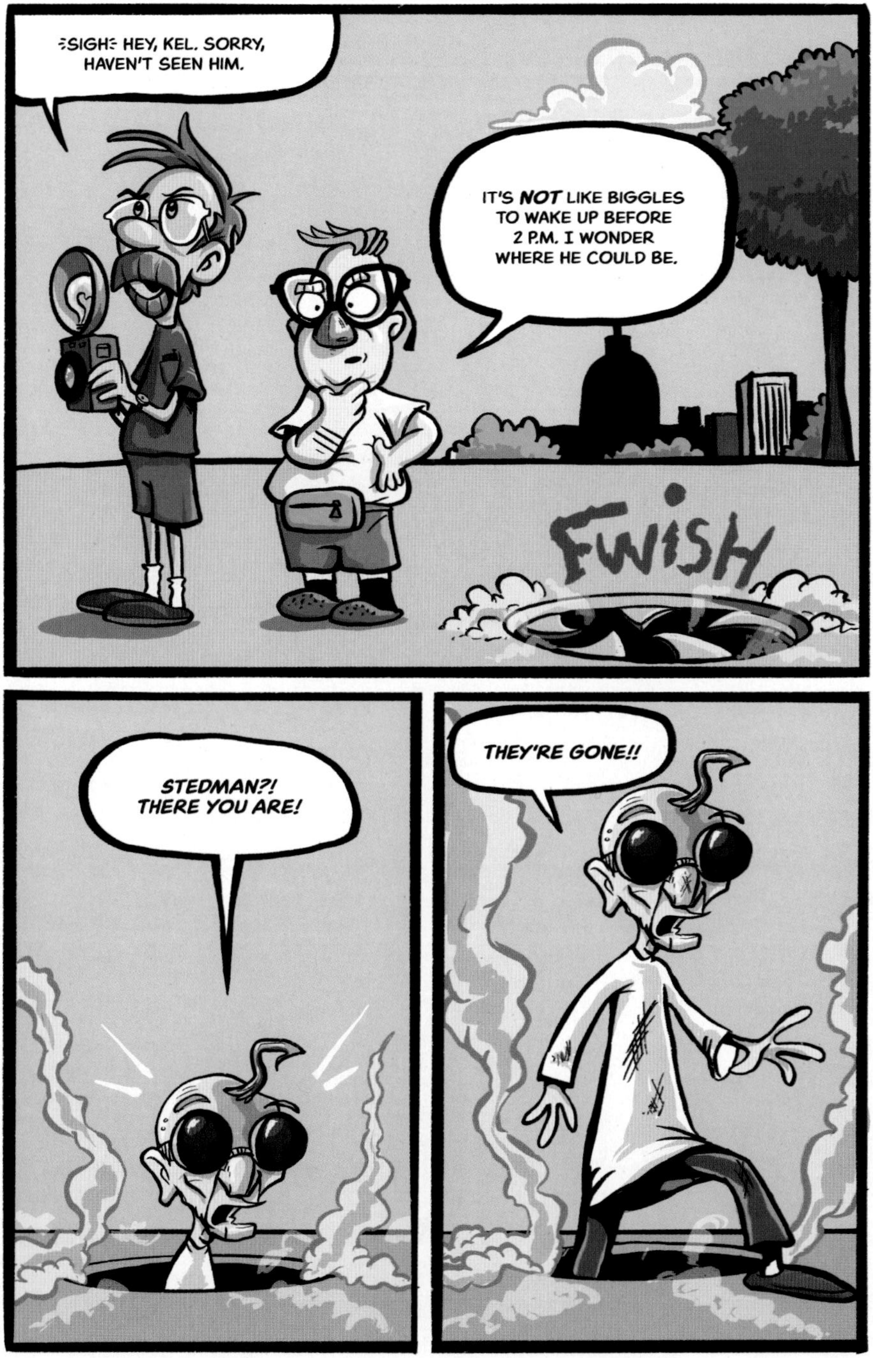

=SIGH= HEY, KEL. SORRY, HAVEN'T SEEN HIM.
IT'S NOT LIKE BIGGLES TO WAKE UP BEFORE 2 P.M. I WONDER WHERE HE COULD BE.
FWISH
STEDMAN?! THERE YOU ARE!
THEY'RE GONE!!

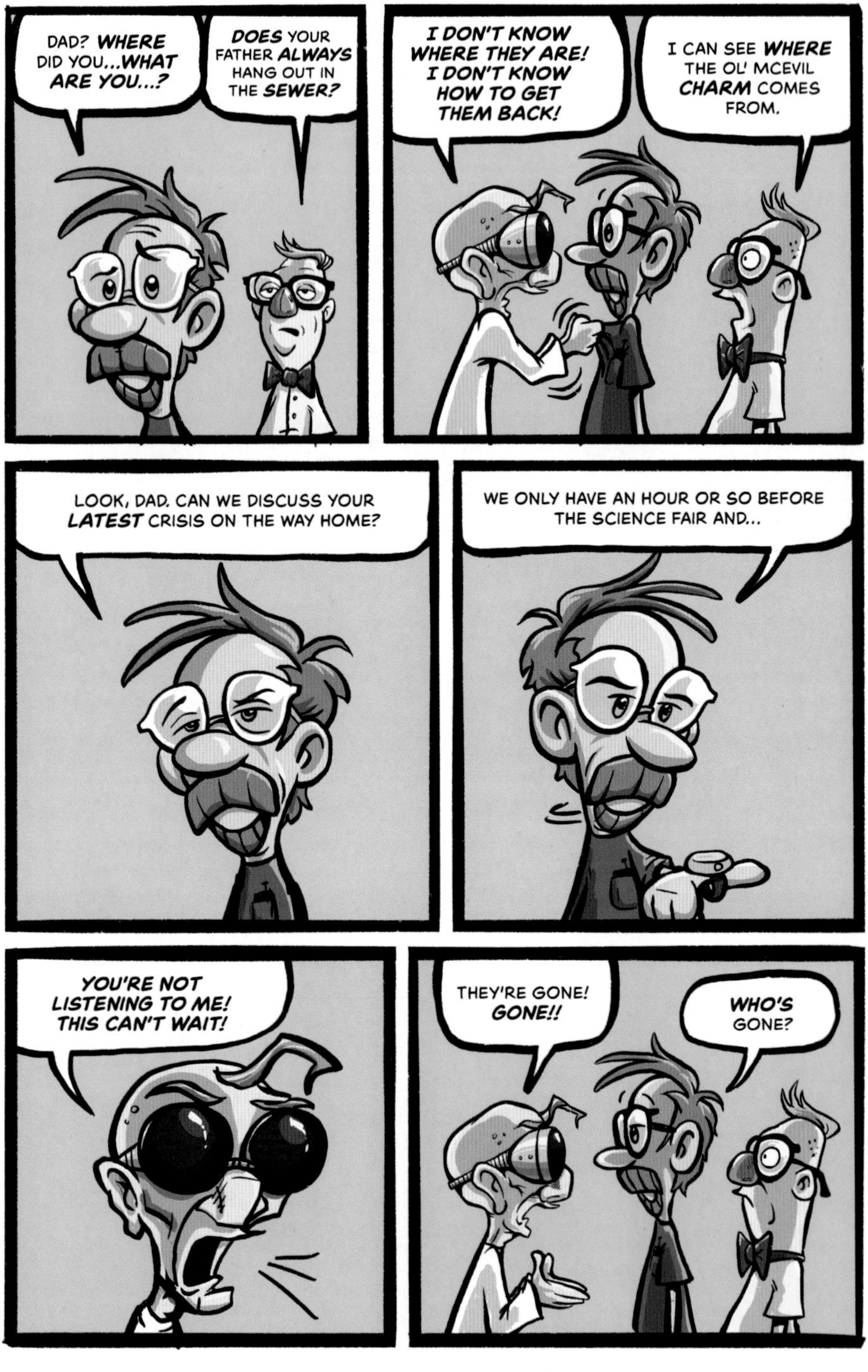
DAD? WHERE DID YOU...WHAT ARE YOU...?
DOES YOUR FATHER ALWAYS HANG OUT IN THE SEWER?
I DON'T KNOW WHERE THEY ARE! I DON'T KNOW HOW TO GET THEM BACK!
I CAN SEE WHERE THE OL' MCEVIL CHARM COMES FROM.
LOOK, DAD, CAN WE DISCUSS YOUR LATEST CRISIS ON THE WAY HOME?
WE ONLY HAVE AN HOUR OR SO BEFORE THE SCIENCE FAIR AND...
YOU'RE NOT LISTENING TO ME! THIS CAN'T WAIT!
THEY'RE GONE! GONE!!
WHO'S GONE?

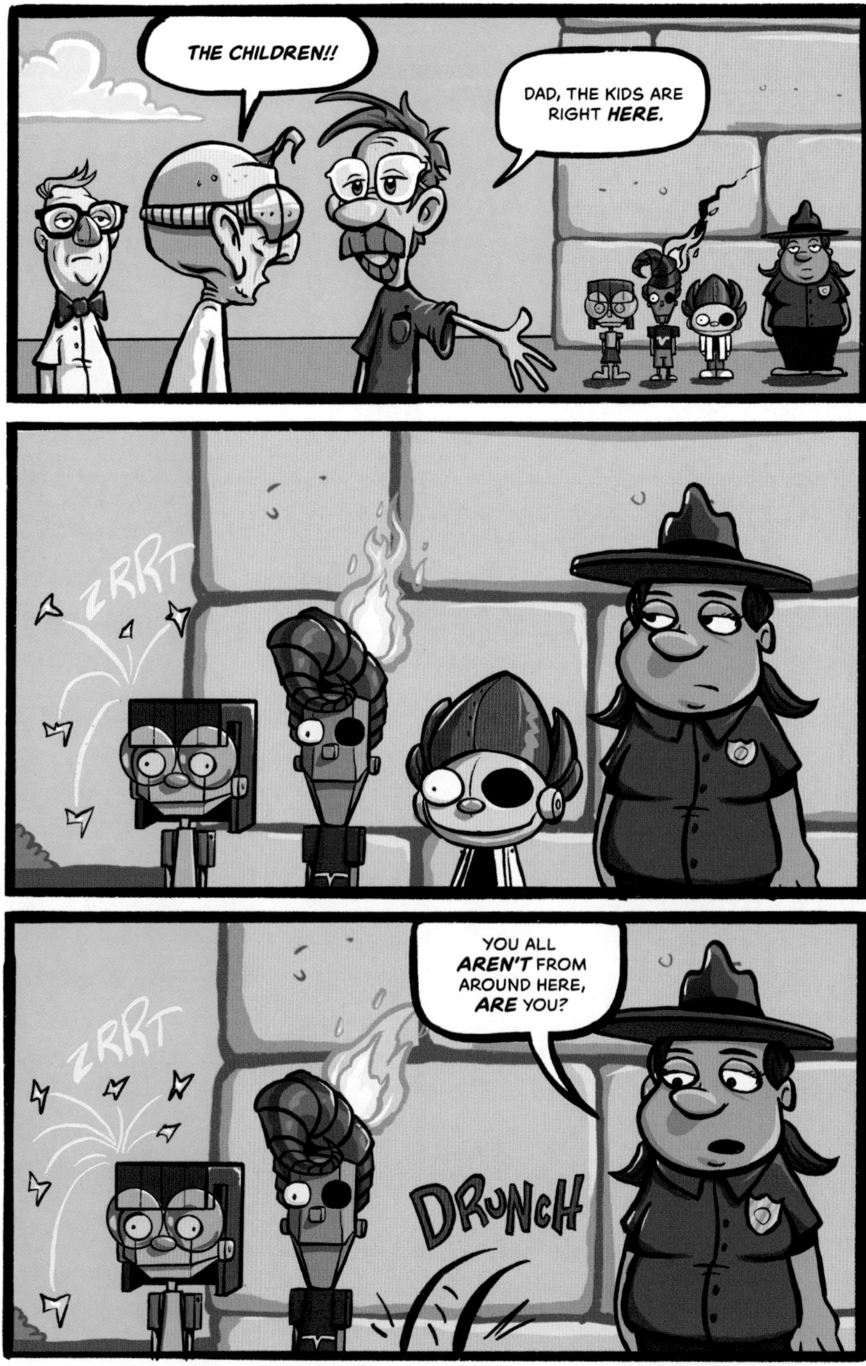
THE CHILDREN!!
DAD, THE KIDS ARE RIGHT HERE.
ZRRT
ZRRT
YOU ALL AREN'T FROM AROUND HERE, ARE YOU?
DRUNCH

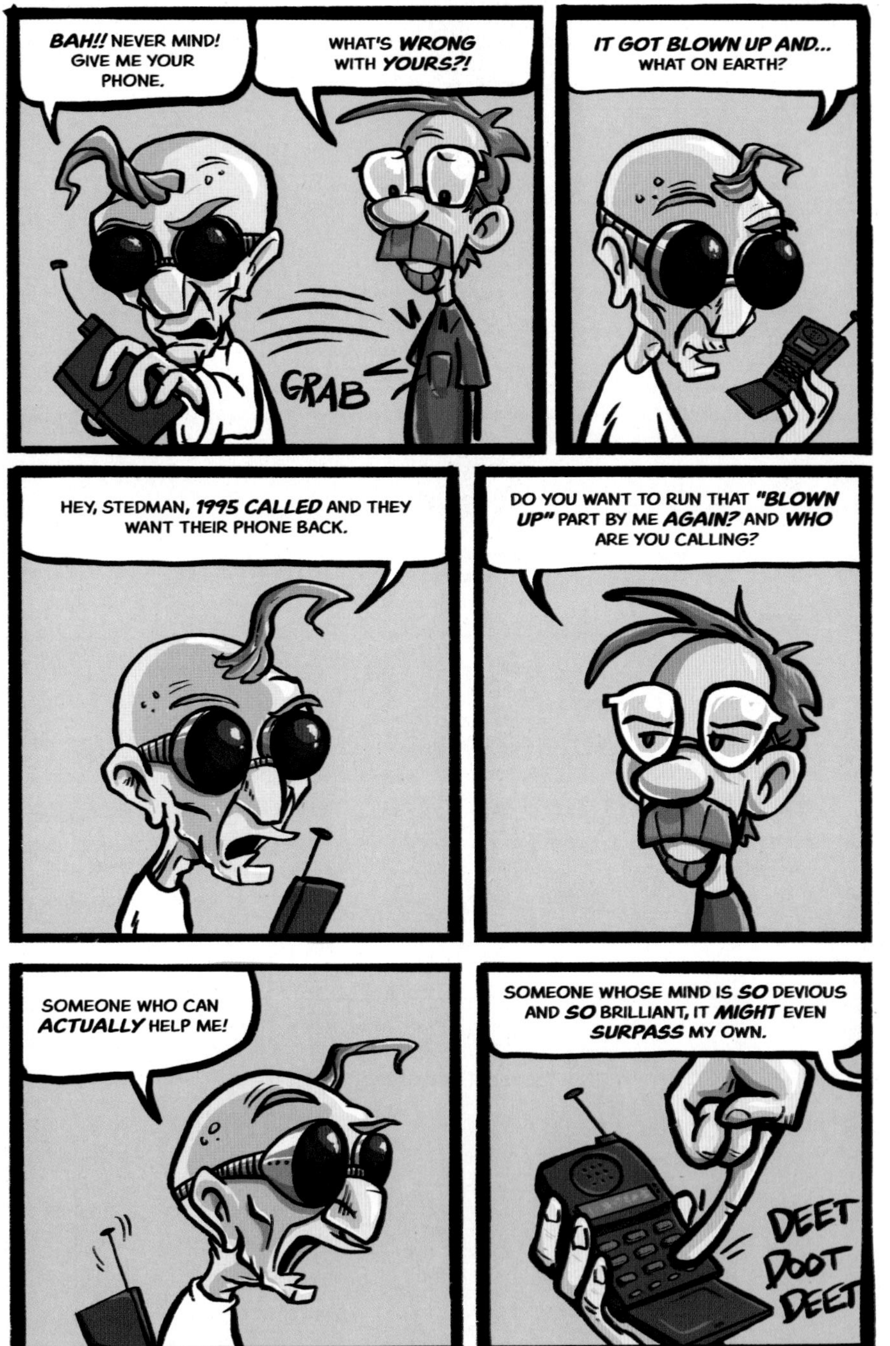
BAH!! NEVER MIND! GIVE ME YOUR PHONE.
WHAT'S WRONG WITH YOURS?!
GRAB
IT GOT BLOWN UP AND... WHAT ON EARTH?
HEY, STEDMAN, 1995 CALLED AND THEY WANT THEIR PHONE BACK.
DO YOU WANT TO RUN THAT "BLOWN UP" PART BY ME AGAIN? AND WHO ARE YOU CALLING?
SOMEONE WHO CAN ACTUALLY HELP ME!
SOMEONE WHOSE MIND IS SO DEVIOUS AND SO BRILLIANT, IT MIGHT EVEN SURPASS MY OWN.
DEET DOOT DEET

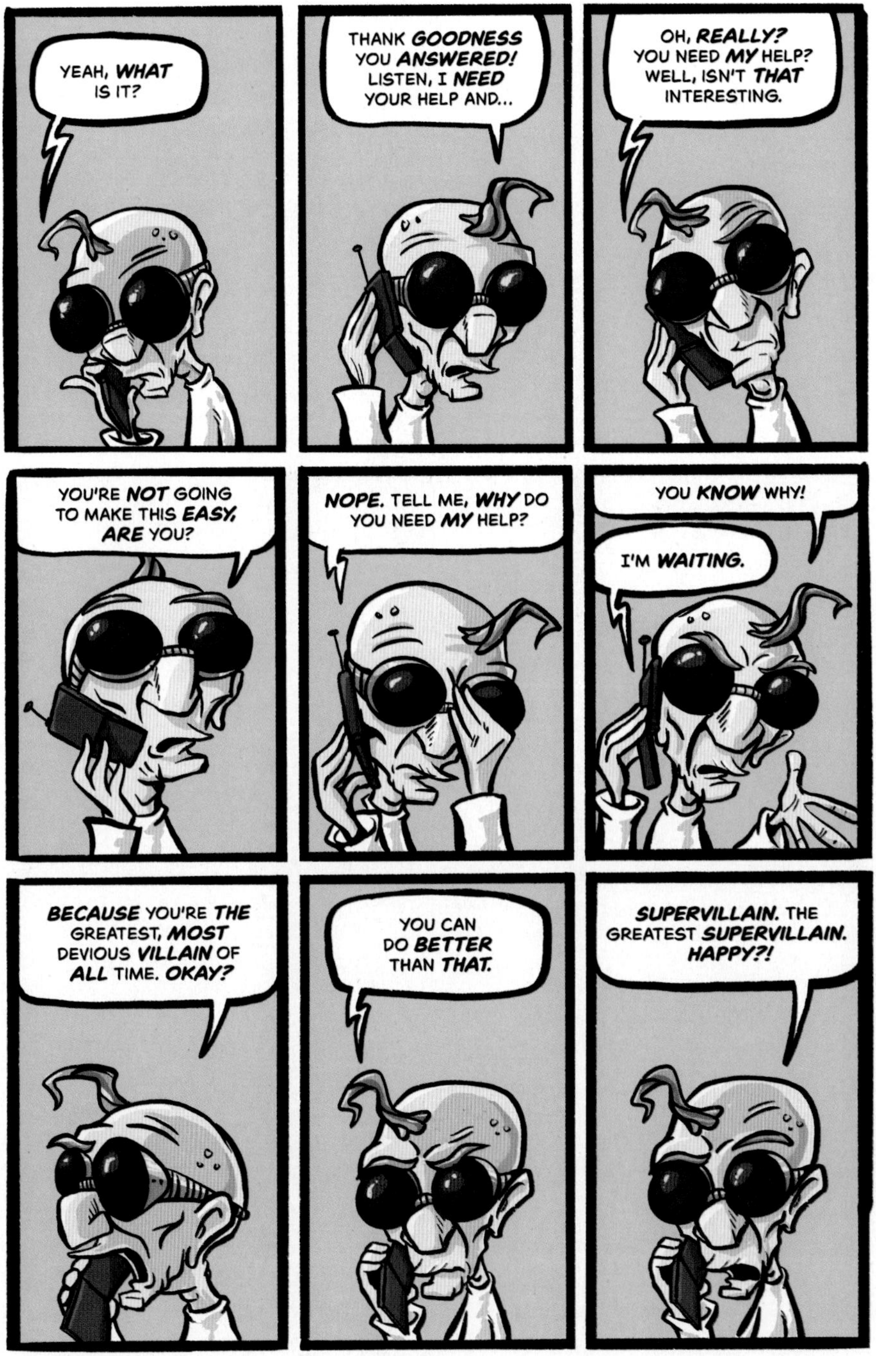
YEAH, WHAT IS IT?
THANK GOODNESS YOU ANSWERED! LISTEN, I NEED YOUR HELP AND...
OH, REALLY? YOU NEED MY HELP? WELL, ISN'T THAT INTERESTING.
YOU'RE NOT GOING TO MAKE THIS EASY, ARE YOU?
NOPE. TELL ME, WHY DO YOU NEED MY HELP?
YOU KNOW WHY!
I'M WAITING.
BECAUSE YOU'RE THE GREATEST, MOST DEVIOUS VILLAIN OF ALL TIME. OKAY?
YOU CAN DO BETTER THAN THAT.
SUPERVILLAIN. THE GREATEST SUPERVILLAIN. HAPPY?!

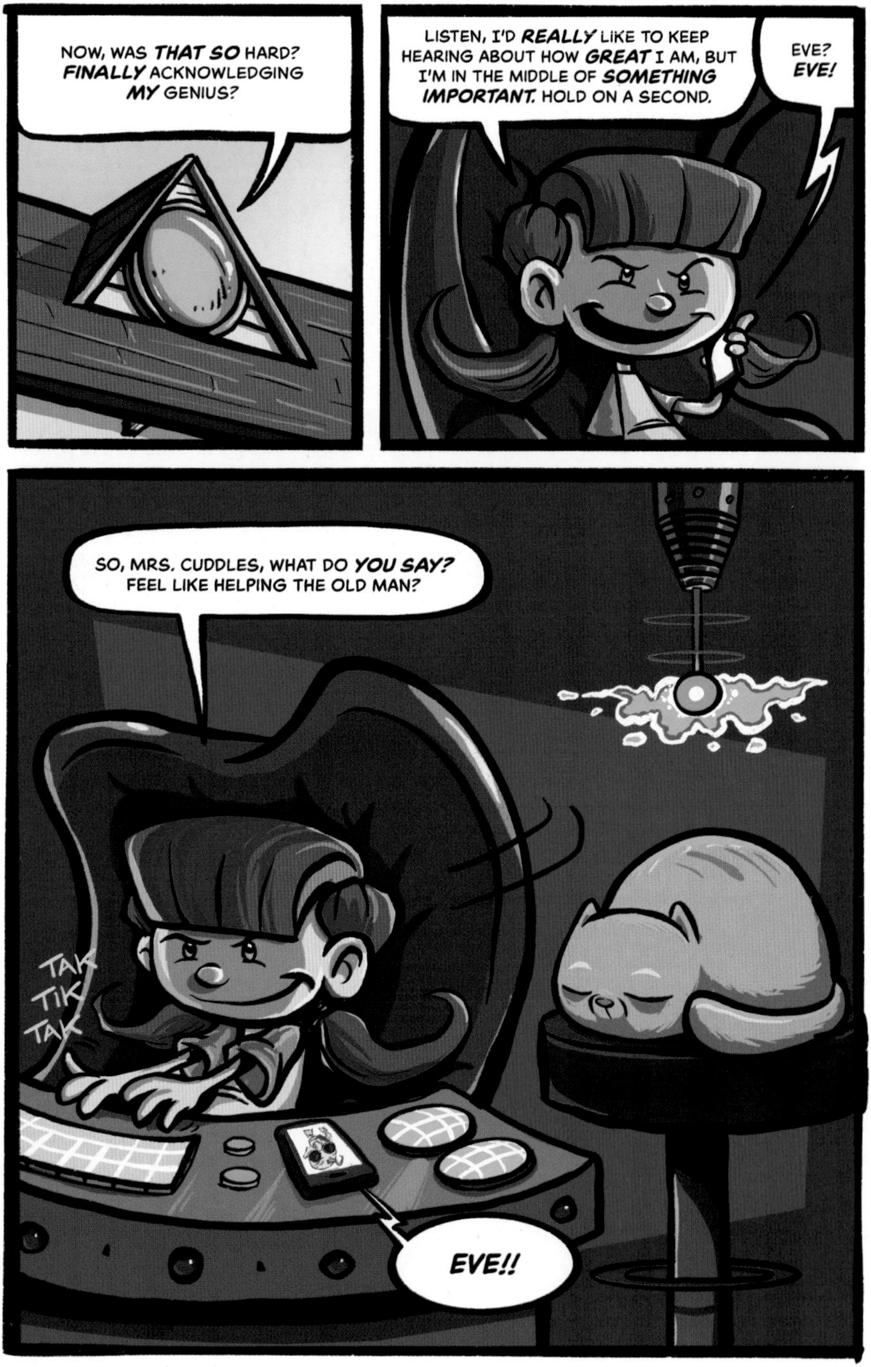
NOW, WAS THAT SO HARD? FINALLY ACKNOWLEDGING MY GENIUS?
LISTEN, I'D REALLY LIKE TO KEEP HEARING ABOUT HOW GREAT I AM, BUT I'M IN THE MIDDLE OF SOMETHING IMPORTANT. HOLD ON A SECOND.
EVE? EVE!
SO, MRS. CUDDLES, WHAT DO YOU SAY? FEEL LIKE HELPING THE OLD MAN?
TAK TIK TAK
EVE!!

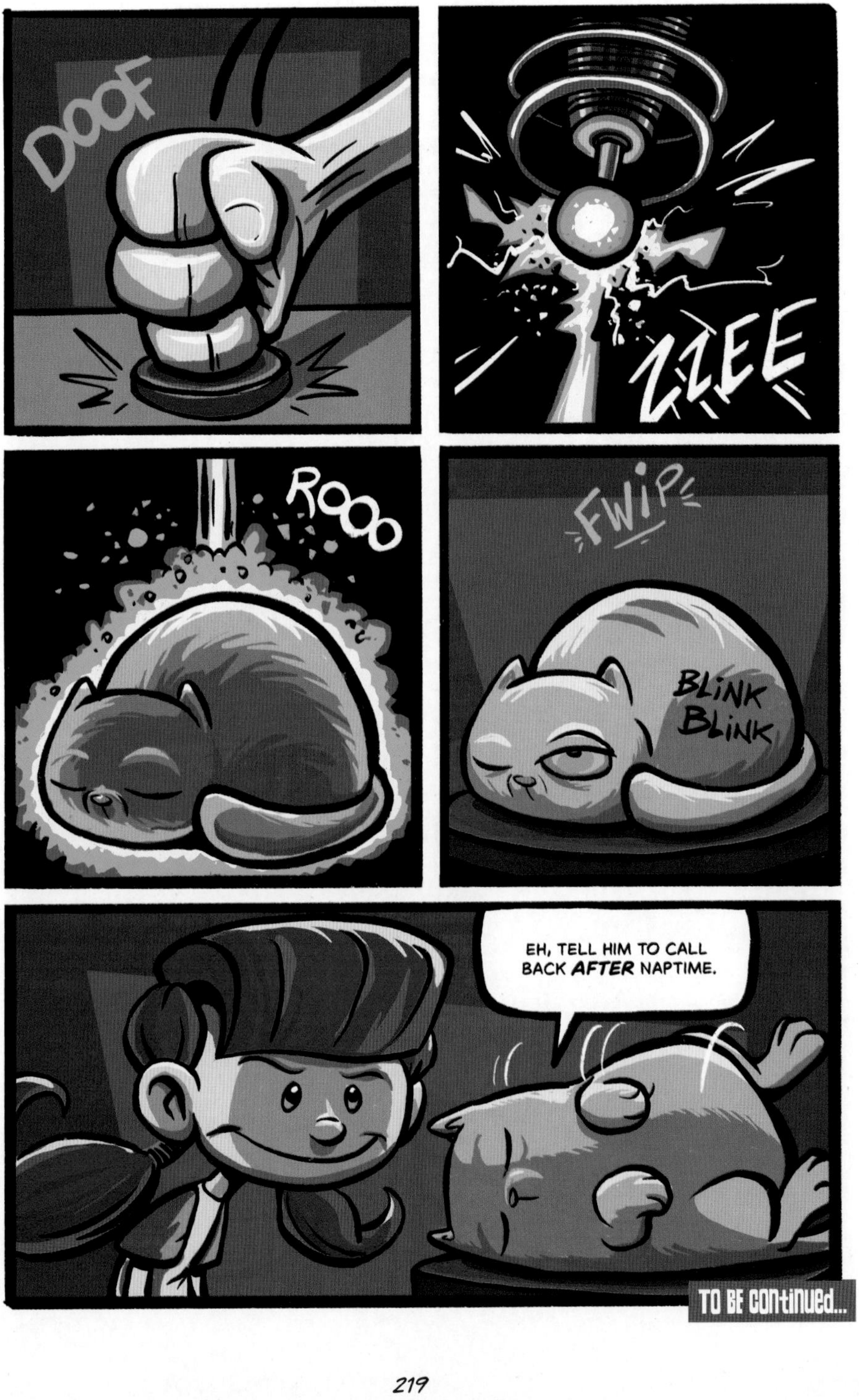
DOOF
ZZEE
ROOO
FWIP
BLINK
BLINK
EH, TELL HIM TO CALL BACK **AFTER** NAPTIME.
TO BE CONTINUED...

Lucas Turnbloom grew up on the shores of Hawaii during the magical era known as the 1980s. There, he spent his days watching stuff like *Star Wars*, *Thundercats*, *Transformers*, and *TMNT*, while also reading comics like *Peanuts*, *Garfield*, *The Far Side*, and *Calvin and Hobbes*. It was during these formative years Lucas realized he wanted to be a professional cartoonist.

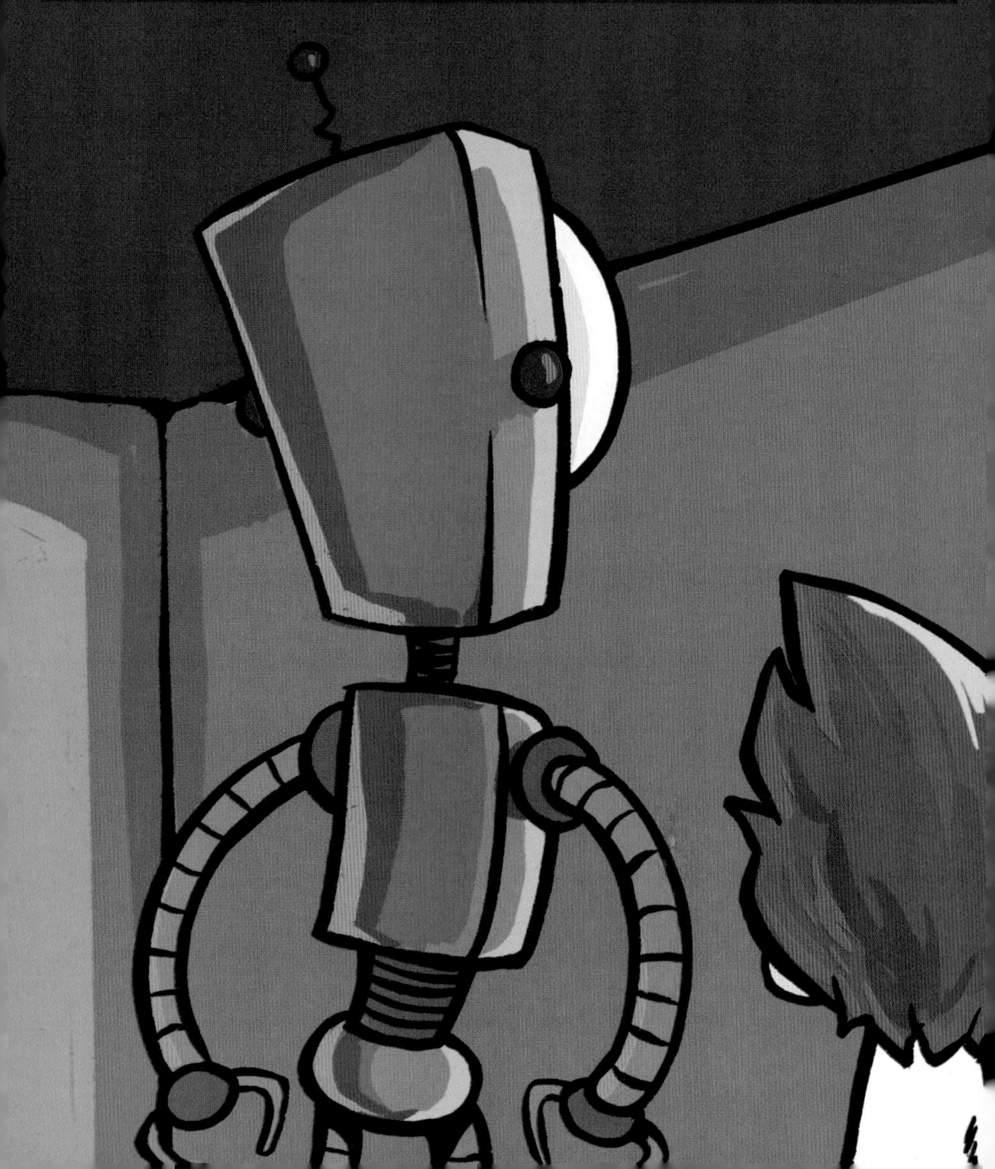

Lucas resides in San Diego with his wife, two sons, and one temperamental cat. When Lucas isn't cartooning, he plays loud guitar, collects embarrassing amounts of action figures, or seeks crucial naps.

Visit Lucas and the McEvil family online at:
McEvilEmpire.com

Or find him on Twitter, Instagram, or Facebook:
@LucasTurnbloom

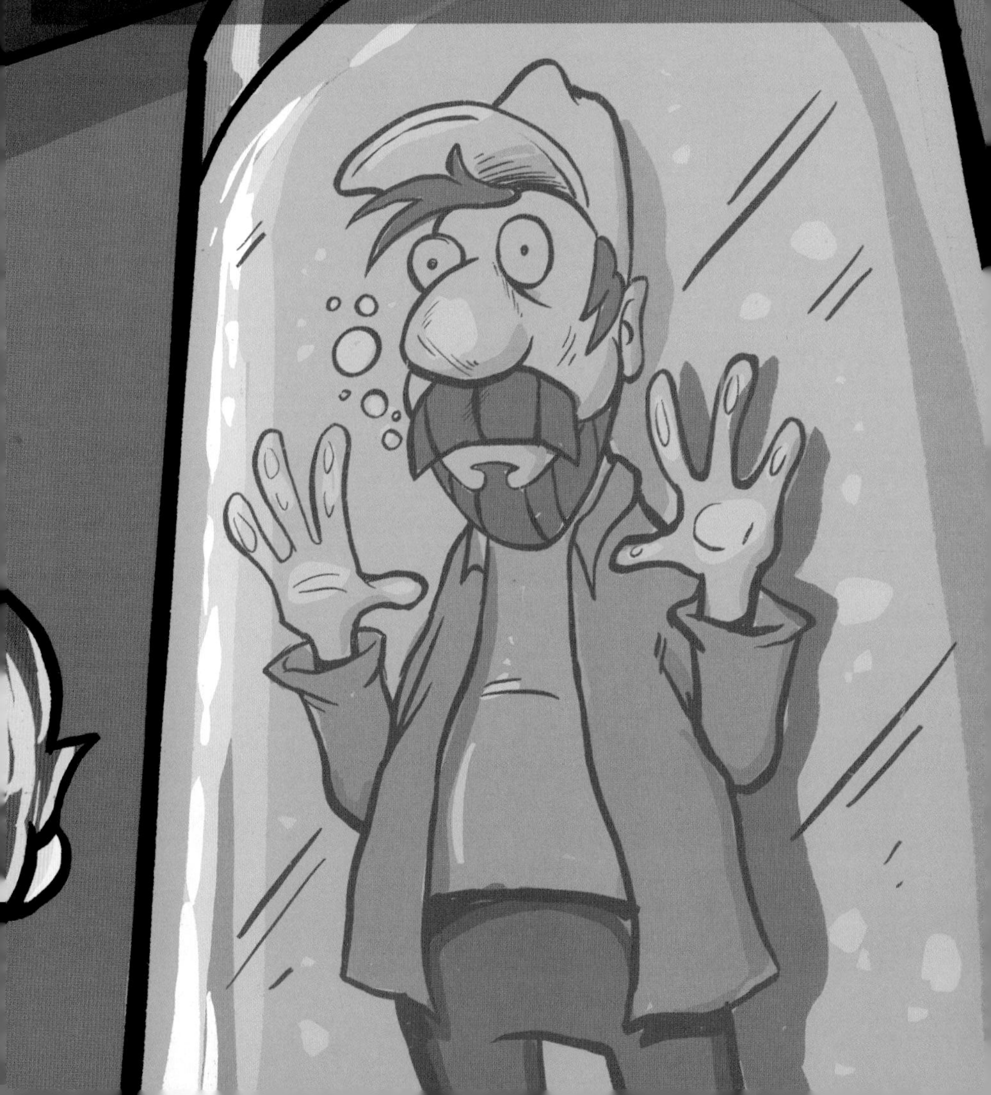

"FELINE FINE"

THE MRS. CUDDLES PREQUEL STORY

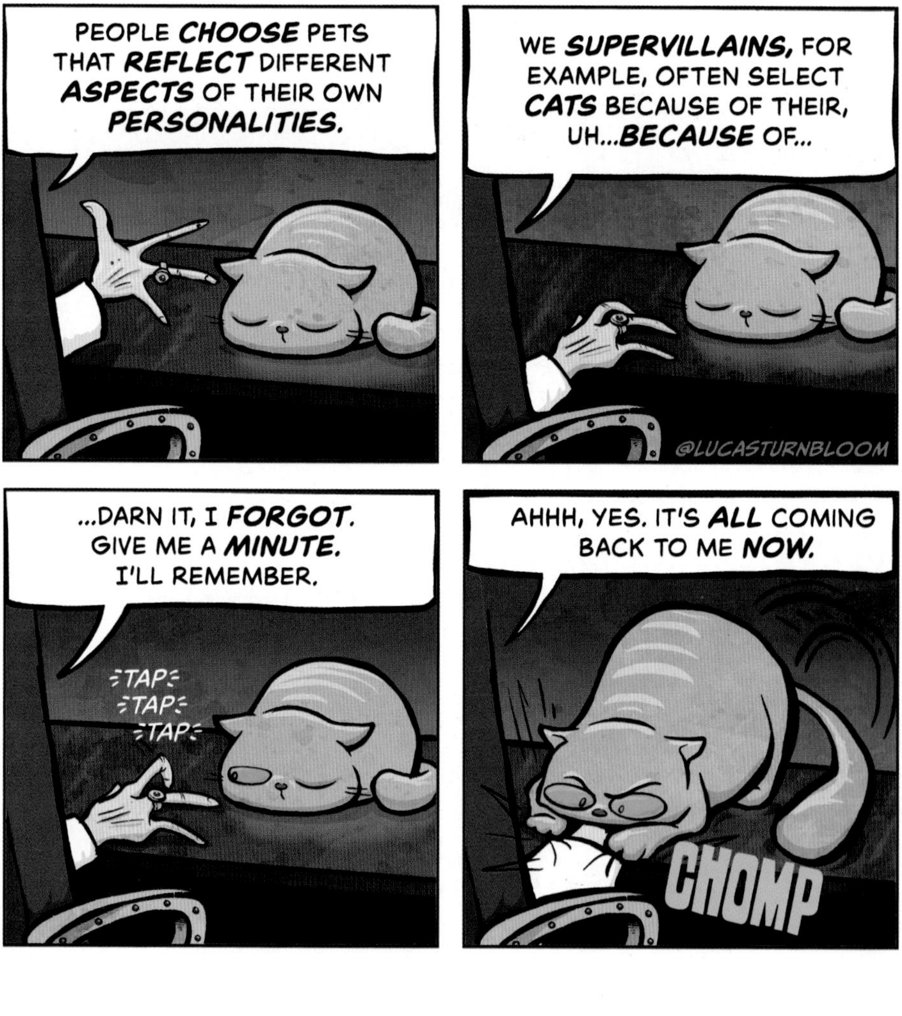
PEOPLE CHOOSE PETS THAT REFLECT DIFFERENT ASPECTS OF THEIR OWN PERSONALITIES.
WE SUPERVILLAINS, FOR EXAMPLE, OFTEN SELECT CATS BECAUSE OF THEIR, UH...BECAUSE OF...
@LUCASTURNBLOOM
...DARN IT, I FORGOT. GIVE ME A MINUTE. I'LL REMEMBER.
TAP
TAP
TAP
AHHH, YES. IT'S ALL COMING BACK TO ME NOW.
CHOMP

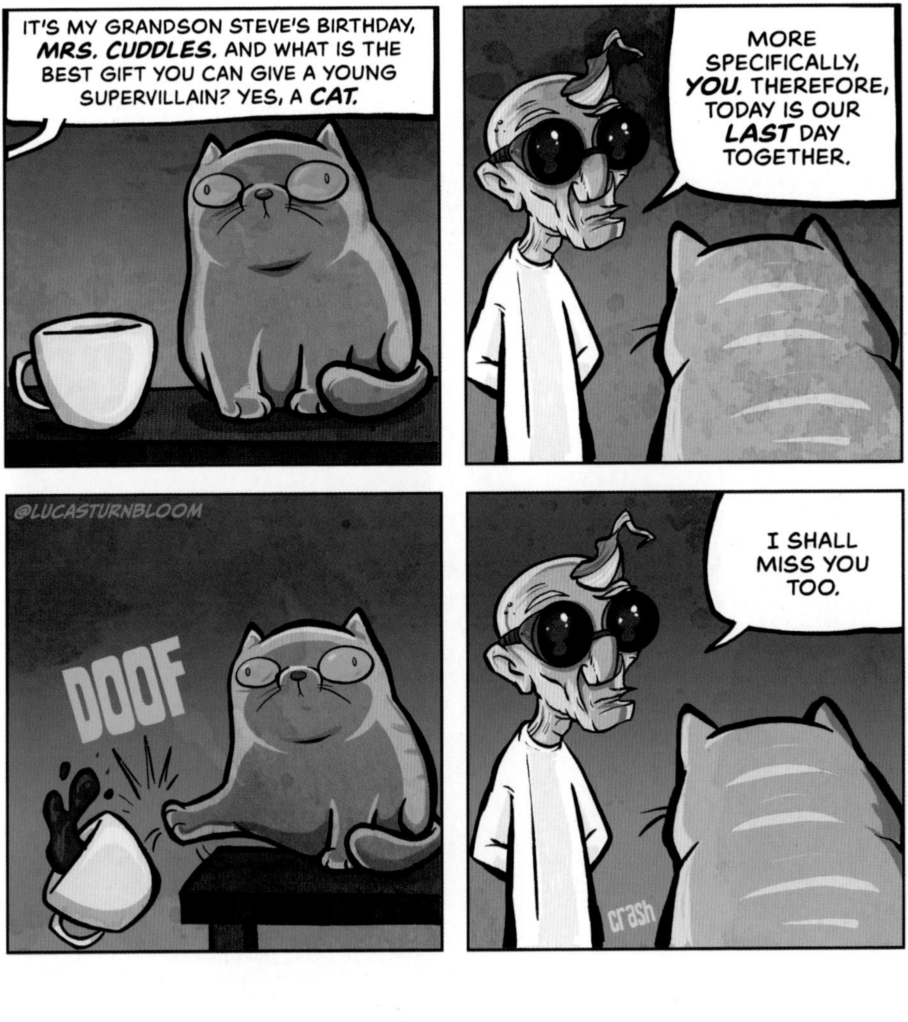
IT'S MY GRANDSON STEVE'S BIRTHDAY, MRS. CUDDLES. AND WHAT IS THE BEST GIFT YOU CAN GIVE A YOUNG SUPERVILLAIN? YES, A CAT.
MORE SPECIFICALLY, YOU. THEREFORE, TODAY IS OUR LAST DAY TOGETHER.
@LUCASTURNBLOOM
DOOF
I SHALL MISS YOU TOO.
crash

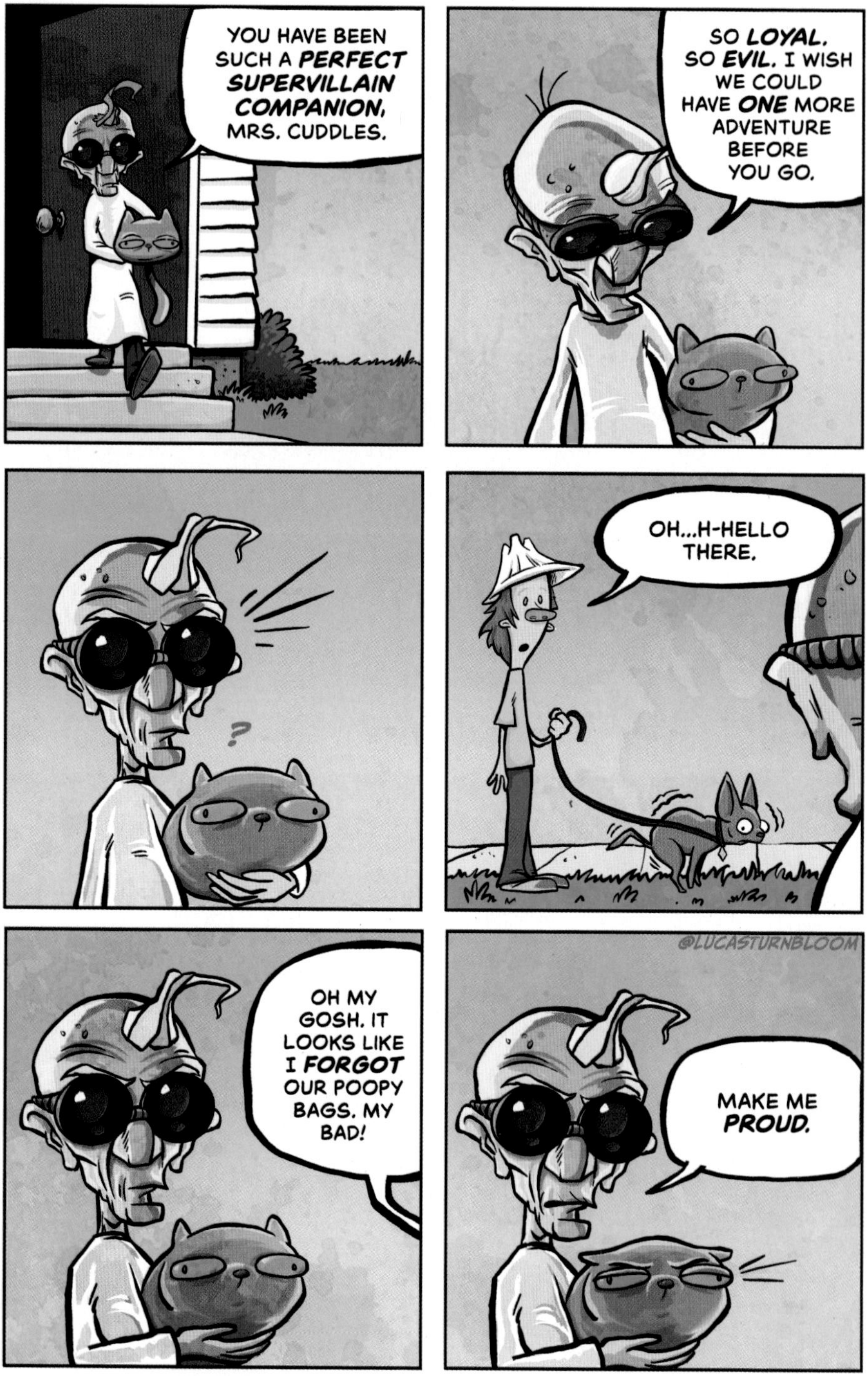
YOU HAVE BEEN SUCH A **PERFECT SUPERVILLAIN COMPANION,** MRS. CUDDLES.
SO **LOYAL.** SO **EVIL.** I WISH WE COULD HAVE **ONE** MORE ADVENTURE BEFORE YOU GO.
?
OH...H-HELLO THERE.
@LUCASTURNBLOOM
OH MY GOSH. IT LOOKS LIKE I **FORGOT** OUR POOPY BAGS. MY BAD!
MAKE ME **PROUD.**

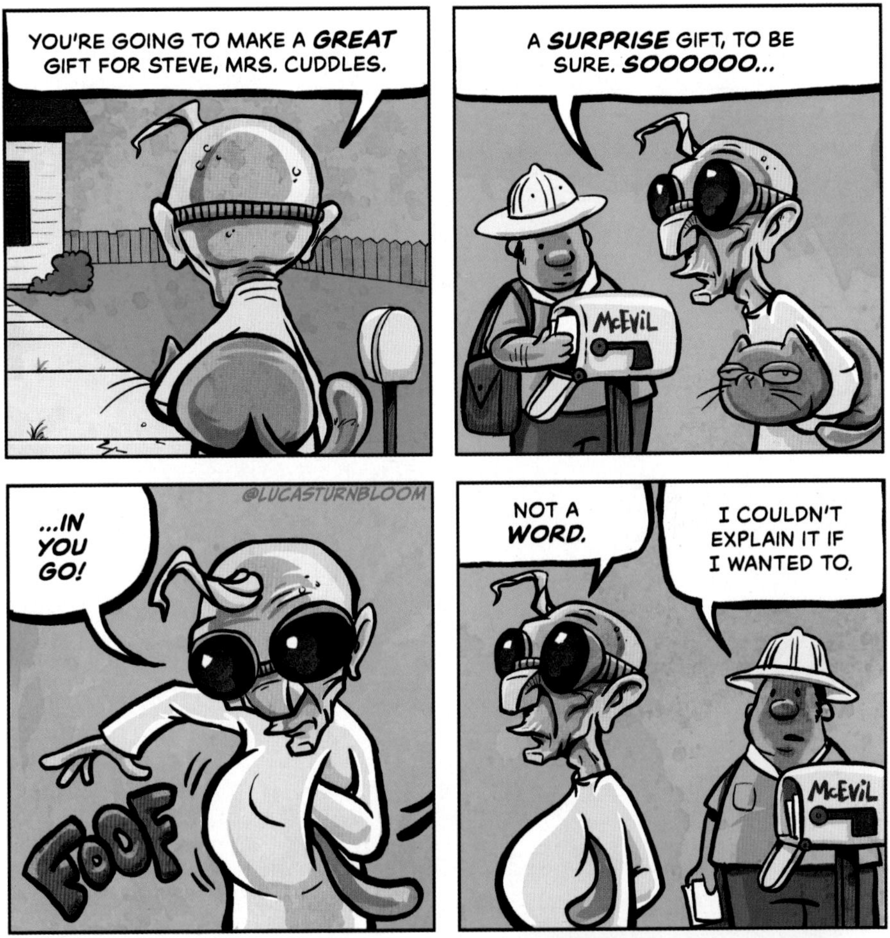
YOU'RE GOING TO MAKE A *GREAT* GIFT FOR STEVE, MRS. CUDDLES.
A *SURPRISE* GIFT, TO BE SURE. *SOOOOOO...*
McEVIL
@LUCASTURNBLOOM
...IN YOU GO!
FOOF
NOT A *WORD.*
I COULDN'T EXPLAIN IT IF I WANTED TO.
McEVIL

PICK UP
STEVE L. McEVIL
TODAY AND LEARN THE
REST OF THE STORY!

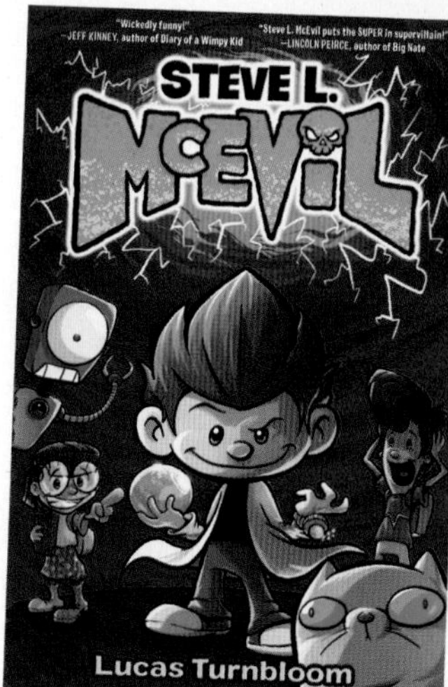
"Wickedly funny!" —JEFF KINNEY, author of Diary of a Wimpy Kid
"Steve L. McEvil puts the SUPER in supervillain!" —LINCOLN PEIRCE, author of Big Nate
STEVE L.
McEVIL
Lucas Turnbloom

HOW TO DRAW MRS. CUDDLES

Grab your PENCIL and let's draw!

TIPS: A) Follow the steps in order; B) Don't press your pencil down on the paper too hard; C) Make lots of little lines to complete your shapes; D) Have fun!

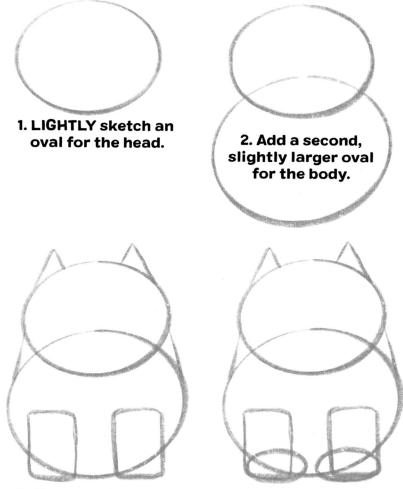

1. LIGHTLY sketch an oval for the head.

2. Add a second, slightly larger oval for the body.

3. Connect the ovals with two lines. Add two triangles on top for ears and two rectangles at the bottom for legs.

4. Draw two small ovals for paws.

**5. Add two ovals for eyes
and a small oval for a nose.**
(Don't forget to dot the eyes
and draw a line under the nose!)

**6. Add a small
swirl for the tail
and toe lines.**

**7. Grab a pen and trace
ONLY over the pencil
lines you wish to keep.**

**8. Erase pencil lines
and you're done!**
(Feel free to add whiskers and
any other small details you like!)

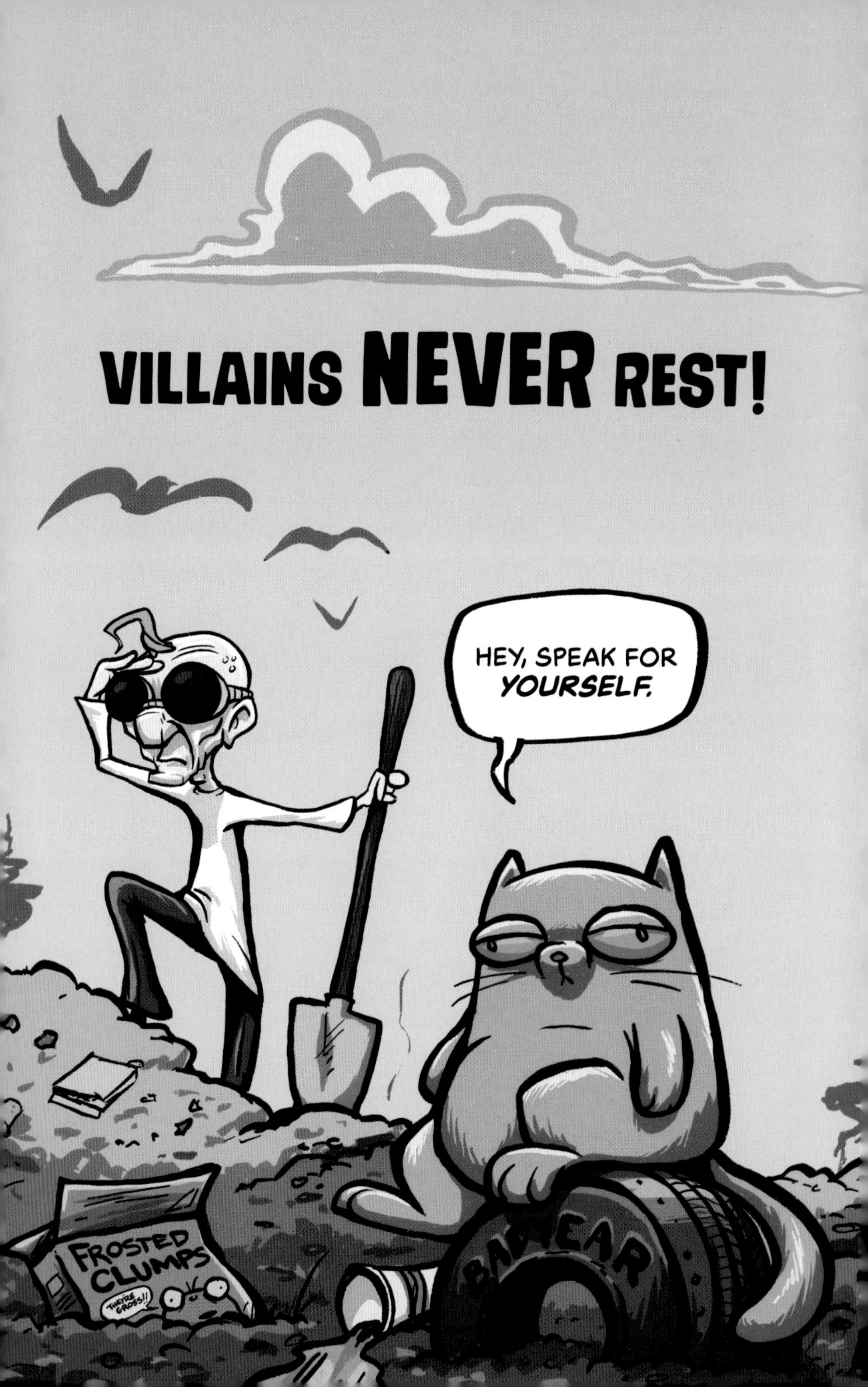
VILLAINS NEVER REST!
HEY, SPEAK FOR YOURSELF.
FROSTED CLUMPS
THEY'RE GROSS!!
BADYEAR

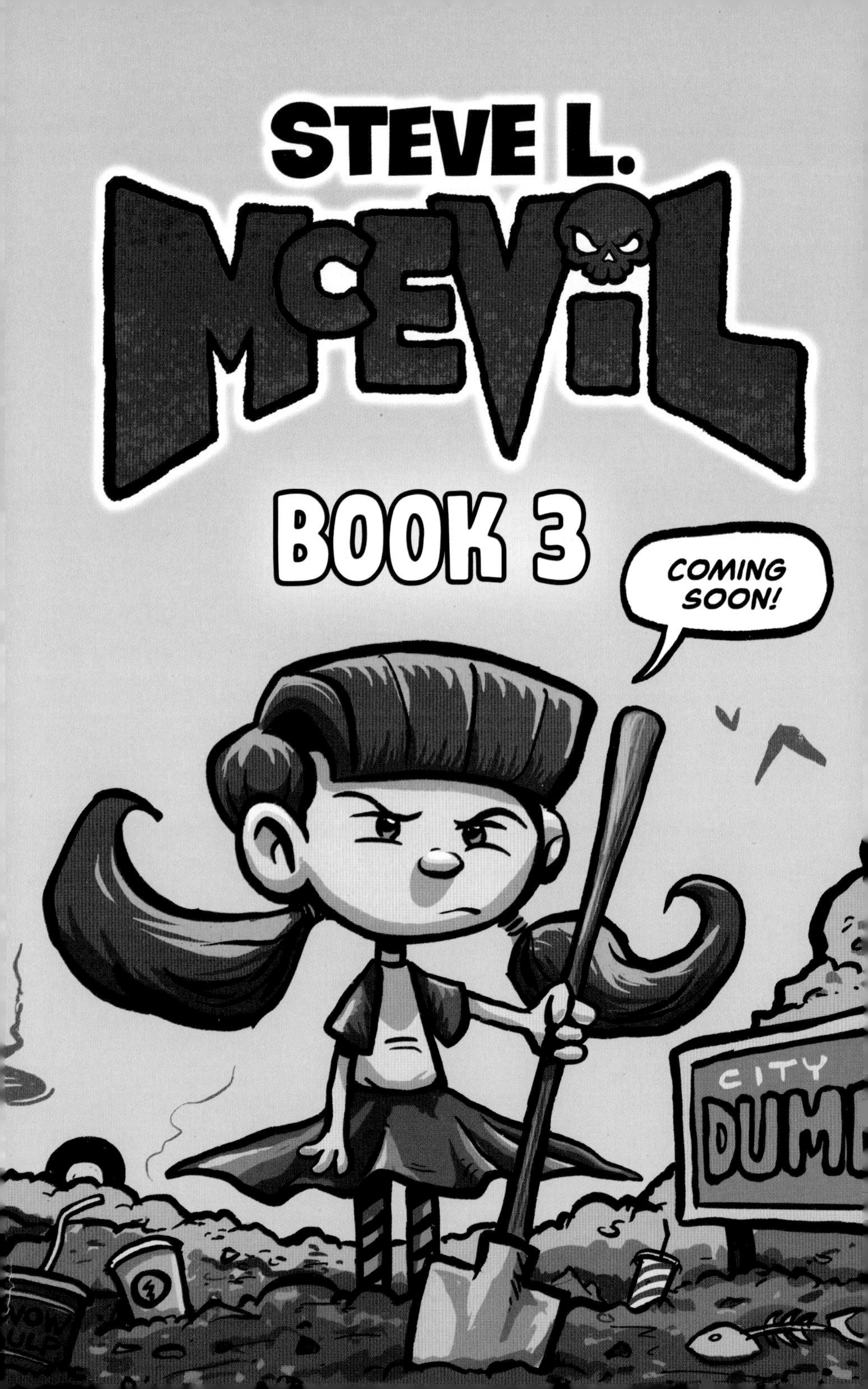
STEVE L.
McEVIL
BOOK 3
COMING SOON!
CITY

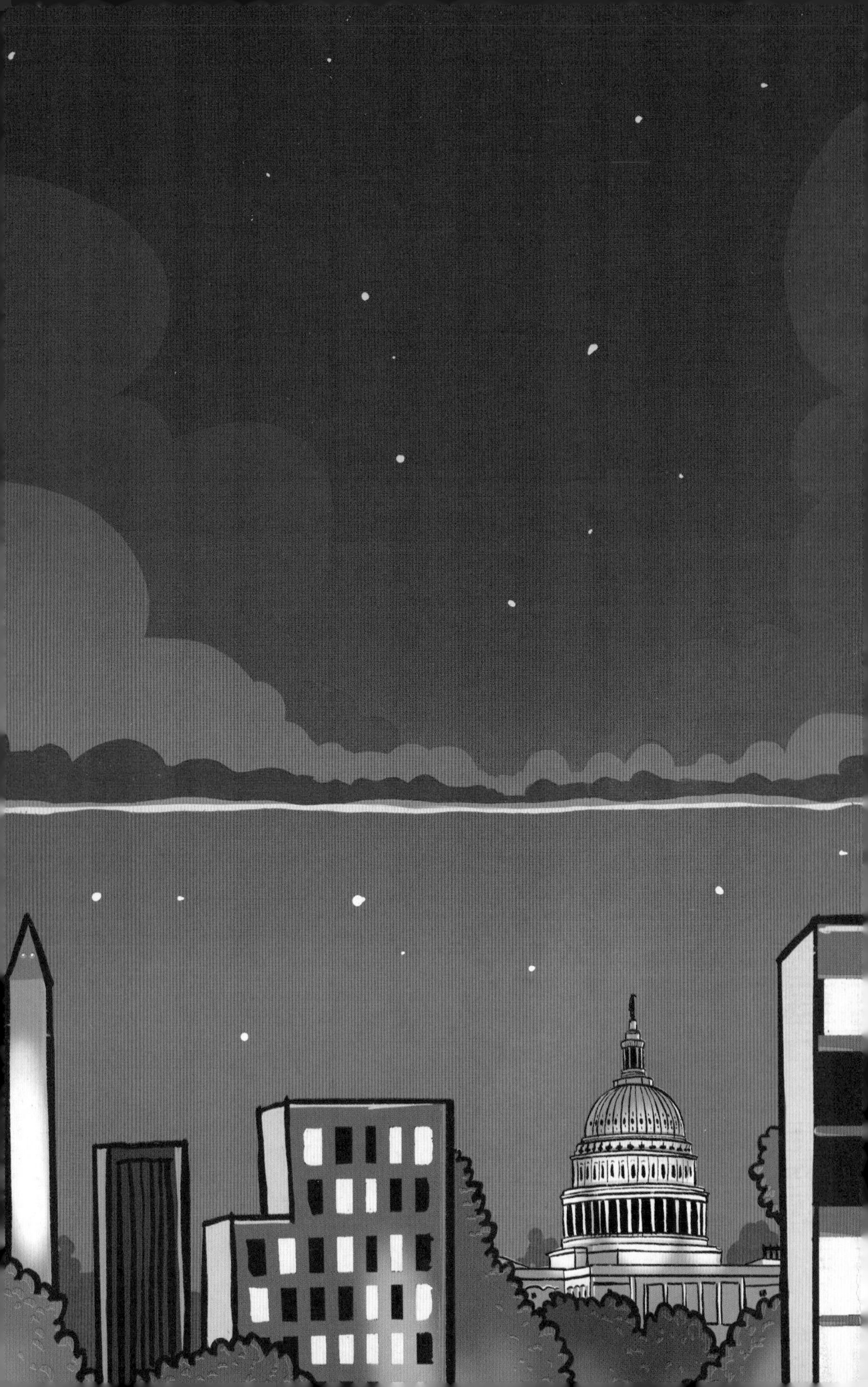